Titles by Karen Rose

DIRTY SECRETS
(enovella)

Baltimore Novels

YOU BELONG TO ME

NO ONE LEFT TO TELL

DID YOU MISS ME?

BROKEN SILENCE
(enovella)

WATCH YOUR BACK

MONSTER IN THE CLOSET

DEATH IS NOT ENOUGH

Cincinnati Novels

CLOSER THAN YOU THINK

ALONE IN THE DARK

EVERY DARK CORNER

EDGE OF DARKNESS

Sacramento Novels

SAY YOU'RE SORRY

SAY YOU'RE SORRY

KAREN ROSE

BERKLEY
New York

BERKLEY
An imprint of Penguin Random House LLC
1745 Broadway, New York, NY 10019

ISBN: 9780451491077

Headline UK hardcover edition / February 2019
Berkley hardcover edition / February 2019
Berkley mass-market edition / August 2019

Printed in the United States of America
1   3   5   7   9   10   8   6   4   2

Cover art: Woman with Windblown Hair by mbot / istock
Cover design by faceout STUDIO

To Claire Zion, my editor extraordinaire, as we begin another series with this, our tenth book together. You make my books better with your keen eye, sharp logic, and generous heart. Your friendship honors me. Thank you.

To Martin. I love you always. Thank you for thirty-six beautiful years.

ACKNOWLEDGMENTS

Terri Bolyard for listening when I get stuck.

Dr. Marc Conterato for all things medical.

Caitlin Ellis for making the biz run smoothly when I'm in the cave.

Sarah Hafer for the research on New Religious Movements.

Jack Harris, WFLA Tampa Bay, for the radio jargon.

Linda Hurtado, WTVT Tampa, for the TV reporting detail.

Firefighter Terence Keenan for helping me put out the fire properly.

Amy Lane and Brenda Novak for introducing me to Sacramento.

Sonie Lasker for the Russian translations and all the self-defense moves. Спасибо большое, я всегда буду любить тебя.

Beth Miller and Sarah Hafer for all the editing.

Amy Schneider for helping to make Brutus a legit service dog.

The Starfish for all the plotting.

Forensic Investigator Geoff Symon for keeping my crime scenes honest and my MEs from going all Quincy on me.

Claire Zion, Robin Rue, and Alex Clarke for your unflagging support. You make it possible for me to do what I love best—making up stories in which villains get their comeuppance, the MCs get their HEAs, and the body counts don't run *too* terribly amok.

All mistakes are my own.

PROLOGUE

Good. She was waking up. *Took her long enough.*

He took a drag on his cigarette and blew the smoke into her face. A coughing fit ensued, and by the time she'd calmed down, her dark eyes were open and staring up at him.

She was scared. This pleased him. He smiled down at her. They were always scared and this always pleased him.

He sat back in his chair, watching as she struggled against her bonds. They always did that, too. But they never got free. He tied a very strong knot. It was one of his best talents.

He waited until she'd given up, until her gaze fixed on his face and recognition set in. "You," she whispered. "From the diner."

"Me," he replied agreeably. From the tired old diner on the outskirts of Portland. Getting her home had been a pain in the ass. She took up much more space than he'd expected. She was curvier than most of the guests he brought home. It would be a nice change.

She yanked on her bonds again, a token effort only. Her lips trembled. "Where are my clothes?"

"Burned."

"Why?"

He stood up, pulled lazily at his tie, aware that she

was following his every move. "Because you won't be
needing them anymore."

She shook her head, appropriately agitated. "Why
are you doing this?"

He unbuttoned his shirt as her eyes flicked all around
the room, looking for help. Looking for escape. There
would be none. He grabbed her hand from where he'd
tied it to the headboard and ran his thumb over her left
ring finger, following the indentation that was all that
remained of her wedding vows.

"Does he know you're gone?" he asked softly.

Her gaze flew to her ring finger and she tried to pull
her hand away, but, of course, she couldn't. Slowly she
nodded.

"Did he let you go?"

Another nod, but her eyes flickered away. He
squeezed her hand hard enough to make her gasp. "Do
not *lie* to me, Miriam."

He was surprised when her eyes flared with a sudden fury. "That is not my name," she ground out. "My
name is Eileen."

"The locket says 'Miriam.'" He held up the heart-
shaped silver charm, letting it dangle between them,
watching it gleam as it caught the low light from the
bedside lamp. He set it to swing, like a hypnotist's
watch. "Did you steal it?"

She swallowed hard, momentarily mesmerized by
the swinging locket. Then her jaw hardened. "No."

"Then, if it's yours, you are Miriam."

She closed her eyes. "No, I am not."

It was really immaterial at this point, but her little show of temper had intrigued him. "Then who is
Miriam?"

A tear ran down her cheek. "Who I used to be."

"Ah. So your husband is looking for Miriam. Not
Eileen."

She clamped her lips shut, giving him his answer.

Good. He hadn't been terribly worried that anyone would be tracking her down. The woman had a solitary, hunted air to her, like she always looked over her shoulder. Like she was hiding. That worked for him.

He ran his thumb over the locket, feeling the etched lines of the engraved *Miriam* on the back, then the symbol on the front. "An olive tree, two kneeling children, all protected by these beautiful outstretched angel wings." She'd winced at the word "protected." If it had been a talisman, it was a piss-poor one. It certainly hadn't protected her. "What does it mean?"

Again her jaw tightened and she looked away. He gripped her chin and yanked her back. "Don't ignore me," he warned.

She clenched her eyes shut, so he covered her mouth and pinched her nose closed. "Look at me," he growled, all fascination with her gone. He was angry again, which was how it was supposed to be. Her eyes flew open, terrified, as she began to struggle to get free. He removed his hand and allowed her to breathe, smiling at her frantic gasps for air.

He gripped her chin again, much harder this time. "Say you're sorry, Miriam." He gave her a hard shake. *"Say you're sorry."*

Stubbornly she clamped her lips together.

His lips curved. Excellent. He'd make her say it before he was through and he'd enjoy every moment of the effort. Because they always said it, sooner or later.

Usually as they begged him to let them die.

ONE

Daisy?"

Daisy Dawson flinched when Trish's finger poked her upper arm. "What?" she asked, knowing she'd been distracted. She returned her attention to her friend, who'd stopped in the middle of the sidewalk, a worried expression on her face. "I'm sorry. What did you say?"

Trish frowned. "What's wrong with you tonight? You're jumpy. Is it because of Gus? Do I need to call Rosemary?"

Daisy rolled her shoulders, trying to relieve the tension in her muscles. It didn't relax her any more than it eliminated the tickle at the back of her neck. Because someone was watching her. Following her.

Again. *Thanks a lot for keeping your word, Dad,* she thought bitterly. She'd thought they'd had an agreement. She'd thought he trusted her. She'd been wrong. *Again.* She wanted to scream, to rage. To call him right now and tell him to stay the fuck out of her life.

A rough, wet tongue licking her fingers had her tamping down her temper. Absently she reached into the pet bag that she wore cross-body like a sling and scratched behind Brutus's enormous wing-shaped ears. "Shh, girl," she murmured, and the dog immediately settled. "It's okay." *I'm okay.* Which wasn't exactly true, not that Brutus would believe her anyway. The little dog knew when she was spiraling, knew when she was on edge, and did what she'd been trained to do—distracting Daisy before her spiral became a meltdown. Drawing a breath, she smiled tightly for Trish's benefit. "No, let Rosemary go home to her family. She's earned it."

Because tonight had been a hard night for all of them, especially Rosemary.

Trish's eyes welled with new tears that she didn't try to hide. It was just the two of them and Trish knew she didn't have to pretend around Daisy. "Poor Gus."

"Yeah." Keeping one hand on Brutus, Daisy lifted her other hand to Trish's face to wipe away the tears. "I guess he just couldn't handle the grief of losing his wife."

"Maybe he didn't want to," Trish whispered.

"I don't know. Maybe you're right." All Daisy knew was that the man's death from alcohol poisoning had hit Rosemary hard. Seeing their sponsor cry like that as she'd told them of Gus's death had left Daisy shaken and feeling helpless. Daisy hated feeling helpless.

Trish bit at her lip. "He'd been sober for fifteen years, DD. Fifteen years. He was a sponsor, even. He was Rosemary's sponsor. How can *we* expect to—"

Daisy cut her off by pressing a finger to Trish's lips. "Stop. You cannot compare yourself to Gus or anyone else. He was grieving. His wife died. They'd been married for fifty years. You said it yourself—maybe he wanted to die. Maybe this was just his way."

Trish nodded shakily. "I know." She straightened her shoulders and took a swipe at each eye with her sleeve. "You're right."

Daisy gave her a one-armed hug. "I'm usually right."

Trish snorted. "You wish."

Daisy laughed. "If I said we needed hot fudge sundaes with extra nuts, would I be right about that?"

"Yes, but that's a given. We always have sundaes after a meeting."

Daisy linked arms with Trish and they began

walking toward the diner where their sundaes awaited. "What were you saying before?"

"Oh. I wanted to know if you were volunteering this weekend at the pet store."

"I am." Daisy smiled up at Trish, who was at least five inches taller. "Are you wanting to volunteer or adopt?"

"Adopt?" Trish said it more as a question. "I was thinking about a cat. Something to come home to, but not something I'd have to walk. Not with my crazy schedule."

"I think that's a great idea. So does Brutus, don't you, girl?" Brutus popped her head out of the sling that doubled as Daisy's handbag, her tongue out in the cutest way possible. "See? She says yes."

Trish laughed. "Of course she does. She's biased, though, coming from the shelter herself. You really lucked out, finding a Chion puppy at a shelter. She *is* a Chion, right? I looked up Papillon-Chihuahua mixes. That's what the article called them."

"Some people call them Papihuahuas," Daisy said. Whatever breed she was called, Brutus was perfect and necessary. "My dad found her, actually, while I was in rehab. One of the therapists had a service dog that helped him control his anxiety, which helped him maintain his sobriety. Dad went looking for a dog that could be trained to do the same for me when I got out. She was the runt of the litter, which was why I named her Brutus. She was so tiny that I figured she needed all the help she could get."

"I wondered about her name. Although she looks like a Gizmo to me."

Daisy laughed. With her large bat ears, Brutus did look like the little creature from *Gremlins*. "She does. Before the gremlins turned evil, that is. Gizmo was my sister Julie's suggestion when Dad first brought her home."

"If I could find a dog this little and this cute, I might rethink a cat, but I couldn't bring a dog to work."

"Well, not where you work now. Which we need to change," Daisy said firmly. "I couldn't work in a bar. You're not being fair to yourself, Trish."

"I know. I'm looking. I've got applications out everywhere. It's not just having the booze all around me. It's also the drunken, grabby assholes who do not take no for an answer. I really hate them."

Daisy frowned at that. "Is somebody bothering you?"

"Not really. There was a guy today who was . . . belligerent. Just wouldn't take no for an answer. I stopped smiling when he 'accidentally' brushed his hand over my ass. Told him that I'd have him thrown out. He got mean after that, insulting me. A real tool, you know?"

Daisy rolled her eyes. "Oh, I know." Because her cohost at the radio station was the same way.

Trish frowned. "Is Tad bothering you again?"

Daisy shrugged. Trish was the only person she'd told about the smarmy Tad. "Same old, same old. Little digs, meant to throw me off my game. I can handle Tad, for now anyway. If the time comes when I can't, I'll report him. Did you report this guy who bothered you?"

"I did. I had to. My manager finally did throw him out. The guy kept baiting me, like he wanted me to react. Normally I'd just wave that off, but I was on edge to start with. I had a big test this morning and I'm not sure how I did."

"I'll help you look at the job listings when I'm done at the pet store adoption clinic on Saturday." A new job for Trish didn't need to be permanent, just not at a bar. When she finished dental assistant school, she'd be able to get a good job. "I checked again at the radio station, but they're not hiring right now."

Which made Daisy wince, because she knew that she'd only been hired because her boss and her father were old friends. It was something that Tad never let her forget. Which was why she hadn't yet reported him. She didn't want to give him any more ammunition against her.

"I appreciate you asking anyway," Trish said. "I'll—"

A sound behind them had Daisy stopping abruptly once again. It was a shuffle, the scrape of a shoe on concrete. A quick glance over her shoulder showed a familiar-looking man wearing a baseball cap ducking into an alley. *Dad's losing his touch.* He used to be able to hire people she couldn't see or hear.

Trish was frowning again. "What's wrong?"

Daisy lowered her voice to barely a whisper. "My dad's having me followed again. I can hear the guy behind us."

Trish's frown deepened. "Again?"

"Yeah," Daisy said grimly. "He hired a guy to follow me when I was backpacking across Europe last summer. Pissed me off so bad that I came back early and Dad and I had it out. He promised never to do that to me again, but I guess he doesn't trust me after all."

"He had you followed?" Trish asked, dumbfounded. "Why?"

"He was worried I'd fall off the wagon. That's what he said, anyway." Daisy still had her doubts, thinking it was more about her father's inability to break from a lifetime of paranoia. It had killed her sister. *It nearly killed me.* It had certainly stolen what had remained of her childhood. She wasn't going to allow it to ruin her life, no matter how well-meaning her father's intentions might have been.

Trish made a face. "Pretty ironic seeing as the guy is following you from an AA meeting. Do you know who it is?"

Daisy rolled her eyes. "Yeah. It's our old ranch hand, Jacob. We grew up together. He's like the brother I never had, but I'm still going to kick his ass." Which she'd done when she'd caught him lurking in the shadows of a Paris alley, much as he was doing now.

Trish's lips twitched. "Can I watch? My cable's been out for two months." She made another face. "The cable people apparently like to be paid."

Daisy patted her shoulder in sympathy. Trish barely made a living wage at the bar. "Go to the diner and put in our order. I'll meet you there."

Trish shook her head. "I don't care if he is your friend. I'm not leaving you alone."

"I'll be fine. Jacob is like a cuddly lamb. A six-foot-two-inch, two-hundred-pound lamb. Seriously, he wouldn't hurt a fly. Go on. I'll meet you there in a few minutes."

Daisy briefly considered confronting Jacob in the alley, but annoyance had her following the path Trish had taken, then veering off to quickly duck into an alley of her own. Jacob deserved to have the shit scared out of him for following her again. He'd promised to let her live her life independently, just as her father had.

She ground her teeth. *Damn them both.* She was not a child. *I wasn't allowed to be one.* She was twenty-five years old, living on her own and doing just fine, all by herself. Well, not by herself, but with the support of people she'd chosen for the job.

She heard Jacob's footsteps seconds before he passed by. Leaping from the alley, she grabbed a handful of his bulky padded jacket and yanked him back. He spun around in surprise, the brim of his baseball cap hiding his face.

"The Giants?" she mocked. "That's the best disguise you could manage? You thought I wouldn't notice you because you're wearing a Giants cap?" Because he'd never be caught dead wearing a Giants anything. They were both Oakland fans.

She reached up and snatched the cap from his head,

realizing only a millisecond later that she hadn't had to reach up far enough. He was too short.

Because he wasn't Jacob.

She took a step back, the gasp stuck in her throat, her pulse instantly going supersonic as the man glared down at her, his dark eyes barely visible behind the nylon stocking covering his face. Distorting his features.

She turned to run, but it was too late. His arm wrapped around her throat, yanking her to her toes, cutting off her air. Instinctively her hands went for his forearm, trying to sink her nails into his flesh, but there was too much padding in the jacket. She panicked, black dots starting to dance in her vision.

And then cold steel was pressing against her temple and he was dragging her into the alley where she'd waited for him. "You'll be sorry you did that," he rasped in her ear. "You'll be begging my forgiveness before I'm done. They all do."

Sharp barking cut through the fog in her brain. *Brutus.*

Her panic abruptly vanished, her focus clearing as muscle memory kicked in and she heard her father's voice in her mind, directing her movements.

Releasing her hold on the man's arm, she twisted her torso, gaining as much momentum as she could before striking his belly with her elbow. Hearing his surprised grunt, she sucked in a breath and grabbed the pinkie finger of his gun hand, yanking it backward. Ducking under his arm, she gripped his hand, digging her thumb into the fleshy area between his thumb and forefinger, just as her father had trained her to do. Ignoring his cry of pain, she shoved the gun away with her free hand.

Then she ran. She'd drawn enough breath to scream when he grabbed her again, covering her mouth with his hand before pulling her against his chest, back into the alley.

"No, no, no." She tried to scream the words, but they were too muffled to be heard. She tried to kick back against his knees, but he was stronger than she was and she couldn't get a grip on anything.

Brutus continued to bark, but nobody came. Nobody heard.

He shoved her hard, her back hitting a brick wall, knocking the breath out of her. He leaned into her space, his forearm pressed into her throat once more, cutting off her air.

"You are too much trouble," he hissed. He put the gun to her head, but paused, looking around in irritation. "Where the fuck is that goddamn dog?" His gaze dropped to Brutus's bag, which she still wore across her body. "Oh, for fuck's sake," he muttered. He hesitated for the briefest moment, then seemed to stiffen as he pointed the gun at her bag.

Brutus. "No." Grabbing handfuls of fabric at his throat, she yanked him forward with all of her might. His hand skittered, the gun discharging with a soft pop. *Silencer,* she thought, as shards of brick rained down on her head. *Brutus.* But her dog was still barking. Fueled by desperation, Daisy brought her knee up sharply, connecting with the man's groin.

She barely heard his curses over the pounding of her heart. She shoved him away and ran for the street. For safety.

"Daisy? Oh my God, Daisy!" Trish was suddenly there, her hands on Daisy's face. "What happened? Oh my God. Your throat. It's red."

"Mugger," Daisy panted, crumpling to her knees. "He was going to shoot Brutus." Her dog poked her head out of her bag and began licking Daisy's still-clenched fist.

But the man hadn't tried to take her bag. *He tried to take me.* She closed her eyes and tried not to throw up, vaguely hearing Trish on the phone with 911. *Safe.* They were safe. It would be all right.

Trish sank to her knees and wrapped her arms around Daisy's shoulders, rocking her gently. "Shh, honey. Shh. It'll be all right. Don't cry."

It was then that Daisy realized she was sobbing. And that a small crowd had gathered. And that Trish's hand was in her coat pocket. "What are you doing?"

Trish pulled Daisy's phone free. "Calling Rafe. The cops are on their way, but having Rafe here will make it easier on you. Here, unlock your phone and I'll call." Voice halting, Trish made the call to Daisy's landlord, who was as much a brother to her as Jacob.

But unlike Jacob, Rafe was also a cop. *He'll know what to do.*

Trish's arms were around her again, carefully rocking her. "Did you scratch him?"

Still crying, Daisy tried to remember. "I don't think so. I don't know. Maybe?" She pulled back enough to look down at her hands, still clenched into fists. But dangling from her left fist was a silver chain and something was pinching her palm. Carefully she opened her fist and sucked in a breath.

It was a locket. A heart-shaped locket. Silver and engraved. Her bewildered gaze lifted to Trish's. Trish closed Daisy's fingers over the locket, trapping it in her fist again.

"We'll show it to Rafe when he gets here," Trish whispered.

||| SACRAMENTO, CALIFORNIA
||| THURSDAY, FEBRUARY 16, 9:55 P.M.

Frowning at the ringing of his cell phone, Gideon Reynolds paused the episode of *Fixer Upper* he'd DVRed. He wanted to groan as he reached for his phone on the end table. He was tired and didn't want to go back into work. Because it would be work calling.

Hardly anyone else he knew actually used a phone for calling anymore.

His frown became one of worry when he saw the caller ID. Rafe Sokolov. His best friend always texted, never called. And never this late. "What's wrong?" Gideon asked, forgoing a greeting.

"Maybe nothing but probably something," Rafe replied. "You know my new tenant? Daisy Dawson?"

Gideon sighed. "Rafe, no. Just no." Rafe's mother had been trying to fix him up with "cute little Daisy" for months. He'd been avoiding the Sokolovs' Sunday dinners because he was tired of Irina Sokolov's unrelenting matchmaking. She'd been trying to find him the perfect mate for more than ten years.

Part of him loved her for it because it meant she cared. Most of him wished she'd just stop. "Tell your mother—"

"This isn't a setup," Rafe interrupted tersely.

Gideon sat up straighter. "What happened to Miss Dawson?"

"She was attacked tonight, down on J Street."

Gideon grimaced in dread. Rafe was a homicide detective. "Is she . . . okay?"

"Yeah. She fought him off. Her and her little rat-dog."

Gideon was confused. "I'm glad she's okay, but her assault isn't my jurisdiction. It's not usually yours, either." Rafe had joined SacPD when they'd graduated from college and had been a homicide detective for a few years. Gideon had taken a different law enforcement path, heading off to Quantico and the FBI. His specialization in linguistics meant that more than half of his work was done from his office.

His recent assignment to Sacramento meant coming home—as close to "home" as he was likely to ever get. "What's going on?" he asked. Because something obviously was.

"She grabbed a chain from the guy's neck right before she kneed him in the nuts."

Gideon's wince was instinctive. "Ouch. Good for her. Did he get away?"

"Yes," Rafe said, disgust in his tone. "He had a gun. Tried to drag her away."

"God. She's got to be shaken up. But—and I don't mean to sound like a jerk, man—what does this have to do with me?"

"The chain she grabbed came with a locket. Silver, heart shaped. Engraved."

Gideon stopped breathing for a moment, then sucked in a harsh breath. A shiver of foreboding prickled over his skin. "What kind of engraving?"

"Two children kneeling under an olive tree—"

"All under the wings of an angel," Gideon finished in a whisper. He swallowed back the bile that burned his throat. "With a burning sword."

Rafe let the silence hang a beat or two. "Yes. The only other time I've seen that design was on your skin, Gid."

Gideon stared at the TV screen, the frame frozen. Just as he was.

"Gideon?" Rafe's voice was quiet. "You still there?"

Gideon pushed out the breath he'd been holding. "Yeah. Was there a name on the back of the locket?"

Rafe hesitated, his reticence palpable even through the phone. "Miriam."

Gideon lurched to his feet in terrified shock, his heart in his throat. *No. It couldn't be. Someone would have told me.* "Where are you?"

"At UC Davis Medical."

He shook his head to clear it. To focus. His Miriam was okay. *She has to be.* "Why are you at the hospital? I thought you said the Dawson woman was okay."

"She wasn't seriously injured, but he bruised her throat trying to shut her up." Rafe sounded . . . brittle.

Clearly rattled. Gideon wouldn't be surprised to find the entire Sokolov clan at the ER. They'd taken the woman under their collective wing since she'd moved into the apartment in Rafe's old Victorian.

Just as they'd done for Gideon when he'd been a lost, scared teenager. He was suddenly fiercely glad the young woman had the family of Russian immigrants at her back.

"We're getting her checked out to be sure she's okay," Rafe went on. "When the doctor's finished, I'll take her to the station to get her statement while it's fresh in her mind. Then my parents are taking her to their house for the night. Mom's going to keep an eye on her tonight because her attacker cracked her head on a brick wall. The doctor didn't think there was any concussion, but you know how Mom worries."

"I know," Gideon murmured. He'd been on the receiving end of Irina's worry many times. It had always made him feel like one of her brood.

Rafe cleared his throat. "I'd like you to come down to the station to look at the locket and tell me about it."

No. No. No.

"I know it's not easy for you," Rafe said quietly. "I really need your help, though. He told Daisy that she'd beg his forgiveness. That 'they all do.'"

Fuck. "You think he's a serial offender?"

"Maybe. Will you come to the station?"

"I'll be there in thirty minutes." Gideon disconnected and stared at his phone for several painful beats of his heart. Then he hit a name on his favorites list. And waited while it rang. It went to voice mail. As it usually did.

He disconnected and redialed, which he rarely did. This time it was picked up on the second ring. "*What,* Gideon?"

His breath rushed from his lungs at the sound of her

voice. *Oh God.* Abject relief had his knees buckling. He locked them, remaining upright as he focused on steadying his racing pulse.

"What's wrong? Gideon? Hello?"

Gideon's stomach hurt, just thinking about how to frame his question.

His sister blew out an annoyed sigh. "For God's sake, Gideon. It's after midnight here. I hope this is important because you woke me up. Tell me what you called for and let me go back to sleep."

"I'm sorry. It is important." He rubbed his left pec through his shirt, remembering how much it had hurt to get the tattoo all those years ago. But he'd been stoic and hadn't complained once. The girls had gotten off easy, he'd thought at the time, clenching his teeth as the artist's needle had marked his skin. They'd just gotten the lockets. How wrong he'd been. None of them had gotten off easy. "Do you have your locket?"

There was a shocked silence. "What?"

"Your locket. Where is it?"

"In my safe-deposit box," she ground out, "where it's always been."

Gideon swallowed hard. "Where's . . . where is hers?" he asked hoarsely.

Another taut silence. "In the box with mine. Why? What's this about?"

"A woman was attacked in Sacramento tonight. Her attacker wore one of the lockets around his neck. She pulled it off him during the attack. It has 'Miriam' engraved on the back. I thought . . . it might be yours." Nothing. Silence. He couldn't even hear her breathe. "Mercy?" he whispered.

Mercy's answer was what he'd expected. "I . . . can't, Gideon." Her voice broke. "I just . . . can't."

"I understand," he said. "I needed to know if you'd gotten rid of it. Either of them."

"No."

A single word. How could one single word be filled with so much pain?

Gideon swallowed. "I mostly wanted to make sure you were all right."

Although he knew she wasn't all right. She would never be. Neither of them would ever be totally all right. How could they be?

"I'm okay," she said, but he didn't believe her. She didn't sound like she even believed herself. "You?"

"Same old, same old." He hesitated, then murmured, "Take care of yourself, Mercy."

"You too," she said sadly. "Good night."

The phone clicked in his ear and Gideon took a moment to calm his racing heart, to settle his churning gut. To fight back the tears that threatened every time he talked to his sister. To wish that things could be different.

He went to the shelf beside his TV, which was still paused on *Fixer Upper*. On the shelf was a polished box made of cherrywood, a gift that Irina and Karl Sokolov had given him for Christmas, at least five years before. Inside the box were his cuff links, a few ticket stubs, and a handful of photos. He riffled through the photos until he found the one he needed. Pocketing it, he retrieved his Glock from his gun safe, got into his car, and headed for downtown Sac.

It looked like he'd finally be meeting Daisy Dawson after all. At least Irina Sokolov would be pleased.

SACRAMENTO, CALIFORNIA
THURSDAY, FEBRUARY 16, 10:30 P.M.

Fuck. Fuck, fuck, fuck. He drew his front door open wider so that he could slam it hard, but his hand stilled as he resisted the urge. No need to call attention to himself. The Neighborhood Watch group kept their eyes and ears peeled for loud noises and signs of domestic disturbances. The nosy neighbors were the only things he truly hated about living in his otherwise perfect little Midtown neighborhood. All he needed was for someone to call 911 on him for something he *hadn't* actually done.

He headed to the basement and slammed that door behind him, effectively closing himself off from the rest of the world. The basement was the one thing he loved the most about his house. It was tied with the fact that he didn't have to share space with Sydney any longer.

He'd soundproofed his basement, bricking over all doors and windows and installing enough insulation to create a little cocoon. No scream would reach prying ears, even those pressed right up against the outside wall. Not that he'd made that simple, either. His rose-bushes had enormous thorns. He'd chosen the varieties for that very reason. Luckily, they were pretty, too. No-body would be able to get close enough to put their ear to the wall, even if they wanted to.

Now he trusted his soundproofing and keep-away thorns to do their jobs because he needed to scream. He did, venting his frustration at the fucked-up mess this night had become. He screamed until his throat hurt and his head throbbed.

But it wasn't enough. It was never enough. Only one thing took off the edge, and one thing only. And that one thing had escaped him tonight.

He glared at the bed in the corner, neatly made up and ready for the guest that would not be partaking of his hospitality. Damn that blond bitch. He hadn't ex-pected her to fight back. At least not successfully. Someone had taught her well.

That fucking dog. Its yapping had distracted him. *I should have just shot the stupid thing.* His hesitation had ruined his plan for tonight, might even have put him in jeopardy. He'd need to take care of the blonde.

He didn't think she could identify him, but he'd spoken to her. And she'd been way too savvy for her own good, no matter that she'd first appeared to be just another teenager.

She hadn't been that young, though. Close up, he'd seen her eyes. The grim determination that came from experience. She had old eyes. And she'd seen enough of him that he needed to be worried about her. He'd have to get rid of her.

Of course, he had to find out who she was first. He'd need to wait until the next morning to look at the log of all the calls taken by 911.

Stripping off his clothes, he shoved them in a bag to be burned. He'd already discarded the stocking he'd worn over his face as well as the coat and gloves. Those he'd soaked in gasoline and set on fire, burning them in the barbecue grill of a deserted park until they were stinking blobs of melted plastic.

The stocking mask had been a huge mistake. He'd known it in the back of his mind the whole time he was buying the stockings, prepping, and dragging the mask over his head. He usually carried at least one disguise in his duffel bag, but he hadn't had it with him when he'd left the house that morning to go to work.

It was just supposed to have been a staff meeting. No big.

But it *was* big. It was a disaster. He hadn't been prepared for the news. For how it would feel, everyone staring at him with pity because his own father was selling the company, putting them all out of a job. That his father hadn't had the nerve to face them himself, sending his assistant to deliver the proclamation that the new owners would be replacing them with their own people, that the current employees would be receiving severance benefits depending on how long they'd been with the company.

He hadn't been prepared for how much it had

ripped him apart. How his world had just collapsed. His rage had taken over and it was all he'd been able to do to escape the meeting without breaking his father's assistant into little pieces.

He'd needed something—or *someone*—on which to vent his rage, and he'd needed it right *then*. Hell, he needed it *right now*. Fucking blond bitch.

He stepped into the bathroom he'd installed in the basement and stared at his reflection. "Goddammit," he hissed as the full impact of what he was seeing hit him hard.

Deep red scratches scored his flesh, which was bad enough. Forensics would have skin samples. *They'll have my DNA*.

But even worse . . . The locket was missing. The moment rushed back, stealing his breath. It had been when the blonde had grabbed for a hold on his coat, right before she'd kneed him in the nuts.

"Bitch." She'd be so sorry she'd done that. Once he got his hands on her . . . He fantasized her on her knees, begging his forgiveness. She'd tell him she was sorry. They always said they were sorry. Eventually.

More pressing was the likelihood that the police would find his fingerprints on the locket. He'd caught himself rubbing the silver heart from time to time since taking it from his last victim. But he'd worn gloves tonight, so hopefully his prints had been rubbed off.

Either way, they'd have to catch him first before using the physical evidence against him. He wouldn't be popping up in any of their databases. *I just won't get caught. Simple enough.*

He started the shower and stepped under the spray, wishing he weren't on duty for the next few days. Otherwise he'd smoke some weed and calm down. But there was always a chance that he'd be chosen for a random drug test, which would pick that shit up.

He ran his hands over the scratches at the base of

his throat, hoping whatever they'd scrape from under the bitch's nails wouldn't be too damning. He needed to figure out how much the cops knew.

He was edgy. Too jumpy. He needed to calm the fuck down. He needed a woman in the basement bed. Now he wished he hadn't dispatched the last one so quickly. He normally kept them alive for a long time, using them to slake his rage, but Miriam had made him so furious. *So get yourself another houseguest.* That he could do.

Tomorrow. After work. You can hunt tomorrow. Take off the edge. And then his mind would be clear and he'd figure out how to eliminate the blonde.

He'd been operating under the radar for years. He wasn't about to allow a loose end to jeopardize that now.

Tonight, he needed to sleep. He left the basement, taking the stairs two at a time. Hopefully, a run would tire him out enough to sleep.

He opened the back door and clucked his tongue. "Mutt," he called softly. "Come here, boy." The Airedale mix trotted in from the backyard, dropping to sit just inside the kitchen door, lifting his paws, one at a time, so that they could be dried off. Mutt was very smart. He'd learned that trick within days of being brought home.

He wondered if Mutt's previous owner had done the same. It was a possibility. Seattle was known for its rain and the woman who'd been walking him had seemed the fastidious type. Janice Fiddler had been her name. He'd been unable to transport Janice to his basement guest room, finishing her off in her own basement instead, but she'd provided him with the best of souvenirs.

Mutt was good company.

TWO

Gideon found Rafe Sokolov leaning against the wall outside one of the SacPD interview rooms, waiting for him. Big and blond with a relaxed air that made him appear far younger than he really was, Rafe always looked more like a surfing frat boy than a cop. But few cops were as smart and there was no one on the planet Gideon trusted more.

Rafe gave him a considering look. "Did you talk to Mercy?"

"Yeah. Right after I hung up with you."

"Figured as much. She okay?"

Gideon shrugged. "As okay as she can be."

Rafe opened his mouth to say something, then shook his head.

"What?" Gideon snapped, but felt instant remorse. None of this was Rafe's fault. The man had been there for him when everything had gone to shit. Had helped him pick up the pieces. "Sorry. It's . . ."

"It's okay," Rafe said quietly. "Talking to Mercy messes you up. I get it. I was just going to say that the two of you would benefit from counseling, but I knew you'd say no, so I edited myself."

Gideon nodded, because that was exactly what he would have said. "Where is Miss Dawson?"

Rafe gestured to the closed door. "In there with Erin."

Erin Rhee had been Rafe's partner for the past year. She seemed sharp. Most importantly, she had Rafe's back. "So you two took the case?" Gideon asked.

"Yes."

Gideon eyed him sharply. "Isn't that a conflict of interest?"

Rafe eyed him right back. "Because?" he challenged.

"Because she's 'like a sister'? Your words, not mine."

Rafe waved his hand vaguely. "She's an old family friend."

"That's what you're going with? What about the fact that you're her landlord?"

Rafe scowled. "I was first on the scene."

"Because she called you, didn't she?"

Rafe's scowl deepened. "Right now we're calling it an attempted abduction and assault with a weapon," he said, ignoring Gideon's question, which was answer enough. "We'll investigate the reference to other victims and see what turns up. I wanted you to see this first." He pulled a small evidence bag from his pocket. Inside was the silver locket, and Gideon's questions about Daisy Dawson evaporated. Rafe's eyes softened, his expression concerned, and Gideon realized the real reason for Rafe's insistence.

To protect me. Because he knows this is going to hurt me. Gratitude welled, leaving Gideon without words, but Rafe clearly understood.

"Daisy pulled this off her attacker's neck," Rafe murmured.

Gideon took the small bag and held it up to the light, clenching his jaw against the sudden wave of nausea that swept over him. Yes, he knew this locket. Well, not this exact locket, but . . . Yeah. He'd seen more than his fair share of them. He'd hated them all once he'd grown old enough to understand what they'd represented. Slavery. Possession. Their wearers pawns in a chess game they didn't fully understand until it was too late.

"It's the same design, isn't it? The same one you had tattooed right here?" Rafe tapped his left pectoral. "It's been so long since I've seen it, I wasn't sure."

Yeah, it was the same design. With the exception of the number of branches on the olive tree. The tree on the locket had twelve branches. The tree on his tattoo had thirteen.

It made him want to throw up.

"Gid?" Rafe softly prompted.

Gideon made himself speak, grateful Rafe had allowed him to see the locket in relative privacy. "Yeah." His voice was rough. Rusty. "It's the same." From his pocket he pulled the photograph he'd taken from the wooden box in his living room. Two teenaged boys, one golden, one dark, both shirtless, arms slung over the other's shoulders, grinning happily. The tattoo on Gideon's chest could be clearly seen.

"I remember this," Rafe murmured. "It was my birthday. We went river tubing."

Gideon remembered the day perfectly, one of the nicest Gideon had ever had. Only a month before he'd found Mercy and his life had been forever changed—again. "Yeah," he said hoarsely.

Rafe looked up from the photo. "The design is exactly as I remembered. What can you tell me about the locket?"

"The original owner's name is Miriam." Gideon hoped she was somewhere safe. "She wouldn't have just taken it off and left it somewhere. It was purposefully removed, the chain cut off her." He spoke dispassionately. It was the only way he knew how to talk about it. About *them*. "With bolt cutters."

Rafe's brows lifted. "Excuse me?"

Gideon pointed to the delicate silver chain in the

evidence bag. "This is not the original chain. The locket would have been hanging from a heavier chain that required a lot of strength to break. Strength none of the women had."

"So every woman who had a locket had a similar chain."

"Not just every woman who had a locket. Every woman. They all wore a locket."

Rafe blinked. "Like a . . . what? A symbol of membership?"

"Ownership," Gideon corrected. "The locket sat at the hollow of their throats, but the chain was never long enough for the wearer to pull over her head. It was, however, long enough to be used as a 'teaching tool.'" He said the two words mockingly.

"Teaching tool?"

"Her husband or any of the other men could grab the chain at the back of her neck and pull until she couldn't breathe."

"Why?"

"Because they could," Gideon said flatly. "There was no clasp. It was welded. The wearer would likely have a scar somewhere on her neck."

"A burn?" Rafe asked, looking appropriately horrified. "From the welding?"

"Yes. At least one. Most wearers would have to be refitted as they grew. Links would be added to the chain. Miriam would have received her locket on her twelfth birthday. How many times she had to be refitted depended on how much larger she grew over her lifetime."

"So this is more like the collar that a dom puts on a sub."

Gideon nodded. "Yes. Although it wasn't seen as a kink to the women who wore them. It was more like a wedding ring, although they wore those, too."

"So she got the locket on her twelfth birthday. Do I

want to know at what age she would have gotten the wedding ring?"

Gideon studied the locket so he wouldn't have to look at his friend's expression. "Also on her twelfth birthday."

Rafe drew a breath and let it out carefully. "And the tattoo you used to have?"

Used to. Because he'd had it altered. Had a new tat inked over it, obliterating that particular reminder of his past. "What about it?"

"When did you get it?"

Gideon swallowed hard, pushing the memory away. Not about getting the tattoo itself, but what had followed later that night, after his birthday celebration was over. The night that still haunted his worst nightmares, seventeen years later.

"On my thirteenth birthday."

Rafe looked like he wanted to ask more, so Gideon plowed forward. "Miriam would have been her given name. She might go by a nickname, though."

"Like Mercy?" Rafe asked.

Gideon nodded again, not wanting to think about his sister. Not here. Not in public. Not when he was barely holding on to his composure. "Or Midge or Mir or Mimi." Miriam had been a popular name. There had been a need for many nicknames.

Rafe was quiet for a long moment. "I know you don't like to talk about this."

Gideon chuckled bitterly. "That's the understatement of the century." But he'd forced himself to do so, the first time to the cop who'd come to see him in the hospital, five days after his thirteenth birthday. Four days after his escape. One day after he'd finally regained consciousness. The cop had been kind. Compassionate.

He might have even believed me. Of that, Gideon still was uncertain.

However, he'd never told Rafe. Not even after finding Mercy in foster care, traumatized and scared. He'd been seventeen. She'd been thirteen. He'd known what had put that haunted look in her eyes. He'd understood. And he'd wanted to rage at God, the universe, the man—or, God forbid, men—who'd hurt her.

She'd never talked about it. Not once in all the years since he'd found her. Maybe he should have pushed her.

But he hadn't wanted to push her away. Which happened anyway. Now she lived in New Orleans, two thousand miles and two time zones away. They exchanged Christmas cards and awkward birthday voice mails. He hadn't actually seen her in two years, and that was only because he'd been "just passing through." He hadn't really been. He'd made the trip because he'd specifically wanted to see her, *needed* to see her, to make sure she was okay. It had been the anniversary of her escape and she'd known he'd been lying about "just passing through."

"You know you can talk to me," Rafe said softly. "Anytime."

Staring at the wall over Rafe's shoulder, Gideon forced the words out. "I know." He had talked about it before, in fact. Once he'd joined the FBI, he'd forced himself to tell his first boss about the community, about the abuse. The boss had opened an investigation and several agents had searched the vicinity where the community had been at the time of Gideon's escape. But they'd found nothing, not on foot or by air. Not even by satellite photos.

The community had been gone.

"I've respected your privacy on this since the day we met, but I need to know more about . . . them." He gestured to the locket that Gideon still held aloft. "I'm sorry."

Gideon managed a curt nod. Rafe had never demanded more information than Gideon had been willing to share, but that obviously was about to change and Rafe was not to blame. "I'll tell you. But not here and not on camera." Because it was going to be hard and Gideon didn't want any witnesses to whatever emotions seeped out. It was going to be bad enough just telling Rafe, even though he trusted the man with his life.

Rafe nodded. "Fair enough. Why would Daisy's attacker have had this locket around his neck?"

"That is a very good question. Did you open it?"

Rafe shook his head. "No. I tried, but I couldn't find the mechanism. I figured I'd ask you before I forced it open."

"There's a trick to it." There'd been a trick to everything there. Everything and everyone had hidden behind a facade. He handed the evidence bag to Rafe. "Let's take it to the lab and I'll show you."

"Forensics will be here in"—Rafe checked his watch—"less than a minute to take it to the lab. We can check it out, but I've got to get Daisy's statement first so that she can go home." He looked up at the sound of footsteps. A woman in her midforties approached them, her head tilted in question.

"You done with it?" she asked.

"For now," Rafe told her, giving her the small evidence bag. "Cindy, this is Special Agent Gideon Reynolds. He has some knowledge about the locket and may be consulting with us. Gideon, this is Sergeant Cindy Grimes of the Forensic Investigation Unit."

Gideon shook the woman's offered hand, then watched her as she studied the locket.

She looked up, a sparkle in her eyes. "I love these things."

Gideon's brows rose. "You've seen one before?"

Cindy shook her head. "Not this exact locket, no, but ones with this basic design. There's a trick to the mechanism."

"Can you open it?" Gideon asked.

"Eventually, sure. Do you know how?" She looked a little disappointed, like a kid who'd had her toy taken away.

"I won't spoil it for you. I've never seen one that was booby-trapped, so if you get it wrong, it's not likely to self-destruct."

She made a face. "The responsible thing to do would be to just open it. Show me," she said with a put-upon sigh.

Gideon pointed to the two children kneeling in prayer. "Push the boy first, then the girl. Then the angel. It should pop right open."

Cindy met his gaze, hers sharp and discerning. "Patriarchal religious movement?"

Gideon blinked. "Yes. How did you know?"

"Olive tree and an angel. People praying. Boy first? That's not a hard puzzle." She gave Rafe a hard nod. "I'll let you know if I find anything inside."

"Thanks, Cindy." Rafe waited until she was gone, then pointed to the interview room door where Daisy Dawson was waiting. "You want to join me?"

Gideon didn't really. But then he remembered that the Dawson woman's attacker had said, *They all do.* If they had a serial rapist or killer on their hands, he wanted to know. And if he could aid in the investigation in any way, he'd ask his boss to lend him to SacPD first thing in the morning. No matter how uncomfortable it made him. Because deep down he doubted that Miriam the locket owner really was okay. That she'd willingly handed the locket over to . . . anyone. He doubted she'd have had the inner strength.

Mercy hadn't, after all, and she was the strongest woman he knew. Mercy had escaped with her life but still hung on to that little piece of silver. Not because it brought back good memories, because it most certainly did not.

The locket had power. Not the power they had

claimed, of course, but it held power all the same. He hoped he was wrong, that Miriam did have the strength to have tossed the locket into the nearest dumpster, that Daisy Dawson's attacker had just happened upon it, but his gut didn't believe it. And Gideon trusted his gut.

He squared his shoulders. "Sure. Lead the way." He followed Rafe through the doorway of the interview room and . . . just stopped.

Stopped walking. Stopped breathing. Stopped thinking about lockets and Mercy and women named Miriam.

Because Irina Sokolov was wrong. The woman sitting at the table next to Detective Rhee was . . . not cute. Nor was she little. She was . . . *Wow.*

A soft pink cashmere turtleneck sweater molded to wicked curves, cupping breasts that were the perfect size for a lover's hands. Blond hair hung past her shoulders in loose waves, framing a face that was too wholesome, too pretty, despite a slightly red nose and swollen eyes. Eyes that caught his attention. Blue. Like the sky on a beautiful day.

Those eyes widened in a moment of surprised recognition, spurring his feet to move. She abruptly schooled her features as he approached her side of the table, one blond brow arching. "So you are the *esteemed* Special Agent Gideon Reynolds," she said dryly, and he had to fight a shiver because her voice was husky. Sexy. And strangely familiar.

"Irina has shown me more photos of you than all of her children put together," she went on before he could place where he'd heard her voice. "I've heard a lot about you."

Smiling politely, she rose with a grace that belied any residual pain from her attack. She was so composed, so poised, that he might have believed nothing had happened at all.

Except that her face still bore evidence of recent tears. And her hand trembled ever so slightly as she extended it for him to shake. Miss Dawson wasn't as cool and collected as she wanted to appear. But she was faking it well and Gideon respected the hell out of that.

"Yes, I'm Gideon," he said, relieved his voice didn't crack like a teenager's, even though he oddly felt that nervous. He took her offered hand, giving it a gentle squeeze. Her skin was too cold, he thought, resisting the urge to sandwich her hand between his own, letting her go instead. "'Esteemed' is a bit of a stretch, though," he added, trying to return her smile but suspecting he'd come up short. He had never been good at faking a smile. "It's nice to finally meet you. I wish it were under better circumstances."

Her polite smile faltered and she flicked her gaze to Rafe. "True enough. I'm going to assume you aren't doing your mother's bidding and arranging a setup because that would be completely unprofessional, which you are not. So why is he here?"

"He's here to help me with the case," Rafe said, which was actually true.

Daisy frowned. "He's federal." Then her eyes widened again, this time in dismay. "Oh my God. He said they all begged forgiveness." She looked up at Gideon, true despair written all over her face. "Are there others? Are you here because there are other victims?"

Gideon found himself needing to soothe her, the words escaping his mouth before he'd thought twice about any repercussions. "I don't know. I'm here because of the locket."

SACRAMENTO, CALIFORNIA
THURSDAY, FEBRUARY 16, 10:50 P.M.

Daisy stilled, blinking up at him. His startlingly green gaze was fixed on her face, his expression kind. Sympathetic. His voice soft and comforting.

And then his words made it through the haze in her head. *Wait. What?* She'd assumed a federal agent was there because her attacker really was a serial rapist. Or killer. Because Daisy had certainly felt her life flashing before her eyes in the moments before muscle memory had taken over her movements. "The locket? The one he was wearing?"

She clamped her jaw tight, holding back the next words because she didn't want to hear them out loud. Words that nevertheless screamed through her mind. *The one I ripped off his throat when he was trying to choke me to death?*

Gideon nodded cautiously, having no doubt noted her tension because he was watching her through eyes that narrowed. "Yes."

Forcing herself to relax, she tilted her head to one side, watching him back. Studying his face. His very handsome face. He was far younger than he'd appeared when he'd first come through the doorway. It was the threads of silver in his crisp black hair that had her forgetting for just a moment that he'd gone to school with Rafe, so they were of a similar age. Thirty, plus or minus a year.

There was something here, she thought. Something in the set of his mouth, framed by a neatly trimmed goatee, which was also threaded with silver. Something . . . personal.

"Why?" she asked. "What's so special about the locket?"

Other than that it was a delicate thing worn by a brute. Other than the fact it said *Miriam*. Other than that he'd rasped *They all do* in her ear as he'd dragged her into the alley.

Curiosity prickled across her skin. Or perhaps that was awareness because Gideon Reynolds was still staring at her with an intensity that left her trembling inside.

Daisy didn't like that. *It's curiosity. Nothing more.*

Go on thinking that if it makes you feel better, the snide voice whispered in her mind.

Yes. Yes, it does, she answered back. Firmly, because the snide voice had to be nipped in the bud. It was the same voice that tempted her to have "just a taste" when her anxiety started to overwhelm her. Like right now. *Just a little taste. Beer. A sip of beer wouldn't be so bad, would it? One little beer?*

No. She gritted her teeth. *Nip it in the bud.*

He hadn't answered her, she realized. He was still watching her and she wondered how much of that little internal chat had been broadcasted from her expression.

"Well?" she pressed. "Why is the locket special?"

A throat clearing had her turning around to where Rafe's partner, Erin, sat waiting patiently. "Let's get your statement, Daisy," Erin said levelly, and Daisy didn't miss the flicker of gratitude in Rafe's eyes. Evidently Agent Reynolds had made a bit of a slip.

So she'd focus on that. On the locket. On the mystery. Not on the fact that tonight was her father's worst nightmare coming to life and that he'd probably be on the next flight to Sacramento as soon as he found out. *Fan-fucking-tastic.*

Daisy gave them a terse nod and retook her seat next to where her bag sat on the tabletop, Brutus nestled comfortably inside. She could hear the dog's gentle snores if she listened hard enough. It grounded her.

Rafe and Gideon took their seats, Gideon on her right and Rafe on the other side of the table. Erin Rhee was still on her left, having not moved since Rafe had stepped out, saying he'd had to make a call. Which had presumably been to Gideon Reynolds.

Because of the locket. Her skin quivering with nervous energy, Daisy reached into her bag, giving Brutus a gentle stroke before withdrawing an emery board from one of the inside pockets. "They clipped my nails in the ER," she said, filing away the sharp edges of her newly cut nails. Because she'd scratched her attacker as she'd managed to escape.

"They'll grow back," Rafe said soothingly.

"I don't think I want them to. They got in the way tonight. My nails, I mean. I did a joint lock on his hand but my thumbnail was so long that it kept me from digging in as deep as I needed to, to incapacitate him. I could be dead because I'd had a mani-pedi," she added lightly.

She needed to stop talking. Her nerves were showing. *Focus on the story. On Gideon Reynolds's face. On anything that's not the memory of* his *arm across your throat.*

"*You* did a joint lock?" Gideon asked carefully, his doubt evident.

Meeting his eyes, she nodded. "Yes, *I* did. Want me to demonstrate?"

Gideon shook his head quickly, seeming unsure if she was serious or not. "No. That won't be necessary."

Rafe bit back a smile. "No, it's really not. She could take either one of us down. It's true," he declared when Gideon gave him a disbelieving stare. "She 'demonstrated' on me when I questioned her ability to defend herself. Not that you ever should have needed to, Daisy." Sober now, he pressed a button on a remote that turned on the video recorder. "Today is Thursday, February sixteenth. It is ten fifty-six. I am Detective Raphael Sokolov. With me are Detective Erin Rhee, Special Agent Gideon Reynolds, and Eleanor Marie Dawson, also known as Daisy. We are here to take Miss Dawson's statement."

Daisy gave Rafe a dirty look. She hated her first name and he knew it. "Thank you for that."

Rafe's expression remained sober, but his dark eyes softened. "What happened tonight?" he asked gently.

Daisy drew a shaky breath. "Where should I start?"

"Wherever you'd like," Erin said. "If we need you to back up, we'll let you know."

"All right." She set the emery board aside. Folded her hands on the table. Then gave up and stuck her hand back into her bag, stroking Brutus's fuzzy ears because her anxiety was clawing at her from the inside out. She did not want to talk about this again. "My friend Trish Hart and I were leaving the community center on J Street, walking toward the Forty-niner Diner." Abruptly she turned to Erin Rhee. "Did Trish get home okay?"

"She did," Erin promised. "I walked her to her door myself and waited until she was safely inside."

"Thank you," Daisy whispered. Trish had been so shaken up, crying with her in the ER until Irina and Karl had arrived to stand vigil. Daisy had insisted Trish go home because hospitals were one of her friend's triggers, threatening her sobriety.

Erin's smile was steady. "You're welcome."

Daisy forced herself to continue, just wanting this part over with. "Trish and I walk to the diner every week." She glanced up at the camera on the wall. *Fuck it,* she thought. Straightening her shoulders, she lifted her chin. "We attend AA on Thursday nights."

Gideon's eyes widened, but he met her gaze evenly when she wordlessly dared him to say a word in judgment. He gave her a steady nod, and that it left her feeling settled inside shouldn't have been a thing. But it was.

"I felt someone following me a few minutes after we started walking," she went on. "Just a tickle at the back of my neck." She shrugged. "I thought it was someone my dad had hired. I never considered someone was actually stalking me."

Gideon's brows rose. "Why would you think your father would have you followed?"

"Because he's done it before," she answered truthfully. "He . . . worries about me." She considered her words, then realized she didn't care. She wasn't hiding anything because she had nothing to be ashamed of.

Keep on telling yourself that if it makes you feel better, honey.

Shut the ever-loving-fuck up.

"My father didn't see the signs of my alcoholism until my sister brought it to his attention. By then, I was pretty fucked up." She glanced up at the camera again, then flicked her gaze to Rafe. "Can I say 'fucked up'?"

Rafe smiled at her. "You can if you want."

"All right, then. I was fucked up. And I had to go to rehab. After that, he watched me like a hawk. Had our ranch hand follow me around everywhere. Back then it was because we were afraid and in hiding."

Gideon's brows shot up higher, scrunching his forehead. "In hiding? Why?"

Why? The question honestly surprised her. "You don't know, Agent Reynolds?" She gave Rafe a side-eye. "I thought your mother would have told him already." The woman had been trying to push them together for months now.

You must meet him, Irina would say in her brusque way, her accent thick, but her sweet nature abundantly clear in the smile that was always on her face. *He's a good man. Handsome, too,* she'd add slyly. Then she'd regale Daisy with stories of when Rafe and Gideon were boys in school, always ending with a frank appraisal. *He'd be good for you, dochka. Let me give him your phone number.* Which Daisy had always politely declined, even though hearing Irina calling her "daughter" always made her feel so safe and included that she'd almost wanted to comply.

"My mother is actually very good at keeping secrets," Rafe said.

Good to know. Irina had gotten the handsome part

right, at least. With his perfectly combed hair and perfectly pressed blue suit that sat perfectly on broad
shoulders, not to mention his perfect face, Gideon
Reynolds could have walked out of a men's fashion ad.
Hopefully he was not only a good man but discreet as
well, because if he didn't know her life story before, he
was about to.

"You want me to tell the whole sordid tale for the
record?" she asked lightly, because she hated this part,
too. Hated airing her family's very dirty laundry. Not
that it would be the first time, but still.

"Maybe just give us the *Reader's Digest* version,"
Rafe suggested.

Her lips twitched, which she suspected was Rafe's
intent. "Okay. I can do that. My father was convinced
that my stepmother's ex-husband was stalking her so
that he could kidnap their child—my stepsister, Taylor.
Dad moved us all up past Eureka and bought a ranch.
All through shell corporations, because he's cagey that
way. He taught us how to shoot and defend ourselves
in case Taylor's biological father came to take her
away. We lived in isolation for twelve years, doing
drills every day like some kind of mini-paramilitary
squad. And then my stepmother died. On her deathbed, she confessed to Taylor that she'd lied about the
whole thing. Her ex had never stalked her, had never
threatened her or Taylor. It had all been a lie. We lost
our adolescence because of a lie."

"And then?" Gideon prompted.

Daisy realized she'd been staring at the wall. Remembering those final days, Donna so emaciated, the
cancer having eaten her up. Taylor had been heartbro-
ken. So had her father. *So was I.* Until they'd learned
what Donna had done to them all. And then Daisy had
hated her with the power of a thousand suns. But it had
been too late. The woman was gone, leaving them all
broken and confused.

It had been three years since Donna's death and eighteen months since they'd learned the truth, but they were finally regaining their lives. Regaining themselves.

She shrugged. "My father felt like shit because he'd believed Donna—she was Taylor's mother. He'd hidden Taylor away from a very good man for all those years because of my stepmother's lies. But then there was no reason to hide anymore. Dad moved to Maryland to live near Taylor and her bio-dad and took our youngest sister with him. Taylor's engaged now, to a really nice guy. My sister Julie is getting the support she needs. She has cerebral palsy," she added, then smiled, remembering the happiness on her sister's face when they'd Skyped a few days ago. "Jules has a boyfriend now. And my father is even dating. I'm happy for them."

"But?" Gideon prompted.

"But I wanted to see the world. So I did. I backpacked across Europe. I was supposed to be gone for six months, but around about month four I realized I was being followed. It was Jacob, the ranch hand who'd grown up with us. My father had paid him to keep an eye on me. And report back. Was I behaving myself? Was I drinking at all?" She sighed heavily. "I know Dad wanted me to be safe, but it pissed me the hell off. So I went home and . . ." She hesitated, because this part of the story was not hers to tell. It was painful and personal and it broke her heart every time she thought about it.

Her eyes burned with tears that she refused to shed because she'd already cried too much for one evening. She scooped Brutus from her bag and, ignoring Gideon's look of perplexed surprise, cuddled her dog under her chin. "My father has his reasons for being obsessive about my safety. But even though I now understand, it's not okay. So I made him promise never to do that again. I didn't really think he'd keep that promise, so when I heard the man behind us tonight, I didn't think twice."

"What did you do?" Gideon asked softly.

She shot him a sharp glare because he was looking at her with pity. *I am not fragile,* she wanted to shout, but bit the words back, answering him in as even a tone as she could muster. "I sent Trish ahead to the diner and I hid, waited for him, then confronted him. Pulled his cap off. He was about six feet tall, by the way. I didn't have to jump up as high to rip the baseball cap off his head as I would for Jacob, who's six-two."

"We found the cap at the scene," Erin said. "It's in the lab for processing. What did he look like?"

"He had dark eyes and no hair." Daisy clenched her jaw, powering through the memory before it could pull her under. "I can't say what his features were because he had a nylon stocking pulled over his head. He was a smoker. I smelled it on his jacket and on his breath. He kept his voice all low and raspy. Like he was trying to whisper loudly. But that wasn't his normal voice. He wore gloves." She frowned. "And black wingtips. With stonewashed jeans." She made a face, sloughing off the mental image of his lower body, all she'd been able to see as he'd dragged her away. "Very bad form."

"No hair just on his head?" Rafe asked. "Did he have eyebrows?"

She thought a moment, forcing herself to picture his features, smashed against the nylon. "No. I don't think he did."

"How much did he weigh?" Gideon asked, and that he'd asked her in all seriousness was a balm to her raw emotions. He had confidence in her observations. Again, it shouldn't have been so settling, but it was, and Daisy was grateful for it.

"About two hundred pounds. He was solid. I don't know if he'd been trained to fight, but he was very comfortable with his movements." Like when he'd tried to choke her with his forearm.

That was the memory that lingered.

Gideon tapped the table to get her attention, but it was actually the scent of his aftershave that reached through her haze. *Because I zoned out again.* She blinked to clear her vision and found him entirely too close. His gaze roamed her face looking for something, which he must have found because he leaned back in his chair.

"And then?" he asked.

"He put his forearm over my throat." She lowered Brutus to her lap, then tugged at the collar of her turtleneck sweater and tilted her head back to expose her throat to the camera. She knew her throat was red and bruised. The bruises would be purple tomorrow. "I'm glad I have a lot of turtlenecks. I'll be wearing them to work for a while."

She righted her collar, then missed a breath at the sight of Gideon's face. His eyes had gone steely hard and a muscle was ticking in his cheek. But he merely nodded.

"He put a gun to my head and that's when he said I'd be sorry for what I did, that I'd beg for his forgiveness." She wasn't able to fight her shudder. "That they all did."

"What do you think he meant, Daisy?" Erin asked quietly. "What do you think he wanted you to be sorry for?"

Daisy shrugged helplessly. "I don't know. Grabbing his hat? Exposing his face?"

"All right," Erin said, then smiled encouragingly. "You're doing great. And then?"

"I . . . I went into autopilot mode, I guess. I bent the pinkie of his gun hand—" She paused. "He was a leftie. Held his gun in his left hand, anyway."

Again Erin smiled. "Good, Daisy. And what happened when you bent his pinkie?"

"I bent it back and used a joint lock. Here." Daisy

pointed to the fleshy area between her thumb and fore-finger. "If I hadn't had such long nails, I could have gotten a better hold. I could have had him on his knees."

Gideon looked unconvinced. Even though he said nothing, Daisy was pissed off.

"Again," she offered sweetly, "I'm happy to demonstrate."

She'd made her point and he had the courtesy to look embarrassed. "Again," he returned, "that's not necessary."

But it would feel awfully satisfying, she thought, still irritated. "I ran, but he caught me." She drew another breath, deeper than she actually needed, just to remind herself that she could. "He shoved me against a wall and used his forearm against my throat again. That's when I grabbed the chain around his neck. I hadn't even seen it. I was grappling for his coat, something to yank him closer. So that I could knee him in the testicles. Which I then did. Hard."

Neither Rafe nor Gideon winced, to their credit. But they did look awfully uncomfortable. It made her feel a little better.

"I ran again and this time Trish was waiting for me. She hadn't wanted to leave me alone with the man I thought was Jacob. She got a half a block away, then turned around and came back to find me. She said she heard Brutus barking and saw me run out of the alley." Daisy closed her eyes, her heart racing too hard. "If she hadn't been there, he might have caught me again. I'm not sure I'd have had the energy to fight him anymore."

No one said anything, but when she opened her eyes, she found all three of them watching her with both concern and respect. That made her feel much better. "Trish started screaming for help, I guess. Before I knew it, a few people had gathered around. I guess the man took off running. Trish called 911

and . . ." She looked at Rafe. "Then you. That's all."
She let her gaze drop to Brutus in her lap, remembering his barking.

She looked up sharply. "He liked dogs, I think."

Rafe had been about to press the power button on
the video remote, but set it back down on the table.
"How do you know?"

"When he was holding me against the brick wall,
with his arm . . . you know."

"Choking you," Gideon supplied tensely.

Daisy swallowed, even though it still hurt to do so.
"Yes. He said I was too much trouble and he was going
to shoot. But Brutus kept barking. He . . ." She searched
her mind. "He asked where that 'fucking dog' was, and
when he realized Brutus was in my purse, he rolled his
eyes. Then he pointed the gun at Brutus. But he didn't
shoot right away. For a second he kind of froze. I went
for his collar and jostled him enough that his aim was
off and he shot the bricks instead of Brutus." She
frowned. "He had a silencer."

"Good to know," Rafe said. "And then?"

"Then I kneed him. And grabbed the locket." *Ah.
Right. The locket.* She narrowed her eyes at Gideon,
who studied her, visibly tense. "Why is the locket so
important?"

Gideon opened his mouth to answer, but before any
words came out, Brutus looked around and barked.

THREE

He jogged up the two steps to his front porch, his body warm and his muscles finally loose. He'd run extra fast, trying to tire himself out. Mutt had not been a fan. He'd had to pull him along the last two blocks. Opening the door, he unhooked the leash and the dog walked over to his bed in the corner, huffing as he threw himself down on it.

"Lazy," he said to the dog.

Mutt didn't respond.

He liked that. He could say whatever he wanted to the dog and always got the final word. Mutt never tried to usurp him. The dog knew his place.

His phone buzzed in his pocket, the fourth time it had done so in the past thirty minutes. Gritting his teeth, he checked the caller ID.

Sydney. All four times.

"I hate you," he hissed, not completely sure if he meant Sydney for being a complete and total asshole or himself for always answering the phone. Schooling his expression, he calmed his voice. He'd answer her call. He always did.

"Sydney," he said levelly.

"Sonny. You were ignoring me."

He could hear the pout she thought was cute. But it wasn't. He hated the pout, too.

"I was running. I just got back." *And I hoped you'd give up and go to sleep.*

But she never gave up. She considered it a strength. He did not agree.

"What do you want?" he asked, more tersely than he'd intended.

"I'm calling to check on you," she said. "I hear you got unsettling news today."

He ground his teeth. "That the old man is selling the company out from under me?"

"You shouldn't talk about your father that way, Sonny," she said, her voice heavy with reproach.

Don't call me Sonny! he wanted to scream, but did not. Because he didn't scream at his stepmother, either.

Don't call him my father! he wanted to shout. Because his "father" had never been anything more than a sperm donor. He'd never been there, working all the time, leaving the raising of his son to babysitters. And then to Sydney.

The old man hadn't cared about anyone but himself. Because any *real* father would have realized that the sex-kitten trophy wife he'd married was really a monster who was destroying his son. Bit by bit. Year after year.

But he didn't say any of those things, either. What he did say was what she'd trained him to say. Trained him like a little dog. "I'm sorry, Sydney."

"That's my sweet boy," she cooed. "Are you worried about your job?"

Hell, yes. He leaned against his front door. "Shouldn't I be?" *Dammit. Do not engage with her.* He wanted to yank the words back as soon as he'd said them, but it was too late.

"Of course not."

He ground his teeth. "The old man's trained dog said the new owners are cleaning house and we're *all* going. He looked straight at me when he said those words. So yes, pardon me if I'm a little worried."

She clucked her tongue. "Silly boy. I've got an in with the new owner."

Which meant she was sleeping with the new owner, too. Sydney could have sex with anyone she pleased, while she expected him to have sex with only her.

And, despite his most determined attempts at any kind of sex with anyone else who wasn't Sydney, that was exactly the way it was. He was so fucking broken that he couldn't get it up for anyone else. And she knew it. *The bitch.* But he didn't say that.

"That's good," he said lamely. "I'm glad."

"You know that I've got your back, Sonny. Stick with me and you'll be fine."

Stick with me. In other words, obey her every command. Every single one. And he would, much to his own shame, even though it tore him up to do so.

"I know," he said dully. "You'll take care of me." Which he'd never wanted her to do. Not even once.

"Of course I will, Sonny, dear. I *should* have been taking care of you *tonight.*"

He winced because he'd forgotten. Deliberately. "I'm sorry, Sydney. I just . . . I needed time to process what happened today." He'd needed to grab a guest for his basement.

"And exactly *where* were you processing? A bar?"

Yes, dammit. He was twenty-eight years old. Not a child. He could go to any bar he chose. But he could never say such a thing to her. "No. Of course not. Look, I really need to go to sleep. I have an early morning."

"I see."

He clenched his free hand into a fist. That icy tone of hers never boded well. "G-g-good night, Sydney."

"Good night, Sonny. Sweet dreams."

He swallowed hard as he ended the call. *Sweet*

dreams. How many times had she whispered those words into his ear as he was falling asleep, feeling so damn confused? He didn't know. He'd stopped counting long ago.

Stomach churning, he stumbled to his bedroom and sank to his knees in front of his stereo. It had been his mother's. His real mother's. The mother who'd loved him and rocked him to sleep and who'd never said *Sweet dreams* in that oily whisper.

The stereo was one of the few things of his mother's he'd been allowed to hold on to. The turntable, the speakers, and a stack of old LPs. Her favorite was on the spindle, ready to be played. It always soothed him, especially when he had an empty basement and for whatever reason needed to wait to fill it. *Like tonight.*

Carefully he lifted the arm, setting the needle at the beginning, then twisted until he was sitting with his back to his bed, his legs crossed. He lit a cigarette and took a deep drag. Sydney didn't like it when he smoked. So of course he did it. Just not where she could see.

He frowned at the pack in his hand, now empty. He'd had half a pack this morning. Yeah, he'd smoked a few while waiting outside the community center, but he hadn't thought he'd smoked *nine*. He usually only allowed himself one per day. He wondered where he'd left the butts. *Great. More of my DNA out there.*

But he wasn't here to worry. He was here to relax. Closing his eyes, he listened to the opening drums of "Copacabana" and remembered his mother dancing with him, her smile wide and just for him as Manilow sang about a showgirl named Lola. He never realized that the song was really about a murder until much later, long after his mother was gone. Not until Sydney had pointed it out, deriding his mother for allowing him to listen to it.

Right before she'd slipped from his bed and whispered, *Sweet dreams.*

He'd known Sydney's ways by then. She would have destroyed the albums while he slept, so he'd hidden them where she'd never find them, not daring to listen to them again until he'd bought this place of his own.

Mine. My home. A place where Sydney had *never* been welcomed.

SACRAMENTO, CALIFORNIA
THURSDAY, FEBRUARY 16, 11:10 P.M.

Why is the locket so important?

Gideon had almost answered Daisy's question. Almost. Luckily that little dog had broken the moment. *Broken the spell.* Which sounded ridiculously dramatic when Gideon was normally anything but.

He forced himself to relax, shifting his gaze away from her face to the ball of fur in her arms. The dog was tiny, possibly ten pounds, if that. And named Brutus. Under other circumstances that would have made him smile. When few things did.

Brutus had the coloring of a collie and the ears of a bat, huge and pointy and covered with fringy hair that stuck straight out. He couldn't decide if the dog was ugly or cute.

Didn't really matter. What *did* matter was that the dog had intervened, stopping him from blurting out a truth that was not appropriate to share.

Isn't it, though? Hasn't she earned it?

No, he told himself firmly. Yes, she'd fought bravely. Shockingly capably, even. Yes, she'd shared everything with them openly, more even than she had strictly needed to. But that did not entitle her to know more. Not about this. *Not about me.*

"I have a few more questions about the man who attacked you," he said instead.

The flash of disappointment in her blue eyes was

unmistakable. As was the glint of determination that followed. She wouldn't be letting the subject of the locket go without a fight. "Okay." She was back to stroking the little dog. "Go ahead."

"Did he have any physical characteristics that stand out in your mind? Any scars that were visible through the nylon, perhaps?"

She shook her head. "No. None that I could see."

"What about on his body? Any markings? Tattoos?"

Her brow arched. "Tattoos? Not that I saw. I didn't see any of his skin. He wore a padded jacket. Like a ski jacket. It must have been open at the throat because I was able to reach the chain around his neck." She stared at the hand that petted the dog and frowned, running her thumb over the pads of her fingers. "I didn't feel any chest hair when I touched him. When I scratched him."

Gideon hoped she'd hurt him. Badly. He hoped the skin they'd scraped from under her nails led to a DNA match. He hoped that the man's balls still ached all these hours later.

"Did your father teach you to fight like that?" he asked, startling himself because it wasn't the question he'd intended to ask.

She looked up at him, blinked once, then nodded. "He'll be annoyed that I didn't take the bastard to his knees. When he finds out." She looked at Rafe. "I don't suppose your mother can keep *that* secret from him. Can she?" she added hopefully.

Rafe ruefully shook his head. "I think she called him on her way to the ER."

"So he'll be here tomorrow," she said with a sigh. "Fabulous."

Erin Rhee had gone still. The woman was normally quiet, although she could move incredibly fast when she needed to, according to Rafe. But most of the time she had this unflappable calm that was kind of eerie. At this moment, though, she was ominously still.

"What will he do when he gets here?" she asked Daisy, and her subtext was loud and clear even though he'd had to strain to hear her voice.

Daisy must have heard it, too, because she turned to Erin with a smile. "Nothing bad. He never, ever physically hurt us. Ever. He'll just . . . fuss over me. And then he'll insist I move to Maryland to live near him. And when I refuse, he'll hire Jacob to follow me again."

Erin nodded once. "All right. I just needed to make sure."

"And I appreciate it," Daisy said, reaching over to pat the detective's arm. "I really do. But you don't need to worry about my father. Or me."

Erin's smile was wry. "Considering that you're here, we do have to worry about you, wouldn't you say?"

Daisy frowned. "Yeah, I guess that's true." She turned to Gideon, that curious glint back in her eye, and he knew she was about to ask him about the locket again.

So he deflected. "We'll need Jacob's last name and phone number so that we can verify where he was tonight, since he's followed you in the past."

"His last name is Fogarty and his number's in my phone. Last time I saw him, he was headed back to his parents' ranch up past Weaverville. That was months ago, though."

Gideon nodded. "What about work? Any issues there?"

He'd expected her to say no. He hadn't expected her to drop her gaze back to the dog. He hadn't expected her to draw a breath before looking up at Rafe, a guilty expression on her face.

"I didn't think it was important," she whispered.

Rafe's confused gaze flicked from Gideon to Erin,

then back to Daisy. "You didn't think what was important?" he asked carefully.

Daisy was stroking the dog so fiercely it was a wonder the poor thing had any hair left. "I've gotten a few calls," she admitted. "And e-mails. Tad said to ignore them. That he gets stuff like that all the time. I was handling it."

"Who is Tad?" Gideon asked.

"And what kind of stuff?" Erin added.

"Tad is my cohost," Daisy said. "At the radio station. KZAU. I work the morning show—you know, *The Big Bang with TNT*. That's Tad."

Oh. Now Gideon remembered where he'd heard her voice. He listened to *The Big Bang with TNT* on his way to work every morning. Mostly because of their new DJ. Which would be Daisy. Except she didn't go by that name on the air. "You're Poppy Frederick."

"That would be me," she said. "My father's name is Frederick. His pet name for my mom was Poppy."

That made sense. Rafe's father, Karl, owned a number of businesses, most of them making money hand over fist. The radio station was the exception. Gideon knew it was perpetually in the red because Irina was always chiding Karl to sell it. Then the two would smile at each other because they knew Karl never would. It had been his first business and where he'd met Irina.

KZAU held sentimental value, pure and simple. That Daisy worked there was no surprise. Irina had told Gideon this when she'd first started singing him the praises of the "cute little blonde," the daughter of one of Karl's oldest friends.

Karl gave jobs to a lot of people starting out. Gideon's first paycheck had come from Karl Sokolov's radio station, as a matter of fact, and for that he'd always be grateful. That Daisy worked the morning show was a bit of a surprise, however.

"I thought you did sales," Gideon said, because that was what Irina had told him.

"I did at first. But . . ." She shrugged. "Right place, right time."

"Not true," Rafe said. "Daisy was doing the vocals for some of the ads and the station manager liked what he heard. The old cohost had to take emergency sick leave about three months ago and Daisy's been filling in. Ratings have never been higher."

He didn't doubt it. He'd tuned in just to hear her more mornings than he cared to admit. Her husky, sexy voice was perfect for radio. That she'd garnered unwanted attention was an unpleasant corollary.

"What kind of calls and e-mails?" Gideon asked.

Another shrug. "Just the normal, I guess. 'You make me hot. You sound so sexy. Let me take you home with me. Meet me for drinks.'" She rattled them off quickly, her cheeks growing flushed. "Some were a bit more explicit."

Gideon had to bite his tongue against a sudden surge of fury. He had no reason to be so angry on her behalf. She was nothing to him, just an acquaintance. Still, no one deserved to be the recipient of sexual harassment. Daisy had not initiated any of it. The morning show was not sexual in any way. It was drive-time morning banter, family friendly. Karl insisted on it.

Gideon blinked, abruptly appalled at himself. Daisy hadn't deserved any of this. Even if she'd told dirty jokes, acted the part of a sex vamp on air, or even shown up stark naked for events, she wouldn't have deserved any of the suggestive calls or e-mails.

Of course, the mental picture of her stark naked sent his mind in an entirely different direction, and he quickly tamped it down. *Not now.* Not now? *What's wrong with me?*

"Why didn't you tell the station manager?" Rafe asked, clearly biting back his own anger. "I'm not mad at you, Daisy. You get that, right? It's just that we could have helped."

"I get it. I do. But Tad said that everyone gets e-mails like that. The really explicit ones came and went. If they'd been steady or grew threatening, I would have told the manager. I was handling it. Or I thought I was." She bit at her lip. "I didn't put the e-mails together with what happened tonight. The man said, 'They all do.' I figured I was one of many, that tonight was a random thing. But . . . maybe it's not." She pointed to her cell phone on the table next to her enormous handbag. "I saved the e-mails and the voice mails. The e-mails came to my account at the station but I can access that on my phone."

"The calls came to your cell phone?" Gideon asked, his own anger reemerging. "How did they get your number?"

"Wouldn't be that hard," she murmured. "I do events at a lot of the places where I've been volunteering for six months—long before I got the morning show. All of those places have my cell number. I imagine someone was either tricked or convinced to give it out."

"That changes tomorrow," Erin said grimly. "New cell phone. Nobody has the number but us. And your family."

Daisy's expression was glum. "I already figured that."

"We'll also check your phone for tracking software," Rafe said. "It could have been embedded in any of the e-mails."

"I never clicked on an attachment." She drew herself up, her frown more than irritated. "I'm not stupid, Rafe."

Rafe's voice was even when he replied. "Never said you were. But I'm going to make sure that nobody has been able to track you using your phone. And I'll be having a talk with *Tad* about what kinds of e-mails are reportable."

"Good luck with that," Daisy muttered.

Clearly Tad was not a cooperative coworker. Gideon filed that away for later inquiry. "Who had your number?" he asked now. "Where do you volunteer?"

Rafe smiled good-naturedly. "Where doesn't she?"

Daisy's chin lifted and, to Gideon's surprise, anger sparked in her eyes. "I do a lot of work for local charities," she said coolly. "For reasons of my own."

Rafe held up his hands in surrender. "I'm not saying you shouldn't. It's just a lot."

"I have a lot of time to make up for," she said quietly, her anger softening to something Gideon couldn't identify. "And amends to make."

"It's a twelve-step thing?" Erin asked, respect in her tone.

"Partly. It also keeps me too busy to want a drink. But mostly because I don't yet know what I want to do. So I'm doing it all."

Gideon wondered if those were all of her reasons or just the tip of the iceberg. Daisy Dawson had layers he hadn't expected.

"Where do you volunteer?" he asked again, his pen poised and ready to make a list.

"The animal shelter, especially on adoption days. I got Brutus at a shelter." She lifted the dog, dropping a kiss between her enormous ears, and Gideon found himself envious of the ridiculous animal. "I also work at the cerebral palsy rec center and at a few of the local nursing homes. I've done some fund-raising for a veterans' group. Multiple good causes there." A shadow flickered across her face, but she forced a cheerful smile. "And the radio station is sponsoring a 5K run for leukemia research, which I'm in charge of."

Gideon stowed his question about the veterans' group for another time. "I'm running that 5K."

She arched a brow. "So am I. I bet I beat your time."

He chuckled. "You're on." Then he sobered. "Someone at all of these places has your cell phone number?"

"Probably several someones, most of whom wouldn't think twice about passing it on, especially if the person asking for it claimed to need me to do something for the community."

That wasn't going to help at all. He looked at Rafe with a frown. "Detective Sokolov, will you be able to trace the e-mails and phone messages?"

Rafe nodded. "We'll certainly try."

Daisy pushed her phone across the table to Rafe. "Can I get it back later? Just to copy my contacts list and calendar?"

"You don't use the cloud?" Erin asked.

Daisy snorted, but it was a soft sound. "No. There's enough of my father's paranoia left in me to nix that idea. Never store your information anywhere you don't have total control of. I have no idea who controls the cloud."

"Nobody does," Erin murmured, but her lips twitched a little, making Daisy's do the same. "What about Tad? Mr. TNT himself?"

Daisy blinked. "Well, Tad isn't . . . mean. Exactly. He never lets me forget that I got my job because I know the boss. Which isn't one hundred percent true, because I do have a degree in journalism. He never does it on the air, but . . . yeah. I'd say he's just determined I know my place. Which is behind him, wherever he happens to be."

A degree in journalism? That explained the gleam of curiosity. Gideon suspected she'd sunk her teeth into finding out more about the locket and was biding her time.

"Has he ever expressed an interest in you that you considered sexually harassing?" Erin asked.

Daisy's cheeks flushed once more. "Not really. It's

usually just a compliment on my clothes or my hair. He makes it sound friendly, so I didn't think anything about it. A few times he's asked if I was free for lunch. I keep telling him no. I don't particularly like him, to be honest. But he's never been blatantly inappropriate or even hinted at the kind of violence I saw tonight."

Erin nodded like this satisfied her, but Gideon wasn't happy with that at all. Tad sounded like a condescending jackass who needed to be taken down a few notches.

"What about your neighborhood?" Erin asked. "Any trouble?"

Daisy looked amused at the question. "Only when Sasha drinks too much and comes home singing at the top of her lungs. I rent from Rafe," she explained.

Gideon knew that. Rafe had bought out his siblings' share in the Midtown Victorian they'd all inherited from one of their grandparents. He'd gone on to completely renovate it, creating three apartments. Rafe lived on the third floor and rented the second to his sister Sasha. Daisy would be renting the first-floor studio.

Gideon knew her studio apartment well. He'd lived there when he'd first come back to Sacramento after years of assignments in other cities, just until he could get himself settled. He'd recently bought his own home near the Bureau's field office. It needed renovation, so he'd been taking his time about moving, but then Rafe told him that his father's old friend's daughter needed the space.

"What about your neighbors?" Gideon pressed. "Has Brutus made any enemies?"

Her brows lifted. "Brutus? No. She's sweet and hardly ever barks, unless I'm being attacked by a masked man in an alley."

Sarcasm then. He was oddly impressed. "Who knew you'd be at AA tonight?"

The smile on her face abruptly disappeared. "My friend Trish. My sponsor, Rosemary Purcell. Everyone in my AA group, I guess. I don't usually leave from the station, but I did tonight because I had to work late. He could have followed me, I suppose."

"Why were you working late tonight?" Erin asked.

"I needed to finalize all the other sponsors of the 5K. I can give you a list of the calls I made. I didn't use my cell phone. I made all the calls from the landline at the station manager's office. Anyone I called would have known I was there. The station's caller ID would have flashed on their phones. I made thirteen calls. I remember thinking it was either very lucky or unlucky. I guess it was the second one."

"I'd like to listen to the voice mails you mentioned," Erin said. "And I'd like to know why you kept them."

Daisy made a face. "I was handling Tad, but if that changed, I guess I wanted to show what he was asking me to ignore."

Rafe slid her phone back to her. "Unlock it, please."

She tapped in her passcode. "It's 071490. If you need to unlock it again. Don't tell my father I gave you the code. He'd have a fit."

"Why?" Gideon asked.

"Because he'd invoke my constitutional right against search and seizure and yada yada." She waved her hand. "He's also a defense attorney."

A paranoid, paramilitary defense attorney. That was interesting. But not what Gideon was after. "No. Why is that number your passcode? It seems like a date."

She turned to look at him, her extreme weariness suddenly evident. "That was my sister Carrie's birthday," she said very quietly.

Was. He could only nod. "Thank you."

Her throat worked as she swallowed. She handed her phone to Rafe. "What are you going to do with it?"

"Right now, I'm going to play the voice mails," Rafe told her. "I want to know if any of the callers' voices are the same as the one you heard tonight."

She closed her eyes for the briefest of moments and Gideon had the feeling that the messages would be much more serious than she'd led them to believe. "Okay," she whispered, then opened her phone app to messages and hit PLAY.

SACRAMENTO, CALIFORNIA
THURSDAY, FEBRUARY 16, 11:30 P.M.

"Copacabana" had segued into "Somewhere in the Night" when his phone buzzed in his pocket once again. Like Pavlov's dog he responded, checking the text. He'd known it would be Sydney, but seeing her name on his screen had him swallowing hard.

You were quite rude tonight, Sonny. I expect an apology or I might not use my influence to allow you to keep your job.

He swallowed hard again. Did she have the influence? Could she keep him employed? He couldn't lose his job. He'd lose his home.

He'd lose his basement.

Her next text hit him far harder. *I'd hate for you to lose your home, Sonny. Of course, you're always welcome to move home with me.*

No. No, no, no. His gut turned to ice. *I can't go back. I won't go back.*

His fingers trembled as they typed on the screen's tiny keyboard. *I'm sorry, Sydney.*

That's better. My sweet boy. You'll always be my sweet boy. Sweet dreams.

He lurched to his feet, pacing the length of his bedroom. That he could actually get fired after *years* of kowtowing to that prick's every demand, after being told that the company would be his? Selling it out from under him was a huge blow, professionally and personally. He'd been betrayed, plain and simple.

Not by Sydney this time. She was merely using the situation to her own benefit. This was all on the old man.

And on me.

Because I trusted him. Again. I believed him. Again. My mistake. Again.

Because he lied to me. Again.

He would not lose his job. He would not lose his house. He would not lose his basement. He especially would not move home with Sydney. Not ever again.

New rage thundered through him, because *he didn't have anyone in his basement.*

And he *would* have had someone in his basement if the blonde hadn't surprised him. If her fucking dog hadn't distracted him.

Sitting on the edge of his bed, he hung his head, his hands fisted on his thighs. His brain was ping-ponging. He *hated* this. Hated not being able to *think.*

He tried deep breathing, but that didn't help at all. He was never going to get any sleep and he absolutely *needed* to sleep.

He had to be sharp for work. His partner would notice and turn him in to the boss. Which was all he needed. He was on thin enough ice as it was. He would not give that prick a reason to fire him any sooner than it would happen anyway. It would be just like the old man to look for reasons to refuse his employees any severance.

Unless Sydney was serious and she really could influence the new owner to allow him to keep his job. *But am I willing to pay her price?* Hell, who was he kidding? He'd pay Sydney's price regardless. He always did. Always asked *How high?* when she demanded he jump.

Because I'm a coward. Which made him *so damn*

angry. Sydney would take advantage of his situation, even though it was unlikely she could do anything to help him, despite her claims. His hands twitched, a sudden craving rising within him like a rogue wave. He could *feel* his hands around her skinny throat. *A* skinny throat, he corrected himself. Never Sydney's, but by the time his guests were dead, at least he wasn't as angry anymore. *I should have had a guest in my basement. I should have had a way to feel better.*

A cold, wet nose nudged his knee and he sneered down into the adoring brown eyes looking up at him. "I blame you," he ground out. "I should have shot that damn yipping . . . *thing* when I had the chance. Before it distracted me. Before you, I could have."

Mutt licked the inside of his arm. He would have liked to believe it was in apology, but Mutt was rarely sorry for anything he did, even the truly bad stuff.

"You could have eaten her mutt in one gulp. Just calling that thing in her purse a dog is a crime," he told Mutt, who gave him a doggie smile, trotting behind him happily as he went to his closet for some clothes.

He knew what he needed tonight and he was unsettled enough to take the risk. He put on his dress slacks and a nice shirt, buttoning it up one more button than usual so that the scratches from earlier were hidden. *Bitch,* he thought, irritated.

He snugged the wig over his bald head and applied a mustache and bushy eyebrows with spirit gum, then checked his appearance in the mirror over his dresser and gave himself a nod. He wasn't gorgeously handsome, but he wasn't a troll, either. He was ordinary, in that in-between where women sometimes noticed but never remembered him.

Just like his old man. If his father hadn't had money, Sydney never would have given him a second look. She'd been a classic trophy wife.

With a predilection for young boys.

He scowled at the mirror. He wasn't going to think about Sydney. He was going to get another guest, hammer out the worst of his rage, and then figure out everything else.

SACRAMENTO, CALIFORNIA
THURSDAY, FEBRUARY 16, 11:35 P.M.

Daisy turned off her phone, willing her hand not to tremble. "I didn't remember there being so many," she murmured when the last voice mail was played.

Or so awful. Because many of them *had* been awful, degrading and humiliating. Some downright terrifying. Different phone number, different voices. All male.

"I bet you have great knockers."

"You got a boyfriend? I'm better than he is. I guarantee it."

"Your voice alone makes me come." That one, or variations on the same theme, had been left by multiple callers over the last few months, at least three a week.

"Can't wait to feel you squirming under me while I show you who's the boss."

"Gonna hold you down and make you scream my name in that sexy voice while I pound that pussy of yours."

The final two were the only ones left by the same caller. *"Loved how you filled out that T-shirt at the ribbon-cutting today."* That had been two weeks before, when she'd attended the opening of a new grocery store.

"Where'd you go after the grocery store thing? I wanted to take you out to dinner. Stick around next time," the caller said with a hearty laugh, then added with forced levity, *"Don't make me follow you home."*

Daisy swallowed hard. "That last one . . ." They all scared her, but the last one had been so much . . . creepier. More personal. "I hadn't heard it yet," she confessed. "I listen to the messages from people I know right away, but I sometimes let the others pile up."

She glanced up to find Rafe glaring at the notes he'd taken as they'd listened. From the corner of her eye she could see that Gideon's face had grown dark with anger, his hands clenched into fists. On the other side of her, Erin Rhee looked grim.

"Did you actually play these messages for your co-host?" Erin asked quietly.

"The first few." Daisy stroked Brutus a little too desperately, but the poor dog simply snuggled closer. "They were . . . worse than I remembered. I may have downplayed them in my own mind. The ones about the caller . . ." She felt her cheeks heat. "You know," she said awkwardly.

"Coming?" Erin supplied gently.

Daisy nodded. "Yes. To the sound of my voice." She swallowed again, bile burning her throat. It was overwhelming, hearing the calls all at once. One at a time she could dismiss. Three dozen calls in total she could not dismiss. And the threat to follow her home from the next event? That one she would have definitely reported, no matter what Tad had said. "I played one of those for Tad and he shrugged and said he still gets a few of those a week. He thought I should be . . . grateful."

"Grateful," Gideon murmured, his voice harsh. "Right."

"I'll report them from now on," Daisy said, lifting her chin. "I'll also get a new phone number first thing in the morning."

"And a new phone," Gideon ground out. "Or at least a loaner until the lab is sure that yours is a hundred percent clean."

She winced. "God, that's gonna be a pain in the

ass." But it was necessary for her safety, and after to-night, she would take appropriate precautions. "And a loaner phone," she promised.

Rafe wrote her a receipt for the phone. "I'll take your phone to the lab. Not sure how long it'll take to get it back to you."

"I know," Daisy grumbled. She started to ask who'd be handling her phone and her personal information when Rafe's phone buzzed with a text.

He typed something, then handed the phone to Erin, who nodded once she'd read it. "Forensics opened the locket," Rafe said. "There's a photo inside. I'd like you to take a look at it, Daisy, to see if you know the person in the picture."

"In case the guy picking me tonight was something other than random," Daisy said, steeling herself for who-ever the pictures were of. Because he'd implied there were others. *Please don't let me know them. Please.*

It was purely selfish on her part, she admitted. If she knew them, she'd mourn them. She'd also have to admit that this was personal. Believing that it was a random thing was somehow easier.

Beside her, Gideon Reynolds went rigid. She stud-ied his profile, the tightening of his jaw, the twitch in his cheek. He was glaring at Rafe, who didn't seem terribly upset by his friend's ire.

Daisy found herself patting Gideon's knee before she realized she was going to touch him. He was tense. She could feel it even with her slight touch. They shared a long glance and after a few moments, Gideon seemed to relax, his shoulders lowering.

Gideon's gaze dropped to her hand and she snatched it away as if she'd touched something hot. And she had. He was so warm under her palm. A shiver rippled over her skin because she was so cold. She wanted to cozy up to his warmth just like Brutus cuddled up to her.

But he didn't seem annoyed that she'd touched him.

He seemed . . . grateful. And tired. He definitely knew something about the locket. Whatever it was, was personal. And unpleasant.

She wondered what it was about the locket that made him so sad. It had been a simple silver locket with an engraving on the front. She wasn't sure that she even remembered what it was at this point. The back had said *Miriam*.

"Do you know her?" she asked him softly.

He frowned. "Who?"

"Miriam."

He flinched, just slightly, but Daisy had been watching him carefully. He met her eyes directly. "Why?"

She wasn't sure how to answer. "I guess because you seem sad," she murmured. "I hate to see people sad. I tend to want to fix things. Sorry."

"It's all right." Again he seemed grateful. "I don't know if I know her," he added, and she got the feeling that he was being honest.

The door opened and a woman entered carrying a small evidence bag and a folder. Both Rafe and Gideon rose. "Sergeant Grimes, this is our witness, Miss Dawson."

The woman's expression was sharp and sympathetic at the same time. "I'm sorry to hear that you were attacked tonight, Miss Dawson." She sat next to Rafe and placed the folder and evidence bag in front of him.

Rafe examined the contents of the folder for a few moments, then placed it on the table and spun it around so that Daisy could see. She could feel Gideon tensing again, but tried to ignore him, focusing instead on the photo.

It was an enlargement and grainy because of it. It was of a young girl, maybe thirteen. She wore a simple white dress, held a bouquet of flowers, and stood beside a much older man in a dark suit who was seated in a straight-backed wooden chair.

Daisy frowned. "The picture looks recent, but the style of the clothing looks old. Like it's one of those old-timey Gold Rush photos you get taken in Old Sac."

"Do you know either person?" Rafe asked.

Daisy pulled the photo closer and studied it carefully. The girl had a sweet face, her dark hair pulled back into a neat bun. "I've never seen the girl before. She looks way too young to be married." But young girls were forced to get married. She was aware of this, as repugnant as it was.

"What about the man?" Rafe pressed.

Daisy hesitated, staring at the man's face, willing herself to look when she really wanted to run away. There was something stern about the man. Something harsh. Something that said his word would be law. "This might be the man who attacked me tonight, but . . . I don't think so. This guy here in the photo, his eyes are spaced differently. Closer together, maybe. Bridge of his nose is wider. But the man I saw tonight had a nylon stocking over his face. His features were flattened, so I can't be certain."

She glanced over at Gideon, who'd grown very still, staring at the photo with a combination of horror and denial.

"You know them, don't you?" Daisy whispered, but he didn't tear his gaze away from the photo.

Gideon let out a long breath. "This man can't be tonight's attacker."

"Why not?" Rafe asked, his voice just audible enough to be heard over the blood pounding in Daisy's head. Because Gideon Reynolds continued to stare at the photo, his expression stricken. Something was very, very wrong.

Gideon finally looked up, his eyes hard. His jaw harder. "Because he's dead."

FOUR

He's dead, Gideon thought, looking at the photo on the table. *Because I killed him.*

The words hovered on the tip of his tongue, but he bit them back. Because murder was a crime. *Except when it's self-defense.* Which it had been. *Which I can't prove.*

The hell of it was, it wasn't even his darkest secret. Or his deepest shame.

I'm sorry, Mama. He could still hear her crying over him. Could still hear her pleas for him to hold on. *Just a little longer, baby. Just a little longer. I promise. It'll be okay. You'll be okay. I promise.*

She'd promised. She'd delivered. And then she'd walked away.

He'd wanted to hate her. But he'd known what it had cost her to walk away. To go back. He'd known why she'd returned, why she'd left him. *Mercy.*

His mother had been forced to make an unimaginable choice. But Mercy had needed her more. He'd understood it then, even as he'd bitterly begged her not to leave him. He understood it now and regretted the words he'd flung in fear. In desperation. In pain.

But it didn't matter because she was gone again. Permanently. He could never take back the words he'd said, could never beg her forgiveness. *I'm sorry, Mama. I'm so sorry.*

"Agent Reynolds? *Agent Reynolds.*"

Gideon looked up with a jolt, the moment broken by Rafe's sharp voice. But it wasn't Rafe's voice that occupied his attention. It was the small hand that covered his fist, squeezing tightly. Daisy Dawson.

Gideon slid his gaze to Daisy's face. She was watching him with a mixture of grim realization and compassion. Slowly she released his hand and went back to stroking her dog, never breaking her gaze.

What had he said? Suddenly panicked, he looked to the others. Both Erin Rhee and Cindy Grimes looked puzzled. Maybe a little concerned. But not upset.

Rafe gave him a wry smile that said more than words could. *You didn't say anything. It's okay.* "Thought you'd fallen asleep on us there. I asked if you were sure he was dead."

Gideon slowly exhaled, hoping he hid his relief. He couldn't believe he'd said that much, but he'd been shocked. Part of him wanted to hurt Rafe for putting him in this situation, and then he remembered that Daisy's attacker had mentioned others. He would have done the same thing in Rafe's place.

"Yes," he said, without explanation. He tapped the folder. "Was there anything more in the locket?" he asked because his brain was finally beginning to kick in.

He'd killed the man in the wedding photo. Miriam— or Eileen, as the girl in the photo had preferred to be called—wouldn't have been allowed to be single afterward. She would have been given to another man.

Or she escaped shortly after I did. Which seemed unlikely. There would have been another wedding photo, inserted over the first.

"There was," Cindy said, surprised. "A layer of shredded paper, cut into tiny pieces. I think it was another photo, but I'll have to try putting it together."

"You know the girl in the picture?" Erin asked.

"A long time ago. I haven't seen her in seventeen years. Her name was Miriam. The locket would have been hers."

"And the scraps of paper I found?" Cindy asked.

Not here. Not now. He'd already said too much. He aimed a pointed stare at Rafe.

Rafe stood up. "I think we're done for now. Daisy, come with me. Mom, Dad, and Sasha are all waiting to take you home."

Daisy looked abruptly frustrated. "You're kidding."

"Sorry," Rafe said with real apology behind it. "You can't be here anymore."

Daisy rose, her blue eyes flashing. "Rude," she muttered. "Just when we were getting somewhere."

Gideon had to clear his throat because a laugh had come bubbling from nowhere. She looked so righteously angry. But he instantly sobered because she was right. They *were* getting somewhere and that was nowhere she needed to be.

"Come on, Brutus. We're being thrown out. Just when it was getting good." She settled the little ball of fur into her purse, adjusting it so that the side expanded, revealing mesh netting.

Gideon reached out and touched her hand before he could talk himself out of it. He could have controlled his need to touch her once more, but he didn't and he wasn't sure why. Okay, that was bullshit. He knew why, but he wasn't going to think about it. Daisy Dawson had given him comfort when she hadn't had to. And he'd found himself dropping his guard around her. It should have appalled him, but it didn't.

"Thank you," he murmured when she looked at him in surprise. "Be careful."

Her lips curved into a sad smile that hurt his heart, and he wondered what she'd seen when she'd watched him with such compassion. "I will. Be well, Agent

Reynolds." She shouldered the bag and followed Rafe to the door. "I can find my way out."

"I bet you could," Rafe said, his voice thick with amusement. "And I'm sure that you'd come upon many interesting conversations to 'accidently overhear' while you were pretending to get lost. So this nice officer here will walk you upstairs."

She glared up at Rafe. "You don't have to be so smug about it." She turned her glare onto the uniformed officer waiting patiently in the hall. "How long has he been there?"

"Since about a minute after I walked through the door with Agent Reynolds, because I know you too well." He gave her hair a brotherly tug. "Tell Mom that I'll call when I can."

"I will." She grew serious, her glare disappearing. "I assume I can go back to my normal life tomorrow. Like work? And all my events?"

Rafe hesitated. "One of us will drive you tomorrow. Don't go anywhere by yourself."

Daisy's brow lifted delicately. "One of you?" She indicated the interview room with a gesture. "Or one of the Sokolovs?"

Me. The thought hit Gideon hard. It was unexpected and ridiculous. The woman had a lot of people to watch out for her. His services were definitely not needed. Or even wanted, probably.

"Not sure," Rafe said. "What time are you expected at the station?"

"Five A.M.," Daisy told him with the slightest bit of satisfaction. "We go live at six. From your parents' house, I need to leave by four twenty-five."

Rafe winced. "Ouch. I'll let you know who'll be accompanying you."

"Babysitting me, you mean." Her shoulders sagged dejectedly. "I know you're just trying to protect me, but I thought I'd finally gotten my independence and now some asshole takes it away from me again."

Rafe gave her a quick hug and Gideon had to bite back a growl. *Settle down,* he barked to himself. *Honestly.*

"Hopefully it won't be for too long," Rafe said. He met the officer's gaze. "You'll follow them home, right?"

The older man nodded. "Of course. I'll call you when they're inside and safe."

"Thank you." Rafe closed the door and returned to the table. "Officer Taggert is a friend of my parents. I think he's hoping for a slice of my mom's *medovik*. She always has one on the sideboard."

Gideon didn't blame Officer Taggert. Like anything Irina made, the honey cake was well worth the extra hours on the treadmill to run it off.

"Then why are we here?" Cindy asked with a smile. "We need to go to your mom's."

"I'll bring you some cake," Rafe promised, then turned back to Gideon. "Okay, now that it's just us, what about the scraps of paper Cindy found in the locket?"

Gideon wanted to apologize, excuse himself, and run home. But he knew he couldn't. This was the lead he'd been waiting for, ever since he'd escaped that hellhole. A connection to the community. To the men who'd raped his sister and killed his mother. He'd get justice for them if it was the last thing he did.

I'm sorry, Mama.

SACRAMENTO, CALIFORNIA
FRIDAY, FEBRUARY 17, 12:00 A.M.

"You're sure you're okay?" Karl asked for what had to be the twentieth time since Officer Taggert had delivered her to the lobby of the SacPD, where the Sokolovs had been anxiously waiting.

"I'm *fine*." Sliding into the backseat of the Sokolovs' Tesla, Daisy gave Karl a smile that she hoped dispelled his fears, but that she knew probably wouldn't. He'd promised her father that he'd keep her safe and considered Daisy being hurt on his watch to be a personal failing. "Nothing a cup of tea won't fix."

His smile was small and wary. "All right, then. Buckle up, Daisy. You too, Sasha."

Sasha Sokolov folded her nearly six-foot self into the backseat from the other side of the car and rolled her eyes. "Yes, Dad. Not like I'm twenty-five years old or anything," she added in a mutter that was loud enough for him to hear.

"I know how old you are," Karl said. "I was there when you were born."

Sighing, Sasha made a grand production of buckling her belt. Daisy followed suit, but more sedately. When they were both secured, Karl brought the wing door down, which always gave Daisy a silly little thrill. It was just a door, but it was very cool.

Irina called the Tesla "Karl's toy," but fondly. The man had earned his money, his wife always said. He had the right to spend it as he pleased. After all, Karl spent much more on his family and charities than he ever spent on himself, Tesla included. He was a very generous man who'd opened his heart and home to Daisy despite not having seen her in over a decade. Daisy's father had asked for his help and Karl hadn't blinked.

She wanted to ask if they'd called her father, but wasn't sure she was ready for the answer.

Karl helped Irina into the front seat, then leaned in to kiss his wife's cheek before gallantly closing her door. Irina turned in her seat to fix Daisy with a stare that missed nothing. "You are not fine," Irina informed her, her accent thick, her worry thicker. "You were attacked tonight. You cannot be fine."

Daisy shrugged. "Then I will be fine?"

Irina waved a hand in irritation. "Of course you will be fine. We will see to it. You will stay with us—"

"Tonight," Daisy interrupted. "Only tonight."

Karl chuckled as he started the car, the Tesla's engine eerily silent. "And after we had the dungeon specially prepared for her," he said to his wife. Karl had no trace of an accent. Unlike his wife, who had come to the United States as a teenager, he was the son of immigrants but had grown up in California. He met Daisy's eyes in the rearview mirror, his twinkling. "Irina even changed out the manacles to the ones we save for company."

Irina swatted him playfully. "You weren't supposed to let her know I went to all that trouble for her."

Daisy laughed. "Okay, fine. I appreciate you taking care of me. It's just that I'm enjoying my independence. I don't want to be . . . hovered over. Not anymore."

"Good luck with that," Sasha muttered and Daisy laughed again. Sasha was seventh of the eight Sokolov children, but only by a few minutes. Cash, her twin, never let her forget that he was older. The two of them had been Daisy's playmates when their families had gotten together for the holidays or birthdays. Get-togethers that had come to an abrupt halt when Daisy's father had whisked his family off to the ranch in the middle of nowhere.

Sasha had been one of the first friendships that Daisy had rekindled when she'd been freed a year and a half ago and the two of them had kept in touch over social media while Daisy had been in Europe. It had actually been Sasha's idea for Daisy to move to Sacramento, but Daisy had managed to make her father believe it was his idea, prompting Frederick Dawson to ask Karl's help in getting Daisy settled with a job and a place to live. Despite the missing years, she and Sasha had effortlessly fallen back into a close camaraderie.

"You don't have to stay with me at your parents' house," Daisy told her. "You'll just have to wake up early to get to work." Sasha was a social worker with CPS, her office much closer to the house they shared with Rafe in Midtown than to the Sokolovs' family home in Granite Bay.

Sasha shot Daisy a reproachful look. "I'm not going to let you be alone tonight. Not after the experience you've had."

Daisy patted her hand. "Thank you. Can I use your phone, please? I want to call Trish and check on her. She was as shaken up as I was."

Sasha handed her phone over. "What happened to your phone?"

"I had to give it to Rafe. He's checking it for tracking devices."

"Why?" Karl asked sharply.

Damn electric cars, Daisy thought, irritated. Too much silence allowed for easy eavesdropping. "I wanted to tell the station manager first, but he'll just tell you, so whatever. I've been getting . . . suggestive voice mails and e-mails from listeners."

"What?" The shouts came at Daisy from all directions.

Irina turned in her seat again to frown at her. "What kind of suggestive voice mails?"

"Oh, you know. Ones saying I'm pretty and they want to do . . . things. You know."

Karl's eyes were narrowed as he glanced at her in the rearview. "No, I don't know, because you never told me!" he thundered.

"I'm sorry!" Daisy thundered back, then sighed. "I . . . should have. Sorry."

"*Why* didn't you tell us?" Sasha asked quietly.

"Because Tad said it was nothing. That everyone gets messages like that. I'm getting a new phone. Don't worry. Rafe's going to try to trace the messages."

"They think your attacker was a listener?" Karl demanded.

"They're exploring all possibilities." Including the locket—with its photo that had Gideon Reynolds looking so haunted. "They booted me before I learned anything I didn't already know. Which isn't anything more than I already told you at the ER," she finished firmly, because Karl and Irina had questioned her more thoroughly than Rafe and Erin had.

She could feel the combined force of three Sokolov stares as she bent her head to Sasha's phone. "Stop looking at me like that," she told them without looking up. "I need to remember Trish's number and you're making me nervous."

"I have it in my contacts," Sasha said, shaking her head. "We will talk about these messages later."

"You'd better believe it," Karl declared.

Sighing, Daisy found Trish's cell number and dialed. Unsurprisingly, Trish answered on the first ring. "Hello? Sasha? Where is Daisy?"

"I'm here," Daisy said. "I'm just using Sasha's phone. I just got done with the cops and I'm going back to Karl and Irina's. Are you okay?"

"Yeah. That lady detective made sure I got in my apartment okay. Not sure I'm going to sleep tonight, though. If there was ever a night I wanted a drink, this is it."

"Me too," Daisy confessed quietly. "If the urge gets too bad, call Rosemary. I'd say call me, but the police have my phone. I'm getting a new one tomorrow."

"You finally told them about the creepy calls like I've been telling you to?"

"Yes." Daisy sighed. "I'll text you when I have my new phone number."

"Was that locket important?"

"I think so, but I don't know why." She had a sudden thought. "Listen, can you send the pictures you took tonight to my e-mail address? I'd like to have them for my files." Trish had had the presence of mind to take photos of her throat, the scene, and the locket. If Rafe was going to block her from all of the good information, she'd have to look on her own.

"Sure. Call me tomorrow so I'll know you're okay. Say hi to the Sokolovs."

Ending the call, Daisy gave Sasha back her phone, met the family's collective stare, and asked the question she'd been dreading. "Did you tell my father about tonight?"

"No," Irina said, surprising the hell out of Daisy. "We knew the ER was a precaution. It would have frightened your father more to hear it from us. He'll need to hear your voice when you tell him, to know for certain that you are unharmed."

"Thank you. I was planning to call him." She was. Mostly. "I'll call him before I go on the air tomorrow." She tilted her head, eyes narrowing when it looked like Irina would argue with her about going to work. "Rafe said someone would take me in to the station. I assumed that meant him or Detective Rhee."

"Karl?" Irina asked. "Is this acceptable?"

He shrugged. "Not really, but we're going to have to trust Rafe to keep her safe."

Daisy shared a side-eye with Sasha, who was biting back a smile. "Welcome to my life," Sasha whispered loudly.

"As long as I keep my freedom. Everything else is negotiable."

SACRAMENTO, CALIFORNIA
FRIDAY, FEBRUARY 17, 12:00 A.M.

It's time to talk about them, Gideon thought. He'd tried to find them. Tried to bring them to justice. He'd failed. *But I was just a kid then.*

The FBI had also tried and failed. The community had hidden itself far too well. They also hadn't had any leads. He hadn't known of any escapees other than himself and Mercy, but now Eileen had escaped. She had to have—otherwise her locket would still be around her throat while she toiled in the community.

And that you killed a man? He wasn't going to share that. *Duh.*

And Mercy? Are you going to tell them about her? No. He couldn't do that. Not without her permission. It would be like violating her all over again.

"Gid?" Rafe prompted.

Gideon sighed. "Just . . . processing. Seeing this photo was a shock."

"We could tell," Erin said dryly, but not unkindly. "Why?"

"Do you have the photo I gave you?" Gideon asked Rafe.

Rafe pulled it from his pocket and laid it on the table, next to the locket, turning the silver heart so that the etching showed.

"Wow," Cindy said quietly. She glanced up. "This tattoo . . . This is you?"

"Yes." He'd had the tattoo covered as soon as he'd found Mercy. It had served its purpose, quickly connecting them as kin when there'd been no documentation for either of them. A DNA test had confirmed Gideon's claim later, but at the time that had taken months.

"They're the same," Erin murmured, gesturing between the tattoo and the locket. "The designs. Why are they the same?"

"They're not exactly the same," Gideon corrected. "The olive tree on the tattoo has thirteen branches. The locket's olive tree has only twelve. It's the symbol of a new religious movement in Northern California."

"A cult," Erin said flatly. "You lived in a cult."

"Yes," he answered simply, then explained the purposes of the locket and tattoo and the ages of the recipients.

"They married off twelve-year-olds?" Erin asked, visibly repulsed.

"No. Only twelve-year-old girls." Gideon proceeded carefully. There were too many personal details he didn't wish to share. "Boys became men at thirteen. They took on more responsibility in the community and entered . . . special training." The words stuck in his throat and he had to force them out. *Special training.* It had sounded so amazing. And for some of the boys it must have been, because they'd continued to smile and joke. Or maybe those boys had just been better able to shove the truth down where no one could see.

"Special training?" Rafe asked, as if he was afraid of the answer.

"In the church," Gideon said and it came out far more curtly than he'd intended. God, he hated this. Hated exhuming this vile pus. "They'd study the scriptures and the church policies. Thirteen was also the start of apprenticeships." *Apprenticeships.* His stomach threatened to heave at the memory. "There was a smithy, a tanner, a cobbler . . ."

"Like a TV western," Cindy murmured.

More like a horror movie. "Thirteen was also the start of inclusion in the hunting trips. It was a self-sustaining agricultural community. They kept chickens, pigs, a few head of cattle for beef, and a few dairy cows. And there was venison when hunting was successful."

"Electricity?" Cindy asked.

"Only in certain areas. Specifically the church office and the homes of the pastor and a few of the higher-ups. They had generators."

Erin was frowning. "So when did the boys marry?"

"When they'd built a house of their own. Boys started building when they were eighteen. It was done in their spare time, after their normal chores and daily work. Some finished sooner, especially if their apprenticeships were construction-based."

Erin studied him. "What was your apprenticeship?"

Gideon's lips curved bitterly. "Metalsmithing. I was to make the lockets, among other things."

"You *were*?" Cindy asked. "What happened?"

"I escaped."

"Lucky you," Cindy breathed.

Yeah. Lucky. I'm so sorry, Mama.

Erin leaned in. "How?"

"I hid in the bed of a truck that was going to town. Slipped out and hid behind a bus terminal." Almost true. Gideon drew a breath and let it out. *Just stay chill. You've done nothing wrong. Well, other than kill a man.* "I was thirteen." *And one day.*

"And then?" Cindy asked, her eyes soft with compassion.

"I was sucked into the foster system." And that was all he planned to share about himself. He tapped the photo of the girl. Of Miriam. *Eileen.* "She was in my class at school in the compound. We were friends. She turned twelve a few months before I did. She was married to him." He pointed to the enlarged wedding photo. "His name was Edward McPhearson. Or that's how I knew him. Names were kind of fluid in the community. She dropped out of school on her twelfth birthday. All the girls did. They were to be wives, not scholars." He said that last part mockingly, remembering Eileen's tears when she realized she would have to quit school. "Eileen loved learning. She was so smart."

"Eileen?" Rafe interrupted.

"That was her birth name. The name she preferred to be called." But only by those she trusted. Her mother. *And me.* "'Miriam' was the name given to her by the community. We had a lot of Miriams."

"You said she was so smart," Erin said. "Why 'was'?"

Because the Eileen he'd known died the day she'd been forced to marry Edward McPhearson. She'd become a shell, her eyes vacant. "I don't know if she's dead or alive. That this locket was around another man's throat means she's either dead or has escaped and the locket somehow left her possession."

Rafe chimed in. "Gideon told me earlier that this chain was not the original, that the original would have been heavy and welded to her so that she would have had to cut it off."

"My God," Erin murmured. "Like a slave."

Gideon only nodded. *Exactly like a slave.*

"The locket's silver," Cindy said. "She could have pawned it. If she escaped."

"Maybe." Gideon stared at the locket, McPhearson's handiwork. It would have been one of the last lockets the bastard made. "I guess it depends on how long it took her to get out. If she was there a long time, the locket would have been difficult for her to part with. It's hard to explain. For the women, the locket became a charm. Kept them safe. Kept them spiritually connected to the rest of the body. That's what the community called itself, the body."

"That's creepy," Erin said.

Gideon shrugged again, not sure how else to describe the locket's importance. "Of course it is. But that's how it was. Like the rabbit's foot you happen to carry and then one day you're in a car accident. You're okay and part of you attributes that to the rabbit's foot. You're afraid that if you take it off, the next accident will kill you."

"I had a necklace like that," Cindy admitted. "It belonged to my grandmother. She always said it was her talisman and left it to me when she died, saying it would keep me safe. I wore it through my entire adolescence." She smiled fondly. "Then the leather cord snapped one day and I lost it. I searched everywhere. Never found it. I kept expecting something terrible to happen. It took weeks before the fear passed. I was seventeen at the time. I can see how a person could build that kind of attachment, especially if that connection is underscored by authority figures."

Gideon nodded. "Thank you. That's exactly what it was like."

She put another evidence bag on the table. "What about this?"

The shredded fragments of the second photo. "After her first husband died, Eileen—or Miriam as she was called by everyone else—would have been given to another one of the men." Gideon pointed to the paper bits. "That would have been the second wedding photo. If she did escape, it's possible that she cut it up herself. Especially if he was abusive."

Not all of the men were violent. But enough were.

Gideon cleared his throat. "If you can manage to put this back together, I'll try to identify the second husband."

"What about this compound?" Erin asked. "Where is it?"

Gideon glanced across the table at Rafe and found his oldest friend studying him sadly, understanding in his dark eyes.

"I don't know where it is," Gideon admitted. "I looked, after I escaped." *And recovered.* "But I never found it."

"We went together," Rafe added. "I never knew what we'd gone looking for, just that taking those car trips up to Mt. Shasta were important to Gid. He didn't have a car, but I did, so I drove. I eventually figured out that it had to do with his family in some way, but . . ." He sighed. "We should have looked harder."

Gideon shook his head. "It was pretty hopeless. Like a needle in a fucking haystack." Back then and every time he'd searched since. He'd never stopped searching.

"What landmarks can you remember?" Erin asked, clearly primed to solve the mystery of the missing community. If it were only so simple.

"Mt. Shasta," he told her. "I remember seeing it in the distance."

"Then we have a general idea of where to start," Erin said with a certainty that seemed like common sense, but that really was not.

Gideon prepared himself to explain, once again. "It might, except that they move."

Cindy's eyes widened. "The whole community? They just move?"

"Yes. They moved twice when I was younger. Each time, I could still see Mt. Shasta, just different views. My mother said it was because the land no longer produced enough vegetables, which was what she'd been told. I was only six at the time of the first move, but I was eight at the time of the second and remember hearing whispers among some of the women that the land was 'cursed,' that we were being punished."

"For what?" Rafe asked, frowning.

"I don't remember anything about the first move, but the second one happened the day after a man was accused of stealing from the food stores. Whether he did or not, I have no idea, but looking back, I'm thinking it's more likely that he tried to escape. The man who'd 'stolen' was brought before the community, all beaten up. He might have been unconscious, but definitely was unable to speak. They announced his crime and that he was being 'banished.' I remember the audible gasp from the adults. Several of them cried—but silently. He was dragged through the gate and into the forest. Nobody ever saw him again. The next morning we woke up to find the community garden was dead. The leaders claimed it was punishment for the man's theft, but it was probably weed killer of some kind."

"Did anyone call them on the bullshit?" Rafe asked.

Gideon shook his head. "Speaking out was punished even more severely than stealing, and after seeing what happened to the man who'd allegedly stolen, no one was willing to risk it. Anyway, we moved and had to prepare new gardens for a fall crop, but it was a lean winter. I remember going to bed hungry a lot of nights and my mother crying about it, but there wasn't anything she could do. The following year, no one stole anything—or tried to escape—and we had a big crop."

"That makes sense," Cindy said thoughtfully. "It would be a way to reinforce control over the community through fear. And subsequent deliverance from that fear."

"It worked. I don't remember anyone else being punished that severely for anything until the night I got away. Later, I went back to the last area I remember, found the view of the mountain, but there was no sign of them."

"Did you tell anyone?" Erin asked.

"Yes." Because even though he might have gone to prison for killing McPhearson, he wanted his mother and Mercy to be safe. Once Mercy got out and their mother was gone, there was no need for truth. Just vengeance. Which was why he'd never given up searching. "I told a cop when I was first found and he couldn't find them, either. It's a big country up there. Lots of places to hide a small community."

Erin frowned again. "How many people were there? Seems like it would be hard to hide a community large enough to have people representing all those trades. Satellite photos would show their homes, their gardens, even. I mean, if we can identify pot growers using Google Earth, we should be able to find a farm community."

"There were about a hundred members, give or take," Gideon said. "Including women and children.

And I *have* searched aerial and satellite photos. The FBI gives me access to government satellite photos. I've questioned law enforcement and store owners in every small town in the search zone. Wherever they shop for supplies, it isn't around Mt. Shasta. They are hidden and take great pains to stay that way."

Rafe looked surprised. "You reported them to the FBI?"

"Of course I did." Gideon wanted to snap it out, but restrained himself. "I wanted them found. I want no more kids to be treated the way we were. I want no more women enslaved like my mother. I wanted the bastards to pay. But I wanted it done *legally.*"

"But the FBI couldn't find them, either," Rafe said, apology in his eyes.

"No." Gideon swallowed. "Then the case went cold." *Until tonight. Until the locket.*

"All right." Erin's expression had softened somewhat, like she'd remembered this was a real story about a real person and not just a case. "How long were you in the truck bed before you slipped out? And what bus station was nearby?"

"It was the Redding bus station—and yes, I've asked about them at the stores in Redding, too. But I don't know how long we drove," he admitted.

Again, Rafe's eyes held understanding. They'd showered in a high school locker room. Rafe had seen his scars. And not once had he asked about them.

Erin's eyes narrowed. "Why don't you remember?"

Gideon swallowed hard. "I was unconscious for most of the trip."

"He'd been beaten," Rafe added.

Both Erin and Cindy gasped. "Got it," Erin murmured. *Finally.* "I'm sorry, Gideon."

"It's okay. It's in the past." And anyone he'd want to find was gone. *I'm sorry, Mama.*

Cindy drew a breath, like she was trying not to

become emotional. "I have sons the age you were then. It's good that I stick to the lab. I'd probably cry all over the victims."

"I have a few more questions," Erin said, her face scrunching up in apology. "What was the name of the 'new religious movement'?"

"The cult," Gideon said flatly, just as she had. "The Church of Second Eden. They called the town Eden, although it's not on any map. Its leader was called 'Pastor.' I never knew his real name."

Erin nodded. "All right. Why were you beaten?"

"I refused my apprenticeship." That was true. In a manner of speaking.

Erin's head tilted curiously. "Why?"

"Because McPhearson had a reputation for being cruel." Among other things.

Erin nodded again. "How did he die?"

Careful. Careful. "He was beaten," Gideon answered. That was very true.

"Why?" she pressed.

Careful. Careful. "Because of what he did to me." True. Technically.

She studied him so closely that he would have begun to sweat had he not been trained to keep his cool. Interesting that he hadn't blurted anything out since Daisy Dawson had left the room. He'd have to think about that later.

"The best lead we have is that torn-up photo," Rafe said. "Can you put it back together, Cindy?"

Cindy's eyes gleamed. "Hell, yes. I've done a puzzle that was one thousand pieces and solid yellow. I can do this."

Rafe grinned at her. "Excellent. By when?"

"Not sure. We're assuming all the pieces are still here. But if she was married at twelve in the photo we have and thirteen in the torn up one, I can use the first one as a guide. Her facial features won't have changed much in a year." Cindy stood up and gathered her things. "Don't call me. I'll call you."

Erin also rose. "I'll write the report. Let me know if I need to take Daisy duty."

Daisy duty. Gideon wouldn't mind some of that. The woman had been kind when she herself was rattled, after she'd been assaulted. She'd calmed him when his mind had churned with things he hadn't wanted to ever remember. She'd smiled at him like she'd understood.

Which wasn't possible, but he'd appreciated the effort. Even more, he appreciated the opportunity she'd dropped into his lap. The locket she'd snatched from her assailant's throat could be a link to finding Eileen. Finding Eden. Finding the men who'd raped his sister and murdered his mother.

When Erin was gone, Rafe turned to him, brows raised. "What's next?"

Gideon frowned. "What do you mean?"

Rafe rolled his eyes. "How many times have you been out to Mt. Shasta in the year since you got back to Sacramento? And don't tell me that you don't know. I'm not buying it."

"Fifteen," Gideon admitted.

"And when you were stationed in Miami and Philly? How many times did you come back and search without even telling me you were back?"

Gideon's cheeks heated at the mild rebuke in Rafe's voice. "Six times. Total."

"Twenty-one times. God, Gid. Why didn't you ask me to go with you? I would have gone, if for no other reason than to keep you company. Have I ever pressed you for information you weren't ready to share?"

"Tonight," Gideon drawled, trying to break the tension.

Rafe's lips thinned, his eyes rolling again. "Besides tonight."

"No," Gideon murmured. "I'm sorry."

"You should be." Rafe glared at him. "You're too smart to be so stupid. Now, I want the goddamn truth. What do you plan to do next? You have the chance to find the men who hurt you. Both you and your sister. To bring them in. To make them pay for whatever they did to you and to Mercy. Don't expect me to believe you're going to sit there and do nothing."

To me and Mercy and our mother. But Gideon had never told Rafe about his mother's part in his and Mercy's escapes. He would, but not tonight. He felt too raw, too exposed. For now, he regarded Rafe soberly as he considered his answer. What could he do? Truthfully, not much. Which sucked more than he could stand.

He felt powerless once again. Thirteen years old and powerless. He thought about McPhearson's photo. Not that powerless, he told himself. McPhearson was dead. One fewer sadist was not a bad thing.

"I can't do much without an ID of Daisy's assailant," Gideon finally said. "What's your plan to find him?"

"Thought I'd start poking around the community center, see what the neighborhood surveillance cameras show. This guy wore a stocking over his face when he attacked Daisy, but he might not have had it on the whole time he was lurking on the street. Someone would have noticed him. Daisy gave a good description of his clothing, so maybe we'll find him on someone's security cam. What's next for you? Are you going to tell your boss about this?"

Gideon nodded slowly. "At this point I have to."

"And if she doesn't decide to lend you to us?"

Gideon met his friend's eyes. "I have leave saved up. I need to see this through."

"I know," Rafe murmured.

"Even if it's not in an official capacity," Gideon added meaningfully.

Rafe nodded, understanding. "I'll do everything in my power to see that you do."

FIVE

"What are you doing?" Sasha asked, having stubbornly insisted on staying at her parents' house to keep Daisy company.

Daisy looked up from Sasha's laptop, happy to see her friend leaning against the door frame of the Sokolovs' spare bedroom, a mug in one hand and a teapot in the other. The cheery room with its whimsical wall murals was where Daisy slept whenever she stayed over.

"Do you need your laptop back?" Daisy asked, hoping Sasha would say no because her search on the locket had resulted in some fascinating reading.

Sasha shook her head. "Nope. I can use my tablet for e-mail." She held up the teapot. "You want a refill? It's that Sleepytime blend."

"I don't think sleep's going to happen anytime soon," Daisy muttered. "Why aren't you in bed? You're gonna be trashed tomorrow."

"I called in, left a message that I'm taking a personal day."

Daisy smiled, holding her mug for a refill after all. "You're gonna be my bodyguard, huh?"

Sasha poured the tea, set the pot on the nightstand, then sat cross-legged on the bed next to where Brutus lay curled up in a puff of fur. Absently petting the dog's ears, she studied Daisy's face for a long moment. "What didn't you tell us earlier? And don't try to bull- shit me, DD. You are really bad at it. Tell me what you were holding back."

Daisy's gaze dropped to the laptop's screen, know- ing exactly why she hadn't shared all the evening's events. Irina had been trying to set her up with Gideon for months and both she and Gideon had been resist- ing. Daisy hadn't told them about Gideon because she simply didn't have the emotional energy to deal with Irina's well-meaning matchmaking tonight. But she trusted Sasha. She always had, even when they were kids telling secrets in a dark tent in the Sokolovs' back- yard, a flashlight their only illumination. They'd told ghost stories, complained about school, and right after her mother had died, Sasha had hugged her while she'd cried her grief.

"I met Gideon Reynolds tonight." Daisy glanced up to see Sasha blinking with surprise. "At the police sta- tion," she clarified.

"Gideon? What was he doing there?"

"Rafe asked him to come." She clicked into her e-mail and brought up the photo of the locket that Trish had taken at the scene. "I grabbed this off the man's neck tonight. The man who tried to attack me."

"Who *did* attack you," Sasha murmured, focusing on the photo. "What is it?"

"A locket. It was engraved. At first I thought Gideon was there because the man had mentioned others and that maybe Gideon was investigating a serial rapist or murderer or something. But he said he was there be- cause of the locket. It . . . hurt him. Somehow. I want to know why."

Sasha's eyes narrowed in thought then abruptly popped wide. "Oh my God," she whispered. "It was his tattoo. I remember it."

That had not been what Daisy was expecting. "Gideon had a tattoo with this design?"

Sasha nodded. "I was young when I last saw it—maybe twelve or so?—but I remember it. Back then I was fascinated by Gideon. I followed him and Rafe around everywhere."

Daisy felt a stirring of something foreign in her chest. Something not very nice. *Something like jealousy?* her small voice asked.

Shut up. I have no claim to him. Don't be ridiculous. And anyway, there was no way Sasha had a thing for Gideon Reynolds, not now or back then.

"Why?" she asked carefully.

Sasha laughed. "If you could see your face right now. Do not play poker, DD. Ever. You realize that I'm gay, right? I was then, too."

Daisy's cheeks heated. "I know that," she said defensively. "Why were you fascinated with him?"

"It was a slight hero worship thing. I mean, all I knew was our family and we're . . . well, we're us. We're loud and crazy and out there."

"I remember," Daisy said with a smile. "I always wished I could live with you." Especially after her father had dragged them into the middle of nowhere. "I had Taylor and I love her to bits, but there was always something fun happening in this house and ours was . . ." She shrugged.

"Rigid," Sasha supplied. "I always wondered if our fathers weren't switched at birth. You hear about stoic Russians, but your dad got all the stoic and mine got none." She sighed. "Everything was always this colorful chaos. Sometimes it would be too loud and I'd crawl off to the attic to hide in my nook. One day—I would have been about nine because Rafe had just started high school—he brings this kid home to work on a science project. He was this dark, mysterious stranger."

"Gideon."

"Yeah. Never said a word, but his eyes said a lot. Most of it didn't seem too good. Nobody ever *said* he'd been hurt, not when I was around to hear, anyway. But it just rolled off him in waves. He was intense and angry. Rafe kept bringing him around and my mom kept clucking over him, making him his favorite treats and just being herself."

Daisy smiled at this. Irina was a treasure, for sure. "You're so lucky."

Sasha smiled back. "I know. I asked her why Gideon didn't just come live with us. I remember thinking, hey, we got eight kids, what's one more?"

Daisy laughed. "Considering Zoya would have been a toddler then, I imagine that went over well. What did your mom say?"

"It *did* go over well, actually. She said that Gideon had a home in foster care, but if he ever wanted to move in, he'd be welcome. I think I was in awe of Gideon because he was so buttoned-down. He wasn't broadcasting his feelings all over the place. I felt like I was the same way a lot of the time, like I didn't belong in this house of craziness. One day I was creeping up to my attic nook and I found him there. Just chilling, you know? I sat next to him and we were quiet together for the longest time. Then he patted my head and thanked me for sharing my space with him. I told him to use it anytime, that I'd keep his secret." Her expression grew sad. "He got this look in his eyes, like I'd punched him in the gut. He just thanked me again and left. The next time I went up there I found a flower from my mother's garden on the window seat and a note that said 'I'll keep yours, too.' I knew it was from him. After that, I'd find a flower there and I knew he'd been there. Sometimes we sat there together." One side of her mouth lifted. "I came out to him, first of everyone."

Daisy smiled sadly, because it was bittersweet. She

was glad that Sasha had had a confidante, but sad that
it hadn't been her. She'd been on the ranch by then.
"Really?"

"Yep. I was fourteen and he was home from college
for Christmas. I trusted him not to tell. The man is a
vault."

"Really?" Daisy asked again, this time in disbelief.
"He let a few things slip tonight. I got the impression
he hadn't intended to say them."

"Like?"

"Like that he'd come to the police station because
of the locket. I don't think he wanted to say that and I
think Rafe was surprised he had as well. I kept trying
to ask about it, but either he, Rafe, or Erin would try
to distract me."

"So you're researching it yourself?"

"Of course," Daisy answered matter-of-factly.

"Of course," Sasha repeated wryly. "What else did
he not mean to say?"

Daisy had no qualms about telling Sasha any of this,
because her friend was also a vault. "The forensics person found a wedding photo in the locket. The girl was
way too young, like twelve or thirteen. Gideon had
known her. He reacted most strongly to the man in the
photo. Blurted out that he was dead. And then he
seemed to . . . go somewhere. In his head."

"Wow. For Gideon, that's a hell of a lot. He must
have been rattled." Sasha returned her attention to the
photo of the locket on the laptop screen. "He had this
tattoo for a long time. Right here." She patted the left
side of her chest, above her breast. "I didn't know he
had a tattoo for the first few years, because he'd never
taken off his shirt around us. One day we were at the
river, tubing, and we all stripped down so we all saw it.
I remember wanting one and my mother said no. I
didn't throw many fits, but I threw one over that.
Gideon told me later, when it was just the two of us,

that I should listen to my mom. That he wished he didn't have the tattoo. When I asked Rafe about it, he said Gideon had had it since he'd known him. So at least since they were fourteen."

Daisy shook her head. "Who would allow a fourteen-year-old boy to get a tattoo?"

"I know, right? But I got the idea that getting it hadn't been his idea. He got it covered when he was eighteen. Something terrible had happened because Gideon was a mess, but I don't know what it was. Rafe knows, but he wouldn't spill. He said it was Gideon's story to tell. But after that, the tat was gone and now he's got a phoenix."

"Rising from the ashes," Daisy murmured. "Not a difficult metaphor to parse."

"Nope." Sasha handed the laptop back to Daisy. "What have you turned up on the locket's design?"

"It's definitely religious in nature. The two kids praying is a dead giveaway, for sure. The tree is an olive tree, I think. The angel has a flaming sword."

"Oh. Like outside the Garden of Eden." She chuckled at Daisy's look of surprise. "I went to CCD every week like every good Catholic girl. I was even confirmed. Do not say what you're thinking. I was a good kid. Things didn't get squirrelly until later."

Daisy dutifully mimed locking her lips, but it was all for show. Sasha's rebellious phase had been intense, but relatively short. She'd never had to go to rehab, at least. Not like Daisy had.

"Olive trees are religiously significant, too," Sasha went on, "but I don't remember how."

"That's what I was reading about. The oil is used to anoint priests and was also used to light the temple. The wood is used for a lot of things. But when you cross-reference the angel with olive trees, it turns out there are some who think the olive tree was the Tree of Life in the Garden of Eden. I'm wondering if the locket wasn't some kind of church thing. I don't know, like maybe a rosary or something. It was significant enough for Rafe to drag Gideon into the station late on a weeknight."

Sasha regarded her seriously. "Why is this important to you? Or are you just keeping your mind busy so you don't have to sleep?"

Daisy shrugged. "It's a mystery, the only lead to the man who attacked me. Who might have . . . I don't know what. Raped me? Killed me? That alone is reason enough. Finding the guy so that he can't hurt anyone else. Or come back and hurt me."

"That's a very good reason. But don't you trust Rafe and Erin to find him?"

"I guess I do. But I'm my father's daughter. I don't like to cede control."

"No," Sasha deadpanned, chuckling when Daisy flipped her the bird. "But I get it. It gives you back some semblance of control, and you must have felt you kind of lost that when you were attacked tonight."

"Yeah. But it's also curiosity," she admitted. "I hate not having the information. Rafe made me leave before they said anything really good. Or before Gideon accidentally blurted out anything else."

"*That* in and of itself is significant. Gideon doesn't blurt. Ever."

"He did tonight." Daisy bit her lip. "When he got lost there at the end—after he said the man was dead—I put my hand over his fist. He'd clenched his hands so hard that his knuckles were bright white. As I was leaving he . . . thanked me. It meant something—you know, to me. I just don't know what."

Sasha nodded knowingly. "Ah. I get it. Someone like Gideon, so self-contained, thanking you. It's nice. Makes you feel like you earned something."

"Yeah." That was it. She'd felt special. "And, if I'm

honest, some of it is that I don't want to go to sleep. I'm afraid of what I'll dream."

"You want me to stay with you?"

"You don't have to." But Daisy wished she would.

Sasha rolled her eyes. "What time do you have to be out of here for work?"

"Four twenty-five." It was less than three hours. "Hardly seems worth trying to sleep at this point."

"Rafe's here," Sasha said. "He came in when I was making the tea. Said he was going to grab a few hours in his old room. If you want to stay up until it's time to leave, I'll stay with you. We can play cards and braid each other's hair. Or Brutus's hair."

"She'd let you, too. Cards would be nice." Daisy logged out of her e-mail and handed the laptop to Sasha. "Thank you."

Sasha drew a pack out of the pocket of her robe. "I thought you'd say yes. Rummy Five Hundred okay with you?" She shuffled and dealt, then waited until Daisy was studying her hand before murmuring, "So . . . Gideon. He's not my cup of tea, but I have to admit he is easy on the eyes, wouldn't you say?"

Daisy thought about the man's strong jaw, clear green eyes, and the threads of silver in his black hair. She wasn't going to even think about what was under that suit he wore like it was made for him. "Enough, I guess. Sure."

Sasha snorted. "Right. He is *very* pretty, DD. You can admit that my mother was right. I promise not to tell her."

Daisy glared at her over the cards. "Be. Quiet." She dropped her gaze to her hand. "Fine. He's very, very pretty."

And he'd blurted out things when that wasn't his norm. She wanted to believe she'd had something to do with that, but it was far more likely that he had been rattled about something else.

She glanced at the laptop. What had she expected to find? A lead to her attacker or a glimpse into the man who'd all but taken her breath away when he'd walked into that little interview room? She still wasn't certain.

A smirk bent Sasha's lips. "Ooh, very *very*? I say the girl is smitten."

Daisy glared daggers. "And *I* say if *you* say one word to your mother, no one will *ever* find your body."

"Fine. Just for that, I'm going first."

SACRAMENTO, CALIFORNIA
FRIDAY, FEBRUARY 17, 4:05 A.M.

He staggered back, breathing hard. His back hurt, his hands hurt, his jaws hurt. He was covered in blood and he didn't give a shit. He stared at the woman in his bed and grinned from the pure joy of it all. Catching a glimpse of his face in the mirror on the wall, he broadened his grin, admiring his own image. Wild-eyed, covered in blood . . .

He looked insane.

He felt exhilarated.

Throwing a fist into the air, he laughed, exultant. *This moment.* This was the best moment. When he'd just finished and the endorphins were running through him like fire . . .

It was like he could fly, all by himself.

He closed his eyes, savoring the feeling for a few moments longer. It would be a while before he felt it again. Yes, he'd fly again, but not all by himself. Not like this.

His breathing began to level off and he opened his eyes. The woman stared up at the ceiling, her eyes open. Glassy. Dead.

Because she *was* dead. He'd gotten too into it, he supposed. He used to make them last. For days. But now they seemed to give up so quickly. Took a lot of the joy out of it, so he had to up his game. Had to get what he needed more efficiently since the women seemed to be growing frailer every time he hunted.

Rolling his head on his shoulders, he shook out his sore muscles and went into the shower to wash the blood off his skin. The hot water felt good on his exhausted body. Between the blonde in the alley and the one in his bed, he'd gotten one hell of a workout. He'd be able to sleep now.

And to think. He *really* needed to think about finding that damn blonde. He had to think about his job. What would he do now? He'd given the best part of his life to one fucking employer. It was supposed to be his only job.

I was supposed to retire with this fucking company.

Fucking bastard. We're watching you, his old man had said. *Just a little more experience. You're next on the promotion list. Take on extra hours, extra shifts. Work holidays so the family men don't have to. Be patient. It'll happen for you soon.*

Soon. Soon. Soon.

More like never, never, never. He winced, realizing he'd scrubbed his skin raw. He turned off the water and got out of the shower, drying himself off, then went to the bed and examined the woman one more time. She'd barely put up any fight at all, saying she was sorry and begging his forgiveness with the very first slice into her skin. She was kind of skinny, her torso so narrow that he hadn't been able to get all the letters carved in.

"S-Y-D-N" sprawled across her stomach. He'd added "E" on the right thigh and "Y" on the left. He made sure he got all the letters in each time, at least on the ones he brought back to his guest room. Otherwise it felt . . . incomplete.

This one had begun to beg before he'd finished the

first curve of the "S." By "D" she was already begging for death.

Miriam, on the other hand, had lasted two whole days. She'd had a will to live that almost made him regret having to break her. Almost. Because that was one of the best parts—when they finally gave up, recognizing that he alone held their lives in his hands.

That moment of surrender was what drove him, each and every time.

But this one was gone. Pulling the plastic sheet from the bed, he rolled the woman up like a burrito and dropped her into the chest freezer against the wall. She'd keep until he could dump her body.

He quickly sorted through her belongings. Her clothing and her backpack would go in the incinerator, as would most of the backpack's contents, including the apron bearing the logo of a local bakery.

Huh. She'd had a day job. It wasn't the first time one of the hookers had had a day job, but it wasn't the norm. That meant someone would be looking for her. He wasn't terribly bothered by this. He'd been driving the beige Chevy, which traced to someone else who wouldn't be answering any more questions.

He glanced at her driver's license, visible through the plastic sleeve in her wallet. Kaley Martell was twenty-nine and resided in Carmichael.

Thank you, Kaley. I really needed this tonight.

He went about cleaning around the bed, disinfecting the floor, the walls, and his tools with bleach. Just in case. Damn forensics were too good these days. But he kept one step ahead. He never left blood behind. Never left fingerprints.

He never left skin samples behind. *Not until tonight.*
Never left a witness alive. *Not until tonight.*

A little of the euphoric peace and satisfaction disintegrated as he once again thought about the blonde. *Tomorrow.* He'd start looking for her tomorrow, after work.

Needing to regain the satisfaction he'd lost, he opened the cabinet on the wall next to his bed. He normally let his guests see the contents because it eroded their resistance, but he'd gotten carried away with Kaley.

The cabinet opened like a triptych, with display shelves covering the back and sides. His souvenir cabinet, ten years in the making. It was impressive, if he did say so himself.

He slid Kaley's driver's license into the next open slot, then scowled at the empty hook beneath Eileen's. He should be hanging the damn locket on that hook, but it was gone. Stolen by the blonde.

But, thanks to Kaley, he had a new trinket—a crystal horseshoe, ironically enough. Her neck was too slim for him to use her chain, so he used a longer chain from his stash. Standing tall, he put the chain over his head, the charm hitting level with his heart. He drew a breath, feeling like himself again as he closed the cabinet doors.

Shutting the basement door, he listened for the click of the lock, then nearly tripped over Mutt. The dog lay on the floor just outside the basement door, just like he always did.

He leaned down to scratch behind Mutt's ears. "Let's go to sleep."

SIX

Gideon straightened his tie nervously. *Calm down.* He'd talked to his boss hundreds of times and never once had been nervous, but it had never been personal before. *Now it is.*

He rapped on the door and entered when he heard a muffled "Come in."

When he did so, he found Special Agent in Charge Tara Molina at her desk. "Special Agent Reynolds. Good morning." She pointed to a club chair and Gideon sat down, willing his hands to be still.

"Thanks for seeing me on short notice." He met her eyes directly. She was about fifty and angular. Every movement she made was economical and he'd never known her to mince words or waste anyone's time. So he wouldn't waste hers. "I have a friend on the SacPD force. He's a homicide detective. Last night he asked for my assistance on a case."

Her brows rose. "Not the usual way SacPD requests help. Why didn't your detective friend go through channels?"

"Because he knew that my connection to his case is personal. My friend is Rafe Sokolov. I'm kind of part of his family. They . . . helped me out when I was a teenager."

One side of Molina's mouth lifted, surprising him. "The family you make, as they say."

"Yes, ma'am. Exactly." Even though he'd decided what to tell her, Gideon still hesitated. "Have you heard of the Church of Second Eden?"

"The cult where you grew up," Molina said, surprising him again. She rolled her eyes. "I read your file, Agent Reynolds. I read the files of everyone who works in my field office. I know you grew up there and escaped. I know you've made allegations of abuse that were substantiated by hospital records. I know that you reported them to SacPD, but they found no evidence of the community. I know you reported them again after joining the FBI, but the search yielded nothing. I know you've made several requests to reopen the investigation in the years since, but there was no new evidence to support reopening the case. Are you asking to reopen the investigation?"

He was impressed. "Yes. I am."

She folded her hands on her desk. "I assume you have new evidence this time?"

"Yes, I do. Last night a woman was attacked on J Street. While fighting off her attacker, she pulled a locket from the man's neck. It was a locket worn by the women of the community. I'm requesting to both reopen the investigation into the community and that I provide security for Miss Dawson, the woman who was attacked. If this man comes back for her, his apprehension could lead us to the location of the community." And, as a side benefit, he'd be watching over Daisy. That would take a load off the collective mind of the Sokolovs. *Yeah. Right. The Sokolovs.* He wanted to roll his eyes at his own bullshitting self but forced himself to focus because Molina was watching him.

"How did you know it was a locket worn by a woman from the Second Church of Eden?" she asked.

"Because I recognized the engraving on the front—two children praying under an olive tree guarded by an angel with a flaming sword."

She closed her eyes briefly, then opened them, nodding. "I remember mention of that in the file. Was there a name on the back?"

"Yes. 'Miriam.'" On his phone he found the photo he'd taken of the locket and the photo inside and passed it to her. "That's the locket and the photo inside."

Molina's eyes flashed with sympathy. "She's so young. Twelve, right? The age that the girls were forced to marry."

"Yes."

"Did you know this girl?"

Gideon swallowed. "Yes. Her real name was Eileen. 'Miriam' was forced on her by the community."

"How did your friend know to call you?" she asked. "Had you told the Sokolovs about the community?"

"Not really. It was . . . painful to remember. I don't talk about it often." Reaching into his pocket, he found the photo of him and Rafe by the river and wordlessly passed it to her.

Molina studied the photo for a few long seconds, then her gaze flew up to meet Gideon's. "They tattooed you?"

He nodded. "On my thirteenth birthday."

"That wasn't in the file."

"I . . . don't like to think about it." The tattoo. The day he received it. What had happened afterward. *I killed a man.* And had nearly been killed himself. "I'd hoped the description of the locket and the abuse and forced marriage of twelve-year-old girls would be sufficient to get the FBI involved. It was, so I kept the rest to myself."

She didn't look away and neither did he, the two of them in something of a standoff until Molina dropped her gaze to the photo of the locket on his phone. "They're not exactly the same," she murmured. "Twelve branches on the locket's olive tree, thirteen on the tattoo's. For the age of maturity?"

"Yes, ma'am," he managed. His throat was thick and swallowing physically hurt.

"You were thirteen when you escaped?" When he only nodded, she sighed. "You'd been beaten badly according to your hospital records." She gave him a scrutinizing look. "Your medical records had been sealed, along with your foster records because you were a minor, but you gave us permission to access them when you joined the Bureau."

"I wanted the community found. Desperately." *For Mercy. For Mama. And for me.* "I've been searching for them for seventeen years."

Molina leaned back in her chair, arms crossed over her chest. "But you left the records sealed from the time you were eighteen until you joined the FBI, six years later. Why, if you wanted them to be found so desperately? Why didn't you report them sooner?"

He'd never been asked this question. He should have known that Molina would catch the small—but critical—fact. "Early on, I guess I figured the SacPD hadn't really believed me. That they thought I was just a kid, making up fantastic stories. I never thought of contacting the FBI on my own then."

"But later? The file from your initial FBI interview says that you always wanted to be a special agent, that you'd chosen your college degree in linguistics after consulting the FBI's Web site. So you thought enough of the Bureau at eighteen to want to join, but you didn't think to report this case?"

Of course he had. But he hadn't reported the community because of Mercy. Because she'd begged him not to. And because he'd been afraid enough for her mental health at the time that he'd agreed. He didn't think Molina would accept his excuses. "Can I expect confidentiality, ma'am?"

She considered it. "Unless you violate policy."

"I didn't even tell my friend this part of it last night. I've never told anyone."

She nodded once. "I understand. You're asking me to keep your secrets."

"Just this one, ma'am, because it's not my secret to share. My sister was also raised in the cult. She didn't get out at the same time as I did."

"So when you searched, you were looking for her."

"Yes. I eventually found her." But not where he'd been looking. Finding Mercy had been the doing of Irina Sokolov. Just one more thing he had to be grateful for. "My sister had also escaped, but she wasn't as lucky as I was. I was beaten. She was . . ." He swallowed hard, cleared his throat. "The words are easier to say when the victim is a stranger."

"She was sexually assaulted?" Molina asked gently.

Gideon's jaw clenched and he fought back the wave of emotion that always followed thoughts of Mercy's ordeal. "Yes, ma'am." *Repeatedly. For years.* "She won't make a formal report. I can tell you this before you ask. She's . . . dealt with it. Kind of." *Not really.*

"But you want revenge?" Another carefully phrased question.

Hell, yes. "No, ma'am. I want justice." Which was also true. "I want freedom for the others that are still being held against their will. I don't want other children to be forced to grow up the way we did."

Molina looked away, studying the view out the window. On a clear day, one could see the foothills of the Sierra Nevada. Today wasn't going to be a clear day. Clouds had already gathered. His boss watched them float by, her arms still crossed, tapping one bluntly manicured fingertip on her upper arm.

Finally she turned back to Gideon. "This is what

will happen. I am officially reopening the investigation. I will have one of my agents do a search of area pawnshops to determine whether the locket was sold by anyone or if a man matching Miss Dawson's description purchased it. In the meantime, you have one week to investigate this lead to the Eden cult. If you find anything—like a place to look for this community—you will bring it to me immediately and we will staff appropriately. Regardless, at the end of one week, you'll report back to me and tell me everything that you've found, even if you don't believe it's relevant."

He could barely believe his ears. She was giving him everything he'd asked for. "Yes, ma'am. And if I'm not finished by then?"

"Let's decide that after one week. I understand your personal mission, but it's easy for a person—let's face it, a person like *us*—to get swallowed up in the quest. You might not be the best person to be searching. You could be so close that you miss something critical. Also, you could easily become obsessed with finding your great white whale. That you've been searching for seventeen years shows me that you won't give up. But do this intelligently."

"That makes sense," he allowed.

Her lips twitched. "I'm glad you think so. Just so that we're clear: If at any time you locate this community, you will inform me. If you locate any specific threat to a specific person or persons, you will inform me. We will investigate and resolve the situation."

Um . . . no. But he simply nodded. "Yes, ma'am."

Her eyes narrowed shrewdly. "I'm serious, Gideon."

She had to be serious. She'd never called him Gideon before. "Yes, ma'am."

She shook her head slightly, as if she didn't believe his promise. "What will you do with your ongoing cases? Where are you on the Chang surveillance tapes?"

"I've translated everything that's come in so far and e-mailed it to you. Nothing of note on the drug trafficking case, but there was some vague conversation about a credit card scam they're starting. Jim Burns has been working with me. He can be brought up to speed quickly. If any new chatter comes in, call me and I can work on it from wherever I am. I'm not going far. I can be reached on my cell in an emergency." Unless he was in the mountains where cell signals were spotty at best.

Molina stood up, extending her hand over her desk again. "Take care, Gideon. I hope you find what you're looking for. If I have to tell anyone what you're doing, I'll keep your sister out of it."

Gideon shook her hand firmly. "I appreciate that, ma'am."

She gestured at the door with a tilt of her head. "Go. Your week's officially begun."

SACRAMENTO, CALIFORNIA
FRIDAY, FEBRUARY 17, 8:25 A.M.

He'd gotten some sleep, but not nearly enough, he thought, stifling a yawn. He'd left too late this morning. When he left on time, he managed to miss rush hour.

If he didn't get there soon, he'd be late for his shift and shit would hit the fan for sure. The old man would like that, he thought bitterly. *He's just looking for any excuse to fire my ass early.* Resisting the urge to lean on his horn, he turned on the radio.

He hated morning radio. Everyone was chirpy. Or trying for witty or sarcastic and missing both. He wished they'd just shut the fuck up and play the damn music.

He'd once had SiriusXM but let the subscription run out. He wasn't in his car often enough for it to be worth the money for satellite radio. So he was stuck with Sacramento's finest. TNT and Boomer. He rolled his eyes, hating both of them as he braced himself for inanity.

"And that was Jeff Buckley's 'Hallelujah,'" a woman's voice said, making him blink. "I love that song," she added wistfully.

She wasn't one of the cranky old guys. She sounded young. Husky. *Sexy.*

"You're not gonna cry, are you, Poppy?" a male asked sarcastically. That was TNT.

Shut up! he thought. *Let the woman talk.* He liked the sound of her voice. Soothing and smooth. He could listen to her talk all day.

"Not right this second, Tad," she answered sweetly, "but if I do, I'll ask for your handkerchief to blow my nose. Of course I'd wash it for you afterward. Maybe even iron it. *My* mama taught me manners."

He snorted, turning the radio up a little bit. *Good for you, Poppy. Set him straight.* Because TNT was usually a dick. She'd dressed him down but hadn't been rude. That was a disappearing art form.

"I do cry over some things," she went on. "Like the animals waiting to be adopted at the shelter. We're having an adoption day at Barx and Bonz in East Sac on Saturday. Come on down. You can meet me and Brutus. Right, Brutus?"

A yip followed and he frowned, thinking of that annoying dog from the night before.

"You tell 'em, Brutus," she said in that baby voice people used for dogs. That he might even have used on Mutt. Once. Or maybe twice. "Come check it out and you might meet your new best friend. Adoption day is sponsored by KZAU and Barx and Bonz, where you can find *everything* your pet needs."

And then she was gone, the feed going into a commercial about the pet store.

He instantly wished she'd come back. But she didn't. TNT had taken over and he was yakking over the music. *Which I detest.* He snapped the radio off, relieved because he was finally at his exit. Speeding the rest of the way, he rolled into a parking place and ran into the small building that housed their offices.

"You're late," Hank said. "Everything okay?"

"Yeah, sure." He didn't hate Hank, but the man was both clueless and irritatingly optimistic. "Traffic was a bear, that's all. Any coffee left?"

"I just made a pot. Customers called to say they're running a little late, too, so you can breathe before they get here."

"That's good." He poured a cup of coffee and turned back to find Hank watching him with pity in his eyes.

"You sure you're okay? Yesterday was a huge shock. I'm still . . . reeling," Hank confessed. "And wondering what the hell I'm going to do. My wife's pregnant again. I don't know how long our savings are gonna last. But it's gotta be hard for you, too. I know you expected to be—"

"I'm fine," he ground out before Hank could say that he had expected him to take over the company. "Worry about yourself. You've got a family. I'll be fine."

Hank nodded, not bothering to hide the hurt in his eyes at his harsh tone. "Fine."

Wonderful. Yelling at Hank was like kicking a puppy. "Look, man. I'm sorry. I'm tired and cranky. I hope you find something soon. That's all I meant."

"Thank you," Hank said quietly. "I've gone over the checklist. You can audit me."

Which was the way they usually did it and the way he preferred. That way he could add in a few odds and ends to their gear after Hank was done and nobody would be the wiser. Made transporting his basement guests so much easier.

"Also . . ." He pointed to the bathroom. "Random test day. You have to pee in the cup."

"Wonderful," he grumbled. "I'll be back in a few." It was good that he hadn't gotten high last night. That shit stayed with you for a long time.

That the random pee-in-a-cup test happened today was no accident. The old man was looking to fire his long-term employees. That way he didn't have to pay severance packages.

I'm going to stay here as long as possible, he decided. Just to make the old man squirm. *Make him fire me. I dare him.*

But even as he mentally spat the words, he knew they were more cavalier than he felt. Without his paycheck, he'd lose his house. And his basement.

He'd do anything to make sure that did not happen, and he wasn't completely without resources. He knew a few secrets that would stay the old man's hand. Secrets the old man would do anything to keep from coming out. Just in case Sydney was lying about having an in with the new owners. He was covering all his bases and taking no chances.

No pink slips for me.

This was the benefit of sleep. He was thinking now. Not panicking. *The best defense is a good offense.* He peed in the cup, then washed his hands and checked the fit of his wig, which was, of course, just fine. It was his everyday wig and would stay on during a hurricane. Well, at least a Category 1. Good thing they didn't live in a hurricane zone.

The less hair he kept on his body, the better. Nothing to fall off, nothing to implicate him. Placing his cap precisely on his head, he left the bathroom determined and confident.

Until his gaze landed on the woman waiting in the customer lounge, sitting in one of the armchairs like it was a throne, elbows propped on the armrests, her long legs crossed. A smug smile curving her lips.

"Sonny, I've been waiting for you," she said in that accent that made her sound like Katherine Hepburn, the one that grated on his nerves. The one that made him want to stick ice picks in his own ears. Or hers.

"What do you want?" he asked, fighting to keep his tone courteous.

"I think you know." Gracefully she rose and quirked her finger. "We need to talk."

Except talking was *not* what she wanted to do. And what she wanted to do made him physically ill. Every single time.

"I'm on shift," he said. "I can't."

Her tweezed brows lifted. "That's what you said yesterday, but I checked. You weren't on shift. You lied to me." She crossed the room to where he'd remained frozen as soon as he'd spied her. Her fingers petted the length of his necktie, smoothing it, smirking when he winced. "Why would you do that to me?" she purred.

Because I hate you and I wish you were dead. He wished he'd killed her years ago. But he hadn't and now he was paying the price.

"I was upset. I told you that last night. I heard that Paul was selling the company." He said "Paul," but he thought "the old man." Pretending to respect his father might assuage some of Sydney's pouting ire.

"Well." She walked her fingers up his tie, then tapped his chin with a manicured finger. He fantasized chopping them off, one by manicured one. "Like I told you last night, I can make sure you come out of this just fine."

She lied. She lied as easily as she breathed. She'd get what she wanted and leave him with nothing. Less than nothing. He might keep his job, but every time he gave her what she wanted, another piece of him died inside.

"Come to my place tonight," she whispered. "We can talk."

No. NO. "Okay," he heard himself say. *Because I'm a coward. A fucking pussy.*

"That's my sweet boy. Have a safe day."

And she was gone, taking all of his determination with her. He closed his eyes, his fury roiling like a tornado. All of the peace he'd achieved with last night's basement guest was gone like mist.

And he still hadn't even started looking for the blonde.

Just get through today. Do your job. And then go home, take a hot bath, walk the dog, and . . . you'll figure it out. You'll find the blonde. You'll keep your job. You'll keep it together. You always do.

"Hey, man, you okay?"

He turned to find Hank watching him with concern.

"Yeah," he said. "I'm fine."

Hank again didn't look convinced. "I can ask Ricardo to take your place if you need me to."

And let that asshole get his hours? *No way.* "I *said* I'm fine."

"Okay, okay." Hank backed away, hands held up in surrender. "Today's group will be arriving soon. I've got the cooler filled. This is a champagne-and-caviar crowd."

"God," he muttered. "Shoot me now." But he hoped they drank all the wine and ate all the fancy finger food because it left the cooler empty. And in his mood, he might need to fill it with something curvy to bring home. The cooler was the perfect size for a size eight. No bigger than a size ten. All soft and pliant. They folded up easier that way.

Hank laughed. "I know, right? But they tip well, and Barb and I need a new crib."

"Then let's do this." He gestured to the door. "After you, Captain Bain."

||| SACRAMENTO, CALIFORNIA
||| FRIDAY, FEBRUARY 17, 10:00 A.M.

Daisy took off her headphones and laid them carefully on the studio console. She'd kept her temper in check for four hours, but it was bubbling over.

Because Tad Nelson Todd—a.k.a. TNT—was a Grade A asshole. He'd started in on her at the beginning of the morning show, little digs at first. The way he always behaved. Those she could ignore or at least manage to laugh off. But the digs got worse and worse as the morning progressed and Daisy was pissed.

Tad wasn't as careful with his headphones, throwing them aside in a clear show of temper. Daisy shouldered Brutus's bag, waiting until Tad followed her out of the studio before turning on him with a scowl.

"What was that about, Tad?"

"What?" he asked flatly, as if he were bored.

"You. In there." She pointed at the studio door. "Calling me 'little girl.' Commenting on my body. Insinuating I'm a wild party girl."

"I just asked what you were doing for spring break," he said, smirking now.

"You asked what size bikini I wore!" And he'd guessed her measurements. Lasciviously. That had truly lit her fuse. She'd almost punched him. Luckily, he'd done the bit about her measurements—as well as his comments on her sexual preferences—during the last two minutes of the broadcast. She'd brushed his boorishness off with a laugh, but if she'd had to hold her temper much longer, she wasn't sure what she'd have done. "You all but gave out my phone number. What the hell was that about? And don't you dare say you were just fooling around." Not after the night she'd had. She was punchy from lack of sleep, too much caffeine, and the feeling that someone was still following her even though she knew it was her imagination on overdrive.

His lips curled in a sneer. "If you had a sexual harassment issue with me, why didn't you say so to my face? Why did you go tattling to the brass? They're considering suspending me. Did you know that?"

She rocked back on her heels, her mouth falling open in shock. "What? Why?"

He took a step forward, leaning into her face. "Because *you* squealed to Karl that I brushed off 'e-mails and voice mails of a sexual nature.'" He used air quotes, then clenched his hands into fists, dropping them to his sides. "It was nothing. Baby shit. Professionals don't whine about shit like that."

Daisy shook her head to clear it. "Let me get this straight. You were reprimanded for enabling sexually harassing behavior this morning, informed you might be suspended, so you decided to go on the air and *actually* sexually harass me? Because that's what *professionals* do? Do I have this right?"

His eyes were a little wild. Desperate. "Why not? Might as well do the crime if I'm gonna do the time. I might have a future as a shock jock."

She blinked at him. "You're an idiot. You know that?"

Anger flared, his jaw going rigid. "And you're a bitch. You know that? Hell, maybe you wanted me suspended."

She almost laughed. "You're joking. Why would I want that?"

"So you can have the show all to yourself."

"What? I don't want the show to myself."

He did laugh, bitterly. "Liar. You waltz in here from nowhere, *sidle up to Karl,* and then the morning show just falls into your lap. Abracadabra. Like *that's* any mystery."

She stared at him, disgusted. It was the way he'd said "sidle up to Karl," all sleaze and innuendo. "You can call me a bitch if you want. God knows I've been called worse. But don't you *dare* insinuate that Karl has been anything but kind and good—to all of us. Including you. Whatever you think about me, don't you dare spread rumors about him. He loves his wife and she loves him." She stopped to breathe, tilting her head when she saw his fury falter. "Did they tell you why I reported the e-mails and voice mails?"

Which she hadn't yet, actually, not technically anyway. She'd told Karl of their existence on the ride to the Sokolovs' last night and had been relieved when he hadn't pressed. *Guess that relief was premature.* Karl had obviously talked to Rafe and then the station manager. All before dawn.

"No." Tad's brows furrowed. "Why?"

"Because I was attacked last night." She tugged at her turtleneck collar, drawing it low enough that he could see the marks on her throat. It was the same sweater she'd worn the night before. There'd been no time for her to go home and change before work since Rafe had needed roughly sixteen cups of coffee to wake up enough to drive her into the city. "Some guy tried to strangle me and drag me away. I . . ." The memory hit her hard and her voice broke. Ruthlessly she steadied it. "I got away."

His gaze dropped to her throat, where the red marks had bloomed into dark black and blue bruises overnight. "Oh my God. Are you okay?"

She resettled the collar high on her throat. "Yes. Rafe Sokolov has the case. He and his partner asked if I'd been threatened, so yes, I told them about the e-mails. When Rafe asked why I hadn't told anyone, I said you'd assured me they were part of the business. That I should be flattered. Because you did say those things and last night I was scared and shaken. But I should have reported the messages when they happened. I knew better." She lifted her chin. "I'm responsible for my bad judgment, not yours. I'll tell them that."

Tad frowned, looking skeptical. "You will?"

"Yeah. I may be a bitch, but I'm an honest one, and I take responsibility for my own choices. But what you did in there today? You're on your own for that. I'll be filing a grievance against you." She turned on her heel, rounded a corner, intent on finding somewhere to chill and collect her thoughts before finding the station manager.

Instead she was abruptly stopped in her tracks. Actually, she was bounced backward when she collided into a hard chest. Strong hands reached out to steady her and angry green eyes glared down.

"Miss Dawson?"

Gideon Reynolds. She stared up for a moment, caught off guard and not prepared for his face. Or the rest of him. *Very, very pretty, indeed.* Her eyes narrowed as her brain caught up. "Why are you here? And why are you mad at me?"

"I'm not." He looked over her shoulder pointedly. Tad had followed her, and the sight of him had Gideon jutting his chin out and breathing like a raging bull.

Daisy looked from Tad back to Gideon, then to Rafe and Arnie, the station manager, who were right behind him. Everyone looked furious. She was guessing that they'd heard Tad's final on-air smears. Just like every listener in Sacramento had.

She pressed her palm to Gideon's chest when he started to go around her toward Tad, who was slinking away, retreating to the studio. "Wait," she murmured. "Please." Because he looked like he wanted to break Tad into little pieces. While part of her found that hotter than hell, it was a very bad idea.

At her touch, Gideon sucked in a sudden breath and

Daisy shivered. Later, she decided. She'd consider this later.

Pulling her hand away, she shifted her bag on her shoulder, shushing Brutus, who'd begun to whimper. "I'm filing a grievance, Arnie. I'm okay. Nobody needs to be this upset."

"Did he touch you?" Gideon asked in a low growl that made Daisy want to whimper along with Brutus, but for very different reasons.

This caveman possessiveness of his shouldn't be hot. But it is.

"No. He was just"—*a dick*—"unprofessional on air. How much did you hear?"

"That he wants to be a shock jock," Rafe answered, one brow lifted. He was still angry, but handling it far better than Gideon, the reputed vault. "I, for one, am hoping that dream will come true. But Arnie, we'll get out of your hair and let you handle things. It's okay if we take Daisy home? She can file her grievance later, can't she?"

Arnie nodded. "Not like we lack evidence. It's all recorded. Was he like that for the whole program? I only caught the last few minutes, but I heard him guess your measurements and your . . ." He winced. "Preferences."

He'd goaded her about whether she liked boys or girls and her preferred sexual positions. Right before he asked the listeners if they'd like her phone number. The switchboard had lit up.

"He wasn't that bad the whole way through," she assured him. "Just general"—*dickishness*—"um, un-professionalism."

Rafe snorted. "Look at who's all diplomatic this morning."

"And without sixty-two cups of coffee," she replied tartly.

Arnie gave her shoulder a squeeze. "See you

tomorrow at the pet adoption thing?" he asked her. Arnie Townsend was a nice guy. Somewhere close to sixty, he'd been the station manager at KZAU for at least a decade, maybe two.

"Absolutely." She smiled at him. "You'll be there, too?" He attended some of the station-sponsored events but had never come to the adoption center.

Arnie glanced at the two men standing like silent sentries. "I think so. Just in case. I'm so sorry about what happened last night, honey."

"I'm okay."

"If it was one of the listeners, I'll do everything in my power to find him," Arnie promised. "I've got our IT guy looking at all those threatening messages and we'll trace them ourselves, because heaven knows when SacPD will get to it. No offense, Rafe."

"None taken," Rafe told him. "We're backlogged everywhere."

Arnie patted her shoulder. "Until then, we're upping security in the parking lot."

"I walk to work," she reminded him. "But it'll be good for everyone else to be covered."

"You don't walk to work anymore," Gideon said behind her.

Oh, really? It made sense and Daisy would take the precautions they suggested, but she wasn't going to let them tell her what she was and wasn't going to do. *Nipping this in the bud, right now.* Eyes wide and deceptively innocent, she looked at him over her shoulder. "I don't? Says who?"

Gideon's grim mouth opened to reply, but Rafe cut in. "She's baiting you, Gid." Rafe put on his best puppy-dog expression. "For now, I'm ever-so-humbly asking you not to walk to work, DD. Please. For me and Dad and Mom and Sasha and—"

She laughed. "Okay, fine." She shook her head. "We'd be here all day if you listed the whole family."

Fighting back a yawn, she pushed past all of them. "Actually, going home to take a nap sounds really good. Let me get a few things from my desk and shut my computer down. I'll meet you in the lobby." She paused at the door to the office cubicles, realizing Gideon hadn't answered her original question. "And then Special Agent Reynolds can tell me why he's here."

SACRAMENTO, CALIFORNIA
FRIDAY, FEBRUARY 17, 10:10 A.M.

Gideon watched Daisy go, frowning. She was . . . "Different," he muttered.

Rafe laughed. "She is. She always was, though. Even when she was a kid she marched to her own drummer."

Gideon followed him to the lobby to wait. "You knew her as a kid?"

"Yeah. Our dads served in the army together and stayed fast friends, so we spent holidays together, celebrated birthdays, went on vacations, all that. Dad is DD's godfather."

Gideon lifted his brows. "So her coming to stay with you all makes sense."

"Wouldn't have made a difference if Dad was her godfather or not. The Dawson girls were like our cousins. Dad was devastated when they disappeared. Daisy was only eleven when her dad packed it all up and went north to that ranch."

"Because of her stepsister?"

"Yes. Taylor. Mom never really liked Donna—Taylor's mother—but she didn't have anything more than intuition."

"She said last night that her stepmother told her that Taylor's biological father wanted to take her away."

"It was worse than that. Donna claimed he was a

homicidal lunatic who'd raped and beaten her and that she'd barely escaped with her life. Frederick believed her."

"She must have been one hell of a convincing liar."

"Must have been, but Frederick was always the protective type. Always knew where all the girls were at any given time." Rafe chuckled ruefully. "My dad used to pity any man who tried to date one of Frederick's daughters. Sasha was devastated when they moved away. She and Daisy had been close."

"I don't think I ever met them."

Rafe absently scratched at the stubble covering his jaw. "I don't think you did. You and I met when we were fourteen. That was about the same time that Frederick married Donna. His first wife had died in childbirth with Daisy's baby sister, Julie. My mom jumped in to take care of the girls, but when Donna came on the scene, all that changed. Donna was territorial. Didn't like my mother's interference. We stopped seeing them as often. Frederick kept his kids in Oakland for holidays and the vacations stopped happening. Mostly because Donna and my mom couldn't be in the same room together without the claws coming out. When they disappeared, my folks were out of their minds with worry."

Gideon frowned. "He didn't tell your father where they were going?"

"Nope. Made a clean cut. Didn't hear from them again until about a year or so ago."

"Because Frederick discovered Donna had been lying all along?"

"Not Frederick." Rafe sighed. "It was Taylor. Donna did some deathbed confession and Taylor decided she needed to go to Maryland to meet her biological father, to see for herself if he was bad or good. Turns out he's a great guy. Taylor moved out there to be near him, and

Frederick moved to be near Taylor. Taylor and her father have so many years to catch up on. She was twenty-three when they finally met."

"Poor guy," Gideon murmured. "Taylor's biological dad, I mean. And your father. Did Frederick just up and call one day?"

"Out of the blue," Rafe said, shaking his head. "My father was so hurt. He won't admit it, but he's still hurt that Frederick didn't trust him enough to tell him the truth. Frederick still hasn't visited in person. Just phone calls and e-mails."

Gideon thought of the bighearted Karl. "But your dad forgave him?"

Rafe shrugged. "I guess so. Frederick still has some bridges to rebuild in my opinion, but my dad understands a father's need to protect his kids."

Gideon nodded at that, because he'd been lucky enough to experience Karl's protection. And affection. Rafe was so damned lucky and fortunately he seemed to know it.

"Plus," Rafe added, "my dad said that if Taylor's biological dad could forgive Frederick, then so could he."

"He forgave him? Really?" Gideon said, then heard the clacking of heels as Daisy joined them in the lobby. "That's pretty unbelievable."

"You're talking about Clay?" she asked. "Taylor's bio-dad?"

Gideon nodded. "It had to be hard for Taylor's father to forgive yours."

Daisy's face softened into a sweet smile. "Not really. Clay forgave Dad almost right away. Basically said life was too short to be bitter. He and Dad have become good friends. It's kind of amazing to watch them together. Speaking of, I need to call my dad. Which means I have to go to the phone store for a new cell. Unless your lab guy is finished with it," she added hopefully, looking up at Rafe.

Rafe produced a phone from his pocket. "They aren't, but I took care of it. This is an old one of mine. I had it wiped and your contacts and stuff transferred over. Use it as long as you need to."

"Thank you." Gratefully she took the phone and slid it into one of the front pockets of her bag, before reaching in and producing the ball of fur she called Brutus. Snuggling the dog up under her chin, she met Gideon's eyes. "Why are you here, Agent Reynolds?"

"Gideon," he corrected without having planned to. He'd planned to keep it formal. He frowned at that, so hard that his forehead pinched.

"Are you sure?" she drawled, sounding amused. "I can call you Agent Reynolds if you want me to."

His frown deepened. She kept him at a disadvantage and he didn't like that. "That won't be necessary."

She regarded him levelly, a mix of curiosity and compassion in her eyes that was both compelling and unsettling. Like she knew something he would have preferred to keep private. "Why are you here, *Gideon*?"

"I'm your . . ." His words failed because her blue eyes were narrowing in displeasure.

"My *bodyguard*?" she snapped.

"That's as good a word as any," he said, fighting the need to wince. A small woman with a ridiculous dog should not be so intimidating.

Rafe sighed. "Look at it as a mutually beneficial business arrangement," he said, and Daisy closed her mouth, silencing what would no doubt have been objections.

Gideon noted this. Rafe was very good at corralling Daisy to do what he wanted her to. He had the feeling he himself would not be so lucky.

"All right," she said suspiciously. She pointed to Gideon. "You explain. Rafe's got some silver-tongued pact with Satan going on. Tries to distract me."

Gideon snorted a laugh before he could stop himself. "That's accurate," he said, and when she smiled back at him, something settled in his chest. "It's pretty simple. The guy who attacked you connects to the locket. I want to trace that locket. If he comes after you again, I can keep you safe and get some information at the same time."

She watched him for a long moment. "So let's say I agree. How long will this mutually beneficial business arrangement last?"

"A week for now."

"And if he doesn't come after me? Especially considering I have a *bodyguard*?"

Gideon exchanged a glance with Rafe, who wore an I-told-you-so smile. *Bastard.* But Rafe *had* warned him that Daisy wouldn't take well to a bodyguard. After her father hiring someone to follow her around Europe, Gideon couldn't say he blamed her.

Still, he was a little offended. "I am quite capable of following you in a way that no one will know I'm there, Miss Dawson. Including you."

"Then why tell me at all?" she asked innocently.

Rafe covered a laugh with a cough. Gideon forced his expression to remain passively neutral even though in his mind he was grinding his teeth. "I thought you'd like to know you're being protected. I was *trying* to be *nice*."

She smiled at that. "Okay."

It was his turn to be suspicious. "Okay what?"

"Okay, you can be my bodyguard," she said graciously, dipping her head like a queen might. "And you may call me Daisy. Well, if we're done here, I'd like to go back to my apartment to go to sleep. Is that acceptable, Gideon?"

He found himself smiling yet again. "It is. My car's parked in the lot in back."

I have a fucking bodyguard. Un-frickin-believable.
Daisy was still silently fuming as Gideon pulled his car
into the driveway of Rafe's house, where she rented a
studio apartment. But she was not too stupid to live,
and thus grateful not to be alone after last night's attack. So she'd bitten back her irritation and smiled
sweetly, offering no overt resistance. It seemed to work
because Gideon Reynolds had finally relaxed, his mysterious, growly, bad-boy vibes settling into something
resembling grim competence.

He didn't seem to be any happier about the arrangement than she was. Although he *had* been furious with
Tad. More like he wanted to take the prick apart.

Which really wasn't that surprising. Irina had been
insisting for the last six months that Gideon was one of
the "rare good guys."

A good guy who apparently had programmed
Rafe's garage door into his own car. Gideon pressed a
button on the overhead light panel and the garage door
slid up.

"How can you open Rafe's garage?" she asked him.

He spared her a quick glance. "I used to live here."

She blinked. "When?"

His smile was wry. "Until six months ago," he said.
"When Rafe told me to hurry my ass up and move because he had a new tenant."

Daisy's mouth fell open, genuinely horrified. "I
kicked you out of your apartment? But Karl said it was
available, that Rafe needed the rent check. I never
would have—"

"Daisy," Gideon interrupted, his voice deep

and . . . authoritative. *Which should not be so enticing. Because I hate authority. I really do.* But she couldn't deny the shivers that ran over her skin at the sound of him saying her name.

He was watching her warily. *Because I probably sound insane.*

She lifted her chin, met his eyes. "Yes?"

"I'd bought a house and it was sitting empty because the thought of moving was exhausting. I was griping loudly every day about the commute from Midtown to the field office and the fact that I was paying rent *and* a mortgage. Rafe was about to kill me."

She smiled, relieved. "So my moving here kept Rafe from a homicide charge?"

He frowned as he pulled into the garage. "*And* kept me from being murdered."

She chuckled. "Okay. That's good, too."

He shut off the engine, then turned to give her his full attention. Which was a little overwhelming, Daisy thought, feeling her pulse ratchet up.

This could end up being very, very good or very, very bad.

"I won't bother you," he said quietly.

"Too late," she murmured, then bit her lip as her cheeks heated. But it was true. Gideon Reynolds bothered her on so many levels. Still, it was rude and that was not okay. "Sorry. I'd intended to keep that to myself."

One side of his mouth lifted. "I know having someone watch over you is not what you want."

"But right now, it's what I need. I really do appreciate it." She made a face. "Part of me hopes the guy will try again so that you'll get what *you* need. How insane is that?"

His smile was so gentle that it stole her next breath. "Incredibly insane. And very generous." He cleared his throat abruptly and the moment was gone. "This is how I thought we'd work this. I'll sleep on your sofa and drive you to and from work."

"What about my commitments? I'm doing the pet adoption clinic tomorrow." She knew she sounded a little childish and a lot defensive, but she couldn't make herself care. "I don't want him to steal my life, Gideon. I've lived that. For years. It was like prison. I can't go back to that. I won't."

Understanding flickered in his eyes, but it was more than empathy. It was a lot more personal than that. Like maybe he really *did* understand. She wondered about the locket once again. "I know," he said before she could probe for answers. "I respect that."

"But?"

"But nothing. You'll go about your life as if nothing is wrong. I'll discreetly follow you. If someone does happen to notice me and asks, tell them I'm a friend from the East Coast or from the ranch, like that Jacob person you mentioned last night."

She lifted a brow, the downsides to this plan all too apparent. "And if I'm going about my life, it's more likely that the guy from last night will try again."

Gideon shrugged. "It's more likely he'll try again if you're out there than if you're holed up somewhere safe. Make me a copy of your schedule. I'll research the setups ahead of time to figure out how to best remain out of sight."

"And at the end of one week you'll be gone?"

His left eye twitched. Just a hair. *A tell,* she thought, filing the discovery away for later. "How about we renegotiate terms when the time comes?"

Her cell phone buzzed, saving her from answering one way or the other. She winced when she saw her screen.

"What is it?" Gideon asked.

"A text from Irina. Asking if I've called my father yet."

"Ah. I take it that you've been putting that off."

Daisy laughed unhappily. "Oh, you could say that."

"I understand his concern in this situation," Gideon said carefully. "But I think I get your concern, too. He seems prone to take drastic action very quickly."

Daisy frowned. "Don't—" *Don't criticize him,* she'd been about to say. But Gideon had it right.

"I'm sorry," Gideon murmured. "I should have kept that opinion to myself."

"No. It's okay. Dad does make quick decisions. Most of them have been good ones because he's smart and careful, but the ones that haven't been? They *really* haven't been."

"Like whisking you all away to a ranch in the middle of nowhere."

"Yeah. But . . ." She sighed. "My dad has reasons for his paranoia." She swallowed hard, wanting to cry as she thought about those reasons. "Dad was in the military."

"With Karl. Rafe told me."

"Yeah. Well, I'm not sure if their experiences were the same. Dad was . . . changed."

"PTSD?"

"Big-time." Prisoner-of-war-survivor PTSD. *I'm so sorry, Dad.* "I never knew, not until this past summer. I mean, I knew he'd been in the military, but not what happened to him there. Finding out was a big shock." She shrugged. "He didn't even tell me. He told Taylor and I overheard him. And I didn't ask a lot of questions, because I was still upset that he'd had me followed. I'm still upset, but now I feel guilty about feeling that way. Which sounds crazy."

"No, it doesn't. You understand the 'why,' but that doesn't make his behavior okay."

"Exactly." She studied his face, shadowed in the semidarkness of the garage. He no longer looked grimly competent. He looked . . . lost. "Why do I think you're talking from experience?" she asked softly.

He blinked and the brusque Fed was back. "You should call your dad. Irina will just keep nagging you until you do."

She unbuckled her seat belt. "I will. Let's go in. Brutus will catch cold."

SEVEN

Gideon came to a dead stop in the living room of Daisy's studio apartment. His old apartment. Which had looked normal then. Now it looked like a craft store had exploded.

Holy fucking shit, he thought as he slowly turned, trying to take it all in. Every wall surface was covered with paper. Bright colors were splashed everywhere, some in random bursts, others as part of murals, landscapes, or portraits of people. And dogs. Lots of dogs.

A spinning wheel occupied the corner where his TV had once sat. Four different easels held more paintings, all in various stages of completion. Bolts of fabric—all bright colors with shiny textures—leaned against the walls in the dining nook, where a sewing machine dominated half of the table. The other half held a . . . he wasn't entirely sure what it was, but lopsided clay vases surrounded it. None finished.

He did another turn around the room. Nothing was finished. Not one single thing was finished. He turned to find Daisy scooping stacks of paper from the sofa. Her arms full, she slid open the coat closet's door with her hip, set the papers on the floor, and closed the door.

But not before he saw all the sports equipment the

closet held. Gideon saw a field hockey stick, a tennis racket, two soccer balls, and a pair of ice skates.

Daisy was now watching him with twitching lips. "Go ahead. You can say it."

"I . . . I honestly don't know where to begin."

She laughed. "You should see all the stuff I took back to the store."

He blinked at her. "Why?"

"Why did I take some of the stuff back?" She shrugged when he nodded. "Because it wasn't as much fun as I thought it would be."

He opened his mouth, then closed it again, crossing the room to one of the murals. It was a neighborhood, he realized. *This* neighborhood. He recognized the colorful homes and the businesses. Children played and people walked dogs along the streets. He could almost hear the shouts of laughter and the murmured hellos as people passed one another.

"Wow," he said softly. "It's . . . alive."

"Thank you." She came to stand beside him, staring at the mural fondly. "That's one of my favorite ones. I did it right after I moved here. I was so happy because there was so much of everything. Colors and scents and activity. A sensory feast."

The joy in the painting was unmistakable. "Because you'd come from isolation."

"Yes. Well," she amended, "not exactly. I'd just come from Europe and it was better than I'd always hoped. I could have stayed a lot longer."

"If you hadn't discovered your father was having you followed."

"Right. It took the fun out of it. I was so angry with him."

"Was he at least sorry?"

"Oh, of course. He felt really terrible. Like I said, my father is a good guy." She sighed. "Who I need to call. Make yourself comfortable. But be aware, if I get cornered, I'm totally saying I've got a Fed on body-guard detail."

"That's fine." At least he hoped so. He hoped Mr. Dawson didn't ask to speak to him because Gideon did not have a good opinion of the man based on what he'd heard to date.

He busied himself checking the security of her windows and doors while she put a kettle on the stove and dialed her father.

"Hi, Dad," she said as she added kibble to Brutus's bowl. The dog pranced up to the bowl and Daisy gave her fur a stroke with a hand that trembled.

Gideon tried not to eavesdrop, but the apartment was small and he had good hearing. Or maybe he was just looking out for her. She'd been upset enough, first by the attack and then that prick she had to work with.

She and her father exchanged a few pleasantries, Daisy's stiff and awkward, but she seemed to relax when she asked about her sisters. Julie apparently had a boyfriend named Stan. Taylor was planning a wedding for the summer.

Gideon wondered which of Taylor's fathers would be walking her down the aisle.

The kettle whistled and Daisy made two cups of tea. She handed him one of the mugs, grimacing as she asked her father about his latest cardiology appointment.

Her dread made a little more sense now.

"Well, that's good to hear," she said. "You're taking all your meds, right?" Sitting on one of the kitchen island stools, she slumped, elbow on the table and forehead in her palm. "So, Dad, I need to tell you something and I need you not to freak out on me, okay?"

Something about seeing her looking so small had Gideon pulling up a stool next to her. Sitting down, he sipped at his tea and nudged her cup a little closer to her.

She looked up, surprised appreciation in her eyes.

He gave her a tentative smile and a nod of what he hoped would be encouragement.

"First of all, I'm okay. But . . ." She proceeded to give him the bare facts of the attack, glossing over the voice mails and e-mails. She began massaging her temples, wincing in pain at whatever her father was saying.

Brutus padded over and, swatting Daisy's ankle with a paw, barked once. Daisy picked her up, settling the dog on her lap. "Of course I reported it. I was at the police station all evening. Rafe's on the case." Her fingers dug into her temple. "No, I do not need you to put Jacob 'on the job.' I have personal protection." Her eyes darted to Gideon's face in a bit of a panic, and he nodded calmly even though inside he was hoping like crazy that her father didn't ask to speak to him. Daisy had been tired and stressed before, but now she looked defeated and that pissed him off. "He's with the FBI. Special Agent Gideon Reynolds."

She winced again then held out her phone to him. *Sorry,* she mouthed.

"It's fine," he said quietly. Squaring his shoulders, he put her phone to his ear. "Mr. Dawson, this is Special Agent Reynolds. How can I help you today?"

"Why is the FBI watching my daughter?" Dawson demanded, but his voice trembled.

Gideon felt a stirring of pity. The man's hypercontrolling ways had created a lot of problems, but they spoke clearly of his love for his daughters. It had to be difficult for Dawson to hear what Daisy had been through in the last twenty-four hours. "I'm here in case her attacker makes another attempt."

"Why do you think he'd do that? He was some random guy. She fought him off. Why would he try again?" There was desperation in the man's tone but also an awareness that had Gideon paying more attention. Frederick Dawson might be overbearing and paranoid, but he was also very sharp.

"We don't know what his motive was."

"Don't try to snow me, Agent Reynolds. The FBI doesn't use its resources to guard every woman who gets attacked. What are you not telling me?"

Gideon sighed silently. The man was right. *And I'd want to know in his place.* "Daisy removed a piece of evidence from her attacker last night. There's reason to believe that that evidence connects to a previous crime."

Cuddling the dog under her chin, Daisy stared at him, eyes narrowing in interest as soon as he indirectly mentioned the locket.

Now I've done it. Although he'd been prepared to tell her at least a little about the locket. It only seemed fair.

"Which is why you're with her now," Dawson said. "How long will you be there?"

"At least a week."

Dawson exhaled. "I see." He was silent for a long minute. "I imagine I'm the last person she wants to see right now."

Gideon met Daisy's eyes directly when he answered, "I don't know about that. I do think your calmness in this situation would go a long way in helping *her* stay calm. She's had a traumatic experience and doesn't need to be worrying about what you'll do or that you'll have a stress-induced heart attack."

There was a long moment of silence. "I'd like your badge number," Dawson said quietly. "I need to know you're who you say you are."

Gideon rattled it off. "My boss is Special Agent in Charge Molina. I've also known the Sokolovs for sixteen years. Please call them if you want a personal reference."

"I'll do that. May I give you my cell phone number and ask that you call me if anything happens to Daisy? I won't interfere with her independence, but . . ." A shuddering sigh. "I'm still her father. I need to know she's okay."

"I promise." He noted Dawson's cell phone number when the older man rattled it off. "I'll try to text you updates regularly. Here's my number in case you need to reach me." He gave Dawson his number. "She's really all right, sir. She did all the right things last night. Said you taught her how. You've obviously taught her well."

Daisy's eyes went soft. *Thank you,* she mouthed.

You're welcome, he mouthed back.

"That's . . . good," Dawson said hoarsely.

"You want to talk to her now?" Gideon asked him, trying to sound kind.

"No," Dawson said. "Tell her to get some rest, but to call me later, it doesn't matter what time it is here. I'll have my phone by the bed. And tell her . . ." He cleared his throat. "Tell her I'm damn proud of her. And that I love her."

"Will do. Do you have someone with you? I think she'll feel better if she knows you're not alone, because this is stressful. For both of you."

"Tell her that Sally is here. She makes sure everything stays okay."

"All right. Good-bye, sir."

Gideon ended the call and gave the phone back to Daisy, who sat staring at him wide-eyed.

"Can I say I'm impressed?" she said with a smile. "You talked him right down from the ledge. Only Taylor's able to calm him down that fast. He and I always butt heads."

"He said to tell you that he's proud of you."

Daisy sucked in a startled breath, her eyes filling with tears. "He told you that?"

"Yes." He fought the urge to touch her face. To wipe those tears away. "Also that he loves you. And that Sally's with him, whoever that is."

Tears spilled down her cheeks. "His girlfriend. Dammit, I'm not going to cry."

Gideon snagged a napkin from the holder and handed it to her. "I see no tears. Just allergies."

She snorted inelegantly. "Fine. We'll go with that." She slid off the stool and laid a hand on his. "Thank you. For being here and for taking care of my dad for me."

Gideon stared down at her small hand resting on his. It felt nice. Too nice. He looked up and met her serious blue eyes, still a little damp. Neither of them said a word and the moment stretched out, thinning until it snapped and was over.

Gideon swallowed. "Go to sleep." He cleared his throat because the words had come out raspy and rough. "But not too long. I need to see the place where that pet thing is going to be held tomorrow morning so that I can plan. We'll drive over before it gets dark."

She nodded once, removing her hand from his, leaving him feeling cold. "All right."

He sat unmoving as she carried the dog to the back of the small apartment that served as a bedroom, then heard her say, "Shazam, Brutus." But he had only seconds to wonder at her words before the shower turned on, making him visualize images that were entirely inappropriate.

Stop it, he commanded himself harshly, pushing away from the kitchen counter to pace. He was here to work. To protect her. Nothing else could happen. Still, he drew a grateful breath when the water shut off, leaving the apartment blissfully silent.

‖ EAGLE, COLORADO
‖ FRIDAY, FEBRUARY 17, 11:45 A.M.

"Is this seat taken?" he asked the woman sitting alone at the bar. Hank had accompanied their guests on the shuttle into Vail, which was about forty minutes away.

They did this route often enough that they knew the limo and shuttle drivers.

Hank always volunteered to ride along with the shuttle here in Vail, claiming it was because the shuttle driver was too "little" to haul all those heavy bags.

He doubted it, though. He'd seen the way Hank looked at the woman, like she was a pork chop and Hank a starving man. Hank looked at all the female drivers that way.

He didn't care if Hank was being unfaithful to Barb. It was sleazy, especially with Barb being pregnant, but a lot of men in their line of work had a woman in every port. What was important was that he had two hours to kill and he knew just what to do with them.

The woman at the bar looked up at him wearily. "Look, hon," she said in a voice that dripped of magnolia and mint juleps. "I don't want to be rude to you, but I'm having one helluva bad day. My ex-husband is being a jerk and I have cramps to boot. You're welcome to sit here, but I'm not going to be good company and I don't want to ruin your day, too."

He found himself smiling at her, which was a little disappointing. If she'd been rude, she would have been perfect. But . . . he didn't invite nice women home to his basement. "I hope you feel better. I've got ibuprofen if you need it."

Miss Mint Julep smiled back. "That's so sweet of you, but I've already taken some." She lifted her glass, which appeared to be full of bourbon with a mint garnish. She was actually drinking a mint julep. "A few more of these and I won't care about the cramps." She pointed to the other end of the bar, where a younger woman sat putting on lipstick. "She might be more to your liking."

Dropping her lipstick in her handbag, the woman in question sneered at both of them. "Like I'd ever," she snapped and hopped off the stool. "I've got a plane to catch."

"How rude," Miss Mint Julep said with a frown.

"Indeed," he murmured. Rude, thus perfect. She was wobbling on precariously high-heeled boots. "Looks like she's had too much. I'm going to make sure she gets to her car."

Miss Mint Julep smiled, popping her dimples. "Aren't you just the sweetest thing?"

"I try, ma'am." He followed Miss Rude from the bar, feeling for the sedative in his pocket. He liked this bar because it had really old cameras. And it didn't matter anyway. He'd switched out his everyday wig for what he liked to call his "rock star" look. With a few facial prosthetics, his own mother wouldn't have recognized him.

Miss Rude was staggering to her car, obviously tanked. He'd be doing the world a favor by getting her off the street. Hell, he could be saving lives, right now. He chuckled at that and jogged a little to catch up to her. "Miss?"

She spun on her high heels, teetering. He couldn't have asked for a better setup.

"I said, fuck off," she said, managing to be withering while incredibly intoxicated. She grew more perfect by the moment.

"No, you said 'Like I'd ever.' And that you had to catch a plane."

She blinked. "What? Leave me alone." She flicked her hand, as if he were a bug.

"Let me help you." He stepped up, pulled the syringe from his pocket, and plunged it into her neck. He really hated the winter. Not a lot of visible skin, so he had to stick his needle as best he could. To any onlooker, it would appear that he was helping her to his car. Or the car he'd "borrowed" from the shuttle driver. She wouldn't be needing it for a while since she was doing the horizontal tango with Hank.

He lowered the woman onto the backseat of the

shuttle driver's four-by-four, folding her into the large duffel bag he'd positioned specifically for this purpose. The woman fought initially, but he'd slapped duct tape on her mouth and bound her hands and ankles within thirty seconds.

He was getting better at this. Years ago it had taken him a full minute and a half. He'd learned shortcuts over the years—like positioning the duffel bag and leaving precut strips of duct tape on the seat. Choosing a victim of the right height was key. Choosing one that was drunk was good. One having consumed GHB was even better.

The one requirement they all had to have was rudeness. If they were nice, he wasn't interested. It was the rude ones that had to go. It was a fucking public service, just like taking a drunk driver off the streets.

He'd given her a hefty dose of the sedative because he didn't want her waking up before they got back to Sacramento. She needed to stay asleep for a good five hours. Six would be better. He'd stash her in the giant cooler he'd bought for the company years ago. Hank had thought him crazy, but he'd told him that he liked to bring home quartered elk if they had an overnight and he'd gone hunting.

Hank was an avowed vegetarian. Just the possibility of red meat in the cooler ensured he'd never even look. *If he only knew.*

He zipped up the bag, straightened his wig, then checked the time, pleased. He was ahead of schedule. He actually had real time to kill. He headed back into the bar, where Miss Mint Julep was ordering another bourbon. He sat next to her and ordered a club soda.

"What happened to the bitch?" she asked companionably.

"She was going to drive her rental to the airport." He rolled his eyes. "She was three sheets to the wind, so I called her a cab. The rental agency can fetch the car later."

Miss Mint Julep lifted her glass. "To gentlemen."

He smiled at her and did the same. "To nice ladies."

SACRAMENTO, CALIFORNIA
FRIDAY, FEBRUARY 17, 2:15 P.M.

The sound of male voices speaking in low tones woke Daisy from her nap. She wasn't a sound sleeper under the best circumstances. Being raised by a paranoid father had seen to that. They'd always been on alert, always ready to take up arms or run.

It had been exhausting. And a hard habit to break.

Pushing her hair from her face, Daisy rolled out of bed and straightened the sweats she'd put on after the shower she'd taken after calling her father.

After witnessing Gideon handle and comfort her father. *Holy cow.*

She was sure that he didn't realize what a feat that really was. Frederick Dawson had always seemed indomitable. Unbreakable. A force of nature. Someone she'd both admired and . . . feared a little, if she was being honest. He'd carried an intensity that had been, at times, overwhelming.

But he'd always loved her. She'd never doubted it. He'd loved them with a fierceness that she'd accepted but never quite understood. Not until recently. Maybe it was time, maybe maturity, maybe even the fact that she'd gotten a few hours' sleep, but Daisy woke thinking of her father in a much more compassionate light.

How much guilt must he have carried on his shoulders for robbing them of ten years of their lives? She needed to call him. Put his fears to rest. She loved him, no matter what.

She pushed at the accordion-style screen that separated her bed from the rest of the open-plan apartment. The only interior door led to the bathroom, so it only took a blink to see that the two men talking were Rafe and Gideon.

Funny, though. She hadn't been even the slightest bit frightened at waking to male voices. She could take care of herself, as she'd shown last night, but it was nice to not need to. For a little while. And that was what Rafe and Gideon had given her—that bubble of safety.

The two were sitting at a card table that Daisy recognized as Rafe's. They'd moved her sofa and chairs so that there was room for the table, which was covered in bits of paper.

Gideon sensed her first, whipping around to look at her over his shoulder. He scrutinized her, toes to face, then nodded, seeming satisfied with whatever he'd seen.

"You slept," he said.

Rafe looked over and smiled lazily. "Hey, DD. Sorry if we woke you. I wanted to do this upstairs where we could be quiet, but the Fed insisted we keep an eye on you."

Daisy smiled back. "I'm grateful to the Fed. I was able to sleep a little because I knew he was here."

"The Fed is sitting right here," Gideon said, rolling his eyes. "The cop brought food."

Rafe opened the plastic container and the aroma of meat pie tickled Daisy's nose. *"Pirozhki,"* he said.

Daisy's stomach gave a sudden growl and she plucked the container from his hands. They were the bite-sized meat pies that had been her favorites when she was a little girl. "Your mom was busy this morning," she said with a fond smile.

"She wanted to make you feel better," Rafe said gruffly. "She felt helpless."

Daisy stared at the little pies for a moment, remembering. "She made these for me after my mom died.

She'd hold me on her lap and sing to me, then she'd feed me *pirozhki*."

"I know," Rafe said gently. "I didn't know if you remembered."

"I remember everything your folks did for me back then." She blinked back tears, because she was not crying in front of Gideon again today. "What was your favorite?" she asked him. "What did Irina make for you when you were sad?"

Gideon looked startled. "Um . . ." Then he smiled. "Honey cake. Luckily she always has one made."

"That's good, too." She narrowed her eyes at Rafe. "Any news?"

"Only that we found your friend Jacob. He was on his ranch and had been at the time of the attack. It was verified by the local vet. They were birthing a foal. All night."

"At least Jacob doesn't have to worry about SacPD breathing down his neck." She pulled a stool over to the card table and sat down to see what they were doing. Munching on Irina's offering, she studied the hundreds of pieces of paper that covered the table. Some were squarish, most were rhombuses. *Or rhombi?* she wondered. "Rhombi," she decided aloud. "Definitely. Why are you—?" She cut off her own question when she realized the answer. "The cut-up photo from last night. These are the pieces?"

Gideon nodded, respect flickering through his eyes that made her want to preen. "Yes," he said. "Cindy Grimes, the forensics investigator from last night, is working on putting the pieces back together."

"So that she can get fingerprints," Daisy said absently. "Can you pass me a napkin, Rafe?"

Rafe leaned sideways, the apartment small enough that he could reach the dining nook table from where he sat. "We thought about clearing your stuff from the table but I wasn't sure if you were in the middle of a project, so we brought a card table down."

Daisy glanced at the sewing machine and pottery wheel that took up her entire dining area. "In between projects," she said, then returned her attention to the scraps of paper spread across the card table. "How long did Cindy think it would take to assemble the pieces?"

"Several days at least," Rafe said, "because she'll need to do it under a microscope. But she made a copy of them for us. Said if we wanted to help, she'd be grateful."

Daisy wiped her fingers on the napkin that Rafe put in her hand. "Thank you," she said to him, and then began rearranging the pieces. "Cindy enlarged them."

"She did," Gideon said. "What are you doing?"

Daisy didn't look up. "The puzzle."

Gideon put his hand over hers. "Stop it. I had those pieces sorted."

She blinked up at him, momentarily riveted at the sight of his face, only inches away from hers. His green eyes had grown dark with irritation. He was very, *very* pretty, but apparently not so good with puzzles. "Um. No, you didn't." He opened his mouth to protest and she popped a *pirozhki* between his lips. "Eat and watch. I may appear to be a little flaky." She gestured to the clutter of the apartment, which she suspected he'd only seen as an unfinished, undisciplined mess. He wasn't entirely wrong, but he wasn't entirely right, either. "I may not be good at pottery or a lot of other things, but there are some things I rock at. Puzzles is one of them. Now hush and let me work."

Rafe took the bowl of meat pies from her hand, leaving her free to rearrange the pieces twice as fast. "Living on a ranch in the middle of nowhere affords few recreational opportunities," she murmured, her gaze focused on the hundreds of pieces, looking for color variations and shadows. "We did a lot of puzzles."

She sorted and squinted and sorted some more, losing track of time as she moved the pieces around until a portion of the picture started to come together. The woman's face. "Miriam," she said softly.

"Eileen," Gideon corrected in a whisper.

She glanced up at him. He was watching her, and this time his respect was unmistakable. "I thought her name was Miriam."

He frowned, then nodded. "Right. You'd left by then."

"I was thrown out," she said petulantly.

Gideon's lips twitched. "Sorry about that. Her church name was Miriam, but her mother called her Eileen. That was the name on her birth certificate. She hadn't been born in the community. She was renamed once her family entered."

"Community," Daisy repeated. "You mean the Eden church?"

Gideon sucked in a breath, his head jerking around to stare at Rafe. "You told her?"

"No," Rafe said firmly. "How did you know that, Daisy?"

Daisy frowned at them, because they were both aiming accusatory stares her way. "It wasn't all that hard. God, you people must really think I'm stupid." She dropped her focus back to the table and began sorting the remaining pieces with a vengeance. Until she felt a warm hand covering hers. She looked up to see Gideon's expression filled with apology.

"I'm sorry," he said. "The last thing I think you are is stupid. How did you know?"

She didn't say anything for a long moment as the heat of his hand seeped into her skin. It felt so good because she was so cold. "I Googled 'angel with a flaming sword' and 'olive tree.' Lots of biblical references. The Garden of Eden is a commonality."

"Eden," Gideon said, his voice strangely muted, "was where I grew up."

"And where Eileen grew up?" she asked.

"Yes."

"Where she got a locket and you got a tattoo?" she pressed on when it didn't seem like he'd say anything more.

His eyes widened so abruptly she might have smiled had this moment not felt so ominously heavy. Again he glared at Rafe, who again shook his head.

"I did not say a word, man."

Gideon sighed. "Sasha."

Daisy nodded. "I didn't think it was a big secret. She didn't seem to think so. She said you got it covered up by a phoenix."

"When I was eighteen."

She tilted her head to study him. "Why?"

Gideon looked away and Rafe's mouth tightened. "It's a long story, DD," Rafe murmured. "It's . . . hard to talk about. And not really our secret to share. Either of us."

"Okay." She didn't like being kept in the dark but respected keeping the secrets others had entrusted her with. She returned her attention to the table, sorting and connecting pieces until a man's face began to emerge. The top part anyway. No features were visible. Yet.

The sound of a cell phone intruded, but she dismissed it. It wasn't her ringtone. One of the chairs pushed back from the table.

"Gotta go," Rafe said.

Daisy flicked her gaze up. "New case or mine?"

"New one. Text me a photo as soon as you finish his face," Rafe said tersely.

"Of course," she said. "Be safe."

Rafe gave her a nod and was gone, leaving her and Gideon alone in the quiet. She resumed searching for the rest of the man's face, getting lost in the rhythm of "sort, seek, compare, discard." And sometimes "find." She couldn't have asked for a much more perfect way to manage the stress of the day.

That she could detect the scent of Gideon's aftershave each time she took a breath? That was just a bonus.

EIGHT

You sure you don't need help with that thing?" Hank asked, pointing to the cooler, which contained a certain Miss Rude.

He shook his head. "I got it. You go on home. Barb's waiting." They'd picked up a headwind and had arrived back in Sacramento a half hour late.

"Thanks. I need to stop by the store and pick her up some ice cream. She says she's craving vanilla. Who craves vanilla?" He shrugged, his easy smile reappearing. "But I don't ask her that question. She doesn't ask for much, so I don't mind indulging her."

You do that, he thought sourly. *Indulge your pregnant wife after you've cheated on her with the shuttle driver.* Because the scent of perfume on Hank's uniform had been unmistakable when he'd finally returned from escorting the passengers to their ski holiday. And Hank had that relaxed look that was like a blinking neon sign: *I got me some.*

And I don't really care because I have what I need in the cooler. "See you on Sunday."

Hank frowned. "Right. It's a long one on Sunday."

"New York City," he replied, knowing full well that the reason for Hank's frown was not the length of the flight, but the fact that he didn't know any of the shuttle drivers at the New York City airport. Poor Hank.

He rolled his eyes. The guy was just going to have to make do with his own wife for a few days. *Tragic.*

He watched Hank head for the locker room, where he'd shower and change into clothes that didn't smell like another woman. Then Hank would drop his uniform off at the dry cleaners and get it back all de-perfumed and no one would be the wiser.

Except me. He saw all the actions of the people around him, most of which he was sure they'd prefer to keep secret. Including the old man who thought he was getting away with selling the company and leaving them all jobless and destitute. He wondered if the old man would be so quick to sign on the dotted lines if his affairs became public. Like Hank, his father had cheated on his wife. To be fair, Sydney cheated, too, but that wasn't the issue.

Paul Garvey had also cheated on his employees, stealing from their retirement fund. It was only a little every year, but over time it added up. To a lot.

He'd been prepared to be quiet because he'd been promised big things. Paul had promised him control. Ownership, even. But Paul had lied. Now he just had to figure out how best to expose the old man for the lying cheat he really was. *Then I'll be in charge.*

His phone buzzed with a text. He rarely got texts, so this wasn't likely to be good. Sure enough . . . His teeth ground together as he stared at his phone's screen. *Sydney.*

I understand you're back. Hurry, sweet boy. I'm waiting.

He closed his eyes. It was like she knew. She always knew. Just when he was getting his confidence, she obliterated it. *Tell her no. Just tell her no. Tell her to fuck off.*

But he knew he wouldn't and he hated himself more than he hated her. *I am a coward. Sniveling, even.* That was what she called him when he was too young to know what she really was. Sniveling. *Yeah. That's me.*

Ignoring the text, he made his way to his Jeep. A few minutes later he was parked in the hangar at the base of the plane's stairs. He boarded, his eyes immediately focusing on the cooler. He was going to need Miss Rude tonight.

He lifted the lid, which he'd left cracked so that she didn't suffocate, and saw that Miss Rude was starting to wake up. He needed her to stay quiet for a little longer, so he injected her with a bit more sedative.

She blinked at him sleepily. "Hold on," he told her. "This next part gets a little bumpy." Yanking the cooler, he dragged it down the stairs, hefting it into the back of his waiting Jeep in a practiced move. He lifted weights for this exact reason.

Miss Rude barely weighed anything, so he wasn't even winded when he returned to the plane for cleanup. He'd taken care of most of the Vail group's mess while he'd waited for Hank to return from his afternoon delight, picking up the discarded cups and bottles of champagne. There was very little food on the floor. The passengers had paid for good caviar and hadn't let a single egg go to waste. A quick vacuum and he was ready to go home. To unload Miss Rude and get her situated in his basement guest room.

Then he'd deal with his nightmare. He'd be in trouble for not hurrying, but he didn't care. When she finished with him he was going to need his new guest.

What about the blonde? When will you deal with her? He grimaced. He needed to figure out who she was and what she'd been able to tell the police. He didn't have the slightest clue where to start. He'd checked the online police blotter before he'd left for the bar where he'd met Miss Rude. The altercation had been mentioned, but the blonde's name hadn't been listed. Nor had the name of the woman she'd been walking with.

He got in his Jeep and leaned his head back, ignoring the dull throb in the base of his skull. He needed a drink to settle his nerves.

Oh. The realization struck him and he laughed out loud. *Duh.* It was so obvious. He didn't know the blonde's name, but he *did* know where to start looking.

SACRAMENTO, CALIFORNIA
FRIDAY, FEBRUARY 17, 4:55 P.M.

Daisy Dawson was fascinating. It was difficult for Gideon to focus on the e-mail he was trying to compose because he couldn't tear his eyes away from the woman who was putting the pieces of Eileen's locket photo together like she was some kind of computer.

Daisy's eyes flicked back and forth between the pieces and the face she was assembling. The man's face was doubly hard to reassemble because it had been cut into much smaller pieces.

Not that surprising, all in all. Eileen had to have been unhappy with her second husband because she'd escaped. It was always a dramatic event. Nobody just walked out of the place. Nobody but the upper echelon of the community.

The cult.

He'd planned to tell Daisy as much as he could while she put the puzzle together. Anything not to have to see her face when he told the story. But he hadn't. He'd tried, but he couldn't make the words come. He did not want to see pity in her eyes. Ever.

He wanted to see interest. Respect. Gratitude wouldn't be bad. He'd liked seeing that in her eyes after he'd talked to her father. Who'd texted him three times this afternoon, apologizing every time he'd asked if his daughter was all right. Gideon didn't mind answering. He could be a buffer for Daisy, at least for today. She had too much on her mind to be stressed out by her father, even if he really seemed to care about her.

Daisy made a small sound of delight—the same sound she made every time she'd fitted another piece of the puzzle together. But she didn't stop to celebrate. She kept going, her blue eyes barely blinking.

He found himself wondering if she made that sound at other times. If she'd make that sound with him. In the bed that took up the back wall of the apartment. He closed his eyes, willing his body to stand down, because that noise she made lit up every nerve he had.

He needed to stop torturing himself. She was off-limits. Period. In another situation, he might have felt okay with asking her out. *Like if you'd gone to Irina's Sunday dinner and met her like Irina wanted you to.* But he hadn't and now he was meeting her when she was vulnerable.

As am I. He was dreading the moment when she pieced the man's face together. Dreaded knowing who had married Eileen after Edward McPhearson was dead. He hoped it would be one of the kinder men, but his gut was telling him it wouldn't be.

Gideon forced himself to look away from her to his laptop, where he'd been composing an e-mail. He was calling in a favor, pure and simple. If his former colleague couldn't help him quickly, he'd have to get into the sketch artist's queue at the field office and that could take forever.

Hi Tino—I hope you are well. I have a favor to ask. I've attached a photo of a twelve-year-old girl. She's a person of interest in my investigation, who could be in danger. She's currently thirty years old. Can you work your magic and send me a rendition of what she'd look

like now? I need this ASAP, of course. If you're too
backed up to turn it around quickly, can you let me
know? I'll find someone else to do it, but your work is
the best I've seen.

Thanks,
Gid

He'd scanned the photo of Eileen from her first
wedding, editing out the man at her side. Seeing
McPhearson's face wasn't necessary for Tino to do his
age progression, and Gideon didn't want anyone asking too many questions about Eileen's first husband.

Because I killed him. And he was not sorry. Not
even a little bit.

▌▌▌ SACRAMENTO, CALIFORNIA
▌▌▌ FRIDAY, FEBRUARY 17, 5:55 P.M.

Daisy blinked at the sudden flood of light. Gideon had
rolled her crafting light to the table. A look over her
shoulder showed the sun had dropped below the horizon.

She lifted her eyes to Gideon's face. "Oh no. We
were supposed to go to the pet store so that you could
scope it out before dark."

"It's okay," he said. "This is more important. We
can leave early tomorrow morning. Did you know your
stomach's been growling?"

Daisy felt her cheeks heat. "Sorry. I get . . . sucked
into stuff like this."

He shook his head, then went to the microwave. It
smelled like he was heating up the *pirozhki* and her
stomach growled again, loudly.

"Don't you dare apologize," he said, taking the food
out of the microwave. "Watching you work a puzzle is
better than ninety-eight percent of the shows on TV."

"What shows are the two percent that are better?" she asked, teasing him.

"*Fixer Upper* and . . ." He turned to face her, bowl in hand, hesitating. His wince accentuated an epic blush that was far too attractive. "*Buffy.*"

She grinned at him, because his being a fan of the vampire slayer was the last thing she'd expected. "Another blonde who's not too stupid to live."

His expression grew pained. "I never said that about you."

She softened her tone, so that he'd know she'd been teasing. "No, you didn't." Sliding off the stool, she stretched her back. "Although sitting on that stool wasn't smart. Now my back is killing me." She replaced it with the chair Rafe had vacated. How long ago, she wasn't sure. Sinking into the chair, she flashed Gideon a grateful smile when he handed her the bowl of *pirozhki* and a fork.

"So your fingers don't get messy," he said, gesturing to the puzzle. He moved his chair so that he sat next to her instead of across. "You're making progress."

She hadn't yet finished the man's face. She had his eyebrows and forehead, his left cheek and half of his mouth, his right eye, and his chin. But she was close.

"The light's going to make it easier to put the rest of his face together, so thank you," she said, her gaze back on the table. "I didn't even realize it had gotten dark. What time is it, anyway?"

"Almost six. You were sucked into it for three and a half hours."

She frowned. "I should be done by now. I can do a six-hundred-piece puzzle in two hours. To be fair, though, this is not a normal puzzle." She sorted through the remaining pieces that went with the man's face. "I just hope we aren't missing any."

"We have software we can use to extrapolate," Gideon said. "Do what you can."

A soft bump to her ankle had Daisy looking down to where Brutus gazed up, all bat ears and hopeful eyes. She scooped her up and nuzzled her. "Are you feeling ignored, girl?"

Gideon frowned. "*Girl?* She's a girl? Why did you name a girl dog Brutus?"

"I couldn't think of a girl name that was as mean. She's little and sweet. I wanted her to feel big and tough on the inside."

Gideon didn't look convinced. "If you say so."

"Don't diss the dog," she said lightly. "She helped me fight off that man last night."

He nodded once, one side of his mouth bending up. "Fair enough."

Wishing she could see him really smile, she set Brutus on the floor and forced her eyes to the puzzle. She tried to find the man's left eye, but there were no more eye-type pieces. "I think we're missing an eye."

She felt Gideon's response before she could lift her eyes to his face, which had grown abruptly pale.

"Gideon?" Daisy slid her hand over the exposed skin at his wrist. He'd taken off his suit jacket, but his shirt was still buttoned to his throat, sleeves buttoned at the cuffs. His tie still knotted tight.

She contemplated loosening the tie if he didn't snap out of it. "Gideon?" She gave his arm a hard shake. *"Agent Reynolds."*

He looked down at her, his eyes strangely . . . off. "Look for a patch," he murmured.

It took her a second. "Oh. I said we were missing an eye. I meant the pieces." She studied him cautiously. "But you didn't. You meant that he's actually missing his eye. Because you've just figured out who this is."

He swallowed hard. "Just see if there is a patch. Please."

The *please* had been uttered politely. Formally. It broke Daisy's heart, because Gideon *did* know who this man was and he was afraid. The big strong man sitting next to her was afraid.

She focused on the remaining pieces, quickly finding the patch now that she knew what she was looking for. She should have figured it out sooner, she thought, mentally chiding herself. There was a dark diagonal line over the man's forehead. She'd thought it was a flaw in the photo, but now she knew that it was the cord that held the patch in place.

"Yes," she said, putting the pieces together and sliding them into place on the man's face. "You know who he is," she repeated.

He nodded, then opened his mouth, but no words came out. He tried again and finally answered. "His name doesn't mean anything, though, because it isn't real. Finish his face and we'll get him out on the wire."

That this man terrified Gideon years after he'd known him was significant. It was another wedding photo. With the girl he'd once known. "Why did Eileen tear up this picture?" Daisy asked as she searched for the man's nose.

"Why do you think?" Gideon asked hoarsely.

"Because he abused her," Daisy said, anger flattening her voice. She sorted and matched faster, putting together the pieces of what Gideon had left unsaid. *Did he abuse you, too, Gideon?*

God, she hoped not, but it might explain the sick pallor on his face.

"He's not the man who attacked me last night," she said, not looking up from the table. "He had both his eyes."

Gideon said nothing so she let him be, putting together the nose, then starting on the mouth. It had been important before, but now the need was urgent.

She sat back, regarding the face that stared up at her. He was stern, unsmiling, his mouth turned down into a near scowl. He did not look friendly.

"What's the name you knew him by?" she asked Gideon quietly as she pulled her phone from the pocket of her sweatpants. She snapped a photo and texted it to Rafe.

Gideon's jaw had grown hard and unyielding, but that was preferable to the lost, panicked expression he'd worn before. "Ephraim Burton," he said through gritted teeth.

Daisy texted that to Rafe as well, then added: *This is likely an alias. Our friend knows him.* She didn't use Gideon's name because she wasn't sure what he wanted kept secret. He'd been so upset when he'd thought Rafe had told her about Eden.

Rafe's response was instantaneous. *Is our friend ok?*

Curious choice of question. Rafe obviously knew Gideon's backstory. *Yes, but shaken up. This is not the man I saw last night. He had both eyes.*

Got it. Good job, Poppy ☺

Daisy sent Rafe a thank-you, then turned her attention to Gideon. He looked wrecked. "I wish I had some booze," she said. "I'd offer you some."

He laughed bitterly. "I'd take it." Standing, he paced to the kitchen and back. He stopped, meeting her eyes, his intense. She thought he might tell her who the man was to him, but he didn't. "Tell me about the hobbies," he blurted.

Daisy respected self-distraction. It had been one of the strategies of her sobriety. "I've always painted. I can remember my mom painting with me, before she died."

"How old were you?"

"Four, so my memories are sparse. I remember spilling a big cup of purple paint on the sofa and crying because I thought I was in trouble. Mom gave me a brush and helped me spread it around on the cushion. It became 'art.'" She smiled fondly. "She got a new cushion and gave me the painted one."

"She must have been nice."

"Yes." She'd considered using a mention of her mother as a springboard to learn more about his, but his response had been so stilted that she decided against it. "My father encouraged my painting after Mom died. I've always used it as an escape."

"But you majored in journalism, not art."

"I'm not good enough to paint professionally. And I didn't want to lose my joy in the one thing I loved by making it a job."

He didn't answer for a moment, instead pacing to the wall that she'd converted into a giant canvas. "I think you are good enough, but I get wanting to keep something for yourself that makes you happy."

Daisy glanced down at the face of the scary man in the photo, wanting so badly to ask what he'd done to Gideon. But she didn't. She wanted to ask him what made him happy, but she didn't do that, either. He'd regained some of his composure and she wouldn't deny him that.

"Have you ever tried to paint?" she asked.

He shook his head. "I don't think I'd be good at it."

"Doesn't matter. Sometimes it's just the doing that's important."

He started pacing again, circling the little table in the dining nook. "Why pottery?"

She chuckled, embarrassment creeping onto her cheeks. "I saw the movie *Ghost* and always wanted to try the pottery wheel. I took a class at the community center."

He smiled at that, and her heart eased, just a bit. His smile grew rueful as he inspected a misshapen lump of clay that was supposed to have been a vase. "Harder than it looks, huh?"

She laughed. "Much. The stuff I made at the center was better. I just got the wheel for home to practice technique. And because I like the feel of the wet clay."

He looked up with a puzzled frown. "Why?"

She frowned back. "I'm not sure. I just do. It makes me . . . calm."

"Calm is good," he murmured, stroking the edge of the misfit vase, then staring at his clay-covered finger, the lost look returning.

Daisy got up to get him a towel from the kitchen, gently cleaning the clay from his finger. Earning her a long, probing stare from those green eyes. There was a question there, but she didn't know what he was asking, so she didn't try to answer.

"I'm better at sewing," she offered, unsure now of whom she was trying to distract—him or herself. "I made costumes for the drama club at the community center. They're doing *Little Mermaid*. I did Ursula and all the mer-tails." He said nothing, so she added lamely, "It was a lot of mer-tails."

For several pounding beats of her heart, he stood there in silence, staring down at her. But when he spoke, her pounding heart stuttered.

"He beat me," he said quietly.

For a second she couldn't breathe, trying to wrap her mind around his words. "The man in the photo?" she asked, even though she knew the answer. She didn't know what else to say. "Ephraim Burton?"

He nodded once, but that was plenty. He didn't turn away from her as she'd expected, but continued to stand there, staring at her. As if he wanted something from her. Or needed it.

Tentatively she reached for him, cupping his jaw in her palm, feeling the soft brush of his beard against her flesh. Closing his eyes, he shuddered out a breath and leaned into the contact.

She, too, released the breath she'd been holding. "How old were you?" she asked in the quietest murmur she could muster, because she was afraid he'd pull away. She needed this connection, just as much as he did. *Maybe more.*

He swallowed audibly. "Thirteen."

More silence. More pounding of her heart. Finally she ventured, "It was bad?" She asked, even though she knew the answer to that question, too. It had to have been severe to cause such an extreme reaction. But then, Gideon Reynolds had seemed off-balance since he'd walked into the interview room the night before.

He nodded. "I almost died."

His reaction to seeing the man's face made a lot more sense. "Was he punished?"

"No," he whispered.

"So he's still out there."

Another nod. Then he covered her hand with his, pressing her palm against his face before letting her go and stepping back, his expression gone blank.

She let her arm fall to her side, waiting for him to speak. Allowing him to regain control. She knew what it was like to feel helpless, to be subject to the control of others.

"You sent the photo to Rafe?" he asked briskly.

She was unsurprised that he'd steered them back to the case. "I did. I didn't mention your name."

"I appreciate it."

"Now what?" she asked him.

He tugged on the cuffs of his shirt and checked the security of his still tightly knotted tie. "How do you feel about Thai?"

She smiled up at him. "Very favorably. I know a good place. Let me change out of these sweats and we'll go."

NINE

Daisy came back into the room wearing well-worn jeans and another turtleneck sweater. That she needed to cover her throat made Gideon angry all over again, but he bit it back because she looked . . . apprehensive. He wouldn't have minded so much except that the look was aimed at him. He'd nearly lost it there for a moment, seeing Ephraim's face.

Of course, when he'd last seen the bastard, he'd had two functioning eyes. The knife had plunged into Ephraim's eye after Gideon's had swollen shut.

That he hadn't been *trying* for Ephraim's eye was kind of immaterial.

And he wasn't going to think about the bastard anymore. He was going to go out and have dinner with a woman who'd made him smile more than once today.

Who'd grounded him when he'd found himself back in the terrified mind of his thirteen-year-old self. She hadn't pushed. Hadn't asked questions he didn't want to answer. She'd simply been there, providing him with human contact when he'd needed it most.

So he was going to get his shit together so that he could do what he came here to do—keep her safe. "How do you want to do this?" he asked.

She looked up at him, a twinkle in her blue eyes. "Um, chew, swallow, repeat?"

He grinned. "Smartass. I meant how should we get there?"

She pulled her coat from the closet where all the sports equipment was stored. "We should walk. It's like two blocks, Gideon. Plus parking's a bitch on Friday nights." She perked up. "Unless you get ticket forgiveness as an FBI agent."

"Nope." He laughed, although he had used his badge to slide around speeding tickets once or twice. Not that he'd admit that to her. "It's supposed to rain. You need an umbrella."

She moved some of the sports equipment around. "Found one."

It was, of course, neon green with glitter hearts, and Gideon found that made him happy for no good reason. "Did you make that?"

She smiled fondly at the umbrella. "No. My sister's little stepsister made it for me as a going-away gift when I left Baltimore to come here. Cordelia is the queen of glitter."

"Your sister's stepsister?" he asked slowly.

"I guess she's technically my stepsister's stepsister. Taylor's bio-dad got remarried and Cordelia is his stepdaughter."

"Oh. That actually makes sense."

"I'm glad you think so." She turned the fond smile on him. "Any other questions?"

He glanced in the closet. "Why do you have all the sports stuff?"

Her smile became an offended frown. "Because I play sports."

He held up his hands. "Sorry."

"It's okay. I know I don't strike anyone as the athletic type."

"But you are," he murmured. "You fought off that guy last night."

"I did. Just . . . don't judge so quickly, okay?" She

clucked her tongue before he could respond. "Brutus!" The little dog came running and she scooped her into her arms.

"You can't take him—I mean, *her* into the restaurant," he said, then winced again because her frown had returned. "Can you?"

"She's a service dog," she said quietly. "I've had her since I left rehab. She senses an oncoming anxiety attack and is trained to distract me, to get me out of my head. If that fails, she'll bring me medication and call 911 if I need her to." She proceeded to take a tiny service vest from her bag and slip it over Brutus's body, before gently settling the dog in the bag. The patch on the vest read *Service Animal* and *Some Disabilities Aren't Visible.* "Time to work, Brutus," she said, then glanced back at Gideon. "I've never needed the call, but I have needed the medication. Mostly she keeps me from spiraling to the point where my sobriety is threatened."

"Oh." He sighed. "I'm sorry, Daisy. I keep putting my foot in my mouth."

She adjusted the bag's strap on her shoulder, then patted his arm. "It's okay. You've had a rough afternoon. I'll cut you some slack. Plus I didn't have her vest on earlier, so that's on me. The radio station knows she's allowed to be there, so I don't always have her wear it."

"So the vest and 'Time to work' tell her she's on duty?"

Daisy nodded. "And 'Shazam' is her release word. Tells her that she's off the clock."

He chuckled. "I wondered about that. I heard you say it to her earlier."

"Some people use 'Release' as the release word, but the man who trained her liked 'Shazam.'" She closed and locked her door behind them, then looked up sharply. "You don't have a key to my apartment anymore, do you?"

"No. Just the garage door code."

"Oh." She pocketed the key and started for the front door of the house. "Not that I'm suggesting you're a serial killer or anything," she added with a wince of her own.

His lips twitched. "Good to know."

She looked appropriately chagrined. "I think Rafe changed the locks anyway."

"Wouldn't have mattered. I didn't give anyone the key."

She stopped a few feet from the door. "No one?" she asked, uncertainty in her voice.

He knew what she was asking, so he met her eyes directly as he answered. "No. No one. I had a girlfriend back in my last posting, but we broke up a year before I was transferred to Sacramento."

He hoped he wasn't imagining the satisfaction in her expression. Maybe, when everything calmed down, he would ask her out. On a proper date. Not as a body-guard.

"Where were you before here?" she asked, not moving from where she stood inside the door. The only light came from the streetlamp through the leaded glass in Rafe's front door, creating an intimate little bubble in the semidarkness.

"Philadelphia. Before that I was in Miami."

She kept her gaze locked on his. "Irina said you're a linguist and are fluent in six languages. One of them is Russian. What exactly does a polylinguist do in the FBI?"

"A lot of translating. I work in the organized crime division."

Her eyes widened. "That sounds dangerous. But I guess all those law enforcement jobs are. What languages do you speak?"

"Russian first, then Chinese, Japanese, Spanish, and French." He smiled at her. "Any other questions?"

She nodded slowly. "Did you ask to come back to Sacramento?"

"Yes. I missed the Sokolovs." They were the only family he had, other than Mercy, and he feared he and his sister would never truly be family.

"And now I'm here and you won't come to Sunday dinner anymore," she murmured sadly. "And don't say it wasn't because of me. I know Irina asked you to come every week."

He wanted to say that sharing Sunday dinner with her no longer sounded like a hardship, but his voice was not cooperating with his brain.

"We can do a rotating schedule," she offered cheerfully when he continued to stand there silently. "We'll each go every other week. That way you don't miss out."

"Daisy," he managed to grind out, and she abruptly stopped talking. "You should go to Sunday dinner. They were your family before they were mine. And when I can, I'll join you. If that's all right."

Her smile lit up their little bubble. "That would be fine." She opened the door and stepped into the light drizzle, opening the umbrella and motioning him under it.

He remained on the porch. "I thought I was going to follow at a discreet distance."

"You'll get wet."

"I'll live," he said dryly.

She shook her head. "Get under the damn umbrella, Gideon. Please."

He obeyed, fighting the urge to lean in and sniff her hair. She smelled like almond cookies. He took the umbrella from her hand, holding it a little higher so that he fit beneath it. "What will you tell people when they ask who I am?"

She stopped and looked up at him. "Who do you want to be?"

A dangerous question. "I'd suggest a friend from

SAY YOU'RE SORRY   163

out of town, but there will be people at the restaurant who know me. I lived here for nine months before I moved to Rocklin."

"That's where you live?"

"Stanford Ranch area. It's close to the office."

She bit her lip, making him want to lick the indentations left by her teeth. Which was not going to happen. *Get a goddamn grip. And fucking pay attention!*

He scanned the area belatedly. Anyone could have jumped out and hurt her and he would have been off in la-la land, daydreaming about licking her. *God.*

She let out a slow breath, seemingly oblivious to his mental disarray. "Let's just say we're on a date, okay? That Irina set us up. That's close enough to the truth that we won't have to remember details."

And welcome back, Mental Disarray. His brain was forming all kind of images now. None of which approached appropriate.

"Is . . . is that okay?" she asked cautiously.

"Yes," he said too quickly. "It's fine. Let's go." And before he could talk himself out of it, he switched the umbrella to his right hand and slid his left along her back. Just to guide her. The pavement got slick when it was wet.

You are such a fucking liar.

A car door slammed across the street and Gideon was instantly alert. "Take the umbrella," he said, shoving it into her hand so he could more easily reach his gun.

She complied, warily watching the young man crossing the street toward them, a large black bag over his shoulder. His car was a blue Prius and Gideon committed its license plate to memory.

"Are you Eleanor Dawson?" the man asked.

"For God's sake," she muttered. At normal volume she said, "Who wants to know?"

The man's smile was charming enough. If one liked

snakes. Gideon swallowed what would have been a legit growl.

"My name is Elliott Scott. I'm with Action News, Channel 7. I was wondering if I could talk to you about what happened last night."

Daisy stiffened beside him but Gideon wasn't terribly surprised. He was more surprised that it had taken this long for the press to approach her. Keeping his left hand firmly on her back, he held up his right. "That's far enough, Mr. Scott."

The man adjusted the hood of his raincoat to better see Gideon. "And you are?"

"A friend," Gideon replied curtly. "You need to stop right where you are. Now."

"Miss Dawson?" Elliott persisted, coming a few feet closer despite Gideon's warning. "Is it true you were attacked on J Street last night?"

"No comment," she said, the strength of her tone giving the man pause. Or it could have been Gideon's glare. "Should we go back inside?" she murmured to Gideon.

He bent his head to whisper in her ear, working hard to focus on the situation at hand and not how warm her skin was. "We can call for takeout, but this probably isn't the last reporter you're going to have to fend off."

She leaned up on her toes to get closer to him. "Do you think I should talk to him?"

"It's up to you. If you do, you might get unwanted attention. On the other hand, you might also ask if any of their viewers was a witness."

Her brows knit together. "You're no help."

He chuckled. "At least he's getting rained on while you're making up your mind."

She glanced at Elliott Scott, who waited patiently. "He doesn't seem intimidating."

"He's a reporter. They're like chameleons. He can be whoever he wants to be."

"I could talk to him on the porch. I'm not allowing him inside."

Gideon wouldn't have allowed it, even if she had. "Sounds like a plan. Keep it short. We have reservations."

She blinked up at him. "We do?"

"We do. I made them while you were changing." He turned back to the reporter. "She'll talk to you, but only on the porch."

Elliott ignored him, replying to Daisy. "Thank you, Miss Dawson." He followed them up to the porch, where he withdrew a camera from the shoulder bag. "Can I film you?"

Daisy hesitated. "You won't show my address, right?"

"Of course not. I'll show you what I've recorded before I leave, if you want."

She squared her shoulders. "Okay. Let's get this done, Mr. Scott. My friend and I have dinner reservations."

Scott set the camera on a tripod and turned the lens to Daisy while Gideon edged away enough that he was not in the picture. "Miss Dawson, can you tell us what happened last night?"

"I was attacked by a man wearing a nylon stocking over his face. He'd been following me for several blocks. When I confronted him, he grabbed me around the throat and dragged me into an alley. He had a gun. I fought him off and a friend called 911. If anyone was in the area last night, please let the authorities know if you have seen my attacker. The man is about six feet tall, bald, has dark eyes, and wore a blue nylon ski jacket and jeans with wingtip shoes. Oh, and a Giants cap."

"It must have been terrifying," Scott said sympathetically. "How did you fight him off? Weren't you scared?"

"I was petrified," she admitted. "But I've trained in self-defense and martial arts. I was able to injure him enough to run away."

"That's lucky," Scott said, sympathy now admiration.

"No, sir, that was preparation," she corrected solemnly. "I *was* scared—that's the point. But I'd practiced over a period of years, and my muscle memory kicked in. I encourage women to choose a self-defense option and stick with it. Don't think that because you've taken one class that you've mastered self-defense. Even the most seasoned martial artists can get scared in a real-life situation. It's the practice that counts more than anything." She looked straight at the camera. "If you know anything about this, please call either Detective Rafe Sokolov or Detective Erin Rhee with SacPD. Thank you."

Scott turned off his camera. "Well, that was simple. You've made my editing job a million times easier. You must've had practice in front of a camera. You're a natural."

"Thank you. You won't mention my address, right?" she repeated.

"No, ma'am," he said kindly. He turned the camera so that she could see the screen and replayed what he'd recorded, showing that there was no sign of a street name or house number before slipping the camera back in his bag. "Thank you for talking to me. I'll let you get to your dinner now."

"Wait," Gideon said when Scott started down the steps to the sidewalk. "How did you get Miss Dawson's name?"

"From her friend, Trish Hart."

Daisy's brows shot up. "How did you get Trish's name?"

"Right place, right time. I was in the bar where

she works and heard her telling one of the other servers about the attack. I'd read about the incident on the blotter this morning but didn't know who the victim was." He flashed the same charming smile that made Gideon want to punch him in the mouth. "I would have gotten your name sooner or later. Your friend just saved me time. I'll put the phone number for the SacPD switchboard at the end of the segment. Hopefully someone saw something that will help you."

"Thank you," Daisy said again. "Stay dry."

"Too late for that." Then he jogged to his car, got in, and drove away.

"Do you really think he'll put my address in the segment?" she asked fretfully.

"I think it doesn't matter. If someone wants to find you, they will. But you need to tell your friend Trish to shut her mouth."

"I was planning to use language that was a little more colorful," Daisy said grimly.

Gideon put the umbrella up and held out his arm. "Dinner?"

She moved into his side easily, leaning her head on his shoulder for a moment that was far too brief. "Thank you. I was freaking out a little there."

He let his arm slide around her waist. Because it felt right there. "I never would have known. Scott was right. You're a natural."

She laughed, husky and deep, and this time he didn't fight the shiver that raced over his skin. "You wanted to punch him," she fake-whispered.

"In the face," he confirmed.

She looked up. "Thank you. For wanting to. And for not doing it."

He hugged her a little closer. "You're welcome. Let's hurry. I'm starving."

SACRAMENTO, CALIFORNIA
FRIDAY, FEBRUARY 17, 6:45 P.M.

He stepped back, breathing hard. Miss Rude had been playing possum, pretending to still be out when in reality she was ramping up for a fight.

He'd given her one. Now she lay tied to the bed in his basement, breathing just as hard as he was, tears and sweat causing her mascara to run down her face. "You look like a reject from a goth festival," he said. "You'll be sorry for making me work so hard."

Because now he had to go to *her*. She'd already texted three times. *Where are you?* Then, *I'm getting annoyed.* Finally, *If you're not dead, you're going to wish you were.*

One of these days she'd wish *she* were, he growled inside his head. But he didn't say the words aloud because he was afraid he'd never be able to go through with it. Somehow hearing the empty threats in his head made him feel like less of a loser.

Miss Rude sneered up at him even as the tears continued to roll down her cheeks. "I won't be sorry for anything, you sonofabitch."

The back of his hand hurt when it came into contact with her jaw, but her cry of pain went a long way toward soothing his discomfort. "You need to apologize for that."

Her chin jutted out. "No."

He smiled down. "I'm glad to hear you say that," he murmured. "You'll be so much fun to break. Nothing like the last one. She broke like a cheap chair." Watching her pale, he leaned in, his smile widening. "Relax. You'll need your strength. I'll be—"

He jerked back when her spit landed on his face. His fist had connected with her cheekbone before his movement registered and he got a grim satisfaction from her low moan. He wiped his face on his sleeve and grabbed his knife.

He needed to shower and change before meeting Sydney anyway. What was a little more bodily fluid? Miss Rude's one working eye widened in fear.

"No," she whispered.

"Say please," he countered lightly.

She clenched her jaw. "Please," she gritted out.

"Say you're sorry," he pressed in a singsong voice.

Her good eye closed. The other was swelling shut on its own. "No."

He blinked, a little surprised. "Why not?"

Her eye opened again and she stared straight up at him. "I've said 'I'm sorry' for the last time. To you or to anyone else. You're going to kill me anyway. So just do it."

He had to hand it to her. She was good. She almost had him backing away. "You've been someone's boss," he said, letting her hear his admiration. "That is a very good power-reversal tactic."

He rubbed his palm over her stomach, felt it quiver, then clench. He took the knife and traced the tip over her skin, just deep enough to draw a thin line of blood.

"S."

She was panting when he straightened, her good eye filled with new tears she was valiantly trying not to shed. She had guts, he had to admit. He cleaned his hands, then searched his pocket for her ID. He'd left her purse and phone next to her rental car in the parking lot of the bar in Eagle, taking only her driver's license.

"Miss Zandra Jones of Providence, Rhode Island. You were far from home this afternoon, Zandra."

She said nothing, the breath sawing in and out of her lungs.

"What I'd started to say before you so rudely

interrupted is that I'm going to leave for a little while, but I'll be back." He walked to the door, then turned to smile at her again. "Scream as much as you like. No one will hear you. No one has heard any of my guests."

He heard a sob just as he was closing the door. Then his phone buzzed and his mood plummeted. *Where ARE you? If you don't call me in the next 30 seconds I'll be making calls you don't want made.*

It was like a switch flipped in his brain, taking him back to his most vulnerable self. He dialed, his hands shaking, even though he knew—he *knew*—that she wouldn't go through with her threat. He knew she had as much to lose as he did.

But his body was moving, ignoring the shouts from his brain to stop. *To think.*

"Where in the fuck are you?" she sniped at him, forgoing any greeting.

He stepped over Mutt, making him think of Pavlov and his dogs once again. *That's what I am. When she says heel, I heel.* He nearly looked down to make sure he still had his balls, because it sure felt like she'd cut them off years ago.

Wasn't like she hadn't ever threatened to. *Bitch.*

"I had some car trouble," he lied.

"You should have called."

His feet kept moving, Mutt on the stairs behind him. "I know. I'm sorry. I'll be there as soon as I can."

"See that you are." The call abruptly ended and he sighed heavily.

I need to kill her. I need to drag her Botoxed ass over here and kill her.

But when push came to shove, he knew he would not. He'd had hundreds of opportunities over the years. Maybe thousands. Every time she lay sated in her bed.

He considered it every time she did so, but he'd never raised a hand to her.

Mind games. He'd cleared the stairs when his cell phone buzzed yet again. Dreading what he'd see, he forced himself to peek at his screen. But it wasn't a text.

It was a Google Alert for J Street. He'd set it up that afternoon after searching for the incident on the news and finding nothing. But there it was now. He sat on the edge of his bed and clicked on the browser link to Action News and some reporter named Elliott Scott.

Scott stood at the entrance to the alley where he'd dragged the blonde last night. He held his breath, waiting to hear the latest on the case.

Her name was Eleanor Dawson. Eleanor. That was a nice name. Old-fashioned. Except the woman from the night before had been anything but old-fashioned. She'd fought like a tiger. His balls had hurt for hours.

And there she was. The blonde. Wearing a black wool coat, her hair pulled over one shoulder. Her hair had smelled good. Like almonds.

She was standing on the front porch of a house. Using two fingers he tried to zoom in to see the address, but there was no house number visible. And then she started to talk in a husky, raspy voice he felt like he'd heard before. He hadn't heard her all that well last night. She'd only said a few words, and those had sounded strangled.

Because he'd been strangling her.

"The man is about six feet tall, bald, has dark eyes, and wore a blue nylon ski jacket and jeans with wingtip shoes. Oh, and a Giants cap," she said clearly into the camera, showing not one iota of nerves, like she talked into a camera every day.

She'd noticed a lot about him, he thought, mildly alarmed. *Right down to my shoes.* He stared down at the wingtips on his feet. *Shit.*

But she didn't have a description of his face, so the stocking had achieved its purpose. So far, so good.

And then she was talking about practicing her
self-defense until she'd developed muscle memory. *No
fucking shit.* He rolled his eyes. He had not been expecting that.

When the reporter finished the segment, he opened
a new browser window and typed in "Eleanor Dawson." Wow. There were a lot of Eleanor Dawsons out
there. He didn't have time to check out all of these
results. He had to get to Sydney.

He showered and shaved and put on nice clothes,
every action bringing him closer to the moment he'd
dreaded every single time he'd been forced to do her
bidding.

For sixteen years.

By the time he gave Mutt's head a pat, his gut was a
trembling mess. *Someday,* he promised himself. Someday he'd kill her and let Mutt clean her bones.

"Watch the house, boy," he murmured. "I'll be back."

SACRAMENTO, CALIFORNIA
FRIDAY, FEBRUARY 17, 6:50 P.M.

Zandra stared up at the ceiling, willing the panic back.
*Stupid, stupid, stupid. How could I have been so phe-
nomenally stupid?*

She never drank. Not enough to get drunk anyway.
The one time . . .

And that was the story of her life. The one time she
exceeded the speed limit, she got a ticket. The one
time she'd risked her money in stocks, they'd tanked.
The one time she'd risked her heart? She forced the
sob back. *Not now. Later.* When she got free.

But the mental image of James and Monica . . . She
could still see them writhing in the bed. *My bed.* Hers
and James's. Her fiancé and her best friend. *It's the
opening scene of a romcom,* she thought bitterly.

And now I'm in a horror movie. The panic began to rise in her throat and she swallowed hard. *You will not panic. You will get away. And then you'll see that the psycho bastard's put away for the rest of his life.*

After six years of trying cases with the prosecutor's office, she certainly knew how to maximize his chances for a lengthy sentence.

Say you're sorry. "Like hell I will," she muttered. Those had been the words that had fallen from her lips as she'd stood frozen in the doorway to the chalet's bedroom. When James had had the nerve to yell at her for walking in on him.

I'm sorry. I'm sorry? Really? Fuck that. It was my room!

She tugged on the ropes that bound her to the bed. The knots were expertly tied and she was feeling tired again as her adrenaline crashed. Everything got woozy and muddy and she blinked back tears.

There had to be a way to get out of this . . . place. Wherever she was. Whatever she did, she wasn't going to tell him she was sorry. She had the feeling that would be the man's trigger. That once she said that, he'd have no use for her anymore. Then he'd kill her. Because he'd done it before. *No one has heard any of my guests.*

Reality barreled through her brave facade, breaking it into bits, and terror filled her heart. *God. I'm going to die. Please don't let me die.*

▌▌▌SACRAMENTO, CALIFORNIA
FRIDAY, FEBRUARY 17, 7:00 P.M.

The restaurant was packed by the time Gideon opened the door for Daisy, getting them both out of what had become a steady rain. Storing her glitter-covered umbrella in a stand by the door, he turned to give the hostess their reservation.

"Gideon! Daisy!"

They turned at the same time to see Rafe and Sasha waving at them from a booth against the wall. With their blond hair, dark eyes, and identical devious grins, that they were siblings was indisputable.

And now they've seen us together, my hand on her back. Unwilling to let Daisy go, Gideon braced himself to be teased unmercifully. It was one of the lesser perks of being adopted by the Sokolov family.

"What are you doing here?" he asked when they'd reached the table.

Sasha looked pointedly at her plate. "It's this new thing called eating, Gideon." She patted the seat next to her. "Sit down, DD."

Gideon hid his disappointment in having to share Daisy with the Sokolovs and sat next to Rafe, who slid his phone over so that Gideon could see.

It was the interview with Elliott Scott.

"Wow, he got that online fast." Gideon met Daisy's eyes across the table. "You are officially a minor Internet sensation."

"I figured it wouldn't take him long," she said philosophically. "He seemed to have his act together. He was slick." She appeared unaffected but the menu shook in her hands as she opened it. "I want the Drunken Noodles. If I can't get drunk, at least my noodles can."

"You sounded good," Sasha said, patting her arm. "Hopefully this will keep the rest of the vultures away."

Gideon shared a glance with Rafe, seeing that his friend didn't believe that any more than he did.

"Did you take care of that case you got called away on?" Daisy asked Rafe, clearly wanting to change the subject away from her interview.

Rafe shook his head. "I just took a break for dinner. I have to go back out."

"It's a homicide?" Sasha asked sympathetically.

"Missing person," Rafe said tersely. "Turns out this single mom was turning tricks to supplement her income from her day job at a bakery. Her family had no idea. She'd told them she'd taken the night shift at a grocery store. When she didn't show to pick up her little girl, the victim's grandparents started calling around to her friends, the hospitals, even the morgue. They finally talked to the one friend who knew what the victim had been doing. She searched the area where the missing woman was working and found her backpack with her purse and phone still in it. She called it in."

"Poor family," Sasha murmured. "To be hit twice in one day—her disappearance and her prostitution. Poor little girl."

Rafe nodded grimly. "The kid's tears tore me up. She's sick, too. Cystic fibrosis. She needs a lung transplant."

Sasha made a pained noise. "Dammit. Was that why the mom was hooking?"

"Probably. Thing is, without the kid this wouldn't have hit our radar. That she didn't come for the kid was the only thing that kept this from being deemed a simple runaway situation or a hooker strung out on meth somewhere." Rafe pushed his food around on his plate. He hadn't eaten much of it. "I got surveillance videos from the businesses in the area of her disappearance, but I'm not hopeful. Most of the cameras were at the wrong angle and the one that picked anything up is so old that the footage is shit. The lab is cleaning it up for me right now. It's always so hard on the families. They want answers, but I don't know if I'll have any to give them."

"They'll sit and wait and hope," Sasha said sadly. "It doesn't look good for her."

"No." Rafe's voice scraped on the single word. "And

most of the time when I do get news, it's what the family's been dreading."

Gideon had worked his share of those cases. They rarely ended well. He gave Rafe's shoulder a squeeze, then noticed that Daisy had grown very quiet, her mouth pressed tight. "What's wrong?"

Sasha's hand flew to her mouth and both she and Rafe looked uncomfortable. And guilty. "I'm sorry, DD," Sasha whispered. "I wasn't thinking."

Daisy shook her head and forced a smile. "No sorries needed." She let out a shaky breath. "My family waited for two months for news when my sister Carrie went missing. She'd run away and we didn't know where."

"She didn't come home," Gideon murmured, remembering her use of the past tense the night before when she'd told them her phone code was her sister's birthday.

"No," Daisy said softly. "It ripped our family apart. I miss her so much."

"I miss her, too," Sasha said, then chuckled suddenly. "Remember the camping trip when she shone a flashlight on that Captain Hook hand we got at Disneyland?"

Daisy's eyes lit up, a wicked grin curving her lips. "On the boys' tent. They thought it was the hook-man from the legend. They ran out screaming, in their underwear."

Sasha was full-out laughing now. "And Meg . . ."

Daisy joined her and they laughed until they cried. "Meg had the hose ready and sprayed them all as they rushed out of the tent. Your sister corrupted mine, I think. It was Carrie's hook-hand."

Rafe was not smiling. "It wasn't funny. We could have gotten pneumonia."

"It was August," Sasha scoffed. "Omigod, Meg got in such trouble from Mom for that."

"As she should have," Rafe said, but his lips were twitching now.

"And now Meg's a cop with three kids of her own." Daisy wiped at her eyes.

"May her children be as bad as she was," Rafe said solemnly.

"I think you should be careful that your wishes don't boomerang back at you," Gideon said to Rafe, glad Daisy's eyes were happy again. Or at least not so sad. "If you ever have kids they'll be ex-cons by kindergarten."

"I was an angel," Rafe insisted. "The only one who is actually named after an angel, I'll have you know."

Sasha snorted. "You keep on thinking that, but the universe keeps score, Raphael."

He grinned at his sister. "Then *you're* doomed." His phone buzzed and he checked the screen with a sigh. "Work's calling. Gotta go."

Gideon got up so that Rafe could slide out. "Anything on Daisy's case?" he murmured so that she couldn't hear.

Rafe shook his head, whispering his reply. "We canvassed the area, but nobody remembers seeing a man matching Daisy's description. There were no surveillance videos. I don't know if he knew that in advance or he got lucky. He must have pulled the stocking off as soon as he ran, but we didn't find it. Lab's backed up. It'll be at least a week before we get the skin from under her nails analyzed. Tad got fired from the station for the shit he pulled on this morning's show, so at least that's progress."

"That is good news. The guy's a dick." Gideon hesitated. "I sent the photo of Eileen to a friend who's a police artist."

"Age progression? Good. I did the same, but I've got to wait my turn and it could be days before our artist gets to it. Send me what your guy comes up with."

"I will. What about the man in the photograph? The one Daisy put back together?"

Rafe's eyes met his. "Who was he?" he asked under his breath. "And not his name. Daisy sent me that. Who was he to *you*?"

Gideon glanced around him, but no one was paying them any attention. "Do you remember the scars on my back?" he asked, knowing that Rafe certainly would.

Rafe stiffened. "Got it. I'll ask the lab to run it through facial recognition in case he's shown up somewhere else, but again, I have to wait my turn. Cindy says it'll be a few days until she has the thing put together so that she can try for a fingerprint. She's doing it before and after her normal work."

Gideon completely understood. So much of his job was waiting for other people to process information. He hated waiting. He was hating it more than usual because it had quickly become personal. Even if there had been no locket, Gideon felt the overwhelming need to protect Daisy Dawson, this woman who made him smile.

"Tell Cindy I appreciate it," he said. Rafe waved his good-bye and Gideon slid back on the seat, waving over a server. Once they'd ordered, Sasha laid a few bills on the table.

"This will take care of my and Rafe's dinners," she said. "If you'll excuse me?" She made a shooing motion at Daisy.

Daisy stared at her. "You're leaving? Why?"

Sasha nodded at Daisy, then winked at Gideon. "I know better than to be a third wheel. Plus, I have a date."

Daisy let her out. "With whom?" she asked suspiciously as she sat back down.

Sasha waggled her brows. "Sexy school librarian. We're going rock climbing at the gym." Sasha dropped a kiss on Daisy's cheek, then on Gideon's. "You two kids have fun. Don't do anything I wouldn't."

"There's very little you wouldn't do," Gideon said dryly.

Sasha winked again. "I know."

Daisy exhaled when Sasha was gone. "Well. I feel like I just survived a tornado."

"Hurricane Sasha," Gideon said with a small grin. "She's like lightning in a bottle."

"She wasn't before we went away to the ranch." Daisy looked a little sad. "I missed her emergence."

An odd word choice, Gideon thought. "What?"

"From her cocoon. She's like this amazing butterfly now, but then she was quiet and reserved." Daisy tilted her head. "She told me that the two of you would sit up in her little attic hideout. And that she came out to you first."

"It was . . ." One of the most special moments of his whole life. He'd felt included. Part of the Sokolov clan. Trusted. "Nice," he finished. *Nice?* He rolled his eyes at himself.

She smiled at him, as if hearing the words he couldn't seem to form out loud. "She kind of idolizes you, you know. She claims it was only when she was a kid, but I'm pretty sure nothing has changed. Just so you know. You were the brother she needed you to be."

Gideon swallowed hard. "Thank you. That's . . ."

Her smile widened. "Nice? Yes, it is." Her smile dimmed as her phone began to light up with texts. "My world has seen the news story. Irina, Karl, my dad, Taylor. Wow. Even my sister Julie." One side of her mouth lifted. "Her texting skills are really improving."

"That's your sister with cerebral palsy?"

"Yes." Daisy found a photo on her phone. "That's us this past summer."

Three women and a little girl smiled for the camera. Daisy had her arm around a tall brunette who cuddled the little girl close. The three of them crowded around the third woman in a wheelchair. "Taylor, Julie, and Cordelia?"

"Yes. Taylor's fiancé took that picture." Her phone buzzed some more and she sighed. "Now I'm getting texts from all the people I volunteer with. And my sponsor. They all want to know how I am." She looked up at him, a bewildered look in her eyes. "But I don't know what to tell them."

"Maybe for now just tell them that you're safe and processing," Gideon suggested.

"That's good. Safe and processing."

He watched her answer the texts, her lower lip pulled between her teeth. She was concentrating, but not the same way she had as she'd put the puzzle together. That expression had been one of joy. This was not.

"I hate that they worry about me," she said, lifting her eyes to his. "They're worried I'll fall off the wagon, but nobody but my sponsor asks me. They just dance around it."

"They love you," he said quietly.

"I know. And I know I'm lucky."

"Or deserving."

"I hope so. I want to make them proud of me. I want to make *me* proud of me."

That was a feeling he completely understood. She returned her attention to her phone, answering the remaining texts, cutting and pasting the same message into each one, then adding "I love you" to her sisters and her father. But she didn't look up, instead swiping at her phone screen and frowning at what she saw.

"I hope you're not reading the comments on that article about you," Gideon said. "That is never healthy."

She shook her head. "No. I was looking for information on the case Rafe was telling us about. The missing woman with the little girl. But there's nothing." She looked up, her eyes filled with devastation once again. "Why?"

He shrugged. "Maybe the parents didn't want the publicity. Maybe the reporters haven't heard about it yet."

"Or maybe because she's a prostitute," Daisy said flatly.

He nodded, because that was probably the best explanation. The public didn't care about missing prostitutes, even ones trying to raise money for their child's health care.

The server brought their meals and they ate in silence. Not an awkward silence. Just . . . thoughtful. Daisy pushed her plate away when she was finished and folded her arms on the table. "What are we going to do next, Gideon?"

"Go back to your place and watch TV."

She shook her head. "I didn't mean that."

He hadn't thought so. "Which thing then, Daisy?"

She looked him directly in the eye. "What are we going to do to find Eileen? And Ephraim Burton?"

He flinched, just thinking about the man. Then he exhaled slowly and reminded himself that he wasn't thirteen and terrified any longer.

Her fingers brushed at his hand and he realized he'd balled it into a fist. And that he'd dropped his gaze to his empty plate. *Fuck.* Humiliation heated his cheeks.

I am not a child. I am not afraid. I am going to find him and . . .

And what, Gideon? the quiet voice in his mind asked. Not mockingly. More . . . curiously. *I'll make him pay.* Of that fact he was one hundred percent certain.

How he'd accomplish it, he had no fucking clue.

Daisy moved his plate aside so that she could lean forward and cover both of his hands with hers. Her skin was warm, her hands so small. But so capable.

This was not a woman who ran from danger or from life. She threw herself in headfirst, wore her heart on her sleeve even when it hurt.

He wanted some of that heart. Staring at her hands on his, he wondered what it would be like. To have someone to ground him when he needed it most.

"Gideon," she whispered.

He looked up. The pity he'd feared he'd see wasn't there. Instead there was a determination that should have come as no surprise. "I'm not sure," he whispered back. "I don't know where to start." And that scared him to death.

He always knew where to start. He felt like he'd been dropped into a desert during an endless night with no compass. He never felt like this.

Not since he'd been dumped behind that bus station seventeen years before, broken and bleeding, with no family, no ID, no money. And wondering what was going to happen to him.

And suddenly he knew the answer.

"That's where we're going," he murmured.

"Where?" she asked gently.

"To the bus station. In Redding."

She blinked. "Why?"

"Because that's where I was taken."

"Taken," she repeated carefully. "After what?"

"After I escaped a cult." He closed his eyes on a sigh. *Fuck it.* He hadn't intended to say that. Why was this woman able to pull words from his mind?

He opened his eyes to find her unsurprised gaze locked with his. "Eden?" she asked.

He nodded. "Yes. It was a religious community."

"That married off girls when they were twelve years old," she said, her jaw clenched, "and allowed grown men to beat teenagers."

Among other things. "How did you know I was a teenager at the time?"

"Because you told my father that you'd known the Sokolovs for sixteen years. If you'd met them any earlier, I'd probably have met you myself. Sasha said you met Rafe in school, and he's thirty. I can do simple math."

He almost smiled. "I bet you can do more than simple math. You put all that together like another puzzle." She didn't answer, just tilted her head, waiting for him to tell her more. "I escaped when I was thirteen. Ended up at the Redding bus station before I was . . . moved to Sacramento." By a medevac helicopter, but he wasn't going into that here. Not in such a public place. Not when her questions would draw out more information that he wished to keep private.

She nodded once. "Then Redding it is."

Releasing one of her hands, he flagged down the server. "Miss? Check, please."

TEN

Daisy looked up at Gideon, the umbrella giving them the illusion of privacy as they walked back to her house. The way his arm circled her back, encouraging her to lean on his shoulder as they strolled, made her want to forget why he was actually there.

Because someone tried to kill me last night. And that someone was somehow connected to Gideon's past by the locket.

Redding. Eden. A cult. She hadn't been surprised to hear him say the words. He'd seemed more surprised that he'd said them.

The man was *not* a vault. A small part of her wanted to believe that he was only that way with her, but she couldn't let herself believe that. Not just yet.

This was an artificial situation. They'd been thrown together at a time of high stress and vulnerability—for both of them. Getting emotionally attached to the man was not a smart thing to do right now.

Daisy wanted to believe she was smart, but deep down she knew the long glances they'd shared, the little touches that seemed to soothe them both, were not insignificant. Maybe Irina had the right idea. Maybe they would be a good fit.

Not that Daisy was going to admit that to the

matchmaking woman, no matter how good her *pirozhki* were. *Pirozhki*. "Shit," she muttered.

Gideon went on immediate alert, head whipping from side to side. Not like he hadn't been on alert before. She'd been aware of his gaze taking in everything and everyone around them from the moment they'd left her apartment earlier. But now he was shoving the umbrella into her hand. "Take it," he bit out and reached for his gun.

She obeyed, but countered, "Whoa, Mr. G-man. Nothing's wrong. I just remembered that I left Irina's *pirozhki* out, which sucks because now I'll have to throw it out and I could have warmed it up for at least one more meal. So you can be at ease or whatever."

He relaxed a bit, taking back the umbrella. "Mr. G-man?"

She shrugged. "Special Agent Reynolds takes too long to say."

"I suppose so. Don't worry. I put the food in the fridge so you wouldn't get *E. coli*."

The word "E. coli" was delivered in so dire a tone, she had to smile up at him. "That was nice of you. Thank you."

"You're w—" He paused, his jaw going hard. "You have company."

They'd just rounded the corner to her street to find two news vans parked across the street from Rafe's house.

"Shit," she muttered again. "I don't want to talk to them. The more times I do, the more likely it is they'll figure out my day job. I was hoping to keep the two separate."

"Why?"

"I lucked into my job at the station because Boomer got sick, but I really like it. I don't want to be Daisy Dawson, the victim. I don't want that to be the first

thing people think of. I want them to think, there's
Daisy Dawson and she's damn good at her job."

He nodded, his eyes serious. "I get that. What do
you want to do? We could turn around and try to run
or I could push you through the gauntlet."

"One way I look like a coward, the other I confirm
I needed a bodyguard."

He waited patiently, saying nothing as the rain beat
down on the umbrella.

She squared her shoulders. "I gotta go home sometime."

His arm tightened around her waist and he handed
her the umbrella once again. "I'll clear you a path. I
don't want any of those reporters coming too close.
Especially any who are male and six feet tall."

She understood the implication. Her attacker could
hide in plain sight and she'd never know, which was
why he'd freed his gun hand. "Let's go."

She dug the house key from her coat pocket as he
led her up the sidewalk to the house, ready to make a
run for it if she needed to. The barrage of questions
came fast and furious as two reporters, one male and
one female, ran from the shelter of their vans. The reporters were under umbrellas, but their cameramen
were not so fortunate.

"I hoped the first interview would be enough," she
murmured. "How stupid was I?"

"Never stupid." Gideon hugged her even closer so
that they were pressed together, shoulder to thigh.
"Maybe a little optimistic."

She chuckled, but sobered quickly, halting on the
first porch step when the male reporter called out,
"Poppy Frederick, how did you escape your attacker
last night?"

She allowed herself a heavy, silent sigh. Straightening her spine, she held herself taller. "Stay with me,"
she murmured to Gideon.

"You got it."

She tugged, and he followed her lead, turning them so that they faced the reporters, him keeping his arm around her waist and his gun hand free.

"Hi, guys," she said, motioning the news teams to come a little closer. "I'm going to tell this one more time, but first I want to ask why I'm getting this attention. Yes, I was attacked and I appreciate you all getting the word out so that hopefully a witness will come forward. But I'm here. I'm okay. I'm safe. There are victims all over this city that don't get this kind of attention from you who could use it a lot more. People who disappear and don't come home. Prostitutes and drug addicts go missing in this city—in every city—every day and nobody pays them any attention. So yes, I'll answer your questions, mostly in the hopes that you'll leave me alone, but I want you guys to do better. I want your viewers to do better, too, to demand more from you."

She quickly recounted what had happened in the alley, once again giving the description of her attacker and Rafe and Erin as the detective contacts.

"Were you being stalked at the radio station?" one of the reporters asked.

Daisy frowned, wondering for just a moment where that line of questioning had come from. But then she knew. Tad Nelson Todd, Mr. TNT himself. *Bastard.* "All I can tell you is that the police are investigating all leads."

"It's been rumored that you set this up," the same reporter called out. "Is this some kind of publicity stunt to improve your ratings?"

Tad, you sonofabitch.

Beside her, Gideon stiffened but continued to say nothing, allowing her to run the show. For now. She had no doubt that if either of the reporters came closer, he'd be on them before they could blink.

The other reporter, a woman who had kind eyes, stared at the loudmouth in surprise before stepping forward. "Miss Frederick, do you have any words of advice for women who might be nervous walking the streets at night alone?"

Daisy smiled at her. "I trained in martial arts and self-defense for years, but that's not possible for a lot of women in your viewing audience. There are moves they can learn, but the truth is, when you're in that situation, you get scared. You forget. Some training is better than none, and if they can take just one class, by all means do that, but realize the limitations. Take the class again, every year or so. Renew your skills."

"Do you have any recommendations?"

Daisy shook her head. "I'm new to the city. But I'll find out and I'll share those on my morning show, if my management agrees."

The woman studied her shrewdly. "Do you know of a specific person who's disappeared in the city?"

"I'm sure you have ways of getting all that information," Daisy told her. "Now, if you'll excuse me, I'm super tired." She smiled at them politely. "And if you come back, I'll call the police and report you for trespassing. Have a good evening."

Gideon sent her up the stairs, waiting in the rain at the sidewalk until she'd opened the front door. He backed up, keeping his eyes on the group below, not even pausing when the obnoxious reporter shouted, "Who's the muscle, Poppy? Why do you have a body—"

"You have thirty seconds," Gideon barked at the man. "Vacate the property or you'll be under arrest for trespassing." To the nicer reporter he said, "Take your time, ma'am."

He pushed his wet hair away from his face when he came into the house. "That fucker you *used* to work with has been spreading those rumors."

Daisy began to tremble the moment he shut and

locked the door, closing them off from the rest of the world. "I know," she whispered.

Gideon took the umbrella from her hand, collapsed it, and set it in the umbrella stand by the door before removing his coat and then hers and hanging them on the coat tree to dry. "What's wrong?" he murmured. "You were amazing out there."

Shaking her head hard, she took a step forward and his arms came around her, drawing her close. "Daisy, honey," he murmured. "It's okay. It'll be okay."

The tears started to come and she couldn't hold them back. Her teeth were chattering, so she clenched them and burrowed her face into his chest. "I'm sorry."

"Don't you say you're sorry," he ordered softly. "That was hard, but you were wonderful. Just wonderful."

"Tad is a bastard," she whispered.

"I should have punched him in the mouth when I had a chance this morning."

"I wish I'd let you. Dammit, Gideon, I didn't even get that jerk reporter's name." She'd been far too rattled.

"It's okay. I got the station call numbers of both vans and their license plates, plus photos of all of the reporters and their cameramen. Rafe has security cameras as well."

"I know. That's why I asked them to come closer. They weren't in camera range."

He chuckled, low and deep, and she wanted to hear that sound forever. "Remind me never to get on your bad side."

She tilted her head, something he'd said just sinking in. "What do you mean, the fucker I *used* to work with?"

"Rafe said that Tad got fired."

"*Good*. I'm *glad*." She burrowed closer, sliding her arms around his waist. "Thank you for having my back out there."

His arms tightened around her. "Thank you for having my back when I had my little meltdown earlier." He laid his cheek on top of her head and she wanted to sigh because it felt so damn good. "What are we going to do now, Daisy?"

There was only one answer to that question. "We are going to paint."

"*We* are?"

She could feel him nuzzling the top of her head with his cheek, his beard catching on her hair. "Yes, *we* are. We'll paint and you'll tell me about Eden. Okay?"

His chest pressed against her as he drew a deep breath. "Okay."

SACRAMENTO, CALIFORNIA
FRIDAY, FEBRUARY 17, 10:15 P.M.

His skin hurt. He winced as he pulled his shirt on. It always hurt when he left Sydney's bed. His back burned from where her nails had dug deep trenches. His chest and arms were raw because he'd scrubbed a layer of dermis off in the shower.

She'd marked him once again. And he hated her. So much.

Why do you always say yes? he asked himself for the one-millionth time. *Just tell her no.* But he never did. And probably never would.

I wish I'd killed her when I'd had the chance. He stared at his reflection in her bathroom mirror, knowing the truth in his mind. He'd never really had a chance. Not with her. He'd been too young. She'd been too . . . much. Too much of everything.

But the truth had never seemed to make a difference. He always came back. He always said yes. And he always hated himself afterward as much as he hated her.

"Sweet boy." Her voice drifted to him through the open door. Because she didn't permit him to close it. She never had.

It wasn't an endearment, her "sweet boy." It was a call to heel. *Because I'm her personal dog.* Still he answered dully, "Yes?"

There was a beat of silence and he felt her disapproval, even from the next room.

"Yes, Sydney?" he amended.

"Come here."

He obeyed, buttoning his shirt as he walked from the bathroom into her bedroom, where she lounged in a peignoir, looking like a movie star from the 1940s. "Yes, Sydney?"

Her lower lip pushing out in a pout, she held out her hand. "You broke my nail."

No, she'd done that while laying trenches in his back. His feet kept him moving to the side of her bed because he knew what she expected.

And he always ended up doing what she expected. *Just get it over with and you can leave.* He sat on the side of the bed, careful not to touch her anywhere, then leaned in and pressed a kiss to the finger with the broken nail.

"I'm sorry, Sydney," he murmured.

Her eyes narrowed. "You're lying to me. You're not sorry."

But he was. He was so sorry. Sorry that he couldn't break away from her. From whatever invisible chain bound him to her. Sorry that he couldn't be a real man and strangle her the way he wanted to. The way he dreamed of doing.

"I'm sorry," he repeated with more force. He swallowed, then kissed her finger again. "Really sorry, Sydney."

It was her finger today. It had been her hip last time, because he'd held on too tightly and left a bruise. The time before he'd "made her" knock a wineglass from her nightstand to the floor, staining the carpet red.

How he'd wished it had been her blood.

Each time there was something he'd done. For as long as he could remember. Each time he'd dutifully apologized. In the beginning he'd even meant it.

In the beginning he hadn't known anything. In the beginning she'd held all the power. In the beginning she'd been in control.

Not much had changed. She still had the upper hand.

She patted his cheek. "I forgive you," she said as she always did, then relaxed into a mountain of pillows. "I'll have it fixed by the manicurist tomorrow. Lock up on your way out and set the alarm. Paul won't be home until late."

And he was dismissed. No *thank you*. No words of affection. She never uttered them. Not that he'd have believed them anyway.

He stood up and tucked his shirt in his pants, stuffing his tie in his pocket and grabbing his shoes and socks from the floor, his rage beginning to boil. "Yes, Sydney."

SACRAMENTO, CALIFORNIA
FRIDAY, FEBRUARY 17, 10:20 P.M.

Daisy leaned into Gideon's arm, peeking at his painting. "You're not half bad for a G-man," she teased. "Getting rid of the tie allowed oxygen to the creative area of your brain."

He laughed gruffly. After much encouragement—and a little bullying—on her part, he'd finally picked up a brush and begun to cover the canvas she'd set up on one of her easels with cheerful daisies, which made her happy.

He'd added a little girl to the painting, but she wasn't blond with blue eyes. She appeared very young, with dark hair pulled into pigtails. And green eyes. "Stop peeking," he said, "or I'll stop painting."

She knew it was a real threat, despite his delivering it in an equally teasing voice. She returned to her own easel, back-to-back with his. She'd started a portrait. She didn't normally do portraits, but at the moment, his face was all she could see. Literally. Because he was standing in her field of vision, his head bowed, his handsome face set in a scowl as he concentrated. But when she closed her eyes, it was also his face she saw and that brought her comfort. Earlier in the evening it had been Carrie's face she'd seen when she closed her eyes, and that hurt. So goddamn much.

She'd been waiting for him to begin his explanation of Eden, but he'd been so silent she worried he was never going to. "So," she prompted quietly. "Eden."

He cleaned his brush, then started with a new color. "I don't like to talk about it."

"I gathered that."

One side of his mouth lifted, but only briefly, and then he was scowling again. "My mom . . . She thought she was raising us right." He painted furiously for a full minute before his arm went still. "She was a single mother with two kids and no husband. Her family had shamed her, told her to leave. So she did." His throat worked. "She didn't have a high school diploma and ended up hooking, but she had a few friends. Other hookers she'd met. They shared an apartment and would watch each other's kids while they worked."

Two kids. Gideon had a sibling somewhere. She thought of the dark-haired girl with green eyes that he was painting so soberly. A sister? "Co-op daycare," Daisy murmured.

He nodded. "Everything changed when a social worker visited one evening. Someone in the building had called, worried that we were being neglected. But we were clean and fed. My mom hadn't gone far from home, still in the same city, so she still had a library card. She checked out children's books for all of us and was teaching us to read."

"She loved you."

His swallow was audible in the quiet of her apartment. "Yeah," he said hoarsely, then cleared his throat. "My mom was on duty the day the social worker came. She was so scared the woman would take us. It was close. She didn't, but she did report my mother for operating a daycare without a license. She had too many kids. The social worker threatened to take us if my mother didn't get a better job."

"Could she have?"

"I don't know. Neither did my mother. But she was scared, so when the other moms came back the next morning, my mom took us and ran. She had enough money saved to get two bus tickets, so she held my sister on her lap for two and a half days."

Daisy wanted to ask more about his sister, but held her tongue and let him continue.

"We started out in Houston. Ended up in San Francisco because that's where she thought my father was, but he'd given her a fake address. Maybe a fake name, too. So she was alone in the city at nineteen with two kids and no one to help her. No resources."

"How old were you?"

"Five."

"Wow," she whispered. "Your mom was a very young mother."

"She was only fourteen when I was born. She told me that my father was a salesman who passed through, that she'd told him she was eighteen." He shook his head. "I saw photos of her when she was fourteen. No man on earth would have believed she was eighteen. The fucker was a pedophile, plain and simple." He cleaned his brush again and changed colors. "We lived with her parents until she told them she was pregnant again."

"With your sister."

"Yes. By the same man. She kept sleeping with him, every time he blew into town. He'd bring me a cheap toy and leave her some cash. I think she really loved him. Or thought she did. I mean, she was a child. My grandparents made sure we got food and took me to church. We were always going to church. They hoped to stamp me with family values so that I wouldn't 'turn out like her.' Their words. Not mine."

"They gave up any right to family values when they threw out their daughter and her two babies," Daisy said, trying to keep the anger from her voice.

Gideon's eyes lifted and met hers over their easels. "I agree. But my mother was a churchgoing girl and so she sought out a church for help and for a while things were okay. The people there were nice. I remember that. They fed us and gave her some clothes to keep us warm because it was San Francisco in July. She hadn't thought to bring jackets."

"But things changed?"

"One of the men in the church gave my mom a job cleaning his house."

Daisy's brows went up. "Just his house?"

A nod. "He told her that he was renting, but I think he was a squatter. Anyway, he told her that he had a farm with a nice house, that he'd take her there and she could find work. That there would be fresh air and vegetables for us. That she could make a life there."

"Which must have sounded like her prayers being answered."

"It did. My mother was smart, but trusting. The kind you'd say, 'Oh, honey,' to."

"Was there a farm?"

"Yes. The whole community was a farm. It was a

commune of sorts. Really it was a cult, built around the personality of Pastor."

"Pastor what?"

"That was his name. That's what everyone called him. Pastor. My mother was accustomed to that. That's what all the members of her parents' church had called their minister. The man who brought us there was gone after the first night. He'd come back from time to time with new families. Sometimes single moms like mine, sometimes whole 'nuclear' families. They were given housing until they could build their own. Sometimes they were just young women with no family. Never a young man alone. If a male entered the community, he was older. He either had a family or a skill."

He dropped his brush in the cleaner and stepped back from the canvas. She watched him go into the kitchen, where he searched the drawers, returning with the deck of cards she'd found there when she'd moved in. Cards he must have left there.

He sat on the sofa, shuffling cards and laying out a game of solitaire. Mindlessly he began playing. Finally, she turned her back to him and continued working on the portrait.

Behind her, he shuffled again. "We were only there for one day when Pastor came to meet us. He was . . . unassuming. Like a regular person. He smiled and joked, then sent me outside to play. I remember thinking how pretty it was. You could see Mt. Shasta in the distance. A little girl came over to me, offered me a cookie."

Daisy wanted to turn around and look at him, but she didn't dare, fearing that he'd stop talking. "Eileen."

"Yes. She was the first person my own age who I met there. We ended up the best of friends. But eventually I was called back inside. My mother was pale. Trembling. She told me she was getting married."

"To the guy who'd brought you there?"

"No. To a stranger. She said that Pastor had informed

her that single women weren't permitted in Eden. Too much temptation to the men."

Daisy couldn't stifle the sound coming out of her throat. She jabbed her brush at the canvas a little too hard. "Sorry. Go on."

"My mother had been raised with similar values. Don't wear this, don't do that, don't be a harlot, all those things. She didn't fight it. She was given to Amos."

She turned around at that. "Given to?"

"Yes." He didn't look up from the cards. "He wasn't a bad man. Strict, but not . . . evil."

Evil. Like Ephraim. Who'd beaten him until he'd nearly died. "Were you happy?"

He shrugged. "I was five years old. I got a toy, a bed of my own, hot food, and a dog."

"What was his name? The dog?"

He looked up. "Boy. I wasn't an original child."

She smiled at him. "I think it's nice."

He nodded, not smiling back. "He was a good dog."

Her smile faltered. "What happened to him?"

His gaze dropped back to the cards. "I don't know. He . . . stayed behind."

"When you escaped."

"Yes." He drew a deep breath and released it on a shudder. "I loved that dog. I don't know how much longer he lived. He was old when I was thirteen. White muzzle. He was a golden." He sighed. "My mom got her locket the next day. It was her wedding day."

"She got married two days after arriving?"

His broad shoulders shrugged. "A day and a half, technically. We moved into Amos's house. Men couldn't marry until they'd built a house, and then it was a lottery of sorts. They put their names in a hat and Pastor picked one whenever a new woman arrived or a girl came of age. Older men were allowed to put more slips with names on them than the younger men, so the deck was stacked against the younger men. Amos had been waiting for quite some time for his name to be chosen from the hat."

It was . . . barbaric. But Daisy bit the words back. "Tell me about the locket."

"Every female was given one on her wedding day. But the chain was different than the one you yanked off your attacker last night."

Last night? Had it only been last night? Daisy felt like she'd lived a month of Fridays. "How was it different?" she asked when he didn't elaborate.

"Stronger. You never would have been able to pull one of those chains off. The Hulk wouldn't have been able to, not without strangling the woman. They had to be cut off. The locket sat in the hollow of the wearer's throat. The chains were forged right there in Eden." He chuckled bitterly. "Metaphorically and literally."

"So it was more like a mark of ownership."

"That's exactly what it was. A photo of the happy couple was placed inside."

"Like Eileen. Even though she was only a child." *My God.*

"She was twelve. That was the normal marrying age."

Daisy remembered the details of the locket's engraving. "Twelve branches on the olive tree."

His gaze flew up, locking on Daisy's. "How did you know that?"

"Trish took a photo of the locket before the police got there last night. She took photos of me, too, my throat, the scene, all that." Her smile was small and rueful. "She watches a lot of cop shows on TV. Anyway, I asked her to send it to me. I wondered at the twelve branches. I thought that it was maybe the twelve tribes of Israel."

"That may have been one of the meanings. But it was the age of womanhood."

Daisy sighed. "Twelve. Just babies."

"We grew up fast in Eden."

"I guess you must have." She dropped her brush into the cup of cleaner. The face in the portrait she'd been painting wasn't recognizable yet, for which she was grateful. She wasn't sure she wanted Gideon to know she was painting him. Not yet, anyway. She didn't want to scare him away by appearing too eager. "I'm going to sit down now, but I can sit in the chair if you need your space."

He held her gaze for a very long moment. "No," he finally said. "Sit next to me."

She did, folding her hands in her lap. "What happened to boys when they turned twelve?"

"Nothing. Manhood was achieved at thirteen."

"Bar mitzvah."

He shook his head. "They adopted some elements of Judaism, but they weren't Jewish. They called it 'ascension.'"

"Got it."

She stole a glance at him. "Sasha said you had the locket's design tattooed on your chest, but that you covered it up with a phoenix."

He frowned. "Sasha was awfully observant for a girl who didn't like boys."

"She liked you. You're like her brother."

"So you said at dinner." He was sitting on the sofa's edge, his knees spread wide, leaning toward the cards he'd dealt on the coffee table. He began a new game, sorting and pairing, the muscles of his back rippling with each movement.

She hesitated, then figured she'd go big or go home. Easy to say, since she was home already and she knew he wouldn't leave her, not until he had someone to take his place so that she'd be safe. *So maybe I'm a horrible person for pushing this, but . . .*

She wanted to touch him. So she did, spreading her fingers wide over his back and caressing him gently. He didn't jerk away. Didn't react at all. She guessed he'd been watching her from the corner of his eye, so she hadn't surprised him. She kept up the soft touch, and after a few tense seconds, he relaxed under her palm and returned to his game.

"Tell me about the first tattoo," she murmured.

"I got it on my thirteenth birthday. Happy, happy," he added sarcastically.

"Did it hurt?"

"Like a fucking bitch. But I'd lived in the community for most of my life and I knew what happened to sissy-boys. I did not want to be a sissy-boy."

Not stopping her caress, she asked, "You said you were thirteen when you escaped. How long was it after your birthday?"

"The very next day."

She wondered which of the questions swirling in her mind she should ask next. *How? Why? What about your sister? What about your mother? Why were you beaten? What happened to make you cover up the tattoo with a phoenix when you were eighteen? Why was the man who beat you not punished? Where was this place?*

Finally she simply said, "Tell me."

ELEVEN

*T*ell me. Gideon's gaze was angled at the cards he'd dealt, but he'd closed his eyes, absorbing the feel of Daisy's hand on his back. He wondered how much to tell this generous woman who wore her heart on her sleeve. She'd looked up at him like he was some kind of hero, had trusted him to keep her safe. Had grounded him when he needed her most. What would she do if she knew the truth?

She would say you were thirteen and did what you had to do. She would be happy that you protected yourself. That you made it out alive. She would say you shouldn't feel guilty. And she wouldn't look at you any differently.

All of that was probably true. Probably. He wasn't sure if he was willing to risk it, though. To risk her looking at him like he was a monster. Or worse. With pity.

"I'm a vault," she murmured. "I will keep your secrets."

He didn't doubt that. But would she still look at him like he was a hero?

He wasn't sure what he'd tell her when he opened his mouth. But he had to tell her something. She was connected to this mess through that damn locket and the man who'd attacked her.

"The thirteenth birthday marked the rite of passage

to manhood. We were assigned to a craftsman in the town as an apprentice. I was given to Edward McPhearson."

Her hand paused for a second at the word "given," but then resumed the caress.

"He was the smith. He forged the chain. Made the lockets. He was one of the founders." He swallowed hard. "He'd been given Eileen in marriage the year before."

"He's the man in the first photo. The one you said was dead."

"Yes. Eileen was his fourth wife."

"What happened to his other three wives?"

"They were still around. It was a polygamist community."

She released a slow breath. "I see."

No, she really didn't. "He'd had his eye on Eileen for a while. She cried the night before her birthday. He terrified her. Watched her like a wolf. I was old enough to understand why and I was afraid for her, too. We plotted together, she and I, on how we could get away, how I would save her."

"But you couldn't," she said softly.

"No, I couldn't. She got her locket and married McPhearson. The next day, after the wedding, my friend was gone. She was still breathing and existing, but her eyes were dead. I thought about the other girls I'd seen after their wedding nights. Some had worn that same vacant expression while others had seemed okay. But not Eileen."

"He hurt her."

"She had to go to the community doctor. I heard some of the women talking and they said he'd torn her up." His voice broke.

Daisy leaned her cheek against his upper arm, continuing to rub his back. "I'm sorry, Gideon. I'm so sorry."

He forced the emotion back. "She was called Miriam

SAY YOU'RE SORRY 203

after that. It was her given name. Many of the girls were named Miriam. Those who weren't often took that name on their wedding days. I often wondered why, but I got my answer when I was given my first walk-through of the smithy. There were a dozen lockets that said 'Miriam,' just waiting for their wearers to turn twelve. Only a few with other names. Rachel, Sarah, Rebekah, Hannah. Mostly Old Testament names. He had templates, each made a different name. It made his engraving job easier, I guess."

"Did you want to be a smith?"

"No. But I knew if I was around, I could watch out for Eileen." He let his head fall forward, stretching his neck, remembering to breathe again after her hand ran up his back to pet the back of his neck.

"But that's not what happened."

"No." His body went rigid, his muscles tightening painfully, as he allowed himself to recall what had happened. The hand on his neck began long sweeps down his back and up his neck, over and over. She wrapped her other hand around his biceps, turning so that her forehead was pressed to his shoulder.

"You don't have to tell me what happened," she whispered.

Her forehead pivoted as her chin lifted, her lips brushing his arm. He could feel the soft movement through the fabric of his shirt, and suddenly he wished the shirt were gone so that he could feel her lips against his skin.

"McPhearson was an equal-opportunity abuser," he bit out.

She didn't gasp, didn't stiffen, didn't do anything other than to continue brushing kisses over his upper arm. But he heard her swallow, so he knew she'd understood.

"On their thirteenth birthday, the boys entered special training. I'd always believed that meant the beginning of the apprenticeship and the beginning of church training. It might have been for some of the others, if their master didn't care for boys. When McPhearson took me to his home that night, I wasn't expecting what he tried to do."

She swallowed again. "Tried?"

"I . . . resisted." He'd resisted so hard that McPhearson died. "I got away from him." And left him bleeding on the floor of the smithy, his head busted open on the anvil.

Gideon hadn't meant to kill him. He'd just been trying to get away.

But he hadn't been sorry. Until he'd seen Ephraim Burton's face on Daisy's card table. Then sorry was all he'd been able to be. Because then he'd known who Eileen had been forced to marry. She'd gone from a degenerate pervert to a violent man with very big hands that he knew how to use to inflict the maximum pain.

"How did McPhearson die, Gideon?" she asked, so very quietly. "Because if you tell me that you didn't kill him, I'll be disappointed."

He flinched in surprise, then pulled away so that he could tip her face up. She met his eyes, hers filled with tears and defiance. She didn't look away and he couldn't, either.

"Did you?" she whispered. "I really hope you did."

All he could do was nod.

"Good," she said fiercely, a blink sending the tears down her cheeks. "I hope that bastard suffered."

"No," he said, and incredibly enough, he almost smiled. The urge was quickly quelled, though, and he tugged her so that she resumed her earlier position, her face against his arm. *Keep kissing me. Please.*

She did one better, moving the hand on his arm to thread her fingers with his. She had her arms around him now and she started kissing his shoulder again.

"We were fighting and I pushed him down. He hit his head on the anvil."

"So it was an accident. Too bad."

That Daisy was a little bloodthirsty came as no great shock. There was a core of steel in the woman. He hoped to see more of it. More of her.

"When did Ephraim Burton beat you?"

He steeled his own spine. "About five minutes after I ran out of the smithy. He saw me running and came to check on McPhearson. He gave this roar that I could hear across the compound. Like a wounded bear."

"Where were you?"

"I'd hidden in Amos's barn."

"Your mother's husband."

"Right. I knew where he kept his wood-carving knives. He was a carpenter. I'd grabbed one of the knives when Ephraim busted into the barn, a couple of the other men with him. Ephraim was McPhearson's best friend. He claimed the right to deliver justice."

"He was going to kill you."

"Yeah. He nearly did."

Her grip on his hand tightened. "Did you fight back?"

"Yes."

"But you didn't kill him."

"No," he whispered. "But I tried."

She reared back, understanding clearly dawning. "You stabbed him in the eye. That's why he has a patch."

He could only blink at her. "How did you . . ."

"It was the look on your face, Gideon, when you saw him with the patch. You did that to him? Well, good. I wish you'd buried the knife in his throat."

Bloodthirsty indeed. But Gideon had to shake his head. "He apparently got first dibs on McPhearson's wives, because McPhearson had no blood brothers, at least within the community. Ephraim was ten times worse than McPhearson from a cruelty standpoint."

"Oh," she breathed. "Poor Eileen."

He nodded miserably, forcing back the bile that

burned his throat. "I can't even imagine her surviving that man. But she must have."

"Because her locket made it out of the compound. What would have happened to the locket if she'd died?"

"It would've been melted down to make a new one or given to another Miriam."

She lifted her hand from his back to cup his face, just as she'd done earlier in the day. Her thumb brushing over his beard, she asked, "How did you get away?"

"My mom," he whispered. "I have a vague memory of Amos rushing into the barn after the men carried Ephraim to the healer. I think Amos truly believed in the community's teachings. My mother wasn't *un*happy with him. She begged him to help her get me out. The next day was Saturday, the day that the truck made the trip for supplies—the things we couldn't grow or make. It took vegetables and some of the products we made. Stuff from the smithy and some stuff that men like Amos made in his carpentry shop, furniture and things like that. The women made quilts and baked goods. Stuff like that."

"You hid in the truck?"

"My mom hid with me, in the back. I have this vague memory, more like a dream, of her holding me under a blanket, crying so quietly. Telling me to hold on, to be brave. That she . . . she . . ." His throat closed and his eyes and nose burned.

Daisy pulled his head to her shoulder and, sinking back against the arm of the sofa, pulled him down with her and wrapped her arms around him. "That she loved you," she whispered, and he nodded, helpless to stop the tears. Daisy held him, stroking his hair, not saying another word.

Daisy didn't tell him it would be all right. She didn't tell him not to cry. She didn't make any soothing noises or promises that meant nothing. She just lay back against the arm of the sofa, holding him until he could breathe again.

He sighed, exhausted. "I'm sorry."

"Don't be," she murmured into his ear. "Please don't be."

"Rafe doesn't know any of that."

"He'll never hear it from me. I promise."

"I believe you." He wasn't sure why he did, but he knew it beyond a shadow of a doubt. "I need to wash my face." No way did he want her to see him like this.

He should feel shame at having cried on her but he didn't. And he wasn't sure what to think about that.

"In a minute." She still stroked his hair. "Let's just finish this so you don't have to talk about it again. How did you get to the bus station? The one in Redding, right?"

"That's what I was told when I regained consciousness. I didn't know how I got there. I was told that I was found behind the building by a cop doing patrol. My pockets were empty and my shoes were gone."

"You were robbed while you lay there."

"That's what the cops thought. I was airlifted to the hospital at UC Davis. It's a level one trauma center."

The hand stroking his hair faltered, then resumed its soothing movement. "Because you nearly died."

"Yeah."

She was quiet for so long that he considered getting up. But it felt so good to be held. It had been a long damn time. He relaxed a little more, nuzzling into the curve where her neck met her shoulder. She smelled so good.

"You said you didn't know how you got to the bus station," she said abruptly.

He didn't want to move. "What?"

"You said you *didn't* know how you got there. Does that mean you found out later?"

He stilled, stunned that she'd pulled that out of everything he'd said. Although he shouldn't have been. The way she'd methodically put that puzzle together demonstrated how her mind worked.

You won't ever be able to get anything past her.

Won't ever be able to. The phrase had his brain momentarily shorting out. That was a future tense. That it wasn't scaring the hell out of him was something else he wasn't sure what to think about. He'd worry about it later. At the moment, she was waiting for an answer.

"I found out later. My . . . sister Mercy got out. She told me." Eventually. Mercy hadn't told him much of anything else, though.

The deep breath she drew lifted his head, lowering it gently when she exhaled into his hair. "But not your mom?"

He shook his head, unable to say the word "no," but he didn't have to because she drew another deep breath that sounded suspiciously wet.

"I'm sorry, Gideon. I'm so sorry."

I'm sorry, too, Mama. So sorry.

She tilted his head up enough to kiss his forehead and he felt the wetness on her cheeks. "Thank you for telling me," she murmured before releasing him.

He nodded against her, not trusting his voice. He lay there on the sofa, half on top of her. His arm was around her waist, his cheek having found a resting place between her breasts. He'd rarely felt so drained. Or so . . . safe.

She was humming to him now. Something low and husky. Sexy. But also sweet. A lullaby, he realized hazily. "Shh, just let go, Gideon. Go to sleep. I've got you."

She held him close, brushing kisses on the top his head, her hand petting his beard. His brain began to shut down even as his body woke up. She was soft and curvy and smelled so damn good. He turned his head, pressing his lips into her palm. He nuzzled, wanting her, but only briefly registering his sexual frustration before he drifted off.

SACRAMENTO, CALIFORNIA
FRIDAY, FEBRUARY 17, 11:15 P.M.

"Hey, Trish, isn't that your friend? The radio chick?"

His head snapped from his phone screen, his gaze zeroing in on the TV that hung over the bar. It was her. *Eleanor Dawson.* The segment on the news was the same one he'd been watching on his phone, but the TV over the bar had closed captioning so he could actually see what she said. He hadn't been able to hear it on his phone.

The noise in the bar was deafening. He could barely hear himself think. And he needed to think.

Especially because Eleanor Dawson was talking about missing prostitutes.

How did she know? Who else knew? *Holy fucking shit.* He wanted to scream, but he did not. Instead, he repositioned himself on the bar stool so that he could fully see the screen.

Nobody knows anything, he told himself. *Nobody has any idea that you're the one who snatched the hooker. Nobody has any idea that you have her stashed in your basement freezer.* And nobody knew that he'd stolen Miss Rude from the airport in Colorado.

Nobody knows. You're safe. You've been smart.

Nobody knows.

"Do you know of a specific person who's disappeared in the city?" the reporter was asking, and the Dawson woman looked sad.

"I'm sure you have ways of getting all that information," she answered.

She does not know. If she did, he'd be sitting in a jail cell right now.

So chill. Enjoy your beer. Find out when her friend gets off work. Because he was going to follow the unfortunate waitress and find out where Eleanor lived.

He frowned. *Wait a minute.* Radio chick? He restarted the video on his phone and held it up to his ear. *Aha. That's where I heard her voice before. She's the radio chick on* The Big Bang with TNT. Who'd been a royal dick that morning.

Poppy Frederick, the reporter called her. *That's her.* Excitement had him sitting a little straighter. Maybe that was why he hadn't been able to find Eleanor's address. Maybe she went by Poppy. Although Eleanor was a much nicer name.

Whatever. He turned off his phone, slid it in his pocket, and proceeded to enjoy his beer. Soon he'd know everything he needed to know about Eleanor Dawson, a.k.a. Poppy Frederick.

Everything was going to be just fine.

TWELVE

Finally the waitress was going home. He'd been wait-ing across the street from the bar in his car for two hours. Covering his head with the hood of his slicker, he locked up his car and followed her. It was still rain-ing cats and dogs, which worked in his favor because the waitress kept her head down the whole way. She never looked up, never noticed him.

He waited until she'd entered the apartment build-ing, relieved that there was no lock on the door. There was a plate glass window next to the entrance and he stood there, watching as she checked her mailbox be-fore starting up the stairs, her head still hanging low. He slipped through the door and followed her as she trudged up three flights of stairs, a heavy backpack on one shoulder. Staying back a flight, he waited until she'd unlocked all three locks and pushed the door open before making his move.

Sprinting up the remaining stairs, a wadded-up cloth in hand, he shoved her inside and in one move stuffed the cloth in her mouth and wrapped his arm around her throat. She hadn't had time to scream.

Quickly he bound her hands and feet with zip ties and rolled her to her back. Her eyes were wide with terror. *Good.* He wanted her to be very afraid.

"This is how this is going to go," he murmured,

leaning close. "You're going to tell me where your friend lives. You know, the blonde who was with you last night."

Her eyes grew even wider.

"Nod if you understand," he commanded, and she jerked a fast nod. "Trish, right?"

Another nod as her eyes began to fill with tears.

Sydney's eyes did that. Filled with tears that meant nothing. Tears were manipulative. He'd learned never to be moved by a woman's tears. They just made him angrier. Crouching beside her, he flicked his switchblade open and pressed the tip to her throat. He cautiously removed the gag, ready to shove it back in if she made a sound.

"Where does she live?"

"I don't know," Trish rasped. "I really don't."

"You're besties. You don't go to her place? Ever? You expect me to believe that?" He pressed the tip of the blade a little harder, and she cried out. "Tell me."

"I don't know," she insisted, but she was lying. He could always tell.

They always lied.

He shoved the gag back in her mouth and dumped the contents of her purse on the floor beside her, sorting until he found her phone. It was unlocked, so he opened her contacts. No Eleanor Dawson. But there was a Daisy Dawson.

There was only a phone number next to her name. No address.

He clicked on the call log. Trish had received a call from Daisy a few hours before the attack, but the only texts were from earlier in the day when the two agreed to meet at the community center for their AA meeting.

He glanced at the bound woman, whose eyes were closed, tears steadily sliding down her face. That was why she and the blonde had been at the community center. AA.

Wish I'd known. I'd have brought booze as a little temptation.

She might have a bottle stashed somewhere, though. Some alcoholics did. Leaving her on the floor, he went into the kitchen and riffled through cabinets and the small pantry, looking for her emergency stash. Then he stopped when he passed the refrigerator, where a flyer was attached with a magnet. At the top of the flyer was the grainy photo of a woman.

It was her. Poppy Frederick a.k.a. Eleanor a.k.a. Daisy Dawson. He leaned closer and scanned the flyer. It was for a pet adoption clinic that Poppy was "hosting" at Barx and Bonz. That meant she'd be there in person. Tomorrow, from ten to two.

I can take it from there. Relief rolled over him in a wave. That took care of that concern. Now he could finish what he'd started Thursday afternoon. When he'd stumbled into the bar, full of rage, after getting the news that Paul was selling the company.

When he'd first laid eyes on the waitress who should have been nicer to him.

‖ SACRAMENTO, CALIFORNIA
‖ SATURDAY, FEBRUARY 18, 3:05 A.M.

He slowed his step, tugging on Mutt's leash when the dog would have kept walking. Because they were here. A pretty Victorian house in the middle of Midtown.

Trish had never divulged Daisy's address, claiming until the bitter end that she didn't know where her friend lived. He had to admire that kind of loyalty.

Too bad she'd been a bitch to him on Thursday. The bitter end for her had been bitter indeed. And he felt so much better.

Lady Luck had smiled on him. Twice.

The first time had been when he'd taken a break

from his work, sitting on her sofa to watch her writhe on the floor. To give her an opportunity to reconsider her lie about not knowing where Daisy lived.

He'd picked up her backpack, curious as to why it was so heavy. It had been filled with textbooks. She'd been a student, it seemed. He'd taken each book from the backpack, stacking them on the coffee table next to some magazines. He'd been pretty sure which trinket he was going to take to remember her, but sometimes he found the coolest things in the bottom of a woman's purse—or backpack.

Unfortunately, the only thing at the bottom of Trish's backpack was a bunch of pencils and pens. He'd tossed the backpack aside—and that was when he'd seen it.

A magazine on her coffee table. But it wasn't the face of the celebrity du jour that had caught his eye. It was the mailing label. *Eleanor Dawson*. With an address. And now he was standing in front of this pretty little Victorian.

Which—second stroke of luck—was only three blocks from his own house.

He'd taken the magazine with him, ripping off the mailing label before tossing the magazine in his fireplace. He hadn't wanted anyone to know he'd seen Daisy's address, or they'd be back on their guard.

He studied the three-story Victorian. He'd wanted one like that, but they'd been too expensive. This one, though, had a trio of mailboxes out front. So the place was separated into apartments. Daisy's was number 1. So perhaps she was on the ground floor? That made it more convenient. He hated climbing through second- and third-story windows.

At that moment a car stopped in front of the house. He turned his back, pretending to be watching Mutt, but a glance over his shoulder revealed a woman getting out of the car and jogging up to the front door. She was tall with a long blond ponytail. Definitely not Daisy. This woman moved aggressively, even though she was clearly inebriated.

She also sang aggressively, he thought, wincing at her butchered tune. Queen. "Bohemian Rhapsody." Her serenade abruptly ended as she switched to calling out, "Sasha's home!" Then she slammed the front door.

He'd been tempted to peek in the lower windows and see if Daisy was in her apartment, but he feared the drunk songstress had woken her up. The last thing he wanted was for her to report a Peeping Tom to the police.

He tugged on Mutt's leash. "Come on, Mutt. Let's go home."

SACRAMENTO, CALIFORNIA
SATURDAY, FEBRUARY 18, 4:00 A.M.

Daisy woke slowly, her neck slightly sore from falling asleep on the sofa, but she didn't care because her body was weighted down by Gideon's, his even breaths warming her breast. Her arms tightened reflexively around his broad shoulders, but he didn't respond. He was solidly asleep.

She didn't have to check the time to know that it was about four A.M. Her body had become accustomed to waking at four within a week of her starting with the morning show. Tad had complained about it every day and he'd been doing the show for five years. She had to wonder now if he was trying to get her to complain as well so that he could report her to the station manager.

Asshole. Spreading lies that she'd faked the attack for ratings. *Bastard.*

But she wasn't going to think about Tad the Bastard now. Not when she had her arms full of a sleeping Gideon Reynolds.

Gideon. *God.* The things he'd endured. Her throat hurt at the memory of his voice breaking, the way he'd cried on her shoulder. Waking up in a hospital like that, at thirteen years old. In pain. And alone.

He must have been so scared. Her heart hurt just thinking about it.

The pain in her chest began to give way to a burning fury as she thought about the men who'd so cruelly tormented his family. Eileen, too. She'd like to get her hands on them. Show them some real pain so that she could get answers for Gideon.

Where was Eden? Where was Ephraim Burton? How many of the men there had watched Ephraim beat a thirteen-year-old boy nearly to death? Of course, first they had to find Eileen. She might know where to find Eden since she'd also escaped. *I hope she escaped. I hope she got away. I hope she's safe somewhere.*

And if they never found Eileen? If she was alive, she might have deliberately lost the locket, wanting to separate herself from the community of Eden as much as she could. *I know I would, in her place.* She'd likely gone under.

Gideon's sister had gotten out, but Daisy assumed that she'd also been unable to tell them where to find Eden, or Gideon would have already uncovered the community and delivered the abusers to the police. And there was nobody else to ask.

Unless . . . The thought made her blink in surprise. What if there were others who'd escaped? Others that Gideon knew nothing about?

How would they even find each other out in the real world?

Absently she stroked his hair, like silk under her fingertips. A cult like Eden wouldn't allow its members to know that they could get out. She wondered what the leaders had told the members when Gideon disappeared.

Probably that he'd died.

So what if others had managed to escape? Where would they go?

As far away as they could, was her first instinct. But Gideon hadn't. Instead he'd stayed in Northern California, requesting an assignment here after his job had taken him away.

To be with the Sokolovs, he'd said, and Daisy was sure that was true.

But he's also been looking for them, she realized. She was somehow positive of that fact. A man like Gideon couldn't allow such evil to continue to exist. Which explained why he'd been so interested in Daisy's attacker. The locket was a lead, maybe the first he'd had.

And if that lead went nowhere, a solid plan B was to search for others. Other lockets. Other tattoos. *A hunt.*

Excitement rippled over her skin as she eased her body out from under his. Tempting as the warmth of his body was, Daisy loved a good hunt.

He made a rough noise as she tried to move, the arm he'd wrapped around her waist tightening. But he continued to sleep. Gently she pried his hand from her waist and kissed his knuckles. Then she rolled away, sliding to the floor as she pushed him back on the sofa. She got a pillow and blanket from her bed and made him more comfortable.

He was beautiful, she thought, brushing her fingertips over his beard, which was softer than she'd imagined. Leaning in, she pressed a kiss to his temple, wishing she were kissing his mouth instead.

There was something between them, call it chemistry or whatever. But she could soothe him. And he her. She could take care of herself, but it was so nice not to have to.

So nice to have someone to walk with in the rain, even if they had battled reporters.

So nice to have strong arms around her when she was shaken and for him to trust her enough to do the same. That had been the most powerful thing of all—that Gideon trusted her with his story, with his pain.

She was going to do whatever she could to help him. And maybe try out some of those investigative journalism skills she'd studied in college, what seemed a lifetime ago.

Sitting in the armchair with her laptop, she opened a browser window and typed: *tattoos olive trees angels with flaming swords.* Saying a prayer, she hit ENTER.

THIRTEEN

Gideon woke with a start, his hand going to his hip, his heart skipping a beat. *It's gone.* His gun was gone. And it was dark.

And he had a raging hard-on.

His mind raced, trying to remember where he was. He lay on a sofa, a light blanket draped over his body, a soft pillow under his cheek. He bolted upright, the blanket sliding down to pool in his lap.

"It's on the coffee table."

The husky voice was like a caress, soothing his racing pulse, but making his cock even harder. *Daisy.* He'd fallen asleep on her while still wearing his gun. He never did that. He always secured his weapon while he slept.

I've got you. She'd whispered it in his ear right before he'd drifted away.

He'd fallen asleep. *On her.* He never did that, either. He'd slept in the company of only a handful of people in his life since leaving Eden, and that had always been in a bed all by himself. He'd slept in the other twin bed in Rafe's room, but it had taken years for him to be comfortable enough to do that. After that, just the roommates he'd had at Quantico and on missions or stakeouts thereafter.

He didn't sleep with people. The women he'd dated

had never been invited to stay the night. They knew it up front—he'd never been anything but brutally honest— and while many of them had wanted more, they'd been satisfied with what he'd been able to give. And when they'd stopped being satisfied, they'd moved on. No harm, no foul. No hurt feelings for the most part.

He'd known Daisy Dawson less than forty-eight hours and he'd already slept with her. *On her.* He'd spilled his guts to her. And cried on her shoulder.

He knew he should feel ashamed, but he still didn't. A bit . . . unsettled, maybe. But no shame. With what he hoped was a surreptitious move, he adjusted himself, then pushed the blanket aside and swung his sock-clad feet to the floor. His shoes were placed under the coffee table, his holstered gun atop.

She sat in an overstuffed armchair that hadn't been here when he'd rented from Rafe, her feet tucked beneath her, her pretty face illuminated by the glow of the laptop on her knees. Brutus was snoring softly on the arm of the chair.

"What time is it?" he asked, rubbing the back of his neck. The pillow wasn't bad, but he'd much preferred when his head had been pillowed by her breasts.

"Six fifteen."

"Wow. I slept a long time."

Her lips curved. "You needed it."

He guessed he had. Yesterday, rehashing his past with Daisy, had been draining in the extreme and he hadn't slept a wink the night before, worrying about his conversation with Molina. And worrying about what it meant that Daisy had caused him to blurt out truths he hadn't intended to share. "Did you sleep at all?"

"Yep. I did wake up once when Sasha came in. She was singing 'Bohemian Rhapsody' at the top of her lungs."

He chuckled. "She was drunk, then."

He could see her eyes rolling in the glow of the

laptop. "She can only hit the high note when she's plastered. But I fell back asleep until four. My body wakes up at four every morning, even on weekends. I'm in the studio at five on weekdays, but I don't try to change my wake-up time on days off. It's too hard to get back to it on Monday. I'll need a nap after the adoption clinic."

He frowned. "Right. That's today."

Her brows lifted. "Yes, that's today. Why are you frowning?"

"Because I need to go up to the Redding bus station today."

Her face fell. "To look for Eileen. Of course. I can ask Rafe to come with me, or even Damien or Meg."

Rafe's oldest brother Damien was a cop in West Sac, his sister Meg a deputy with the county sheriff's department. Any of the Sokolov cops would be acceptable replacements, but he didn't want anyone to replace him.

He wanted to be the one to protect her. Which was ridiculous. But real.

He found his cell phone still in his front pocket. She apparently hadn't been brave enough to remove anything but his shoes and holster. That he'd slept through that was testament to how exhausted he'd been.

Or maybe how much you already trust her.

Checking his e-mail, he found the reply he'd been looking for. It wasn't what he'd wanted to hear. But it also was, because he didn't want to leave her. Which was also ridiculous. He sighed, frustrated with himself.

"What's wrong?" she asked.

"I sent an e-mail to a friend in Philly, a police artist. He also worked with the Bureau field office, which was where I met him. I sent him the photo of Eileen."

"So he could do an age-progression sketch. Good idea. What did he say?"

"That he can't get to it until this afternoon. I don't want to ask around up in Redding without a more up-to-date sketch, in case she escaped recently."

"I can leave the adoption clinic early," she offered. "Maybe we could arrive up there by the time you get the sketch?"

He shook his head. "That's not necessary. The ticketing office at the bus station closes at one this afternoon and it'll take us two and a half hours to get up there, so we can't make it up there in time today. We'll have to wait until they open tomorrow, which means we can leave anytime after the pet thing is done."

Her eyes widened and even in the dim light he could see that he'd delighted her. "You're actually going to take me with you? I figured you'd be all"—she dropped her voice to a rusty, commanding bass—"'No way, you must stay!'"

He laughed. "I figure you're safer with me up there than staying here alone."

That the Sokolovs would never allow her to be alone went unsaid.

Her smile dimmed as she studied him in the semi-darkness. "Did you ever tell the police what had happened to you once you woke up in the hospital?"

He went still, his insides freezing. Which also took care of his hard-on. "Yes. But they couldn't find the community. I didn't know where they were and the cops weren't going to authorize an all-out air search for a group no one had ever heard of on the word of one beaten-up teenager. I told them it was a town called Eden. I didn't know then to call it a cult. I think the detective believed me, but he said that there was no town called Eden anywhere nearby. He said they sent out someone to search, but . . ." He shrugged.

"So you searched for them on your own." She'd said it as a statement, not a question.

"You sound sure that I did," he said.

"I am. You wouldn't have let your mother and sister suffer if you could have stopped it. I take it you couldn't find them, either."

"No," he said, humbled by her confidence in him. "I've been searching for seventeen years. All I know about the location is that I could see Mt. Shasta in the distance."

She grimaced. "That doesn't really narrow it down, does it? You can see the mountain for a hundred miles on a clear day." Her brow wrinkled. "That's, what? About thirty thousand square miles of search area? What about your view of the mountain? Which way did the sun rise or set? That will narrow it down."

He hated having to go through this again. But he'd do it for her. "It changed a few times. The community moved a few times before I was thirteen. The mountain was to the west when I left, but they could have moved again before the cops got out there to look."

"What about satellite photos?"

He shook his head. "I've spent countless hours poring over them, comparing the images season to season, year to year. I've seen no settlements that aren't accounted for on existing maps."

"Then they're camouflaged somehow," she murmured.

"That's what I think, too," he said. "The homes were small, just a few rooms each. Some had lofts where the kids would sleep."

"Very *Little House on the Prairie*," she said wryly. "Except, of course, for the slavery, the polygamy, and the rampant pedophilia."

He almost smiled. "Exactly."

"Could they have earth homes?"

"They might now. They didn't then. The homes were basic plank construction. Concrete foundations. They'd break down the houses and move the used lumber to the new site and rebuild."

"And the foundations would be easy enough to cover with dirt when they moved on. How many homes? And were they grouped close together?"

"Maybe twenty or twenty-five homes, and yes, they were very close together. My mother used to complain that she could reach out her window to borrow a cup of sugar from the woman next door."

Daisy shrugged. "It wouldn't be all that hard to hide under a camo tarp. Most of that land up there is heavily forested wilderness, a lot of it evergreen."

"You know that area?" he asked, surprised.

She nodded. "It's not too far from where our ranch was. Can I see your map later?"

"My map?"

"The one you've used to mark off the places you've checked."

Again she sounded certain that he'd have one, and she was right. "It's at my house. We can go there and pick it up on our way."

She smiled at that. "I get to see your house?"

He felt a thrill of anticipation at being able to show it to her. He was proud of the renovations that he'd done so far. "Do you want to?"

"Yes. I do." She tilted her head, her eyes narrowing curiously. "Did your sister remember any of the details of her escape?"

His gut abruptly tightened again, and he sucked in a pained breath. "No."

She went quiet. "Not your story to tell?"

"No. I'm sorry."

"It's all right, Gideon. Can you at least tell me how old she was?"

"Thirteen."

"She would have been married for one year."

He swallowed hard. "Yes."

"Okay," she murmured. "I can imagine the rest." She raked her fingers through Brutus's fur, petting the dog gently, and Gideon couldn't tear his eyes away. He wished that she'd pet him that way. Again. Because she had the night before. She'd stroked his hair and his beard and his back. So very gently. Nothing in his life had ever felt so nice.

"Gideon? Gideon?"

He yanked his gaze from her hand petting Brutus to meet her eyes. "What was that?"

"I asked if you've talked to any of the other escapees from Eden?"

His mouth fell open. "What?"

"Other escapees. Have you connected with them?"

It was like a sucker punch, leaving him breathless. He shook his head. "There weren't any others. Only me, Mercy, and Eileen."

She unfolded her legs from beneath her and came to sit next to him, putting her laptop on the coffee table. "I found two, both boys. Well, they're young men now."

He stared at her, openmouthed. "How? How did you find them?"

She gave him a serious side-eye. "I majored in journalism, Gideon. I know how to find stuff. This wasn't even that complicated. Just time-consuming."

"You've been awake for two hours."

Her eyes softened. "And you're an FBI agent who's been free for seventeen years?"

"Well . . . yes."

"Have you ever looked for other . . . escapees or survivors or whatever you want to call what you are?"

"Yes, many times. I searched online for tattoos like mine and lockets like my sister's, but I never found anyone."

"All right." She covered his hand where it rested on his thigh. "I know you can't share Mercy's story, and I'm not asking that. But did she tell you how they explained your disappearance?"

"Yes." It had been one of the few things she *had* told him. "Pastor told them that I'd attacked McPhearson and murdered him and they'd banished me as punishment."

"What did that mean exactly?"

"That they took me into the wilderness, tied me to a tree, and left me there to die. Ostensibly I would have been attacked, mauled, and consumed by animals."

Daisy gasped. "Dear God."

He shrugged. "Pedophilia was apparently A-okay. Murder was not."

"Was . . ." She hesitated. "Was your mother punished for getting you out?"

Yes. He had to bow his head against the sudden pain. *I'm sorry, Mama.* "How did you find the two escapees?" he asked, his voice hoarse and heavy.

Her eyes filled with sudden tears, because he'd answered the question without saying a word. "I searched newspapers in the Northern California area for teenagers with tattoos. Also a generic search for specific tattoos with olive trees and cross-referenced Eden." She grimaced. "There are a lot of olive tree tattoos."

"So you just searched manually . . . with your eyes." He blew out a breath when she grinned at him.

"With my eyes?" she asked, chuckling.

He rolled his own. "I know I'm not making sense. I meant, do you have software to search picture files for details?" Because he *had* used software and had still found nothing.

"No to software, yes to eyes. I can focus on things faster than most people."

"And for longer," he murmured, thinking about the puzzle she'd zoned in on for hours the day before. He straightened abruptly, turning to see her laptop screen. "Show me the two you've found."

"I haven't actually tracked them down to a current location yet. One of them could have changed his name by now. I can e-mail these links to you."

"Please," he murmured, hoping like hell that there were really others. Every escapee was one more person who no longer lived in hell.

||| SACRAMENTO, CALIFORNIA
||| SATURDAY, FEBRUARY 18, 6:30 A.M.

Mutt gave a little shake when they came into the house, marched straight to his bed, and curled up with what sounded like an irritated grunt. He liked to walk, but maybe not this much. They'd done the path to Daisy's house twice more.

She was home, because both of the last two times he'd walked by, there had been lights on in her apartment. But there had also been lights in the third-floor windows and he'd seen a man walking around up there. He hadn't even attempted to approach the house. He had no interest in breaking and entering to grab Daisy Dawson, especially if a scream would draw the attention of whoever lived upstairs.

He'd been tempted to park his car near Daisy's house and wait for her to come out, but the Neighborhood Watch kept a lookout for cars that didn't belong to the residents. Dog walkers were kind of ubiquitous, but Mutt was tired.

So am I. He'd worked yesterday, brought Zandra home, and taken care of Trish Hart. Plus his evening with Sydney, he thought with a shudder. At least taking care of Trish had loosened up his mind. He could think clearly now.

And, thinking clearly, he'd begun Operation Overthrow the Old Man. With Manilow crooning in the background, he sat on his bed, studying the photos and documents he'd been sorting between walks with Mutt. He'd been collecting proof of his old man's dalliances for years. *Years.* But even more powerful was the evidence of the old man's association with the drug cartels. He had pictures and letters and even a few taped conversations from the times he'd bugged Paul's phone, all proving the old man had used his charter planes to transport drugs. He was confident that there was something among them that would give Paul pause. Something that would be enough to save his job.

But what he really wanted was for Paul to fulfill his promise—that if he worked hard, he'd someday own the place. *The company should be mine.*

He needed the salary. He needed the *planes.* Without flying, how would he keep his abductions under the radar? Nobody had noticed him. Nobody knew that he brought his guests home. His abductions, spread across time and numerous cities, hadn't raised any flags, but if he was forced to hunt locally, he'd quickly establish a pattern for law enforcement to follow. And he'd likely be caught.

He tidied the piles of paper, putting each one into a Ziploc bag so he wouldn't have to sort them again. Then he put the bags into a box and slid it under his bed. He needed to find out if the sale of the company had been finalized and, if not, when it would be. That would tell him how long he had to act.

He'd catch a few hours' sleep before walking Mutt again. If he couldn't catch her coming out of the house, he'd see her at the pet store later. However he did it, she needed to be silenced. She was the worst kind of loose end—vocal and articulate.

SACRAMENTO, CALIFORNIA
SATURDAY, FEBRUARY 18, 6:30 A.M.

Bracing his arm along the back of the sofa, Gideon leaned in to see Daisy's laptop screen, his beard brushing against her cheek. Sitting with her in the quiet darkness was . . . intimate. He drew in her scent and let it settle his agitation as she clicked on a browser tab.

He squinted at the small picture of a bare-chested

man showing off his new tattoos. "Expand it, please."
She did so and he slowly exhaled. "Oh my God. Judah."

"You know him?"

He nodded. "He was younger than me by a few
years. Closer to Mercy's age."

"I found this photo on the tattoo artist's Instagram."
She pointed at the fire-breathing dragon on the
younger man's right pec. It was aiming its fire at the
Eden tattoo. "We can contact the tattooist. This is a
pretty unique tattoo setup and it was only a few months
ago, so he'll probably remember the tattoo itself. We
can ask if he remembers the client."

A few months ago. He hadn't searched for tattoos like
his in at least six months. "*If* he's willing to talk to us."

"That's a big one," she allowed. "He might not talk
to you, but he might talk to me."

"Why you?" He frowned, afraid he didn't want to
know the answer.

"You look like a cop, and I don't. And I have an
unfinished tattoo. I can ask about it."

His brows shot up, as did something else he'd rather
have stayed down. But the idea of a tattooed Daisy was
hot as hell. "What and where?"

Her cheeks dimpled. "Brutus and none of your business. Focus, Gideon." She clicked on the second photo.
"I'm less sure of this one because the tattoo is not exactly the same." She brought it up and enlarged it.

Focusing, Gideon shook his head at the young
man's photo. "Never seen him before. And you're
right, the tat is different."

"This photo comes from an article on the swim team
of a university in SoCal. His name is Lawton Malloy.
He's only nineteen, so if he did come from Eden, he
would have been a toddler when you left and it makes
sense that you wouldn't have known him." She zoomed
in on the tattoo. "See, the praying children look different and the olive tree only has ten branches."

"A copycat, then." Gideon stared at the tat. From a distance it would look very close to the real thing. "But if so, he would have had to have gotten the idea from someone. Maybe he'll tell us who."

"I was thinking that."

He frowned. "But . . . why wouldn't these guys have spoken up?"

"Maybe they're afraid. Or maybe they had the same bad experience that you did with abuse and it's just as hard for them to talk about it. It's hard enough for you and you're trained as an investigator."

"You could be right. I guess we'll find out when we talk to them. Did you find any more?"

She shook her head. "Not yet. But I'll keep looking."

"Please do. I'll call this in to my boss." He needed to tell her about the second wedding photo anyway. "This will be enough to increase staffing. She can have a search run using recognition software—for lockets and tattoos."

They sat in silence for a long moment that seemed to grow even quieter with each beat of his heart. Her scent filled his head and his body abruptly kicked into overdrive, his erection throbbing to the point of being painful. He needed to do something or he was going to combust. Stay or go? Move away or closer?

If she turned her head the smallest bit, their lips would brush, but she sat staring at her laptop, so still that he wondered if she was holding her breath. He needed to know what she was thinking. What she wanted.

"Daisy," he whispered. "Look at me."

She turned her head then and, just as he'd thought, their mouths were just a breath apart. She looked up at him and he saw the same thing in her eyes that he was sure filled his own. Desire. Need. And a yearning for something more.

If he kissed Daisy Dawson, it was with the full awareness that it would be more than one kiss. It would mean more than a quick hookup. He knew without asking that she'd want it to last longer than one night.

So did he.

Slowly he lowered his head to hers, giving her time to pull away. But she didn't. Her eyes closed as she leaned in, and then he was kissing her, softly and far more sweetly than he wanted. What he wanted was to drag her against him, to lay her down on the sofa and plunder. He wanted to touch her soft skin all over. Wanted to know if she smelled so good everywhere. Wanted to see her eyes go dark with lust and heavy with satisfaction. He wanted to mark her so that pricks like that reporter would know she was his.

But she's not yours. Not yet. So he kept his touch gentle, his kiss chaste, even though his body vibrated from the effort of holding back.

She smiled against his lips. "I won't break, Gideon," she whispered, shattering his self-control. He shoved his hands into her hair and yanked her closer, the kiss becoming instantly hot, rough, and hard. Her arms circled his neck and she hung on, humming against his mouth, opening to him when he licked at her lips.

Yes. This. This was what he'd wanted, what he'd longed for, what he'd dreamed about as he'd slept on the sofa. Her. Just like this.

Blindly he put her laptop on the coffee table next to his gun and pulled her onto his lap so that she straddled his thighs. He sank back into the cushions, carrying her with him, not breaking the kiss.

Her mouth was soft, her curves lush under his hands as he slowly caressed from her hips up her sides. She whimpered in the back of her throat and he had to grip her sweater in both fists to keep from taking what he wanted, because at some point in the two hours that she'd been awake, she'd taken off her bra. The only thing between him and skin was a thin layer of soft cashmere.

She ripped her mouth away from his, breathing hard. "Yes," she whispered. "Please."

Please. Delivered in that husky voice, it was like an engraved invitation to everything he wanted. But he needed her to be perfectly clear. He wanted no mistake. "Please what?" he asked hoarsely.

"Touch me." Reaching behind her back, she tugged his fists free from her sweater and brought each one to her lips, kissing his fingers, then opening his fists to kiss his palms. First one, then the other. Holding his gaze, she placed his palms on her breasts. "Please."

His heart was thundering in his chest as he cupped her breasts, testing their weight, the way they filled his hands just right. Even with the sweater in his way, she was perfect.

"You're perfect." The words came out as a growl.

Her shiver was impossible to miss. "I watched you sleep," she confessed, flattening her hands against his chest. "I wanted to touch you like this."

"Anytime," he managed, wanting her hands on his bare skin, but he didn't want to let go of her breasts long enough to take his shirt off. She fixed that for him, her nimble fingers pulling the buttons free and yanking the shirt from his pants until she'd bared his chest.

For a few seconds she simply stared while he wanted to shout for her to *touch him, goddammit.* Then her hands were back, gliding over his skin, gentle and almost reverent. It felt so good. *She* felt so good.

"Gideon," she whispered. "Look at you."

He'd rather look at her, at her face as she explored his chest. Her fingers were tracing the phoenix tattoo on his chest—the tat that covered the Eden tattoo. "Beautiful."

Swallowing hard, he skimmed his thumbs over her nipples, cursing the soft wool that stood between his fingers and her flesh. She sucked in a breath, her eyes closing as her head fell back, her hands stilled, and her hips began a slow, subtle grind against his groin that was driving him out of his mind.

And then her hands were moving again, now mimicking his, her thumbs teasing his nipples. He groaned, his hips bucking up in a reflexive move that had her breasts bouncing in front of his face.

"Daisy." His voice was hoarse. Ripped up.

"Mmm?" She didn't open her eyes, her hips maintaining their slow rocking, adding in an occasional shimmy, like she was dancing. On his cock. *God.*

"I want to touch you."

She opened her eyes. "Yes." Then leaned in to kiss him again and his brain detonated. Crunching forward, he came off the sofa and rolled them until they were horizontal, and he was yanking the sweater up and over her head. She grabbed his shoulders as her hands came free of the sleeves, and then his mouth was on her breast, sucking a stiff nipple into his mouth.

A low cry escaped her throat and she arched against him, her hands in his hair, holding him close. "God . . . That feels . . . Don't stop, Gideon. Not yet."

Stop? He would in a heartbeat if she asked, but until then he had no intention of stopping. *Ever? How far are you going to let this go?*

As far as she'll let me. She was sweet and hot, her body undulating against him, and for this moment she was his. And he couldn't get enough. His hips rocked against her and her legs parted, letting him settle between them. He released her breast and took her mouth in another blistering kiss.

He lifted his head enough to mutter "I want you" against her lips.

She moaned again, deep and husky, and he shivered,

head to toe. "Same," she whispered. "But I don't have anything."

Anything? The word finally permeated his sex-hazed brain, bringing with it a hard hammer of disappointment. "Me either."

Her fingers gentled in his hair. "Fuck," she cursed, disgruntled.

He stiffened, then buried his face in her neck, snorting a surprised laugh. "Not this morning, apparently."

She laughed, too. "Bad choice of words." Her chest lifted and fell as she sighed, continuing to play with his hair. "Thank you."

He lifted his head, looking down at her with a smile. "For what?"

"Making me feel good."

"I think it was pretty mutual."

Her cheeks pinked up. "I . . . I don't do this very often."

He kissed her forehead. "Neither do I. It's been a while for me. Even if I'd had a condom in my wallet, it would probably have been expired by now."

She smiled. "Is it horrible of me to be happy about that?"

"Not at all." He lowered his head to her shoulder, kissing her chin. He traced lazy circles on her breast, simply because he could. He was still hard as a rock, but it wouldn't kill him. Probably. "When do we have to leave for your event?"

"I have to be there at nine to get things set up, and you wanted to go early. To . . . scope it out or whatever. It's after seven now, so we should leave in an hour or so. If you let me up, I can make you some breakfast before I take my shower."

He groaned. "Stop saying that."

"Breakfast?" she asked cheekily.

"Smartass," he grumbled. "What if I don't want to let you up?"

"I become hangry and possibly homicidal," she said solemnly. "It's not pretty."

He nuzzled against her skin. "Five more minutes then."

She kissed the top of his head. "Okay."

"Daisy?"

"Hmm?"

He hesitated. Because he was nervous. He hated feeling nervous. "When anyone asks today who I am to you, what do you plan to say?"

Her fingers faltered, lying still in his hair. "What do you want me to say?"

He opened his mouth to speak, but the words were stuck in his throat. *Dammit.* He hated this. He wanted to say *Never mind*, but she'd gone abruptly stiff, like she was on her guard, too.

Way to fuck this up, he growled at himself. He'd managed to fuck it up without actually fucking.

It wouldn't have been fucking. And dammit, the little voice in his head was right. There would have been nothing hurried or rushed or . . . temporary about sex with Daisy.

Because he cared. Which made his brain stupid.

"Well," she started when he said nothing. "We could say you're my cousin, but I'd get called on that, because I'd forget to not look at you like you're *not* my cousin."

He scrunched his brow as he considered the construction of that sentence. "Meaning you'd look at me as something other than your cousin."

"Yes," she said, sounding relieved.

He smiled at that and relaxed. And when he did, she did.

"I could say you're an old friend, but . . . same issue," she added.

"So . . ." He kissed across her collarbone. "You're left with bodyguard or boyfriend."

"I don't want to admit I have a bodyguard." Her voice was amused as she continued the game. "The reporters will keep following me."

"All right, then. Boyfriend it is."

FOURTEEN

Back again this month?" Daisy smiled up at the couple with the four-year-old boy. She'd been sitting at the table where she was processing adoption applications since ten A.M.—after Gideon had moved it so that her back was against an interior wall of the pet store. It left one less area he needed to protect.

"We keep looking for the right fit," the man said and his wife rolled her eyes.

"He keeps looking for the dog that won't shed on the rug," she corrected tartly.

"That's an important consideration," Daisy said. "If shedding is a deal breaker, you need to make sure it's a dog that is less likely to do so, otherwise you'll end up getting mad at him for something he can't help. You might check out the shih tzu–poodle mix. He's a real sweet dog. Already housebroken."

The family went off to meet the dog in question and Gideon perched on the table's edge. The clinic was nearly finished and so far, so good. No one had shown any animosity toward Daisy. There'd been some attention that Gideon had considered unwanted, but that was because one man couldn't keep his eyes off her breasts and another kept wanting to engage her in conversation.

"Will those people adopt the shit-poo?" Gideon asked in a whisper.

Daisy laughed. "It's shih-poo. Although your way is funnier."

He scanned the people in the store, watching the crowd of both potential adopters and Saturday shoppers. "Where's that guy?"

"Which guy?" she asked, although she was pretty sure she knew.

"The one who was trying to pick you up." He lifted a hand when she started to protest. "He asked you out for coffee. Twice. He is trying to pick you up."

She shrugged. "He's an out-of-work drama teacher trying to get a job in radio, but whatever. Besides, he has a really nice dog. He can't be that bad."

Gideon snorted. "Do you really mean that?"

"What, that killers can't love dogs? No, of course not. But I do think you're overreacting. However—" It was her turn to raise her hand. "You are here to keep me safe. I will not meet with him alone, if at all, if that makes you feel better."

"It does," he said grumpily, scowling until she smiled at him again.

"I'm not stupid, Gideon. I promise. I'll take your advice. At least for now."

"That's honestly more than I thought I'd get." He leaned in to press a kiss to her forehead. "I'm going outside for a few minutes. I'll be back."

He'd been going outside periodically to check for anyone suspiciously loitering outside. So far, the coast had been clear. Daisy didn't think her attacker would bother them here. There were too many people milling around. No deserted alleys to yank her into. But she appreciated Gideon's vigilance, all the same.

"We love him," a man said, and Daisy jerked her gaze away from Gideon's retreating back—and backside, because it was *very* nice—to see that the young couple and their son had returned. The husband held the white curly shih-poo in his arms, the wife beaming as she tried to keep the little boy from grabbing at the dog.

"He's perfect," the wife added.

Daisy leaned over the table to smile at the little boy. "What's his name?"

"Spike," the boy announced with no irony whatsoever.

Daisy chuckled, because the dog looked no more like a Spike than her pup looked like a Brutus. "That is a very good name." She handed a clipboard with paperwork to the mother and a list of necessities to the father. "A few things you'll need. You can sit down to fill that out, if you like," she said to the wife as the husband and the boy went off to shop.

"Thank you." She sank into the chair and rubbed her back. "I'm glad we picked a little one. I'm not going to be able to see my toes soon, much less handle a big dog."

Daisy smiled at her. "Congratulations!"

The wife smiled back. "I could say the same to you." She looked over at where Gideon stood, just inside the doorway, arms casually crossed over his chest as he leaned against the wall, scanning the crowd in a way that made it look like he was idly observing.

He was . . . wow.

"Um, Poppy?"

Daisy looked at the woman sitting next to her, who had pursed her lips to keep from laughing. "I'm sorry, what did you say?"

"I said that your boyfriend is very handsome. But I think you already know that."

Daisy's cheeks heated, but she couldn't stop the smile that spread over her face. "He is, isn't he?"

"He is. And he looks at you the way a man should." She gave a decisive nod, finished filling out the paperwork, then went to the register to pay the adoption fee.

Another satisfied customer, Daisy hoped, waving as the family took their new pet home.

"Oh, good."

Daisy spun in her chair to see that the man wanting to get a job in radio had slid onto the chair beside her. Gideon was not going to like this.

"Good what?" Daisy asked cautiously.

He smiled at her flirtatiously as his Airedale curled up at his feet without being told. "I wanted to talk to you without your pit bull hovering."

And Gideon had been right. The guy was trying to pick her up. She pasted a kind smile on her face. "How can I help you, sir?"

His expression fell. "I'm so sorry. I didn't mean to be offensive, but I clearly have been. He seems like a nice pit bull," he added lightly, as if trying to mollify her. "I was just hoping I could ask you some questions about your job. To see how I can get into the business. I know this isn't the time because you're busy with the adoptions, but I was hoping you'd call me to set something up. We can meet anywhere you'd like, wherever you're most comfortable." He frowned suddenly, all lightness disappearing from his eyes. "I'm sorry to bother you, but I'm getting desperate. I'm about to lose my home. I'd have to give George away." He looked at his dog, devastated. "If I have to move, I won't be able to find a place that'll take a dog as big as he is."

Daisy's heart squeezed in sympathy. "Why don't I give you my e-mail address at the station?" She wrote it down on one of the flyers for the adoption event and handed it to him. "I'm happy to answer all your questions that way. I can even forward you a job application." They were going to have a hole in the lineup due to Tad being fired for his diatribe the day before, so maybe, once the existing employees were moved around to fill the gaps, there would be a place for this guy. "I'll put in a good word for you with the station manager. He's over there by the cats. I'll introduce you when the event is over and you can demonstrate your radio voice."

His gaze softened. "That's really nice of you."

"I hate to think of you and George losing your home. George is such a nice boy, aren't you?" She leaned down to scratch the dog's ears and he gave her hand a lick. "You are nice."

"I can't stay any longer, but I'll be sure to e-mail you. I'd still love to meet you for coffee or tea sometime. George has taken a liking to you."

"Send me an e-mail, and I'll be sure to answer back right away. If you don't want to wait, you can download a job app from the station's Web site, but it's not very user-friendly." She dug into the big jar of Milk-Bones and pulled out a large one for George. "Is it okay if I give him a treat?"

He nodded, a faint smile on his lips, but worry in his eyes. *Poor guy.*

Daisy leaned over to give the dog treat to George, who took it gingerly from her fingers. "What a polite boy you are." She looked up and smiled at the man. "You've trained him so well."

"Thank you." He rose and offered his hand. "I appreciate your time."

She shook his hand firmly. "I only hope we can find you a job. I have a few friends who are teachers. I'll ask them about openings in their schools' drama departments, too."

"That's . . . nice of you." He tugged on the dog's leash. "Come along, George. We have to go."

When he was gone, Gideon sat in the chair he'd vacated. "I don't like him."

She kissed his cheek, next to the clean line of his goatee. He'd showered and shaved at her place and his skin was soft and smooth. "I know. I didn't offer to meet him. I just gave him my work e-mail address, which is available on the station's Web site anyway. But I wasn't going to be rude. That's just not nice."

"All right." Gideon checked his watch. "It feels like things are winding down."

"We can start cleaning up now." She frowned. "Trish was supposed to have come today. She was talking about adopting a cat."

"Maybe she got busy. Or she knows you're peeved that she told that reporter about you yesterday."

"I never talked to her. I don't call or text her when she's working. Her boss gets annoyed. And then we fell asleep."

His lips curved into a wicked smile. "And then we woke up."

She had to smile back. "That we did." She took out her phone. "Let me call her now. I was hoping you could meet her." She dialed and frowned when her call went straight to voice mail. "That's not like her. I hope she's not sick." Then a more horrible thought struck her. "Oh God. I hope she's not drinking. We were upset on Thursday night even before the attack. One of the men in our AA group died. He was special. One of our leaders. Trish had known him for years."

"We can check on her when we're done here, if you want to."

She nodded, trying to put her panic aside. "Okay. Have you gotten back the sketch from your friend in Philly?"

"Not yet. So we're not on a clock."

"And the swim team kid in SoCal?" she asked. "The one with the almost-tattoo? Should we head down to San Diego first?"

"No, I think finding Eileen is more critical at this stage, both to your case and mine. I need to know if she's all right and if she was also attacked by the man who hurt you or if she parted with her locket willingly. If we find her, I'm also hoping she knows where the community is now. I told my boss about the photos of the other Eden tattoos. She called the San Diego field office and they're going to the university today to make sure he's still there so that I can arrange to interview him. I haven't heard back from them yet, either."

"And the tattoo artist who did the dragon on your friend, Judah?" she asked, thinking of the other Eden tattoo she'd found.

"The tattoo shop is in San Francisco. I called them to set up an appointment with the artist, but they said he'd moved away. They claimed he left no forwarding address. I'll track him down once I've found Eileen. Or at least once we've traced her locket's chain of ownership if she sold it."

"All right, then." Things were at least progressing. "We can check on Trish, go to your house for that map, then head up to Redding. Sound good?"

He gripped her chin and kissed her mouth soundly. "Sounds perfect."

▌▌▌ SACRAMENTO, CALIFORNIA
SATURDAY, FEBRUARY 18, 2:00 P.M.

He sat unmoving in his car for several minutes after buckling Mutt into his safety harness. Mutt, who'd taken to the Dawson woman like a kid to Santa, who'd eaten from her hand and licked her fingers. Like she was the best thing since sliced bread.

"Traitor," he muttered to the dog, who sat there panting happily.

And yet . . . spot on, he had to admit. Mutt had been right. Daisy Dawson was nice.

Dammit.

"Why'd she have to be so nice?" he growled. There

had been no trace of the tigress who'd fought him on Thursday night. No sign of a bitch.

Just a nice woman who helped dogs in her spare time.

And talked to supposed out-of-work high school drama teachers, trying to help them back on their feet.

He'd watched her for a long time, under the pretense of shopping for Mutt's needs. She'd been genuine with each person who'd come to the table, going out of her way to make them feel welcome and at ease with choosing a pet. Several of them had called her Daisy, because she'd apparently volunteered there before.

She'd been *so damn nice*.

Frankly, he wasn't sure what to do and he hated the feeling. Hated indecision. Hated insecurity. It made him weak. He hated being weak.

He'd hoped to draw her out, to get her talking about radio, and then he'd ask her about the experience she'd had on Thursday, about what she'd seen. About any leads the police had. He'd seen it on the news, he'd say. Just like half of Sacramento, because the videos of both of her interviews had gone viral. The radio station had chimed in, declaring their support for "Poppy Frederick" and their commitment to stop violence against women in the city.

So he'd had a lot of stuff he could have said to start the conversation. But not in the pet store. Not with her bodyguard hovering.

It was clear that the guy was a cop. It was like a blinking neon light over his head. He was the same guy who'd been with her the night before, when the reporter had caught her going into her house. Definitely a cop.

Bastard. He had that tall, dark, and mysterious thing going. And it totally worked for him. Women all over the store were purposely shopping the same aisle over and over just to get another look at him. Some of the men, too.

I just wanted him gone. Because he hovered over Daisy or Eleanor or Poppy—or whatever the hell her name was—like he owned her.

What he'd really wanted to know was how much she knew about the man who'd attacked her Thursday night. And about the dead hooker. Kaley Martell.

The woman in my fucking freezer.

Daisy had been so confident with that woman reporter yesterday. Confident enough that he was still rattled.

He glared at Mutt. "What the fuck am I supposed to do now?"

He couldn't strap Daisy to the bed in his basement and kill her. Not now. Number one, he already had a woman there. But mostly because Daisy didn't deserve it. It was a fine line, he knew, but he'd never killed anyone who hadn't *deserved* it.

And now there's no need. She hadn't recognized him from Thursday. He now knew that for sure. If she had, he'd have been in cuffs before he could say a word.

"At least the nose worked," he muttered, glancing up in the visor mirror at the prosthesis on his face. The only part of his face she might have recognized were his eyes and he hadn't altered them. He wasn't going to worry about Daisy Dawson right now.

His higher priority was to find out what was known about Kaley the hooker. He thought he'd been careful that night, but he had been distracted, edgy, the static in his head too loud. It was possible that someone had seen him talking to the hooker, guiding her to his car.

It's possible that Daisy was talking about someone entirely different during that interview.

That's very possible. He needed to know.

Bringing up a browser window in his phone, he

typed: ***hooker baker disappeared from South Sac.***
Then pressed ENTER.

And . . . *Fuck*. There she was. He let out a breath as
Kaley Martell's face stared up from his phone's screen.
She'd gone missing Thursday night from Stockton
Boulevard, the article stated. Her parents were insist-
ing she was not a runaway, that she had a four-year-old
daughter with a terminal illness.

God. He stared at that sentence until the words
seemed seared into his retinas. Four-year-old daughter
with a terminal illness. *Terminal illness.*

Way to go, asshole. Leaving some sick kid motherless.

This was why he never looked back. *This* was why
he didn't get to know his victims. *This,* right here.

He drew a breath and forced himself to keep reading. Police were "exploring all leads." And there was a
number for anyone who'd witnessed anything to report
it to SacPD.

There were comments attached to the article. All
sympathetic for the motherless child and her mother,
who'd been trying to earn money for her daughter's
medical expenses.

God. What have I done?

A few commenters said that Kaley had gotten what
had been coming to her, that she knew the risks when
she took to walking the streets, but they were in the
minority. There was, instead, a swell of public insistence that the police find the monster who had done
this vile action, no matter what.

I have to do something. But what? He couldn't
un-kill Kaley Martell.

And what leads were the cops following? *I need to
know.*

He needed to plan. He needed a clear head. What
he needed was some time with Zandra, a.k.a. Miss
Rude, who was, fortunately, still in his basement, and
who, even more fortunately, he *could* kill.

And if she's a single mother, too?

It didn't matter. He wasn't going to look to find out.

He glanced over at Mutt as he started the engine. "Let's go home, boy. I've got things to do." He was about to pull out of his parking place when Daisy Dawson walked out of the store with the cop.

He knew where they were going. As he'd been leaving the store, he'd overheard her say that Trish was supposed to come to the clinic and adopt a cat. The cop assured her they'd check on her friend when they were finished at the pet store.

At least they'd soon know that Trish had been the true target on Thursday night. *And, if I'm lucky, Daisy will think she's no longer in danger and the fucking cop will go away.*

He'd go home now. Clear his mind with Zandra. And he'd figure out exactly how much trouble he was in with the hooker.

SACRAMENTO, CALIFORNIA
SATURDAY, FEBRUARY 18, 2:20 P.M.

Gideon frowned up at the apartment building in a very unsavory part of town. "Your friend lives here?"

Daisy shot him a reproachful look, complete with raised brows. "Not everyone can afford a house in Rocklin, Gideon. Trish can barely make ends meet with her waitressing job at the bar. She's taking classes to be a dental assistant, but until she gets her diploma, money is tight."

"I wasn't suggesting she wasn't a hard worker. I was suggesting that this is not the safest part of town." His frown deepened when the building door opened without a key. "The lock is broken?"

"Has been since I've known her."

He scowled. "Do you come here often?"

"No. She usually comes to my place. Irina has taken her under her wing, too. She's shown Trish how to make birds' milk cake."

Gideon followed her up three flights of stairs, the stairwell murky because three of every four lightbulbs needed to be replaced. "Trish must have made a good impression, then. I've been asking Irina for that recipe since I was a teenager."

Daisy knocked on the door. "Trish!" she called. "It's me! Open up!" She looked over her shoulder at Gideon. "Irina mentioned that you'd asked about the recipe. She said if you'd have bothered to come to Sunday dinner, she'd have shown you, too."

"That's just some bullshit right there," he said mildly. "She's just mad I didn't come so she could matchmake."

Daisy smiled, her dimples appearing. "Are we going to tell her that we went on a date?"

He smiled back at her, unable to resist. "Eventually. She'll be unbearable for a while afterward, telling us how right she was."

Daisy held on to the smile for a few seconds longer before it dimmed, her mouth curving down in worry. "Trish? Open up! It's me—Daisy! Are you okay?"

"She might be gone."

"Maybe. I hope so." She hesitated, then pulled a set of keys from a side pouch of Brutus's bag. "I'm going to check on her." From inside the bag, Brutus whimpered, and Daisy reached in to soothe her. And herself. "It'll be okay. Please," she whispered, "be okay. God, please don't let her be drunk."

Gideon turned on the flashlight app on his phone and handed it to her. "Shine it on the locks," he said, taking the keys from her hand when her hand trembled too hard to fit the key in the lock. He made quick work of them, two dead bolts and the lock on the door-knob. About the level of security he'd require in this neighborhood, especially as the main door had a broken lock.

Looking up at him with open apprehension, Daisy knocked again. "Trish," she called, opening the door a crack. "I'm coming in."

She pushed the door open and flicked on the light. Then Brutus began barking. A split second before Daisy screamed.

"No. No. No, no, no." She rushed into the room before Gideon could stop her, dropping to her knees next to a brunette who lay on the floor. Nude and covered in blood.

Fuck. Two attacks in as many days was no coincidence. "Daisy," he barked. "Stop."

Daisy's hand froze in midair, her face alarmingly pale. Slowly she lowered her hand, clutching the edge of her bag with a white-knuckled grip. "Is she dead?" she whispered.

The woman was most certainly dead. She'd been stabbed multiple times. At least seven that he could see. There could be more under all the blood. Nonetheless, Gideon pulled a pair of disposable gloves from his pocket and dragged them on as he crouched by the woman's side. "Call 911," he said tersely.

"Is she dead?" Daisy repeated, her voice growing shrill.

He glanced up long enough to meet Daisy's terrified, shocked gaze. "Yes, honey," he said as gently as he could. "She's dead."

The blood covering the woman's torso was dry, her skin gray. Her ankles were bound with duct tape and Gideon assumed her wrists, hidden behind her back, were also bound. Lying on her back, her eyes stared at the ceiling, unseeing, petechiae mottling the whites. The bruises around her throat were familiar—they were the same that Daisy wore. Only those on Trish's throat were wider and accompanied by smaller oval bruises. Those and the petechiae indicated strangulation.

Daisy's hands shook as she searched her pockets. "Wh-wh-where did you get the gloves?" she choked out.

"I keep a pair of gloves in my pocket," he told Daisy calmly, because she was still patting her pockets frantically. "Take a breath, honey."

"Oh my God." A woman gasped behind them. "Trish."

Gideon held up a hand to keep the woman from running into the apartment as Daisy had done. "Stop, ma'am. You can't come in here." He pulled his badge from his pocket. "Special Agent Reynolds, FBI. Please step back."

The woman nodded and backed away, clearly shaken. Gideon turned his attention to Daisy as he dialed 911 on his own phone. She was staring down at Trish, her expression blank. Brutus was fervently licking Daisy's fingers and bumping her hand with her head, but it didn't appear to be distracting her back to awareness. Daisy was going into shock. Gideon rose and was carefully walking around the body as the 911 operator answered.

"This is Special Agent Reynolds with the FBI." He gave the operator the address and asked her to send the police and an ambulance, as was protocol. Then he crouched next to Daisy, pulling off his gloves before gently urging her to her feet. "That's my girl," he murmured when she followed him up robotically. "I've got you. Come on, honey. Come with me."

Leading her out into the hallway, he stood sentry against the curious tenants who had begun to congregate. Pulling the door almost closed, he turned Daisy so that she hid her face against his chest. After texting Rafe the address, he dialed his cell. "I just texted you an address. Get over here now."

"On my way," Rafe said. "Why?"

"Daisy's friend Trish is dead."

Rafe sucked in a harsh breath. "Fucking hell, Gid."

"I know. You need to hurry. I've called it in to 911 and the cops should be arriving soon."

"I'll call in, make sure they don't touch anything until I get there. How is DD?"

"In shock." She was shaking with silent sobs, her teeth chattering, the dog whimpering. "It's . . ." Gideon trailed off, unwilling to give the avidly curious bystanders any more gossip.

"Got it," Rafe said grimly. "Be there in fifteen."

Gideon dropped his phone into his pocket and wrapped his arm around Daisy, pulling her closer. "Please stand back," he said to the waiting group of tenants. They'd crowded the small landing and the stairs, both up and down. "The police will need room to work."

Surprisingly, they obeyed and so he stood there, holding Daisy until she looked up at him, her face drenched with tears. "Her necklace was missing."

He frowned. "What?"

"Her necklace," Daisy whispered. "A turquoise cross. It belonged to her mother. She never took it off. It wasn't around her neck."

A souvenir. Like the locket that had belonged to Eileen.

Her hands clutched at his jacket, her eyes desperate. "He wasn't after me that night, Gideon. He was after Trish."

Gideon wasn't so sure about that, but he didn't refute her words. Not right now. He could only hold her while she fell apart in his arms. Because they'd all been wrong. They'd all misjudged the threat. The danger hadn't been only to Daisy. Now her friend was dead. And they were no closer to the identity of her killer.

He'd brutally killed Daisy's friend and he would have done the same to Daisy if she hadn't gotten away. He still might if he believed Daisy could identify him.

And he'd killed Eileen.

One look at Trish's body had shredded any remaining hope Gideon had of finding his old friend. *You'll be begging my forgiveness before I'm done,* Daisy's attacker had said. *They all do.*

There were definitely others. This changed everything. And nothing at all. The goal was the same. They needed to stay their course, needed to trace Eileen's steps.

Daisy lifted her face, her tears still falling unchecked. But her eyes were hard, her jaw set. "We need to go to Redding," she whispered.

He didn't marvel that she'd all but read his mind. He could only answer, "Yes."

||| SACRAMENTO, CALIFORNIA
||| SATURDAY, FEBRUARY 18, 2:35 P.M.

Zandra was jerked out of a restless sleep by the sound of a key turning in the lock. *He's back. Dammit, he's back.*

She closed her eyes, unwilling to participate in his game. *He's going to kill me either way.* She was not going to give him the satisfaction of seeing her fear.

Because she was afraid. So damn afraid.

"Hello, Zandra," he drawled, then closed the door behind him. "Have we been thinking about our behavior?"

She wanted to roll her eyes but refrained.

"No?" he asked. "I was hoping you'd say so. I like your spirit, Zandra. I'm going to have such fun breaking you."

No. No, you won't. She wasn't going to give him any pleasure.

He leaned over her, running his lips across her cheek.

"If I take out your gag, will you tell me that you're sorry?"

She didn't respond. Didn't open her eyes. But her eye twitched as he licked a trail along her jaw.

He laughed delightedly. "You are exactly what I needed, Zandra Jones. I've had a difficult few days, but you are a breath of fresh air, I have to say."

She heard the jangle of keys, followed by the creak of . . . hinges? She lifted her lashes enough to see what he was doing, relieved to find his back to her.

He was opening a cabinet. She sucked in a breath through her nose as the contents became visible. Driver's licenses. Dozens of them. And jewelry hanging from hooks.

He was placing a driver's license in what had to have been a groove in the shallow shelf because the plastic license stood straight up.

"There you go, Trish," he murmured, giving the top of the license a quick stroke with his thumb. "You did good. Protected your friend until the bitter end, no matter what I did to you. And now for the changing of the guard." With dramatic flair, he removed the chain he wore around his neck and hung it below the second-to-last license. Hanging from the chain was a horseshoe, made of crystals. He gave it a tap, sending it swinging.

Then he pulled another necklace from his pocket and held it up so that the turquoise cross hanging from the chain spun in the air. He put it around his neck and gave the turquoise a stroke.

"Did you enjoy my little show, Zandra?" he asked, turning to her with a smirk. "You think you're hiding from me, but I've had a lot of guests on that bed. I know all the tricks. Now . . ." He opened a drawer, and when he turned, he held a thin blade. "It's time for me to get to work. The 'S' that I scratched into you yesterday is starting to heal already. I'll just go over it again. And then you'll be ready for the 'Y.'"

He removed the gag from her mouth and she coughed until her head pounded and her chest ached. "How loud can you scream, Zandra? I'm betting pretty loud. I hope you won't disappoint me."

I won't scream. I won't.

But she did.

║║║ SACRAMENTO, CALIFORNIA
║║║ SATURDAY, FEBRUARY 18, 2:45 P.M.

Daisy only resisted the compulsion to rock her body because of the crowd gathered in the doorway of Trish's neighbor, Mrs. Owens. Even though Daisy's eyes were tightly closed, she knew that they watched her every movement, cell phones at the ready, waiting for anything newsworthy.

Because Trish was dead.

No. No, no, no. Daisy wanted to scream it, wanted to scream that it was a mistake. A trick. An awful joke. But it wasn't a mistake. She'd seen the body. With her own eyes.

The body. Trish's body. All bloody and—

Oh God. Trish.

Daisy heard a sharp keening sound, then felt a warm palm cup her cheek.

Gideon. "Hey," he murmured. She turned into it, drawing Gideon's scent into her lungs, needing it to fill her head. "Look at me, honey."

She forced herself to open her eyes, blinking away new tears when she saw his face, inches from hers. He was crouching in front of where she sat on a folding chair on the landing outside Trish's door. The chair had been provided by one of Trish's kinder neighbors—not the nosy woman avidly watching from her doorway along with the majority of the building's occupants.

Gideon tugged at her hand. "Let Brutus breathe, honey. You're holding her too tight."

Horrified, Daisy dropped her gaze to Brutus, who, now that she could breathe, was desperately snuggling up under her chin and licking her fingers. "I'm sorry," she rasped. "I didn't know."

"She's fine," Gideon assured. "She was just whimpering a little." He studied her face, frowning at whatever he saw there. "Rafe called Sasha and Damien. They're coming to get you. Okay? You know Damien, right?"

She nodded. "He used to give us piggyback rides," she whispered. "Sasha and me. When we were little." Now the oldest of the Sokolovs' children was a big, burly cop with little girls of his own. "He gave us rides home from Irina's Sunday dinner a few times. Me and Trish. He fussed at Trish for living in a building with no locks on the front door." A sob forced its way out. "I wish she'd just moved in with me. She'd still be here."

He came to his feet, standing between her and the crowd. Blocking their view, she realized. She looked up at him numbly. "I keep wanting to wake up."

"I know," he said quietly, keeping one hand on her cheek, taking her free hand in his.

"He . . . stabbed her," she whispered. "So much blood."

He brought the hand he held to his cheek and nuzzled her gently. The faint scrape of his stubble grounded her. It was real. *He* was real. Not like the nightmare they'd stumbled into.

She choked on a sob. "Why?"

"I don't know. But we're going to find out."

"He . . ." She was crying now. Weeping. "I saw the marks," she whispered, hyperaware of the crowd waiting for any tidbit they could gossip about. "On her throat. I did, didn't I?"

He hesitated, then nodded. "Yes."

He'd strangled her. God. "When?"

He sighed. "I won't know until the ME—"

"Estimate," she interrupted on a hiss.

He shook his head slightly. "Maybe eight hours. Give or take."

"She was supposed to get off work at one this morning."

"We'll call her boss, okay? I promise." He gave her hand a little squeeze. "Do you have any photos of Trish wearing the necklace with the turquoise cross?"

"On my phone." He let go of her hand so that she could find her phone in the side pocket of Brutus's bag. She fumbled with it one-handed and he took it gently, tapping in her passcode. She frowned for a moment, then remembered she'd given it to him on Thursday night. Less than forty-eight hours ago. How was that even possible?

He held the phone so that she could swipe through the photo files until she found a selfie that she'd had taken with the two of them at the radio station's New Year's Eve party. The turquoise cross hung between Trish's breasts, plainly visible against the pale cream of the sweater she'd been wearing that night.

"This one," Daisy whispered. She'd never see Trish smile like that, not ever again.

"I'll just e-mail it to myself and Rafe, okay?" Gideon said quietly. He did so, then slipped Daisy's phone back into the side pocket of Brutus's bag.

A door slammed several floors down and heavy footsteps echoed up the stairs. Two uniformed police officers had arrived.

"I'll be back," Gideon said softly, swiping his thumb over her cheeks to dry them. "Stay here." He pressed a kiss to her forehead. "I have to talk to these officers.

Make sure they don't disturb anything until Rafe gets here."

She nodded, still numb. Unable to do a thing. Except sit. And wait. And try not to think about what she'd seen. How Trish had suffered. *God.*

The crowd had dispersed. Rafe arrived, along with the woman Daisy had met at SacPD on Thursday night. The forensics woman. Cindy Grimes. Cindy gave her shoulder a sympathetic pat and Rafe gave her a hug, before they disappeared into Trish's apartment.

Where Trish lay on the floor. Dead. It was . . . impossible. But it was true.

Trish is dead. Because she'd been the target after all. *Not me.*

Although if Rafe had asked Damien to come with Sasha . . . *They still think I need protection.* And that was something her mind couldn't process at the moment.

If we'd only protected Trish like they've protected me. I'm sorry, Trish. So goddamn sorry.

FIFTEEN

Did they leave?" Erin Rhee asked when Gideon joined her and Rafe in Trish's small apartment. Cindy Grimes from Forensics was taking photos of Trish's body, her mouth set in a firm line as she worked.

"Yeah." Gideon pinched the bridge of his nose, fighting back a headache. "Sasha and Damien took her to your parents' house, Rafe."

Rafe nodded, staring down at Trish's body with a carefully blank expression. "She was stabbed and strangled."

Erin squeezed Rafe's shoulder. "We can hand this one off," she murmured.

Rafe shook his head, his blank expression remaining unchanged except for the twitch of a muscle in his cheek. "No. We're going to find the fucker who did this."

"Okay," Erin agreed. "But say the word and we'll back off."

"You knew Trish well?" Gideon asked.

Rafe's nod was terse. "She's been a regular at Sunday dinner for the past six months. Ever since DD moved in. My mom . . . liked her."

"I'm sorry," Gideon murmured, but Rafe didn't respond, continuing to study Trish's body with angry concentration. Gideon crouched next to the body, careful to stay out of Cindy's way. No one had touched Trish since the coroner hadn't yet arrived. "He strangled her. Just like he tried to do to Daisy."

"And the others," Erin said quietly. "'They all do.'"

Rafe pointed to a pile of clothes next to the body, neatly folded, but jagged slices in the fabric were visible. "He cut them off her. That's her work uniform. I hope he wasn't as meticulous about cleaning the crime scene as he was with her clothes."

"I think he was," Erin said. "I checked the kitchen. It's very clean, except for a single butcher knife washed and left in the dish drainer. I smelled bleach on it. I haven't been able to find any bleach anywhere in the apartment. Not even a bleach-type spray bottle. Nor are there any empty bottles. He may have brought it with him or at least taken the bottle with him when he left if he used Trish's. My money is on him bringing it with him. This was planned."

"Agreed," Gideon said. It was impossible to tell whether the knife had made the incisions, but it seemed likely. He hoped the coroner would be able to hazard an opinion. Pivoting, his gaze swept over the apartment, falling on the coffee table.

He rose, frowning. "Look at the stack of magazines." The blood spatter on the top magazine had abruptly stopped, leaving a clean edge.

"He took the top magazine," Rafe said flatly. "Why?"

"Souvenir?" Erin waved Cindy over. "Can you get this from every angle, Cindy?"

Gideon stepped back to let Cindy take the photographs. "Possibly a souvenir," he said. "Daisy thinks he took Trish's necklace. Turquoise cross." He found the photo he'd e-mailed to himself. "I sent it to your e-mail, Rafe. I didn't have yours, Erin." He passed Erin his phone so that she and Rafe could examine the necklace. "Daisy said that Trish always wore it."

Erin studied the photo. "He took her necklace, like he took Eileen's locket."

"We should have been guarding them both," Rafe said heavily. "This may have had nothing to do with Daisy specifically. Nothing to do with her e-mails or voice mails. He might have simply followed them from the community center on Thursday night, but Daisy surprised him by confronting him."

Gideon agreed. "Which means he might come after her, too. Especially if he's afraid she can identify him."

"We can put her in a safe house," Erin said.

Rafe's laugh was grim. "We can try. After twelve years in hiding, she's not likely to agree to being hidden away again."

"Then we don't let her out of our sight," Gideon said. *A.k.a., I don't let her out of my sight.* So basically, nothing about her protection plan had changed.

SACRAMENTO, CALIFORNIA
SATURDAY, FEBRUARY 18, 4:45 P.M.

"Excuse me, ma'am. I'm so sorry to bother you at this time." He smiled sympathetically at the woman who'd answered the door at Kaley Martell's house. This would be her mother and her eyes were red-rimmed and swollen from crying. *Poor lady.*

It honestly hadn't been anything personal toward this sad old woman. Her daughter had been in the wrong place at the wrong time and had been unforgivably rude, refusing to get into his car when he invited her nicely. Something about her "policy." She'd tried to convince him to get out of his car.

He might have cut Kaley some slack and moved on to another hooker had he known she was a single mother with a sick kid, but he'd been in a crisis of his own that night.

"I don't have anything more to say to you reporters," the woman said wearily. "Please go away."

He was glad he'd prepared a plan B. "No, ma'am, I'm not a reporter. My name is Johnny Steves and I live over on the next block. I saw the report on Kaley on the news. She . . . I'm a customer. At the bakery. She always had a smile for me." A common theme of the people the reporter had interviewed. Kaley was always smiling. "We were . . . well, we're friends."

Mrs. Martell's expression grew softer and more pained. "You know my Kaley?"

"Yes, ma'am. We talk. Every day. I . . . wanted to do something to help. She loves Amelia so much." Amelia had been mentioned not in the article, but in the comments on the Martells' Facebook page. People really needed to be more mindful of the information they simply gave away.

He swallowed hard, laying it on thick. "I hate that her little girl might never know her." He held out the shopping bag he'd stuffed full. "I got some things. For Amelia. Some toys. Stuffed animals and crayons, that kind of thing."

Tears filled Mrs. Martell's eyes, and her grip on the front door loosened. "That is so nice of you. Thank you. Would . . ." She held the door open wider. "Would you like to come in and give Amelia the toys yourself?"

He smiled. "That would be nice."

GRANITE BAY, CALIFORNIA
SATURDAY, FEBRUARY 18, 5:45 P.M.

"Here, honey." Sasha set a cup of tea on the Sokolovs' kitchen table next to Daisy's laptop and sat next to her, expression anxious. Shocked and grieving.

Irina was baking. Tea cookies. Trish's favorite.

The atmosphere in the kitchen was oppressive as each of them processed what had happened.

Trish was dead. *Dead.*

Sasha had brought her to the only place it made sense to be. Irina's kitchen. There was love here. And safety. And, at the moment, great sorrow.

Daisy still couldn't believe her friend was gone. "I know this isn't my fault," she murmured, staring at the images on her screen without really seeing them. She'd opened her laptop because she'd needed to *do* something. But when she'd found herself staring at the tattoos from her Eden search, she'd just sat.

Because all she could see was Trish's body. Bloody and broken.

"Of course it's not your fault," Sasha said, making Daisy blink up at her friend's tear-streaked face. The Sokolovs had embraced Trish as one of their own. It had been the first time Trish had had a family since her mother had died when Trish was seventeen. They'd loved her, too. "But?" Sasha added softly, knowing Daisy well.

"But if she'd had the guard instead of me, she'd be alive right now." Not dead. Not bloody and mutilated and . . . dead.

"Maybe," Irina said, sliding a plate of cookies onto the table and sitting on Daisy's other side. "But you cannot know that. Maybe he went after her because you were guarded. Maybe had Gideon not been with you, this man might have . . ." She swallowed hard. "He might have hurt you as well."

Daisy sighed. Her head ached and her eyes were sore. "Maybe."

Irina patted her hand. "Drink your tea, Daisy. It's getting cold." She looked over Daisy's shoulder at her laptop and frowned. "Why are you looking at tattoos?" Her eyes narrowed. "You're *not* thinking of getting one?"

Daisy realized that the images on her screen would raise more questions than she could answer. She'd promised Gideon her silence. "I already have one," she said, casually closing the browser window. "I have to get it finished. After that, maybe."

"When did you get a tattoo?" Sasha asked.

"In Paris. I came home before it was finished." Because her father had hired their old ranch hand to follow her.

Sasha grinned at her. It was kind of a fake grin, because she wasn't happy by any stretch, but she was sincerely trying to be. "I'll show you mine if you show me yours."

Irina tsked. "I already know about yours."

Sasha's mouth fell open. "But . . ."

"But it's on your butt cheek? *Psht.*" Irina flipped a hand, scoffing. "I see and know all, child. Don't forget it just because you think you are grown."

Daisy snickered, happy for the distraction. "Who blabbed?"

Irina smiled sadly at that. "Trish. How do you think she bribed me for my birds' milk cake recipe?"

Her own smile faltering, Daisy glanced at Sasha, who'd closed her eyes. New tears seeped from her eyes. "Oh, baby," Daisy murmured, wrapping her arms around her friend. "I didn't know." She'd known Trish was bi. She'd never known Trish and Sasha . . . "I'm so sorry. Here I am, crying like I'm the only one hurting."

"It was just a few dates," Sasha whispered. "It was never going to be permanent. We broke up before Christmas. But . . . dammit, DD. I liked her. We were still friends."

"I know, honey." Daisy's throat closed as new tears clawed their way out. "I just can't believe this. I saw her with my own eyes and I can't believe it."

"Have a cookie," Irina commanded, shoving the plate into Daisy's hands.

"Okay," Daisy mumbled, grateful for the distraction that kept her from going off on another crying jag. But her gratitude was short-lived when Irina took advantage of her full hands, leaning over her to commandeer her laptop's track pad. With a swipe and a click, she'd restored the tab Daisy had deleted and tattoos filled the screen once again. "Irina! What the fuck!"

"Mom!" Sasha seconded, agape. "You just don't go around—"

"Hush," Irina snapped. "I'll apologize later. Maybe. First Daisy tells me why she's searching tattoos like the one my Gideon had years ago. That tattoo was . . . wrong. I was glad when he got it covered up. It made him sad."

Daisy sighed and gently closed the tab again. "Irina."

Irina's brows lifted into her hairline. "Eleanor."

"I can't tell you," Daisy told her earnestly. "It's not my story to tell. I . . . promised, Irina. I can't break that promise."

"To Gideon," Irina said quietly.

Daisy held her gaze, neither confirming nor denying. But her nonanswer was enough for Irina, who nodded. "I'm sorry, Daisy. I shouldn't have pried into your computer."

"It's all right," Daisy said softly. "You love him."

"I do. That boy's like one of my own." Irina's head tilted. "He trusted you with information that he's never told me?"

"Mom," Sasha warned.

Irina ignored her. "It's true. He did. That's good." Her eyes became sly. "I was right, wasn't I? He is perfect for you."

Daisy felt her cheeks heat but tried for an eye roll. "Irina, just stop."

Irina winked at Sasha. "She didn't say no."

Sasha's laugh was teary. "No, she didn't. Plus they had a date last night."

"Sasha." Daisy frowned at her. "Really?"

Irina popped a tea cookie into her mouth, not bothering to hide her delight. "Tell me all."

"Well, Rafe and I were having dinner and I saw them coming up the street before they got to the restaurant. At first, I didn't know it was them. They were under an umbrella and I thought, 'Wow, that's so sweet how he's holding on to her,' and then when he put the umbrella down, I realized it was them." She fluttered her lashes and sighed.

"Sasha had a date with a librarian," Daisy blurted before Sasha could say more.

Irina turned her inquisition on her daughter, who gave Daisy a dirty look. "A librarian?" Irina said. "This is good. She is smart then?"

Sasha's glare softened minimally. "Very smart, Mom. Now back to Daisy and Gideon—"

"Or not," Daisy interrupted, relieved when her cell phone chimed. Until she saw the caller ID. Both Sokolovs ceased their chatter.

"Take it, honey," Irina said, the momentary respite from their grief over.

Daisy answered, her hand suddenly trembling. "Dad?"

"Daisy." Her father sounded . . . terrified. "I . . ." He shuddered out a breath. "There was a body found in Sacramento. A young woman. I . . ." Another shuddered breath. "I thought it was you."

"Oh, Dad, I'm sorry." Daisy's eyes stung. "I didn't know it would get out so quickly. I was going to call you. I've just been in shock."

He was quiet for a moment. "You knew her, then?"

"Yes. She was my friend. Trish."

"Oh no. Your friend from AA?"

Daisy nodded, then remembered she had to speak. "Yes," she whispered hoarsely.

"I'm so sorry, honey. The news said . . . they said

there'd been a murder and they speculated that it was connected to the attack against you on Thursday night."

"I should have expected they'd make the connection," Daisy muttered. "Enough of the people in Trish's building saw me there tonight and they knew Trish was with me Thursday. I should have called you right away. I'm sorry, Dad."

"Stop apologizing," he said gruffly. "You were there?"

Daisy drew in a breath, then let it out when Irina's arm slid around her shoulder and tugged her close. "I found her. Gideon and I."

"Gideon? The FBI agent I talked to?"

"Yes. He hasn't left my side until now. He's with Rafe now. I'm with Irina and Sasha. Karl's here, too, somewhere."

"And my Damien, too, Frederick," Irina said loudly. "Your Daisy is protected."

Her father chuckled. "I heard her. Tell her thank you."

"I will. I just wish we'd protected Trish, too. She wouldn't have been in her apartment all alone."

Her father was quiet for so long, Daisy could practically hear his mind working through the details. "How did he know where she lived?"

That was a very good question. "I don't know. She was at work last night and would have come straight home. She was supposed to come to a pet adoption clinic with me today." Daisy rubbed her sore head. "I guess he could have followed her home from work."

"Who knew where she worked?"

Daisy didn't want to think about it, but her father was a smart man and was thinking all the things she should have been thinking herself. "All her friends. Her coworkers, of course. All the members of our AA group. She worked in a bar. It was hard for her to stay sober. She was looking for another job."

"Did any of the news reports list where she worked?"

"I don't know. Hold on." She turned to Sasha. "Did any of the reporters say where Trish worked or lived?"

Sasha shook her head. "I don't think so. Put your dad on speaker, DD."

Daisy did and her father greeted the Sokolov women. "We don't think they said where she worked, Dad," Daisy said, "but the first reporter who found me said he'd overheard Trish telling someone about the attack at work. So the reporter knew where she worked."

"He didn't mention her in the news story he up-loaded last night," Sasha said quietly.

Daisy squeezed her hand. Then forced herself to think. "On Thursday, we'd just left the community center when I noticed we were being followed. We'd been to AA. Rafe wondered if he'd followed us from there or if he'd been waiting—for me. I told them that he could have followed me from the radio station. But Trish came straight from work, too. Maybe he followed her from work both times—Thursday and last night."

Which underscored Daisy's initial gut feeling that Trish had been the man's target.

"Maybe he did," he said. "Maybe you should get that Fed to look at surveillance tapes from the bar where she worked."

Daisy's mouth curved up, just a little. "I should. Thanks, Dad."

"Anytime," he said gruffly. "Listen, baby. If you need anything, you let me know. I'll be on the next plane."

Daisy's first inclination was to say no, but she stopped herself. Her father loved her. She knew that. *And I love him.* She knew that, too. Her throat closed up and she had to clear it. "She didn't have any family." No father who'd loved her, even though he went way overboard sometimes. No mother who'd rocked her to sleep and let her paint the sofa. Trish's mom had been an alcoholic, too. "I'm . . . going to have to bury her."

The thought ripped the sob from her throat and she covered her mouth to try to stifle it. "I can't do this."

"You want me there?" he asked, sounding so hopeful that it made her cry even more.

"Please," she whispered. "Please come."

"I'll send you my travel arrangements. Stay with someone at all times, Daisy. Please. I know I'm overprotective. Just . . . humor me," he added with a stilted laugh.

Daisy wiped at her eyes. "I promise."

"We will stay with her until Gideon comes for her, Frederick," Irina stated.

"Thank you, Irina." Frederick's voice had grown soft. "Thank you and Karl for everything."

"You are family, Frederick," was all Irina said.

"Thank you," he whispered. "I'll be there soon."

"Bye. Love you." Daisy ended the call, then immediately dialed Gideon, this time not on speaker.

He answered on the first ring. "Are you all right?"

"I'm fine. Still with Sasha and Irina. I just talked to my dad."

His voice became wary. "And?"

"And it was good. We talked about Trish a little and he recommended checking out the surveillance tapes in the bar for both last night and Thursday. I think he's right."

"You think her killer followed her to the community center from work on Thursday?"

"Yeah. She said she'd had an altercation with a customer. She downplayed it, but that she mentioned it at all was unusual." Now that Daisy was remembering, more details were coming back. "She was used to rude men. She got propositioned all the time. This guy, though . . . He was belligerent. Kept baiting her until she lost her temper. She called him a tool. Had to report him to the manager, who tossed the guy out."

"I'll tell Rafe. I'm about to join him at the—" Gideon stopped himself. "In the investigation."

But she thought she understood his self-edit. "At the morgue?"

"Yeah," he admitted. "I'm almost there."

"Okay." She wasn't going to think about the morgue. About poor Trish lying on a cold slab. "Have . . . have you heard from Philly?" She was as careful as she could be, very aware that Irina and Sasha hung on her every word.

"Not yet. But he said he's nearly finished. Do you have a bag packed? We may end up spending the night in Redding if we get a lead."

"I'm still coming?" That made her feel better somehow.

"Yes, of course." A slight hesitation. "I need to know you're okay. I don't want to leave you alone. Even with the Sokolovs, although I know you're safe there. I'll get to you as soon as I can."

"I'll be waiting."

SACRAMENTO, CALIFORNIA
SATURDAY, FEBRUARY 18, 5:55 P.M.

He snugged his tie up against his throat, his step a hundred times lighter. The cops had nothing on the disappearance of Kaley Martell. No leads. Nothing to aid them in finding her—or whoever had taken her. That had come straight from Marlena Martell's mouth as she'd tearily served him weak tea and stale Oreo cookies and prayed for her daughter's safe return.

I have absolutely nothing to worry about.

But he did have an excellent disguise that he didn't want to go to waste and some remaining questions about Daisy Dawson. The crowd around Trish's apartment had thinned, but there were still a few reporters and rubber-neckers milling about.

The reporters were gathered around an older lady who appeared to be holding court. Someone had brought her a folding chair and she sat there answering questions.

So he listened.

Her name was Mrs. Owens, he learned, and she'd discovered Trish's friend Daisy and "that FBI agent" crouching over the body. Okay, so he was a Fed, not a cop. It was splitting hairs, in his opinion. He had to fight back a smile as the older woman dramatically spun her tale, making it sound like Daisy and the Fed had killed Trish.

Now that's not right. She needs to be giving credit where credit is due.

Daisy had been "distraught," sobbing in the arms of the FBI agent.

That made him frown. *In his arms?* No. He was just her bodyguard.

It doesn't matter. Daisy Dawson was nothing to him. She was not a threat. He'd be giving Daisy-Poppy-Eleanor Dawson—and her Fed—a wide berth.

But she was so nice. He almost wished he really were an out-of-work drama teacher looking for a job at her radio station. It would be nice to work with her every day. She was no more like Sydney than day was like night. Just thinking about Sydney made him sick to his stomach. But Daisy? It would be nice to have a woman like her to come home to.

Really, really nice. His stomach fluttered, but not with revulsion this time. This time it was . . . what? Desire? Was that what that was? He'd never felt it before. Not ever.

Certainly not for Sydney, and all he felt for his guests was rage. Not desire.

He let himself picture it—Daisy Dawson in his bed.

Not the one in his basement, but the one in his bedroom. The bed that Sydney had never defiled. No one had. She'd lie in his bed and smile at him the way she'd done at the pet store.

She'd take off her clothes for him. Without being forced to. And she'd smile at him. And he'd never have to tell her he was sorry for anything. Ever. The mental image of Daisy naked in his bed was more than nice. It had his dick taking interest. On its own.

Without pills. Without Sydney.

This was . . . huge. Mind-blowing, even. That he could have something normal, like everyone else? It was almost too much to consider.

He'd thought that Sydney had ruined him for any kind of normal relationship. He'd honestly thought there was no one for him. But then there was Daisy, smiling at him and being so damn nice.

It was about time he got something really, really nice. Right?

Yes. He deserved something nice. He deserved a woman in his bed, like everyone else. He deserved Daisy Dawson.

It was definitely worth thinking about. And now it was all he *could* think about.

And her bodyguard? The one who held her in his arms while she cried? The Fed.

He has to go. It was as simple as that. With him out of the picture, she'd need someone else to hold her when she cried. *Which would be me.*

"What was the agent's name?" one of the reporters called out, yanking his attention back to the old woman holding court in the parking lot.

Yes. I'd like very much to know.

"Special Agent Reynolds," Mrs. Owens said with an emphatic nod. "He showed me his badge."

"Where is Daisy, ma'am?" another reporter called out.

Another very good question.

"Her friend came to get her, the one who was friends with them. Sasha something. I didn't catch the last name, but I've seen her around before. Told the FBI agent that she was taking Daisy to 'Mom and Dad's house.'" She quirked her fingers for air quotes.

"Do you know where that is?" the same guy asked.

"No," Mrs. Owens said, clearly sorry that she did not have this information.

"Can you describe the body, ma'am?" a third reporter called.

The woman shuddered. "I don't want to think about it, but . . ." She leaned forward, expression avid. "It was awful. The woman had been stabbed at least twenty times. Maybe thirty! And her head . . ." She swallowed hard. "He'd slit her throat. Nearly cut her head off."

Now that's just not true. He'd strangled Trish. His knife had never strayed above her collarbone. He *always* strangled them. If they died of their wounds, it just felt . . . empty somehow.

But the audible gasp from the small group seemed to satisfy the woman, who sat back in her chair with a nod. "She ran wild, that girl."

"Ma'am," a female reporter called out. "Are you suggesting that the victim brought this on herself?"

The old woman shrugged. "He certainly didn't break her door down. How else would he have gotten in if she hadn't brought him home willingly?"

He was starting to feel sorry for Trish. Too bad the old biddy wasn't his type. He'd take care of her for the simple pleasure of it.

The female reporter's lips had pinched into a straight line. "Thank you, ma'am." She started to walk away and he followed, hoping the woman could give him some more information. Like where the Fed was now. It was likely that wherever the Fed was, Daisy would be there, too.

"Excuse me," he said softly, fixing his expression into one of shock and sorrow.

The reporter turned and took him in in a glance. "Can I help you?"

"I hope so. I . . . just heard about Trish. We . . ." He closed his eyes. "God. We were dating." He let a sob escape his throat.

The reporter took a few steps closer, patting his arm. "How long were you dating?" she asked, her tone compassionate, but he wasn't fooled. There was a gleam in her eye that said she was looking for a fresh angle.

He'd give her a story. He just had to make sure he wasn't photographed. Couldn't have his face in the newspaper. Mrs. Martell might recognize him as her daughter's "friend."

"Not long," he told the reporter. "About a month."

"And what's your name, sir?"

"John," he murmured distractedly. "John Senegal. I need to talk to the FBI agent who was with Daisy, Trish's friend. What that woman said about what was done to her . . ."

"I don't think the woman was telling the truth," the reporter said kindly. "I don't think it was that . . . extreme."

Yes, it was. It was totally extreme. I just didn't cut off her fucking head.

"I need to talk to the agent handling the case," he repeated more forcefully. "The old woman said it was being handled by the FBI."

"Well, an FBI agent happened to find the body, but a pair of SacPD homicide detectives is on the case. Sokolov and Rhee."

"Sokolov and Rhee," he murmured, pretending to be taking his leave. "I'll go to the station right now. Thank you."

"They weren't going to the station," she said when he turned to go back to his car.

He pivoted back to face her. "Where did they go?"

Her expression became intensely sympathetic. "To the morgue."

He sucked in a breath. "Oh. Thank you." He made a show of squaring his shoulders. "All of them? The FBI agent, too?"

"Yes, he was with them. If you hurry, you can catch up to them. They only left a short time ago. I'm so sorry for your loss," she added softly, then handed him her business card. "My cell and my e-mail are on there. Please contact me if you learn anything new. I'll make sure your story is told with dignity."

Sure you will, he thought sarcastically, but he took the card. "Thank you," he breathed, then hurried to his car, waiting until he was behind the wheel to bow his head and let his grin take over his face.

Excellent. He tapped Maps, found the county coroner's office, and started driving.

Fifteen minutes later he was slowing as he drove by the coroner's offices—just in time to see the Fed park his car in between a blue Range Rover and a red Subaru, then hurry inside.

Daisy had been in that man's arms. He really didn't like that.

He'd given the subject some thought while driving to the morgue and realized that not one of the women he'd ever met—and that included his guests, passengers, everyone—had made him feel the way Daisy had today.

Not one had made him want her. Like a normal man wanted a normal woman. Not like Sydney, that was for damn sure. No one until Daisy Dawson. He might not ever find this feeling again, so he was going to make sure he held on to her.

He needed to see if this was real or something he'd only imagined. Of course he knew that she was very attractive. He'd seen that today. He knew she was nice. He'd watched her be kind to everyone she saw today, including himself. He'd watched her smile, and watched others smile back. He knew she was generous with her time, volunteering with the animal shelter.

She was the kind of woman a man brought home to meet his mother. *Unless the man's mother is dead and he has a vicious stepmother that makes Cinderella's stepmom look like freaking Mother Teresa. Then . . . no.*

If she'd only been "nice," he could have kept walking. He could have ignored her. But it was his body's response that had floored him and that was what he needed to explore. She made him feel sexual.

That was it. *Sexual.* For the first time *ever.*

That decided it for him. He'd find a way to take Daisy home with him, so that he could take his time finding out if this feeling was real. If it wasn't, he'd kill her quickly and painlessly.

Because he'd have to keep her. Once he took her home, he could never let her go. He'd have to reinforce his doors and windows, probably even locking her in the basement so that she couldn't escape when he was gone to work.

But he'd make her happy. And in return, she'd make him very happy indeed. He could keep a woman alive. He'd done it before. He didn't kill *all* his guests right away. He'd kept Susan for almost a year. He'd have kept her longer if she hadn't gotten fucking pneumonia. If he kept Daisy, he'd have to do something about the dampness of his basement guest room.

He'd also need to get rid of that Fed who hovered over her like she belonged to him. Then he'd figure out what to do with her. If she proved a problem, he'd have to kill her, no matter how nice she was.

He parked a half a block down and put money in the meter. Just in case. He did not want to be delayed by an overzealous meter maid.

He'd tail the Fed when he came out of the coroner's. Because if the man really had held Daisy in his arms, he'd go to her at some point.

I just have to be patient.

SACRAMENTO, CALIFORNIA
SATURDAY, FEBRUARY 18, 6:10 P.M.

Gideon found Rafe and Erin waiting for him outside the door to the autopsy suite. "How is Daisy?" Erin asked.

"Holding up," Gideon said, then told them what she'd said about the customer who'd been bothering Trish on Thursday.

"Shit," Erin murmured. "I should have asked her that. I took her home from the ER on Thursday. I should have asked."

Gideon sighed. "You couldn't have known, Erin. We all thought he was after Daisy."

"He did grab her," Rafe said, "and try to abduct her."

Erin shook her head. "Only after she confronted him, thinking he was her friend Jacob. He must have figured that it didn't matter which of them he took. Except that he tracked Trish to her apartment. If he comes after Daisy, too, we need to be ready. We can't let our guard down."

Gideon had already thought of this—several times. It still made his gut tighten painfully. "I won't. What does the coroner have?"

"Not sure," Rafe said. "Let's find out."

Gideon followed Rafe and Erin into the autopsy suite just as a man came out of one of the offices, gowned and goggled. He gave a nod when he saw them coming.

"Dr. Sifuentes," Rafe said, "this is Special Agent Reynolds. He's working with us on this investigation."

"Good to meet you," Sifuentes said, his rich voice echoing off the white tiles.

"And you." Gideon looked to the body covered by a sheet. "This is the victim?"

"Yes. I haven't started the examination yet. I won't get to her until late tomorrow, but I thought you would want to see what we found when we prepared her." He lifted the sheet from her face, folding it back at her abdomen.

With the body washed of its blood, more stab wounds were visible.

"Oh God," Rafe murmured. "Trish."

Gideon had nearly forgotten that the Sokolovs had befriended the woman. But he was abruptly paying no attention to anything except the pattern of stab wounds on her lower torso. "He marked her," he said, leaning in for a closer look.

The stab wounds in her upper torso were random slashes, but those in her lower abdomen were in the shape of the letters "S" and "Y."

Erin, too, had leaned in closer and now looked up with a frown. "'SY'? What does that mean?"

"I don't know," Gideon said. "But I'm betting he's done this before."

"Very precise cuts," Dr. Sifuentes agreed. "No hesitation on the lower abdominal wounds."

The stabs and slices that formed the letters were more like puncture wounds, stylized with curly ends and cuts that looked like asterisks in between and around.

"'They all do,'" Rafe said quietly, and they stood quietly, staring down at the letters that appeared to have taken an inordinately long time to create.

"I can run a search in the Bureau database," Gideon said, "to see if there are other cases of victims found with these letters carved into their torsos."

"We'll do the same," Erin said. "Is there anything more, Dr. Sifuentes?"

"Not visibly," he said sadly. "She'll have to tell us any other details during the examination."

"We found a butcher knife in her dish drainer," Erin told Sifuentes. "Could that have made both sets of wounds?"

"It's certainly possible that a butcher knife made the lower torso stab wounds," Sifuentes said. "But I assume he'd need a smaller knife for the letters. It would have been awkward to use the butcher knife in such a fashion. But I can't categorically say."

"There was a smaller knife in the knife block," Erin said, "but it didn't seem to have been used. Perhaps he brought a finer blade with him along with the bleach."

Sifuentes's forehead bunched above his goggles. "I'm sorry. I wish I could give you the answer you want."

"We'd rather get the right answer," Erin told him with a wistful smile.

"Thank you for calling us in," Rafe said, taking a final look at Trish's body before Sifuentes pulled up the sheet. "Let's take our discussion outside."

Gideon had to agree. The autopsy suite always made him slightly ill. He couldn't imagine what Rafe was feeling at the moment, having known Trish.

Gideon knew what he was feeling, just imagining Daisy's body with all those stab wounds. If she hadn't gotten away . . .

Stop. You can't think like that or you're no good to her or anyone.

If only it was that easy.

The three of them left the morgue, each of them drawing a deep breath of the crisp outside air. "You okay?" Rafe asked him. "You're looking a little green."

"I'm fine," Gideon lied. "I don't see the morgue every day," he added truthfully. "I'm a linguist."

"Nor do you have to imagine those wounds every day on someone special," Rafe murmured, ignoring his deflection. "I get it, Gid."

"We need to get back to the scene," Erin said. "I want to finish interviewing all the neighbors to see if anyone saw anything last night. We've got Latent taking prints. As for the knife, it was washed and bleached, but I'm hoping we'll get something off it that we can use. Some nook or cranny that he missed, assuming that was the murder weapon."

Gideon nodded. "It might have been the murder weapon, but I'll lay down cash that he has another blade he used for the letters, one that he brought with him and took away. He's done the letters before. He showed no hesitation. He trusted his tools."

"I agree," Rafe said. "So we look for similar cases."

"Agreed," Erin said with a hard nod. "Where are you headed, Gideon?"

"Back to the Sokolovs' to pick up Daisy and then we're heading up to Redding to, hopefully, track down Eileen. Tracing Eileen's steps since her escape is going to be key to finding Eden."

Rafe nodded. "Because you were left in Redding. Good thinking."

"I hope so. I've got to call my boss with an update. I'll also ask for a review of the database, looking for similar MOs."

He was going into this assuming that they'd find something, because the bastard had been cocky enough to leave them a clue. He must have believed he was safe from discovery.

He'll discover that he's wrong.

▌▌▌ GRANITE BAY, CALIFORNIA
SATURDAY, FEBRUARY 18, 8:10 P.M.

He was pretty damn proud of himself. It hadn't been easy, but he'd managed it. He'd followed Agent Reynolds's black Toyota all the way from the coroner's office to Granite Bay—with a detour to both a home and a drugstore in Rocklin—without once garnering the agent's notice.

The bonus was, now he knew where Reynolds lived, too.

Reynolds had parked in the driveway of one of the massive houses that were commonplace in Granite Bay. This one, however, had a lived-in look to it. There was a basketball hoop over the garage and whimsical gnomes hiding in the garden. A flag with Valentine hearts fluttered on a pole attached to a porch pillar.

Reynolds had walked in the door like he lived there.

As for who *did* live there, all it had taken was a quick search of the address to see that it was the residence of the Sokolov family. The first names were all a single initial followed by a string of asterisks—specifically K***** and I*****, who were both in their fifties, and one Z*****, who was only seventeen. But first names didn't matter because a search on Sokolov immediately produced their connection to Daisy Dawson.

Karl Sokolov owned KZAU, the radio station where Daisy worked. And now, there was every indication that Daisy was inside the house.

He settled into his seat to wait. The Fed had to come out sooner or later.

SIXTEEN

Gideon glanced in the rearview mirror. The car was still back there. It appeared to be a Chevy sedan, based on the headlight configuration. He'd yet to get behind the car because every time he slowed, the car did as well.

It could merely be a cautious driver. Or a driver who used others to keep their pace. Driving slower than the traffic pack leader was a strategy some used to avoid tickets on the interstate.

"I have to be home by seven tomorrow night," Daisy murmured from the passenger seat.

Gideon glanced over at her, surprised she was awake. She hadn't said a word since he'd picked her up at Karl and Irina's house, except to confirm she still wished to make the trip to Redding with him. At first she'd sat silently, petting poor Brutus bald. And then he thought she'd fallen asleep when she leaned her head against the car window, but now he realized she must have just been staring out the window.

He could have left her at the Sokolovs'. He knew that they'd keep her as safe as he could. But he'd wanted her with him because he thought it was better to get her away from the city. Away from the reporters and the story of Trish's murder, which was now front and center at every media outlet in town.

Mostly, though, he wanted her with him because he needed her. He needed the sound of her husky voice and the smell of her hair to calm him. To keep his mind from playing the reel of Trish's body, except with Daisy lying there. Dead.

Daisy is alive. He kept telling himself that. Kept drawing her scent into his head.

"Why seven tomorrow night?" he asked.

"My father's coming." Her phone glowed in the darkness as she turned it on to check. "He texted me that he's arriving at six thirty tomorrow night. Karl said he'd pick him up at the airport, but I don't want to keep Dad waiting since he's coming to see me."

Well, okay. "Are you all right with him coming?"

From the corner of his eye he saw her nod slowly, like she was running at a slower speed than normal. "I asked him to come." She was quiet for a very long moment. "I'm going to have to plan Trish's funeral and I've never done that before."

"I understand," he said softly.

She shrugged. "I know Irina and Karl could have helped me."

He was thinking that. "Or me."

She swallowed hard. "I still need you," she whispered.

His heart swelled at that, and she looked at him with warmth in her eyes. "Good."

"My dad . . . takes over. But he loves me. And Trish never had that. I . . . just needed him," she finished, sounding almost apologetic.

"You don't have to apologize for anything, Daisy." He reached for her hand, bringing it to his lips for a kiss before lowering it to the center console. He was relieved to find her skin warm, not clammy. She'd been stroking Brutus almost manically up until he'd arrived. That tidbit had been shared by Irina, who'd given him an I-told-you-so look after telling him that Daisy had visibly calmed every time he'd called her on the phone.

Gideon hadn't minded Irina's smugness one bit.

But Daisy wasn't calm now, and Brutus whimpered until she nuzzled the dog under her chin with one hand and clutched Gideon's hand with the other.

"I . . ." Daisy's swallow was audible, and she gripped his hand tighter. "I never saw a body like that before today. So . . . bloody." She stared out the window again. "Losing Trish. It feels almost like losing Carrie all over again."

Her older sister who'd run away. "Carrie didn't take to the military life your father imposed at the compound?"

"Or life on the ranch in general. She *hated* it there. She was older than Taylor and me and had left a lot more of her life back in Oakland. She begged Dad to take us back and he refused. They . . . had words. Terrible words." She hesitated and he remained quiet, waiting for what came next. "Sasha says you're a vault. Is that true for me, too?"

"Yes," he said simply.

She nodded once. "I don't want any of the Sokolovs to know about this."

"Rafe said your father disappeared without telling Karl where he was going. That it hurt Karl deeply."

"Which is why I don't want them to know." Her shoulders lifted in a slight shrug. "My dad's coming tomorrow and I hope it will help heal their relationship. I know they've been trying since we came out of hiding, but it's hard, I know. I mean, to trust Dad again. But it hurt him, too, leaving Karl and Irina. Hurt all of us."

"I won't tell them," Gideon promised.

"Thank you," she whispered. "Dad doesn't know that I overheard their fight."

Gideon's gut tightened because this wasn't sounding good at all. "Your father and Carrie?"

"Yes. My stepmother was there, so she knew, and of course Carrie knew, so Dad thinks his words died with them."

"But you overheard."

"Yes. They were in the kitchen and I was standing in the hallway, out of sight." She twisted in her seat, pinning him with her gaze. "My dad is a *good* man," she declared vehemently. "He *never* raised a hand to us. *Ever.*"

Gideon was marginally relieved. "I'm glad. What did they say, Daisy?"

She had to clear her throat, and a glance her way showed that she'd clenched her eyes shut. "Carrie accused Dad of loving Taylor more than the rest of us. He said he . . . was ashamed of her. That she didn't care about Taylor enough to 'sacrifice.' That family meant loyalty, and loyalty meant sacrifice." She drew a breath, letting it out as Gideon squeezed her hand just enough to show his support. He sensed Daisy had kept this bottled up for a long time, with no one to share her burden. "He said he used to be proud of all of his daughters, but he couldn't be proud of her anymore. She just froze, Gideon. She had this look on her face, like he'd hit her."

"She felt betrayed."

"I guess she must have. I was too shocked to move. Carrie ran out the back door. Slammed it so hard that the house shook. My father . . . He was horrified at what he'd said, as soon as the words had come out of his mouth. He just whispered, 'What have I done?' and he started to go after her, but Donna held him back. She said to let Carrie calm down. That she shouldn't be allowed to get away with tantrums like that. I ran to my room and cried. Things were so damn tense, all the time."

"And then?" he asked.

"Then . . . Carrie was just gone."

"She ran away? That night?"

"Yes. She eventually sent a postcard to my father's PO box in McKinleyville. He went to get the mail every two weeks, which was when he and Jacob would pick up supplies. She told him she'd gone to Oakland."

"That's where you'd come from."

"Yes." She sighed. "She started out staying with friends, but that changed at some point. She hung with the wrong crowd. Started living with some guy who was older and an addict. She followed him to L.A. and . . ." She went so still he couldn't hear her breathing.

Gideon squeezed her hand hard. "Breathe, Daisy."

Daisy sucked in a lungful of air, let it out on a shudder. "And then she died," she finished. "She was only sixteen. My father has to live with the fact that the last thing he said to her was that he was ashamed of her."

"Shit," he murmured. "How did she die?"

"She OD'd. Before we heard about it, he went to Oakland to try to find her. He looked and looked, but he never did. He didn't know she'd gone to L.A." She went too still again and her next words were uttered in barely a whisper. "He didn't report her missing to the police."

Gideon frowned, then understood. "If he had, he would have had to come out of hiding to file the report."

"Exactly. He did send photos of her to the shelters with the number of a disposable phone listed in case someone did see her. But no one ever called. He checked all the places homeless kids hung out. When he finally did get a call, it was to bring her ashes home."

Gideon couldn't imagine that kind of pain. "If you were all hidden, how did he know she was dead?"

"He'd started calling around to hospitals and morgues after he got the postcard. He said he had a feeling. My stepmother told him he was buying into Carrie's drama. That if he went after her, she'd know she could manipulate him. To leave her be and she'd come home with her tail between her legs."

He was quiet a moment, thinking about that. "And all that time your stepmother knew she was lying, that there was no reason to hide because Taylor's biological father wasn't the predator she'd made him out to be."

Daisy's laugh was bitter. "Yeah. Donna was a piece of work."

"That had to have made her betrayal that much worse when your father finally found out."

"It did," she said, and he was silent again, for longer this time. A question burned the tip of his tongue, but he was afraid to ask it.

Daisy frowned at him. "I can *feel* you hesitating. Just ask your question, Gideon."

"When did you start drinking?"

She nodded, as if she'd been expecting him to ask. "Right after Carrie died."

"How old were you?"

"Fourteen."

He wasn't able to swallow his gasp. "Daisy."

"Yeah. It was like we were all stretched with stress, taut like a rubber band, and when it finally broke, it snapped back and hit us in the face. My father withdrew. I started drinking. And Taylor became Superwoman, doing her chores, plus Dad's and mine."

"Your sister must have felt horrible, since you'd moved to protect her."

"She did. I don't know if she heard the argument Carrie and Dad had, but she did know that Carrie blamed her. It was horrible. It was like we were in this little fishbowl filled with acid. We couldn't get away from each other and we were disintegrating. Taylor was the one to see my problems, probably because she was the only one leaving for a while. She'd go out and ride fences or do outdoorsy things. I . . . didn't. I was too drunk, or hungover, or just too angry. Not with her. Never with her."

There was something more she wanted to say. He could sense her warring with herself. "But?" he murmured.

She shrugged helplessly. "I thought it, too. I thought Dad must love Taylor more and I resented her. But I wasn't mad at her. And that doesn't even make sense."

"Yes, it does." He thought about Mercy and how she resented him still. She didn't hate him and she wasn't angry with him, but she resented him and he didn't know what to do about it.

"I was just . . . mad at everything and everyone. And nothing and no one at all."

"You were grieving and everyone does that differently."

"I know. I figured that out in rehab."

"When did you go?"

"Eight years ago, when I was seventeen. Taylor noticed my drinking first. At first I wasn't sure how Dad didn't notice, because I was drinking his booze, but then I saw Donna refilling the bottles. He never knew I'd been guzzling."

"Wait." Gideon shook his head. "Your stepmother hid your alcoholism? Why?"

"I don't know. I mean, I wasn't going to tell anyone because it left me free and clear to drink all I wanted. It was Taylor who started keeping track of my hangovers and drunken stupors. I think she just thought Dad was so withdrawn that he simply didn't notice."

"Did you ever tell her that her mother was refilling the bottles?"

Daisy nodded slowly. "I spent this past summer with Taylor and her new bio-family, in between Paris and moving here. Gave me a chance to see Julie, too. My dad, not so much. I was still mad at him for having me followed across Europe."

"What did Taylor say when you told her about her mother and the booze?"

"She believed me and was horrified. I mean, once Taylor figured out that her mother had lied about her bio-dad all those years, all bets were off. My sister is a smart cookie. And insanely practical." She made a face. "So the opposite of me."

Gideon frowned. "Did your father tell you that? That you're not practical?"

"Didn't really have to. Taylor liked to ride, and rope, and was a natural on the ranch. She's an equine therapist now—she uses horses to help kids with emotional trauma."

"She sounds very special."

"She is."

"But does she volunteer all over the place and paint and put together puzzles like a computer brain? Can she defend herself against a man who was almost twice her size like you did on Thursday night?"

Daisy tilted her head, appearing to truly consider the question. "No?" Then she smiled, beautifully, and his heart gave a little tumble. "Well, she can do the self-defense thing, but she's at least six inches taller than I am, so I'll take your point and thank you." She brought his hand to her lips and kissed his knuckles. "Thank you, Gideon."

"You're welcome," he said gruffly. "But you and Taylor are close, right?"

"Yeah. We were all we both had there on the ranch. She's this bright light, you know? She was always like a little mom, taking care of me and Julie. I love Julie, too, of course. She's just a few years younger and her disability widened that gap. She's got cerebral palsy and needed therapy all those years—physical and occupational. Dad hired a live-in physical therapist for a while, but Jules never got what she needed back then."

"She's getting it now?"

Her smile was fond. "Yes. She's going to a special center and she even has a boyfriend. Dad just about lost his shit when he found out about that." She chuckled, then sighed wistfully. "Dad finally found someone, too. Her name is Sally and she's a nurse. I like her. She's nothing like Donna! She reminds me more of my own mom. She's good for him and now Julie has a real mom."

"Donna didn't take care of Julie?"

"She wasn't bad to her, but . . . when I think about the hardships we went through because of her lies. Julie needed help that she wasn't getting."

"And you blame your father for that?" He glanced over to see her expression pinch. "It's okay with me if you do. I think I would, too."

"Yeah, I do. He does, too, though, so my being angry with him about that is kind of pointless. He beats himself up more than any of us do. I just wish he wouldn't worry so much. But I understand why he does."

"You said he experiences PTSD. From the military?"

"Yes. That isn't my story to tell, though. Oh. Speaking of which," she said, and it was clear that she was changing the subject, but that was okay, "I'd opened my laptop to do some more research on the tattoos and Irina saw the page."

Gideon sighed. "Shit."

She winced. "I'm sorry. She demanded to know why I was looking at tattoos like you used to have. I told her it wasn't my story to tell."

"She accepted that?" he asked, finding that hard to believe.

"Well, in a manner of speaking. She was happy that

you'd chosen to trust me with something you hadn't trusted her with. She got all I-told-you-so on me. And then Sasha started telling her that you and I had a date last night."

"So what did you do?"

"The only thing I could do," she replied without skipping a beat. "I told her that Sasha had a librarian girlfriend."

He laughed. "You're evil."

"I know." She gave his hand a squeeze and was quiet for a few moments. "Did you get that age progression from your friend in Philly?" she finally asked.

"Yes." Tino had come through with a sketch that exactly captured the sad eyes of the girl Gideon had once known. "I printed twenty copies on my printer when I went home to pack a bag and get my map." He'd intended to take her with him, but when he'd called Irina after leaving the morgue, she'd told him that Daisy had fallen asleep. He'd take her to his house when they got back.

"What will you do if no one at the bus station remembers her?"

"Ask around in some of the other towns around Redding. Redding was the closest large town, but there are a number of smaller towns within and just outside the radius I drew around Mt. Shasta. Someone in a smaller town might be more likely to remember her. I've been to most of them, asking in general about Eden and specifically about the man who'd go for supplies, but I figured that the guy probably went to Redding for our supplies because nobody knew anything. But I didn't have a photo of Eileen then, so it's worth trying again."

"Or they might even remember one of the other men with the Eden tattoo."

He nodded. "I thought of that, too. I made copies of the tattoo photos." He saw the sign for Redding and put on his turn signal. A glance in his rearview showed the Chevy sedan to be exiting as well. Except when he turned right at the end of the exit ramp, the sedan turned left. *Good.* "If no one at the bus station remembers her, I'll check the pawnshops to see if the locket was pawned or purchased."

"If she pawned it, she might still be alive," Daisy murmured. "God, I hope so."

Gideon's chest ached because even though he hoped so, too, he didn't think the odds were very good. "If the pawnshops are a bust, then we can start on the other towns."

REDDING, CALIFORNIA
SATURDAY, FEBRUARY 18, 11:20 P.M.

It had been a risk, turning left at the end of the Redding exit. The Fed had tried a few times to get behind him, to get his license plate number, but he'd managed to keep him from succeeding. It wouldn't matter if he had, though. The plates had never been reported stolen. He'd made sure of that.

The plates—and the car—belonged to one of last year's guests, a woman from a small town in southeastern California who he'd met in a Vegas casino. She'd been playing slots, something she admitted to always wanting to do. She was on her bucket-list tour. Had just quit her job as a professor and had embarked on what was to have been a two-year trip around the world. All alone. She was craving the privacy, the ability to be accountable to no one. She'd been the perfect guest. No one had come looking for her. No one ever would.

So he'd kept up the payments on her car's registration, and voilà, he'd had the perfect car to use whenever he wished to be someone else. As he had today.

Hooking a quick U-turn, he went in search of the

black Toyota Camry. They'd been on the road for three hours and it was getting quite late. He hoped that the first place the Fed would stop would be one of the exit's many gas stations or fast-food places—

Or motels. Because there it was, coming to a stop under the awning of a moderately priced motel. The Fed got out and went around to help the woman he recognized as Daisy, holding her hand as she got out of the car. And continued to hold her hand as they went inside.

The Fed was holding her hand. And she was letting him.

He pushed the annoyance aside because he was certain the two hadn't come to Redding to simply bang one out. The Fed had a home. In Rocklin. So if they just wanted to be alone, they could have driven twenty minutes from the Sokolov house in Granite Bay, not nearly three hours to Redding.

Something was up. Something important.

He waited impatiently because they'd left the car under the awning. After ten freaking minutes, Reynolds came out alone and parked the Toyota.

He considered using the gun under his seat to take care of the Fed there and then, but hesitated too long. Reynolds went in through a side door using his key card.

It seemed they were turned in for the night. Together. The two of them.

They could be here to see Trish's family, he allowed. That would make sense. Except Trish had had no family in her contacts list.

His gut was telling him that this trip was important.

Of course, his gut also told him to kill Sydney, but he obviously hadn't listened to it.

And see where it got you? You're dancing like her puppet on a string. And you came all this way, had a shot at the Fed, but you wussed out. Pussy. Now Daisy is sleeping with him. Or not sleeping.

He blew out an angry breath, furious with himself.

He'd wait until morning, to see where they went from here. And when he got a shot at the Fed, he'd take it. Then Daisy would be alone again. She'd talk to him about radio and maybe even get him a job.

Which was ridiculous. He didn't want a job in radio. He needed to keep the job he had.

Oh. Shit. He was supposed to fly to New York City tomorrow with Hank.

Panic seized his already roiling gut and he had to force himself to calm down. He'd . . . call in sick. That's what he'd do. Hank did it sometimes. .

Not when he's afraid of being fired.

No, no, no. He had dirt on the old man, he reminded himself. All those photos of him, both with his women and his drug-smuggling clients. Photos that would keep him from getting the ax. Not that he should have had to stoop to such extremes. The company had been promised to him. So many times.

He needed the company. He needed the planes. Flying was the reason he'd never been caught. Why he'd never even been a blip on law enforcement's radar. Anywhere.

But he had the pictures. He had the proof. He wasn't going to lose his job. He could take a goddamn sick day. He'd never called in sick before. He was allowed.

He eyed his gas gauge. He was nearing empty. Since it appeared the Fed and Daisy were down for the night, he'd fill up, get some coffee and snacks, then come back here and wait.

REDDING, CALIFORNIA
SATURDAY, FEBRUARY 18, 11:35 P.M.

Daisy left the hotel room's bathroom, her spine stiff with uncertainty. She'd known on some level that going to Redding meant spending the night. She'd even known, on that same level, that it meant staying in a hotel room and that Gideon wouldn't let her out of his sight.

She hadn't thought about the logistics past that and she should have. Especially given what had happened between them on her sofa this morning, which now seemed like a lifetime ago.

She was in shock from finding Trish. From *losing* Trish. She got that. Still . . . She looked down at the plain shorts and camisole set that Sasha had packed in her overnight bag. The clothes belonged to Zoya, the youngest Sokolov, but fit pretty well since she and Zoya were about the same size.

It would have been nice to have worn something prettier for Gideon. Not that anything would happen tonight. It was presumptuous of her to think so. Especially since she still hadn't picked up any protection. On the other hand, the room was a small suite, with a bedroom and a separate sitting room and kitchenette. But just one bed.

Her heart pounded harder when she rounded the corner to see the bed. The one bed. It looked huge and looming, its only occupant a snoring Brutus.

But then her pounding heart skittered in her chest when she saw him.

Gideon leaned into the window, arms crossed over his chest, his forehead pressed against the glass. He'd changed into black sweatpants and a gray T-shirt that stretched tight across broad shoulders that were stiff but seemed to sag at the same time. He looked as exhausted as she felt.

Without overthinking it, she went to him, wrapping her arms around his waist. She pressed her cheek into his back and felt his muscles flex slightly as his arms released the hold he had on himself, dropping to cover hers.

"Is something new wrong?" she asked quietly.

"No." He laced their fingers together over his hard

stomach. "I was just thinking about your sister. Which made me think of mine."

"Mercy," she murmured. "Will you tell me about her?"

He sighed. "She . . . doesn't hate me."

That was a curious way to begin, she thought and waited for him to say more. "But?" she prompted when he remained silent.

"But she resents me."

"Like Carrie and I resented Taylor?"

"Something like that. She doesn't want to. She tried not to. But she can't help it. So she left."

He sounded so bleak, so very hopeless. She squeezed his middle tighter. "Where did she go?"

"Lots of places. But she ended up in New Orleans."

"Do you see her?"

"Last time was two years ago. I . . . well, I lied. I told her I had business there, but I really just went to see her. She looked . . . better." The last word was a hoarse whisper that broke her heart.

"Better than what?" Daisy whispered back.

"She didn't get away from the community until she was thirteen."

An indirect answer to her question, but she understood. "You told me that. It means she was married for a whole year. Did her husband hurt her?"

"Yes." Another hoarse whisper. "Badly. She also almost died."

Daisy swallowed hard. "You don't have to tell me if you don't want to. You don't owe me quid pro quo, Gideon."

He shuddered. "I don't want to tell you." He straightened and moved away from the window. "But I need to. Not all of it. Some of it . . . I can't."

She took a step back, releasing him to sit on the edge of the bed. "Tell me what you can," she said, scooping Brutus from the bed and settling the dog on her lap.

He unexpectedly slid to the floor, his back against the bed, his shoulder against her thigh. Holding Brutus with one hand, she gently toyed with Gideon's hair with the other, admiring how the light caught the threads of silver among the inky black.

"My mother left me at the bus station," he said abruptly.

"Because Mercy was only nine years old and needed her." Daisy kept her voice soft. "Not because she didn't love you."

"I *know* that," he bit out, his vehemence startling.

Okay. So I put my foot in that. Shutting up now. "Sorry," she murmured.

"No." He sighed. "I get tense when I think about this and when I talk about Mercy. See, my mother went back for Mercy, but I don't know if she understood what life was going to be like—for her or for Mercy—when she returned. Or maybe she did, I don't know."

"She was punished."

"Yes." There was an eternity of misery in that one little word. "Pastor knew that she'd smuggled me out, but before he could punish her, her husband gave her an alibi."

"He protected her."

Gideon's laugh was bitter. "Not exactly. He was forced to pay Ephraim Burton restitution because I'd stabbed him in the eye. My mother was the payment."

Daisy's eyes filled with hot tears. "Oh, Gideon."

"My mother's husband took on another wife and my mother was transferred to Burton."

Daisy continued petting his hair, not knowing what to say. The guilt he carried was so very obvious in that moment.

"The man who drove the truck . . . he'd gotten his payment also. Several times on the way to Redding and, I presume, on the way back."

Daisy couldn't swallow back her gasp. "In front of you?"

His shoulders moved in a sad parody of a shrug. "I was nearly dead. I guess he figured it didn't matter."

"Wasn't he . . . well, wasn't he worried about getting in trouble for smuggling you?"

"I never knew what was going on with that guy. He left the compound every week, so he could have run, but he never did. And he kind of did what he wanted, when he wanted. I always wondered what he'd had on the leaders."

"You think he had incriminating information on them?"

"Yes. Something strong enough to give him the plum job of driving wherever he went for supplies every week. Whatever it was, he wasn't punished for smuggling me out. Mercy told me that much. And she said no one else got out between her escape and mine. I've hoped others were able to get away. I even searched for lockets and similar tattoos but found nothing. Not until you found Eileen's locket."

"How did Mercy get out?"

"My mother got Mercy out. I'm not sure what she used to bribe the truck driver again, but she and Mercy made it to the bus station just like I had. Mercy was in bad shape and our mother wouldn't leave her. She insisted on being left behind. Started to scream and raise a fuss. I guess she was hoping someone would help her."

"Nobody did."

"No. The truck driver shot her."

Daisy couldn't contain the cry that escaped her throat. "No. In front of Mercy?"

Gideon stared straight ahead at the dingy beige wall. "He shot Mercy, too."

Daisy couldn't speak. She just stroked his hair with one hand and wiped tears from her face with the other.

"He took my mother's body back with him," he

went on stonily. "He left Mercy there. She nearly bled out. They airlifted her to UC Davis, just like they'd done me. A nurse noticed her lockets and remembered my tattoo."

"Wait. Lockets?"

He nodded once. "Somehow Mercy had my mother's locket, too. She was found with her locket and my mother's hidden in her clothes. I asked her how their chains were cut, but she always shakes her head and refuses to answer me."

"Her trauma runs deep," Daisy murmured, then shifted the conversation when he shuddered. "Was Irina the nurse who noticed her lockets?"

"No, but the nurse was a friend of hers. By the time news got to Irina, Mercy was in foster care. I got to her as soon as I could. She'd gone mute, wouldn't speak to anyone. But the foster mother told me that Mercy had been found at the Redding bus station. I begged Mercy to tell me where our mother was, but she just stared at me, her eyes so empty. And then I knew. I asked her if Mama was dead. She nodded."

"What did you do?"

"Rafe carried me out. I was . . . a mess. He'd driven me there. I made him promise that he wouldn't tell anyone. Mercy had been through enough. I didn't want everyone else to know what had been done to her. I didn't want anyone to know she'd suffered because of me."

"Did you think Irina and Karl would stop loving you?"

He sucked in a harsh breath. "Rafe promised me and kept my secret to this day. Irina knows I found Mercy, but she thinks the foster family adopted her and moved away."

He hadn't answered her question about the Sokolovs loving him, which was an answer nonetheless. An answer that broke Daisy's heart in two. She wished she had words of comfort, but she had none that wouldn't sound wrong or condescending. "You said she ended up in New Orleans. What happened to her between the time you found her in foster care and today?"

"She stayed in foster care until she was eighteen, but she only agreed to see me a few times. Once she'd aged out of the system, she went to Houston."

"Where your mother had come from."

He nodded. "I think she wanted answers. I know she met our grandparents, but I don't know what she said to them, if anything. I had no interest in seeing them again. But between Houston and New Orleans was a string of towns. I'd get a postcard every so often from a different place saying she was alive. No calls, texts, or e-mails. Only the postcard. I never even knew her cell phone number. I'd try to track her down to wherever the card had been postmarked, but I'd always miss her. When I got the card from New Orleans, I tracked her down immediately. Lurked outside the address I'd found until she came home. She wasn't happy to see me. She agreed to meet me for dinner and finally gave me her cell number if I promised to only use it in an emergency. Otherwise, we've had no contact."

"Why does Mercy resent you so much?"

"I think it was because our mother suffered after getting me out. And Mercy suffered, too. She was treated terribly by whoever she'd been married to."

"You don't know?"

"She wouldn't tell me. To this day. She won't talk about it."

"What happened to Mercy's locket?"

"She said she put it in her bank's safe-deposit box. Along with our mother's. I'm not sure how she got Mama's locket. She's never told me. I've never seen either locket."

Because Mercy resented him. *Oh, Gideon.* Daisy slid off the bed to the floor beside him, then straddled him and wrapped her arms around his neck. "I'm sorry."

He held on to her with a ferocity that stole her breath, burying his face into the curve of her shoulder. "I wish I could go back and change it. I wish I could go back and not stab Ephraim Burton in the eye."

Her heart hurt for him. "He would've killed you, Gideon."

He went very still. "There have been times that I wish that he had."

No. No, no, no. She held him tighter. "Recently?"

He nuzzled her gently. "No."

She let out a breath. She wanted to tell him that it wasn't his fault, that he'd only been a child, fighting for his own life. Fighting not to be raped. *Just like I fought Thursday night.*

She wanted to tell him that if anyone was to "blame," it was his mother for allowing them to be taken to a cult to begin with. But his mother had been little more than a child herself.

Daisy wanted to rail at his grandparents for kicking his mother out to begin with, starting the spiral into homelessness, prostitution, and despair.

But she said none of those things, because she didn't think he needed to hear any of that tonight. She loosened her hold on his neck enough to kiss his cheek. "Come to bed with me, Gideon. Let me hold you there."

SACRAMENTO, CALIFORNIA
SATURDAY, FEBRUARY 18, 11:40 P.M.

Zandra Jones stifled a sob. *Don't cry. Do not cry.* Her nose would get stuffed up and she'd suffocate.

He'd left her tied and gagged, and as hard as she pulled, she couldn't get free. Each tug merely tightened her bonds. Her wrists were bleeding now and they burned like fire.

She wasn't thinking about the cuts. The way he'd

carved letters into her body. They hurt, but it was more a dull throb. The cuts weren't going to kill her. She knew that now.

He'd tended her wounds. Even stitched up a few that had gone deeper than he'd intended. The suture supplies had been in one of his drawers, his hands steady and horrifyingly practiced as he'd closed the worst of the wounds made by his fine-tipped detail knife.

He'd done this before. Many times. One of his victims was still here. In the freezer behind her. He'd taken a photo of the woman's body and had shown it to her to frighten her. And it had. The body, all wrapped in bedsheets. The woman's face wasn't visible in the picture, but Zandra had seen her hair. Dark and long. He'd strangled her, the dead woman in the freezer.

He'll strangle me, too. He'd already done it several times, but he'd let up right before she passed out, allowing her to suck in air that felt like knives scraping her lungs and throat. One day soon, he wouldn't let up.

And I'll be dead.

I'm not supposed to be here. She'd lost track of time, but he'd said it was Saturday. *I'm supposed to be getting married today. To James. In Vail.* But she'd run away so abruptly that no one knew where she'd gone. If James traced her to the airport, all he'd know was that she'd gone to a nearby bar and left too intoxicated to drive. She'd told both James and Monica to go to hell after finding them in bed together, that she was leaving and never coming back. To not come looking for her, that she didn't want to hear anything they'd have to say.

All this as they had lain there, watching her wide-eyed. And coitus-interruptussed.

Stupid James. Stupid Monica. Stupider me. She'd trusted the bastard, only to have him sleep with her "best friend"? *Yeah, right.*

They can both go to fucking hell. At this point, she'd be seeing them there soon enough. *Because no one is looking for me.* Everyone at work thought she was on her honeymoon. Everyone at her wedding figured she'd flounced off to lick her wounds.

No one would miss her. Tears pricked at her eyes again and she ruthlessly held them back. *Not gonna cry.*

Instead she focused her attention on the interior of the cabinet he'd left open. Trying to freak her out. It was working.

After studying its contents for hours on end, she now knew that there were all kinds of trinkets and jewelry mounted on hooks—a number of necklaces, a few bracelets, an old rabbit's foot, a few coins, and what looked like dog tags. All were small enough to fit into a pocket. Each was mounted beneath a driver's license. There had to be thirty of them. Maybe more. Each was a woman. A person.

A dead person.

Not me. I'm not going to die.

But she wasn't sure how to make that happen. She was an attorney, not an escape artist or a magician. Her only superpower was the ability to talk her way out of anything.

Except this. Unless something radically changed, she wasn't going to talk her way out of this one. She'd seen his face. He was never letting her go.

There has to be something I can do. There has to be. I'm not ready to die.

SEVENTEEN

Come to bed with me, Gideon. Let me hold you there. He'd obeyed and she'd been as good as her word, holding him much as she had the night before, his head between her breasts, her fingers gently sifting through his hair, one arm curved protectively around his shoulders. Giving him comfort when she was the one who'd suffered the loss.

She had a generous heart and he wanted it. He wanted her generosity and gentleness for himself. *You have it,* he told himself. *For tonight at least.* But he knew without a shadow of a doubt that one night wouldn't be enough.

She stilled him somehow. Calmed his mind. Filled the spaces he hadn't known were empty. She understood him in a way that no one had ever understood before.

To be fair, you didn't give anyone else a chance. He'd shared things with her that he'd never shared with Rafe. Never shared with Karl and Irina and they were as close to family as he had.

But he'd spilled his story to Daisy in just days and he wasn't sure why. Maybe it was how she made him feel . . . normal when he was with her. They'd both grown up prisoners, in a way. Maybe that was it. Whatever it was, he knew that he wanted more.

He knew that he wanted her. So much so that he'd angled his body away from her so that she wouldn't know how hard he was. She didn't need demands tonight. She needed comfort.

Pressing a kiss to the hollow of her throat, he lifted his head, propping himself up on his elbow, their faces only inches apart. "I'm sorry," he murmured. "I'm being selfish."

He could see her eyes widen in the semidarkness. "What?"

"You've lost your friend, but I made it about me."

One side of her pretty mouth lifted slightly. "But it *is* about you. That's why you're here, Gideon. Whoever killed *my* friend connects to *your* friend." She cupped his cheek, brushing the lines of his beard with her thumbs. "Don't apologize. Besides, I like comforting you." She shrugged. "It makes me feel useful."

"Like you're doing something," he said softly. "Because being helpless sucks. I get it."

Her small smile faded as she held his gaze. "I figured you would."

"What can I do for you?" he whispered.

Her gaze flickered away and she bit her lip. "Nothing. I'm . . . I'm good."

With his forefinger on her chin, he turned her head so that she faced him again. "Tell me, Daisy." He lifted one eyebrow. "Or I'll feel helpless, too."

She swallowed hard, then slid her hands into his hair. And pulled him down, taking his mouth in a tentative kiss, a mere ghosting of lips that sent his heart instantly pounding in his chest. She ended it far too soon, releasing her hold on his hair. But he didn't retreat.

"Is this what you want, Daisy?" he murmured against her mouth. "Me to kiss you?"

Breathlessly, soberly, she nodded.

"Like you kissed me? Or more?"

She closed her eyes. "More," she answered, but it was barely a whisper. She looked . . . ashamed and that made his heart hurt, even though he thought he understood why.

"Daisy, look at me." He waited until she'd opened her eyes. "You're feeling guilty because Trish is gone?"

She nodded again, her eyes filling with tears. "It feels wrong to want to feel . . . good, I guess, although Trish would have been the first person to tell me that was stupid. It's just that . . ." She blinked once, and the tears streaked down the side of her face, into her hair.

She was quiet for so long that he felt compelled to help. "Do you want to just forget for a little while?" Which made him feel even more selfish, like he was trying to convince her to do what he wanted when she was in a vulnerable place. But to his surprise she shook her head hard.

"I'm not going to forget. Every time I close my eyes I see her . . . lying there." She shuddered and he tightened his hold around her waist, drawing her tighter to his body.

He kissed her temple. "Then it's just what?"

"It could have been me," she said, and he sucked in a breath.

"*No.*" The denial was out of his mouth before he could stop it.

"*Yes,* Gideon. That man tried to drag me away on Thursday. I would have ended up like Trish." Her hands were back on his face, stroking his skin, his beard, as if to soften her words. "It could have been *me.*"

He dropped his head until their foreheads touched. "Please tell me that you aren't thinking that it *should* have been you."

She reared back into the pillow, her eyes blinking wide as she stared up at him. "No! Of course not. It shouldn't have been anyone, Gideon. But it was. And I just . . . I guess after everything that's happened, I want to feel . . . not scared for a little while. You know, to feel good. You make me feel good. But I feel selfish asking. Like I'm . . . using you."

It was his turn to blink. "Oh. Well." That was honestly not what he'd expected. He'd thought she'd say it was because she needed to wait for a mourning period. Or worse, that she feared she'd be next and didn't want to die without having one final fling. That she'd be using him? Wow.

Part of him wanted to tell her that he'd be happy to be used by her anytime, but that wasn't true. What he was feeling was more than an itch to be scratched. He'd scratched itches in the past and he'd been satisfied. But this was different. *She* was different.

"Tell me this," he said, because she still looked troubled. "If someone else were here guarding you, would you still want to do . . . whatever?"

She thought for a moment, then shook her head. "No." She traced his lips with her fingertip. "It's because it's you. I like you. I can let my guard down with you. I . . . trust you." Her gaze flicked away for a few seconds before resolutely returning to his. "And I want you. More than any man I've ever met."

His pulse went into overdrive, even as he wondered how many men that had been. Ruthlessly he shoved the thought away. It didn't matter. Tonight she was with him.

"Yeah?" he asked, feeling almost shy, for God's sake. Like a goddamn teenager. Which he'd never really been allowed to be.

Her mouth curved as she brushed a lock of hair from his forehead, her touch tender even as her eyes invited. "Yeah. So if you'd kiss me again, I'd be very grateful."

"That I can do." He took her mouth in what started as a simple kiss but quickly heated when she opened to him. He tasted her, a little minty, a little sweet, and so hot. He still lay on his side, his erection a safe distance away. At least until he knew how far she wanted this to go.

A moment later—or maybe minutes, he wasn't sure—he had his answer as one of her small hands came up to grip the back of his neck, the other clutching a handful of his shirt. She tugged and, schooling his features so that his disappointment didn't show, he lifted his head, breathing hard.

Her mouth was red and wet, her eyes glazed, and the breasts that had cradled his head rose and fell with her panted breaths. She looked slightly dazed. And so beautiful he had to force himself to back off.

Suppressing a shudder, he pressed his lips to her temple, then kissed down to her ear. "Too much?"

She tugged on his shirt again. "Not enough. You're too far away, Gideon."

He shuddered again, a full-body shudder that he couldn't hide. He buried his face in the curve of her shoulder. "Thought you wanted to stop."

"No," she whispered, the hand on his neck sliding up to pet his hair, the hand on his shirt sliding down to grip the waistband of his sweats. "Don't stop." She tugged again. "Please."

He shifted, settling between the legs she parted in welcome, his cock finding her softness, and he couldn't stop his hips from rolling against her. Humming, she arched her body, pressing her head back into the pillow, exposing the line of her throat. Resting his forearms on either side of her head, he kissed up her throat to her jaw.

"This okay?" he asked.

"Very okay." Her voice was huskier than normal, sending shivers over his skin. She closed her eyes on a throaty sigh. "You feel so good."

He brushed her mouth with soft kisses, gratified when she tried to follow him up when he lifted his head again. "What do you want, Daisy?"

Her lips curved wryly. "More than I'm going to get. I never did get a chance to stop by the drugstore. But this is nice, too."

Nice was not what he wanted her to feel. Over the moon and out of her mind with pleasure is what he wanted her to feel. "I did," he admitted. "Stopped at the drugstore."

Her eyes blinked open. "You did? Whe—" She stopped herself before she could finish asking him *when*. Realization flickered in her eyes and she drew a deep breath, because the only time they'd been apart was when he'd gone to the morgue. She nodded once, a grim acknowledgment. She closed her eyes again. "Thank you."

"We don't have to do anything," he whispered. "I didn't expect anything. I just figured . . . Well, I hoped we'd need them sooner or later."

"Tonight." Her eyes opened and he saw desperation mixed with raw yearning. "Unless you don't want this."

He barked out a laugh. "No, that's not a problem." He rolled his hips again, drawing a gasp from her lips. "In case you didn't notice."

She arched into him again, her eyes drifting closed. "I noticed." She hummed more. "I totally noticed and I want this. I want you. Inside me. Is that clear enough?"

His hips jerked, a groan rumbling from his chest. "God. Yes. That's plenty clear." He pressed a hard kiss to her now-smiling mouth. "Don't go anywhere. I'll be right back." He knelt between her legs, not wanting to tear his eyes away from the sight of her body, spread out before him. Her nipples had grown hard and were now starkly visible through the camisole that would have been completely modest otherwise. Her hips undulated, lifting to where he'd been seconds earlier. Where he couldn't wait to get back to.

Forcing himself from the bed, he dug in his duffel

until he found the box of condoms. Hands trembling, he ripped at the plastic, then at the top of the box, sending strips of condoms.

Behind him, she laughed, a purely joyful sound that he hadn't heard nearly often enough. She eyed the strip he'd snatched in midair, one brow lifting. "I'm not sure if that's optimistic or ambitious, Gideon."

He looked at the strip of three in his hand and grinned. "A little bit of both?" He tossed them to the nightstand and started to take off his shirt, but she scrambled to kneel at the edge of the mattress, stopping him.

"Hold on. I want to do it." Then she surprised him by switching on the lamp. "I want to see you."

God. He fisted his hands at his sides so that he didn't rush her. "Okay."

She came up on her knees, her teeth biting into her lower lip as she pulled his shirt over his head and dropped it to the floor. She made a sound of appreciation as she looked at him for long seconds that had him growing even harder.

"Touch me," he managed in a guttural voice that he didn't recognize as his own, shuddering when her hands spread out over his skin, caressing him with a slow reverence that tested his control. She dragged her fingertips through the hair on his chest, tracing the wings of the phoenix tattoo before following the line of hair to the waistband of his sweats.

He sucked in a breath when her seeking finger dipped below his sweats and the boxer briefs he wore beneath. "Daisy," he rasped.

She lifted her eyes to his. "You're beautiful."

He couldn't hold back any longer. He thrust his fingers into her hair, dragging her to him as he plundered her mouth until they were forced to break apart for air. He dropped his hands to his sides again. "Take your top off," he gritted out.

Keeping her gaze locked to his, she did so and he groaned when her breasts came into view. "You're the beautiful one." Gently he cradled them in his hands, his thumbs softly flicking the nipples he couldn't wait to taste.

Her head fell back, her mouth falling open on another of those throaty sighs that made him want to plunge inside her. But he held on to his control. This would be good for her. For them. He'd take his time. He'd—

"Fuck, Daisy, fuck," he snarled when she delved under his briefs, her fingers closing around him. He pulled her to him again, this kiss openmouthed, primal, and absolutely raw as she pumped him, squeezing on the upstroke. And then her hand was gone, but before he could protest, she was pushing his sweats down his hips and wriggling from his hold. He wanted to drag her back, wanted to throw her on the bed and suck on her breasts.

But all those thoughts were driven from his racing brain when she took him in her mouth and all he could do was stand there, his legs shaking as he was enveloped in hot, wet . . . heaven. He watched her blond head bobbing up and down, the sight the most erotic he'd ever seen, until the pleasure became too much and his head fell back.

He was close. Too close. He gripped her shoulders, pulling her off him, kicking off the sweats and briefs. Carefully he pushed her to the pillow, stripping her shorts and panties down her legs.

And he stood there and looked his fill, wishing he had a better word than "beautiful." Bracing one knee on the mattress next to her hip, he drew a line from the hollow of her throat, down her chest, between her breasts to her stomach, feeling it quiver. Watching the goose bumps spread across her flesh. Watching her arch expectantly when he paused.

"Gideon." His name on her lips was both plea and

command. Her knee bent, falling to the bed, leaving her open to his hungry gaze. "Do it. Touch me."

He trailed his finger down, dipping his fingertip into glistening . . . perfection. She cried out, her back and hips coming off the bed as if he'd shocked her.

He'd known she'd be this responsive. Somehow he'd known.

He explored slowly, deliberately, earning more curses and pleas. When he slipped his finger inside her she writhed helplessly. "Please, please, please," she chanted in a whisper. Impatient, her arm flung backward, blindly searching the nightstand for the strip of condoms. When she had them in her hand, she shoved them into his. "I need you. Now."

He didn't want to stop touching her. Fascinated with the way her body was moving, he withdrew his finger and added a second.

With a snarl she grabbed the strip of condoms from his hand and ripped one off herself. She fumbled the packet, cursing again. She finally ripped it open and, with an upward glance that promised retribution, she lifted up on her elbow and managed to slide the condom down his length, stroking him as she'd done before.

He closed his eyes, letting himself steep in the sensation. It had been so long since anyone had touched him like this. *Like this?* Maybe never.

"Please," she said, so quietly he nearly missed it. Opening his eyes, he saw she was on her back, her arms open. "Now, Gideon."

He pulled his fingers from her and brought them to his mouth. His tongue gathered up the flavor that was all her. "Next time I want to taste you."

"Next time you can do whatever you want. This time I need you down here."

He moved between her thighs, sliding down so that he could suck on her pretty breasts. Her fingers were in his hair again, her head thrown back, her hips pressing against his chest in a rhythm that was slowly driving him insane.

He gave each of her nipples a lick before bracing his hands beside her head, lifting his body so that he hovered at her entrance. "Look at me," he demanded.

Her eyes opened and his chest squeezed so hard that it almost hurt. There was hunger in her gaze, but also trust. They mixed with the yearning that had been there before and he knew that, whatever happened between them, he'd never forget the way she was looking at him now.

"Tell me you want this," he ground out, needing to hear her say it once more.

Her hands skated down his back, gripping his ass. "I want this. I want you."

He let go of his control and slid inside her, groaning at how amazing she felt around him. Tight, wet heat. Shuddering, he dropped his face to her neck. "God."

"Yes," she whispered. "So good, Gideon. I can feel you . . . throbbing inside me."

Her words were like an electric shock. "Fuck," he growled, the rest of his words nowhere to be found. He began to move, pushing up so that he could see her face.

Her eyes were still open, still hungry. Watching him. She licked her lips and dug her fingers into his glutes, meeting him thrust for thrust as their eyes locked in a way that was more than simple sex.

He'd known she'd be perfect. But she was better than his wildest imagining. Tighter, hotter. Like she'd been made for him. *For me. No one else.*

Mine. She's mine. It might be a foolish thought, but he wasn't dismissing it because this was the best he'd ever felt. Ever.

This was pure pleasure. But it was also comfort and affirmation. That this thing between them was very, very right.

Her legs wound around his, holding him to her, drawing him impossibly deeper, and his train of thought jumped its rails. He began to thrust harder. Faster. He hooked his hands under and around her shoulders, trying to pull her closer. And still she watched him, her gaze never wavering, her hair spread on the pillow, golden in the low light.

"More," she mouthed, and he lost the last of his control.

He pounded into her, his mind wiped of everything but how she made him feel. She made him *feel*. She made him alive. "Come," he hissed. "Come for me. Now."

Throwing back her head on a fractured cry, her eyes closed as she went over, her wet heat spasming around him, pulling him with her.

Burying his face in her hair, he followed on the most powerful release he'd ever experienced, the shout in his throat completely silent.

Boneless, he collapsed, his lungs unable to take in enough air. Gradually he became aware of the scent of almond cookies. Her hair. And gentle fingers stroking up and down his back. He pushed up on his elbows to find her face relaxed like he hadn't yet seen it. Eyes closed. Lips smiling. She looked . . . serene. Blissed out. Well loved.

He kissed her forehead, trying to think of something to say, but no words would come. Her eyes opened and he couldn't look away.

"Don't go yet," she whispered.

"Okay."

Her hands continued to stroke his back and he wished they could stay like this forever. But he had to deal with the condom, so he reluctantly pulled out of her. He kissed her mouth softly. "I'll be right back."

When he rounded the corner after leaving the bathroom, she was exactly where he'd left her. Watching him with a smile that made all the pieces of his heart come together.

He climbed under the sheets, holding his arm out. She rolled over, her head on his chest, her hand over the tattoo on his chest.

And he realized he hadn't seen her tattoo yet. He curved his arm around her, bringing her even closer. "You never showed me your tattoo."

She laughed. "Tomorrow, okay?"

"Okay." He twisted, reaching for the light switch, plunging the room into darkness.

She sighed, a sweet sound. "Thank you, Gideon."

He kissed the top of her head. "It was my pleasure. Really."

She laughed again, sleepily. "Good. Sleep now. I set an alarm for us to go to the bus station."

The bus station. *Right.* The reason they were here. He held her a little tighter, hoping the morning would bring them answers.

REDDING, CALIFORNIA
SUNDAY, FEBRUARY 19, 2:30 A.M.

He turned into the hotel's parking lot, holding his breath, then letting it out on a rush when he saw the Fed's black Toyota exactly where it had been before. He pulled into the adjacent parking slot and got out of his car, relieved to find the Toyota's engine cold to the touch and frost spreading over the windshield. The car hadn't been moved. Both the Fed and Daisy were still in the hotel, the light still out in their second-floor room.

What they were doing at the moment . . . he didn't want to think about.

Earlier, he'd seen the Fed standing in front of the window, his head against the glass, staring outside. At first he'd been afraid, worried that the Fed had seen him. He'd had his gun in his hand, aiming for the man in the window, when he'd glimpsed Daisy coming up behind him, sliding her arms around the man's waist. They'd stood that way for some time, and then they'd both disappeared from the window. They hadn't seen him at all.

So he'd put his gun away, feeling unsettled and angry because the relationship between the two was obviously more than bodyguard and victim.

But he'd also been feeling hungry. And cold. And needing to use a restroom somewhere. So he'd left the hotel, for just a little while. Long enough to grab a bite from a twenty-four-hour McDonald's drive-through and run into Walmart for a blanket, some thermal socks, and a few snacks.

And a tracker. He'd been surprised to find one there, but he'd snatched it up and put it in his cart. He didn't delude himself into believing that the tracker was anywhere near the top of the line, but it should suit his purposes. He didn't want to fall asleep and miss the Fed and Daisy's departure to whatever had brought them to Redding.

Walking between his car and the Fed's, he crouched and hid the device in the Toyota's wheel well, frowning a little. He doubted the adhesive holding the tracker to the metal would last long, but he didn't need it to. He just needed it to stick there until morning.

Climbing back into his car, he moved to the far side of the lot where he could still see the Fed's car, but where they wouldn't notice him. He downloaded the tracking app to his phone, wincing because he'd likely just overshot the limits of his data plan, but he couldn't worry about that now. He was pleased to see the blinking dot on the app's map, exactly where it should be—exactly where the Toyota was. Then he pulled the blanket from its package, put his seat back, and fell asleep.

EIGHTEEN

Daisy woke slowly, reaching for Gideon, but the bed was empty, the sheets cool to the touch. The first time she'd woken had been at her normal four A.M. to find that they'd shifted in sleep. She no longer lay with her head on his chest, but they'd been on their sides, him spooned behind her, his arm around her. Protecting her even in sleep.

Or claiming her. Either was completely acceptable, she thought, stretching her very well-used muscles. Remembering the way he'd held her. The way they'd come together.

Daisy wasn't inexperienced, but she hadn't been with that many men. A few at college when she was able to ditch a class and meet up somewhere close. Jacob had been her bodyguard back then, hers and Taylor's, accompanying them to their classes. He sat with Taylor in hers, though, giving Daisy a few free hours a week.

She'd made good use of them.

There'd been a few men in Europe, but she'd been picky. And always safe. She was grateful for every one of those meager experiences because they'd enabled her to pleasure Gideon last night. And she *had* pleasured him. She could still feel the resulting twinges and she was grateful for every one of them, too.

He was here. She could hear the soft rumble of his

voice in the sitting room and it settled her, down deep where she shoved all the chaos. Right now there was a lot of chaos.

Trish was dead and her killer might have killed others. *He'd have killed me, too.* Her stomach gave a sick twist every time the thought entered her mind. She'd only gotten away because her father had made her into a soldier. The skills she'd so resented being forced to learn had saved her life.

Thank you, Dad.

She reached for her phone to check the time. Seven thirty. Less than twelve hours before her father arrived in California. *Because I said I needed him.* That Frederick Dawson loved her wasn't in doubt. She needed to make things right with him. Except she wasn't sure where to start. *I'll figure it out later, once we're done at the bus station.*

The sun was up and her stomach was growling. She needed coffee desperately. She was usually on her fourth cup by this time of the morning.

Swinging her legs to the floor, she checked her texts and blinked. There were a lot of texts. Most asking how she was doing. Some were from her and Trish's mutual friends, asking if it was true. If Trish was really dead.

Daisy shoved away the memory of Trish's battered and bloody body. Her eyes staring sightlessly at the ceiling. The bruises around her throat.

Yes. Trish was really dead. But Daisy didn't answer those texts. She wasn't in the frame of mind to deal with their friends yet. There was a text from her father, saying all of his flights appeared to be on time. And telling her that he loved her.

She swallowed hard at that one, not even hesitating before texting back. *Love you too.* Because she did. Nothing had changed that. Nothing could.

The final text was from Sasha, sent just a few

minutes before, probably the buzz that had woken her up. *Checking on you. Everything ok?*

Not really, she texted back. *But it will be, right? How are you?*

Sasha's reply was immediate. *Couldn't sleep. Went to office to do paperwork. Needed to be busy.*

Daisy sighed. Poor Sasha. She was grieving Trish on a whole other level. *I get that.*

The dot-dot-dot bubble appeared and hung there, indicating that Sasha was typing a long reply, but when the answer appeared it was quite short. *Get busy w/G.* And was followed by a gif of a man winking exaggeratedly.

Daisy wondered what Sasha had really typed and deleted but let it go. *Yes ma'am,* she texted back, then smiled when Sasha's reply was about fifty question marks. That would at least give Sasha gossip material when she next saw Irina and Karl.

She got out of bed, brushed her teeth, and went in search of Gideon, but when she approached the door to the outer sitting room she heard two voices—Gideon's and a woman's. Daisy assumed he was talking on the phone but cracked the door to be sure before she barged in there stark naked.

Sure enough, he sat on the sofa with his back to her, hunched over his laptop, which sat on a coffee table. His phone was next to his laptop, on speaker.

"—Redding bus station," Gideon was saying. "But I doubt you called for an update on my plans for the morning. Especially since I sent them to you in an e-mail already."

"No," the woman admitted. Gideon's boss, Daisy assumed, trying to remember if Gideon had ever said her name. "We got hits when we ran the search you requested."

What search?

Gideon's back stiffened. "How many?"

"So far, three," the woman's voice said. "There is an

open investigation on these three. It's being led out of the Seattle field office."

Gideon's shoulders sagged. "Three," he said, sounding defeated. "Including Trish Hart?"

Daisy opened the door a little wider. She should make herself known, but this involved Trish and she needed to know.

"No," the woman said softly. "Three additional. All were strangled, two were found with bleach-cleaned butcher knives in the dish drainer. All had letters carved into their skin. One had an 'EY,' one an 'N,' one had a 'D.'"

"Like Trish Hart," Gideon said grimly.

Daisy gasped. Letters? Carved into her skin? Trish had *letters* carved into her *body*? She thought about all the blood, how it had covered Trish's stomach. Which meant she'd been carved up while she was still alive, she realized.

Gideon twisted around, his eyes widening in dismay when he saw her standing there. "Shit," he muttered. "I have to go now," he said to the woman on the phone. "I'll call you when I'm done at the bus station."

Ending the call, he rose, coming around the sofa to take her hands in his. "I'm sorry," he said. "I'm sorry you heard that. I'm so sorry, Daisy."

His face was blurry when she looked up at him, clearing when she blinked, only to grow blurry again. "He carved her up?" she asked, her voice breaking.

Gideon's eyes closed. "Yes." He drew her close and wrapped his arms around her and she realized she was shivering.

"When she was still alive?" she asked in a small voice.

"Yes," he said again. "I'm so sorry, Daisy. I should have made sure you were still asleep."

She wished he had, but not really. "I needed to know."

"No, baby. You didn't." He let her go long enough to pick up her phone from the carpet. She didn't remember dropping it. Then he was guiding her back into the bedroom. He sat on the bed, his back to the headboard, and pulled her into his lap, holding her as her tears started anew.

"Did he . . ." She clutched at his T-shirt, barely able to breathe, wondering how she hadn't thought to ask this question the night before. *You were in shock.* She felt like she was again. "Did he rape her, too?"

"We don't know. The coroner is supposed to start the autopsy this afternoon."

God. Trish. Her jaw clenched as a wave of fury layered over the shock. "I want to kill him, Gideon," she hissed fiercely.

"I know, baby. I know. I wanted to just for putting his hands on you. Now . . ."

"He's killed four women. Maybe five if he got Eileen, too. So far."

"Yes." Because his gut was telling him that Eileen was dead. He kissed Daisy's forehead. "I know this is hard, but try not to visualize what happened."

She huffed bitterly, not sure how *not* to visualize it. "I'm trying. But . . ." She closed her eyes. "She died all alone. Scared and in pain and all alone."

"I know." He gathered her closer. "Visualize him behind bars. Scared and alone."

She pressed her ear to his chest, hearing the steady beat of his heart. Trying to let it calm her. But her anger was a live thing. She wasn't practiced at handling it. Her skin bristled from it. "And in pain?"

"Yes. If that's what you need to do. It's how I survived after I found Mercy. Pictured the man who'd hurt her in great pain."

She wiped at her eyes, sore from crying. "Were you inflicting the pain?"

"Oh, yes," he said, very quietly. Very earnestly.

She nodded then, picturing exactly that. It helped a little, but it still hurt. *So much, Trish.* But she was also so very angry. *Use it. Channel it. And when you find him, end him.*

Visualizing him behind bars? *To hell with that.* When she got the chance, she was going to kill the bastard. She drew a breath, finding a measure of peace in her resolution. "All right. Let's get breakfast and go to the bus station."

He drew back, studying her face, wiping her cheeks with gentle fingers. His frown was troubled. "Daisy?"

She met his gaze head-on, lifting her chin. "Yes?"

"I don't want to lose you. Don't do anything that puts you in his sights. Please."

"I'm already in his sights. Look, I won't take any unnecessary chances. How's that?"

He sighed wearily. "That's the best I'm going to get, isn't it?"

"Probably." She narrowed her eyes at him. "Short of locking me away for my own protection, anyway."

His surprise was genuine. As was the hurt in his eyes that she would suggest it. "I would never do that to you. We both know what it means to be confined."

Her heart eased, just a little. Just enough for her to breathe. "Thank you."

He rested his cheek on the top of her head. "I had other plans for this morning, but it's getting late. The bus station opens at nine."

REDDING, CALIFORNIA
SUNDAY, FEBRUARY 19, 9:00 A.M.

Daisy gripped Gideon's hand when his step faltered in front of the Redding Greyhound bus station. "Come on," she urged softly. "You need to know."

"I know. But I keep thinking, what if they never saw her?"

His tension was so palpable that Brutus whimpered inside her bag. Daisy gave her a pet with one hand while tightening her hold on Gideon with the other. "Then we'll try towns within a hundred-mile radius of Mt. Shasta. But first we'll show them the photos of the other escapees. You and Mercy might be the only ones to have made it to this bus station, Gideon. But there are other stations and other ways out of the area. The FBI will keep looking. You'll keep looking. *We'll* keep looking. I promise."

"I know. But thank you." He squeezed her hand. "Really."

She smiled up at him, encouragingly, she hoped. "You're welcome."

He let go of her hand and slid his arm around her waist, tugging her close. "Let's do this."

An older man sat behind the Plexiglas ticket counter, reading a paperback novel. He looked up as they approached, then straightened his spine, his eyes growing sharper.

Because Gideon walked like exactly what he was—a career cop. Didn't really matter which badge he carried. "Excuse me, sir. We'd like to ask you some questions."

We. That felt . . . nice.

The man pushed his glasses up his nose. "You can ask." His tone clearly said that he might choose not to answer.

"I'm Special Agent Gideon Reynolds," Gideon said, pulling out his badge.

"With the FBI," the man said mildly. "Ask your questions, Special Agent Reynolds."

Gideon slid a copy of the aged photo of Eileen through the slot in the Plexiglas. "I'm looking for this woman. She's missing."

The man tilted his head, squinting now at the photo while Daisy held her breath.

After what seemed like an eternity, the man slowly nodded. "Yes. I think so. She didn't look exactly like this, but . . . the eyes. Same eyes." He slid the photo back to Gideon. "Would have recognized her sooner if you'd added bruises on her face and a black eye." He tapped his right eye. "This one."

Gideon flinched. "She was bruised?" he asked, his voice harsh and hurt.

The man nodded, again slowly. "You might also add on the necklace she was wearing."

"What kind of necklace?" Daisy asked.

The man gave her a long measuring look, almost as if gauging her trustworthiness. "A locket," he finally said.

Daisy released the breath she'd been holding. "Did you notice the chain?"

"Hard not to. It was thick. Like those rappers wear."

"Heavy, like a security chain? On a door?" Daisy asked.

"Yeah. About."

Beside her, Gideon tensed. "Do you remember where she went?"

The man gave Gideon the same appraising look. "Why do you want to know?"

Gideon swallowed. "Because she's missing and I'm afraid she's met with foul play. You can make a copy of my badge if you like. My boss will confirm I'm who I say I am."

"I think I will."

"Ask for Special Agent in Charge Tara Molina. I know she's in because I talked to her earlier this morning."

They stood there waiting while the man behind the Plexiglas made his call, inquiring about Gideon to his boss, his head bobbing occasionally as he talked. Finally, he hung up and inclined his head to Gideon.

"She speaks well of you. Says I can be confident that you'll handle whatever I tell you with 'integrity and discretion.'" He folded his hands. "She bought a ticket to Portland. One way. This was about three months ago."

"Oh." Gideon grasped Daisy's hand. "Portland."

"Was she alone, sir?" Daisy asked.

"No. She was with a fella from . . ." He scratched his head. "You got a few minutes?"

"We have as long as you need," Daisy said firmly.

They waited again as the man searched his computer. It took him ten minutes to find what he was looking for, mainly because he had to break twice to sell actual tickets to actual customers.

"Got it," he announced. He printed something up, then slid it under the Plexiglas to Gideon. "This is the guy that purchased her ticket. His credit card, anyway."

"Gale Danton," Gideon read. "How do you remember him so clearly?"

One side of the man's mouth lifted. "The card belongs to a man who lives outside Macdoel, which is barely a dot on the map."

Daisy found Macdoel on her map app. "Northwest of here, on Highway 97." She glanced up at Gideon. "Within view of Mt. Shasta."

Gideon's chest rose and fell, the only indication he'd felt the impact of her words. "And you remember this man, why?" he asked.

"Because he bought her a ticket with his credit card and she was arguing with him. Said he'd already been too nice, giving her a ride. That she didn't want to owe him money."

Gideon nodded, as if this made perfect sense. "She wouldn't want to borrow from anyone. Why did he? Give her a ride and buy her a ticket?"

"I think he was just a genuinely nice guy," the old man said. "He was worried about her. Gave her his phone number and some cash. Told her to take her time paying it back. And if she was forced to do anything she didn't want to do, that she should call him and he'd help her."

Gideon frowned. "How old was he?"

"My age." He sighed. "I was worried, too. Like maybe he was setting her up to meet a pimp or something. I shut down my register and took a break. Just happened to sit behind them, so's I could hear what they said. The guy told her that his daughter had run away once and a stranger had helped her get home. He was paying it forward."

Gideon was holding the paper with the man's credit card information in a white-knuckled grip. "Did she get on the bus for Portland?"

"She did. She almost went south to Sacramento, but she got heads."

Gideon had gone silent, so Daisy asked, "Tails would have been Sac?"

"Exactly. I never saw *her* again."

His emphasis on "her" was startling. "Did the nice man come back? Mr. Danton?"

"No. Not him."

Daisy had a terrible sense of dread. "Was it a man with an eye patch?"

The old man nodded. Just once.

Daisy felt Gideon tense once again. She put her arm around his waist and leaned into him, more to hold him up. "Did you tell him where she went?" she asked.

"No. I got a bad vibe. He was . . . menacing. I remembered the girl's bruises and thought maybe he'd been the one to put them there."

"He was," Gideon said grimly. "You did the right thing. Thank you."

"Thank you so very much," Daisy echoed.

"I hope you find her," the man said.

"Us too," Daisy said, but she didn't have much hope. Neither did Gideon, not after seeing what Trish's killer had done to her.

She waited until they were back in Gideon's car before turning to him. "Where to next? If she still had the locket when she arrived that morning, it's likely that she was still wearing it when she got on the bus. She probably didn't hock it here in Redding."

"Probably not." He started the car. "We're going to see Mr. Gale Danton."

"I thought as much. He might be able to tell us where she came from. Or at least where she was when he found her. That could dramatically reduce your search area for Eden."

He nodded. "Yes to all that. But he'll also know where she settled after arriving in Portland."

"How do you know?"

"Because Eileen borrowed money from him. She wouldn't have been able to rest until she'd paid it back. He would have received some communication from her, even if it was a money order or wired money."

Daisy didn't want to point out that he hadn't seen Eileen in seventeen years and that people did change. Talking to this guy was worth a shot and she could get behind it. "Money orders or wires we can trace. Excellent. Who are you calling?" she added when he punched a screen on his cell phone.

"My boss." He put the phone to his ear and waited, clearly not wanting her to hear the whole conversation.

Daisy couldn't begrudge this, given how upset she'd been at overhearing his last conversation with the woman. *Oh, Trish, I'm so sorry. Marked like that. Tortured like that.* She scooped Brutus from her bag and cuddled her under her chin. Turning to look out the window, she tried not to cry again, focusing instead on a man striding to a beige car parked at the far end of the lot.

He'd been one of the people to buy a bus ticket while they waited for the man behind the glass to find the record of Eileen's bus ticket purchase. Idly she wondered why he was leaving again. *Maybe he forgot something in his car.*

"It's Reynolds."

Gideon's voice brought her back and she turned from the window to watch his profile. This had been devastating for him, too. Seeing Trish. Wondering if his friend had undergone the same fate. Finding out she'd been battered and bruised when she'd arrived at the bus station.

"Yes," he said into the phone. "Thank you for vouching for me. He gave us some useful information." He told his boss what they'd learned. "Can you run a check on Gale Danton of Macdoel?" He listened for a few seconds. "Thank you, I appreciate it."

Ending the call, he leaned his head against the headrest. "Macdoel had a population of 133 in the last census."

"I know. I looked it up, too. Your boss is going to do a background check?"

He nodded. "I don't want to walk into an ambush. Especially if you're with me."

Daisy reached for his hand that gripped the parking brake like it was a lifeline. "Gideon." She kissed his knuckles. "I'm not going to ask if you're all right because you're clearly not. But what can I do to help you?"

"You're doing it." He brought her hand to his cheek and held it there. "Thank you for back there, at the ticket counter. I hope I didn't break your fingers."

"I'm tougher than I look."

He glanced over at her as he pulled out of the lot. "I know."

And that was one of the nicest compliments she'd ever received.

▌▌▌ REDDING, CALIFORNIA
▌▌▌ SUNDAY, FEBRUARY 19, 9:40 A.M.

Well, shit. At least he knew why they'd come to Redding. Searching for little Miriam, who'd insisted her name was Eileen.

I knew that locket was important. Dammit.

He'd stood behind them in line at the ticket counter for as long as he'd dared, agreeing to buy a ticket to the next stop when the man behind the Plexiglas had asked if he could help him. He hadn't wanted to arouse suspicion.

It hadn't been a terribly expensive fare and well worth the price to hear what Reynolds was up to. The Fed was chasing that damn locket.

Chasing me.

Reynolds had to be stopped. And if that meant Daisy died with the Fed, he'd have to make himself okay with that. But he'd avoid that if he possibly could.

He found the town of Macdoel on his map app. *Excellent.* There was lots of open land in between here and there—and only one road to get there. And even *if* there were a decent cell phone signal, it would take forever for help to arrive. If the man survived.

If not, there was a helluva lot of land to hide a body. Or two, if he had to. He'd done it before.

And no witnessing bystanders to be loose ends, except for Daisy. It was perfect.

GRASS LAKE, CALIFORNIA
SUNDAY, FEBRUARY 19, 11:25 A.M.

Eileen might have come to Sacramento, but for the flip of a coin. The words kept circling in Gideon's mind. Had she searched for him? Hoped he'd help her?

Had she escaped the nightmare of Eden only to have fallen prey to another? *God. Please let her be alive somewhere. Please.*

"Gideon?" Daisy's voice broke into the turbulent stream of his thoughts.

He glanced away from the road, surprised to see a laptop resting on her knees. He hadn't even noticed her taking it out of its case. Of course, the sight of Brutus curled up in the open collar of her coat was no surprise at all.

"Yes? What's wrong?"

"Your phone is buzzing."

He hadn't noticed that, either. God. He had to get his head back in the game. He grabbed his phone from where it was charging, not taking the time to look at the caller ID. "Reynolds."

"This is Molina." His boss's voice was calm on the surface, but there was an undercurrent of urgency that immediately sharpened Gideon's focus. "I ran a check on your Mr. Gale Danton of Macdoel, California."

"And?" he prompted when she let the answer dangle.

"He has no criminal record. He appears to be exactly as he described himself—a man whose daughter once ran away and was returned by strangers. He filed a missing-person report on his sixteen-year-old daughter nine years ago. She returned home by bus about three weeks later. She was unhurt, but had been helped by 'kind strangers.' That's all the police report said."

"Good to know. Thank you, ma'am." He was about to end the call when she cleared her throat. "Is there more?"

"Yes. I had Agent Schumacher run a search on crime scenes where a bleached knife was found. So far she's come up with three additional victims, bringing the total to six—seven including Miss Hart. The three she found did not have letters carved into their bodies, though. So far, they're the earliest victims, so perhaps he hadn't started carving them yet."

"I see." Gideon glanced at Daisy, who was watching him with careful eyes. She'd nearly fallen apart when he'd told her about the marks on Trish's skin. He did not want to hurt her any further. "I'm driving right now. Is it possible for you to e-mail me the information?"

"I already did. I figured you'd be driving. I wanted to let you know that these victims were also women between the ages of twenty and thirty-five."

"And like Trish," he murmured. "And Eileen." *And Daisy, if she hadn't gotten away.*

"And Miss Dawson, had she not escaped," she said, echoing his thoughts. "So far we know of seven victims, including Miss Dawson's friend, Miss Hart. There could be more who have not been found, like Eileen. These additional three have been added to the open investigation. So far, we've found no reports of any women who've gotten away other than Miss Dawson. They came from different cities, disappearing from various places—work, home, bars. One was last seen in the park walking her dog. All were found in their homes with the bleached knife in the drainer. All lived alone. Half had letters carved into their torsos and all had a bleached knife at the crime scene, but there were no other obvious similarities between the victims."

"Which cities?"

"So far we have Seattle, Chicago, Miami, and then some small towns like Niagara Falls, New York; Carlisle, Pennsylvania; and Ellicott City, Maryland."

"Over how much time?"

"Five years so far. They have different body types, different hair color, different ethnicities. The bleached knife left in the dish drainer was the only commonality between all seven."

"'SY,' 'EY,' 'N,' and 'D,'" Gideon murmured.

Beside him, Daisy blinked hard. "Sydney?"

"Yes," Molina said. "That's what we've assumed."

Gideon pulled the phone away, glancing over to find Daisy looking resolutely grim. "Do you know anyone named Sydney, Daisy?"

She shook her head. "Sorry."

"It's okay," he assured her, then returned his attention to his boss. "We got nothing on Sydney."

"It was too much to hope for, I suppose." Molina sighed. "We have a multistate serial on our hands. I'm joining our field office with Seattle's open investigation. I'd like you on the team. When can you come back?"

Gideon frowned, torn. He didn't want to leave Daisy unprotected. "Daisy still needs protection. She won't be safe until the man who's already murdered seven women is caught. But the Sokolovs will pick up guard duty for now, I'm sure." Plus her father was coming to town. Gideon was certain that Dawson wouldn't let Daisy out of his sight. "I'll be back in the office first thing tomorrow. I'll need to go to Portland ASAP. Eileen is still our best lead, and Portland was her last known address."

"I'll ask my clerk to book your flight. Agent Schumacher will go with you. Tomorrow afternoon?"

He'd worked with Joslyn Schumacher on cases in the past. She was a solid agent. "Thank you. Tomorrow will be fine."

"This is interstate now, so the FBI will lead the investigation. But you'll be teaming up with Detectives Rhee and Sokolov."

"Yes, ma'am. I'll be in your office first thing in the morning. I'll be back in the city by this evening, so I can come in earlier if you need—" He swallowed a surprised grunt as the car hit ice on the road and fishtailed.

"Agent Reynolds?" Molina asked sharply. "Gideon?"

He got the car back under control, but his pulse was pounding in his head. "Sorry. It's icy here. I thought my car could handle it without chains, but I should have put them on." They were actually lucky the road was still as passable as it was this far into the mountains. Hell, he was lucky to have a signal at all. "I need both hands for this."

"Then go, but call me when you finish with Mr. Danton."

"Will do." He ended the call and pocketed his phone with a sigh. "Dammit."

"You have to go back?" Daisy asked.

"By tomorrow. They've found more victims."

She was quiet for a long moment. "I figured they would."

"I'll make sure you're protected."

She smoothed her palm over his knee. "I figured you would."

He covered her hand with his. Her skin was cold. "We'll find him."

She only nodded. "How many more, Gideon?"

He didn't pretend to misunderstand. "Three more, in addition to the three we knew about this morning from the open investigation. Adding Trish and Eileen makes eight altogether."

She shuddered out a horrified breath. "Where were they found?"

"Why?"

"Because I found three more while you were driving."

"Through newspaper articles?"

"Through a true crime forum, actually. Conspiracy theorists are buzzing about them. I'm hoping they're part of the eight."

He told her the names of the cities and towns that Molina had mentioned. "Are they the ones you found?"

She nodded. "Yes, thank goodness. The victims in the articles were found in Niagara Falls; Carlisle, Pennsylvania; and Miami. It makes no sense. Big cities and small towns, all over the country. There doesn't seem to be any pattern."

He frowned. "There *is* a pattern. There has to be. We just haven't found it yet."

"We will," she murmured. "We have to."

He turned the data over in his mind. "Clearly this is someone with the means to travel. Or it's his job."

"A truck driver maybe?"

Gideon nodded. "It would make sense."

She closed her laptop and turned in her seat, one hand cradling Brutus. "So this guy Danton. Your boss says he's on the up-and-up?"

"She couldn't find anything on him. Which doesn't necessarily mean he's good. You'll still stay with me, and if I say run, you take the car and go."

"Okay."

He glanced at her, expecting to see her jaw hardened in opposition to his command. But she simply sat there, petting the dog. "You will?"

"You'll be smarter about protecting yourself if you're not worrying about me."

"That's true. We're nearly there." He swallowed hard, acknowledging the eels that were slithering through his gut. What if this guy knew nothing? Worse, what if he was really some kind of degenerate who'd taken advantage of Eileen?

Her hand closed around his arm. "If he doesn't know where Eileen went after she got off the bus in Portland, you'll find another way to trace her steps, okay?"

"Okay."

MACDOEL, CALIFORNIA
SUNDAY, FEBRUARY 19, 11:45 A.M.

Gale Danton's home was a plain, single-story structure with an oversized couch facing a big picture window that looked out onto his view of the mountains. This was where he seated the Fed and Daisy.

Which was very lucky because it meant their car was unattended.

He lugged the two jugs of bleach to the Fed's car and pried open the gas cap cover. He had experience with this maneuver, having stopped several of his guests on the side of the road this way. Plus, bleach was a staple.

One never knew when one would have to clean up the scene of a nasty altercation. He had experience with that, too.

He thought of the one time he'd been disrupted by a guest's angry boyfriend, just as he was forcing the woman into the trunk of his car. He'd had to shoot the man, right there in the deserted parking lot behind the restaurant where the woman had worked. There had been a lot of blood that he'd needed to clean up after disposing of the man's body.

And the guy had been heavy! That had not been an easy evening. He'd needed to run to the all-night grocery and buy bleach to decontaminate the scene. Ever since then, he'd carried bleach with him wherever he went. Always in a laundry basket along with a box of fabric softener sheets, just in case someone asked.

It took him only a few seconds to pour the bleach into Reynolds's gas tank, first one bottle, then the other, because he'd fitted the mouths of the jugs with vortex breakers. No swirl, no wait. It was a trick he'd picked up watching pit crews on race day.

He then slunk back down the driveway to his car and drove for fifteen minutes before stopping. He'd wait here. The Fed's sedan wouldn't make it more than fifteen or twenty minutes before his engine locked up.

Once that happened, he'd have nowhere to go. He'd be a sitting duck.

He checked his gun, made sure there was a bullet chambered. All set.

All he had to do was wait.

MACDOEL, CALIFORNIA
SUNDAY, FEBRUARY 19, 11:45 A.M.

"You have quite a view," Daisy murmured, staring out Gale Danton's big picture window at the mountains in the distance.

"Thank you." He handed her a mug of steaming coffee. "This should warm you up."

Daisy wrapped her hands around the mug, nearly sighing at the heat seeping into her palms. It wasn't the weather that had her hands so cold, even though the temperatures had dropped as they'd made their way north through the mountains. It was fear, plain and simple. She was terrified that Gideon would be disappointed.

And that they'd lose the trail that connected them to Eileen's killer.

And Trish's. But she couldn't let herself dwell on that right now. She could fall apart later. Right now she needed to focus on Gideon, who sat next to her on a flannel sofa, his back ramrod straight. She let her body lean into his, just enough that he remembered he wasn't alone.

"So." Danton sat in a chair kitty-corner to the sofa. He was a tall, thin man with a smile that seemed to cover his whole face. He'd shaken her hand and immediately declared that her hands were like blocks of ice. After which he'd leaped into host mode, leaving them alone in his living room.

He hadn't asked for ID. Hadn't asked them anything other than if they wanted coffee. Tilting his gray head, he studied Gideon. "How can I help you, Agent Reynolds?"

Oh, I hope you can, Daisy thought.

"Thank you for welcoming us into your home," Gideon said a little stiffly. Because he was nervous. Because this was important. "I'm here because I'm a friend of Eileen's."

If Daisy had thought Danton would look surprised, she'd been wrong.

"So you're *that* Gideon," he said with a sad smile.

Gideon stared at him. "She mentioned me?"

Danton nodded. "Oh, yes. She was hoping to find you. Someday, anyway. She called you by a different last name."

"Terrill," Gideon murmured. "That was my mother's husband's last name."

"Yes, that was it. She was aware that you'd probably changed your name. She still hoped to find you. I take it that she didn't."

Gideon shook his head, then swallowed audibly. "She's missing."

Danton abruptly frowned. "What do you mean, missing?"

"She . . ." Gideon pursed his lips and started again. "Her locket was found a few days ago. By Miss Dawson."

Daisy looked up at him and he nodded slightly. She turned to Danton. "I was attacked Thursday night."

"Oh my!" Danton leaned forward. "Are you all right?"

"Yes, thank you. I was able to get away, but I grabbed at the man's throat. I didn't realize I was holding a locket in my hand until I was safe."

Danton frowned again. "Eileen's locket? No way. That chain would never break." His expression became pained. "It was welded on her. She had a burn mark on the back of her neck."

"She'd replaced the chain at some point," Daisy said. "Or someone did it for her."

Danton paled. "You suspect foul play?"

"It's possible," Daisy said. "The night after I was attacked, the man attacked a friend of mine." She closed her eyes for a moment.

"Daisy's friend was murdered sometime on Friday night," Gideon said softly, keeping her from having to say it aloud.

She opened her eyes when Danton made a small choking sound. His eyes had filled with tears. "Oh, Miss Dawson, I'm so very sorry. You think the same person hurt Eileen?"

"It's possible," Daisy said. "We hope she's still alive."

"But you don't think so," Danton murmured.

"No, sir," Gideon told him. "We don't. I didn't know Eileen had gotten away from our community. I've been trying to find it for seventeen years."

"Since you got out." He wiped at his eyes unashamedly. "She wasn't sure if you'd survived. The rumor was that you'd died. Or that you'd been exiled to the wilderness, which was the same thing."

"Do you know where the community is?" Gideon asked, going so still that Daisy knew he was holding his breath.

"No, son, I surely don't. I asked, but she wouldn't tell me. She was terrified I'd make her go back."

Gideon's shoulders sagged, just a little. Only recognizable if one was looking. And Daisy was looking.

"Can you tell us how you met Eileen?" she asked. "All we know is that you bought her a bus ticket in Redding, for Portland."

"I met her at the beginning of November. She was staggering along next to the road. We'd already had some snow and I barely saw her head as I went by. She'd heard me coming and was trying to hide. I only saw her because I was driving slow, searching for a lost cow. One of my pregnant ones. I stopped and Eileen was . . . so scared. And half-dead."

Daisy held Gideon's hand. "The man at the bus station said she was bruised," she said. "Were there other injuries?"

Danton swallowed, then nodded. "She was bleeding." Then he clenched his jaw.

"She had . . . female injuries," Daisy said gently.

Danton jerked another nod. "Yeah. That. I wanted to take her to the hospital. Wanted them to do one of those kits. You know," he said helplessly.

Daisy kept her voice gentle, both for Danton and for Gideon. "A rape kit?"

Danton nodded again, miserably. "Yeah. One of them." He met Gideon's pained gaze. "I'm sorry. I know you don't want to hear this."

"But I need to know," Gideon said, almost soundlessly. "I'm sorry to ask you to tell it. But what did you do?"

"My daughter came over. Took care of her. She's a vet, my daughter. Not an army vet. A veterinarian." He rubbed the back of his neck. "She told Eileen that she needed to go to the ER. The closest clinic's in Yreka, and that's a good hour away when the weather's good. Eileen wouldn't go. She was afraid that they'd call her husband. We tried to tell her that there was no way they'd do that when they saw what had been done to her, but she became hysterical, so . . ." He shrugged. "My Sammie stitched her up as best she could. By the time the man at the bus station saw her, Eileen had been with us for two weeks. She was still so hurt." His sigh was wet, like he was holding back more tears. "Sammie stayed here with us for those two weeks, so Eileen wouldn't feel so alone. Or afraid. She was afraid of me at first." He looked a little ashamed at this admission.

"I hope you know that it wasn't personal," Daisy told him. "Not really."

"I know. I just hated the thought that she'd be afraid of me." He wiped his eyes with his shirtsleeve. "How long has she been missing?"

"We don't know," Gideon said. "We were hoping you'd communicated with her after she arrived in Portland."

"I did. But after a month she stopped calling and I didn't get any more letters."

"But you heard her voice? You know it was her?" Daisy asked.

"I did. She called to tell me she'd gotten a job and found a place to live. It wasn't fancy, but it was clean and she felt safe. She rented a room at a boardinghouse and waited tables. Cash only. Sammie visited her once, up there in Portland. Just dropped in and surprised her."

"How did Eileen react to that?"

"Sammie said she was upset at first. She was afraid Sammie had been followed, but my girl is smart. Sammie told Eileen to settle down, that she needed to check the stitches she'd put in, to make sure Eileen wasn't getting an infection. She came home saying that Eileen seemed 'okay.' Whatever that means."

"So your daughter knows where she lives? And works?" Gideon asked, a sliver of hope in his voice.

"She does." Danton's eyes narrowed. "She'll take you there."

"I'm not going to hurt Eileen," Gideon protested.

"I know, son. I wouldn't have told you had I thought you were the type. But you're also a lawman, and I don't want Eileen getting into trouble for anything she's done to simply survive. So Sammie will take you."

"I'm flying into Portland from Sacramento tomorrow," Gideon told him. "I have to get Daisy home tonight."

"That's fine. Sammie can meet you at the airport."

"Let her, Gideon," Daisy murmured. "You'd want the same in his place."

Gideon relaxed. "You're right. I would. Thank you, Mr. Danton. And I'll thank your daughter when I meet her. I'm glad Eileen had you to care for her."

"It was kind of you to take her in," Daisy added softly.

Another shrug. "I'm sure the bus station guy told you what I told Eileen when I dropped her off. That I was paying it forward because someone had helped my Sammie when she was a teenager and alone and a runaway. I know he was sitting behind me. I figured he was making sure Eileen wasn't being trifled with. You know."

"I know," Daisy murmured, "and that's exactly what he did say. But it was still kind of you. How did Eileen call you? Did she have a phone?"

"We bought her one, me and Sammie. One of those prepaid ones from Walmart. She and I stopped at the one in Redding before I took her to the bus station. She picked out a few necessities."

Daisy swallowed hard. "You are very kind, Mr. Danton. We appreciate it. Gideon appreciates it."

Gideon cleared his throat roughly. "I do. I truly do. Did . . . anyone come looking for her? Other than us?"

Danton shook his head warily. "Like who?"

Gideon showed him the photo of Ephraim Burton. "Him. He'd be a little older."

Danton studied the photo carefully. "This looks like it was ripped up once and put back together."

"It was," Gideon said. "It was found in Eileen's locket, ripped up."

"Her husband," Danton said flatly, his anger clearly close to the surface. "This is the one who beat her up?"

"Probably. He's dangerous." Gideon held up his hand when Danton tried to give the photo back. "I have more copies of it. Keep it, in case he comes by. Don't tell him anything and be careful. He went to the bus station asking about Eileen, but the man there didn't tell him anything. This man is violent."

"I will. I'll warn Sammie, too. Thank you, Gideon." He pulled a notepad and pen from an end-table drawer and wrote down three phone numbers. "The top one is my Sammie's cell. I'll tell her to expect a call from you. She can arrange a meeting place and time in Portland. The middle number is my cell phone. I got spotty coverage here, but the bottom number is the landline. I'm not here much during the day, but you can leave a message."

"Thank you," Gideon said, standing up and helping Daisy to her feet. "We'll let you get back to whatever you were doing. Thank you for the coffee, too."

"My pleasure," Danton said, walking them to the door. "Once you know for sure, can you tell me what's happened to Eileen? We didn't have her here with us for long, but we grew very fond of her."

"I will," Gideon promised, then drew a breath. "Either way."

NINETEEN

Why did the men move there?" Daisy asked, breaking the silence in the car. Neither of them had spoken since leaving Danton's house fifteen minutes earlier.

"What do you mean?"

"The men of Eden. I get why your mother ended up there. She was alone, trying to raise two kids and someone promised her a better life. But the men . . . did they grow up there? If not, what drew them there? It was a hard life. Lots of manual effort. No electricity. No sports on TV. Was it just the sex with multiple wives anytime they chose?"

"For some, that was enough," Gideon said seriously, because it was a very serious question. "Some were drawn by the whole back-to-basics concept."

She stared out the window thoughtfully. "This area isn't too different from where I lived on the ranch with Dad and my sisters. Remote. Rough terrain. Makes for a hard life."

"Where was your ranch?"

"West of Weaverville."

She was quiet then, so long that he glanced over to see her biting on her lower lip. "What?" he asked. "What are you thinking about?"

"That we went to the middle of nowhere to hide. I wonder if any of the people in your community did the same." She shifted in her seat to meet his eyes. "And if they did, what—or who—were they hiding from?"

"That's a damn good question. I've thought of that, but—" A loud rattle of the engine cut off what he'd been about to say, right about the same time he smelled—

"Is that bleach?" Daisy asked, her brow furrowing.

"Yes," Gideon said grimly, because the engine's rattle was growing louder. And now plumes of smoke were rising from the edges of the hood. "Shit."

They were only twenty minutes from Gale Danton's house. But that might as well have been in the middle of freaking nowhere because his car had been sabotaged, leaving them vulnerable. Very fucking vulnerable.

Gideon did a U-turn and pulled the car to the narrow shoulder facing back toward Macdoel. This way he could look at the engine and Daisy would have some protection from whoever had intended to stop them here. The drop-off was steep, but it could have been far worse. "If bullets start flying, slide down the hill there and keep your head down."

Daisy was sliding Brutus's bag over her shoulder. "What about you?"

"Just do it," he snapped, feeling true fear for the first time in a long time. If anything happened to him, Daisy would be . . . dead. Like Trish. And Eileen. And six other women.

He drew his weapon from its holster as he got out of the car and popped the hood. Smoke billowed from the engine, the stench of burned rubber and bleach enough to make his eyes tear. Someone had put that bleach in his gas tank while they'd been in Danton's house. Someone who'd wanted them to stop *here*.

And if it was Danton himself? No, the man couldn't have done it. He'd been in the house with them, within their sight except for the moments he'd stepped away to get their coffee. *Not long enough to dump anything into my gas tank.*

Didn't mean he didn't have someone else do it, though.

Gideon moved to the trunk to get his rifle. He needed to be ready. Just in case.

The shot registered as burning pain shot up his right arm into his shoulder. "Fuck," he bit out, grabbing the rifle, then rolling to the ground, off the road. He slid down the hill, where Daisy waited anxiously.

The hill was covered in snow. So now he was bleeding and wet. *Great.*

"You're hit," she said.

"Not badly." It wasn't quite a lie. It hurt like a bitch, but he'd had worse. He got the rifle into position, but it was awkward using his left hand. Because the fingers of his right hand were slippery with blood and . . . not moving. *That's not good. That's not good at all.*

It was then that he realized his handgun had slipped from his fingers. He'd lost his service weapon. *Fuck it.* He shifted the rifle to his left shoulder, using the embankment to prop up the barrel. But the angle was going to be wrong.

"Give it to me," Daisy commanded, then snatched the rifle away. Before he could blink, she was pushing her way back up the hill on her stomach, commando-style through the snow, her Brutus bag slung around to her back.

"Daisy!" He scrambled behind her, grabbing at her leg. "Do not do this!"

"You're hit," she said calmly. "I'm not. Let go of my leg, Gideon. I'm a good shot."

He remembered what she'd said about her father training her to shoot. He wasn't sure how far away their shooter was, much less how good she actually was.

A car roared by, spraying a volley of gunfire through the open passenger window.

Gideon held on to her leg tighter, pulling her down the hill, and she kicked at him, startling him enough that she was able to yank herself free. He grabbed her again, and she kicked at him again, harder this time, sending him sliding a few feet down the hillside, dragging her with him.

"I'm not going to dance in the fucking road, Gideon. For God's sake, let me go!"

Another shot came flying over their heads, this time from the far right. The shooter had turned around and was coming back for another attack.

Gideon let Daisy go, wiping the snow from the rocks so that he could get a decent grip, and started the rather daunting task of hauling himself up one-handed. He'd done this in training, but he hadn't been shot then. He tried clenching his right hand into a fist, but his fingers hung limply at his side. *Shit.*

He watched as she regained her position at the top of the hill, steadying herself on a small outcropping of rock so that she was just able to see over the edge, the rifle against her shoulder. "He's driving a beige car. I saw it in the bus station lot," she said.

Shit. Motherfucking shit. "I saw it following us last night, but it turned the other way when we exited at Redding."

"Well, he somehow found us," she said grimly, still holding the rifle in ready mode.

Gideon edged upward until he could finally see. The beige car was coming closer, slowing to a crawl as it weaved dangerously along the road. The driver wouldn't be able to see them from this angle as they were shielded by Gideon's car.

He could just see a handgun being held out of the open driver's-side window, but the person inside had ducked down—thus the dangerous weaving. "Are you waiting for something special to happen before you shoot him?" he asked with exaggerated patience. "Or maybe you're waiting for him to drive off the road and let the hill take care of him? Just give me the damn rifle already."

She didn't spare him a glance. "I want to get his gun out of his hand. Be quiet. You're distracting me."

"The gun," he muttered. "Out of his hand. You realize that only happens in movies?"

"I said, *be quiet,*" she hissed.

He glanced away from the approaching beige car to study Daisy's profile. She was truly beautiful, all ferocity and focus. She held the rifle like an extension of her own arm.

He contemplated grabbing the rifle, but there was no way he was going to be anything but awkward with his right arm useless and his feet slipping in the snow, and she was cool, collected. Ready.

So he bit his tongue and stayed quiet. But not still. Hiking up his knee, he drew his backup from his ankle holster. Not as powerful as his service weapon, but it would do. He hoped.

"Can you shoot with your left hand?" she asked, still calm.

"Not as well as with my right, but still proficient." Drawing his weapon, he aimed at the shooter's window as the beige car approached, hoping to get the man's head or upper body in his sight. But the man stayed down, somehow navigating the car so that it didn't hit his own as it passed by.

Gideon shifted, positioning his body, so that he'd get a view of the driver's-side window when the beige car cleared his Camry, but it was Daisy who pulled the trigger first.

He held his breath. And his mouth fell open. To his utter amazement the handgun was on the asphalt and blood dripped down the side of the car, which had turned sharply.

She pulled the trigger again and the windshield turned to opaque pebbles. She'd fired through the open window, hitting the windshield from the inside, the view through it completely blocked. Her third shot hit the back window, shattering it as Gideon watched the car for the moment the shooter tried to escape, but the man was still hunkered down.

She lowered the rifle to the tires and he added his own aim. Together they fired, each shooting the tires on the driver's side, back and front. Each hitting the tires, all four shots connecting.

"FBI!" Gideon shouted, barely hearing his own voice over the ringing in his ears. It had been a while since he'd fired a weapon without ear protection. "Get out of the car!"

He grabbed on to the tire of his own car and hauled himself up the hill and over the edge of the road, intending to approach the shooter in his car and drag him out of it. Instead he was gritting his teeth against a sudden spear of pain and he felt his body sway.

Get up. Dammit. He pushed himself to stand, his knees seriously wobbling. But it didn't matter because his demand was answered by the squeal of tires as the beige car sped away, heading toward Redding.

Daisy swung herself up onto the road, and scrambling to her feet, fired several more times at the retreating car. "Goddammit!" She turned to him, frustration all over her face. "I hit those tires. I know I did."

He breathed through the burning in his arm. "Runflats," he gritted out. "They're—"

"I know what they are," she spat. "Tires with reinforced sidewalls. He'll be able to drive for fifty miles on those things. At least he won't be able to see where he's going." Then her eyes widened as her gaze took him in. "Oh shit. Gideon. You said it wasn't bad."

He tried to smile, but only managed a grimace. "I've had worse."

She glared at him, but her touch was gentle as she led him around his car, opening the back driver's-side door. "Sit down before you fall down."

He obeyed wordlessly. His head was spinning. He

didn't need to look at his arm to know he was bleeding. Badly. "My gun. I dropped it on the road. Near the trunk."

"I'll get it in a minute." Laying the rifle down on the floor of his car, she grabbed her phone from her pocket and punched some numbers, then put the phone on speaker.

"This is 911. What is your emergency?"

"We have a gunshot victim on California 97, about twenty miles southwest of Macdoel. How fast can we get medical assistance?"

"I'll call it in," the operator said but sounded doubtful. "Let me see who's available."

Daisy handed him the phone. "You want to talk to them, Agent Reynolds?"

He shook his head. "You do it," he said quietly, because now that the danger to her was past, his adrenaline was crashing fast and he was quickly becoming light-headed.

"Agent Reynolds?" the operator asked. "Who is that and what's happening?"

"The victim is FBI Special Agent Gideon Reynolds. The shooter is driving a damaged beige sedan—I'm not sure of the make—"

"Chevy," Gideon interrupted. "Chevy Malibu, 2010."

"I got that," the operator said. "Did you get the license plate?"

"No," Gideon said quietly. God, he was cold. Really cold. *This is bad.*

He wasn't surprised to hear Daisy rattle it off. "The car has a shot-out back window, a completely pebbled windshield, and at least two shot-out tires. They're run-flat tires, so he can go a fair distance, but I don't see how he can without a windshield. Also, he's injured. I shot his hand."

"Got it," the operator said. "I've contacted the sheriff's office in the next town. They're on their way."

"That's thirty minutes east of here," he muttered. "Twenty if they floor it."

"I know," Daisy said evenly, but she'd grown pale, her gaze fixed on the rapidly growing dark stain on his coat. "Agent Reynolds is bleeding very badly," she told the operator. "I can call someone who's closer who may be able to help. I'm going to do that now. I'll use Agent Reynolds's phone. I'll leave you on speaker for now, okay?"

She put the phone on the road next to the rifle, then turned to him. "Where's that piece of paper that Mr. Danton gave you?"

"My jacket pocket. Inside my coat. But first we need to stop the bleeding. Help me out of my coat."

"Where are you shot?" she asked.

"Arm. Must have hit an artery. Not good."

"I figured that out myself." Carefully she removed his coat, tossing it so that it rested on the back of the driver's seat. She grimaced at the sight of his suit jacket. "You wear too fucking many clothes, Gideon."

"Tell me that later," he said breathlessly.

She glared at him, tears in her eyes. "Shut up," she whispered. "I'm not going to let you die."

"I hadn't planned to. Get the jacket off."

She obeyed, taking off his suit coat faster than his overcoat, moaning herself when he grunted in pain. "I'm sorry. I'm so sorry," she murmured.

"Get my belt. We'll use it as a tourniquet."

"Okay. I can do this," she said firmly. "I can."

"I know you can."

"I don't," she shot back. Fingers clumsy, she unbuckled his belt and slid it free of his pants, then looped it around his arm, above the bullet hole. "How tight should I pull?"

"Tight," he grimaced, then groaned when she obeyed again, the pain sending little black spots dancing across his vision. "Like that. Stop for now. Thread the end through the buckle, then loop it under the belt to secure it."

Hands trembling, she did as he instructed then searched his jacket pocket for the piece of paper with Danton's phone number and then his overcoat pocket for his phone. "Code," she demanded, unlocking the phone when he gave it to her, and dialing the man whose house they'd just left. "Hi, it's Daisy. We were just shot at. Gideon needs your help." She explained his injury, then listened for another minute, nodding as if Danton could see her. "We applied a tourniquet already. Please get her here as soon as you can. We're only twenty minutes from your place. Thanks." She ended the call and pocketed his phone.

"Her?" he asked, too exhausted to demand she give it back.

"Sammie, his daughter. The vet."

"Not a military vet," he said with a small smile.

"No." She wrapped his coat around him. "You're shivering."

He was cold through to his bones. "Keep me warm?"

Gripping the rifle in one hand, she rolled her eyes as she carefully pulled his jacket and coat over his shoulders, then pressed up against his left side, sliding her arm over his back. "Does that line ever really work for you, Agent Reynolds?"

"You're snuggled up against me, so I'd have to say yes."

She shuddered out a harsh breath. "That was scary," she whispered.

"And you were a pro." Ignoring the throbbing in his arm, he kissed the top of her head. "I still can't believe you shot the gun out of his hand."

She chuckled weakly. "My father will be proud."

"So am I."

She stretched up to kiss his cheek. "That's more important."

GRASS LAKE, CALIFORNIA
SUNDAY, FEBRUARY 19, 1:00 P.M.

She'd shot the fucking gun out of his hand. He stared
at his fingers disbelievingly. They were all still there,
but he couldn't move his thumb. The bullet had taken
a chunk out of his flesh between his thumb and forefinger. He was spurting blood like a broken hose.

Sitting there, in the car, in shock, he'd wrapped the
wound in his scarf. And it was good he'd dipped his
head to do so because the next shot came through the
windshield, the one after that through the back window. He'd thought the shooter was the Fed. He'd been
cursing the damn Fed.

Until Daisy had appeared, rifle in her hands.

She'd shot him?

He was still stunned as he raced down the highway
on two good tires and two flats. He'd never been so
glad to have invested in the run-flat tires. Otherwise he
would have been dead in the water.

*She was trying to get me out of the car. She was try-
ing to kill me.*

That was not nice.

That was rude. The very rudest.

He laughed, still in shock. *Yeah. The very rudest.*

Daisy had to go.

He laughed again, this time scornfully. "But not today," he murmured. She'd definitely outgunned him.
He should have expected a rifle.

But there was no way anyone should have expected
that woman to shoot like that. Every bullet went exactly where she'd wanted it to go.

She shot the gun out of my fucking hand.

*Yes, she did. Now sit up straight and figure out what
the* fuck *you're going to do.*

He sat up as straight as he could, considering he was leaning his head out the window to be able to see. There was cell signal here. Sooner or later a cop was going to respond, because Daisy and the Fed would have, *of course,* called for help by now.

There was no way any cop would miss his car now. Not with both windows shot out. *Fucking Daisy Dawson.* The first thing he needed to do was ditch this car and find another.

You should have gone home last night. You could have been on a cushy flight to New York City. But no. He'd just *had* to see what they were up to.

Almost there. He'd noted the Grass Lake rest area on the way in, but he hadn't wanted to lose the Fed and Daisy. Now, it was his only hope of getting out of this clusterfuck a free man.

Slowing his car, he eased it to the other side of the road, hiding it behind a group of trees. If he was lucky, no one would see it until he'd procured another.

But his prints were all over it. And his blood.

Not a problem. Your prints aren't on record with the police. But his DNA was. He was certain they'd scraped Daisy's fingernails Thursday night. *They have my skin.* Neither fingerprints nor DNA would matter— unless he got caught. Then it would matter a lot.

The car needed to go, too. *Shit.* He didn't have time for this.

Take the time, asshole. Or when you're sitting in jail, you'll wish you had.

Think. He had no gasoline in the trunk. No booze. Nothing that would burn.

Nothing but the gas in the tank itself. He had a lighter, but no matches. And dropping a match into the gas tank was insane anyway. He wanted to get away, not immolate himself.

I need a fuse. He did a quick mental inventory of everything he had in the car, which wasn't much. Just the now-empty bottles of bleach and the laundry baskets . . . *And the dryer sheets.*

Retrieving the box of dryer sheets from the car, he spread a few on the floor of the trunk and lit them with the lighter. Then he stuffed all that were left into the gas tank and lit the tail he'd left hanging out.

He stood back for a moment, watching the fire eat at the sheets, then kicked himself back into gear. *Move it, asshole.* His left hand was still bleeding. It dripped down, spattering the snow. He quickly unwrapped his hand and rewrapped it with the scarf, pulling it tighter and hiding the bloodstains as best he could before kicking at the snow to cover the blood spatter. Then he found a good-sized rock and hefted it in his right hand. It would do. He hoped.

Crossing the highway, he made his way to the rest stop and waited in the shadows. There were only two cars there, a Honda four-door sedan and a Ford Mustang. Both were empty. It looked like the occupants of one of the cars were taking photos of Mt. Shasta. It was a very nice view. He hoped it kept them busy a little longer.

Because walking out of the ladies' room was an older woman with a cane. She should be easy pickings. Then again, Daisy should have been, too.

He waited until she'd approached the Honda, taking her keys from a gigantic purse. Slipping up behind her, he brought the rock down onto her head, ignoring her cry of pain when she fell to the pavement. He grabbed her keys and her purse and got into the car.

Exiting the rest stop, he stomped his foot on the gas, speeding back to the highway—just as an explosion splintered the air. His car was now just a memory. It'd burn until someone came to put it out, and by then, his prints would be no more.

"Yes," he hissed triumphantly. "I did it."

Plus, a fire was a handy way to keep all the cops busy. *So they're not looking for me.*

About two miles later, he passed through another group of trees. Slowing down, he tossed the woman's purse into the thicket. He hadn't wanted her to have her phone or her ID. Her car could be too quickly identified that way and he needed a head start, until he could find somewhere to dump this car and get another.

At the same time, he didn't want anyone tracking her phone, either. So he'd taken care of both problems.

He checked his rearview mirror, relieved to see no one behind him. No one followed him. Except . . .

His heart stopped. Just . . . stopped.

"Holy fucking shit."

MACDOEL, CALIFORNIA
SUNDAY, FEBRUARY 19, 1:15 P.M.

"*You* shot the gun out of his hand?"

Daisy was getting damn tired of answering this question. Danton had asked. His daughter had asked. His daughter's husband's cousin—a park ranger with EMS training—had asked. This time it was the sheriff from the next town up.

"Yes, sir, I did," she said, not taking her gaze off Gideon, who was being settled onto a stretcher by the park ranger/EMT. From the corner of her eye she saw the sheriff's deputy moving to pick up the gun, which still lay in the middle of the road. "Don't touch it!" she shouted, finally looking away from Gideon, who was actually smirking at her.

The deputy straightened his spine and glared at her. "Who are you to be telling me how to handle a crime scene?"

"I'm nobody. But *he's* Special Agent Reynolds with the FBI and that gun may have been used in other crimes."

"What she said," Gideon called out.

She gave him an irked look even as she gently pushed his hair away from his eyes. "You need to keep still. Plus you're not helping anyway."

Although he did look a lot better. Sammie Danton had done a good job stopping his bleeding and applying a dressing. At least Daisy thought it was a good job.

But you let him get away.

Fuck off.

"Daisy?" Gideon tugged on her sleeve.

She blinked down at him. "Sorry. What?"

"Call Molina again," he suggested. "Hopefully she'll answer this time."

Daisy did as he asked, dialing up his boss with his phone.

"What is it, Agent Reynolds?" a woman snapped.

Daisy had heard her voice before, that morning when she'd overheard Gideon and the woman discussing what had been done to Trish . . . so matter-of-factly.

Which is how they cope, she reminded herself.

"This isn't Agent Reynolds," Daisy blurted out. "This is Daisy Dawson. Gideon's been shot, but he'll be okay. He asked me to call you."

"Is he conscious?" Molina asked sharply.

"Yes. We're waiting for the helicopter." Sammie's husband's cousin—the EMS guy—had immediately radioed for one.

"Where are they taking him?" Molina demanded.

"To UC Davis."

"Let me talk to Reynolds. Please," she added in a tone of forced courtesy.

Daisy put the phone to Gideon's ear. He was securely wrapped in blankets, but he was still shivering. "She wants to talk to you."

Gideon rolled his head to get closer to the phone. "I'm a little . . . indisposed at the moment." A few seconds ticked by as he listened, then gave his boss the CliffsNotes account of what had happened. "Please tell the sheriff that your team is coming to deal with the crime scene." He rolled away from the phone. "Give the phone to the sheriff."

Daisy did, nodding politely when the sheriff met her eyes with a bit of apology.

"Yes," the sheriff said into the phone, "we'll make sure the scene is secure as long as someone gets here soon. There isn't much traffic through here this time of year, but it is the only road and we're blocking it off." He handed the phone to Daisy. "She wants to talk to you."

"Yes?" Daisy asked.

"You're going with him in the helicopter."

"Yes. I'd planned to."

"You will. Call me when you get to the hospital."

"Yes, ma'am. I'll call you." She heard the sound of the helicopter's approach. "His ride's about to land. I need to go."

"Miss Dawson," Molina said, her tone still terse. "Thank you for stepping up and protecting Gideon the way you did."

"Yes, ma'am." Ending the call, she called good-bye to the Dantons, who waited beyond the helicopter's landing range. "I'm not sure what's going to happen tomorrow," she told them. "If it's one of the other agents who goes to Portland, will you still help them?" she asked Sammie.

Sammie nodded. "If you vouch for them, sure. I'll be going anyway. I need to try to find Eileen. If she's hurt . . . I just need to make sure she's okay. My husband's already said he'll go with me, so Dad doesn't have to worry."

Daisy gave Mr. Danton an abrupt hug. "Thank you. For everything."

"We didn't do anything that anyone else wouldn't have done," he murmured, patting her back. "Call us.

Let us know you're okay. Go on now. They're ready to load you up."

"I will." She'd turned for the helicopter when the sheriff tersely ordered his deputy to secure the scene, then got in his squad car and took off in the direction they'd be going.

She glanced up at the EMT who was helping her up into the back of the rig. "Is he clearing a path for us?"

The man shook his head. "No, he just got a call from Dispatch. A guy just knocked out an old lady at the rest area and stole her car."

"Mr. Beige Chevy?" she asked, although she already knew the answer.

"Sounds like. There's a car vaguely matching that description parked off the road across from the rest area. But it has the same license plates, so probably."

"Probably? It's a beige Chevy with a shot-up windshield and shot-out back window. How hard can it be to ID it?"

"It's on fire. Gas tank exploded. He got away in the stolen car."

"Then they can catch him," she said with relief. "Hopefully they're better shots than I was and they actually flatten his tires."

"There's no way they can get off a better shot than you did," Gideon said with a pride that made her smile. Until the EMT spoke again.

"I don't think anybody's gonna be shooting at that car, ma'am. There's a child in the backseat."

Any color still in Gideon's face drained away. "Oh my God," he whispered.

Daisy's stomach pitched. "Oh no."

They'd seen what the monster had done to Trish. What would he do to an innocent child?

▌▌ GRASS LAKE, CALIFORNIA
▌▌ SUNDAY, FEBRUARY 19, 1:15 P.M.

He threw on the brakes and turned around to see big brown eyes staring from the child's car seat strapped in behind him.

His heart simply stopped. "Holy fucking shit," he repeated in a whisper. "It's a kid."

A toddler, to be exact. Wearing pink. *So probably a little girl.*

What the hell was he supposed to do now?

Just drive. Fucking drive. Ditch the car as soon as you can.

But it's going to get cold tonight. I can't just leave her. Alone. What if some pervert steals her?

You fucker. You *stole her.*

Not on purpose! And I'm *not going to hurt her.*

Idiot. Just. Drive.

He pressed the accelerator to the floor, peeling out with a squeal of tires. "What the hell now?"

But the kid didn't answer.

▌▌ SACRAMENTO, CALIFORNIA
▌▌ SUNDAY, FEBRUARY 19, 1:15 P.M.

Bellamy, Anna. Pennsylvania. Zandra Jones squinted at the driver's licenses mounted on the inside of the cabinet door, barely close enough for her to see. *Fiddler, Janice. Washington.*

She'd been repeating the women's names in her mind, over and over again.

Because I'm going to get out. I'm going to tell someone who they were. That they're dead. Because I will get out.

She had no idea how she'd make that happen. But she would. She was not going to end up as an addition to his collection of trinkets. And licenses.

She'd get out and she'd make sure this monster paid for his crimes. And she'd make sure the families of all the women he'd killed got closure. So they could grieve.

Orlov, Nadia. Illinois. Stevenson, Rayanna. Texas. DeVeen, Rosamond. Minnesota. Borge, Delfina. California. Oliver, Makayla. New York. Danton, Eileen. Oregon.

Her gaze faltered on the next license, then flicked to the freezer against the wall. A sob started to rise and Zandra battled it back. She couldn't cry or she'd suffocate, saving him the trouble of killing her. But the bastard hadn't even buried the poor girl. He'd just shoved her in a freezer. *Like he'll do to me if I don't find a way out.*

Resolutely Zandra redirected her attention to the display of licenses. *Martell, Kaley. California.* With the horseshoe crystal hanging from the hook below it.

And the very last one. *Hart, Trisha. California.*

Then she began again. Again and again until she had them memorized. Because these were fewer than a third of the names in the cabinet. She'd memorize every one that she could. *Bellamy, Anna. Pennsylvania. Fiddler, Janice. Washington.*

Orlov, Nadia. Illinois. Stevenson, Rayanna. Texas. DeVeen, Rosamond. Minnesota. Borge, Delfina. California. Oliver, Makayla. New York. Danton, Eileen. Oregon.

Martell, Kaley. California. Hart, Trisha. California.

And again and again.

And if he came back and showed her more of the licenses in the cabinet?

I'll memorize them, too.

‖ WEED, CALIFORNIA
SUNDAY, FEBRUARY 19, 1:20 P.M.

"There," he muttered, slowing to turn right. It was a lonely parking lot—a viewing area for Shasta—and there was only one vehicle parked there. A Ford F-150. That was an engine he knew well. There was an ancient one at the airfield, owned by the old man. Nearly twenty years old with more than two hundred thousand miles, it still ran like a dream.

He'd learned to hot-wire the thing before he could legally drive.

Finally, something was going his way. Slowly he pulled into the lot, looking for the driver. *Ah, there he is.* Standing at the edge of the lot, staring off toward the mountain, was a middle-aged man with a camera around his neck.

And probably a cell phone in his pocket. He'd call the cops to report the theft of his truck in a heartbeat. *And I'm all outta rocks.*

But he did have a car. In a pinch, it was a very good weapon.

But the man hadn't done anything. Not like the guests he brought back to his home.

He has a vehicle you need.

But . . . that's . . . wrong.

He laughed out loud. Literally. *Wrong?* Hell, yes. All of this was wrong. "I've got a fucking *baby* in the goddamn backseat." Which was *so* far past wrong.

He glanced in his rearview. The child was so quiet, it was unnerving. The kid just stared at him with wide brown eyes. Then she stuck her thumb in her mouth and closed her eyes.

And went to sleep.

"You've got to be kidding me," he muttered.

Well, at least she was quiet. She could be screaming and breaking his eardrums.

The man moved forward a few feet, climbing to stand on top of the low rock fence around the parking lot. He lifted the camera to his face and adjusted the lens. Then stepped off the fence and turned around, looking down at his camera as he replaced the lens cap. Walking toward his car.

If you're going to do it, then do it now.

God.

Pointing the car toward the man, he rammed his foot on the gas, narrowing his eyes until they were almost closed. Because he didn't want to see—

A thump had him gasping. He'd done it. He'd taken the guy out.

Cautiously he backed up until he could see the man on the ground. The guy rolled over, arm stretched over his head, hand grasping at the asphalt.

Not enough. He needed the man unconscious. Not dead. Just unconscious.

So he backed up, closed his eyes, and punched the accelerator once again, flinching when the car made contact. Carefully he nudged the car backward far enough to see the man. Who was no longer moving.

Oh God. He drew a breath and shuddered it out, then looked around to be sure no one else had seen. There was no one there.

There might be security cameras, but it didn't matter. He'd changed his whole look that morning while waiting for the Fed and Daisy to emerge from the hotel. Plus, the cap he wore would hide his face.

Cautiously he slid from the old woman's Honda and approached the man, who lay still. He was breathing, so that was good. Crouching beside him, he rolled him over so that he could take his wallet out of his pants, then got his car keys and phone.

No identification. No tie to the truck. No way for him to call to report the theft if he did wake up.

Hurry. Before the word got out and the cops set up roadblocks. Although he hoped all emergency personnel were tied up with the fire he'd set in his car.

He got back in the car and parked it over the man's unmoving—but still breathing—body. It would hide him from view and even shelter him from the wind. In case he survived long enough to be saved.

All right then. He locked up the old woman's Honda and started for the man's truck. Then . . . stopped. And turned to look at the back window. Where the baby sat, sound asleep.

How had the kid slept through that? Would she even cry to tell someone she was in the car if help did come?

What if she froze to death? What if animals came and attacked her?

She was like Mutt had been. Helpless. Defenseless. Innocent.

"Fuck me," he muttered, going back to the car, opening the back door, and unbuckling the straps that held the car seat in place. He yanked the car seat out, baby and all.

"Holy shit, kid. You weigh a frickin' ton." He unlocked the man's truck with its old-style key. No fobs for this guy, which was good. Because key fobs could be tracked by the cops. He'd read that in the forensics magazine he had delivered to his Kindle each month.

It was always good to keep ahead of developments that could land him in prison.

Opening the door to the backseat, driver's side, he shoved the baby onto the floorboard, car seat and all, wedging it between the back of the driver's seat and the back bench.

The kid woke once, stared up at him, then made a snuffling sound like she was about to cry.

"Uh, no. Just . . . no." He ran back to the Honda to see if there was a diaper bag, and sure enough, there was a pretty pink bag with bears printed on it. He grabbed it, locked the car, and ran back to the truck, frantically searching for something to keep the kid quiet.

"Oh, good." He pulled out a pacifier, which was exactly what the kid wanted. She sucked on it contentedly and he let out a sigh of relief.

He'd figure out where to leave her on his next stop.

Weed, California, was the next town. It had shopping centers where he'd find another car to steal and somewhere he could leave the kid. That would be best.

You should have left her in the Honda. The thought scratched at his mind as he drove away in the man's truck.

No. I couldn't have. She doesn't deserve to be abandoned.

The voice in his head turned sly. *Like your mommy did to you?*

He gritted his teeth. "She did not abandon me," he said aloud. "She died."

But the effect had been the same. She'd been gone and then . . .

Sydney had come.

Sydney had come and stolen everything good in his life away.

Sydney had ruined everything.

Just like she ruined me.

TWENTY

K arl, stop pacing." Irina glared at him across the waiting room. "You are making Daisy crazy."

"I'm fine," Daisy protested. Brutus was nearly bald from being petted, but a dog's fur would grow back. She was pretty sure. *God, I hope so. Poor Brutus.* But Gideon was going to be fine, too. It wasn't a serious wound. They were just going to stitch him up.

"Way to blame it on DD, Ma," Sasha said, her arm around Daisy's shoulders protectively. "Stop projecting your feelings onto her."

"Fine," Irina admitted. "You are making your wife crazy, Karl. Please sit down."

Karl sat next to Irina sheepishly. "I'm sorry. I can't seem to help it."

"Our Gideon will be fine," Irina assured.

Whether she was assuring Karl or herself was anyone's guess, Daisy thought with a fond smile for the woman who'd been a mother to Gideon. Irina had been a mother to her, too. She reached over Sasha to pat Irina's arm. "Of course he'll be fine. He's getting worked on by the best vascular surgeon in the place."

So Molina had told them and Daisy didn't dare question her. But she didn't blame Karl for pacing. They'd all engaged in some form of stress management. Sasha's choice was chocolate and Daisy had been all too happy

to share her bag of M&Ms. She'd ask for more, but all
the sugar had her feeling slightly sick. Or that could
have been the stress, because even though she told herself that Gideon would be fine, he'd been in surgery for
almost two hours already and it was supposed to have
been a quick repair, an hour tops.

"If he's so damn good," Rafe grumbled, "what's
taking him so long? It was a damn through-and-
through."

"He'd lost a lot of blood," Daisy said quietly, still
remembering it on her hands and clothes. A kind nurse
had offered her a set of scrubs when she'd arrived.
Washing Gideon's blood from her hands had triggered
the first crying jag. Seeing his blood mixing with the
water and swirling down the drain had been like . . . losing a part of him.

Which was ridiculous. He was going to be fine.

Whether he'd be able to work in law enforcement
again was another question. It was a through-and-
through, she told herself for the millionth time. Hopefully there would be no damage to his nerves. It had
taken her nearly two hours after the shooting to get
him here, and it would have been three times as long if
the Yreka facility hadn't called for the helicopter to
take them to UC Davis.

And the whole way he'd lain there, holding her hand
so tightly under the warming blanket that she'd
thought he'd broken her fingers for the second time
that day.

One day. It was hard to believe it had only been one
day since she'd found Trish. Even less since she'd lain
in Gideon's arms and felt such peace after he'd taken
her to the moon and back. It seemed like a year.

"Miss Dawson?"

Daisy turned in her seat to see Gideon's boss coming through the door and popped to her feet. "Agent
Molina. Have you heard anything?"

"Not yet," she said, not unkindly. "I understand you have Agent Reynolds's phone and laptop."

Daisy's hand darted into her pocket, closing around his phone as if it were a part of him. Brutus let out a little whine and she realized she was squeezing her too hard as well. She loosened her hold on Brutus but kept her hand clamped around the phone.

No, I don't have either of them, she wanted to say. But she knew that wouldn't be okay. "Why do you want them?" she asked instead.

"They have his work e-mail on them. There are classified items there." Molina held out her hand. "May I have it, please?"

Like I have a choice. Daisy handed over Gideon's laptop case, which she'd taken from the car while they'd waited for the helicopter.

Molina's brow lifted. "And his phone?"

Daisy brought it out of her pocket, then hesitated, a thought striking her so hard it hurt. "Can I make one call first? You can watch and listen if you like. Then I'll be able to give it to you."

"Let's go into my consultation room."

Her consultation room. It was really one of the small rooms the doctors used to talk with the patients' families. Daisy wanted to roll her eyes but refrained. The woman exuded power, after all. *She could squash me like a bug.*

But Molina didn't, merely holding the door open so that Daisy could pass through.

"Make your call, Miss Dawson."

Daisy fumbled with the code, remembering how bloody her fingers had been when she'd tapped it in on the side of the road. She pushed the memory aside, focusing on the names in his contacts list, scrolling to the *M*'s.

Mercy Callahan. Daisy wondered where Gideon's sister had taken her last name from. For that matter, she wondered where Gideon had taken Reynolds from.

"Terrill" had been the name he'd used while in the cult community.

She tapped Mercy's name, unsure of what to expect. *She doesn't hate me,* Gideon had said. Which was not a glowing endorsement. It was entirely possible that Mercy would tell her to go to hell.

"Hello, Gideon." The words were uttered with ill-disguised impatience.

"Hi," Daisy said. "Don't hang up, please."

"Who is this?" Mercy asked sharply.

"My name is Daisy Dawson. I'm a friend of your brother's. He's hurt. In surgery. I thought you'd want to know."

There was a moment of abject silence. Then, "Is he going to live?"

"Yes," Daisy said firmly. "If you want to come, he's at UC Davis. I know he called you about the locket. The shooting was related to that."

"Oh God," Mercy whispered, then cleared her throat. "Thank you for telling me. Tell him . . . that I hope he doesn't die."

Gideon's sister ended the call, leaving Daisy to frown at the phone screen. *That she hopes he doesn't die?* What the hell kind of message was that, anyway?

"She's not coming, is she?" Molina asked. "Gideon's sister, I mean."

Daisy shook her head. "Didn't sound like it." Quickly she entered Mercy's phone number into her own contacts list, just in case, then turned off the screen and handed Gideon's phone to his boss. If she didn't have the code, Daisy wasn't going to give it to her.

"Thank you," Molina said with a wry smile. "I don't plan to use his phone, but I can appreciate your loyalty. And your marksmanship."

"You're the only person who hasn't said, '*You* shot the gun out of his hand?' So thank you for that."

"I checked you out. Checked your family out, as a

matter of fact. You and your sister have done some impressive shooting. And you have a high-ranking special agent in Baltimore who personally vouches for all of you."

That made Daisy smile. Special Agent Joseph Carter had become a friend to both Daisy's father and Taylor's bio-dad. "Agent Carter's a nice man. It was kind of him to speak well of me." It was then she remembered what time it was. Her father's flight from Baltimore would be getting in soon. Karl was supposed to go get him.

She slipped Brutus into her bag and stuck her hand out to Molina. "I need to go. My dad's flying in tonight." She breathed through the tightening in her chest when she remembered why he was coming. "He's coming to help me with the burial arrangements for my friend."

Molina shook her hand. "I'm very sorry for your loss," she said and it sounded . . . genuine, but then she was back to business.

"Thank you. I'll be back as soon as I can." Daisy hesitated at the door. "The missing child. Is there any word?"

Molina shook her head again. "Not yet. We've got multiple agencies searching. When I have something to share, I'll let you know."

Daisy backed out of Molina's little makeshift office, only to see a familiar male frame hovering just outside the door to the waiting room. Tall, his broad shoulders a little stooped, he wore his favorite tweed jacket with patches on the sleeves. Frederick Dawson.

"Dad?" Her father turned and Daisy flew into his arms. "You're here." And for the second time since arriving at the hospital, she burst into tears.

Her father's arms came around her, holding her so tightly that she almost couldn't breathe. "Daisy, baby. Are you hurt, too?"

"No, not me." Still she couldn't stop crying. "Just Gideon."

"Honey, I'm sorry. Is he going to be okay?"

"Yes," she said, still firmly, although as the minutes passed she was feeling less sure.

"Good." He pulled back to study her face, his expression darkening when he saw her throat. "Who did that to you?"

Daisy had forgotten she no longer wore a turtleneck. "The same man who shot Gideon this afternoon. I shot him in the hand. Got him to drop his gun, but he got away."

Her father nodded grimly. "But he's shot a Fed now. The Bureau will be on him like white on rice."

"I think they would have been on him before he shot Gideon. They think he's killed a lot of women, Dad." She swallowed hard. "He killed Trish."

"Your friend. Baby, I'm sorry."

"Me too. She was a good person. It still hasn't sunk in yet, you know?"

"I know," he murmured.

She dashed away the tears on her face. Because he did know. She had a fuzzy recollection of her father's sorrow after her mother had died. He'd been inconsolable for a few weeks. Until one day he'd gotten out of bed and made them breakfast, just how their mother had done. He'd loved them and protected them as best he'd known how.

She wondered what kind of father he'd have been had he never been in the military. If he'd never been captured. If he'd never been a POW.

But she couldn't say that. Not to him. She didn't want to hurt him. So she said, "You're early."

"I was able to get an earlier flight, but the connection was iffy. I figured I'd get here when I got here."

"How did you know to get to the hospital?" she asked.

"I went to Karl and Irina's first. Straight from the airport. But only Zoya and Damien were home."

"Zoya wanted to come to the hospital, but she's got a big chemistry test tomorrow. Damien is staying with her until all this has blown over."

Frederick smiled, but sadly. "Damien used to be a skinny kid, but he isn't any longer. Now he's this big, burly cop. I pity any criminals who try to cross him. And Zoya? She's grown so much. She was barely in kindergarten when we left. I missed . . . so much." He gave his head a little shake. "Anyway, Zoya told me that there was a shooting, that you were here, that you were 'fine,' but that Gideon was not. I barely heard anything after 'shooting.' It seems I always find you girls after you've proven your skills."

"Well, I'm fine." She hesitated. "But I've been thinking."

His brows furrowed warily. Almost fearfully. "About?"

He was afraid. Her fearless, take-charge father was afraid. *Of me?*

No. But of my opinion of him. She pushed the topic of his PTSD behaviors aside for the present and smiled up at him. "That I'm so glad you're here. I've missed you so much."

His relief was tangible. "I'll always come when you need me."

She slipped her arm through his. "I know. Let's go see Karl and Irina. They've missed you, too."

He hesitated. "I . . . I've got a hotel room. I'll just go check in and come back."

She looked up at him again, softening her words with a smile. "We still have some differences to work out, you and me. But there's one thing about you that I've always admired and that's your integrity. And courage."

His face flushed with embarrassment. "That's two things."

Shaking her head, she patted his arm. "If you made a mistake, you admitted it and asked for forgiveness. Even to us kids."

He closed his eyes and sighed. "I hurt him. Karl. He was my best friend and I just walked away. I didn't trust him."

She took his hand, lifted it to her cheek. "Dad, does Karl know about what happened to you in Central America? That you were captured? And everything else?"

He nodded, his face flushing again, but this time with shame. "He was the one that got me out," he whispered.

Daisy's chest constricted. *Thank you, Karl. Thank you, a thousand times.* "So, on one hand, you should have known you could trust him. That you didn't wasn't a good thing. On the other hand . . ." She trailed off, ducking low so that she could meet his downcast gaze. "He, of all people, should understand why you made the decisions that you made. You felt cornered and scared."

Her father swallowed hard. "You got really smart," he said hoarsely.

"Yeah, well." She squeezed his hands. "Go in there, Dad. Tell Karl you're sorry. He'll forgive you. I know it."

Frederick drew a deep breath. "I know it, too."

"Frederick?" a man asked.

Together they turned—and froze. Because Karl stood in the doorway to the waiting room, watching them, his face uncharacteristically unreadable.

Frederick reached out a tentative hand. "Karl," he whispered. "It's good . . ." He cleared his throat. "Good to see you."

Then Karl closed the distance between them, wrapping his arms around Frederick and holding him tight. "Frederick. Welcome back."

Her father exhaled and Karl met her eyes over Frederick's shoulder. "Give us a few minutes, Daisy. Rafe has good news from Gideon's doctor."

Daisy gave her father's back a light pat but had to keep herself from running into the waiting room. Rafe and Sasha stood when she hurried in.

"Gideon's come through the surgery," Rafe said. "He's in recovery."

Daisy's shoulders sagged in relief. "Oh, thank goodness. And his hand? Will he regain use of it?"

"The doctor didn't say," Sasha answered, linking her arm through Daisy's. "But we'll be able to see him in a few minutes. Everything's okay."

Daisy leaned her head on Sasha's shoulder. "Thank you."

SACRAMENTO, CALIFORNIA
SUNDAY, FEBRUARY 19, 5:45 P.M.

Zandra flinched. She'd felt the little shake rattle through the room. The front door. He was home.

No. Please no. The sound of her own whimper had her eyes stinging.

She clenched her jaw. *No,* she mentally repeated much more firmly. Gathering her strength, she straightened her spine.

Bellamy, Anna. Pennsylvania. Fiddler, Janice. Washington. Orlov, Nadia. Illinois. Stevenson, Rayanna. Texas.

A key rattled in the lock. *DeVeen, Rosamond. Minnesota. Borge, Delfina. California. Oliver, Makayla. New York. Danton, Eileen. Oregon.*

Zandra closed her eyes. *Martell, Kaley. California. Hart, Trisha. California.*

She braced herself for the first strike, but it never came. Instead, she heard a slight beeping sound.

Cracking her eyes open just enough to see, she watched him open a safe.

And withdraw a gun. And a silencer.

No, no, no. Not yet.

At least it'll be quick. Please, God, let it be quick.

But he didn't shoot her. He merely checked the magazine and nodded once before dropping the gun into his coat pocket.

She didn't notice the scarf wound around his hand until he began to take it off.

Bloody. It was covered in dried blood.

Oh. Wow. His hand. It looked . . . like he'd been mauled by an animal.

That had to hurt.

Which made her feel triumphantly, ridiculously happy.

He tossed the bloody scarf in a trash bag, then rummaged in a drawer, coming up with gauze pads and medical tape. Just like he'd used on her.

Because he hadn't wanted her to bleed too much. He wanted her to stay alive. Wanted her conscious.

Say you're sorry, he'd chanted. *Say you're sorry.*

Fuck you, she snarled in her mind.

He continued to rummage in the drawer, bringing out a pack of sewing needles. Big ones. And more of the suture thread he'd used to close her own wounds. The wounds he'd carved into her body.

She watched as he attempted to bandage his left hand with his clearly less dexterous right. He ended up using too much tape to secure one of the gauze pads, leaving his thumb looking like a mess.

He then wrapped tape around his fingertips and the pad of his thumb. *He's covering his fingerprints.* He finished by sliding his uninjured right hand into a black glove, using his teeth to pull it on. A final search of the drawer yielded a hat with a wig already attached. He put the hat on and adjusted the hair of the wig in a small mirror, then slid on a pair of wire-framed glasses, lenses tinted a light brown.

He looks like someone else. That was how he'd never been caught. *Not yet, anyway.*

"Nice of you to join me," he said quietly.

Too late, she realized she'd opened her eyes fully.

He was smirking at her. "Don't worry, Zandra. I haven't forgotten about you. I'll be back later and we'll have some more fun."

Then he gathered the suture materials and left the small room. She could hear the turn of his key in the lock. A minute later, the slight rattle shook her again.

He was gone.

But he would be back.

Bellamy, Anna. Pennsylvania. Fiddler, Janice. Washington.

||| SACRAMENTO, CALIFORNIA
SUNDAY, FEBRUARY 19, 6:25 P.M.

He pulled into the parking lot of one of the hospitals in the farthest east of Sacramento's suburbs, idling his minivan next to the employee exit. He'd traded the truck for a minivan in a grocery store lot just south of Chico, about an hour and a half north. He'd sat in the grocery store's parking lot waiting for an employee to leave their minivan and enter the store to start their shift, hoping that would buy him at least a few hours before anyone realized the vehicle was gone.

But no one had been available in the parking lot to take care of a baby, so he'd moved the car seat into the minivan and kept driving down the back roads, avoiding the interstate, and no one had given him a second glance.

Just another dad driving the family minivan.

Now, he was ready for the last phase of his getaway

plan, having armed and disguised himself again after his quick visit home. His wound was still gaping and bleeding. He needed stitches but didn't trust the dexterity of his right hand.

He waited, watching for someone in scrubs to leave the employee exit. Many would have changed into street clothes in the hospital's locker room, but he was hoping at least one medical professional would still be wearing identifying scrubs. He didn't want to grab an administrator by mistake.

He'd prefer a doctor, or even a physician's assistant, but he'd take a nurse in a pinch. He wasn't picky. He just needed to have his hand stitched up.

Excellent. He spied the woman coming out of the hospital, her head down as she walked his way. She was searching her handbag. Maybe for her keys. It didn't matter. As long as she wasn't searching for a gun, he didn't care.

Leaving the motor running, he got out of the minivan and slid the side door open, revealing the kid, still sleeping. It was pretty awesome, actually, how good this kid was on the road. He leaned over the car seat and muttered, "Sorry, kid," before easing the pacifier out of her mouth.

Her lips bent into a sleeping pout, but she didn't wake up.

He was beginning to think there was something wrong with her, actually. Kids weren't supposed to sleep so much. She hadn't even woken long enough to cry for food.

Whatever.

This child was a means to an end. Nothing more.

The woman was almost to his van, so he went into action. Pulling the cap he wore low on his face, just in case there were cameras, he "stumbled" from the van into her path, making his expression panicked.

"Excuse me! Excuse me!" He kept his head low,

which worked because she was short. Not even five feet tall, if that. "Are you a doctor? I need a doctor."

Her spine straightened. "I'm a nurse. I can call you a doctor."

"No! No, please," he pleaded. "There's no time. My baby isn't breathing. Please. Can you please help me?"

She sprang into action. "Where is your baby?"

"Right here." He led her to the van, where both the driver's-side door and the sliding door behind it were still open. "Please, help me. She just started making choking sounds and—" He cut himself off, bringing the gun out of his pocket and pressing the barrel to her side. "Don't scream and I won't hurt you."

She gasped and froze. "What are—"

He jabbed the gun into her side. "Get in the driver's seat. No sudden moves. *Do it.*"

She was shaking. "Don't shoot. Please, don't shoot."

"I won't. Get in. But if you try to run, I will kill you."

She slid behind the wheel and he climbed into the backseat next to the kid, crouching behind the driver's seat.

"Excellent," he said. "Now, pull the door closed."

She obeyed. "I have money. I'll give you all my credit cards."

"I don't need your money. I need your help. If you help me, I'll bring you back," he lied smoothly. "Don't look at my face and I won't have to kill you." He pulled the sliding door closed. "Give me your purse."

Hands shaking, she did. He dug through it, finding her phone under a ton of junk. Holding it in his gloved hand, he said, "Put your seat belt on. I don't want any cops stopping us. Good girl. Now pull out slowly and turn left."

"Wh-where are you taking me?"

"Just drive. Turn left on Auburn and follow it west. We're not taking I-80."

She drove, exiting the lot. Her face was deathly pale. "Is your baby really sick or was that a lie?"

"Just drive," he snarled. When they were on Auburn Boulevard, he opened his window and tossed her cell phone out. Now no one could track her.

SACRAMENTO, CALIFORNIA
SUNDAY, FEBRUARY 19, 6:30 P.M.

Gideon glared at the fingers of his right hand, bleary-eyed. "Move," he muttered. "Fucking *move*." But his arm just lay at his side. Useless.

"Give it some time."

His chin jerked up and he blinked hard at the doorway, where Daisy waited, her blond hair reflecting the blinding fluorescent lights. She looked a little like an angel, standing there.

A sharpshooting angel who'd defended him with her own life.

"Hi," he said, then tried to roll his eyes at his own lack of smoothness. Except his head ached and eye rolling was not on the program for today.

She smiled at him as she crossed the room to stand next to his bed. "I get two minutes alone with you before Rafe comes in." She brushed the hair off his forehead with gentle fingers and he closed his eyes, remembering how she'd done the same thing in the helicopter. And in bed the night before.

Then all he felt was warmth as she leaned over the rail and brushed a kiss over his lips. Very sweet. Very chaste.

And very much not enough. With his left hand he clasped the back of her head, ignoring the bite of the IV needle as he dragged her closer for a deeper kiss. She opened for him and he tasted her—chocolate and

Daisy. She hummed against his mouth, cupping his cheek in her palm.

Until a loud beeping had her backing away with a guilty jerk.

The kiss had left him breathless. So much so that it had apparently set off the heart monitor. He struggled to look back at the monitors behind the bed, only to see Daisy grimacing as she pulled something from her hair.

"Your monitor." She showed him the finger-clip device. "It came off your finger and got stuck in my hair. Let me put it back on you before the nurse comes to throw me out."

She slipped it back on his finger, quelling the alarm. Then she brushed another kiss across his mouth. "Hi." She pulled back far enough to see his eyes. And he hers. He'd locked on the bright blue sky of her eyes in the helicopter as she'd clasped his hand under the blanket the EMS guys had tucked around him. "We've been so worried about you."

"I'm okay," he said quietly, and it sounded like a promise.

"I know. I knew you would be, but it's still . . ." She lowered her forehead to his. "God, I'm so glad that's over."

He glanced down at his hand. "It's not over yet."

She jerked back again, her wide eyes filled with horrified guilt. "I'm sorry. That was insensitive of me. I just meant . . ." She sighed and sank into the chair next to his bed, wrapping her hands around the rail. "What did the doctor say about your hand?"

"I'm not really sure, to be honest." He reached for her hand, careful not to dislodge the finger monitor again. "I was a little out of it when he came to speak to me."

"I'll have Rafe find out," she told him. "He's the only one they'll talk to, because he's listed as your next of kin."

He nodded, a wave of exhausted sadness washing over him. "Because I didn't think Mercy would come if they called her." Daisy winced at that, dropping her gaze to their joined hands. "You called her? My sister?"

She nodded, seeming to brace herself before she met his eyes again. "I did. She sent her . . . best personal wishes."

He sighed heavily. He was way too tired for this. "I think they put some pain meds in that IV and I'm starting to drift. Just tell me what she really said."

"She said to tell you that she hopes you don't die."

His lips quirked up at that, grim amusement mixing in with the sad exhaustion. "She told me that the last time I saw her in the foster home. She was thirteen and . . ." He shook his head, grimacing when it hurt. "Shit."

"And what?" Daisy asked softly.

"And angry. Bitter. Mostly grieving and still in shock."

"Because of your mother."

He started to nod and thought better of it, holding his head still on the pillow so that he could look up into Daisy's sweet face. "Yeah. I visited her in the foster home where she'd been placed. She didn't talk at first, but I kept visiting. She'd give me one-word answers. But this time I was there to tell her it might be a while before I came back. I was starting college and I didn't know when I'd have time to make the drive out to where she was living. I tried to hug her and she didn't want to be touched. She didn't want to talk to me. She didn't want any part of me."

She brushed the hair off his forehead. "That must have hurt."

It had nearly killed him. "Yes," he answered simply. "I was only seventeen. I didn't know what to do. I don't know if I would have known what to do if it'd happened today."

"What did you do?"

"I told her that I was sorry. That I loved her. That I'd missed her, so damn much. That I'd tried to find her. And our mother. All the things I'd told her before." He swallowed. "I told her that I'd always be there for her if she changed her mind. And then I wished her a really good life and started to leave. She stopped me at the door. Called my name." His eyes stung at the memory of Mercy's face, at the pain in her haunted eyes. "She said she'd thought I'd been dead all that time. She just stared at me, then told me to please not die. Then she turned her back on me and walked away."

"And then?"

He shrugged his uninjured shoulder. "For the last thirteen years I've called her on her birthday, Christmas, Easter, and our mother's birthday. I've seen her in person only once, when I tracked her to New Orleans."

"Does she talk to you on the phone when you call?"

"Not really." And now the pain in his chest was almost as bad as the pain in his arm. He brought her hand to his lips and kissed her fingers. "New topic. Have they found him?"

"No. I talked to your boss and she said no one's found the child yet, either."

He closed his eyes. "Dammit."

"Hey. Okay if I come in?"

Gideon blinked his eyes open to see Rafe in the doorway. "Please. What did the doctor say about my arm?"

Rafe pulled up another chair. "A lot of words I don't remember, but the gist of it is, it's not abnormal for you to have lost movement in your fingers and that it appears to be temporary, because your nerves are 'squashed.'" He used air quotes.

Gideon frowned. "Squashed? How?"

"He said that the energy wave from the bullet 'disrupted' the tissue in your hand, which basically means the tissue got compressed and squashed your nerves. When the tissue settles down, movement and control should return. They won't know for a few days whether you'll regain all or only partial use, but he was optimistic that you'll get back most of it."

Gideon felt light-headed again, this time from relief. Daisy squeezed the hand she held lightly and he kissed her fingers again. "Thanks," he said gruffly.

"Don't mention it." Leaning forward, Rafe rested his forearms on the rail and sighed. "I'm going to tell you what I know, okay? Then you need to get some rest."

"When can I leave?"

"Tomorrow probably," Rafe said. "They'll keep you overnight for observation."

"I need to go to Portland tomorrow."

"Um, no," Daisy said firmly. "That is not happening."

Gideon opened his mouth to argue, but Rafe cut him off.

"She's right," Rafe said. "I'm going."

"You are?" Daisy asked while Gideon just stared up at him.

"I am." Rafe's eyes went hard. "Rhee and I are going up with Agent Schumacher."

"Schumacher is good," Gideon said grudgingly. "Where are you going to look?"

"I told your boss about Mr. Danton and Sammie," Daisy said. "Gave her their contact information. Sammie said she'd cooperate with whoever I endorsed. I'm glad I can endorse you, Rafe."

Rafe's smile flashed across his face. "Me too." Then he sobered. "Listen, Gid, before you hear it from someone else, there've been a few other casualties. The child in the car? She was with her grandparents, who'd stopped at a rest area a few miles west of where you were shot."

Gideon frowned. "Why the hell did they leave a baby in the car?"

Rafe sighed. "Grandma got out to pee and Grandpa waited with the kid. But Grandma was taking a while and Gramps figured she'd be back in seconds and he really had to go, too. He didn't think the baby would be alone that long."

Daisy made a choked sound. "He's got to be blaming himself for this, too."

Too? Gideon's gaze flicked to her face. She looked too pained for simple compassion. "You're not blaming yourself, are you, Daisy?"

Daisy shook her head, but without much conviction. "No. Not really. It's like this nightmare of cause and effect. I shot up his car, so he was forced to steal another." She lowered her voice to a barely audible whisper. "I should have tried harder to kill him."

"No," Rafe growled. "This is not your fault. You did everything right. It was his choice to shoot Gideon and to shoot at you. It was his choice to steal that woman's car. And to hit the woman on the head with a rock."

Daisy flinched. "Did he kill her?" she asked, still in a whisper.

Rafe shook his head. "No. But she lost consciousness for a little while. Her husband came out of the bathroom to see her on the ground and immediately called 911."

"The sheriff left our scene to rush to the rest area," Daisy said.

"They must have put out a BOLO right away," Gideon added. "Did they find her car?"

"Yes." Rafe hesitated. "He'd used it to run over the owner of a truck. He died of his injuries."

Daisy covered her mouth with her hand. "Oh God."

Rafe nodded. "I know. It took them a while to ID him. His name is Ryder Young. He was on his way north and took a detour for some Shasta photos. Luckily, he'd told someone where he'd be, and when he didn't show up at his next stop, they called the state police, looking for him. He had no ID."

"The shooter took it to give himself some time," Gideon murmured. "And the child wasn't in the stolen car?"

"No. We can only assume that the shooter took the child with him. Ryder Young's truck hasn't been found yet. It's too old to have GPS, so no way to physically track it. State police are out looking. Everyone's looking. Photos of the little girl are being posted everywhere, all over the Internet. Amber Alerts. You name it. Right now our best lead is tracing the shooter's steps through Eileen."

"I gave your phone to your boss," Daisy said to Gideon. "She said that your e-mail was on there, so it was classified. I didn't think to check first to see if you'd heard from your colleague in San Diego."

Gideon frowned for a moment, trying to place the detail. It was in his brain somewhere.

"The college swimmer with the almost-Eden tattoo," she said softly, reminding him.

"Oh, right." He shot her a grateful glance. "Maybe he knows where the community is."

She kept stroking his hair and it felt so nice. "Or knows someone who does."

Rafe must have looked confused because Daisy was telling him about the tattoos she'd found online.

Rafe made a frustrated sound. "Given what they did to Eileen, Mercy, and Gideon, it's fair to assume they were too scared to report the cult," he said. "Hope they talk to us."

Rafe's words flooded Gideon's mind with images of

Eileen's battered face and the other injuries Sammie Danton had repaired.

And, of course, Mercy. *I should have been searching harder. I should have found them by now. Mercy would get justice and Eileen might still be alive.*

"Whatever you're thinking," Rafe warned, *"don't.* You just went somewhere bad."

Gideon exhaled. It was true. "I'll try."

Rafe pushed to his feet. "I'm going now. I have work to do to prep for tomorrow. Gid, please do what the docs say to do. Don't be yourself."

Gideon found he could still laugh. "Okay. Is your mom here?"

Rafe rolled his eyes. "Of course. But let her do her thing. She needs to."

"Rafe," Gideon called as his friend turned to leave. "Tell me what you find? Even if it's bad."

Rafe nodded once. "Okay."

When he was gone, Gideon looked up at Daisy. "You're going to the Sokolovs' house, right? Please don't argue. I need to know you're safe and getting some rest yourself."

"I'll leave when the nurses throw me out," she promised. "And I probably will end up at Karl and Irina's. My dad, too."

"Oh, right. He's here." Gideon wasn't sure if this was a good or bad thing until she smiled.

"Yes. He and Karl are patching things up. If I stay with them, it'll give Dad and Karl more time together, because Dad won't leave my side for a while."

"I can't blame him."

She stroked his cheek. "Me either. Today was intense."

He lifted one side of his mouth, the pain meds dragging him under. "You saved my life. Went all Rambo on the guy's ass."

She caressed his lip with her thumb. "Not Rambo. Try Lara Croft. I always wanted to be her."

He grinned, but sleepily. "Rather try you."

She snorted. "Go to sleep, Gideon."

"Will you stay?" he murmured.

She pressed a soft kiss to his temple. "I'll be here when you wake up in the morning."

TWENTY-ONE

O ver there." He pointed to their office, adjacent to the hangar that held all the old man's planes. The airfield was deserted, as he'd known it would be. The only flight they had today was the charter to New York City, and Hank and whoever they'd gotten to fill in would be spending the night there and flying back in the morning. "Park in the first space. Don't touch those wires." He'd hot-wired the van when he'd stolen it up in Chico. The procedure had been an enormous pain in the ass given his thumb and first two fingers on his left hand were basically useless. He did not want to have to do that again.

The nurse, Amber Shelton, obeyed. He'd been pleased with her obedience. If she stitched him up quickly, he'd give her the same consideration.

He slid the side door open and climbed out, opening the driver's door. "Get out."

"What are you going to do to me?" the nurse asked, her voice shaking.

"Like I said, if you do as I ask, I won't hurt you." He closed the driver's door and the slider, hiding the kid from view. It was twenty-five degrees warmer here than up in the mountains. Plus he'd leave the engine running. There was still a quarter of a tank of gas, enough for where he needed to go to dispose of the nurse and drop off the kid.

Pressing the barrel of his gun to her back, he walked her into the office and shut the door. He swung his backpack to the counter. "Get the suture kit out."

Her eyes widened. "What?"

"Get the suture kit out," he repeated slowly. "You'll need to clean, disinfect, and stitch up my hand. If you hurt me on purpose, I'll kill you. If you try to escape, I'll kill you. If you do as I ask, I'll take you back to the hospital."

She looked up at him, her skepticism clear. But she didn't have much choice, did she? No, she did not. She must have figured the same thing because she reached into the backpack and began to assemble what she needed to fix his hand.

She unwrapped the bandage. "This already looks infected. You need an antibiotic."

"I know," he murmured, grateful that she was being gentle.

He almost wished she'd be a jerk. But she wasn't. She cleaned out the wound and stitched it quickly and competently. Then rebandaged it.

She took a step back, not meeting his eyes. He scooped up the remaining suture supplies into the backpack, making sure he packed the bloody gauze pads in the front pouch. He wouldn't leave them behind.

"Thank you," he said again. "Let's go."

He gestured for her to get back behind the wheel and resumed his place behind her seat. After closing the doors, he directed her to go north, past Sacramento International Airport. "Continue on this road."

She complied, turning when he told her to, her body shaking with terror as they got closer to the river. She brought the minivan to an abrupt stop on the two-lane access road.

"No," she declared. "I'm not going to make this any easier for you. You're going to kill me and dump me in the river. You can drag me the whole way. I'm not driving up to the water's edge."

He had to respect her guts. But it didn't change what he had to do. "Okay," he said. "Suit yourself." Leaning forward, he released her seat belt and, sliding the forearm of his injured hand behind her head, quickly knocked her off balance and over the console.

He put his gun to her head and pulled the trigger, grateful for the silencer. A mild pop later, she fell over the console into the passenger seat.

He drove to the river's edge and found a portion of road with nothing nearby. No one coming or going. No one to see what he was doing. He opened the front passenger door, pulled the nurse's body out and to the ground, then kicked her into the river.

She'd end up on shore eventually, but hopefully not before morning.

Then he got back into the van and drove back toward the city.

SACRAMENTO, CALIFORNIA
SUNDAY, FEBRUARY 19, 7:45 P.M.

Daisy found her father and Karl in the waiting room. Talking. And smiling. Both men's eyes were red and Daisy considered that a promising thing. Both stood when she entered. "Did you get kicked out?" Karl asked.

She hugged them both and took the empty chair between them. "I did," she said when they'd sat down. "Irina told me to let someone else have a turn. Which meant her." She held her father's hand. "So did you guys kiss and make up?"

Karl chuckled. "We did."

"Except Irina did the kissing," Frederick added. "How is Agent Reynolds?"

"Annoyed that he can't go back to work tomorrow,"

she said with a shrug. Leaning her head on her father's shoulder, she closed her eyes on a sigh. "I'm tired."

"You have a right to be," Frederick murmured, kissing her forehead. "You've had an eventful few days."

Now that she knew Gideon was all right, her mind was awake and spinning even though her body was weary. "Indeed."

"I'll take you to Karl's house," Frederick said. "You should sleep."

Daisy shook her head. "I'm staying." She held her hand up to stop her father's disapproval. "He asked me to stay. I promised him I'd be here when he woke up."

Frederick sighed. "All right then. You should stay."

Now that she knew Gideon was all right, all her mind could see was Trish's body, covered in blood on her living room floor. "Trish has been dead for almost forty-eight hours. The morgue's had her for twenty-four. How long before they release her body?"

Frederick wrapped his arm around her shoulders. "I don't know."

"Rafe will know," Karl said. "I'm so sorry, honey. She was a nice young woman."

"Yes, she was," Daisy agreed sadly, her chest suddenly heavy and tight. "I'm listed as her next of kin. She had no family. I have to plan her . . . what to do with her."

Karl reached over and tilted her chin up until she looked up at him. "She had family, Daisy. She had us. We'll help you with the arrangements. Don't worry. If Rafe doesn't know when her body will be released, I'll call the morgue. Irina and I have friends in the funeral home business. We'll find one who'll take care of Trish, okay?"

Daisy's eyes stung. "Thank you. I've never planned a funeral before."

"Is that what you want?" Karl asked. "A traditional funeral?"

"I think she would," Daisy murmured.

"Well," Frederick said with a sigh, "she won't know. You will. Funerals are for the living, honey. It's the opportunity for her friends to get together and remember her life."

"Then that's what we'll do," she whispered. "Trish has a lot of friends." She winced. "*Had* a lot of friends. She grew up around here, so she had a lot of friends outside of work and school and AA. People I've never even met. We'll get the word out and have a party at the community center. That's what she would have wanted. I'll ask Rosemary for help in reserving a room. She's my sponsor and manages the room reservations for AA. She'll know who to ask to get a room big enough for Trish's friends."

Both men went still. "What?" she asked, looking from one to the other.

"We'll need to get security," Frederick said. "In case he tries to get you again."

Because the bastard was still out there, walking around with a piece of his hand missing. "I agree that we need security, but not that he was after me. He shot at Gideon."

"And if he'd killed him?" Frederick asked quietly. "He would have killed you next."

Once again, the image of Trish's mutilated body flashed through her brain. "You're right," she murmured. *That could have been me. He would have done that to me.* "We'll ask the FBI and SacPD to provide surveillance, just in case he crashes Trish's service."

"How will we know him?" Karl asked. "Other than a basic physical description, nobody knows what he looks like. And if you make it an open invitation, you won't know who's supposed to be there versus who's just there to either gawk, report on the story, or . . . hurt you."

"He'll have an injured hand, for starters." Daisy

thought of the bare skin below the hollow of Trish's throat. "And he'll probably be wearing her necklace."

SACRAMENTO, CALIFORNIA
SUNDAY, FEBRUARY 19, 8:40 P.M.

He pulled the minivan into the parking lot of the hospital nearest to his house. It didn't have a special unit for kids, but it had a general ER and that would have to do. His hand throbbed, his head ached, and he was utterly spent. He'd slept fitfully in his car the night before, waiting for Agent Reynolds and Daisy to emerge from their hotel, then that clusterfuck on the mountain, and then the drive home.

Throw in killing the nurse and he'd had a fucking busy day.

Almost done. Almost home. He got out of the car and looked around for anyone who'd see him. Finding no one, he turned off the ignition, leaving nothing but blissful silence. He popped the locks, got out, and opened the slider door.

The kid stared up at him, all blinking brown eyes. "See you around, kid. Sorry about all this." Then he made sure his hat was on straight and the wig was covering his face.

He started walking toward his own house. All he wanted was a shower and his own bed. And after a good night's sleep, he wanted Zandra. Fortunately, he still had her available, because he'd have a helluva lot of stress come morning.

He'd gone five blocks when he saw a pay phone. Snugging the cap down to cover his face, he lifted the receiver and dialed 911.

"What is your emergency?"

"I saw a baby abandoned in a car in the parking lot of the hospital."

"Which hospital, sir?"

"The one at J and Forty-first." He hung up before the operator could ask any more questions. "Okay, kid," he muttered under his breath. "That's the best I got."

He still had a mile to go before he got home. He'd done this route a hundred times on his morning jog, but he hadn't been bone tired with a shot-up hand then.

He also hadn't been one step away from life in prison before, either. The real danger of being caught gave him the extra burst of energy he needed to make it the rest of the way.

He let himself in, then let Mutt in from the backyard. "Sorry I left you outside. I bet you're hungry." He gave the dog some food, then staggered off to the shower.

He let out a sigh of relief. He'd done it. He'd gotten himself home, where the cops would never find him. He'd dealt with the baby. Tomorrow, he'd deal with the Fed and Daisy Dawson. For now . . . sleep. That was all he wanted.

||| SACRAMENTO, CALIFORNIA
MONDAY, FEBRUARY 20, 2:10 A.M.

The throbbing pain in his arm pulled Gideon from a fitful sleep, but it was the sniffling that fully woke him. He turned to see Daisy sitting in the chair next to him, her head bowed, her arms crossed tightly across her chest.

Her shoulders shaking with sobs she was desperately trying to keep quiet.

His heart crumbled, watching her. She'd been through so much the past few days, yet she'd continually held herself together. "Hey," he said, his voice coming out gravelly.

She looked up through her hair, one hand clamping over her mouth while the other wiped at her eyes.

Turning her head so that he couldn't see her face, she shuddered out a breath. "Sorry. I didn't mean to wake you up."

"You didn't. My arm did. Why are you asleep in the chair? You should be at Karl and Irina's, in a real bed."

"You asked me to stay."

He frowned. "I did?"

She nodded. "You did." She dashed away a few more tears. "You were on some good drugs, I think. You were falling asleep."

"That was kind of selfish of me to ask," he said. "But I'm finding it hard to feel regret for my actions." He could get used to waking up to her pretty face. "Come here." He patted the edge of the bed. "Put the railing down and come here."

She looked over her shoulder. "I think the nurses will yell." But she got up to lean over the rail to place a kiss on his forehead. "You should go back to sleep."

"I can't." He patted the bed again. "I don't want any more pain meds, so come here and take my mind off things." He blinked what he hoped were pitiful puppy-dog eyes. "You'd be doing a humanitarian act of kindness."

Her lips twitched. "Humanitarian, huh?"

He nodded soberly. "Come lie with me for a little while. If the nurses yell, we'll apologize profusely. Please?"

She lowered the rail. "I don't want to hurt you."

"You won't," he said firmly.

She looked doubtful but carefully climbed into the bed, snuggling down until her head was on his left shoulder. She cuddled close, resting her hand over his heart.

"This okay?" she asked softly.

He sighed, contented. "Perfect." He kissed the top of her head. "Where's Brutus?"

"Asleep on the floor. I think she needed a break from me. I've kind of petted her a lot today."

Because it had been a pretty horrible day. Still, he held Daisy against him and it was so nice. "She's got to be hungry by now."

"Sasha brought some food for her. Don't worry." She patted his chest. "Go to sleep."

He didn't think he could. "Are you okay now?" he murmured, hoping he could give her the same comfort she was giving him.

"Of course."

Stupid question, Gideon. Of course she's not okay. She was just crying her eyes out. He hummed deep in his throat. "Okay, I'm going to try that again. Are you okay now?"

She lifted her head to glare at him. "If you didn't want my answer, you shouldn't have asked the question."

"Fair enough," he said. She rested her head on his shoulder and he nuzzled her hair, liking the feel of it getting caught in the stubble covering his jaw. "Why were you crying?"

She was quiet for a long moment. "Trish," she finally said. "I only knew her for six months, but she and I . . . we fit. Sasha and I have been friends forever and I love her like my own sister, but Trish was the first friend I'd made on my own since we went into hiding." Her voice dropped to a tortured whisper. "I can't believe she's gone. I don't want to think about how she suffered, but it's all I can think about."

He wanted to tell her it would be all right, wanted to promise that they'd catch the man who'd killed her friend. He wanted to tell her not to think about the way Trish had died, but she'd seen the body herself. Telling her to simply "not think about it" was neither fair nor reasonable. But he could try to distract her. Unfortunately, not the way he'd distracted her the night before. Hopefully it would be as helpful, though.

"Tell me about her. How you met her. Tell me about the things you did together."

"We met at AA," she began, "and we just hit it off." She kept talking, then she started crying, soaking his hospital gown with her tears. After a while, her words slowed, grew slurred. And then she was asleep on his chest, just as she'd been the night before.

He wasn't sure how much time had passed when the nurse came in to check on him, because he'd fallen asleep, too.

"Agent Reynolds," the nurse said quietly, and he jerked awake.

He looked up at the nurse pleadingly. He'd learned the woman was something of a softy and had a son who was a cop. "Let her sleep," he murmured. "Please."

"I wish I could, but I have to check your vitals and she's in the way."

Daisy stiffened, sucking in a startled breath, and he knew she was awake. She lifted her head, narrowing her eyes before they flared almost comically wide. "Oh. I'm sorry."

"Stay," he said firmly, but she shook her head.

"It's okay," she said, softening her words with a smile. "I got what I needed, so thank you. The nurse needs to do her job and I need to walk Brutus." She slid from the bed and picked up the furball who'd curled up on her big bag.

His pulse skyrocketed. Walking Brutus. Outside? No way in hell. *"Daisy."* Her eyes snapped back to him, wide and alarmed.

"What?"

"Agent Reynolds," the nurse cautioned. "Take it down a notch."

He dragged in a harsh breath. "You can't go outside, Daisy. Ask someone else to walk her. Please."

Understanding dawned in her eyes. "Oh, right." She

laughed bitterly. "I almost forgot. How messed up is that?"

He forced his muscles to relax. "You had other things on your mind."

She huffed her frustration. "I'm sorry. I didn't mean to do that." She pointed at the monitor, where his pulse was slowly decreasing. "I'll be careful. I promise. I won't go outside. I'll be back soon."

Sighing, the nurse did all the necessary checks. "That poor girl," she clucked once Daisy had gone. "She's been through the wringer these past few days. Hated to wake her up. Don't worry. There's plenty of extra security here tonight."

"Because of us?"

She shook her head. "Well, not just because of you. That little girl that got kidnapped after you were shot? She was found at Mercy."

Gideon sat up abruptly, sending new pain shooting down his arm. "Mercy? Where?"

The nurse took a half step back. "Mercy Hospital is only ten minutes from here."

"Oh." His lungs emptied on a rush. "I'm sorry. Mercy is my sister's name and I—" He stopped himself from rambling. "I didn't mean to startle you." He pulled his thoughts back under control. "Was she okay? The little girl?"

"She was fine. A little dehydrated, maybe. From what I heard through the grapevine. The police haven't made any statements yet."

"How did they find her?"

"A 911 call. Again, from what I heard."

911 call? What the hell? "Does the grapevine know who made the call?"

She shook her head. "Not that I heard. If I pick up any new intel, I'll let you know. Anyway, they've beefed up security around all the hospitals in the area, just in case he's nearby. We can't turn around for tripping over a cop. Your girlfriend will be fine."

Yes, she would. Because he was getting out of this place. As soon as possible.

"You're due for some pain meds," the nurse said. "Let me know when you want them."

That'll be never. He couldn't go nodding off again. "I'm okay without them."

"I kind of figured you'd say that. You cops are all alike. You know how to get me if you need me."

"I need to make a phone call," he said.

She pointed at the remote that controlled the TV. "On the other side is the phone."

When she was gone, he flipped the phone and dialed his boss's number. "It's Gideon," he said when he got her voice mail. "My laptop was in my car up in Macdoel. I assume someone from your office retrieved it. Can you have it brought to me at the hospital?" He gave her the room number. "I'll also need my phone back. Thanks."

He had work to do.

TWENTY-TWO

Good morning, A—" His boss broke off her greeting when Gideon tapped his finger to his lips, then pointed to Daisy, who slept in the chair next to his bed. "Agent Reynolds," Molina continued in a whisper.

Gideon pointed to the empty chair on the other side of the bed. "Good morning," he murmured. He nodded to the laptop bag over Molina's shoulder. "Mine?"

"Yes. With your phone." She laid them carefully on the bed beside him. "You're not supposed to be working. You're officially on medical leave until you're healed and cleared to return to duty."

Gideon gave her his best innocent look. "I won't. I promise."

She snorted. "Right." She sat in the chair and glanced over at Daisy. "She needs to go home and rest."

He sighed. "I apparently asked her to stay when I was on pain meds last night."

"I doubt she would have left, even if you hadn't. She's loyal. And smart. She called me last night."

Gideon blinked. "She did?"

"She did. She asked us to place surveillance cameras at the rec center where they'll do Miss Hart's memorial service. Told us to look for a man with an

injured hand who might be wearing her friend's necklace. We will, of course."

"Good," Gideon murmured.

Molina gave Daisy a sympathetic look. "I don't
think it's sunk in yet. That her friend is gone, I mean.
She seemed too . . . rational."

"She is rational." And loyal and smart. And fearless. The memory of her scrambling up that hillside
with his rifle, of her going after that car on foot . . . they
still made his gut turn to water. "And the death of her
friend is starting to sink in."

His hospital gown was still a little damp from where
she'd cried all over him. And then she'd let him hold
her. He'd been the one to give her comfort. It felt too
damn good.

Too damn right. Whatever it took, he was keeping
that feeling.

"I heard that the little girl was found," he told his
boss. "My night nurse told me."

"It's all over the news, so I'm not surprised."

"She's still okay?"

"Unhurt. Her grandparents admitted to giving her
a large dose of Benadryl. They were on a long drive
and wanted to keep her quiet."

"Lovely," he said sarcastically.

"Yeah, well." She shrugged. "Not sure if they'll be
charged or not. The kid being quiet might have saved
her. If she'd screamed, he might have killed her, too."

"Too?" Gideon asked quietly. "You mean besides
the man at the rest area?"

"I hope he's the only one. He grabbed a nurse from
another hospital's parking lot. The nurse hasn't been
seen since." She grimaced. "The interior of the minivan the kid was found in was covered in blood." She
sighed. "And brain matter."

God. "He shot the nurse."

"It appears so."

"He needed medical attention," Gideon said grimly. "At least Daisy hit him hard. Hopefully this slows him down a little. What's next?"

"Agent Schumacher and Detectives Sokolov and Rhee go to Portland."

That detail he vaguely remembered from the night before. "Did you get a hit on the license plates of the beige car?" Because Daisy had reported them when she'd called 911. He vaguely remembered that as well.

"They're registered to Delfina Borge. California DMV says she lives in Blythe. That's near the Arizona border. She's never been reported as missing. We're going to contact her employer as soon as their office opens. She was a professor in a small college. The last post on social media said she'd quit and was about to go on a two-year trip around the world. That was over a year ago."

"What about the other victims? What have we done to connect them?"

Irritation flickered in her eyes, but Gideon didn't sense that it was directed toward him. "The team's working on it," she said. "So far they haven't found any commonalities. Even where the victims' last movements were traceable, there's no pattern. A few were last seen at bars. One at a movie theater. She'd just seen a horror movie. One at a concert."

"Who was performing?" Gideon asked.

Molina shook her head, bewildered. "Barry Manilow, of all people. The venue's security has been very cooperative. They're sending us tapes today."

Tapes. Gideon stilled, his brain reconnecting with an almost audible click. The pet store from Saturday. The shopping center's security staff had also been cooperative. They'd given him a digital file of the surveillance tapes of the parking lot outside the pet store during the adoption clinic.

The beige car had followed them up to Redding. What if it had been following them even longer?

"Daisy volunteered at a pet store Saturday," he said. "They were hosting an adoption clinic for an animal shelter."

"You think he might have followed you from there?"

"It's possible."

"I'll get the tapes from the shopping center," she said. "Thanks."

He gave her a brisk nod. "You're welcome." He didn't offer her his copy of the tapes. The Bureau would, he reasoned, have to get their own anyway. Chain of evidence and all that. Especially now that he was involved as a victim. *Asshole shooter. Making me a fucking victim.*

But I can tell them where to look on the tape if I see him first. He was pretty certain he'd see the beige car. Seeing who was driving it would be the icing on the cake.

Molina stood up, studying his face intently. "You're to rest, Agent Reynolds."

He nodded soberly. "Yes, ma'am."

She rolled her eyes. "You're so full of it, Gideon."

She surprised a laugh out of him. "I can't do much else but rest from here," he said.

"Uh-huh. You're on medical leave until you're cleared to return."

"I know."

She sighed. "I'm serious. Do not get yourself hurt any worse. Okay?"

"Hey, I was just on a drive with a pretty girl," he said lightly. "It's not my fault some asshole shot me."

A slight sound came from the chair where Daisy slept. Something between a cough and a laugh. Okay, so she wasn't really asleep. "Daisy?"

She sat up, rubbing at her eyes. "Sorry. I really was asleep until you laughed, Gideon. I mostly caught the 'not my fault' line."

And the "pretty girl" line, he thought. Her cheeks were a charming pink.

Daisy stood up. "I'll wait outside if you want to finish your meeting."

"No," Gideon said.

"Not necessary," Molina said at the same time. "I'm on my way out." Holding the door open, she turned to point her finger at Gideon. "I'm serious," she said, very soberly. "You are on leave. You will have an agent assigned to your protection detail."

That was good. They'd keep Daisy safe. "Thank you."

Molina narrowed her eyes, as if not trusting his easy acceptance of a bodyguard. "You are not to investigate this case. Are we clear?"

He nodded. "Yes, ma'am. Crystal."

She rolled her eyes again. "Or you will face disciplinary actions."

"I understand."

"Oh, for fuck's sake," Molina muttered, shutting the door behind her.

Daisy blinked, rolling her head side to side. "What was that?"

He smiled at her. "Nothing you need to worry about."

She stood up, shouldering Brutus's bag. "I'm going to get coffee. You want some?"

"Yes, thank you." He hesitated. "And thank you for staying. I didn't realize how much I needed to see you when I woke up, until I did and you were there."

Her smile lit up her eyes. "I wanted to." She cupped his cheek, her thumb riffling through the day-old growth as she stroked his jaw. "I needed to. I needed to see you when I woke up, too." She brushed a kiss over his lips. "Now do the thing you were planning to do while you were saying all those 'Yes, ma'ams' to your boss."

He snorted. "Yes, ma'am."

SACRAMENTO, CALIFORNIA
MONDAY, FEBRUARY 20, 7:25 A.M.

He squinted at the light flooding his bedroom. He'd ne-glected to pull the shades last night and his damn win-dow faced east. Rolling over, he pulled the pillow over his head, only to peek out when he heard a whimper.

Mutt was pawing at his mattress, a sure sign that the dog needed to go out.

It was the worst part about having a damn dog. But if he didn't take Mutt out, he'd be cleaning up a pile of shit.

He groaned, swinging his legs over the side of his bed. He needed to walk off this stiffness in his joints. He'd been in a car too much yesterday. And his hand throbbed.

At least he didn't have to go into work this morning. Hank and the substitute pilot would be flying back from New York City today.

He checked the calendar on his phone for his next shift. Wednesday, round trip to Salt Lake. His hand would not be better by Wednesday. He needed at least a week before he could handle the flight duties safely.

He'd have to call in sick. He'd spend the time finishing what would be a beautiful portfolio of photos for the old man. Lots of photos of him with very bad people. And some very beautiful people. The bad people—notable drug dealers who hired him to carry product in his planes—would get him in trouble with the cops. The beautiful people would get him into trouble with Sydney.

Which will get me *into trouble with Sydney.*

You're already in trouble with Sydney. She's owned your ass since you were twelve years old. You should have killed her then.

Because Sydney had compromising photos of him, too. Of them together. And even though it had never been his choice, the photos made it look like it had been. Once his father saw them, any hope he had of forcing the old man's hand would be gone. *I'll be lucky if the old man doesn't order me killed for fucking his wife.*

The only good thing to come of the photos Sydney had taken was that it had given him the idea to begin collecting his own blackmail fodder. So at a minimum, they'd all be at a stalemate.

If he was lucky, the sale wasn't yet finalized and the portfolio he'd gathered would put the brakes on it.

He wanted the airline. He deserved it. He'd *earned* it. Every time he'd let the old man walk all over him. Every time he'd allowed Sydney to . . .

To fuck me up. To ruin me. I earned *it.* Again and again and again.

He slapped the sides of his head, hard. "Not having this conversation today." He'd deal with Sydney at a time of his choosing.

Grabbing the remote on his nightstand, he turned on the TV on his dresser, tuning in to CNN. He was interested to know what the media was reporting on the events of yesterday. And, if he was honest, if it had made the national news yet.

He pulled on his track pants, searching for his shoes as he listened to the anchor welcome them to the "bottom of the hour" and prattle on for a moment about the newest congressional scandal and the war in the Middle East.

"And now for the latest news out of Sacramento," the woman on-screen said soberly. "The man suspected of killing twenty-six-year-old Sacramento native Trisha Hart has been linked to the deaths of at least six more women, this according to our sources, and is the subject of an ongoing FBI investigation.

Many of the victims were found with letters carved into their torsos. Common to all of the victims was a knife found at the scene—washed, bleached, and left to dry. The victims have been found in seven different states over the past ten years. It's the opinion of one source at Sacramento PD, who requested anonymity because he wasn't authorized to comment on this case, that this is the work of a serial killer."

Abandoning his shoe search, he slowly lowered himself to the bed. "Fuck," he muttered at the TV, where the abduction and safe return of the big-brown-eyed kid was now being discussed—and attributed to the same man, who had left a "trail of death" in his wake.

They'd put it together, he thought grimly. He hadn't expected that they would. *It was the letters. I never should have started that.*

But it was done now. *At least they can't trace the victims to me.* He'd never been fingerprinted and his DNA had never been analyzed anywhere, so the skin samples that the cops took from under Daisy's nails could not implicate him. Nor could any prints he'd left on the beige Chevy, if any of the car was even salvageable after being burned up.

He found his shoes, shoved his foot into one, then leaned over to tie it. But he paused once again when a new photo popped up on-screen. And he heard himself growl.

"Special Agent Gideon Reynolds," the anchor said, "one of the lead investigators on the serial killer case, was shot and hospitalized yesterday. It is believed the shooter, the serial killer, and the kidnapper are one and the same. Special Agent Reynolds should be released from the hospital later today and is expected to make a full recovery. The FBI and Sacramento PD will be holding a joint press conference later this morning. This is a developing story, so stay tuned for further updates." She then turned to her left. "And now, the weather."

The Fed won't make a full recovery, he thought. *Because I'm going to kill him. But at least while he's in the hospital, he won't be hovering over Daisy.* He glared balefully at his bandaged hand. *Who shot me, the bitch.*

It was bizarre how he'd been fantasizing about keeping Daisy as his own less than twenty-four hours ago. Now all he could think about was making her suffer for shooting his damn hand and ruining his car.

He wondered where Daisy was at the moment. It was Monday morning. Turning off the TV, he switched on the radio next to his bed and set it to *The Big Bang with TNT and Poppy*—a.k.a. Eleanor, a.k.a. Daisy. He could at least find out if she was at work or home. That way he'd know where to go to shoot her, for God's sake.

The station was actually playing music for a change instead of talk, talk, talk. He applied a mustache and eyebrows and smoothed a wig over his bald head, finishing as the song was over, and poor Mutt was spinning in circles next to his bedroom door. He paused, leash in his right hand, when the DJ started talking over the music.

"And that was a blast from the past," the man said. "Kansas with 'Dust in the Wind.' I'm Alfred, substituting for TNT and Poppy. TNT's taking a vacation and Poppy's out sick, so send her good thoughts, okay?"

He switched the radio off and slipped both his gun and his switchblade into his coat pocket. Not at the radio station? He'd find out if she was home, and if so, he'd create a disturbance so that she came outside. He could force her back inside her place, slit her throat, and be gone in under a minute.

With one hand?

Fine, I'll shoot her. His gun was silenced. Even if her upstairs neighbors were home they wouldn't hear anything. He'd prefer to bring her home and make her a guest in his basement, but if that wasn't possible, a fast kill would have to do.

"Her home it is, Mutt." Mutt panted his approval.

And if she wasn't home, she was probably at the hospital with Reynolds. If so, he'd hide outside and shoot her as soon as she was visible.

And then when Reynolds was released, he'd do the same thing to him.

SACRAMENTO, CALIFORNIA
MONDAY, FEBRUARY 20, 7:25 A.M.

It didn't take Gideon long to spot the beige car on the shopping center's surveillance tape. It had already been parked in the lot when he and Daisy had arrived.

A shiver of cold ran down Gideon's spine. *He'd been waiting for her.*

He fast-forwarded in bursts until the car was gone, then rewound until he saw it again. Then he waited.

And clenched his teeth so hard that his jaw popped. A man approached. With a dog.

Gideon recognized the man. He was the unemployed drama teacher who'd hit on Daisy. The one Daisy had been kind to.

"Son of a mother*fucking* bitch," he snarled.

And the pulse monitor began to beep just as Daisy entered with two cups of coffee and a fast-dwindling smile. "What happened?" Sitting in the chair farthest from the monitor, she set one of the coffees on the table next to his bed but out of his reach. "The nurse is going to be here any—"

"Agent Reynolds!" the nurse scolded. "What are you *doing*?" She forcibly took the laptop from his hands, closed it, and handed it to Daisy. "You are *resting*. Not working."

Gideon closed his eyes, trying to relax, but all he

could see was that man, sitting less than an arm's length from Daisy. He could have hurt her then. Could have shot her. Could have touched her.

But he hadn't. He'd waited. He'd followed them, all the way to Redding, then Macdoel. *He shot at me. Not Daisy.*

Because he wanted me gone. He wanted her. And then? Gideon didn't have to imagine what the bastard would have done to Daisy had he been successful in killing Gideon.

He'd already done it to Trish Hart.

But he didn't. *Because Daisy can take care of herself.*

Gideon was finally able to drag in a breath. Then another. The memory of Daisy's face as she'd taken aim at the bastard's shooting hand . . . She'd been strong. Intense. Focused. Confident in her abilities.

And as sexy as that was, it was more comforting at the moment. Little by little he calmed himself, reining in his racing pulse, until the nurse finally made a noise of approval.

He opened his eyes to find Daisy watching him, her coffee clutched in one hand, Brutus in the other. She held Brutus up to her face, nuzzling her cheek into the little dog's fur. When he smiled she seemed to breathe again.

"I'm okay," he assured her. He glanced up at the nurse. "Really."

"That's because now you are not working," the nurse said tartly.

He chuckled. "Yes, ma'am."

The nurse shook her head. "You are not fooling me with that one, not again anyway. You 'Yes, ma'am' to make people leave you alone."

Daisy snorted into her coffee.

He raised a brow at her. "You're supposed to be on my side."

"I am," she said. "Which is why I'm agreeing with her."

He sighed. "I'm sorry."

The nurse glared at him as she backed toward the door. "I'm watching you."

Daisy snorted another laugh when the woman was gone. "You're a piece of work, Agent Reynolds."

"But you like me," he said smugly.

Her grin softened to the sweetest of smiles. "I do. Tell me what had you so angry."

He swallowed hard. "What was the name of that out-of-work drama teacher who talked to you on Saturday? At the adoption clinic?"

She frowned. "Really, Gideon? You're not still worried about—" She suddenly paled and set her coffee on the table, her hands trembling. "That was him?"

He nodded. "He left the store and got into the beige car. The shopping center's surveillance camera got part of his plate. It matches the one you saw yesterday."

She was nuzzling poor Brutus again, but the dog wasn't complaining. "I don't think he told me his name. His dog was George, that's all I remember." She was breathing fast and hard. "Gideon, he sat right next to me."

"I know," Gideon said grimly. "Cocky sonofabitch."

She covered her mouth with her hand, rocking herself slightly. "Oh my God."

He patted the bed. "C'mere."

He didn't have to ask her twice. She climbed on the bed, resting her head on his uninjured shoulder as she had in the wee hours of the morning, except this time she cuddled with Brutus as well. He kissed the top of her head, stroking her back as best he could reach with his other hand, mindful of the IV.

"He tried to hurt you," she whispered. "He would have killed you."

He blinked at that. "He wanted to get to you, honey."

"I know. But he would have killed you to do it."

For some reason that made him smile. "Lucky I had you to protect me."

She lifted her head to glare at him. "I'm not joking."

He kissed the tip of her nose. "Neither was I."

She narrowed her eyes slightly. "Well, all right then." She resettled her head, placing Brutus on his chest and her own hand over his heart. She was quiet for so long he thought she'd gone to sleep. But then she whispered, "What are we going to do, Gideon?"

He sighed. "We're going to track him down and put him away."

"He had a dog. He seemed good to it. The dog didn't seem afraid of him."

"Maybe it's a good lure. Gets his victims to let their guard down. A guy walking his dog can't be bad, right?"

"Yes," she said sadly, "you're probably right. It's just . . . when I think what he did to Trish and then I think about how he treated his dog . . ." She stiffened. "That night in the alley, he hesitated. He was going to shoot Brutus because she kept barking. But he hesitated. I used it to knee him and get away."

"He didn't dump the baby, either. He brought the kid with him. Changed cars at least twice along the way. Then left her at the hospital."

"He has . . . standards? How do we reconcile a man who's kind to dogs and babies with a monster who could do that to Trish? It's so different. How can he be so different?"

"I don't know," he said honestly. "I only know he's never getting his hands on you."

She shuddered. "Or you."

He kissed her head. "Or me."

"You need to tell Agent Molina."

"I know," he said glumly. "She's going to be pissed off."

The clearing of a throat had Gideon glancing up at the door to see Rafe grinning at them. Daisy wriggled like she was going to slide off, but Gideon pressed his hand into her back, ignoring the sharp pull of the needle in his hand. "It's just Rafe," he murmured. "Stay. Please."

She relaxed again, earning another kiss to the top of her head. He didn't care if Rafe saw or not.

"Why is your boss pissed off at you?" Rafe asked, crossing the room in two strides. He took the chair Daisy had slept in and put his feet up. "What did you do now?"

Gideon told him about the man at the pet store and Rafe instantly straightened, lowering the recliner footrest and leaning forward in the chair. "You're kidding."

"I wish," Gideon muttered. "Now I have to tell my boss."

"He wasn't supposed to be working on the case," Daisy said. "He disobeyed a direct order."

"Which I'd do again in a heartbeat," Gideon inserted.

Daisy lifted her head, talking to Rafe even though her gaze remained locked to Gideon's. "But now he's worried about facing the consequences."

"Yes," Gideon had to admit. "I am."

"Don't tell her," Rafe said. "I'll tell Agent Schumacher when I meet her at the airport for our flight to Portland. She can tell your boss that she found it."

"She'll go for that?" Daisy asked.

"Why not?" Rafe said with a shrug. "I get the impression that she likes Gideon and that she's ambitious enough to use the information for her own benefit."

Daisy grew stiff in Gideon's arms. "She likes him? Exactly how?"

Rafe laughed. "Withdraw your claws, DD. She's married."

"That doesn't stop some people," Daisy said darkly.

Gideon was working very hard to keep a stupid grin from his face. "It takes two to tango, Daisy. I'd have to want to be caught for her to have any chance of success. And I don't. I've worked with her on a few cases. She's good at her job and she does love her husband, so chill." He met Rafe's gaze straight on. "I heard about the nurse."

That Daisy didn't react at all made Gideon wonder exactly how long she had been awake when he and his boss had been talking.

Rafe sighed. "Yeah. Her body hasn't turned up yet. We know now that he drove the truck he stole from the rest area near Macdoel to Chico and stole the minivan from a grocery store employee there. The woman had just gone on shift, so she didn't even know the vehicle was gone."

"He's smart," Gideon muttered. "He waited for her for just that reason."

"I agree."

"Talk to area vets," Daisy said suddenly. "Veterinarians, I mean." She sat up, shifting to sit cross-legged near Gideon's knee. "He had a dog with him on Saturday. The dog had tags. I didn't examine them, but I remember that they clinked when I petted him. Maybe someone will recognize the dog from whenever he got his shots."

"And his owner," Gideon said. "Nice."

She smiled. "Thank you."

Something was nagging at the corner of his memory. Had been, he realized, since Daisy had mentioned the dog a few minutes before Rafe arrived. He frowned, thinking hard. Then tried to snap his finger, wincing when the IV needle reminded him of its continued presence. "The dog. Have Schumacher check out one of the victims. She was walking her dog in the park. Maybe he was, too."

Daisy's eyes widened. "Or maybe that's her dog. He takes souvenirs, Gideon."

"Shit." That, Gideon thought, was cold. And very much in line with this killer. "Maybe he did."

"Will do," Rafe promised, then checked his watch. "Gotta go. Have to be at the airport soon. If you think of anything else while you're not working, give me a shout. You guys stay safe today, y'hear?"

"Will do," Daisy promised, scrambling off the bed to give Rafe a hard hug. "You too."

When Rafe closed the door behind him, she returned to the chair next to the bed. "What now?"

He pointed to Brutus, who lay on his chest, quietly snoring. "Now I want you to take your dog and give me back my laptop."

She complied, glancing at the door. "If I get into trouble from the nurse, I'm going to say you coerced me."

"If she comes back in, I'll be playing solitaire," he promised. He clicked on his e-mail, nodding when he saw the one he'd been waiting for. "Dabney answered. My colleague in San Diego," he added when she looked confused.

"Oh, yeah. Did he find the swimmer with the almost-Eden tattoo?"

He scanned the e-mail and let out a relieved breath. "He did."

"What will you do?"

"Schedule a meet." He started a reply, hunting and pecking at the keys with one finger.

Daisy lifted his laptop from his lap with a sigh. "Let me type it. You'll take all day with one finger."

The brush of her hand against his stomach as she

took his computer made his body wake up. He inhaled, the scent of her shampoo nearly gone, but
enough remained to remind him of the shower
they'd taken Saturday night after the best sex he'd
ever had.

"I can do a lot with one finger," he whispered.

She froze, color flooding her face, and he knew she
was remembering, too. "Oh," she breathed. "Yes. Yes,
you can."

"When I get out of here," he promised. "As soon as
you take me home with you."

She drew a deep breath. "You are a dangerous man,
Gideon Reynolds."

He grinned up at her. "That's not a no."

She laughed breathlessly. "Definitely not a no. But
we're not going to talk about that now, because it's
almost visiting hours and Irina promised she'd be
back." She glanced at his lap where the sheet was definitely tented. "So think unsexy thoughts." She sat in
the chair, his computer on her lap. "Like how you
want me to answer your friend about meeting the
swimmer."

That did the trick. His erection abruptly gone, he
settled back into the pillows and closed his eyes.
"'Dabney, thanks for the quick reply.'" He paused
to give Daisy a chance to keep up. "'I was shot
yesterday and am still in the hospital, but should
be out later today. I could fly down to meet you
tomorrow or the next day. Let me know.' Sign it:
G. Reynolds."

She read it back to him and he noted she'd eliminated "tomorrow," amending the message to read
"Wednesday or later in the week." That was probably
best. He nodded, sudden fatigue smacking him like a
ton of bricks. "Send it, please," he said, then let himself
drift off.

"Good morning."

He nodded to the woman walking a corgi, forcing his lips to curve. "Morning."

It was a nice enough morning, although a bit chilly for his tastes. Seemed that folks in the neighborhood didn't agree because he'd passed at least a dozen people walking their dogs. At least there was no danger of sweating through his facial prosthetics. And the chill gave him an excuse to wear a form-hiding bulky coat.

He approached Daisy's house, slowing his step so that he could see if she was home. He stopped a house away, letting Mutt sniff around on the grass. Surreptitiously he studied the windows of her apartment. All dark.

She could still be asleep.

Or she might have gone elsewhere. Like the house in Granite Bay, where she'd gone Saturday after finding her friend's body. He'd take a drive out there later.

He frowned. But he needed another car. At this point he wasn't driving his own car anywhere. He didn't want any activities traced back to him. The Chevy was a burned-out, bullet-riddled mess, probably in some evidence garage somewhere getting picked over by forensics experts.

He snapped to attention when the garage door opened, then sighed with disappointment when he saw it was the tall blonde who'd come home so late Friday night, drunkenly singing Queen at the top of her lungs.

He nudged Mutt a little closer to the driveway as the blonde dragged the trash cans down from the garage to the street. She was muttering something about lazy brothers and lazier landlords.

The home was owned by Raphael Sokolov, the same detective that was on the case, so this was probably his sister, Sasha. A simple Google search had yielded information about all of the Sokolovs. If this was Sasha, she was a social worker. She wore her hair up in a loose twist, her slacks were tailored, and her shoes were comfortable-looking flats. Comfortable enough to allow her to jog back to the garage with athletic grace.

She'd look nice on the bed in my guest room.

"Woof," he muttered to Mutt, who took the hint and barked happily.

The woman turned toward the noise and he made a show of hushing Mutt. "Chill out, boy. She doesn't have time to play."

"Aw." The woman stopped, dropping to one knee to pet Mutt's head. Mutt lifted a paw to shake and she laughed, clearly charmed. "You're a flirt, aren't you? A cutie, for sure. What's your name?"

"Rolfe," he lied.

She looked up, eyes dancing. "Like on the Muppets?" She scratched Mutt behind his ears. "The piano-playing dog was Rolfe."

Actually, the piano-playing dog was Rowlf. Rolfe was the Austrian boy who betrayed the Von Trapp family at the end of *The Sound of Music*. He'd always liked Rolfe.

But Sasha's mistake was forgivable, so he smiled at her. "Exactly."

She gave Mutt a final pat on the head. "Bye, sweet boy. I'd rather play with you all day, but I've got to go to work."

No! he wanted to shout. He needed information, so he kept himself calm and casual. "Rolfe was hoping to see his little friend. Little powder-puff dog."

She smiled. "Brutus. She's not home right now. But maybe later today she'll be out." Waving good-bye, she jogged to her car, got in, and backed out of the garage.

She hit a button on her car to lower the garage door, gave Mutt another wave, and drove away.

She was nice. So as good as she'd look tied to his bed, he'd leave her alone.

Daisy was another story altogether. "Okay, Mutt. Looks like you'll get walked again later today." Tugging on the leash, he headed home.

And when Daisy was home? *What are you going to do with her?* A fast kill would be the smartest thing. Hopefully, he'd wounded the Fed badly enough that he hadn't survived. And if he did, he'd be in the hospital for a while. Leaving Daisy all alone.

He'd thought about this on his walk over. The best of all scenarios was to catch Daisy walking her dog. He could pretend to be surprised that they were neighbors and he'd remind her that he was the out-of-work teacher at the pet store. Her powder-puff dog could play with Mutt a little bit. Get her to let her guard down. It was preferable to bring her home, where he could keep her for a while—but not because she was nice. She'd be very sorry she'd shot him, for sure. If he had to, he'd just shoot her on the spot, but if there was any chance of bringing her home, he'd do it.

If he could just get her alone . . . *I can handle the rest. Either way.*

He spent the walk home planning all the things he'd do to her if he was able to bring her home. He'd definitely keep her for a while. Which meant he needed to be finished with Zandra Jones sooner versus later. He needed the space for Daisy.

He'd made it home and was in his kitchen, feeding Mutt, when his phone buzzed with a text. Immediately his good humor disappeared like mist in the sunlight.

Sydney. *Fucking Sydney.*

I called into the office to find out when you would be home from NYC. They said you'd called in sick. What's wrong?

Shit. Shit, shit, shit. He put the bowl of food on the
floor, whistling for Mutt, then sat at the kitchen table.
Texting with his nondominant hand was taxing but
possible. He picked the excuse that was most likely to
keep her far, far away.

*I have the flu. Probably contagious. Fever and
chills.*

Poor thing. I can have chicken soup delivered.

He huffed a sarcastic laugh. "Because you'd never
be caught dead being a caretaker," he said aloud, but
like always, no one heard. He clearly remembered the
time he was ten and she'd made him clean up his own
sick after vomiting. He'd cried out for help, but he
hadn't been heard then, either.

He was certain that piranhas were more maternal
than Sydney.

Then again, she was exactly what she'd purported
herself to be—a trophy wife. Her job was to keep
her figure trim, her makeup flawless, and the house
party-ready.

Oh, and to fuck her rich husband.

And his young son.

His phone buzzed again. *Sonny? Do I need to pay
you a visit?*

He *hated* when she called him Sonny. Hated when
she threatened to "visit." This was his space, goddammit. His. She was not welcome here. It was bad enough
what they did in her bed. In the old man's bed.

But not in my *bed.*

Breathe in, hold, breathe out. His pulse began to
slow so that his head no longer felt like it was going to
explode.

I was throwing up.

The text shut her up for a few minutes while he did
more yoga breathing.

Sorry. A green sick-face emoji. *Go rest. I'll check
on you later. Maybe I'll stop by and take care of you.*

His stomach did an actual slow roll and he suddenly did feel sick. "Taking care of him" had an entirely different meaning to Sydney than it did to the rest of the world. Rage bubbled up through him, mixing with the dread.

No. She was not coming here. She was not humiliating him in his own home. His hands shook with fury as he typed his reply.

Not a good idea. I don't want to give this to you. It's miserable. He sent it, but he was still damn *angry.* He pocketed his phone before he threw it across the room.

He pushed away from the table. If he was going to prepare space for Daisy, he'd better start now. Zandra was waiting. He'd break her today, then end her.

TWENTY-THREE

hanks, Rosemary," Daisy said into the phone as she paced around the waiting room down the hall from Gideon. "Trish didn't have a church and she spent so much time at the community center."

She was alone for the moment and wishing she had Brutus in her hands. But one of the nurses was walking her. For which she was very grateful, but . . . agitated. Beyond agitated. She was poised on the edge of a panic attack.

God, I need a drink. She stopped dead in her tracks. *No. No booze. You do not need a drink.* Perhaps it was good that she was talking to her sponsor. She cleared her throat. "I appreciate the help. Truly. The Sokolovs and my father are dealing with the funeral home and getting a reverend, but I told them I'd find a place."

"I'm . . ." Rosemary sighed. "I don't know the right word for what I am. I guess I'm honored to do it. Trish was special. Everyone at the community center knew her. When we add in her friends from work and school, we'll need the biggest room for her memorial service. Do you have a date set?"

"Not yet. The coroner hasn't . . ." Daisy drew a deep breath. Released it. Fought back the tears that were closing her throat. "The coroner hasn't released her body yet. I don't know when that will happen."

Rosemary was quiet for a long moment. "Daisy, are you all right?"

Daisy sank into one of the chairs, her right hand gripping the arm while her left held the phone so tightly she was surprised it hadn't shattered. "No," she whispered. "I'm not okay. I'm not okay at all."

"Where are you, honey?"

"In the hospital. In the waiting room. I can't leave by myself. I can't get any fresh air. I can't even walk Brutus. Someone's doing that for me right now."

"Why are you in the hospital?"

"Oh." She hadn't talked to Rosemary since Saturday night, when she'd told her that Trish was dead. She'd been Trish's sponsor, too. "I guess I've got some details to fill in."

"I guess you do. I've got my morning coffee and a cigarette. Start talking, honey."

So Daisy did. She told her about her trip to Redding with Gideon—excluding the night they'd spent together and the actual reason for the trip—and the shooting at Macdoel, the helicopter ride back, and the knowledge that two more people were dead because she hadn't stopped the shooter.

"You saved Agent Reynolds's life," Rosemary said, sounding a little awed.

"But not the guy at the rest area or the nurse."

"You're not responsible for their deaths, Daisy. You know that, right?"

"I know," she whispered. "In my head I know."

"But the heart twists things sometimes. Especially when we're under stress. You have been under tons of stress this week, Daisy. I thought the worst thing you were going to tell me was that you quit your job."

Daisy blinked. "Why would I tell you that?"

"I listened to your show this morning. There was another guy doing the show. Said TNT was on vacation and you were out sick. I figured TNT had been suspended over his remarks on the show on Friday."

Daisy blew out a breath. "I'd totally forgotten about that. Tad was a dick and he mouthed off to the station manager after Friday's show, which got him fired. I didn't even think about the show. I didn't ask for a replacement or time off or anything."

"Daisy," Rosemary chided gently. "You work for Karl Sokolov. He's your godfather, for heaven's sake. And he certainly knows what's going on. I'm guessing he and/or his wife have been at the hospital with you. You really think you needed to ask for time off?"

Daisy huffed a small laugh. "I guess you're right. That seemed like such a big deal on Friday. And then everything else happened."

"Like Agent Reynolds?"

Daisy's cheeks heated. "Yes. I really like him. A lot."

"I figured that out for myself," she said dryly. "How much longer will he be in the hospital?"

"They're supposed to discharge him this afternoon. He fell asleep, so I came into the waiting room to call you. I want to get a location for Trish's service before something else horrible happens."

"Normally I'd say not to expect the other shoe to drop, but you have a pretty good excuse. Now . . . let's return to the topic of Agent Reynolds. Don't think I missed that very skillful attempt to change the subject."

Daisy laughed, a real laugh this time. "You're too smart for me, Rosemary."

"Tell me about him," Rosemary said, a smile in her voice.

So Daisy did—excluding any of Gideon's secrets, of course. And she remembered once again why she'd known Rosemary was the right sponsor for her as soon as they'd been introduced. Rosemary had the ability to instantly connect with people, to ask the right questions.

"He knows about your sobriety?"

"Yes. He knew the first night we met."

"Which was what? Three days ago?"

Daisy frowned. "Three and a half," she said defensively.

Rosemary chuckled. "Okay. And those three and a half days have been highly chaotic. I'm not saying he's wrong or bad for you. He sounds pretty wonderful. Just be careful, honey. I've seen this too many times, two people falling in with each other too quickly."

Daisy heard the love in the woman's voice. "I'll be careful. And I'll introduce you to him as soon as I can. How's that?"

"A good start. How are you feeling now?"

"Better." And it was true. The door to the waiting room opened and a smiling nurse entered, nuzzling Brutus, grinning when the dog licked her cheek.

"She's walked," the nurse said with a final nuzzle. "But she's missing her mom."

"Thank you," Daisy said fervently, reaching for her lifeline. Brutus immediately snuggled up under her chin, as she did when she sensed Daisy's distress. "Thank you so much."

"Anytime. I had to fight the others for walking rights." Giving Daisy a wave, she left her alone.

"I've got Brutus back," Daisy told Rosemary. "I'm better now."

"Good. Now you know what I'm going to say next, right?"

"To take in a meeting and see a counselor."

"Exactly. You could be a sponsor, Daisy."

"Not me. Not yet." She shuddered at the thought of taking on that kind of responsibility. "I can't come to a meeting until this dies down. I'll put everyone in danger. Which brings me full circle back to Trish's memorial service. There will be security. And cameras."

"Why?" Rosemary demanded, clearly peeved.

"Because I'll be there. And Gideon. And because the man that killed her might show up."

Rosemary sighed. "That's going to keep some of the folks from coming out. Especially our AA group. They won't want the association, in case someone asks how they knew her."

"I know. If they catch him before the service, then we won't need it. If not, then maybe you can have a separate service, just for the AA group."

"Okay. I don't like it, but I understand it. Once you know when we can hold it, tell the police or FBI or whoever to contact me. I'll make sure it happens."

"Thank you," Daisy said again. "Thank you so much."

She ended the call and headed back to Gideon's room, unsurprised to find him on his laptop again. "You're gonna get in trouble."

He looked up and smiled. His hair was a mess and he needed to shave and trim his goatee, but he still looked like a movie star. "I thought you'd gone home."

"Nope. Just making some calls." She sat next to his bed, Brutus remaining in place under her chin. She could feel her little chest expand and fall with every breath she took, and the steady cadence calmed her. "What are you doing?"

"Did you eat?"

"Yes, the nurse gave me your breakfast when you were too asleep to eat it. She'll bring you another. I wouldn't eat the eggs. The sausage wasn't bad. What. Are. You. Doing?"

He tilted his head, staring at his laptop screen. "I had a quasi-dream."

"A quasi-dream? What exactly is that?"

"I think it really happened, but it's in that twilight area of my brain right now. Stuff's fuzzy."

"The anesthesia does that. What did you remember?"

He met her concerned gaze. "Did you suggest that

the men of Eden were there because they had something to hide?"

She blinked at him. "I truly don't know. When
would I have said this?"

"Right before the car locked up and died yesterday."

She frowned, rubbing her cheek over Brutus's fuzzy
bat ears as she searched her memory, nodding when she
found it. "Yes. I was saying that my family had moved to
our ranch to hide. I wondered why the adults in Eden
chose to live in such a primitive environment when they
didn't have to. Your mother's reasons I understood. I
think I was questioning the men in charge. You said
you'd given it some thought. And that's when the engine
started to lock up." She paused, studying him. "Why?"

"I woke up thinking about that. Maybe because it was
the last thought I had before going into survival mode."

"And?"

"I'd wondered if they were hiding. The men like Edward McPhearson and Ephraim Burton."

The man who'd tried to molest him, who'd died
as they'd fought. And the man who'd tried to kill him
afterward. Who now was missing an eye thanks to
thirteen-year-old Gideon's knife skills.

"What would they have been hiding from?"

"That's a very good question. I've run their names
through the database, but nothing popped up, which
didn't surprise me. That they changed their names
when they reached the community makes sense."

"And then?" she prompted.

"Well, now we have photos. I didn't have those before. I sent their photos—the two wedding photos from
Eileen's locket—to my friend in Philly."

"The one who age-progressed Eileen. You want
him to age-regress the two men."

He nodded. "I figured you'd understand."

She smiled at him, pleased with the compliment.
"And?"

"Well, he has to Photoshop Ephraim Burton's photo to give him back an eye. He said he'd have them back to me ASAP," he added, clarifying. "He knows this is a Bureau case now, so he can rush it."

"How far will you regress them?"

"At least ten years. I was in the community for eight years and they were there when I got there. They'd been there awhile. And then I'll ask that their photos be checked against the database with facial recognition software and see what pops up."

"Good job, Gideon," she said with a nod.

He grinned at her. "Thank you. What calls were you making?"

Her smile slipped. "I was trying to find a location for Trish's memorial service. The Sokolovs and my father are going to do the rest."

He instantly sobered. "I'm sorry, honey."

The endearment soothed her heart, just enough. "Thanks. Rosemary's going to plan most of it at the community center because I can't get out and do anything right now."

"Who's Rosemary?"

"My sponsor. She was Trish's sponsor, too."

He nodded slowly. "Are you having cravings, Daisy?"

She closed her eyes. "Yeah. And it's bad. Rosemary helped a lot, but . . . God." She swallowed. "I need to do something else. Something to take my mind off . . . *it*. And don't tell me to leave. I don't want to leave. I need to be here. With you. But . . . God, Gideon. I just . . . I need a distraction. I don't want to call Karl and Irina to come get me. One, I don't want them in danger. But mostly, my dad will see me like this and think I've fallen off the wagon. I haven't. I'm not even close, but . . ." She trailed off, having run out of words.

He patted the bed at his side. "Come on up. Bring Brutus. She likes me now."

"She liked you before," Daisy said. Carefully she

climbed up, snuggling into his side, laying her head on his shoulder, gripping his laptop when it threatened to slide off his lap. "I'm not hurting you, am I?"

"Not at all. Close that e-mail window," he directed, nodding at the screen. "My arms are occupied."

One was in a sling and one was lightly resting along her back. She did as he requested. And grinned when the screen filled with the opening credits of a TV show. "You were watching Buffy?"

"I cued it up, just in case I got bored. Or caught working again. Hit PLAY and we'll be distracted together until they spring me from this joint."

She laughed softly. "Thank you." Leaning back a little, she kissed his jaw. "Really."

"Anytime. Start it up and we can see the first episode of season one. It's best to begin a binge at the beginning."

"We could fast-forward to the part where she meets Angel."

"Nope. And please don't *tell* me that you're Team Angel."

"Don't *tell* me you're Team Spike," she replied dramatically.

"Ask me no questions, I'll tell you no lies," he said lightly.

She hit PLAY. "Deal."

SACRAMENTO, CALIFORNIA
MONDAY, FEBRUARY 20, 10:15 A.M.

He'd struggled to get the surgical glove over his bandaged hand, but there was no need to get the dressing bloody if he didn't have to. "Ah." It was finally in place. "Here we go."

Zandra glared up at him defiantly. She said nothing because she was gagged. Gingerly he removed the gag, jerking his fingers away from her mouth as her teeth came down hard.

"If you'd bitten me, I would have killed you."

"You're—" She coughed and coughed. He let her gasp for air, then dribbled a little water down her throat. Greedily she drank the thimbleful, chasing the bottle when he pulled it away. "More," she rasped.

"Say you're sorry," he said with a smile.

"Go to hell," she snarled. She might have tried to spit at him again, but she had no moisture in her mouth.

"Not today," he said with a smile. "You, on the other hand . . ." He gave her an earnest look. "Do you need anything special to meet the requirements of your religion? Last rites, anything like that?"

She stubbornly remained silent, but there was fear in her eyes. He wanted to hear her fear. He wanted to hear her respect.

"Say you're sorry, Zandra."

She closed her eyes, turning her face away.

His temper snapped, and winding her hair around the ring finger and pinkie of his left hand, he yanked her head up and slapped her face with his right, hard enough to dislocate her jaw. He shoved it back in place, earning him a low moan.

"Say you're sorry, Zandra," he hissed.

She drew a breath, sobbed it out. And said nothing, her eyes still closed.

He threw her head back to the bed, earning another low moan. But it wasn't enough.

"Open your eyes." He gripped her chin and dug his fingers into her skin. "Open. Your. Eyes."

She didn't reply. She didn't open her eyes, either.

Frustrated, he found a roll of tape in his supply drawer. Awkwardly, he cut two lengths of tape and attached them to her eyelids, forcing her eyes open and taping them in place.

"You had to choose the hard way." He was panting already. Both energized by her and furious with her. But not aroused. Never aroused.

That had only happened with Daisy. The nice Daisy at the pet store. Not the bitch Daisy who'd shot his hand. Not the whore Daisy who'd protected the Fed. Who'd slept with him.

He wanted the nice Daisy. He *needed* the nice Daisy. He eyed the bed, the restraints. The blood that Zandra had shed. Perhaps once Daisy had experienced a little negative reinforcement, she'd be more inclined to be nice.

He'd make her say she was sorry, too. Just thinking about Daisy apologizing—on her knees—stirred his blood. Made him hard. Made him *want,* when none of the others had.

He'd have her here, he promised himself. He'd keep her for a very long time.

But first he had to break Zandra. He gave himself a firm stroke, renewed. He might not even need his blue pills this time.

"Let's try this again, Zandra." He leaned over until she was staring straight into his eyes. "Say you're sorry."

She jerked her chin to one side, staring at the cabinet with all his souvenirs and trinkets. She was trembling, which was just how he liked it.

"You really want the hard way, don't you?" He pulled out the drawer of knives, arranging them on the table next to the bed. "So far you've got an 'S,' a 'Y,' and a 'D.' I've been kind to you. Have given you recovery time. Not today. I don't have anywhere to go but here and nothing to do but this. You are the recipient of my undivided attention."

He grabbed the first knife, frowning because it felt wrong in his right hand. "You remember this one from last time, don't you?"

Tears rolled from her open eyes. She said nothing.

"Say you're sorry, Zandra."

Her throat worked, like she was trying to speak. "Fuck you," she whispered.

"Oh, we'll get to that," he promised. "Don't you worry."

SACRAMENTO, CALIFORNIA
MONDAY, FEBRUARY 20, 1:55 P.M.

"Reynolds," Gideon murmured in answer when his cell buzzed, careful not to wake Daisy, who'd fallen asleep during the fifth *Buffy* episode, cuddled into his side. His arm hurt too much to sleep, but his mind was clearer without the pain meds, so he'd deal.

The nurse had removed the IV an hour ago. She'd managed to do it without waking Daisy and for that he was very grateful. He had to lean his head up from the pillow to put the phone to his ear, but it was a small price to pay to keep holding the woman he'd come to rely on in a terrifying short time.

"It's Molina. I've assigned your protection detail. Agent Hunter will be accompanying you everywhere for the next few days. We'll reevaluate at the end of the week or whenever we catch this suspect, whichever comes first."

"I don't know him," Gideon said with a slight frown.

"He's new. This is his first placement, but he comes highly recommended by his superiors at Quantico. Don't be difficult with him."

Gideon blinked at that. "I hadn't planned to."

"You're just the type to ditch him and do your own thing."

Gideon looked at the woman sleeping in his arms. "I won't. I promise. Because he'll be keeping Daisy safe, too."

There was a beat of silence. "All right," she said, her tone softening. "Schumacher called me. She found the beige car on the pet store's surveillance tape."

Gideon hoped he sounded surprised. "She did? Where?"

"*Pffft*. You youngsters all think you're so brilliant. I know you found it first, but I'm giving her credit for it."

"That's fine with me. I want him caught. I don't care who does it."

"Hm. That I actually believe." She let out a breath. "The nurse's body washed up on the riverbank. We're looking now at current models to see where she was dumped."

Gideon sighed. "I'm sorry to hear that." And sorry that Daisy would feel guilty. "What else did Schumacher say? Have they found any leads on Eileen?"

"They met the Danton woman, the one who helped Eileen."

"And me."

"And you. For which we are all appropriately grateful."

He almost laughed at her stilted gratitude but realized that stilted was her go-to tone when she cared. "And Eileen?"

"I'm only telling you because Detective Sokolov probably will. They found the diner where she worked. The owner had surveillance tapes but they were grainy. He remembered a man giving her a hard time. He nearly threw the guy out. That was two months ago. When Schumacher and the detectives found the day on the tape, they saw a man who looked like the man on the pet store surveillance tape."

Two months. Eileen's been dead for two months. Gideon's heart tripped, and he focused on staying calm so the nurse didn't come in and yell at them. "So we have a face?"

"Not a great one, but better than we had before. We've put out a BOLO. That's all I have, Agent Reynolds. I'll let you go back to 'not working.'"

She'd said it lightly, trying to make him smile, but he didn't have a smile in him. *Eileen had been dead for two months.* She'd had a single month of freedom between running from the monsters of Eden and falling into the hands of a sociopath. "Yes, ma'am."

He ended the call and let his head fall back on the pillow. Brutus sat up on her haunches and stared at him, head tilted, bat ears sticking out so far it was comical. She looked like a cross between Yoda and Gizmo, from *Gremlins.*

That made him smile. A little. And he was suddenly so tired, he couldn't hold his eyes open.

He woke abruptly, sensing a presence at his side, then relaxed at the sight of Irina and Karl standing together on one side of his bed.

"Hey," he whispered. "Don't wake her up. She was up all night." Crying, but he kept that to himself.

Wearing an impossible grin, Irina pointed to the other side of his bed and Gideon slowly turned his head, dread instantly a live thing in his gut. *Shit.* The tall man bore no real resemblance to the woman using him as a human pillow. Except they shared a certain set of their mouths when they were annoyed.

Which her father seemed to be at the moment as he looked down at the two of them.

"Mr. Dawson," Gideon murmured, somehow managing to keep his voice level and somewhat dignified.

"Agent Reynolds," Dawson said with a nod. He gave his daughter a pointed glance.

"She was awake crying all night," Gideon said quietly. "This has been very hard for her. So if we're going to do the macho handshake thing and the stay-away-from-my-daughter speech, perhaps you can wait until she wakes up."

The man stared down at him for a long moment. Then his lips twitched. "It's nice to meet you, Agent Reynolds," he said, his tone as low as Gideon's had been.

"Gideon. And likewise."

He glanced over at Irina, whose smile was very smug. "You might as well sit."

She did so, like a queen taking the throne. Frederick took the other chair, leaving Karl to perch on the arm of Irina's seat. "We talked to the doctor," Irina whispered. "He'll be releasing you in an hour or so. You'll probably need physical therapy. Cash says to tell you he'll do it."

"Cash" was Cassian Sokolov, Sasha's twin. He was one of the physical therapists contracted by Sacramento's basketball team and traveled with the team. "He doesn't have time for that."

"He says he'll make time," Karl said. "And I feel like we're in a library, all this whispering."

Gideon smiled at that, then turned to see Frederick's gaze locked on his daughter, the man's worry clear. "She talked to her sponsor this morning," Gideon told him. "She's okay."

"She doesn't sleep like that," Frederick murmured. "So deeply. She normally sleeps like an antsy cat."

"Maybe she feels safe with our Gideon," Irina said knowingly.

Gideon rolled his eyes, relieved when the motion no longer sent a spike of pain through his head. "Your Gideon is right here." He lifted a brow. "Did you bring me any food?" He hadn't smelled anything, but there could be all manner of treats in Irina's humongous handbag.

"Brought you some more of the *pirozhki*." She patted her purse. "But you'll have to let her go to eat it."

Well, that was a no-brainer. "I'll wait then."

Irina's smile was so bright Gideon thought he'd

have to shield his eyes. But he glanced over to see Dawson still looking worried.

"What's been done to find the man who did this?" he asked.

Gideon told them what was happening, not mentioning that the man had been within touching distance of Dawson's daughter. "Right now we're gathering information."

"While he's out there, planning his next attack," Dawson growled.

"I'll have FBI protection," Gideon said, mentally thanking Molina again. "So Daisy will have it as well."

Frederick looked only mildly mollified. "I saw what you did there. Capitalizing on my need to see her safe as a way to keep her close to you."

But he didn't look angry. Just scared as hell. *Join the club.*

"Guilty as charged," Gideon said lightly and was saved from any further conversation by the rapping at his door. Dr. Grisham, his surgeon. *Saved by the doctor.*

"Mr. Reynolds?" Grisham asked. "I need to do a recheck before I can release you. Would everyone mind clearing the room? Including the young lady."

Gideon bounced his shoulder, jostling Daisy. "Time to wake up."

She groaned softly. "Don't wanna," she slurred.

Gideon bounced her again. "Eleanor," he said sharply.

Daisy woke in a flash, bolting to sit ramrod straight, her face instantly blushing when she saw that they were no longer alone. "I must have fallen asleep."

Gideon grinned. "Like a log. But the doctor's here, so you'll need to cut out for a few."

Daisy rubbed her hands over her face. "Okay. I think."

"Come on, Daisy." Dawson helped his daughter to her feet, scooping up a yawning Brutus. Brutus went in her bag with no fuss. "We'll get a coffee. That'll wake you up."

Irina leaned over to kiss his forehead. "Come home with us. Let me take care of you."

Gideon wanted to be taken care of. "That sounds good. Thank you."

When the room was empty of everyone but him and the doctor and a smirking nurse, the doctor smiled. "You have a nice family."

"I do." And he'd kept too many secrets from them. Brushing the guilt aside for the time being, he focused on his fingers. "They still don't move. My fingers, I mean."

"Yes, they do. I could see them from the doorway as I watched. You were drumming your fingers when the man in the chair helped move your girlfriend from the bed."

Gideon stared down at his fingers. "I was? Huh. He's her father and this was our first meeting. I guess I might have been a little distracted."

The doctor chuckled. "Some first meeting." He checked the stitches and nodded. "You're looking good. No infection, no tearing. I'll have the nurse reapply the dressing and give you a list of instructions and a prescription for a painkiller."

"No narcotics. They mess with my head."

The doctor looked exasperated. "You law enforcement types. This is the real deal, Agent Reynolds—you need to sleep. If you are in pain, you will not sleep. If you do not sleep, you will not heal. If you do not heal, you cannot go back to work or protect the woman you didn't want to let go of not five minutes ago."

Gideon blinked. "You play dirty, Doc."

The doctor nodded. "You're not my first obstinate patient. I've been on this carousel before. Take the damn pills. And rest. And do not do anything physical."

Wait. That didn't sound good. "What if something physical is done to me?"

The doctor's lips twitched and the nurse coughed to cover a laugh.

"Well, if that's the case, enjoy. Just don't move your arm." The doctor signed off on the paperwork with a flourish. "You and your entourage are going home."

He left and the smirking nurse moved to his side. "Your mom was telling everyone what a hero you are."

Gideon's heart squeezed. Hard. "She's actually not my mom." Like hell she wasn't. Irina Sokolov had mothered him from the moment she'd laid eyes on him.

The nurse looked surprised. "She sure talks like she is." She patted his good arm. "Either way, you've got a great group taking care of you. Now hold still. I'm going to redress your incision."

TWENTY-FOUR

Thank you, Agent Hunter," Daisy said to the special agent Gideon's boss had sent to escort them home from the hospital. "I appreciate you being willing to stop here."

"Not a problem, ma'am," he said. "Just let me go in first to make sure it's safe."

She unlocked the door to her apartment and allowed him to go in, following when he gave the all-clear. Gideon, her father, Karl, and Irina were on her heels. Karl and Irina had their own car, but they'd followed them over, Karl's protective instincts kicking in despite the presence of Agent Hunter.

"Daisy!" her father exclaimed in horror as he turned a full circle, taking in the clutter of her apartment. "What the hell have you done?"

Daisy stood in the middle of her living room, unable to speak. Suddenly she was a child again, unsure of what to say next. A sarcastic answer had sometimes gotten her a laugh. Other times it got her sent to her room and extra chores.

Only Taylor had been able to walk the fine line of her father's moods. Suddenly Daisy wished her sister were there.

Luckily, Gideon had no such issues. "She made it hers," he said to her father. "I love the murals, especially the one of the street outside. She's captured the life of the neighborhood, don't you agree?"

Frederick opened his mouth, closed it, then coughed. "Yes. Of course. The paintings are very good, Daisy."

Daisy wanted to roll her eyes. Her father *was* trying. But not succeeding. Even when he tried to be supportive, he came off sounding condescending and stiff.

"They *are* very good," Karl said with appreciation. "I've seen murals at art shows that aren't nearly this quality. You didn't tell me you could paint like this, Daisy. We need to talk about how to use this talent of yours. Maybe for fund-raisers. Or even a city beautification project. I was talking with the arts council . . ."

"She teaches a class at the community center," Gideon said, gentle pride in his voice.

Daisy's cheeks heated. "It's nothing much."

"It's important to the community," Gideon insisted. "And the fabric over there? She made costumes for the drama club at the same center. They did *The Little Mermaid* and she made all the mer-tails. And Ursula's costume."

"That production raised money for the LGBTQ youth shelter," Irina said. "Sasha and I went to one of the performances. It was wonderful."

Frederick closed his eyes. "I messed up again, didn't I?"

Daisy leaned up to kiss his cheek. "Yeah, but I'm still glad you're here."

"I'm sorry, honey." Frederick winced at the clutter. "This is a lot of stuff."

She smiled up at him. "I know. You should see what I sent back to the store."

Gideon snorted. "She said the same thing to me. I was also a little overwhelmed."

She looked at Gideon over her shoulder and he winked at her. He could handle her father and that made her feel so much better. "Go get your clothes,

Daisy. I want to get out of here and to the big house. I need a slice of Irina's honey cake."

"I made one this morning," Irina told him. "Just for you."

Daisy hurried to the back corner that housed her bedroom, grateful for the screen that closed off the area, giving her a little privacy. She'd felt off-kilter ever since waking up in Gideon's hospital bed a few hours before.

She and Gideon had watched four episodes of *Buffy* and the next thing she'd known Gideon was waking her up from a sound sleep.

And then she'd been promptly mortified to see her father, Karl, and Irina gathered around Gideon's hospital bed. She'd slept through their conversation. She wouldn't have woken at all if Gideon hadn't shaken her because the doctor had come to discharge him.

Karl had brought Gideon a change of clothes so that he could clean up before leaving the hospital, and now he sat at her little dining table, freshly showered and shaved, with his arm in a sling. His jeans and UC Davis sweatshirt made him look so much younger, despite the silver strands threaded among his thick dark hair.

She now knew what it felt like to rake her fingers through his hair. She wanted to do it again. She wanted more of what they'd done Saturday night. A lot more.

But it would have to wait until they were truly alone, if that ever happened again.

She shook her head at her own dramatics. Rosemary was right. It had been only three and a half days. She needed to slow it down. Do it right.

Besides, one of them would have to go to the drugstore for more condoms. She wasn't sure what had happened to the contents of his car. She'd taken both of their laptops, but Gideon's gun, his rifle, and their overnight bags were still AWOL.

Probably in an evidence locker somewhere.

Thus, no condoms. Thus, no fun. Well, maybe they could have other fun.

"Daisy!" Irina called. "Do you need help, dear?"

"No, thank you." She tossed enough clothes for a few days into the bag, then packed her toiletry kit and zipped the suitcase.

"I'll take that," Frederick said. "Karl got food for Brutus. Is everything unplugged?"

Daisy nodded, looking around to be sure she hadn't left anything plugged in or turned on. Her father used to check every electrical outlet three times before they left the house and that was before they'd gone into hiding.

All the signs for anxiety had been there. Why hadn't anyone helped him?

That, she supposed, was a discussion for another day. Because even though he'd shown improvement, he still wasn't whole. And that hurt Daisy's heart far more than his disapproval ever had.

"I'm ready, Agent Hunter," she said, taking another coat from the closet. The one she'd been wearing had been caked with Gideon's blood the last time she'd seen it. She didn't think she'd be able to wear it again, even if the dry cleaner worked a miracle.

He ushered Daisy, Gideon, and Frederick to the SUV he'd parked in Rafe's garage, making sure they were all buckled in before he lifted the garage door. Daisy and Gideon were in the middle seats, her father riding shotgun with their escort.

The Sokolovs were in Karl's Tesla, also parked in the garage.

Both vehicles had begun to back out as soon as the garage door opened, when, from the corner of her eye, Daisy saw a woman running toward them. "Excuse me!" the woman called, waving her arm.

"Down!" Gideon barked, popping his and Daisy's seat belts. As soon as they were free, he grabbed her by the coat and hauled them down.

"I think it's just one woman, Gideon," Daisy said quietly.

"She could be armed," he bit out, his face gone pale. He'd moved his arm awfully fast. He was probably in pain. "You stay down."

"He's right," Frederick said, his voice gone steely. "We'll take care of the woman."

Daisy pitied anyone who got on the wrong side of that voice. "Okay. Just saying." She touched Gideon's face. "Did you hurt your arm?"

"Yeah," he admitted gruffly. "So don't make me have hurt it in vain. Stay down."

Daisy raised her brows. "Guilt trip much?"

Gideon's lips quirked in a fast smirk before pressing together. "Will it work?"

"Probably," she grumbled.

She heard a cough—her father covering a laugh. "Well played, Gideon."

Agent Hunter rolled his window down. "Stand back, ma'am. And keep your hands where I can see them."

"Um . . ." the woman stammered. "You have a gun. Pointed at me."

"Yes, ma'am. I'm Special Agent Hunter. Who are you?"

"My name is Nina Barnes."

"She's from the TV news," Daisy said. "She interviewed me on Friday."

"Get her ID," Gideon instructed. "If her ID's a match, she's legit."

"It's a match," Hunter reported. "It's your call, Miss Dawson."

Daisy sat up slowly, rubbing her neck. Nina Barnes was staring at Agent Hunter's gun with wide eyes. "Can I roll down the window and talk to her myself?"

"No," both Gideon and her father barked at the same time.

Well, okay then. "I can't open the window. Sorry. You'll have to talk loudly."

"What happened yesterday in Macdoel?" Nina asked through Hunter's window.

Daisy sighed. "Look, Miss Barnes, we are exhausted and we need to rest. If you give us your card, I'll call you and give you a phone interview. How's that?"

The woman tilted her head cagily. "Exclusive?"

"For now, yes."

She nodded and gave Hunter her card. He handed it back and Daisy snatched it before her father or Gideon could. "Thank you. I'll be calling you within a few hours."

"Thanks. Look, interview aside, I'm sorry for the loss of your friend. Miss Hart was a really nice person, from all I've been able to glean."

Daisy swallowed. "Yeah, she was nice. Thank you."

"How is Mr. Senegal?" Nina asked.

Daisy frowned at her. "Who?"

Nina frowned back. "Miss Hart's boyfriend. He showed up at the crime scene looking for the police. I told him to contact Sokolov or Rhee."

Daisy's breath caught. "Trish didn't have a boyfriend, Gideon."

Gideon leaned between the two front seats, angling his body so that he wasn't knocking his sling. "Tell us about the boyfriend, please. What did he look like?"

"About six feet tall, red hair, gray eyes. Mustache. He was very upset. Said he needed to find out what was happening. Like I said, I told him to call Sokolov and Rhee, because they were lead detectives."

"Did you see what kind of car he drove?" Gideon asked quietly.

"Yeah. Beige Chevy." Her eyes narrowed speculatively. "This is important."

"Could be," Gideon deflected.

"Tell her to avoid him," Daisy whispered. "Tell her that he's dangerous. Or I will."

Gideon nodded. "Did you give him your card, Miss Barnes?"

"I did. Why?"

"Has he reached out to you?"

"Not yet."

"If he does, call Sokolov or Rhee right away. Don't try to approach him yourself."

Her eyes grew round as saucers. "That was him?"

"We don't know. But he could be dangerous. Please, don't go after him yourself."

Nina nodded slowly. "Got it. You'll give me the interview? For real?"

"For real," Daisy said. "Exclusive."

"We'll both call you," Gideon promised. "Thank you."

Nina stepped back. "Thank you. Be careful."

"You too," Daisy called as Agent Hunter drove them away, Karl and Irina following close behind them all the way to the Sokolov house in Granite Bay.

SACRAMENTO, CALIFORNIA
MONDAY, FEBRUARY 20, 5:15 P.M.

His hot, fetid breath was in Zandra's face, and she didn't even care. Not anymore. At least her eyes could close again. The tape had fallen off long before. As soon as it got bloody, it had stopped sticking.

Bellamy, Anna. Pennsylvania. Fiddler, Janice. Washington. Orlov, Nadia. Illinois. Stevenson, Rayanna. Texas.

"Say you're sorry," he snarled, beyond fury.

She'd begged him to stop, begged him not to hurt her. But *I'm sorry* were two words she would not say. As soon as she did, she was dead. She knew it. She didn't know how she knew it, and she didn't care about the why of it anymore, either.

DeVeen, Rosamond. Minnesota. Borge, Delfina. California. Oliver, Makayla. New York. Danton, Eileen. Oregon.

"Say. It." His voice was guttural. Like an animal. "Say you're sorry."

Martell, Kaley. California. Hart, Trisha. California.

He put his hands around her throat and tightened. She couldn't breathe.

But she couldn't fight. Not anymore.

"Say it. Say it, damn you." He clamped his hand over her windpipe and shook her hard. *"Say it, Sydney,"* he screamed. "Say you're sorry. *Say it!"*

Spittle flew from his mouth as he screamed at her, spraying her face. And she didn't care anymore. She was floating. He was killing her. *I'm dying. Right now.*

And then something clicked, far back in her mind. *Say it, Sydney.*

He'd called her "Sydney." He'd carved most of those letters in her body. He had all of them but the final "Y." She opened her mouth, tried to speak.

Releasing her throat, he backed away, crowing triumphantly. "Say you're sorry. Say it. Say it and I can end it. You'll be done. No more pain."

"I'm . . ." She hacked, her throat dry as a desert and nearly swollen shut. She opened her eyes. "I'm . . ."

He leaned in, smiling. "You're?"

"I'm not Sydney."

His face contorted in vicious rage. He grabbed the largest of the knives and brought it up over her body in a smooth arc.

But then he stopped midswing and dropped the knife back with the others on the table. "No," he said firmly, his voice rough from screaming at her. "You will say you are sorry to me."

"For what?" she asked for the hundredth time, her voice pitifully weak.

"It doesn't matter!" he yelled in her face. "Just say it!"

"No." *Bellamy, Anna. Pennsylvania. Fiddler, Janice. Washington. Orlov, Nadia. Illinois. Stevenson, Rayanna. Texas. DeVeen, Rosamond. Minnesota. Borge, Delfina. California. Oliver, Makayla. New York. Danton, Eileen. Oregon. Martell, Kaley. California. Hart, Trisha. California.*

Shaking from head to toe, he took another step back, then another until he was through the door to the small room.

She heard him lock it behind himself.

Please, God, she prayed. *Please help me. I can't last much longer.*

She began reciting the names again because it was all she could do. She'd lost count of how many times she'd done so when the door opened again.

He was back.

"Hello, Zandra," he said calmly, almost sweetly, and that frightened her more than seeing him unhinged. He'd showered and changed his clothes and now held a bowl of water in his hands. He set the bowl on the table next to her bed and, taking a washcloth from the bowl, washed her body.

The water was warm, his strokes gentle. A moan escaped her throat. It felt so good. So good. He washed her all over, leaving several times to dump the bloody water, returning with fresh. Always warm. Always gentle.

He studied her stomach and chest after she was clean, shaking his head sadly. "I can't suture you up because of my hand," he said, "but I'll disinfect them and bind them up."

The disinfectant was cold and burned like fire. She moaned again, this time in agony, all while he shushed her. "You brought this on yourself, Zandra," he said kindly. "If you'd just said you were sorry, all of this could have been avoided."

He's trying to mess with my head. She blocked out his voice, instead listening to the voice in her mind.

Bellamy, Anna. Pennsylvania. Fiddler, Janice. Washington. Orlov, Nadia. Illinois.

He cut the ropes binding her to the bed and rubbed her raw wrists. Warm water, soothing strokes. Then burning disinfectant. And more sad-sounding admonitions.

Stevenson, Rayanna. Texas, she thought desperately. *DeVeen, Rosamond. Minnesota. Borge, Delfina. California.*

He cut the ropes on her ankles, repeating the motions. Rubbing her legs briskly.

Oliver, Makayla. New York. Danton, Eileen. Oregon.

He lifted her from the bed gently, carefully laying her on the floor as he changed the sheets. Then he lifted her back.

Please don't tie me. Please.

"I have to tie you," he said, and she wondered if she'd said the words aloud. "But I'll use softer cloth," he promised. "This is silk." He slid it over her skin. "It feels so nice, doesn't it? I've got lots of silk."

He tugged her until she was sitting upright, and then he was pulling something silk over her head. It was a sleep shirt. He laid her on the bed and pulled down the gown until it hit her midthigh. Then he tied her wrists and ankles again.

Martell, Kaley. California. Hart, Trisha. California.

He's trying to trick me. She'd read about these tactics. He was reminding her what luxury felt like, only to take it away later. Whatever he planned to do later would feel a thousand times worse because now she remembered what comfort felt like. What hope felt like. *I'm not going to let him mess with my head. I'm going to get away. I'm not going to die. Not like the others.*

"Now, I have to go for a little while. But I'll be back and then we'll chat some more." He pulled a velour blanket from a cabinet and covered her with it. "Until then, stay warm and try to get some rest."

Then he cleaned up his knives and locked them up. He also closed and locked his trinket cabinet so that she could no longer see the driver's licenses and souvenirs. He pressed a kiss to her forehead and left. Locking the door behind him.

Bellamy, Anna. Pennsylvania. Fiddler, Janice. Washington. Orlov, Nadia. Illinois. Stevenson, Rayanna. Texas. DeVeen, Rosamond. Minnesota. Borge, Delfina. California. Oliver, Makayla. New York. Danton, Eileen. Oregon. Martell, Kaley. California. Hart, Trisha. California.

‖ GRANITE BAY, CALIFORNIA
‖ MONDAY, FEBRUARY 20, 5:35 P.M.

Gideon felt a surge of pride as Daisy ended her call with the reporter, turned off the speaker, and carefully placed the Sokolovs' cordless phone on the table. She'd been as articulate and wholesomely believable as she'd been in the on-camera interviews she'd allowed Friday night. She'd also skillfully kept the conversation to facts that were easily verifiable from public sources of information.

She'd also petted poor Brutus within an inch of her life.

She hadn't mentioned Eden or the locket, somehow managing to deftly sidestep the reporter's line of questioning every time it focused on Eileen and why they'd gone to Redding to search for her. She'd never once mentioned Gideon's connection to the case. Never uttered the word "cult."

She'd been honest about how she'd met Trish, how

they'd both attended AA. Her grief over the loss of her friend had been genuine and evident and there hadn't been a dry eye around the Sokolovs' kitchen table, where everyone seemed to gather as Daisy answered the reporter's many questions.

Karl and Irina sat in their usual places at either end of the table. Gideon was closest to Irina, who'd folded her hands on the table in front of her, but her knuckles were white.

Frederick sat directly across from Daisy, who sat between Gideon and Sasha, who'd been waiting for them when they'd arrived. Daisy had held Gideon's hand throughout but let him go when she'd talked about finding Trish's body so that she could put her arms around Sasha.

Because Sasha was weeping soundlessly, her face turned into Daisy's chest while Daisy stroked her hair.

It wasn't until the reporter had asked why she and Gideon were in Macdoel that she truly deflected, saying that she'd lived in the area for years and wanted to see it again.

Given how Daisy had felt about the ranch, saying that she'd wanted to see it again had probably been a lie. She'd ended the call after that, saying that she was tired from the ordeal and needed to rest. That was not a lie. No matter that she'd napped on and off all day, she was pale and drained.

"Well," she murmured. "That's done." She pulled a few tissues from the box and gave them to Sasha, who wiped her face with a dramatic sigh.

"I'm so glad it is," Sasha whispered. "I don't know how you didn't fall apart."

Daisy's gaze flicked to Gideon before returning to Sasha. "I did that already. I'll probably do it again." She kissed Sasha's temple. "Go wash your face."

"Not yet, Sasha," Irina said sharply. She wiped her

own eyes and it was then that Gideon saw that they'd narrowed.

At me. His gaze traveled around the table, noting that Karl was looking at Irina, troubled, and Frederick was watching his daughter with an outright frown.

Daisy picked up Brutus, rubbing her cheek over the dog's bizarre bat ears.

"You lied," Frederick said quietly.

Daisy met her father's gaze, lifting her chin defiantly. "No, I simply used generalizations of the truth and let Nina Barnes believe what she wanted to believe." She lifted one shoulder. "Kind of like you did when you told your ranch hands that you'd grown weary of the city rat race when they asked why you'd come to a ranch in the middle of nowhere. Not exactly a lie."

"I was protecting my family," Frederick said tightly. "Or thought I was, anyway."

Daisy continued to hold Frederick's gaze, unblinking, her fingers deep in Brutus's fur, until her father sat back in his chair and looked at Gideon. "Oh," Frederick breathed.

"Oh, what?" Karl looked between father and daughter. "How did Daisy lie?"

"Generalized the truth," Daisy corrected, and Gideon's lips quirked up despite the fact that Irina was glaring daggers at him.

"Whatever," Karl said, frustrated. "What is going on here?"

"Our ranch was west of Weaverville," Frederick said, "which is *three hours* southwest of Macdoel. You two were nowhere close to our old ranch, which Daisy routinely called the armpit of California."

Daisy winced. "When I was a teenager."

"Sorry," Frederick said sarcastically. "When you were twenty-one you called it a 'pustulent boil on the ass of California.'" He looked at Karl. "All to say there was no way she'd ever go back to walk down memory lane. Why did you go to Redding to begin with? And why Macdoel? Why were you on that road to start with?" He pointed to Gideon. "You tell us. She's way too good at 'generalizing the truth.'"

Karl's brow bunched. "Gideon? What's going on here, son?"

"She's protecting Gideon," Irina said flatly.

Sasha let out a breath. "I didn't say a word, DD. I swear it."

Daisy patted her hand. "I know. Your mama's smart. Dammit," she added lightly.

Irina didn't smile. "This has to do with that tattoo that you had when you first came to us, Gideon. No, I hadn't forgotten about you searching for tattoos on Saturday, Daisy. It was only two days ago. Talk to me. *Now.*"

Gideon rubbed his hand over his face. "I don't want to," he murmured, sounding like a child even to his own ears.

"I can see that," Irina said, her voice trembling.

He chanced a glance and his heart broke a little. Her eyes had filled with tears. She was hurt. Unmistakably. "Don't cry. Please. I didn't want to tell you because I didn't want you to worry." He sighed. "And because there are things I never wanted you to know."

He'd told Rafe some things. He'd told Rafe, his partner, and that forensic investigator more things. He'd told Daisy everything. He'd *only* told Daisy everything.

But he owed Irina and Karl the truth. They were his family. They'd loved him from the moment he'd first entered their home. He could live with not sharing all of this with the FBI. He couldn't live with keeping this from his family. "Where is Zoya?" he asked.

"At her friend's house doing a school project," Irina said. "Why?"

"Because I don't want to fill her mind with things she doesn't need to know." Gideon hesitated. "And because I don't want to burden her with a secret that she's too young to be asked to keep."

Daisy cuddled Brutus under her chin with one hand and held on to Gideon's hand with the other. She gave his fingers a hard squeeze. *You got this,* she mouthed.

God, he hoped so. He drew a breath, let it out. "My mother was a prostitute in San Francisco. Until she met a man who told her about a place called Eden."

He told them everything, ignoring the gasps when he told them that he'd been tattooed at thirteen, that the girls were given lockets and married at twelve. But the power of speech deserted him when he came to his encounter with Edward McPhearson on the evening of his thirteenth birthday, because Irina began to sob, noisy, hiccupping sobs that she couldn't suppress.

"Mama." Sasha got up and walked around the table, wrapping her arms around her mother from behind, rocking them. Sasha was crying, too, silently but steadily.

Karl sat with his eyes closed, his face grown pale.

And Frederick's eyes had clouded with compassion.

Daisy gave him a gentle nudge with her shoulder. "You need to finish the story, Gideon," she murmured. "She thinks McPhearson . . . was successful. That he assaulted you. Hey. Look at me."

He opened his eyes, not realizing he'd closed them. Her blue eyes were clear and full of gentle understanding. "They love you. They will understand. You need to trust them." She brushed a quick kiss across his lips. "Don't leave Irina hanging like this. It's cruel."

Gideon grabbed her hand as she started to pull away, pressing it to his mouth for just a moment. Just long enough to gather his courage.

Then he turned to Irina, who'd covered her face with both hands, sobbing like her heart would break. Because it was. He gently gripped her wrists and pulled her hands from her face, holding them tightly. "Irina. Listen to me. Please."

She dragged in a shuddering breath. "I'm sorry. I'm so sorry. I'm supposed to be strong for you and here I weep like a child."

"No," he said softly. "Like a mama bear whose cub is hurt. But he didn't hurt me, Irina. Not him."

She held on to his hands, her breath coming fast and hard. "No?"

"No. I fought him. Fought him hard." He swallowed, but his throat had closed and he felt like he was going to be sick. He'd told Daisy somehow. But this . . . Telling Irina was killing him. "I pushed him and he fell." He closed his eyes. "He hit his head. And died."

There was absolute silence in Irina's kitchen. Then a chair scraped back and a strong arm hugged his uninjured side from behind. Karl. "Good," Karl rasped. "Because I was going to kill him myself."

Gideon opened his eyes, twisting around to stare at the man who'd been his father since Rafe had brought him home, sixteen years ago. "What?"

"He touched you," Karl growled. "He would have hurt you. What did you think we'd say, son? Did you think we'd *blame* you? Report you? Make you leave?"

Yes. That was exactly what he'd thought. And the admission shamed him. The Sokolovs had never shown him anything but love and acceptance.

The grip on his hands disappeared, Irina's hands lifting to cup his cheeks. "You are *ours*, Gideon," she said firmly, herself again. "Nothing you've done to survive, nothing you will ever do, will change that. You belong to us. To this family. To me. Do you understand me, *sinok*?"

Son. He pursed his lips, trying to keep the tears at bay, but they fell anyway. "Yes," he said hoarsely. "I understand."

He understood that he was the luckiest bastard on the planet.

A glance to his left showed a smiling Daisy. "I told you so," she whispered.

He looked up at Sasha, who still held on to her mother. "You're an idiot, Gideon," she said, but she was smiling, too. "They've always liked you best of all of their kids."

Irina sniffed. "He was the only one who did what I said without argument."

Sasha kissed the top of Irina's head. "That's fair."

Karl hugged him hard, then stepped back. "There's more." Not a question.

"Yeah." Gideon sighed. "It kind of goes downhill from here."

Irina braced herself. "Okay. I am ready."

That made him chuckle. "I'm not." He sighed again, then told them about the chase, the fight with Ephraim Burton. The beating he'd received at the older man's hand, the knife he'd plunged into Ephraim's eye.

The ride from Eden in the middle of the night, the whispered words from his mother. And then waking up in the hospital.

Karl looked confused. "She left you there? Alone?"

"She had to return to her daughter," Irina said softly. "Truly a Sophie's choice."

Gideon nodded. "Yes."

"But your sister escaped, didn't she?" Irina asked. "You were reunited with her."

"How?" Frederick asked. "How did she escape? How did she find you?"

"My mother smuggled her out, too." He wouldn't speak of the abuse Mercy had endured. That was Mercy's story to tell. "But when our mother tried to get out of the truck, the driver shot her."

"Oh, Gideon," Irina murmured.

Daisy threaded her fingers with his. "Breathe, Gideon."

He sucked in a breath, realizing he hadn't been. "Thank you."

She rested her head on his arm. "You're almost done."

He nodded. Just a little more. He could do this. "My mother died. Mercy saw it."

"Oh." Irina covered her mouth with her hand. "She was in shock when she was our patient. Just rocked herself all day. Wouldn't talk to anyone."

"His sister ended up in your hospital?" Frederick asked quietly, and Irina nodded.

"We're the only level one trauma unit for miles. She wasn't my patient. I never actually met her. I only heard about her locket. And I'd seen the same design on Gideon. His tattoo." Irina closed her eyes. "The one you had covered. I should have known it symbolized something painful."

"How could you know?" Gideon asked sadly. "I never told you."

She shook her head. "I should have known."

Frederick turned to Gideon, his eyes calm and kind, and even though they were brown and not blue like Daisy's, Gideon saw the resemblance between them. It was that look. That serenity that Daisy seemed to summon when Gideon needed it most. But not when she needed it for herself.

It was hard to reconcile the man who sat across from him with the man who'd dragged his family across the state into isolation. But in that moment, it was easy to see why Daisy loved him.

"How did you find your sister?" Frederick asked.

"Irina told me that she'd heard of a girl wearing a locket that matched my tattoo. I called the hospital, told them I was family, and they put me in touch with the social worker. It took forever, but I finally got to see Mercy."

He couldn't let himself remember how she'd looked that day.

Like I could ever forget. Her eyes had been empty and haunted, and she'd rocked herself, over and over. It wasn't until Gideon had shown her the tattoo that she recognized him. And then turned her face away, staring at the wall. Only nodding when he'd asked her if their mother was gone.

"She . . ." Gideon shook his head. "She was still in shock when I found her. We don't have a strong relationship. I'm . . ." He sighed. "I'm a reminder."

"I'm sorry," Frederick said softly.

"Thank you."

Karl wore a puzzled frown. "So how did you know to go to Redding?"

"That's where Gideon and I intersect," Daisy said. "When I was attacked last week, I inadvertently pulled a chain from the man's neck. It was a locket, just like Gideon's sister's. It had a wedding photo inside and the remnants of a second photo, cut into slivers. The full wedding photo showed a young girl named Eileen. She was Gideon's friend."

"She escaped, too," Karl murmured. "And you were found at the Redding bus station, Gideon, so you figured she'd go there, too?"

"It seemed like the best guess," Gideon said, "or at least the place to start. I know the compound is somewhere within a hundred-mile radius of Mt. Shasta."

"Redding is the closest big town." Karl nodded. "Smart thinking. And then?"

"The ticket clerk remembered her," Daisy said. "Gideon had the photo of Eileen age-progressed. She'd come into the bus station with a man who'd bought her ticket. He lives in Macdoel. He was a Good Samaritan. He bought her a ticket to Portland."

"Oh," Sasha said slowly. "Portland's where Rafe and Erin Rhee are today."

Gideon nodded. "Because Eileen connects to the locket, which connects to the man who attacked Daisy."

"Who then killed Trish," Daisy said unsteadily. "And shot Gideon."

"And killed a man for his truck near Macdoel,"

Gideon said. "And kidnapped that baby and the nurse whose body was found this morning. And may have killed six other women across the country. That we know of."

Again there was silence.

"Holy shit," Sasha said quietly. "Daisy, he would have killed you, too."

Frederick had gone still. "What is the commonality between his victims?" he asked, so softly that Gideon almost missed the question. The man's eyes had gone from kind to terrified.

Gideon hesitated. "There are certain consistent elements of his MO. But there are more that seem completely random."

"He has a dog," Daisy offered, her tone a mix of sarcasm and hopelessness.

It hurt Gideon's heart. He tipped her chin up. "We're going to find him, Daisy."

She nodded. "I hope so. I'd like to have my life back."

"How do you know he has a dog?" Karl asked.

Daisy sighed. "He came to the adoption clinic Saturday. Gideon found his car on the parking lot surveillance video—the same car he was driving when he shot Gideon."

Frederick had lost all remaining color in his face. He looked waxy. And sick.

"Dad?" Daisy said sharply. She pressed her fingers to his wrist.

Frederick pulled his arm away, shaking his head. "I'm not having a heart attack, Daisy. I'm having a panic attack. Some sick freak is trying to *kill* my *daughter*."

She opened her hand, palm up, and Frederick took it. "It's going to be okay, Dad. I'm taking no chances. Agent Hunter is outside and he goes wherever Gideon and I go. I will behave. I will comply." She squeezed his hand. "I will not fall off the wagon. I promise."

"You can't promise your sobriety," Frederick said.

"But I will accept your promise to behave and comply. And to make every attempt to maintain your sobriety."

"I talked to my sponsor this morning. It helped. A lot."

He nodded weakly. "Good. That's good."

"And the behaving and complying stuff only pertains until this situation is resolved. Then I'm going back to the real me."

Frederick's mouth curved. "I love the real you, Eleanor."

She smiled back at him, shaking her head. "You just can't resist, can you, Dad? You're lucky that I love you, too, even when you call me Eleanor."

Frederick rose out of his chair, and leaning forward, kissed her forehead. "I am lucky." His eyes closed. "I need you to be safe, baby," he whispered hoarsely.

"I know, Dad," Daisy whispered back. "I understand."

"Thank you."

Frederick let go first and looked around with a start, his cheeks flushing as he seemed to realize that he and his daughter hadn't been alone for that exchange.

Gideon figured that Frederick had been kind and calm to him, so he could return the favor. "So why is she called Daisy?" he asked.

Frederick's smile spread across his face. "That's an interesting story."

Daisy dropped her face into Brutus's fur. "Dad," she moaned.

Irina pushed away from the table. "I've got dinner in the warming oven. Sasha, can you set the table? You've heard the Daisy story."

Daisy peeked at Gideon as the somber mood was broken. *Thank you,* she mouthed.

Gideon winked at her, then turned to her father. "So? Daisy?"

TWENTY-FIVE

He'd break her. He would. No woman was getting the better of him.

Bullshit.

Shut up.

You nearly lost it down there. You would have stabbed Zandra to death. And without any satisfaction whatsoever.

It's true. But he'd stopped himself. She had not beaten him. He just needed some fresh air. A walk around the block.

He grabbed Mutt's leash from its hook on the wall, opened the back door, and called to him. Mutt came running, and he clipped the leash to his collar, locked the door behind him, and sucked in the fresh air. It had gotten downright steamy in the basement. Sweat and blood and exertion.

His.

And Zandra's. If he'd been planning on keeping her for the foreseeable future, she'd be perfect. He'd eventually wear her down, but he might need months to do so. But he didn't have months. He had days, if that. He'd be bringing Daisy home any day now.

He started out for Daisy's house, Mutt eagerly leading the way. He was pretty smart. For a mutt.

Probably because that woman petted him this morning. Sasha Sokolov.

Mutt always went for anyone who petted him. But he didn't want to go charging up to Daisy's house, so he pulled on the leash, reining Mutt in. By the time they were approaching the house, Mutt had his nose to the grass, sniffing.

He stopped abruptly. There were news vans in front of the house. Again.

He'd checked the news today. There'd been lots of coverage of the child discovered in the parking lot of Mercy Hospital. And of the missing nurse. And about the shooting up north. And that there was a serial killer out there.

"Crazy, isn't it?" a man asked, coming up behind him. The man walked a Lassie-looking dog, all long, flowing hair. Prissy dog, probably.

The collie and Mutt began sniffing each other's butts, so he turned his attention on the collie's owner. Midforties, medium height, bit of a beer belly, heavy five-o'clock shadow.

"What's happening?" he asked, feigning clueless-ness.

"The woman who lives there has been involved in a shooting. Some Fed was shot. It hit the news this morning."

"Was the Fed okay?" he asked, maintaining his show of ignorance.

"Yeah. Saw 'em a few hours ago. They came home. Two vehicles. One was an SUV, black with dark tinted windows. You know, like you see on TV. The other was an honest-to-God Tesla. A real beauty. Anyway, they stayed for a while, then left, both cars together. There was only one reporter here, then. I guess hers was the story that ran this afternoon."

He'd seen the Tesla on Saturday, parked in front of the Sokolovs' house in Granite Bay. At least now he knew where to go next. But this guy might have some more useful info and seemed to be the chatty type, so he continued playing clueless.

He blinked at the man. "Wow. How'd you know all that?"

"I live in the house next door. The house where the woman lives is generally really quiet. A cop owns it, so I thought, what the hey? At least one of my neighbors won't be throwing parties."

"Do they? Throw parties, I mean."

"Not really. They have a big family. I saw 'em barbecuing last summer. They invited me to join them, but I was on my way out. Seem nice enough. Shame that the woman's involved in this. She's the same one who got attacked last week."

He widened his eyes. "I didn't hear about that," he lied.

The man laughed. "You been living under a rock? It was big news."

"I've been out of town."

"Ah, well. It was no Golden State Killer case, but it's got a lot of press, just the same."

"That one got tons of coverage," he said companionably. "But that killer was awful. He killed like twelve people." He hid a smirk. *I've killed twice that many and haven't even been suspected. It's taken the FBI years to connect my kills.*

The Golden State Killer was eventually caught because he left DNA all over the place. *Which I am super careful not to do.* Although, to be fair, the Golden State Killer had done all his murders forty years earlier, before anyone could have predicted the use of DNA and forensics.

Damn forensics.

Because he *had* left DNA this time. They had nothing to compare it to, but if he got caught? He'd go away for life. The thought had him breathing hard.

He gave Lassie-man a wave, not wanting to hyper-ventilate in front of a stranger. "Well, have a nice evening. I hope the reporters don't trespass on your property."

"Me too," Lassie-man said glumly. "Come on, boy. Let's go home."

Mutt tried to follow him, but he pulled him back. "No, boy. We're going home, too." Pulling on the leash, he and Mutt walked home. He was going out to Granite Bay.

But first, he needed a new set of wheels. Stealing the van from the grocery store lot up in Chico from an owner who had just arrived for her shift had worked pretty well.

He had enough to worry about without fixing what wasn't broken. He needed to get rid of the Fed. Then he'd decide what to do with Daisy.

SACRAMENTO, CALIFORNIA
MONDAY, FEBRUARY 20, 7:30 P.M.

Gideon let Irina fuss over him, tucking him into one of the twin beds in Rafe's old room. He'd have preferred to have Daisy helping him out of his shirt, but Irina had looked so broken after his revelations. He hadn't argued when she'd followed him upstairs after he'd nearly fallen asleep, face forward into his dinner plate.

"Here's something for your arm," she said, shaking a few pain relievers into her palm. "They're over-the-counter, so no sass from you about taking them."

"I'd never sass you," he said seriously.

Her smile was sad. "No, you never did. You were always 'Yes, ma'am' and 'No, ma'am' and 'please' and 'thank you.' Like you were afraid we'd throw you out if you misspoke. I guess now I understand why."

He'd hated telling them about Eden. Hated seeing

the stunned looks on their faces. Hated the hurt in their eyes. *For me. They hurt because I was hurt. Me and Mercy. And Mama.* He'd hated that he'd upset them, but at the same time he'd found he'd really needed the love and support that they'd offered in return.

He hadn't been surprised during dinner when they'd offered to help him search for Eden; it wasn't a huge surprise, either, but that he couldn't allow. He didn't want anyone he loved anywhere close to that place. But he'd deal with that tomorrow. After he'd slept.

Irina shook her head, fast and hard. Gideon wasn't sure if she was trying to shake off her sadness or to banish the images now burned into her mind. She folded the shirt he'd been wearing and placed it on the dresser, then returned to help him put his sling back on, her retired nurse's hands capable and sure.

"You're sure you'll be warm enough? I can find one of Rafe's old sweatshirts," she said.

He didn't want to tell her that he usually slept in the buff. It had been unnerving enough to take off his jeans and boxer briefs while she fussed with making up the bed. He'd stepped into his sweats and had managed to drag them up, then actually blushed when she reached for the drawstring, tying it in a neat bow. The sweats would be all he'd be able to tolerate against his skin as he slept, and he'd only agreed to them in case he had to get up in the middle of the night to use the bathroom. Zoya still lived here, after all, and he'd be sharing the bathroom with her. And with Daisy, who was set up in the spare bedroom.

The thought of Daisy had him hurrying into bed and pulling the blanket up past his quickly growing erection. Not something he wanted Irina to see and the sweats hid nothing.

As for being cold, he hoped Daisy would be joining him soon to keep him warm.

"I'll be fine, Irina. Honestly."

"All right." She pulled the blanket up to his chin, patting his face softly. "I'm glad you're here, Gideon."

"Me too." He smiled up at her when she plumped his pillows. "You used to do this when I was a kid. When I was sick. I pretended I was too old for you to fuss over me, but I really loved it."

She perched on the side of the bed. "I knew you really wanted me to. But you were fourteen and that's such a rough age. And you were in rough shape then." She searched his face. "I worried so much about you back then, Gideon. I still do."

"I'm fine," he assured her. "I just got my wing clipped a little. I'll be healed in no time."

Irina shook her head. "Not that. I know you'll heal. You and Rafe got so many hurts and you always healed. On the outside. I worry about your inside." She tapped his chest. "Your heart."

"It's fine, too," he said, deliberately misunderstanding. "It keeps on beating."

She gave him a quelling look. "Gideon. I'm being serious. We need to talk."

"I'm being serious, too. I'm okay, Irina. Really." He frowned as a concern struck him from left field. "Wait. We need to talk about *what*?" He narrowed his eyes. "Are you upset that I'm seeing Daisy?" Because that would not be okay.

She flinched, her expression shocked. "No. Of course not. I was the one trying to set you up, remember? For *months*."

"Oh," he said sheepishly. "Right. Sorry."

"You should be. *Durashka*." She shook her head, her exasperation with him clear. "Silly boy. I think she'll be good for you. Loosen you up a little bit. You'll be good for her, too. When you took up for her, there in her apartment? She looked at you like you'd hung the moon. And when you told us about Eden she was like a soldier, ready to defend you if we even frowned

at you. I only ask that you take it slow. Strong relationships take time."

"Then why are you worried about me? Why do we
'need to talk'?"

"Why am I worried about you? Other than the fact
that you just told us you were raised in a cult and were
nearly murdered by its members?"

"Well, yeah," he mumbled. "That's over and done."

"I don't think that's altogether true, but we can
tackle that later." Irina hesitated, then sighed. "Your
sister didn't come."

It was his turn to flinch. Because even though he
hadn't expected Mercy to come, he'd wished she
would. "No. She didn't. But it's f—"

"I swear, Gideon Reynolds, if you say 'fine,' I'll . . ."
She sputtered. "I don't know what, but you won't like
it. You love her. I could see that her rejection hurts
you."

He opened his mouth, then closed it again, uncomfortable that he'd let that show. "Yeah," he whispered.
"It does hurt."

"I'm so sorry, *dorogoy moy.*"

Sweetheart. He almost smiled, despite the hurt. "I
am, too. Partly because I'd love to have a sister. I mean,
Sasha and Meg and Zoya are *like* sisters to me, but
Mercy *is* my sister. I . . . miss her."

"Of course you do. How could you not?"

And that might be the very heart of it, he thought,
turning the notion around in his mind while Irina
waited patiently. "That's the thing," he finally said quietly. "I miss her, but she doesn't miss me. She's cut me
out of her life and doesn't look back. I understand it. I
understand that just seeing me brings back a host of
bad memories, but . . ."

"But what?"

He sighed. "That's the bigger part. If she'd turned
her back on me for another family, yeah, it would hurt,

but she'd be happy. But she didn't find another family. She's so *alone*." He took the hand she had resting on his heart and squeezed it. "I'm not. I've got you guys. You've always had my back. If she came here, you'd love her, too. She'd have a family, too."

Irina's eyes grew bright and she dabbed at them daintily. "We would love her. I'm glad you know we love you, Gideon."

He pressed a kiss to the back of her hand. "I've always known that. You and Karl have been my parents since the day Rafe brought me here. You've been the mother that my own mother wasn't allowed to be."

Irina tried dabbing again, but gave up and blinked the tears from her eyes, wiping her cheeks with the back of her hand. "Your mother got you out of that awful place. I'm grateful to her for that. She got your sister out, too. Physically."

"Yeah." Because Mercy was still so damaged, all these years later. Still in a prison, of sorts. "I'll keep working on her." Needing to change the tone, he smiled at her slyly. "She might be bribed with honey cake."

Irina's chuckle was watery. "If you ever want me to bake one for you, you need only to ask, *sinochka*." She leaned in to kiss his forehead. "Rest. We'll be here for you in the morning."

"Thank you," he said gruffly. "For everything."

She blew him a kiss, turned off the light, and closed the door, leaving him all alone.

Alone, staring at the ceiling, and wondering where Daisy was. It had only been three nights, but he'd become accustomed to her sleeping in his arms.

He listened. The TV was on downstairs. Sounded like *Monday Night Football,* to which Karl was addicted. Hopefully that would keep Frederick busy, too, because Gideon planned to find Daisy and ask her to stay with him. Just until he went to sleep.

He'd pulled the blanket away and swung his legs

over the side of the bed when his door slowly opened. Daisy slipped in and shut the door quietly, locked it, then listened, presumably, for anyone who might have seen her.

Like her father. Who'd taught her to shoot and fight like a soldier. It kept occurring to Gideon that Daisy's father should probably scare him more than he did. Although Frederick hadn't seemed too upset that Daisy had been asleep on his hospital bed.

A real bed was probably different.

She turned around and let out a startled *eep* when she saw him, clapping her hand over her mouth after the fact. "You're awake."

"So it would seem," he said dryly. "I think you just erased any benefit of your super secret stealth."

She grinned as she crossed the room. "They're screaming at the TV downstairs. I doubt they heard one little *eep*. And if they did . . ." She shrugged and sat on the bed. "Irina was crying when she left your room. But smiling, too. What happened?"

"I told her that she and Karl are my family."

Daisy's smile was soft. "That'd do it." She stroked his cheek with the backs of her fingers. "I won't stay long. I just wanted to check on you. It can't have been easy, telling them about Eden."

"It wasn't so bad," he said, surprised that it was true. "I think every time I tell it, it gets easier. The hard part was that it upset them." He flattened her palm against his cheek and nuzzled into it. "Can you stay for a little while?"

"I was hoping you'd want me to." Setting her Brutus bag on the floor next to the bed, she placed the dog on top of it, told her "Shazam," then cuddled up to Gideon's side. "Kind of missing the hospital bed's rails," she chuckled. "This is a tiny bed. I might just fall off."

Mindful of his sling, he shifted so that his back was to the wall and he pulled her into him. Not having to worry about the IV needle made holding her so much easier. On the other hand, holding her closer made it harder to hide the fact that he was getting very hard, very fast. "Better?"

"Yeah. Much. Does your arm hurt?"

"Some," he admitted.

"In other words, it's hurting like a bitch, but you refuse to take any more pain meds."

"Pretty much. I took some over-the-counter painkillers Irina brought me."

"Gideon," she said on a sigh.

"Daisy," he mimicked, then kissed the top of her head. "I was coming to find you. I can't sleep without you."

She lightly stroked down his chest. "I like that."

"Thought you might," he muttered.

Her hand continued its downward journey, stroking the crease of his thigh and his groin. He sucked in a breath, his cock starting to throb. Her fingers were so close, and not nearly close enough.

She hummed low in her throat and he held his breath, letting it out on a groan when her fingers finally lightly brushed up his length.

"I like this, too," she whispered.

He choked out a laugh, which morphed into another groan when her fingers gripped him through his sweats. "Daisy. Please."

She lifted her head from his shoulder, sliding her free hand under his head and leaning in to brush her lips over his. "What do you want, Gideon?" she asked, her husky voice and her clever fingers sending shivers all over his body.

Cursing the sling that immobilized his right arm, he arched his hips, needing more friction. "Everything." The word came out sounding desperate. Because suddenly he was desperate. He gripped a fistful of her hair, careful not to hurt her but needing something to hold on to. "Kiss me, Daisy Dawson."

And she did. Slowly and thoroughly she kissed him, until he thought the top of his head would fly off. It wasn't a rough kiss, or raw. But it wasn't gentle, either. When she finally lifted her head, they were both panting and his hips were rolling, his dick craving her touch.

Holding his gaze, she tugged on the drawstring of his sweatpants and slid her hand under the waistband. His body, arched and needy, collapsed back on the bed with a growl.

"Please," he whispered.

She gripped him hard and kissed him, this time with no gentleness. It was dirty and raw and he loved it.

Too soon she pulled back, her lips swollen and red and gorgeous. "No noise," she panted, then slid down his body, kissing his chest, his abs, then disappearing under the blanket. He clenched his eyes closed, waiting for it . . . waiting . . .

Her mouth closed over him, hot and wet and amazing. "Oh God," he moaned. She was alternating a slow, slick glide down with a tight suction on the way back up. It was pleasure, so intense that his brains were . . . gone. *"Daisy."*

The heat and suction abruptly stopped. Her head popped out from under the blanket. "I said, no noise. Got it?"

He nodded, probably too eagerly because she grinned at him before disappearing under the blanket again. And . . . He exhaled in relief when she took him back in her mouth. Gently he threaded his fingers through her hair, holding on as she drove him completely insane.

His orgasm Saturday night had been like a bomb blast, hitting with no warning. This one built slowly, starting at the base of his spine, electricity radiating outward until every square inch of his skin was sensitized and aching.

"Daisy," he rasped. He let go of her hair to pull the blanket away. "Almost there."

She looked up at him through her lashes, winked once—then took him deeper.

"Fuck," he groaned, unable to keep it quiet. What had been a slow build suddenly detonated, his body bowing up as he came, lifting off the bed of its own accord as his abs crunched tight. And it kept going and going.

Until finally he fell back, thoroughly and utterly drained. He stared up at the ceiling, blinking as his brain came back online. Then he laughed.

She crawled up the bed, lying on her side with her elbow propped by his ear. She smiled down at him. Her swollen lips were red and wet and . . . so damn sexy.

She traced his goatee with one finger. "Was that an I'm-so-happy laugh? Just letting you know that the right answer is 'yes.'"

He caught her finger between his lips and sucked it into his mouth for a moment before letting her go. "Well, duh. Yes. But it was also because I was thinking I felt drained. And then the middle schooler that still lurks in my mind said, heh-heh, I *was* drained."

She chuckled. "You should let the middle schooler out to play more often. He's funny."

He closed his eyes. "I think you shorted out some major fuses."

"Good." She sounded amused and . . . content.

He opened his eyes to study her face. "Thank you."

"My pleasure." Her eyes gleamed. "That was truly remarkable, Gideon."

"Yeah. It was. I didn't expect it." He hesitated. "I'm clean. You should have asked."

"You were just in the hospital. I'm sure they tested you six ways to Tuesday, especially since I was covered in your blood."

"Still. You shouldn't be so—" He cut himself off when her brow winged up, a sure sign of annoyance.

"Slutty?" she asked quietly.

"No," he blurted out. "I was going to say trusting. Some men will lie to you."

"I'm not with 'some men,'" she said, way too calmly. "I'm with you."

He'd made her angry and he wanted to kick his own ass. "I never once thought anything negative. I'm sorry. I'm not . . . I'm a little socially awkward sometimes."

Her frown softened. "Yes, you are. I don't trust many people, Gideon, but I won't go through life suspecting everyone. My father did that and . . . I mean I love him, but . . ." She sighed. "It hurt our family."

He rested his good arm over his eyes. "I'm sorry, Daisy. I just took the most amazing gift and smashed it."

"Nah. You just scuffed it a little. It can be buffed out."

He peeked at her from under his arm. "Yeah?"

"Yeah." She ran her fingers over his phoenix tattoo. "I'm not a blushing virgin, Gideon. I enjoyed sex before I met you."

He sucked in a breath at her light touch, weighing his words. "I'm glad."

Again the eyebrow lifted, but this time it was curious rather than angry. "Really?"

"Yes. You were able to connect with people in a way that you needed before I was here."

She smiled. "And now that you're here?"

He met her eyes, hoping she didn't bolt. "I don't want to share you."

"I'm good with that. Same goes. We're exclusive until we decide otherwise. Okay?"

"Absolutely okay." He traced the V of her collar, dipping his finger under her sweater until he traced the lace of her bra. "Irina thinks we're moving too fast."

Daisy made a face. "I know. She told me the same

thing. But then Karl reminded her that he told her that she'd marry him after their first date. She didn't believe him then." She laughed. "She said she's still not sure it's going to work out."

Gideon grinned. "I really love those guys."

"Me too." She kissed him softly and he could taste himself on her lips. And damn if he wasn't getting hard again.

"What can I do for you?"

"Right now? Recover from a gunshot wound. I probably shouldn't have done what I did, in hindsight. But I hope you'll be able to sleep now."

"Like a baby," he predicted. "But you'll stay?"

"Yes." She got comfortable on his shoulder. "Did I mess up your arm?"

"What arm?" he asked and felt her smile.

"Go to sleep, Gideon."

His eyes were already growing heavy. "Okay."

||| GRANITE BAY, CALIFORNIA
||| MONDAY, FEBRUARY 20, 9:30 P.M.

It appeared that he was playing the waiting game yet again. He sat in his stolen minivan, down the street from the Sokolov home. Watching.

He wasn't the only one. There was a black SUV in the driveway whose driver just got out to do a perimeter check. Carrying a rifle. With a scope.

Seemed like the Feds weren't messing around.

You shouldn't be here. It's not worth it. If he checks the license plate, you're toast.

It was a good point. Especially since the minivan he'd stolen clearly did not belong in this neighborhood. He could have stolen a newer model, but they all had GPS. He was basically a blinking neon light saying *SEARCH ME.*

You have time. They don't know who you are. You've left no physical evidence behind. Well, except for the skin scrapings. The car he'd left up in Macdoel had been burned to a crisp. Even if they had found any blood, the heat would have rendered it useless.

But . . .

But what? But you didn't get Daisy Dawson yet? You will. Just be patient. Wait for her to let her guard down. She can't hide like this forever. You know where she lives.

And they did not know where he lived. He definitely had the upper hand here.

Sitting here in a stolen minivan with GI Joe doing laps around the Sokolovs' house was a risk he did not need to take. Especially with all the lights in the house going off, one by one. The family was settling down to sleep.

He stripped the glove off his right hand and the mitten off his left, then held one ignition wire between the working fingers of his injured hand. Using his less dexterous right hand, he clumsily touched the two wires together and the van roared to life. He pulled the glove and mitten back on.

He wasn't going to leave any forensic evidence behind in this vehicle, just as he'd left nothing of his own in the truck or the Chico minivan yesterday. Damn forensics.

He turned the van around and headed back to the city. He'd park it somewhere close to the supermarket from where he'd stolen it and leave a few empty beer bottles on the floor. The cops would assume it had been stolen by teenagers.

He could go home, have a cup of cocoa, and listen to his mother's record collection. And then he could have another go at Zandra. He was kind of hoping she'd hold out a little longer. She was proving to be a very satisfying guest.

SACRAMENTO, CALIFORNIA
MONDAY, FEBRUARY 20, 9:55 P.M.

The ringing of a phone woke Daisy from a sound sleep. Blinking, she rolled over to grab it and—

"Shit." She hit the floor hard. "That hurt."

"Wha—?" Gideon sat straight up in the bed. The very small bed in Rafe's old room.

Daisy scrambled to her knees, grabbed the still-ringing cell phone from the nightstand, and handed it to Gideon. "It's yours."

"Oh God. What time is it?" He tapped the screen. "Hello?" A second later he was fully awake. "Tino, hey."

Tino was his friend in Philly. Hopefully this meant age-regressed sketches they could use to search for the two men who'd abused Gideon in the compound.

"No, don't worry about it. It's not that late here," Gideon said. "I had a little altercation with a suspect and I'm still recovering. What do you have?" He listened for a few moments, said, "Hold on," then opened his e-mail. He stared at his phone for a long moment before putting it back to his ear. "Wow. Thank you, Tino. It's more than I hoped for. I'll be sure to let you know what we find. Thanks again."

He ended the call and handed his phone to her. The photos on the screen had her sucking in a startled breath. Two men, about the age Gideon was now. Both rugged and . . . harsh-looking. There was cruelty in their eyes, an edge that said they'd take what they wanted and damn the consequences. It had been noticeable in the wedding photos if one had known to look for it. Here, though, it was the first thing one saw.

"Wow," she murmured.

"I know," Gideon murmured back.

"Did you tell him who they were and what they'd done?"

He shook his head. "No. Tino just seems to know stuff. Eyes are his specialty."

The light knock on the bedroom door had them both jumping. Gideon grimaced. "We're busted," he whispered. "Yes?" he called.

"I heard a thump," Irina said. "Are you okay, Gideon?"

"I'm fine, Irina," he said.

"Is Daisy okay then?" she asked, sounding amused.

Daisy rolled her eyes. "I'm fine, Irina," she called.

"That's good, dear. I figured you were here when you weren't in your own bed when I went to say good night."

"Not like we're adults or anything," Daisy muttered.

"What was that, dear?" Irina's question was followed by a laugh, deep and rolling. Male.

"Karl," she and Gideon said together.

"Good night, Irina," Daisy said firmly. "Good night, Karl." She gave them time to leave, then looked up at Gideon. "That was close."

"Karl and Irina?" He shrugged his good shoulder. "I figured they knew you were here."

"No." She reached behind her for Brutus. "I almost squashed her."

"Poor girl." He reached down to scratch behind the dog's ears.

Daisy kissed Brutus on the head. "Tomorrow we take over Sasha's old room and make her sleep here. She's got a queen bed."

"*If* we're still here. We don't have to go back to your place. My house has an excellent security system."

"I like that idea even better."

He patted the bed. "Put Brutus on the other bed

and come here." He lifted the blanket for her to crawl under. "I need to forward these photos to Molina."

"Give me your phone. I'll type the message and then you can go back to sleep."

"Maybe," he said, still frowning at the phone's screen.

The photos were exceptionally well done. Gideon's friend had a gift. The photos also represented the worst moments in Gideon's life, moments he'd been forced to relive at the dinner table tonight.

She slipped the phone from his hands and kissed his jaw. "Let me send the e-mail to Agent Molina and then I'll see about helping you sleep."

One dark brow lifted, making him look wicked in the dim light of the moon through the window. "That is an intriguing offer."

"I thought you'd think so. What do you want this to say?"

He frowned again. "Maybe I'll call her before I send her the photos. It'll be easier to explain on the phone. Can you set an alarm for five forty-five? She's usually in the office by six. If I get to her before anyone else does, she'll be in a better mood."

"Considering she told you not to be working, that's not a bad plan." Daisy set the alarm, then put the phone on the nightstand and cuddled up to his side so that their lips were only millimeters apart. "Now. Let's discuss sleeping aids."

His lips curved. "Is that what we're calling it?"

"A Daisy by any other name?"

He laughed. "I'm still shaking my head over the story your father told at dinner, about why you're called Daisy. How you made daisy chain princess crowns out of the arboretum's prized orchids."

She rolled her eyes. "They were flowers, for God's sake. Mom would take us to the park and we'd make daisy chain crowns and pretend we were princesses. Who knew orchids were worth a few hundred bucks? No flower should be worth a few hundred bucks." Then she kissed him softly. "My dad likes telling that story a little too much. But it made him smile, so thank you."

"He sent me a photo of you and your sister, wearing the orchid crowns. I'm going to make it the wallpaper on my phone."

"We were pretty cute," Daisy admitted.

"So now I know why you're called Daisy, but why do you hate 'Eleanor' so much? It's a pretty name."

"I was named for my great-grandmother and there's a photo of her in my grandmother's house that used to terrify me when I was really little, before my mom died. The old Eleanor was sitting in a rocking chair, clutching the arms, you know? And her fingers were like witch's claws. She scared me so much." She shuddered and he chuckled.

"What?" Gideon asked. "It's cute."

"Yeah, yeah, cute me," she grumbled.

"You don't want to be cute?"

"No. I want to be badass."

She watched as his eyes grew dark. Intense. "I'd say there's a wanted killer out there who thinks you are. And I'd have to agree. I hate that you have to protect yourself, but I'm so damn glad that you can. You are very badass, Miss Dawson."

She didn't want to think about the man who'd attacked her twice, who'd sat inches away talking about jobs in radio and his dog. Who'd killed Trish. *And others.* She swallowed hard, not caring that she was blatantly changing the subject. "And sexy. I want to be sexy. To you."

One side of his mouth curled up, his tone growing much lighter. "Oh, you definitely are that." He slid his hand under the hem of her sweater, toying with her skin. "Isn't this sweater uncomfortable?"

"Oh, very," she said with mock seriousness.

His finger traced lazy circles on her back, making her shiver. "I'd hate for you to be uncomfortable."

"You are such a gentleman."

He laughed quietly. "I can't do this with a straight face. Just take it off, Daisy." Sobering, he stared up at her for so long she actually did feel uncomfortable. "Please," he whispered. "I want to feel your skin."

She pushed to her knees, grabbing the hem of the sweater to pull it off . . . when his cell phone rang again.

He let his head fall back against the pillow. "Fuck."

"Or not," she said unhappily. She reached for his phone and frowned. "It's Rafe. Maybe he found something on Eileen?"

"Put it on speaker?" He waited until she did. "Hey. I've got Daisy here. What did you find today?"

"I'll tell you in a minute," Rafe said, his voice tense. "Where are you?"

"Your parents' house."

"Sasha?" Rafe asked.

"Also here," Gideon told him. "Should we get her?"

"No. She just wasn't answering her phone. I need you to get to my house as quickly as you can."

"Why?" Gideon asked, but he was already scooting around her to get out of bed.

"I'm still in Portland. My flight was delayed, but we've boarded now. Listen, I just got a text from my neighbor, Ned Eldridge. He said there's a car sitting in front of my house. He didn't pay attention to it, because there've been so many reporters camping out. But it's been there for two hours. He got a photo of the driver."

"Is it him?" Gideon asked excitedly. He found a folded shirt on the dresser and held it out to Daisy, his brows raised in a request for help. "Our suspect?"

"No," Rafe said. "Gideon, I think it's Mercy."

The shirt fluttered to the floor. Gideon turned to

lean against the dresser, his features slack with shock. "What?"

"I think it's Mercy. I told Ned not to approach her. I didn't want to scare her off."

Gideon didn't say a word. He just stared at the phone, his mouth open.

"Gid?" Rafe asked. "You still there?"

Daisy jumped off the bed, picked up the shirt, and started working on removing Gideon's sling. "Rafe, he'll be on his way as soon as I get him dressed."

"Ohhh. Okay. I . . . I'm not touching that with a ten-foot pole. What do you want Ned to do if she starts to drive away?"

"Stop her," Gideon blurted. "Thanks, Rafe."

"You got it. Drive safely, okay?"

"We will." Daisy ended the call and opened the bedroom door. "Irina, Karl! Can you come here, please?" She had the sling off when the entire household gathered in the doorway. "Can you tell Agent Hunter that we need to go back to my place, right away?"

Gideon grabbed her wrist, halting her as she put his injured arm through the sleeve. "No *we*. Just *me*."

"Yeah? No." She looked over at them, focusing on her father, who'd opened his mouth to no doubt protest. "Mercy's at my house. Gideon is not going alone."

Irina nodded. "No, not alone. You will obey every word the agent tells you?"

"Every word," Daisy promised, putting Gideon's other arm in the sleeve. *Unless he tells me I can't go.* Because Gideon was *not* going to face his sister alone.

Gideon huffed a laugh. "Daisy, I'm getting the distinct impression you were a bit of a handful as a kid."

"You have no idea," Frederick said dryly. "Daisy, take Brutus and go downstairs to wait. I'll help him with his clothes." He glanced at Gideon. "I'm going, too. I'll ride shotgun. Literally."

Daisy was about to tell him no way in hell when

Gideon nodded. "I'd appreciate it, Frederick. Thank you."

Daisy was still openmouthed and staring when Irina tugged her out of the room. "Do what your father says, Daisy."

Daisy exhaled loudly. "Fine." She passed Sasha's room, where her friend stood in the doorway, not even bothering to hide her grin. "Don't start."

"Oh, I wouldn't think of it," Sasha snickered. "I'm too busy laughing my ass off watching you be all obedient and shit."

"I'm obedient," Daisy muttered. "When I want to be."

"Sasha," Irina chided. "Leave her alone. Karl, go back to sleep."

"We weren't asleep," Karl said, waggling his brows.

Sasha groaned. "Stop. I can't do this." She closed her door with a snap.

Irina guided Daisy to the stairs. "My children insist on believing they were brought by the stork. Come, Daisy. I'll make you some coffee to take with you." She paused a few steps from the bottom, her eyes suddenly revealing her true emotions—anxiety and uncertainty. "You'll call me, won't you?" she whispered. "Let me know what his sister says?"

Daisy kissed her cheek. "Of course."

TWENTY-SIX

Bellamy, Anna. Pennsylvania. Fiddler, Janice. Washington. Zandra stared up at the ceiling, desperately grappling to hold on. Not to lose hope. Not to fall apart.

Not to get comfortable in the clean sheets, silk nightshirt, and soft ties around her wrists and ankles. Not to be grateful for the "kindness" because it wasn't kindness at all.

He wants to break me. I won't break.

But she was so damn tired.

Orlov, Nadia. Illinois. Stevenson, Rayanna. Texas. DeVeen, Rosamond. Minnesota. Borge, Delfina. California. Oliver, Makayla. New York. Danton, Eileen. Oregon.

Names on pieces of plastic, hanging in a sadist's cabinet in a cold, silent basement. Where a dead woman lay in the freezer against the wall. *Martell, Kaley. California.*

Hart, Trisha. California. His most recent victim. Zandra remembered when he'd shown her the license, when he'd placed it in the cabinet. When he'd taken off Kaley's lucky horseshoe and replaced it with Trish's turquoise cross in some kind of macabre ceremony.

What day was that?

She didn't know. She didn't know what day this was.

I'm going to die here. And he's going to put my license in the cabinet and no one will ever know what happened to me.

Her eyes filled with tears and, hardening her jaw, she resolutely blinked them away. *No. He will not break me. I'm going to get out of here.*

The doorknob rattled and Zandra tightened her body in dread. *He's back. He's back and he's going to start all over again.*

But the door didn't open and the rattling continued, followed by a banging.

She sucked in a breath, too terrified to hope. Someone was out there. Someone not him.

But then the banging stopped and Zandra's heart sank. They were leaving.

"H—" Her throat was too dry. "Help." She wanted to scream it, but it came out as not even a whisper. "Please." A sob tightened her chest and she fought it back. "Don't go."

But she was whispering. No one would hear her.

No one would help—

The door flew open, revealing a woman standing in the doorway. *"You fucking slut."*

Zandra turned her head toward the door, staring. The woman wasn't young. She wasn't old, either. It was hard to say, at least with the scowl she wore. A scowl and a white satin peignoir. And five-inch heels.

Zandra started to ask for help but the woman burst into the room.

And slapped her.

Zandra stared up at her, tears forming in her eyes. *He did this. He set me up. He wanted me to hope. To think that she'd help me.*

It was too cruel. And too much. No longer able to hold the tears back, Zandra began to cry. Big, huge sobs that racked her body.

He'd done it. *He broke me.*

The woman leaned into her space, her face inches from Zandra's. "Do not think your tears will move me," she snarled. "You're a manipulative bitch, like all the others."

Zandra shook her head, no words forming. Tears flowing.

"Don't tell me no. You're one of his whores. Did you think I didn't know about you? Did you think I'd let you have him?"

She was drunk, Zandra realized. And maybe high. The woman's eyes were glazed, insane. Definitely insane.

"Water," Zandra managed to croak out. "Please."

"You get nothing from me except the fucking door."

To Zandra's shock, the woman began to yank at the ties binding her to the bed. Loosening the knots.

"You're nothing. You come in here and play your little sex games. A little S&M, a little BDSM." She sneered, ripping the first binding from Zandra's wrist. The woman went immediately to the second binding, clawing at the knot with long, elegantly manicured nails. "I made him. He's mine. Gave him the best years of my damn life and you think you can come along and take him from me?"

The second binding came off and the woman moved to the third, shoving the blanket up Zandra's legs. She gave Zandra a furious glance. "What did he promise you? Money?" She snorted. "He's got none. He comes to me for money." She pointed to her own chest. "To *me*. I control his money. I control him. He thinks this is his house. He thinks he has secrets. I know all his secrets. I've known about his little kink for years. You're not the first woman he's brought down here."

She loosened the knot at Zandra's left ankle but used no care, her nails digging into already abraded skin. Zandra choked back a moan.

The woman chuckled. "You like that? You're a pain

slut. He must be a good master." She sounded . . . proud?
"I taught him everything he knows." She was on the
final tie. "You want him? Tough shit. Get your own.
Start him young." She looked up from the knot she was
freeing and smiled, making Zandra's blood run cold.
"Ten is best. Twelve at the latest. They'll eat right out
of your hand. Literally."

Zandra stared at the woman in horror, unable to
move even when the last tie was ripped off her skin.
And then she understood. "Sydney," she whispered
hoarsely.

"Sydney," the name he called when he was in a rage.
Say you're sorry.

The woman straightened, looking pleased. "He told
you about me?"

Zandra couldn't say anything. Not a single word.

"Get up," Sydney snapped.

Zandra blinked rapidly, trying to get enough control
over her body to stand. But she'd been tied too long, her
body too exhausted. Her legs refused to move.

"I said, *get up*!" Sydney grabbed her arm and
dragged her, blanket and all, off the bed onto the floor.

Zandra struggled to stand, her knees like rubber.

"Move." Sydney dragged her out of the room, where
she nearly tripped over a dog.

A dog? Zandra squinted down, not sure she'd seen
right. But it was a dog. Its tongue was out, its tail wagging.

Sydney kicked at the dog. "Get out of my way," she
ordered and hauled Zandra up a flight of stairs. Tangled in the blanket, Zandra stumbled and fell to her
knees, barely able to breathe.

Move, she screamed at herself. *Run. Get away while
you can.*

But her limbs didn't move. Everything was blurry
and the room spun. She retched, but there was nothing
to come up.

Sydney snarled. "I said *move*." Renewing her grip on Zandra's arm, she half dragged, half carried her until they'd cleared the top of the stairs and crossed a small, neat living room. Sydney was breathing hard as she pushed Zandra out the front door.

Zandra crumpled to a heap on the front porch, hitting her head on the concrete. A few seconds later the door opened again and the dog was thrust onto the porch with her.

"Take that sorry excuse for an animal with you."

The door slammed hard.

Zandra lay there, panting.

Get away. Get away.

And then she felt something rough on her cheek. Rough and wet. Heard a whimper. Felt a nudge against her shoulder. Mindlessly she pushed to her knees. The dog leapt off the front porch and spun three times before giving a short bark.

She pushed to her feet and new tears fell. It hurt. Her feet. Her head. All over.

The dog barked once again and walked a few feet, turning to her expectantly.

Move, Zandra. Just a few steps. She forced her feet to move and she shuffled across the porch, holding on to the post for balance.

Bellamy, Anna. Pennsylvania. Fiddler, Janice. Washington.

The dog ran ahead another ten feet, then looked back. Zandra forced her feet to shuffle forward. *Orlov, Nadia. Illinois. Stevenson, Rayanna. Texas. DeVeen, Rosamond. Minnesota.*

She made it to the street and looked both ways. Houses. Lots of houses.

A car stopped in a driveway a few houses up. *Go. Get help.* She lurched forward and tripped on the blanket again.

A woman was getting groceries from her car. She

looked at Zandra with disgust and fear. Hurriedly, she took the bags and ran up her sidewalk. "Go away," she called over her shoulder. "Or I'll call the police. Go sober up."

"Please," Zandra cried. Or tried to. The woman slammed her front door.

Zandra pushed back to her knees. And came face-to-face with the dog. He licked her nose, yipped, then ran ten feet before turning to look at her.

Gritting her teeth, she used a lamppost to pull herself to her feet. She forced herself to move, shuffling down the street, looking for someone who'd help her. Anyone. All she needed was a phone. She could call 911. Get help.

Go to the next door. Beg if you have to. She turned into the next yard with a light on in the front window. She took a step. *Borge, Delfina. California.* Another step. *Oliver, Makayla. New York.* Another step, ignoring the burning of her feet on the cold concrete. *Danton, Eileen. Oregon.*

She got to the door and knocked. And waited. She could hear people inside, but no one came to the door. "Help," she whispered. "Please."

But no one answered and she turned from the door, ready to give up, but felt a brush against her hand. The dog had come back.

Too tired to think anymore, she mindlessly followed him, one foot in front of the other. *Martell, Kaley. California. Hart, Trisha. California.*

||| SACRAMENTO, CALIFORNIA
||| MONDAY, FEBRUARY 20, 10:35 P.M.

His good mood evaporated when he pulled into his driveway. He'd been making plans for Zandra all the way from Granite Bay to the grocery store lot where he dropped off the van. He'd walked to his Jeep, parked in front of a coffee shop, whistling. He'd even left a tip in the jar on the counter when he'd gotten himself a caramel macchiato to go.

But now . . . Dread mixed with fury as he drove past the all-too-familiar Mercedes parked in his driveway. He opened his garage door and rolled in, trying to come up with a way to explain why he'd been out when he'd claimed to be sick and feverish.

And, more importantly, a way to get rid of Sydney.

He sat for a moment, reviewing what he'd already told her so he wouldn't tell a lie that made things worse. After a minute, he nodded, his story fixed in his mind.

Putting down the garage door, he went into the house and stopped short. A soup tureen sat on his dining room table. It was Sydney's china pattern.

She'd brought him the fucking soup after all.

He drew a breath, tamping down the rage that threatened to boil over. She was trying to be nice. He wanted no part of her "nice." He wanted no part of her.

Swallowing hard, he forced himself to call her name in a hoarse, coughing voice. "Sydney? Are you here?"

Of course she was here. Her car was outside.

He began searching for her. The kitchen? No. Bathroom? Empty. He braced himself as he opened the bedroom door. *Please don't let her be in my bed. Please.*

But the bedroom was empty as well. The bed was not as he'd left it—neatly made—but was, instead, turned back with rose petals strewn across the pillows. The sight had bile clawing up his throat.

He wanted to vomit.

But he swallowed it back. Like he always did. Like he had since he was twelve years old. Since the first time she'd visited his room in the night.

Breathe, he told himself. *Just breathe, dammit.* Because he'd gone light-headed. Dizzy. He grabbed on to the door frame with his good hand, hanging on like it was a life preserver. Breathing in and out. Trying not to let the panic take over.

Stand up straight. Be a man, for fuck's sake. Find her. Get rid of her.

Then show Zandra what a real man does to selfish whores.

He walked back through the house, calling Sydney's name. Sounding compliant, just the way she liked it. But she didn't answer. The house was quiet. Too quiet. Something was different. Wrong.

Where was Mutt? "Mutt?" he called. "Here, boy!"

And then he noticed the door to the basement.

It was open.

He never left it open. He was meticulous about that door, *always* locking it and the one at the bottom of the basement stairs. The one to his . . .

He gasped. *Oh God. Oh no. Not the guest room.* It wasn't possible.

He stumbled down the stairs, his heart pounding so hard it was all he could hear.

The door to the guest room was open.

Open. Open. Open. The word echoed in his mind to the beat of his frantic pulse.

He stepped inside and saw her. Sydney. Lying on the guest bed on her side, propped on her elbow, her nightgown all arranged, a pout on her face.

And Zandra . . . was gone.

"Where is she?" he blurted out, shouting the words.

Sydney's pout became an angry glare. "Sonny," she warned.

He took a halting step forward. Then another, both of his hands clenching into fists. The pain in his injured hand just made him madder. "I *said*, where *is* she?"

Sydney sneered. "Your whore? I tossed her ass out."

He started to pant, panic consuming his rage. "Out? Out where?"

Sydney fluttered her hand dismissively. "Outside. Wherever whores go."

Oh God. Oh God. Oh God. He dragged air into his lungs, but it wasn't enough. "When?" he whispered.

She sat up and folded her arms across her breasts. Her expression became haughty and disapproving. "I don't like your tone, Sonny."

He didn't care. "Why would you do this?" he asked, his voice trembling.

"Because you're mine," she said as if that made all the sense in the world. And in Sydney's world, it probably did.

He felt like he would faint. "How did you get in here?"

She scoffed. "I made copies of your house keys years ago. Right after you moved out."

Because he'd wanted to get away from her. Far away. But she hadn't let him go.

"How?" he managed.

She lifted one shoulder. "I drugged you and took them. I told you that you couldn't leave me, Sonny. I've known about your little room for years. I just never discovered a woman in here before. I found your toy collection. And your little blue pills." She smirked. "I wonder why you need those things. Having trouble getting it up for your whores?"

He was hyperventilating and she was laughing at him. "Shut up," he cried. "Just shut up."

"Watch your mouth," she snapped, then, visibly calming herself, came to her feet, all elegance and grace. And rotted, fetid filth. "I told you that there would be no one else but me. I warned you, Sonny. Now, I believe you owe me an apology. Say you're sorry, Sonny."

Say you're sorry. His pulse was thundering in his

ears. Zandra had never said the words. Now she was gone.

Gone.

To the police.

Oh my God. They'll come for me. He looked at the elegant woman who watched him with clear disdain and growing impatience. Her face grew hard and he wanted to throw up.

"Say you're sorry, Sonny," she demanded coldly. "Right now."

Say you're sorry. Sorry? She should be sorry, not me. She's ruined everything. She always ruins everything. I'm going to get caught. I'm going to lose everything.

His anger began to grow, overshadowing the fear, the panic. "You say it," he snarled.

Her face blanched and she took a step back. "Sonny," she snapped. "Watch your tone with me." She softened her voice, but he could hear the fear in it. "Just apologize and it'll all be fine."

"No." He shook his head, advancing on her, step-by-step, watching comprehension fill her eyes. Watching her shrink back as his good hand shot out to shove her backward. She stumbled, falling onto the bed when the backs of her knees hit the frame.

And then he was on her, holding her down with his left elbow and one knee, pounding into her face with his right fist. She screamed, long and loud, and he slapped her.

She fell back, her mouth open in shock. "Sonny," she whispered. "What are you doing?"

What I should have done sixteen years ago, he thought, but he said nothing because he was gritting his teeth, his hand tight around her throat. Watching her eyes grow wide, then bulge. Watching her mouth fall open as she tried to suck in air.

Watching her die. Finally.

||| SACRAMENTO, CALIFORNIA
MONDAY, FEBRUARY 20, 10:50 P.M.

What if she leaves? What if she's gone when I get there?
Gideon bit back what would have been a snarl for
Agent Hunter to drive faster. The man was already
speeding and the last thing they needed was to have a
traffic accident.

Agent Hunter had been pretty cooperative, all
things considered. He'd balked a little at having Frederick carrying a weapon in the front seat with him, despite the fact that he still had a valid California
concealed carry permit—until Frederick had put him
on the phone with one of his friends in the Baltimore
field office. Special Agent Joseph Carter had personally vouched for Frederick's character and marksmanship. After Carter had bitched about being woken up
at one fifteen in the morning.

All that had taken precious time they could have
been using to drive to Rafe's house, where Mercy—
hopefully—still waited, but Frederick had made his
presence a requirement for Daisy's. *And I need her
here with me.*

Gideon's initial response had been no way in hell
was she coming with him, but he was grateful she
hadn't listened to him. She sat quietly in the seat beside him now, holding his hand.

No one had said much as they'd sped down the interstate, and now that they were turning onto Rafe's street,
all Gideon could think was that Mercy had come.

She's here. She came. She really came.

Hunter slowed as they approached Rafe's old Victorian and Gideon frowned. A blue sedan was parked on
the curb, but the driver's-side door was open. Hunter

pulled the SUV into Rafe's driveway and Gideon was out before the vehicle had fully stopped.

Mercy was here. She was still here. She was . . . kneeling on the ground near the curb in front of the blue sedan. A dog sat next to her on the sidewalk.

SUV doors opened behind him, Frederick barking at Daisy to be careful.

"Oh my God," Daisy whispered from behind him. "Is that . . . ? Yeah, it is. That's George, the dog from Saturday. *His* dog, Gideon."

Both Gideon and Frederick grabbed her arms, keeping her from walking to the dog. The dog showed no fear, leaping up to run to Daisy, tail wagging.

Mercy's head whipped around. She was on the phone, giving someone the address. Her eyes met Gideon's and it was like looking in a mirror.

Like looking back thirteen years when he'd found her in foster care. She hadn't changed that much. Her face was fuller, her hair longer. But it was *her*. Here. *For me.*

"I called 911," she said, forgoing any greeting in true Mercy fashion.

Releasing Daisy's arm, Gideon moved to Mercy's side, where a woman lay on the ground, curled into the fetal position. "Who is she?" Gideon asked.

"I don't know. I was sitting here, waiting for you, when she kind of staggered down the sidewalk. I thought she was drunk or homeless or both. The dog kept running a few feet ahead, then running back to her, all the way down the block. And then the dog just sat in front of your house. She caught up, and when he didn't go any farther, neither did she. I think she was trying to ask me for help. She's alive, but not making sense."

Gideon knelt beside the woman, whose face was bruised and battered, her lip split. She was somewhere in her twenties with dirty blond hair. She was shaking uncontrollably and muttering under her breath.

"She's not wearing any shoes, Gideon," Mercy murmured.

Mercy was right. The woman's feet were cut and bleeding. It wasn't cold enough to freeze her extremities, but it wasn't warm enough to be barefoot.

Hunter appeared with a blanket and covered the woman carefully. "Why does she have the suspect's dog?" he asked.

"Damn good question," Gideon said. He sensed Daisy behind him and looked over his shoulder. Frederick stood behind her, shielding her as his gaze constantly searched for danger. "Are you sure that's the same dog from the adoption clinic, Daisy?"

She stood next to Gideon, her leg pressed against his uninjured shoulder. "Well, pretty sure. He seems to remember me."

Mercy looked up at Daisy. "You're the one who called me."

Daisy nodded once. "Yes." Then she smiled at Mercy. "And you came."

Mercy nodded and dropped her eyes back to the muttering woman. "I can't figure out what she's saying. It sounds like names and places, but it doesn't make sense."

Gideon dipped his head, angling his ear closer, trying to listen.

"DeVeen, Rosamond," the woman muttered. "Minnesota."

Gideon sucked in a breath, instantly recognizing the name. "Oh my God," he murmured.

Daisy dropped to her knees. "What?"

"Listen to what she's saying," he said, his heart beating harder. "Names, Daisy."

"Borge, Delfina. California," the woman continued. "Oliver, Makayla. New York."

Daisy's gaze jerked to meet his. "Makayla Oliver

was one of the women with letters carved into her body. She lived in Niagara Falls."

Gideon nodded grimly. "Delfina Borge owned the beige sedan. Her body was never found."

They bent low to hear more just as the woman muttered, "Danton, Eileen. Oregon. Martell, Kaley. California. Hart, Trisha. California."

"Oh." Daisy's hand was over her mouth. "Trish. And Eileen. Gideon, I'm sorry."

He felt like he'd been punched in the gut. He'd known chances were that Eileen was dead, but . . . he'd still hoped.

Daisy frowned. "Wait. Kaley Martell. That's the prostitute who went missing Thursday night. Rafe's case, remember? I read the report Nina Barnes did on her after I talked to her Friday."

"The one with the sick little girl," Gideon whispered. "Holy hell."

"Gideon?" Mercy asked hesitantly. "What about Eileen? What's going on here?"

Gideon turned to find his sister's eyes wary. "There's so much to explain here, Mercy, but . . . I'm pretty sure that she's dead."

"Shh." Agent Hunter had his cell phone next to the woman's face. "Hold this. She's talking again."

Daisy did as he asked while Hunter rose, on full alert. Frederick, to his credit, didn't need to be brought up to speed. "The names are his victims?" he asked softly.

Gideon nodded, standing when he heard sirens. He held his hand out to Mercy, who stared at it as if it would bite her. Finally, she took his hand and let him help her to her feet. He led her to the sidewalk, so that Daisy could record the woman's utterances without their interference.

"I have a lot to tell you," he said quietly. "But . . ." He swallowed hard. "I'm so damn glad you came."

She dropped her gaze to her feet. "I should have come a long time ago."

"No should've's, okay?" He touched her cheek briefly. "Will you stay for a little while? I need to try to talk to this woman."

She nodded, glancing up for only a second before studying her shoes again. "Yes."

He squeezed her hand awkwardly. "I'll be right back. Don't leave, okay?"

"I won't." One side of her mouth lifted. "I promise."

"Okay." He returned to where Daisy was handing the phone back to Agent Hunter.

"She was just saying the same few names again," Daisy explained. "I recognized some of them. Gideon, where did she come from?"

"That's my question." He bent closer. "Ma'am, what is your name?"

She blinked at him, her eyes empty. "Bellamy, Anna. Pennsylvania. Fiddler, Janice. Washington."

Daisy gently touched the woman's shoulder through the blanket. "Hey," she said softly, her husky voice like a caress. "You're safe now. We won't hurt you. These men are with the FBI. We'll keep you safe, and an ambulance is coming. Will you tell us *your* name?"

The woman's eyes filled with tears and she shuddered out a sob. "Zandra. Zandra Jones."

The ambulance was pulling up to the curb. Daisy stroked the curve of the woman's ear—one of the few places she didn't have bruises. "Zandra, I'm Daisy. Can you tell us where you came from?"

She shook her head very slowly. "I walked and walked."

"All right," Daisy said as the EMTs rolled a stretcher toward them. "You're going to the hospital now but I'll meet you there, okay?"

Zandra nodded. "Can't forget them."

"Who, honey?" Daisy soothed.

"The others."

Gideon felt a chill race down his spine at those two little words. *The others.* Some of the names Zandra had recited were ones he had not recognized. Either Zandra had misunderstood or the asshole had killed more women than they'd thought.

"You need to move, sir," the EMT said briskly.

Gideon rose, tugging Daisy up with him. "Where are you taking her?"

"UC Davis."

SACRAMENTO, CALIFORNIA
MONDAY, FEBRUARY 20, 10:50 P.M.

He slid his knee off Sydney's chest, straddling her, then slowly pushed himself back to sit on his heels.

She was dead.

And it had been so easy.

All those years wasted. *I should have done this long ago.* He drew a breath, feeling remarkably . . . free.

Until his reason returned and he remembered why he'd flown into an explosive rage.

Zandra was gone. Sydney had set her free. Had thrown her out.

To go straight to the cops.

Fuck.

He closed his eyes, willing his heart to slow to a normal pace. *What now? What if the police come?*

What if they do? They didn't have anything on him. He'd never left physical evidence on any of his victims. *Except with Daisy.* But his own DNA was still not on record anywhere for them to match it to.

So what if Zandra said she'd been held here? It was his word against hers and she was in pretty bad shape.

The police probably wouldn't have enough for a warrant. Probably. But he was too careful to wager on "probably." If they did come in, he needed there to be no evidence that Zandra had ever been here.

He needed to get rid of Sydney's body for starters. And there was still Kaley Martell in the freezer.

Of course . . . it was possible that Zandra was still out there, wandering the neighborhood. If Sydney had tossed her out with nothing, it was possible that she was still close by.

He blew out a breath, frustrated with himself. He'd wasted valuable time killing Sydney when he could have been looking for Zandra. He'd try looking for her first.

If he couldn't find her, he'd come back and police-proof his house.

He jogged up the stairs, through the house, and to his Jeep. He had no choice but to use his own car in a situation like this. He had a blanket in the back that he could use to cover her up when he found her, just until he got her back.

When he'd simply kill the bitch.

Then he'd take all three bodies to his dumping ground. And he'd be done. From here on out, he'd kill his prey in their natural habitat. No more bringing them home.

He pulled out of his driveway, passing Sydney's Mercedes on his way out. He'd have to do away with that, too. Eventually someone would start looking for her.

He drove down his street slowly, watching for the white nightshirt he'd dressed Zandra in before leaving the house earlier. Watching for anything resembling a crawling, stumbling woman.

He'd gone two blocks before realizing he'd automatically followed the route to Daisy's house. He pulled into a driveway to turn around when an ambulance roared by, sirens and lights going.

No, he thought. *It can't be Zandra. Hopefully some old person just had a heart attack.*

But something told him to follow the ambulance, so he did.

And his gut turned inside out. The ambulance stopped in front of Daisy's house, where a group of people had gathered. He recognized Daisy's blond hair as well as the Fed he'd shot, who now wore a sling. They were huddled around something on the ground.

No, not something. *Someone.*

"Zandra," he whispered. But how? How had she known to come here?

And then he saw Mutt.

He swallowed hard. The damn dog. Mutt had brought her here. *Here.* To the one place that Zandra should definitely not be.

Carefully he turned the car around and headed for home. He hadn't approached close enough to raise any suspicion, but when he got away from Daisy's street, he floored it. He needed to destroy any evidence and then . . . *Get away. I have to get away.*

TWENTY-SEVEN

Daisy walked with Zandra, holding her hand until they loaded the woman into the back of the ambulance. "We'll meet you there," she promised, but she was shaking her head as she stepped back from the ambulance. "I don't think she heard me," she told them once the ambulance was gone.

"She looked dehydrated," Frederick stated, then turned to Mercy. "Hi. I'm Daisy's father, Frederick Dawson. You must be Mercy Reynolds."

Mercy's flinch was barely noticeable, but Gideon saw it because he was watching. "Mercy Callahan," she corrected. "It's nice to meet you, Frederick."

"And that guy over there on the phone is Special Agent Hunter. He works with me at the FBI," Gideon told her. Hunter had stepped away to update Agent Molina.

"He's your bodyguard?" Mercy asked.

"More or less," Gideon said. He looked down at the dog. "How did this dog know to come here?"

Daisy looked at the house next door, waving to a man watching from an upstairs window. She gestured for him to come outside. "That's Ned Eldridge, the guy who texted Rafe about Mercy being here. Maybe he saw something. He's on the Neighborhood Watch committee."

"He's been watching me for two hours," Mercy confirmed.

"Why didn't you call me?" Gideon asked her. "I moved away from here six months ago. I put my new address in my Christmas card in December."

Mercy looked down at her shoes again. "I . . . I didn't notice it."

She hadn't opened it, Gideon guessed, but that was a topic for another time. The dog and its owner were the highest priority now. "It's okay," he said softly because she looked ready to bolt. "Will you stay with me at my new place? I have plenty of room."

She nodded but said nothing. She had that overwhelmed, panicked look in her eyes that he'd seen when he'd found her in the foster home.

The door to Eldridge's house opened and the man rushed out in his bedroom slippers. "Daisy," he said, grasping her hand. "I've been worried about you."

"I'm fine," Daisy said, then introduced the rest of them. "Did you see the woman in the blanket?"

"I did. She came from that way." He pointed behind him. "I was about to come outside when Miss Callahan got out of her car. I called 911." He looked at Mercy. "I saw you on your phone and figured you were doing the same. I didn't come out because Rafe told me not to scare you away."

Mercy smiled tightly but said nothing.

"The dog has been by here before," Ned went on. "I saw him earlier this afternoon. Not too long after you guys left. Some guy was walking him."

"Was he about six feet tall with glasses, dark hair, and a mustache?" Gideon asked, describing the man who'd dared come near Daisy on Saturday at the pet store.

"Height's the same, but nothing else," Ned said. "No glasses, blond hair with a little gray in it, and no mustache."

Daisy narrowed her eyes. "That's what the guy in the bus station looked like. You remember, Gideon, the one who bought a ticket when we were asking about Eileen."

"So he uses disguises." Gideon blew out a breath. "Of course he does. How often did he walk the dog past here?"

"I saw him a few times. I went out to talk to him this afternoon because I saw him lurking. I would have reported him to the Neighborhood Watch if he'd kept it up. I don't like strange people wandering the neighborhood. No offense, Miss Callahan," he added politely.

"None taken," Mercy said with a smile that loosened a knot in Gideon's chest. He hadn't seen that smile in too many years.

"So when Zandra escaped, the dog brought her here." Daisy petted the dog's head. "Good boy." Then her head tilted. "I wonder if he knows the way H-O-M-E?"

Agent Hunter finished his call and joined them in time to hear her question. "Good idea. I need to get him a lead, then I'll try the command."

"I have one," Ned said. "Give me a minute to get it for you." He jogged back to his house.

"Now what?" Daisy asked.

"I'd like you, Mercy, and your dad to go inside and wait for another agent to take you to the hospital," Gideon said. "I'm going with Agent Hunter and the dog. If we can't find where his H-O-M-E is, I'll meet you at the ER."

Daisy frowned. "You can't go. You're still in recovery. If anyone goes, it should be me. I'm a better shot."

Gideon saw Frederick's mouth open, the word "no" already on his lips, but he stayed the older man by lifting his hand. "You are a better shot," Gideon agreed. "Even when I have two functioning hands. But if he can get to you, he'll use you to force our hand. He could get away. With you."

Daisy took a deep breath. "And I would end up like Trish," she said quietly. "And the others."

Frederick visibly paled and Mercy watched them all, clearly confused. *I'll explain to her later,* he thought. Paramount now was keeping Daisy safe.

"And the others," Gideon repeated soberly. He cupped Daisy's cheek. "So you'll stay here? You'll get to the ER faster this way," he added when she didn't respond. "And you did promise Zandra you'd be there."

The side-eye she gave him said he needed to shut up now. So he did.

"Yes," she finally said. "I'll stay. But if he starts shooting, you let Hunter shoot back."

Frederick relaxed, shooting him a grateful glance.

Gideon managed to hide his own relief. "I'll let Hunter do all the heavy lifting," he said. *If I can,* he added silently, and once again he saw he hadn't fooled her. "Thank you. For now, stay together and we'll figure out logistics later. Is that okay, Mercy?"

Mercy nodded. "Although I am getting tired. I pulled an all-nighter before I flew out this afternoon. I'm on Central Time. Maybe I can crash in a waiting room."

She was being very accommodating. It made Gideon a little nervous, if he was honest with himself. "You won't leave?"

Her smile was faint. "I promised. I won't leave until we get a chance to talk."

Ned returned with a collar and leash. "Here you go. It's an extra, so no hurry in getting it back to me."

"Thank you, sir," Hunter said. He put the leash on the killer's dog and handed it to Gideon. "Let me do a sweep of Miss Dawson's house before they go in," he said.

"I'll call Molina," Gideon said, "and ask for backup." Gideon waited on the sidewalk, watching as Daisy, Mercy, and Frederick followed Hunter up to the house, then turned to Ned. "Thank you," he said gruffly. "I appreciate you keeping watch over the house and letting Rafe know there was a car outside. And thank you for watching over her to make sure she didn't leave. I . . . I haven't seen my sister in a long time."

Ned smiled. "My pleasure." His smile faded. "That guy I talked to, the one with the dog? He's the killer they've been talking about on the news? The one that killed Daisy's friend Trish?"

"It's likely," Gideon said. "If you see anyone with that description again, can you call Rafe right away?" He had to fight his own wince, because telling the man to call someone else with information stung. But he was on medical leave and he wasn't going to do anything to jeopardize this case. Not when Daisy's safety was involved. When they caught the bastard, he wanted him put in prison forever and wasn't about to give some defense attorney reason to get the fucker off. "I'm not on the case anymore." He pointed to his sling when Ned looked confused. "He shot me over the weekend."

"I read about that, too. Wow." Ned looked partly horrified and partly fascinated. "I've never stood next to a killer before. I'm not sure how to think about it." He shook himself. "I'm going to have a stiff drink and try to sleep. You have a good night, Agent Reynolds."

"You too."

Gideon stood on the sidewalk, scanning his surroundings for any movement as he phoned Molina. She answered on the first ring.

"Agent Reynolds," she said crisply. "I was just briefed by Agent Hunter. I was about to call him back, actually. I got a hit on Zandra Jones. She disappeared from Vail on Friday afternoon. She'd been in the bar, got into an altercation with a man there, another patron. She was, reportedly, very drunk at the time. Another patron said the man left for a little while, said he was going to call Miss Jones a cab. He came back after a few minutes, saying he'd sent the woman to the airport."

"Airport," Gideon said quietly. "He's not a truck driver like we thought. He works on a plane. A flight attendant maybe. Or maybe even a pilot. That's how he could take victims from so many different places."

"Sounds right," she said. "The woman couldn't have walked far. You say the dog brought her?"

"It looks like it. Daisy's neighbor says he's seen a man walking the dog around here."

"Smart dog."

"Hunter and I were going to see if it knows its way home."

"And Miss Dawson?"

"She's with her father. And my sister."

"Oh? That's . . . very nice," she said, a little stiffly, but not unkindly. "I think Daisy's father can protect them until I get backup to transport them. He and Daisy came recommended by the Baltimore field office."

"Yeah. We had to let Hunter talk to Agent Carter before he'd let Frederick in the car with us."

"Are you able to drive?" she asked.

"Yes," he said immediately, suspecting where she was going with this and not wanting to miss out. "I haven't taken pain pills since this morning."

"I want you to drive Agent Hunter's vehicle, tailing him while he sees if the dog knows his way home, providing backup if necessary. I'll get you new backup as soon as I can. In the meantime, I'm going to get the addresses of any pilots who live in a five-block radius of Miss Dawson's home."

Gideon remembered Trish's body. "SY." "Cross-reference the name 'Sydney.'"

"Just did it," she said, "but thank you. I've requested SacPD backup. They'll be there within three minutes. It'll take a little longer for Bureau backup, but I'll let you know who's coming. If you find the house, inform me immediately. I'll have someone draft a warrant right away."

"Will do. Hunter's coming back. I'll brief him and we'll see what the dog can show us."

"Be careful, Gideon."

"I will be. Thank you." He ended the call as Agent Hunter joined him. He told Hunter what Molina had said and Hunter traded him the keys for the dog's leash.

Hunter crouched in front of the dog, affectionately petting his head. "He's in good shape. Clean, groomed. Good weight. Someone's been caring for him." He leaned in, letting the dog lick his face. "You're a good boy, aren't you? Let's see how good." He rose, lightly tugged on the leash. "Let's go home."

SACRAMENTO, CALIFORNIA
MONDAY, FEBRUARY 20, 11:10 P.M.

He looked around, trying to stay calm as he hurried. He didn't have much time. Zandra had been talking to the FBI. To Reynolds. Of all people.

The last of the gas poured from the can and he shook it before setting it aside. He took a final look at the house that had been the first thing that had been *his*.

But it had to go. He wasn't going to leave them any evidence to use against him.

Damn forensics.

The fire would destroy everything—his DNA, fingerprints, the Jeep he'd moved to the garage. The souvenirs in the basement. Sydney's body. And good riddance to her. Without evidence, it was just his word against Zandra's.

He fumbled with the match, damning his bandaged hand. Damning Daisy Dawson. Ever since she'd fought him off in the alley, everything had gone to shit.

I should have shot her that night. And that yappy dog of hers, too.

But he hadn't and now he was trying—and failing—to light the match to incinerate his own home. He looked over his shoulder, listening for the wail of sirens.

He'd used precious minutes dousing the stairs leading to the basement and the back exterior wall, running out of gasoline before he could soak the rest of the perimeter. But this wall was closest to his guest room. Hopefully he hadn't taken too much time.

But there were no sirens. Not yet. All he heard was silence. *So far, so good.*

Breathe. Just breathe. He flexed his good hand, trying to control the trembling. Gripping the matchbox between his palm and his three working fingers, he gripped the match in his right hand. *Now, light the damn match.*

Finally. The match flared to life and he dropped it onto the gas-soaked ground at the back of the house. Picking up the gas can, he ran to the front of the house, threw it in the garage, then pulled his duffel from the back of his Jeep. It had emergency supplies like water and money. And at least one disguise. He closed the garage door, then hurried to Sydney's Mercedes. Hopefully no one would be able to identify her body for a while. He needed time to get away.

Climbing behind the wheel, he put it in reverse and calmly backed out of his driveway. Then he changed gears and drove.

To where, he wasn't yet sure. But he knew how he'd get there.

▌▌▌ SACRAMENTO, CALIFORNIA
▌▌▌ MONDAY, FEBRUARY 20, 11:15 P.M.

Gideon drove Hunter's SUV slowly, staying even with
the man, who was following a very happy dog. The dog
didn't seem to have been abused. It was almost too
friendly.

It was difficult to reconcile the image of a doting pet
owner with the killer who'd mutilated Trish's body.
And the others.

"Reynolds!" Hunter called. "He's pulling hard toward that house." He pointed at the tidy little ranch-
style house with roses climbing up one side.

Gideon looked up ahead and for a second could
only stare. Because smoke began to billow into the air.
Oh God. "The one on fire?"

Hunter's eyes widened at the smoke rising from the
house. "Shit." He opened the backseat of the SUV and
the dog jumped right in. "There's a fire extinguisher
under your seat." He slammed the door and ran
around to the driver's side, opened the door, and
grabbed the extinguisher as Gideon called 911 and
gave the address to the operator.

Hunter ran toward the house and Gideon followed,
leaving the dog safe in the SUV. He drew his weapon,
clutching it in his left hand, as he approached the
house, where flames were licking up the exterior walls.

The bastard had set the beige Chevy on fire after
fleeing the scene at Macdoel. Now he'd set fire to a
house. Hunter was emptying the fire extinguisher on
the flames, but it wasn't going to be enough.

Fuck. This had to be where Zandra had been held.

Gideon looked around for something to use to fight
the fire, even if just to slow it until the fire department
arrived. He started around the perimeter, stopping

short when he saw the water spigot and a hose next to the climbing rosebushes. And a stack of eight big bags filled with soil.

"Hunter!" he shouted, pocketing his gun and yanking at the hose with his good hand.

Hunter rounded the corner and skidded to a stop. "Let me do that," he said when he saw Gideon pulling the hose toward the flames, which seemed to be confined to only one wall at the moment.

"I've got this. You take the bags of dirt. We can dump them on the fire."

"Will do." Grimly, Hunter hefted a bag of dirt onto each shoulder and followed Gideon around to the back of the house. He ripped the bags open and began hurling dirt at the flames while Gideon soaked the wall with water.

"This isn't going to be enough!" Hunter shouted over the crackle of the flames.

"We don't have to put it out," Gideon shouted back. "Just keep it from spreading. The firehouse is only a few blocks away."

Nodding, Hunter went back for more dirt and returned with two SacPD uniforms who'd just responded. Between the three of them, they threw the rest of the dirt on the flames, and then one of the cops took the hose from Gideon.

He thanked them and dialed Molina. "It's Gideon," he said when she answered.

"What the hell is going on there?" she demanded.

"We found the house. He'd set fire to it."

"Sonofabitch," she spat.

"We may have slowed it down a little, Hunter and I and a few SacPD cops." Loud sirens got louder as the fire truck barreled down the street. "Fire department's here." He gave her the address as Hunter gestured him toward the front of the house. Gideon and one of the SacPD cops followed.

"I'm going in," Hunter shouted. "He could have more victims in there."

Gideon nodded at him. "Get a warrant," he told his boss, "but Hunter and I are going in."

"I heard," Molina said. "I want you to sit this one out, Gideon. You're too close. I will not lose this fucker because you get accused of planting evidence because he fucking shot you. For which you are on *medical leave*. I'm serious."

Hunter gave him a questioning look. Gideon just pointed at the SacPD cop. "You two go. I'm sidelined."

With a sympathetic nod, Hunter turned to the cop. "Ready?" The cop nodded and Hunter kicked in the door. The two disappeared into the house.

Gideon ground his teeth, knowing she was right, but not liking it one little bit. "Hunter's in," he told his boss levelly. "I'm not."

"Thank you," Molina said. "Stay on the line with me. I've got a judge signing the warrant and my clerk just looked up the property record. The home belongs to Carson Garvey. People related to him are . . . his father Paul Garvey and . . . bingo. Sydney Garvey, Paul's wife. Paul Garvey owns a charter air service."

Carson Garvey. Finally a name to put with the evil.

"He won't be here," Gideon said. "He set the place on fire and took off." He looked in the garage window. "There's a Jeep in there. I'll talk to the neighbors to see if he had another vehicle. He may have just stolen one again. I'll call you right back when I know."

He ended the call and crossed the street to where a group of neighbors had gathered. "I'm Special Agent Reynolds. Did anyone see a car leave the property within the last ten minutes?"

They all shook their heads no, but several had seen a black Mercedes parked there a few hours before.

"He never has visitors," one woman said. "I noticed the car because I was surprised to see it there."

Several other neighbors nodded their agreement.

"Thank you," Gideon said. "I'll be right back." He walked away and dialed Molina again. This time he was put on speaker. "Do either Carson, Paul, or Sydney have a black Mercedes?"

"Checking the DMV records," a male voice said. That would be Jerry, Molina's clerk. "Yes," he said a minute later. "There's a black Mercedes Cabriolet, S class, registered to Sydney Garvey, age forty."

Gideon whistled. "Those start at a hundred and thirty grand. Not exactly inconspicuous. We need a BOLO, but make sure any photo comes with the caveat that he uses disguises."

"Done," Jerry said.

The phone picked back up, speaker disconnected. "I'm sending two more agents to the scene," Molina said. "They'll take care of interviewing the neighbors."

Gideon had to bite back his disappointment. "Got it."

"For what it's worth?" she said. "I'm sorry."

"I understand." And he really did. It just sucked.

"Gideon," she said quietly. "You've performed above and beyond. You were just operated on less than thirty-six hours ago. What if he shows back up? And has another gun? He shot you once. I'm not going to lose a good agent because you want in on the action. There will be other cases."

"Yeah, I know. Speaking of which, I'd like to do a facial recognition search on two of the members of the Eden cult. I've had their photos age-regressed."

"Send them to me," she said. "And stay out of the line of fire. Got it?"

He huffed. "Yes, ma'am." He ended the call just as

Hunter came out of the killer's house, looking grim.
And pale.

He met up with Hunter at the SUV. "What did you
find?" Gideon asked.

"If that house had gone up, all the evidence would
have been gone. He'd doused the inside with gasoline,
down the basement stairs." Hunter dipped his head in
a respectful nod. "So fast thinking with the dirt. Looks
like SFD was able to put it out." He rubbed one hand
over his face, leaving behind streaks of dirt. "Two bodies in the basement. Both female. One about forty. She
was on a bed in a soundproofed room. Strangled. The
other was younger, but hard to say. She'd been stuffed
in a chest freezer."

"Shit," Gideon murmured, then cleared his throat.
"The house is owned by Carson Garvey. The forty-
year-old is probably Sydney Garvey, wife of Paul. Paul
owns a charter air service."

Hunter nodded. "All fits." He held out his phone.
"There's a cabinet down there. I pried it open." He
swallowed. "Took photos of the contents."

Gideon dropped his gaze to Hunter's phone. "Oh
my God," he whispered, looking at the rows of driver's
licenses, of the necklaces and bracelets and rings hanging from hooks beneath the respective licenses. His
souvenirs. "How many?"

Another hard swallow. "Thirty-one."

Gideon's horrified gaze jerked up to meet Hunter's.
The other man looked equally shaken. "Thirty-one?"

"Zandra Jones was not one of them," Hunter said.
"Nor was Sydney Garvey. But Trisha Hart is. And Kaley Martell. And Eileen Danton. I'm sorry."

Gideon's chest hurt, and he realized he was holding
his breath. "Thanks." He enlarged the photo and
sighed. "The hook under Eileen's ID is empty."

"So is the one under Trisha Hart's."

Gideon gave Hunter back his phone. "Send those to Molina, if you will."

Hunter nodded. "I was going to after I showed you."

Gideon found a small smile of thanks for the gestures of respect. "Thank you. I appreciate it."

"As soon as our backup arrives, I can take you back to Daisy's house. Then I'll take you both to the ER to see Zandra."

Daisy was no longer Miss Dawson, Gideon noted. He glanced in the SUV's window when a furry paw gave it a smack. *Right. The dog.* "What do we do with him?"

"That's a damn good question," Hunter said. "Maybe ask a K-9 cop? They might recommend a place to keep him. I'd hate to see him go to a shelter."

"We could. But one of the victims was abducted while walking her dog." Gideon rubbed at his temples. "If it belonged to her, her family might want it back. The woman from Seattle. Janice . . ."

"Fiddler," Hunter said quietly. "I heard Zandra say her name a few times. You look like you're in pain, Gideon."

Gideon nodded. "I am. My head more than my arm, I think."

Hunter went to the hatch of his SUV and pulled a bottle of water from a cooler, then fished something from the glove box. "Here," he said. "Water and Advil."

Gideon took the pain reliever and chased it with the water. He met Hunter's concerned gaze. "Thank you . . ." He shook his head. "I don't know your first name."

"It's Tom."

"Thank you, Tom." Gideon drained the bottle. "Hell of a welcome to Sacramento you've had."

Tom gave him a wry smile. "I hate to be bored."

"Then this is right up your alley."

SACRAMENTO, CALIFORNIA
MONDAY, FEBRUARY 20, 11:45 P.M.

He took the exit for the airport, watching for cops but seeing none. He didn't have a lot of time, after all. Once the fire at his house was discovered, they'd be focused on putting it out. Luckily, gas fires burned hot and fast, so by the time the fire department got there, they'd be containing it versus extinguishing it.

But once they'd eliminated the danger of the fire spreading to other houses, they'd figure out he lived there. Then it wouldn't take them too long to figure out he worked for a charter airline.

But by then he'd be in Mexico. He'd have a plane, so he'd have income. Hell, he could even do drug runs like his father had. The only difference was that his father would only risk it occasionally, when they needed a revenue boost.

I'd do it full-time. I'll have a business built in no time. And I'll make a new life.

He'd miss his basement guest room, but it wouldn't be too hard to build another.

He'd put his blinker on and entered the turn lane onto their access road when he saw the flashing lights. *Fuck. Fuck. Fuck.*

There were police cars everywhere. Surrounding his hangar. The doors were open, the planes shining in the hangar's overhead lights. A SWAT van out front. Uniformed men and women walking around in tactical gear with AR-15s.

Oh my God.

Fuck, fuck, fuck.

They know. He whipped back onto the main road, earning a horn blow from the guy behind him. *They know it's me. They know where I work.*

How? How did they know? How had they gotten here so quickly?

His gut roiled. "What am I gonna do now?" he whispered aloud, cringing at the fear he heard in his own voice.

You are not going to lose it. You're going to think.

He needed to figure a different way out of town. He could drive. But it was nine hours to the border and that was if he hit no traffic, which wasn't likely to happen. Keeping to back roads would take far longer. Plus he'd need to buy a fake ID from somewhere. *And* a fake passport. And if he encountered any roadblocks, he'd be fucked.

He didn't know how to cross borders on land. He'd always flown.

I should have killed Zandra when I had the chance. But he hadn't and now she was a key witness against him.

But . . . what if she wasn't? What if she died? His house was burning this very minute. There would be nothing left to incriminate him. He'd burned the car up north, had left no fingerprints anywhere.

They have your DNA. Daisy scratched you in the alley.

Damn forensics.

But . . . there had been no other witnesses to her attempted abduction. He could say she'd been willing. That she'd changed her mind and fought him. That he'd let her go when he realized his mistake. Without witnesses it would be his word against hers.

And she's an alcoholic. Nobody will believe her.

He nodded to himself. That could work.

So basically the only thing between him and freedom was Zandra. It was time to snip off that loose end. But first he had to ditch the Mercedes. It would stick out like a sore thumb.

TWENTY-EIGHT

Daisy, you're making me crazy," Frederick said quietly. "Please sit down, honey."

Daisy paused in the middle of her living room, mid-pace. "I can't." Despite poor Brutus's best attempts. "Those were fire trucks, Dad." She'd heard the sirens, seen the flashing lights as the trucks had passed by at the end of her street. That they were going to the killer's house was a certainty in her mind.

He'd set fire to a car on Saturday to get rid of any DNA he'd left behind. *Like his blood that I spilled onto his car door.* He was hurt badly enough to take that nurse. Then to kill her. And desperate enough to kill the owner of the truck.

And evil enough to murder at least eight women. And still out there, which was why a SacPD cop sat in her driveway and another stood guard at the back door. Because, according to the cop, Gideon and Agent Hunter had found the house, but the killer was gone. *He could be anywhere now. He could be waiting for me or for Gideon. Or his next victim.*

"Gideon's out there somewhere, already hurt," she said, knowing she was headed toward a panic attack, because Brutus was alternating between licking her fingers and patting her arm with his little paw. "Now he's dealing with a fire?" *While I'm stuck here doing nothing.*

"I know," Frederick said calmly. He sat on the sofa, one arm resting on the back, his posture relaxed as if he were getting ready to watch a football game.

She glared at him. "How can you be so calm?"

His lips quirked up. "Meditation."

Her glare turned to an openmouthed stare. "You? Meditation? Really?"

"It calms . . ." He waved his hand in the direction of his head. "The static. Upstairs."

Static upstairs. She wondered what those two little words really meant.

He lifted graying brows. "You don't believe me?"

"Of course I do." The words burst from her in a rush, but abruptly fizzled. "I'm . . . Well, I'm . . . surprised, that's all."

"Meditation helps," Mercy said softly.

And Daisy spun to look at her. Mercy hadn't said a word since they'd entered her apartment. She'd been examining the murals since she walked in.

Daisy tried to think of what to say, then said what was in her heart. "I'm glad."

Mercy's smile was small, but there. "Plus therapy. Lots of therapy."

"Yep," Frederick said, and Daisy looked back at him, even more surprised.

"You're going to therapy?" She walked to her chair and sank into it, the moment having become almost surreal. Cuddling Brutus up under her chin, she added, "Really?"

He nodded, his smile rueful. "Really." He sighed. "After . . . well, after you and Taylor found out about . . . you know." He glanced at Mercy, who was studying him closely. "I was a POW in the eighties," he told her. "In El Salvador. It was . . . unpleasant."

"You were tortured?" Mercy asked her question in a barely audible whisper.

"I was. It changed me. Changed how I thought

about things," he confessed. "How I reacted. Screwed my logic up, like the pathways in my brain became like tangled string."

Mercy only nodded, but her eyes held deep understanding.

"From what little I know, you were also a prisoner," Frederick went on, so gently that Daisy's eyes burned with tears. This man, this kind, gentle, empathetic man, was not the father she'd known.

And she was ashamed to realize she wasn't entirely happy to see him like this. The tense father who'd drilled her and Taylor like they were a paramilitary force—*that* was the father she knew. The father who'd made a snap, rash decision that had led to the death of her older sister . . . *that* was the father she knew.

And, she realized with a small intake of breath, the father she'd never forgiven.

She still blamed him for Carrie's death. And she was certain that he blamed himself.

Which might not be entirely fair. Carrie had somehow managed to lay her hands on drugs when they were hours away from the nearest town. She'd been wild even before they'd gone to the ranch.

Who knew? Maybe, had they stayed in Oakland, Carrie would have run away and OD'd even sooner. No one could know. Yet still Daisy blamed him.

That wasn't fair at all. And it wasn't healthy. It wasn't right.

It wasn't love.

She swallowed hard, pursing her lips against the need to cry. *Later.* She'd cry later. For now, she wanted to observe this man who spoke of meditation and therapy and his past to Gideon's sister—a woman he didn't really know.

Maybe because it was easier to disclose those truths to a stranger. *But in a way that I can still hear. So that I can understand. And forgive him.*

"I suppose I was," Mercy was saying. "There was no war in Eden. Not in a traditional sense. But, yes, it was prison. Yes, there was . . . torture. And yes, it changed me." She dropped her gaze to her shoes. "Hardened me."

Frederick sighed. "Yes. Me too."

Mercy darted a glance at Daisy, who figured she still looked gobsmacked, because Mercy gave her a sad little smile. "Therapy has helped. Took me a while to seek it. Took me even longer to put it into action."

"But you did," Frederick said. "And now you're here. Which is pretty brave."

Mercy nodded unsteadily. "Maybe. I only knew that I needed to come. I have a friend in New Orleans. We work together. She knows . . . everything. She's the one who helped me find the therapist. And she's the one who bought me a plane ticket, reserved me a rental car, hijacked me from work, drove me to the airport, and left me there."

"She's a good friend, then," Frederick said with a genuine smile. "My girlfriend"—he rolled his eyes— "which feels ridiculous to say at my age. She's the one who nudged me to go to therapy. She's a nurse. Pediatric, but she volunteers with veterans. Does equine therapy with them, along with my other daughter. Sally heard one of the vets talking to another about meditation and she did the research for me. It's helping."

He glanced over at Daisy. "Both my daughters give back. Daisy is active in the community here. She gives her time to the community center, LGBTQ youth, animal rescue, and has organized sponsorship of a 5K run for leukemia research. I'm proud of her. Proud of both of them. Not something I can take any credit for, though."

Daisy's heart ached and broke. "I don't know about that," she said, her voice on the rusty side of husky. "You were all about civil rights and protecting the defenseless when you practiced law. You took us to volunteer at soup kitchens and we picked up trash in the park and visited nursing homes." How could she have forgotten those days? She remembered them now. Sitting on her dad's lap as he read to the elderly at their bedsides, standing on a box to stir a stew at the shelter . . .

He shook his head. "All that was your mother."

"No. It was you, too. I remember." Now.

"After she died . . . well, it was hard."

"You had three kids, Dad. A baby with a disability. The oldest was wild. And the middle one, while ninety-nine percent awesome, was an occasional handful."

His lips twitched. "Occasional," he agreed, and then his expression darkened. "And then we went to the ranch, where I put you in prison, too."

"That *was* a bit over the top," Daisy allowed, because it had been a prison. To deny it was to negate this entire conversation that seemed like a giant step forward. "You may have gotten a little obsessed, but . . ." She shrugged. "People say the same about me." She pointed to the mural wall. "At least I come by it honestly."

Frederick blinked at her for a moment, then threw back his head and laughed, a great booming sound that Daisy hadn't heard in so long. Not since her mother died, she realized. Certainly not after Donna had come into the picture. The woman had been poison— to all of them, including her own daughter. At least Daisy had still had her father. Taylor had been denied hers for her entire life.

"I guess you do," he said, wiping his eyes. Daisy wasn't sure it was all from the laughter, so she moved to the sofa, sitting next to him, and rested her head on his shoulder.

"Thank you," she murmured.

He stiffened as if he was surprised, then relaxed, curling his arm around her and hugging her to his side. "For what?"

"Coming as soon as I said I needed you."

He kissed the top of her head. "Always. I will always come when you need me."

"Oh!" The sound came from Mercy, who'd discovered the paintings Daisy had left on the easels from Friday night, when she'd given Gideon a paintbrush.

Mercy lifted the canvas from the easel, her movements slow, her expression stunned. And devastated. "Did Gideon . . . ?"

"Yes," Daisy said simply.

Mercy stood there, staring at the face Gideon had painted from memory. Mercy as a little girl, sitting in a field of happy daisies.

"I remember this day," she whispered. "I was nine. He was almost thirteen. We little kids went on a school trip into the forest, and Gideon was one of the helpers. We were supposed to be learning to pick herbs for the healer, but I got sidetracked and found the flowers. They were so pretty." She looked over at Daisy with a sad lift to her lips. "But the field was of bright red flowers. He made them daisies."

Daisy's heart squeezed. Gideon had included her in his painting, too. "What happened that day?"

"You sound certain that something did," Mercy said, tilting her head curiously.

"Not certain, but Gideon had a look on his face while he was painting. Like it was bittersweet."

"It was the last time I saw him before his ascension. His thirteenth birthday," she clarified. "We'd been told not to go to the flower fields, but I thought they were so pretty and I kind of wandered off. Gideon found me and . . ." She swallowed again and carefully returned the canvas to the easel. "He took my punishment that day."

"Which was?" Daisy asked very quietly, because Mercy seemed very fragile.

"A week in the box."

Daisy exhaled, sensing her father going still. "The box?" she asked.

"It was like a little outhouse. You got water and a little food every day. It would have been a *little* food for me at nine. Because he took my punishment, he got the same amount."

"They starved him," Daisy whispered.

"Essentially, yes. It would get hot in there, even in the mountains. It was summer. When they came to get Gideon, he was so thin. He must have sweated off fifteen pounds that week. They took him out on the seventh morning, cleaned him up, and got him dressed for his ascension party later that day."

He was fighting for his life by the end of that day, Daisy thought, marveling at Gideon's strength, even as a boy.

Mercy sank into the chair Daisy had vacated, her hands clutched tightly in her lap. "It was the last time I saw him. The next morning I found out that he'd killed Edward McPhearson, stabbed Ephraim Burton in the eye, then escaped with my mother's help."

Daisy glanced up at her father. "And then poor Eileen ended up with Ephraim after that. She was 'given' to him. That's the man she ran away from."

"What do you know about Eileen?" Mercy asked sharply.

Daisy hesitated. "I think Gideon wanted to tell you."

"He told me that he thinks she's dead. I wanted to demand to know what he was talking about, but Zandra needed our help. Now I want to know and he's not here, but you are. Zandra said Eileen's name, but she called her Eileen Danton. Her last name wasn't Danton."

"Give me a second." She typed a quick text to Gideon. *All ok here. Mercy asking about Eileen. Okay to tell her what I know?*

His reply came quickly. *Yes. On way back to you. Will take you to ER.*

Relief flowed over her. He was okay. She wanted to get more information, but she could wait until he arrived. And talking to Mercy would be a decent distraction.

"All right then." Daisy resettled herself on the sofa next to her father, Brutus in her lap, and told Mercy about Eileen and the Dantons. "He loaned her the money for a bus ticket. Rafe Sokolov, the man who owns this house, is a major crimes detective for SacPD. He investigates assault and homicide. He went to Portland today, trying to trace her steps."

Mercy's forehead furrowed for a moment, studying Daisy in a puzzled way until she nodded, understanding dawning in her eyes. "Her locket. That's how you knew it was her. Gideon called me Thursday and told me that a locket had been found with 'Miriam' engraved on the back. He was worried it was mine."

"Because your name is also Miriam and he knew you'd escaped," Daisy said, more for her father's benefit.

Mercy's eyes widened. "Oh. Gideon said a woman was attacked and tore the locket from around her assailant's throat. That was you? That's how you met?"

Daisy nodded. "Rafe's mother, Irina Sokolov, had been trying to set us up for six months, but we kept evading her. Thursday night changed everything."

"Gideon's mentioned her a few times," Mercy said. "Irina. He said she mothers him."

"She mothers all of us," Daisy said with an affectionate smile. She almost added that Irina would mother Mercy, too, but she wasn't sure how long the woman would be here.

For Gideon's sake, Daisy hoped she'd stay a good while.

A knock at the door had her running to check the peephole. Gideon. She opened the door and her heart hurt once again. He looked . . . weary. Beaten.

Oh, Gideon. What happened? But she didn't ask.

She took a step forward and, being careful of his sling, looped her arms around his neck. He shuddered out a breath, his good arm coming around her as he buried his face against her throat.

He smelled like smoke. "The fire trucks were going to his house," she said.

"Yes."

Her heart sank. "Was everything destroyed?"

"No. Tom and I beat the flames back until the fire department arrived."

Okay, she thought, mentally clenching her teeth. "You, um, fought a fire?"

"Tom did most of it."

"Who's Tom?"

"Agent Hunter."

"Okay. What did you find, Gideon?"

"I didn't find anything," he muttered against her skin. "I'm benched."

Oh. "All right. Then what did Hunter find?"

He just shook his head and clutched her like she was his lifeline. In that moment, maybe she was. And, in that moment, she was grateful to her father for distracting her out of an impending panic attack earlier. She would have been no good to Gideon that way.

She pulled back enough to see his face. "Are you coming in or are we going out?"

"Out," he said. "Tom's got the SUV in the garage." He backed up and straightened, his green eyes looking dull and pained.

"When did you last have one of your pain pills?" Daisy asked.

Gideon gestured to Frederick and Mercy. "Let's go. We'll check on Zandra and then we'll get you back to the Sokolovs'. It'll be safer there. Especially since he knows where you live, Daisy."

"Don't think I didn't notice you totally ignored me about the pain pill," Daisy said tartly. "But we can talk about that later. For now, understand that he has to know where Karl and Irina live, too. He followed you Saturday, Gideon. Remember what the reporter said yesterday? He was at Trish's apartment building asking where you'd gone. That's how he knew to follow us to Redding."

He rubbed his forehead. "You're right. I'll get you a safe house."

She put Brutus in her bag and shouldered it. Gideon wasn't thinking straight, which was why she wasn't panicking at the thought of a safe house. "Fine. But if I go, you go."

He blew out a breath. "We can talk about that later."

Behind them, her father coughed, but she was pretty sure he was covering up a laugh. Daisy was okay with that. She'd finally heard him really laugh again, after far too many years. She couldn't wait to hear it again. "That's fine. Let's go."

SACRAMENTO, CALIFORNIA
TUESDAY, FEBRUARY 21, 1:05 A.M.

Finally. He'd been sitting in the hospital's parking lot, waiting for a doctor or a nurse or a PA of the right size to come outside wearing scrubs. And a badge. Especially a badge.

He tapped his pocket, making sure he still carried the syringe he'd filled with sedative on arrival. It had been in the emergency duffel bag he'd grabbed from the Jeep. He'd last used the bag in Vail, the sedative on Zandra. There was still enough left to take out an average-sized man for at least an hour. He eyed the man and figured the scrubs would be a good fit. Maybe a little loose in the front, but all the better to hide his gun.

The man was standing alone in the shadows,

smoking a cigarette. Even better, he wore earbuds in his ears, leaning with one shoulder against the wall, gently bobbing to whatever music he was listening to.

He won't see me coming. And he didn't.

He walked up behind the man and brought the grip of his gun down hard on his skull. When the man stumbled, he sprang, using his weight to drag him to the ground and injecting the sedative into his neck. It was clumsy using his right hand, but he didn't need perfect aim.

He continued to press the man into the ground, a knee in his back, his good arm across his back, until his struggles slowed and he slumped, down for the count.

Quickly he undressed the guy, shoved the scrubs in his duffel, took his badge, and dragged him behind some shrubs. Not the best hiding place but the guy was heavy.

And I'm in a hurry. He took a peek at the badge. For the next little bit he was Nabil Halif, RN. *Well, shit.* His disguise didn't exactly go with that name, but he wasn't planning to stop and talk to anyone, either. Using the badge, he entered through the employee door and calmly found the nearest family restroom. There would be plenty of room there to change his clothes and apply the disguise he had with him. Then he'd find Zandra's room.

||| SACRAMENTO, CALIFORNIA
||| TUESDAY, FEBRUARY 21, 1:30 A.M.

"What took you so long?" Agent Molina demanded as their party of five exited the elevator on Zandra's floor. She frowned. "I asked only for Miss Dawson and Agent Hunter."

Because Zandra had been calling for Daisy and Daisy only.

Gideon frowned back. "My sister was at Daisy's

house when we got there. I wasn't going to leave her there. And Daisy's father insisted on coming as a condition of her being here at all. I told you this."

Molina sighed. "Yes, you did. My apologies. We're all tired. But only Miss Dawson and Agent Hunter are to approach Miss Jones in her room."

Gideon was tired and his head hurt. His arm was throbbing. He should have taken the pain pill Daisy tried to force on him on the way to the hospital, but those pills made him too groggy. He was no good to anyone that way. Especially Daisy.

"With all due respect, ma'am," he said, "that's bullshit."

Daisy rolled her eyes at him. "You are super cranky when you're in pain." She turned to his boss with a winning smile. "Agent Molina, Gideon is on medical leave, is he not?"

"Yes. That's why he's to stay in the waiting room."

"Well, if he's on leave, he's here as my companion, is he not?"

Molina narrowed her eyes. "I suppose so."

"Then as my companion, I'd like him to accompany me. I have a service dog in my bag. Gideon is kind of like a service . . . man. My anchor. Without my anchors, I get very bad panic attacks that threaten my sobriety. I'd like to help calm Miss Jones so that you can get her statement, but if I'm not calm, she won't be, either. So I respectfully ask you to reconsider allowing Gideon to accompany me."

Molina's lips actually twitched. "You're trouble, Miss Dawson." Then she was back to business. "All right. I've lost enough time waiting for you. Come with me, the three of you. But the father and sister go to the waiting room. It's around the corner. There's an armed agent at Miss Jones's door and a uniformed police officer at both of the elevators. If you need help, don't hesitate to ask."

Frederick and Mercy headed to the waiting room, Frederick looking like he was biting back a smile.

Gideon, however, didn't think he'd smile again anytime soon. *Thirty-one victims.* They'd only found seven bodies so far, because Eileen hadn't been found. He thought of the body in the freezer. But Kaley Martell had. So eight bodies so far.

The earliest of the victims' driver's licenses had been issued ten years ago. If that first victim had been taken the year her license was issued, it meant he'd averaged three murders a year. But it was clear that he'd sped up in the last year and especially in the last week. He was escalating and he was fixated on Daisy.

Which scared Gideon to the depths of his soul.

"Miss Jones disappeared from an airport in Vail," Molina told Daisy as they walked.

"So not a truck driver," Daisy murmured.

"No. He's a pilot. We confirmed that he and another pilot flew a party to Vail on Friday for a ski vacation. They were there for three hours while their aircraft refueled."

Daisy gave his boss an incredulous look. "So he abducted Zandra and brought her home with him?"

"Yes. It appears he abducted her from a bar a few miles from the airport. Let me give you a few details before you start talking to her. She's a prosecutor in Rhode Island. She was engaged. According to her family, she was in Vail for her wedding, which was supposed to be Saturday. She left early when she found her fiancé and her best friend . . . together."

"Poor Zandra," Daisy murmured. "So she went to a bar?"

"Apparently so," Molina said. "The bar had security cameras inside, but the ones outside had been disconnected."

"By our suspect?" Tom asked.

"Not unless he did it on an earlier trip. We have him

on an internal camera. He looks nothing like his driver's license photo or the man captured on the security video in the bar where Miss Hart worked."

"I've seen him twice," Daisy said, "once at the pet store and once at the Redding bus station, and he didn't look the same either time."

"Which makes Miss Jones's statement so important," Molina said.

"She may be the only one who's seen his real face," Gideon said.

"Exactly," Molina said. "Miss Dawson, I'd like you to help Agent Hunter get as full a description as you can. And a description of everything she remembers about the incident itself. Including how she came to be free."

"I figured the body on the bed let her out," Tom said.

"If she's the Sydney he was carving into his victims' skin," Gideon added, "which is likely considering a car matching hers was in the driveway, then he was obsessed with her at the very least. That Sydney was strangled indicates a lot of rage. If he found Zandra gone and this woman in her place? That may have driven him to kill her."

"That makes sense," Molina said. "But *why*? That's what I want to know."

"What I'd like to know is the extent of Zandra's injuries," Daisy said quietly.

"Bruises on her face and lacerations at wrists and ankles," Molina answered. "He carved letters into her torso. He actually bandaged and stitched her so that she could heal."

"He wanted to keep her longer?" Tom supposed.

"Maybe. I'm hoping she can tell us."

Molina slowed as they approached Zandra's room. She was about to enter when Daisy grabbed her arm.

"Wait." Daisy bit at her lip.

Molina tilted her head, pointedly glancing at Daisy's hand, still on her arm. "Yes, Miss Dawson?"

Daisy closed her eyes, not letting Molina go, almost as if she needed to hold on or fall down. "Was she sexually assaulted?"

Molina hesitated. "It appeared so."

Daisy nodded, her eyes still closed. "And Trish?"

Oh, honey, Gideon thought sadly. Of course she'd been worried about that. But she hadn't said a word, except for the one time she'd asked. She'd just been worrying all alone.

"No," Molina said kindly. "The preliminary autopsy report made no mention of it."

Daisy let out a huge breath. "Thank you. I mean, I called the coroner, but they hadn't finished the report yet. And then all this other stuff happened. So just . . . thank you."

Molina patted Daisy's arm. "You're welcome. This is her room. Good luck."

"Thanks," Daisy muttered. "No pressure here."

Zandra's room was being guarded by an armed agent. Gideon knew the guy well enough to say hello, so he nodded as he passed through the door.

He got a sympathetic look in return. *God, I must look like shit.*

He sure felt like shit. Nevertheless, when Daisy took the chair next to Zandra's bed, he took up the position behind her. Anyone getting to Daisy was coming through him first.

Daisy leaned in, her smile gentle. "Hey, Zandra, do you remember me?"

Zandra latched her gaze to Daisy's face. "Daisy."

"That's right. I heard you wanted to talk to me."

"Only you." She glowered at Molina, Hunter, and Gideon. "Not them."

"Well, this is the thing. Agent Hunter has to take your statement, so that we dot all the *i*'s and cross all the *t*'s so this asshole gets locked up and the key thrown away."

"I want you to do it."

"I would," Daisy assured her, "but I'm not a cop."

Zandra blinked her surprise. "You're not?"

"No. I'm too contrary to be a cop. I just talk on the radio."

"You have the voice for it."

Daisy smiled. "Thank you. *You* sound so much better. Amazing what a little water can do, huh?"

Zandra tried to smile back but flinched when her lip started to bleed. "Can you get me a tissue?"

Daisy passed her the box. "Here you go. Now the guy behind me is my guy, okay? I get bouts of anxiety sometimes and he helps me stay calm. I'm thinking what you went through won't be easy for you to say or for me to hear. I don't want to flake out on you. Is it okay if he stays?"

Zandra dabbed at her bloody lip. "I hope he's not a cheating rat."

Daisy brushed a lock of Zandra's hair from her forehead and continued lightly stroking her hair away from her face. "I heard your guy was a cheating rat."

Tears welled in Zandra's eyes. "I'd never been drunk once before that bar. Not once in my life."

"And that one time, you meet the bastard who hurt you."

Zandra nodded. "Does my family know I'm here?"

Daisy looked over her shoulder at Molina. "Do they?"

"They do," Molina said. "Your parents and sister will be on the first flight tomorrow."

"Good." It came out as a small sob and more tears leaked from her eyes.

Daisy got a tissue and dabbed at Zandra's eyes, then held her hand. "So, Special Agent Hunter has some questions for you. Are you ready?"

"As I'll ever be."

Tom sat in a chair on the other side of Zandra's bed. "Thank you for talking to me."

Zandra appeared to narrow her eyes, but it was hard to tell because they were so swollen. Carson Garvey had done a real number on this woman's face.

But at least she's still alive.

"You look too young to be a special agent," Zandra said.

Tom smiled. "I'm twenty-six and a *half.*" He emphasized the half as if he were a small child. "You got me because the other agent on this case is on her way back from Portland."

Zandra had been smiling at the "and a half" comment, but her smile disappeared. "Danton, Eileen. Oregon," she murmured.

"Yes," Tom said quietly.

"She's dead."

"We know," Tom said in that same quiet tone. It was making Gideon sleepy, dammit. "Can you tell us what he looked like?"

"He was six feet tall. Had an ordinary face. Not handsome, but not ugly. Not the kind to get women at a bar. He had no confidence. His eyes were dark brown. His nose was thin. Sharp. He was bald. All over. No body hair. He gloated about it. Said he'd never left any physical evidence behind him. Oh, and he had scratches on his upper chest." She closed her eyes. "Did you find his house?"

"Yes," Tom told her. "The dog took us there."

She looked genuinely amused at that. "He's a nice dog. What happened to him?"

"We took him to a vet," Gideon said. "The one who takes care of the police dogs. He's going to check him out and then we'll find him a good home. He'll be a hero."

Zandra met his eyes. "Thank you. He is a hero. He

saved me." She closed her eyes. "So if you found the house, did you find the cabinet?"

"Yes," Tom whispered. "You memorized some of the names. How did you do that?"

"I could see a few of their licenses. I just kept repeating their names over and over."

"Why?" Tom asked.

"Because I wanted their families to know what happened to them when I got away. He kept saying that nobody cared what happened to them. That nobody was looking for them. That nobody cared that I was gone. But I didn't believe him."

"Good," Tom praised warmly. "How did you get away?"

She huffed a bitter laugh. "Sydney. God, what a psycho bitch. She busted in the room calling me a whore. Said I couldn't have him. Said she'd put the best years of her life into him, that I wasn't going to just waltz in and take him. I mean, I thought at first she was going to help me, but she gave me the split lip. Did you find her?"

"Not yet," Tom said, which was the right response because they hadn't made a positive ID of the body yet. "So she yelled at you and hit you. What then?"

"She untied me. Said that if I wanted one of my own, I needed to make one myself. To start early." Zandra shuddered. "Said it was best to start them before they were ten years old. Twelve at the latest."

Gideon had a hard time not cringing. Tom blinked once, but his composure didn't crack. Not bad for a probie. Agent Hunter would do just fine.

Daisy, on the other hand, held on to Zandra's hand but stuck a trembling hand in her bag. It was an awkward position and no doubt poor Brutus was getting mauled. Gideon gently pulled her hand from the bag, scooped Brutus out, and put the dog on her lap. Her look of gratitude was unmistakable.

Zandra blinked. "Is that a . . . dog?"

"Yes," Daisy said, a trifle defensive. "She's Brutus and she's my service dog."

A slow smile curved Zandra's lips. "Can I pet her, too?"

Daisy knew that she really shouldn't allow it because Brutus was working, but Zandra had been through so much. "Of course." Releasing Zandra's hand, she removed Brutus's vest. "Shazam, Brutus," she said, and put the dog on the bed so that they could both pet her. Brutus, in heaven, rolled to her back for a belly rub.

"She's cute," Zandra said. "She helps you?"

"Yes. I'm eight years sober. Brutus helps me control my anxiety, which helps me maintain my sobriety. You might consider one for PTSD. You know, once you're home."

"Maybe I will." She drew a breath, then resolutely turned to Tom. "Sydney had a wild look in her eyes. I'm a prosecutor. I see criminals every day of the week. I've seen them high and mentally ill. I honestly couldn't tell you which she was—hell, maybe both—but definitely it was one of them."

Molina took a few steps forward, holding to the rail at the foot of the bed. "Did she tell you her name was Sydney?"

"Well, I figured it out. He . . ." She trailed off, her fingers busy in Brutus's coat. "He kept demanding that I say I was sorry. Over and over but I wouldn't. I had the feeling that that was what he was waiting for. That he *needed* me to say I was sorry. And once I did, he'd kill me. I kept hoping if I could hold out a little longer that someone would find me."

"He said the same thing to me," Daisy murmured. "To apologize."

Zandra's swollen eyes grew a little wider. "You? He got you?"

"He tried. Thursday night. I fought him off and got away. But I'd surprised him, I think. He really wanted my friend. Trish Hart."

Zandra sighed. "Hart, Trisha. California."

Daisy nodded. "Yeah. Did you see her necklace?"

"Turquoise cross? Yes. He was wearing it the last time I saw him. He did this bizarre kind of ritual where he took off a crystal horseshoe and hung it on a hook under Kaley Martell's driver's license. Then he put Trisha's license on the shelf and put the turquoise cross necklace around his neck." She glanced from Tom to Gideon. "Kaley Martell. She's in the freezer. Her body, I mean."

"We found her," Tom said. "But thank you." He drew a breath. "I have a question that's probably going to be hard for you to answer, but we need to understand."

Zandra braced herself. "Yes, he sexually assaulted me. But not with his . . ." She grimaced. ". . . penis. He had . . . implements. Some sex toys. Some were other things. They're in one of the drawers. You'll find them when you search. I got the impression that he couldn't get it up for me. He tried. He really tried." Her eyes narrowed. "He even called me Daisy while he tried, but he kept losing his erection, so he had to use the stuff in the drawer." She glanced at Daisy. "Sorry."

Daisy had visibly cringed. "No, no. Don't apologize. I didn't realize . . ."

Gideon fought to contain his fury, conscious of Molina's steady regard. The man had fantasized about raping Daisy. *But he didn't. Because she fought him off.*

So do not blow this. Do not lose your temper. Just focus on catching the bastard. He forced himself to relax, watching Molina do the same. He'd passed the test.

He returned his attention to Zandra, who was still talking.

"I considered using his impotency," she said, "to throw him off balance, but he had sharp knives and I didn't want him plunging one into me any more than he did when he was . . . you know. Carving." She swallowed. "He carved all the letters of Sydney's name into my stomach, except for the final 'Y.' He was going to come back and do that, but Sydney threw me out first." Her composure trembled, then cracked. "I'm going to have scars."

"I'm sorry," Daisy whispered, her voice breaking.

Zandra pulled a tissue from the box and handed it to Daisy, who wiped her cheeks. "I'm alive," she said grimly. "I'll get through this."

Tom hesitated, then shook his head.

"What?" Zandra snapped. "Don't worry about my feelings now. I think I'm numb."

Tom gave her an apologetic look. "I have a friend with similar scars from an attack when we were kids. She got tattoos to cover them. Vines with flowers. When you're ready, if you're interested, contact me and I'll introduce you to her."

Zandra gave him a long, sober look. "I might do that. I'm running on adrenaline now and channeling my badass lawyer self, but later . . . I'll need something. Support. Something."

"A friend?" Daisy suggested. "Call me, anytime."

"I might do that, too. Thank you."

"You said you figured out she was Sydney," Gideon said when it seemed Zandra was ready to return to the interview. "What happened then?"

"I said, 'Sydney,' and she seemed pleased as punch that he'd mentioned her."

"Can you describe her?" Tom asked.

"Five-eight, forty-ish, had some work done. Blond

hair." She aimed that laser look at Tom, then Gideon once again. "You found her, didn't you? He came home and found her there." She sank back on the pillows. "God. She created that monster. I'm not sure whether to feel pity or satisfaction that she died at his hand." She waved a hand wearily. "Don't worry, I'm not going to tell anyone. No interviews with the inside scoop. This is going to be damaging enough to my career."

Gideon got that. Now that he was a victim of a shooting, it would likely be a point of question anytime he had to give testimony in court. His credibility and impartiality would be called into question. He'd seen it before. How much worse would it be for a prosecutor?

"Can you think of anything else, Miss Jones?" Molina asked.

Zandra petted Brutus for a full minute, thinking, then said, "Oh, yeah. He got shot. Left hand and he's a leftie."

Daisy nodded. "I know. I shot him."

Zandra's lips curved again. "You go, girl." Her smile faded. "She kicked the dog. Sydney did. She was dragging me out of that little room and she kicked the dog for getting in her way. She threw us both out, me and the dog. But he was still friendly. Licked me and danced around until I followed him. To you guys." She lifted a brow. "Also, I asked two different people for help while I was walking and they threatened to call the cops on me because they thought I was drunk and homeless. I wish they had called the cops. I'd like them to know that they turned me away. Just because I want them to feel bad about it."

Daisy nodded. "You write down what you can remember of those two people and I'll take care of it myself. That's my neighborhood, too." She shivered. "We had a serial killer in our neighborhood."

"That'll do wonders for your property values," Zandra said dryly. "One more thing. He wears disguises. I saw a few. He can make himself look like someone totally different."

"I've seen a few, too," Daisy said. "What did he look like Friday at the bar?"

Zandra briefly closed her eyes. "He looked . . . smarmy. He had a shaggy look. Kind of a medium brown with blond highlights. Like a rock star trying to look young. His nose was longer. A little sharper."

"You sound certain," Molina observed.

Zandra opened her swollen eyes, only to narrow them. "You're intimating that I was too drunk to remember. Yes, I was drunk, but I remember thinking that he looked like a boy I dated in high school who'd cheated with a cheerleader. I know what I saw."

Molina sighed softly. "I'm sorry, Miss Jones. I didn't mean it to sound accusatory. You've been through a trauma and we need to be certain."

"Yeah, well, I managed to memorize the names of ten of his victims, too."

Molina inclined her head. "Point taken."

"Thank you," Zandra snapped then slumped, clearly drained.

"You're tired," Daisy murmured. "Are you finished, Agent Hunter?"

"I am." Tom stood up. "Thank you, Miss Jones. I'm going to leave my card at the nurses' station. Please contact me if you think of anything else."

"I will." Zandra drew a deep breath. "Thank you. Thank you for saving me. Thank the woman who got out of her car to help me."

"I will," Gideon said. "That's my sister."

"I can see the resemblance." She closed her eyes. "Thank you for making this easier for me. I'll fall apart later, but . . ."

"The credit goes to Brutus." Daisy put the dog back

in her bag and adjusted it across her body. "I'll leave my number with the nurses' station, too. Please, feel free to call."

And with that, they left Zandra to rest. And hopefully, eventually, to heal.

TWENTY-NINE

He slowed his step as he neared Zandra's room. The door was closed, a man in a black suit standing guard outside.

Don't freak. Stay calm. He'd already passed muster with two other groups of nurses and the cop at the elevator. Luckily, the disguise in his duffel was one of his favorites. No one would recognize him. He'd removed the bandage from his hand and the gloves he wore were perfect with the whole nurse look. *So do this. Now.*

"I need to see the patient," he told the guard. "It's time for her pain medication." Which would come in the form of the gun tucked into his waistband. He'd get in, shoot her in the head, then get out. Quick and simple, then no more Zandra. No more witness.

"You'll need to wait," the guard said gruffly.

He channeled every medical show he'd ever seen on TV, drawing himself taller. "She is my patient. Her care comes first. Let me in."

"Stay here." The guard scowled, cracking the door open enough for voices to emerge.

He tried not to stiffen, immediately recognizing the woman speaking. Daisy. Daisy was in there with her. *Dammit.*

He should have anticipated this. Should have anticipated that Daisy would visit her in the hospital. She seemed . . . kind in that way.

"What did he look like Friday at the bar?" she was asking.

Zandra's voice was much stronger than he'd expected. "He looked . . . smarmy. He had a shaggy look. Kind of a medium brown with blond highlights. Like a rock star trying to look young. His nose was longer. A little sharper."

Smarmy? he thought, indignant. But then he froze as her next words sank in. *Shit.*

She'd just described him. Perfectly. He was wearing the same face that he'd worn the day he'd taken her from Vail. She'd been so drunk. And he'd dosed her up. She shouldn't have remembered anything. But she had.

And now the guard was giving him a suspicious, searching look.

"I didn't realize the police were in there," he murmured. "I'll come back."

He started walking, not too fast, not too slowly. Just a normal nurse doing normal nursing things. He approached the end of the hallway and glanced up at the round mirror hanging in the corner. No one was behind him.

But that didn't mean he was home free. He needed to lose the disguise and get out. Out of the hospital. Out of the country. He needed leverage. Something to guarantee his passage.

Daisy herself would be perfect, but that wasn't going to happen. She had that pit bull Fed who never left her side.

He rounded the corner and came to a waiting room. Losing the disguise was job one. He could do that here. Pausing outside the doorway, he watched the round mirror for the guard while he listened to see if there was anyone inside.

There was, dammit. Two people at least. A man and a woman.

"How long can you stay?" the man was asking.

"For a week," the woman answered. "I had vacation days saved up from the lab where I work, so I took them."

"Gideon will be happy to hear that," the man answered, a smile in his tone.

Gideon? It was not a common name. It stood to reason that if Daisy was here, her bodyguard Fed would be, too.

The woman sighed, sounding frustrated and tense. "I think . . . well, I'm not sure what I think. I just hope I don't hurt him any more than I already have."

"Your brother loves you, Mercy." The man sounded fiercely kind. "I think he'll be happy with whatever you're able to give him."

Brother? A smile curled his lips. A sister might be better leverage than a girlfriend.

Staying behind their chairs, he entered the room, going straight to the coffee machine, pretending to check the supply of cups and creamers. The two didn't turn around. They'd been so deep in conversation that they hadn't seen him come in.

"I don't want him to have to settle," Mercy admitted. "He's been through hell, too."

Aw, poor Agent Reynolds, he thought snidely. He glanced at the pair from the corner of his eye. The woman appeared to be average height, her dark hair pulled back at her nape with a hair clip. He could overpower her if he needed to, even with a bum hand. The man was older, but tall and broad. He'd be harder to take down.

The man patted Mercy's hand. "One day at a time, honey. That's all you can do. That and make amends where you can. You've got a great place to start. But do it now." His voice broke a little and he cleared his throat harshly. "Don't let the past take over your whole life like I did."

Dammit. He wished he had more of the sedative, but he'd used it all on the nurse outside. He'd try knocking the man out first, and if that didn't work, he'd shoot him. Even if the man did sound kind.

Them or me. I choose me.

He'd taken a step toward the older man when the guy abruptly stood. "I'm going to the men's," he said gruffly. "I'll be back in two minutes."

He held his breath until the man was gone, then, still standing behind the Fed's sister, he pulled the wig from his head and stuffed it in his pocket. Drawing his gun, he crossed the room and—

He stopped short when the woman pulled a pack of cigarettes from her purse, her hands trembling. He held his breath, watching as she dug deeper in her purse, coming up with a lighter.

And suddenly it seemed too easy. He slid his gun back into place, tugging at the top of his scrubs to hide it.

"Ma'am," he said, and she jolted to her feet, spinning around to stare at him, her eyes wide and panicked. She pressed her palm to her heart, trapping the cigarettes against her body.

"Oh." She drew a breath, let it out. "You startled me."

He smiled as sweetly as he could. "I'm sorry. But you can't smoke that here."

She nodded, shouldering her purse, clutching the pack of smokes and lighter. "I know. I was going to ask someone where I could go."

"If you give me a smoke, I'll show you where I go," he said, turning on all the charm he possessed. "All my cigarettes are in my locker."

She seemed to relax. "I thought you were going to tell me it was bad for my health."

He shrugged. "It is. But a lot of medical professionals smoke." He should know. He'd flown enough charters of doctors to conventions, having to tell them multiple times that even though it was a private plane they couldn't light up. "Come on. I'll show you."

Mindful that the older man would be back from the men's room any second, he walked out the waiting room door, holding his breath, hoping she'd follow. And she did. He went to the nearest stairwell, simply to get her out of sight.

"These stairs are closest to the exit," he said over his shoulder as he jogged down the first flight. "I have to hurry, though. My break is halfway over."

She followed him, easily taking the stairs as she kept up with his pace. "I need to hurry, too. I should have left a note. They'll be worried about me."

"Well, at least let me show you the spot and then you can run back up to tell your friends where you'll be."

"Okay. I don't smoke often. Just when I'm stressed."

"Me too," he muttered truthfully. "Me too."

They got to the bottom of the stairs, and when he led her into the hallway, he was relieved to find that the nearest door was another employee entry, not a fire exit that would alarm when he opened it.

"Just out here," he said, holding the door open for her.

As soon as she was outside, he closed the door, grabbed her arm, and shoved the gun into her side. "Let's walk, Mercy. If you scream I will kill you. I have nothing to lose."

He thought she'd argue. Maybe fight.

But she didn't. She froze, her eyes going blank. He waited a second for her to do something, but she just stood there, staring. Like he'd flipped a switch or something.

What the hell? Whatever. As long as she didn't fight him.

He walked her around the hospital and she went willingly. Like a doll. Or someone in a trance. It was fucking spooky.

When they approached the van, he glanced at the bushes near the door he'd used to enter, relieved to see that the nurse he'd sedated was still sound asleep. Hopefully someone would find him soon. He'd catch pneumonia if he stayed out here too long.

Mercy stumbled as he put her in the van he'd stolen from an off-site long-term parking lot near the airport. Not knowing if she'd "come to" at some point, he unclipped the nurse's ID from its lanyard, then used the narrow strap to restrain her wrists.

Knowing he was on borrowed time, he ran back inside to the family restroom where he'd left his duffel. He threw it over his shoulder and jogged back to the van.

Then he drove away. He had his leverage. Now he just needed a plane.

ǀǀǀ SACRAMENTO, CALIFORNIA
TUESDAY, FEBRUARY 21, 1:50 A.M.

Daisy kept her composure until she, Gideon, and Agents Molina and Hunter left Zandra's room. Then she turned to Gideon, burying her face against his chest, unable to stop her tears. "That could have been me," she whispered.

"I know," Gideon whispered back, rubbing her back in large soothing circles. "But it wasn't." Still, he trembled as he said the words.

"I want to help her. I want to do something. I want to go back to Thursday and fight harder. Then he wouldn't have taken her. I know that's stupid, but . . . God, Gideon."

Gideon kissed the top of her head. "You can't change what happened to Zandra, but you're supporting her now. That matters, Daisy."

She nodded unsteadily, wiping her tears with the back of her hand as she pulled away. Molina stood watching—but her gaze was on Agent Hunter, who leaned against the wall, head bowed, hands clenched into fists at his side.

"Are you all right, Agent Hunter?" Molina asked crisply.

Daisy's feathers ruffled at the woman's tone, but it seemed to be what Hunter needed. His head snapped up, and he straightened.

"Yes, ma'am." His jaw clenched. "Or I will be. That was difficult to hear."

Molina nodded sagely. "It was. Yet you did well, Tom." She glanced at her watch. "I need to get back to the office."

"Will you add the rock star disguise to the BOLO?" Gideon asked.

"Already did while we were in there," Molina said, holding up her phone. "As soon as we had Paul Garvey's name as the subject's father, we sent detectives and a SWAT team to the airfield where they operate, just in case Carson Garvey showed up there and tried to appropriate a getaway plane. Up until now, he has not."

"Which airfield?" Gideon asked.

"Garvey Airfield, twenty miles north of Sacramento International. Paul Garvey has owned it more than twenty years. We now have Carson's home, his father's home, their hangar at the airport, and the office where he works surrounded. The license plates of the Mercedes registered to Sydney Garvey are also added to the BOLO. We've got aerial searches going on and all

airports have been informed or will be as they open."
She looked at the three of them. "Why don't you go get
Miss Dawson's father and your sister, Gideon, and get
some rest."

"And you?" Daisy asked. "Will you rest, too?"

Molina's brow rose and she looked a bit stunned
that Daisy went there. "I . . ." She gathered herself,
lifting her chin. "It's kind of you to ask. I'm quite capable of deciding when I need rest, Miss Dawson."

Daisy shook her head with a weary smile. "Of
course you are."

Molina managed to look like she was rolling her
eyes even though she didn't. "Agent Hunter, I need you
at the office. We're examining the computer taken
from Carson Garvey's home. I need your expertise.
I've got someone to take Agent Reynolds's protection
detail."

Hunter nodded once. "Yes, ma'am."

"Gideon!"

As a group, they turned to see Frederick running
around the corner, his face pale. Several nurses frowned
at him for shouting in the hallway in the middle of the
night, but he didn't seem to see them.

"It's Mercy," he called out desperately. "She's gone."

Beside her, Gideon swayed. "What?" he exploded.

Frederick reached them, breathing hard. "I went to
the men's room. Two minutes. I was gone two minutes.
When I got back she was gone. I ran to the elevator, but
the cop there said that no one had come that way."

The agent guarding Zandra's door stepped forward, expression grim. "Agent Molina, a nurse—male
Caucasian—tried to get into the victim's room. When
he heard you were in there, he said he'd be back."

"Description?" Molina demanded.

"Brown hair, longish."

"Shaggy?" Gideon asked harshly.

The agent nodded. "Yes."

They stood there for a second as the truth sank in. *No. No, no, no.* It couldn't be.

"Oh God." Gideon's whisper was tortured. "He's got her."

Molina dialed her phone and began giving a description of Mercy to whoever she was talking to. "Do you have a photo, Agent Reynolds?"

Gideon's response was slow. "Yes. But it's old." He pulled his phone from his pocket, but fumbled with it.

Daisy took the phone from his shaking hands, punching in the code he'd given her when she'd called for help in Macdoel. She opened his photo file and held the phone while Gideon tapped on his favorites folder. The photo of Mercy was at the top and it *was* an old photo. The face looking from the phone screen was thinner than Mercy's was now. Her hair was longer now. He tapped a few more buttons, then nodded at his boss.

"I sent it to you," he said. "But she looks different now."

Molina nodded. "I saw her tonight. I'll take care of getting the right info out, Gideon." She laid her hand on Gideon's arm. "Try to stay calm, okay?"

He jerked a nod, then strode to the elevator, the rest of them following close behind him. When he got to the elevator, he jabbed the DOWN button. The officer on guard started to get involved, but Molina shook her head and the man stepped back but stood ready.

"Where are we going, Gideon?" Frederick asked, his tone the one he'd used on restless horses on the ranch.

"To find her," Gideon bit out. "Before he can hurt her. And kill her. Like he killed thirty-one other women."

Daisy sucked in a breath. "Oh my God." She glanced at Hunter, then Molina. And saw that it was true. Thirty-one women.

Frederick sidled up to Gideon, angling himself

between Gideon and the elevator, and Gideon glared. "Do not try to stop me, Frederick."

"I won't. But I will go with you."

The elevator opened before Gideon could respond. Stepping around Frederick, he moved into the elevator, only to be pushed back out by Rafe Sokolov.

"Rafe," Daisy breathed in relief. "Mercy's been taken."

Rafe looked between them all like they were insane. "What?"

"Carson Garvey came into the hospital and took Mercy," Daisy said impatiently. "What are you doing here?"

"I came because I got home and my neighbor had to tell me what had happened. Nobody updated me."

The nurse who'd been standing on the sidelines stepped in. "Ladies and gentlemen, I know you're dealing with some kind of a crisis, but you'll need to do it somewhere else. This is a hospital and you're disturbing the other patients."

Molina held the phone away from her ear. "Tom, go to the office. Your replacement will take them home."

"I'll take them home," Rafe said, his gaze never leaving Gideon's stony face.

It was the expression Gideon had worn the first night they'd met, Daisy thought. She'd become so used to the more open Gideon in the past few days that the hardness of his jaw caught her by surprise.

Ignoring them all, Gideon jabbed the DOWN button again.

Molina nodded. "I'll send Agent Hunter's replacement to your house, Detective Sokolov."

"I'll walk with them to their car," Hunter offered.

The elevator doors opened and, as a group, they got in, surrounding Gideon. Partly for support, Daisy thought, and partly to control him if he tried to bolt.

Because there was sheer terror in his eyes.

Because he'd seen what this killer was capable of. He'd seen Trish's body. He knew about the others.

Thirty-one, he'd said. It was the first she'd heard of it, and Daisy wondered what else they'd find in that house. The house where he'd held Zandra. Where he'd tortured her. Where he'd tortured so many others.

Thirty-one.

Please don't let him hurt Mercy. She'd already been through so much.

And Gideon had just gotten her back. *Please.*

SACRAMENTO, CALIFORNIA
TUESDAY, FEBRUARY 21, 2:10 A.M.

No. No, no, no.

Gideon knew he was getting into the backseat of Rafe's Subaru, but he was too numb to control his own body. He wanted to scream. Wanted to throw his head back and scream until he had no more voice. But that did nothing to help his sister.

Soft hands cupped his cheeks and he looked up to see Daisy's concerned eyes studying him. She said nothing, just leaned in to buckle his seat belt. A minute later she was beside him, holding his hand tightly.

Still she said nothing. No words of comfort. Nothing pithy or wise. No *We'll find her, Gideon* or *It will be all right.* Because she couldn't promise those things.

But she was here. With him. Holding on to him like she'd never let go.

"He might be hurting her right now," he said hoarsely.

She brushed at his cheeks and he realized he was crying. "Gideon, listen to me." She waited until he'd drawn a breath and nodded. "He took her for a reason. He's on the run. He's scared. He's going to try to escape."

Gideon nodded, her words cutting through the haze of panic. "Leverage."

She nodded. "He won't hurt her yet. He hasn't made any demands."

He nodded again, her words like a lifeline. "Okay. We need to find him."

"And now we know who he is and what he does. More than we knew a few hours ago. So breathe. Molina is good at her job, right?"

Another nod. "Yeah."

"Then hold on," she said as Rafe and Frederick got in the front seats, slammed doors, and buckled in.

Gideon saw Tom Hunter walking to his SUV and realized the three of them had been talking. "What were you talking to Hunter about?"

"Comparing notes," Rafe replied. "Seems like SacPD knows stuff and the FBI knows different stuff. They may be sharing info up at Molina's level, but a lot isn't trickling down."

"Like?" Daisy asked.

"The FBI knows the victims' names. Both FBI and SacPD know where Carson works, but SacPD knows who he works with. SacPD surrounded the office where his father operates a charter airline. Erin and I went straight there when we got in from Portland. We got the flight manifests and employee records. Carson's main copilot is Hank Bain."

"Is he a suspect?" Gideon asked.

Rafe shrugged. "It's possible. All the abductions happened when they shared a shift. We searched his house and questioned him, but he swears he knew nothing of Carson Garvey's actions. According to Bain, they weren't friends and didn't hang out together. He didn't object when we did the search and we found nothing indicating he'd brought any victims to his home. Nothing like what was found at Carson's house."

Daisy frowned. "How does he explain the fact that Garvey transported victims—live women—on their flights?"

"He says that Garvey had a cooler in the plane, that he took it home after every flight to clean it. Claimed Garvey said he hunted and would bring home a quartered deer or elk."

"And he never looked in the cooler?" Frederick asked, incredulous.

Rafe shrugged. "He says he's a vegetarian, that red meat makes him sick. And that had he known there were live victims in the cooler, he would have looked. He said that they went their separate ways between legs. He had an alibi for the time that Zandra was taken from the bar. He was having sex with the airport shuttle driver. She confirmed it. He gave us a list of women to call, in fact. He's got a woman in every port. Apparently, this got him into trouble with Mrs. Bain. He was in New York City on Sunday night when one of his women called the very pregnant Mrs. Bain, tearfully told her the truth, and Mrs. Bain left him and took the other kids with her. He was on his way to getting very drunk when we got there, but finding out his copilot was a serial killer sobered him up fast."

"Did he know about Sydney?" Daisy asked.

"He said she'd come by the office from time to time. She'd call Carson 'Sonny,' which he hated, and she'd be all touchy-feely with him—but only when her husband wasn't in the office. When she'd leave, Carson was, and I quote, 'more of an asshole bastard than all the other times.' Bain figured something was going on between them, but he figured Carson didn't say anything about Bain's dalliances, so he wouldn't say anything, either. He didn't seem to know how long it had been going on."

Frederick's brows knit. "What does Bain look like?"

"Six four, blond hair—all his, Erin checked—and no scratches on his chest."

"So not the man who attacked Daisy in the alley," Frederick said. "Is it possible that he's a silent partner?"

Rafe shrugged again. "Anything is possible, but he was eager to distance himself from Carson. Bain showed us his bank account. Let us search every room, even those not covered on the warrant. He had a shed out back and we searched that, too. Everything looked normal. It's possible he's hiding something. But he seemed cooperative."

Gideon's heart sank. "So Garvey won't be hiding Mercy in Bain's house."

Rafe shook his head. "We've had cops all over his place, Gid. Erin stayed to watch Bain to make sure he isn't either a target or an accomplice, but right now? Mercy isn't there." He started the engine. "Let's go home."

PLACERVILLE, CALIFORNIA
TUESDAY, FEBRUARY 21, 2:45 A.M.

He brought the stolen van to a stop, then exhaled slowly. No one had followed him from the city and this property was accessed by a private road, so he wouldn't be noticed by any passersby.

"Where are we?"

He turned to see Gideon Reynolds's sister calmly sitting in the passenger seat, her bound hands resting in her lap.

"You're back," he said.

She just watched him with level regard. It was almost as creepy as the empty-eye thing she'd had going on before. It set him on edge and he didn't like that.

"Why did you go all blank at the hospital?" he asked.

"Defense mechanism. It's how I cope with stress." She didn't blink. Didn't look the least bit terrified. "I guess we all know how you cope with stress."

He wasn't sure if he'd been complimented or

insulted. "This is what's going to happen. You're going to sit here. If you try to run or scream or do anything to get in my way, I will shoot you in the head and toss your body where no one will ever find it."

She swallowed, the only indication that she was affected at all.

"Are we clear, Mercy?" he asked.

She nodded once.

"Good." Shaking his head, he got out of the van and inspected the old road that ran along the rear of the property, which had been in Sydney's family for generations. They'd never built on it. It was a little too far out from both Sacramento and Lake Tahoe to be convenient to either. That was what Sydney had told him, anyway.

It was every boy's dream—there were three abandoned gold mine shafts on the land. He'd explored them all, which in hindsight had been very stupid. Mine shafts were no place for children. It was also a good place to look at the stars, far enough away from the city that there was not so much light interference.

Sydney used to bring him here when he was young. She'd been in her early twenties then, the trophy wife his old man had brought home to replace his mother. He hadn't liked her at first, but she'd won him over with treats and fun outings. Like here.

He'd explore the mines and, when the sun went down, he'd set up his telescope and look at the stars and map them. He'd wanted to fly in space back then. But then Sydney had shown him what she expected. The first time had been right here.

He'd been twelve. When he'd gotten home that night, he put the telescope in the closet and never used it again. He had no idea where it was now.

He shook off the memory. *Enough of that.* He'd taken this place back long ago, using it for his own purposes. To his knowledge, Sydney hadn't been here in years.

Too bad I didn't have more time. She could have made a final visit.

He walked the length of the old road where Sydney had first ruined him, hearing her voice. *I'll make you feel good. Our secret. Nobody else will make you feel like I do.*

And it was true. Nobody could. She'd trained him well.

And now she was finally dead.

I can finally breathe.

Although taking too deep a breath here wasn't advisable. Eileen Danton was still on the fresh side. She'd been dumped down the shaft two months ago. Her body was still decomposing. The door that closed off the mine was heavy, but no door was that heavy.

He'd always fantasized about killing Sydney, then dumping her here. Now her body was burning to ash, which didn't seem quite fair.

The road was still usable. It had a few potholes, but nothing too bad. He'd landed on worse before. Hank Bain was a decent pilot. He'd be able to land a plane here with no problem. Hank would need to be convinced to deliver it, but he had that covered, too.

Unfortunately, he'll be joining Eileen and the others, but I'll make it quick.

He'd brought the relevant photos on his phone. Hank with Sweetie, the shuttle driver in Dallas. Hank with Debbie, the owner of the coffee shop in Tulsa. Hank with Laura, the baggage porter in Minneapolis. He tilted his head. That was actually a very interesting pose. He'd never realized Hank was so flexible.

He'd taken the pictures over the years, just in case Hank got curious and looked in the cooler at the wrong time.

He brought up Hank's number and hit CALL.

||| GRANITE BAY, CALIFORNIA
   TUESDAY, FEBRUARY 21, 3:05 A.M.

Rafe pulled his Subaru into the Sokolovs' driveway
and Daisy was releasing Gideon's seat belt, because he
couldn't reach it with his arm in a sling, when Rafe's
cell phone rang.

Rafe glanced over his shoulder, frowning. "It's Erin.
Wait a minute."

So she, Gideon, and her father sat in tense silence as
they listened to Rafe's side of the conversation. Frederick
was looking kind of gray and Daisy had been worrying
about him when she wasn't worrying about Gideon. Or
Mercy. Her father felt guilty for his role in Mercy's abduction, although Gideon didn't seem to be blaming him.

At least there was that.

"You're kidding," Rafe said. "When?" He listened for
more than a minute, then looked at Gideon, his eyes going wider. "Okay. We'll be there in less than ten."

He ended the call, put the car in reverse, and backed
out of the driveway.

"Well?" Gideon exploded when Rafe said nothing.

"We were driving when I got this call," Rafe answered, which made no sense at all. Then he put the
blue flasher on his roof and took off down the street.
"Because I know you'll want Daisy with you and Frederick won't let her go anywhere without him."

Gideon was shaking. "Dammit, Rafe, what's happened? Did they find her?"

"No," Rafe said. "But Erin was sitting next to Bain
at his kitchen table when he got a call from Carson.
Carson's demanding that Hank bring him one of their
planes."

"To where?" Gideon demanded.

"He wouldn't tell him. Bain told him that he was

crazy, that there was no way he'd be able to get a plane out of the hangar with the police swarming the place. And that even if he did, no airport would let him land. Carson told Bain not to worry, that he had leverage."

"Mercy," Gideon breathed.

"Why did he think Bain would help him?" Frederick asked.

"Carson had photographic proof of Bain's affairs. He's threatening to tell his wife. But Bain's wife already knows. He figures at this point he has nothing to lose. And maybe by helping to catch this guy, he'll be a hero and Mrs. Bain will forgive him."

Daisy rolled her eyes. "I wonder if he's naive or just optimistic."

"I don't know," Rafe said. "Bain asked Carson if he'd actually killed the women he's being accused of. Carson told him no, that he was being framed, falsely accused. That if Bain didn't believe him, he'd send the pictures to his wife right now and get help from elsewhere."

"Does Detective Rhee know about Mercy?" Frederick asked.

Rafe nodded. "I called her before I got into the car."

"Has Erin reported this call to SacPD or the FBI?" Daisy asked, gripping Gideon's right hand when he crossed it over his chest.

"She called me first," Rafe said. "She's probably on the phone with our boss now."

Daisy looked up at the rearview, where Rafe was periodically glancing up to watch them. "You said you were already driving so that Gideon could be there and your excuse would be that you didn't want to take the time to drop him off?"

Rafe nodded. "Exactly."

Gideon's eyes closed. "Thank you."

"I won't regret it, will I?"

Gideon shook his head. "No. I promise."

THIRTY

Seven minutes later they pulled into the driveway of a nice home in Folsom. Gideon's heart was racing in his chest. *Please. Please let us get to her in time. Please don't let him hurt her. Please.*

He wasn't sure Mercy would survive another assault. The four of them piled out of Rafe's Subaru and hurried to Bain's front door. Erin met them there with a scowl. "You brought them with you? What the actual fuck, Sokolov?"

"Carson Garvey has abducted his sister," Rafe said quietly.

Erin's face fell. "I know that. You told me. But, Rafe, Gideon shouldn't be here. You know this."

Yes, I should be here. If anyone's making plans that involve my sister, hell yes *I should be here.* Erin Rhee could *not* make him leave.

She just couldn't.

He took a step closer. "Erin, please." He'd get on his knees and beg if he had to. "You saw what he'll do. Please."

Erin's eyes filled with sympathy. "I know, Gideon. But—"

"I didn't save her the first time," Gideon blurted out. "Please, let me help her now."

Erin looked confused, but Rafe sighed. "What he

didn't tell you Thursday night was that his sister was also in the cult. Gideon didn't escape as much as he was smuggled out by his mother because he'd been beaten nearly to death. His sister was also smuggled out by their mother four years later and Mercy . . . well, she was in bad shape. Gideon searched for that compound the entire time his sister and mother were still in there."

Erin's eyes had widened, but she shook her head. "I'm sorry, Gideon, I really am. You have to wait outside. I'm not going to jeopardize this case because you got close to a witness and tried to force him to talk."

Gideon's mouth opened to beg, but Rafe stayed him with a gentle hand. "Wait," Rafe murmured. "Erin, I want to call in my marker."

Erin stared at him. "Seriously?"

Rafe's normally smiling face was uncharacteristically sober. "Yes. Seriously."

Gideon wanted to know what this marker entailed, but he was holding his breath, waiting for Erin's agreement. She looked undecided, her gaze bouncing everywhere but them. Finally, she nodded and he could breathe again.

"Okay," she said, resigned. "Don't blame me if this blows up in your face."

"I won't."

"Just bring them in," an irritated voice called from inside the house. "You're letting the cold in and giving my neighbors their third show of the night."

Erin held the door open and the four of them filed in.

A disheveled man sat at the kitchen table, staring dolefully at an empty bottle of beer. He looked up at them when they took seats around the table, his expression sad and weary as Erin introduced them.

"I couldn't help overhearing," Bain said. "I'm sorry about your sister."

Gideon nodded. "I need to bring her home."

"I'll do what I can," Bain promised. "Within reason. I don't want to take him a plane. He told me to come alone and I'd like to see my kids grow up."

"He's *not* getting a plane," Erin said. "There's no way anyone is letting him fly out, especially considering he has Mercy."

"Do you know where he'd go?" Gideon asked the man, hearing his own desperation and not caring.

Bain shook his head. "I already told the detectives—Carson and I weren't friends. We didn't confide things. The only personal things I know about him is that he's the boss's son, he was banging the boss's wife, he was expecting to get the company when the old man retired, he loved his roses, and he really got off on listening to Barry Manilow. When he'd get stressed, he'd sometimes listen to the guy's music on his phone."

That fit at least. Gideon remembered Molina telling him that one of his victims was a woman who'd just been to a Barry Manilow concert. The friend she'd gone with said that a man had approached after the concert, angry that she'd stood up and danced. They'd argued and the women laughed it off. Then the friend was never seen again.

He'd also provoked arguments with both Trish and Eileen. *He chooses women who've angered him. Even if he has to provoke them into making him angry.*

Daisy had propped her elbows on the table, her forehead furrowing. "What if you could put him off? Tell him that you can't get him a plane now, but you will when the cops leave the airport. Until then, maybe offer him a car. One that he hasn't had to steal, so the police won't be looking for it."

"And a place to stay until the heat dies down," Frederick added. "Then you'll bring him a plane in a day or two."

"But we'll provide the car," Rafe said, nodding his approval.

Gideon shook his head. "He'll kill her when he sees you."

Rafe looked at Erin. "Not if I can make myself look like Mr. Bain long enough for you to come up from behind and get the shot."

"We need to have backup in place," Erin said with a frown. "Confronting him alone is suicide."

No! Gideon wanted to scream. *No cops. He'll kill her.* But he forced himself to think about it more rationally. Like a professional. "I'd trust a trained SWAT team," he said. "But not a group of local cops or even FBI agents who are untrained in hostage situations."

Erin nodded. "All right. So what car do we offer if he accepts Mr. Bain's counterproposal? Mr. Bain's? No," she answered her own question. "Seeing as how they work together, he might worry that the police would connect the car to him."

"He's been to my house," Rafe said. "So he may have seen mine. It'll need to be yours."

"Okay," Erin said. "And the place? It needs to be a real place, a real address so he can check it online if he decides to."

"I've got a cabin in Lake Tahoe," Frederick offered.

Daisy blinked at him. "You do? Since when?"

"Since you moved to Sacramento and I finally sold the ranch," he answered. "Needed an investment. Can I use your paper and pen, Detective?" Erin slid them to him and he jotted the address and the name "Cadajulor, Inc." "I bought it under the corporate name I used when I bought the ranch." He shrugged. "I don't like to be found. Old habits die hard."

Cadajulor, Gideon thought. *For Carrie, Daisy, Julie, and Taylor.* The man loved his daughters. The pang of sympathy that Gideon felt for Frederick and his rocky relationships with his daughters gave him respite from the overwhelming, oppressive fear that was pressing on his chest. For just a minute, but the respite was welcome.

"The final detail," Rafe said, giving Bain an appraising look, "is to make him think I'm you long enough to distract him while the SWAT team lines up their shot."

"What about Mercy?" Gideon asked, able to imagine the scene all too well. The bastard would hold Mercy at gunpoint. Once Carson realized he was surrounded . . . He shuddered, unable to think it.

Rafe met his gaze, steady and calm. "I'll get her away from him."

Gideon felt a new wave of dread, this time for the man who'd been a brother to him for sixteen years. What was Rafe planning? "How?"

Rafe squeezed his arm. "I'll find a way."

"A safe way," Gideon gritted out.

"Don't worry," Rafe said firmly. "I'm not planning to be his final victim." He turned to Bain, the topic clearly closed. "You're a forty long?"

"Yes. You want one of my uniforms? I'll get you one."

Rafe stood. "No offense, sir. You've been very helpful. But I'll need to go with you."

Bain nodded once. "Of course."

When they left the room, Erin gave Gideon, Daisy, and Frederick a serious look. "You are not going. Are we clear?"

Like hell I'm not. But Gideon held that back, nodding instead. "Yes, Detective."

A few minutes later, Rafe returned wearing a white captain's uniform, complete with the cap. They were the same size, their hair different shades of blond, but close enough that if Rafe dipped his head to hide his face, he could pass for Bain from far enough away. Especially if it was dark.

"Okay," Rafe said. "This is how this is going down.

Detective Rhee will sit with Mr. Bain while he makes his call. I will go into another room with the three of you."

Gideon started to protest, but Rafe held up his hand and kept talking. "From his cell phone, Mr. Bain will call my cell phone first. He'll then call Carson back and merge the calls, so that we are conferenced together. Mr. Bain will have his phone on speaker so that Detective Rhee can hear. I will have my phone muted and on speaker so that you can hear, Gideon, but not interact." He shot Gideon a look of apology. "If that's not acceptable, Gid, the three of you will need to wait in the squad car outside."

Gideon started to object, then realized that Rafe was right. He wasn't sure he could stay silent when he finally heard that sonofabitch's voice. "That is acceptable," he said roughly. "Thanks."

Relief flashed over Rafe's face. "All right then. Let's—"

"Wait," Frederick interrupted. "Won't he see who else is on the call?"

Erin shook her head. "No. He'll only see that Mr. Bain has called him. That's also what Detective Sokolov will see."

"Everybody good?" Rafe asked. When everyone nodded, he turned to Bain. "Make your call, please, and good luck. Just breathe and be yourself. The rest of you, come with me. Mr. Bain has allowed us to listen to the call from his sons' bedroom."

Rafe answered Bain's call as he led them to a child's room with two twin beds and a small student desk. Rafe closed the door, still waiting for Bain to add the bastard to the call.

Gideon slowly lowered himself to the bed with a Pikachu bedspread, feeling a hundred years old. Daisy sat next to him and Frederick sat on the bed covered in a Spider-Man spread while Rafe pulled the desk chair close to him.

Just as Carson Garvey's voice came from Rafe's muted phone.

"Hank," Carson barked. "Where's my fucking plane?"

Gideon couldn't suppress the growl that rose from his throat. Daisy rubbed his back comfortingly and Rafe grasped his forearm and squeezed, his expression sympathetic and without a trace of *I told you so.*

Bain stammered his reply. "I c-can't get you a plane, Carson. Not this minute," he rushed to add when Carson started to curse. "The cops are everywhere at the airfield. It'll be much better if you lay low until I can get you the plane. A day. Two tops."

"I'm listening," Carson said warily.

"My neighbor is gone for the whole month. He's on a job in India. He's not going to be coming back until the middle of March. I have keys to his car and his house. I can get keys to his cabin in Tahoe from his house. It's remote and comfortable."

There was a long, long silence. Then, "All right. Laying low may make more sense. If anyone gives me shit about being in the cabin, I'll send the pictures to your wife. She'll find them most illuminating. You really should use protection, Hank. Who knows what you've picked up and brought home to her."

Bain groaned softly. "No!" he cried. "Please don't."

"He sounds genuinely distraught," Rafe murmured, looking impressed. Gideon was, too—unless the guy was acting with them, too.

God, he hoped not. If so, Rafe and Erin were walking into a trap. And Mercy would be caught in the crossfire. *And they expect me to sit here, helpless.*

"I don't want your mewling pleas," Carson said with contempt. "I want you to do what I said and get me a damn plane. If you're fucking with me, you'll be begging for forgiveness, not mercy." Then the bastard chuckled. "Mercy. Get it?"

Gideon bit back another growl but wasn't entirely successful. Daisy brushed the barest of kisses over his injured shoulder and Rafe squeezed his arm harder.

"I . . . I got it," Bain said, his voice shaking. "Wh-where are you?"

Another long, long pause. Gideon thought his heart would give out from the stress. But no. It kept on beating until Carson blew out a breath. "Placerville. I'll call you with the exact coordinates once you're close."

"Okay," Bain whispered. Then asked, "Carson, I've got three kids and one on the way. I'm coming home to them, right?"

"Of course you will," Carson said smoothly. "You've got thirty minutes. And if you're thinking of involving the police, don't. My leverage is only useful if I have transportation. The cops won't give me a plane or even a car. I know that. They'll pretend to negotiate, but they lie. They only want to buy enough time to take me into custody and that's not going to happen. If I have to make my own way and go on the run, my leverage becomes a liability. I'll kill her and dump her in your backyard and I'll find a way to make it look like you did it. Then the police will question *you*."

Bain made a strangled noise. "You wouldn't do that."

"You have no idea what I'd do," Carson said ominously.

"Then it *is* true. You've . . . you've killed people?" Bain asked with quiet horror.

Gideon figured that Erin must have asked him to ask this so that they could record it.

Carson's laugh was unpleasant. "Let's just say that you don't want anyone to think you've been playing with me after hours."

"Okay, okay. I'll do it. Just . . . don't hurt anyone. Please."

"Then don't fuck this up, Hank. You now have

twenty-nine minutes. Make them count. See you then."
The call abruptly ended, leaving Gideon more helpless
than before. And hopeless.

His emotion must have been clear on his face because Rafe gave his arm a final squeeze. "We've got
this, brother," he whispered.

Brother. They always had been. "Yeah," Gideon
managed. "Okay."

Rafe slid the chair beneath the desk, then held out
his hand to pull Gideon up. "Come on. We have a lot
to do."

The four of them found Erin talking on her phone
and Bain staring at his own. "He plans to kill me if I
show up," Bain said dully.

"Most likely," Rafe agreed. "But you're going to be
here. Protected."

Erin ended her call and stood up, her expression
grim. "I just talked to the lieutenant and he's with
Agent Molina. They're preparing a SWAT team, but
ETA to Placerville is an hour."

Gideon choked back his fear. "He'll kill her by then."

Rafe and Erin exchanged a long, long look while
Gideon held his breath because he knew they were
mentally discussing whether to go or stay. He shuddered out a breath when Erin nodded reluctantly. "I do
believe Carson will kill her," she said quietly. "He really does have nothing to lose."

"I believe him, too," Rafe agreed, his expression
grim. "We can't wait an hour. And even if they
speed, the field office is still forty-five minutes from
Placerville. Anyone SacPD sends *might* make it in
thirty."

Erin rubbed her forehead wearily. "Let's start driving to Placerville. We're thirty minutes out, but we can
get there in twenty. We'll go to the coordinates when
Carson gives them to Bain. We won't act unless it
looks like Mercy is in imminent danger."

"She's already *in* imminent danger," Gideon ground out.

Erin gave him a serious, quelling look. "We are going to do this right. We are not going to knee-jerk our way into a clusterfuck. And you will stay here." She sighed. "You're going to have to trust us, Gideon."

Gideon jerked a nod, knowing she was right. "All right."

Rafe gave his arm a final squeeze before turning to his partner. "Rhee, let's go in your car. If we have to approach, I'll drive, you stay low. I'll drop you off first so that you can make your approach."

Erin didn't move. "How will we know where he is?"

"He said he'd call Mr. Bain when we got close," Rafe said. "Mr. Bain can call us once he has the location."

Bain frowned. "I won't be in the car, though. He'll hear the difference."

"Good point," Rafe allowed. "We'll ask the officer to drive you around the block until you get the call."

Bain did not look okay with that. "My neighbors will think I've been arrested. It'll get on the news and my kids will see it."

"We'll ask the officer to ride along with you in your own car," Rafe said. "Nobody will think you've been arrested. When you get the call from Carson, just call me or Detective Rhee with whatever coordinates he gives you."

"I can check the property from Google Earth," Gideon offered. "Just tell me the coordinates when he gives them to you. I'll describe the lay of the land so you know how to approach."

Erin shook her head. "Nice try, Gideon. No cigar."

"And if he plans to guide you in step-by-step?" Gideon asked.

"Then we do a three-way call again, just like we did here," Erin said. "Another nice try. Still no cigar. I'm not involving you. You are staying *here*."

Rafe gave him a half hug. "Gid, we've got this. Daisy, you wait here for your protection detail. They're probably already waiting for you at Mom and Dad's house. I'll tell them to send your escort here." Pressing his car key in her hand, he leaned down and hugged her, then whispered something in her ear that Gideon couldn't hear.

She nodded up at Rafe, then smiled sweetly. "You too."

Erin paused in the kitchen doorway. "Mr. Bain, one of the officers will come in to escort you. You three"—she pointed at Gideon, Daisy, and Frederick—"*stay here.*"

Daisy made the Girl Scout sign, like she was vowing on her honor.

When they were gone, Gideon put his hand out. "The key. You stay here."

"Um, no." Daisy put the key in her father's hand instead. "How are your driving skills, Dad? Mine are a little rusty."

"Mine are good. And yours were awful *before* they got rusty."

Daisy went to the front window and made a frustrated noise. "For God's sake. Erin's behind the wheel. She's not letting Rafe drive."

"Because she knew he'd let us tail him," Frederick said grimly.

She turned from the window. "Okay, they're gone. If we're quick and slick, we can catch up. Let's go. Dad's going to drive because you're tired and terrified and you'll kill us before we can get to Mercy. I'm going along in case you need a marksman."

Gideon wanted to argue, but he knew they were right. He was one step away from falling flat on his face, holding on through sheer fear for Mercy.

One of the officers who'd been waiting outside knocked, then entered the house. "Detective Rhee asked me to drive Mr. Bain in his car while we wait for his call. Mr. Bain? Are you ready to go?"

Hank pushed away from the table and handed the officer his keys. "You drive. I don't want to add a DUI to this night," he added, his jaw tight.

"We'll wait in our car," Daisy told the officer. "Our escort is expected soon."

The officer in the cruiser outside gave them a curious look as he passed them going into the house, but said nothing. Which surprised Gideon, but he didn't comment until they were buckled into Rafe's Subaru and driving the direction that Erin's blue Range Rover had gone.

"That cop didn't say a word to us," he commented.

"Because he didn't expect us to stay," Daisy said. "Rafe probably said something to him."

Gideon lifted his brows. "What did Rafe whisper in your ear?"

"The combo," she said, "to the gun safe in the cargo hold."

PLACERVILLE, CALIFORNIA
TUESDAY, FEBRUARY 21, 4:15 A.M.

He leaned against the passenger side of the van he'd stolen, watching for headlights. He'd called Hank with the coordinates twenty minutes ago. He was ten minutes later than the thirty minutes allotted.

The asshole needed to hurry. It was cold outside for one, but more importantly, the sun would be up in three hours. He'd like to be safely in the cabin before sunrise. There would be less chance of discovery that way.

Except the road to Lake Tahoe could be treacherous if the weather got bad. If he needed to buy chains for the tires, he'd have to wait until the local Walmart opened at six A.M.

He'd been sorely vexed to find that it wasn't an

all-night Walmart one of the first times he'd dumped a body in the abandoned mine and wanted a snack on the way home.

It would depend on what kind of vehicle Hank was bringing him, he decided. Some SUVs could make it through the mountains without chains. Hopefully he was getting one of those.

He started when the passenger window lowered behind him, his right hand going for the gun in his pocket. He relaxed when he realized Mercy had somehow hit the window switch with her elbow. Her hands were bound and they were a good mile away from the nearest house. Considering that he'd taken her shoes, she wasn't going anywhere.

"Who are you waiting for?" Mercy asked in that quiet way she had.

He was undecided about Agent Reynolds's sister. He wasn't sure if her strange calm was peaceful or just plain creepy. He leaned toward creepy.

"None of your business," he snapped.

"At the risk of sounding trite, you're not likely to get away with this. My brother is very good at his job and he won't stop looking for you, no matter where you run."

He looked over his shoulder at her. She had wide green eyes and she studied him levelly. "Shut up," he said, with a look that had silenced many of his victims.

She, however, didn't flinch. Didn't blink. "Are you planning to kill me?"

"No. But I will if you don't shut the fuck up."

She shrugged slightly as if it didn't make any difference. She was trying to mess with his head. He was sure of it. "What do you do for a living?" he asked, curious now.

"I'm a forensic investigator."

He rolled his eyes. "Of course you are. Damn forensics. So you're like *CSI*?"

She rolled her eyes this time. "No. That is not a factual show."

"So do you go out in the field?" he asked, because forensics had always fascinated him as much as they'd annoyed him.

"No. I mostly stay in the lab."

He tilted his head. "Are you trying to make me like you so that I don't kill you?"

"No," she said easily. "I figure you'll do what you'll do."

"You're not afraid of me?"

"No."

He frowned. "Why not?"

Her lips curved ever so slightly. Ever so mockingly. "I survived a monster far more terrifying than you. No offense."

Now he was very curious. "Tell me about him."

She shook her head. "No. You should have asked Eileen that same question."

"Why?"

She looked out the windshield, no longer meeting his eyes. "She survived the same monster."

"She was stubborn," he said with a fond smile. "She lasted for two days."

"Zandra lasted three," she said mildly. "Until she got away."

His jaw tightened. *Stay calm,* he thought. *She's yanking your chain to threaten your focus.* "If you're so brave, why did you go all zombie robot on me when we left the hospital?"

"I told you. That's the way I cope with stress. I shut down."

"But you're not stressed now?"

"Of course I am. You're probably going to kill me."

He lifted a brow, then touched his face to find that the false eyebrow he'd fixed to it had fallen off at some point. "But you're not afraid."

"Stress is different from fear."

"That's fair," he allowed. "Or you're just crazy. I'm not sure which." When she didn't respond, he asked, "Why aren't you all zombie robot if you're still stressed?"

"The episodes don't last as long as they used to."

"Well, I suppose that's good for you." Not that it mattered. Sooner or later he would be killing her. He turned back to the road, watching for Hank. The man was almost out of time. *And then what? What will you do?*

I'll kill Mercy, dump her, then drive to Mexico. He'd just have to figure out where to get a fake passport. Or where he could cross over without one.

"Why this place?" Mercy asked, surprising him. "Why did you come here tonight?"

He looked at her with a frown. "Why do you want to know?"

"I'm curious by nature. And I smell death."

He drew a deep breath through his nose. Yeah, he could smell it, too. "That would be Eileen," he said. "If my ride doesn't get here soon, you'll be reunited with her."

He shifted back to the road, watching, his sense of dread growing with every second that ticked by. Something wasn't right. Hank should have been here already.

He was now fifteen minutes late.

Heart beginning to pound harder, he pulled out his phone and dialed Hank, fighting back the urge to pace as the phone rang and rang and rang. *He's not answering,* he thought as the call went to voice mail. *Why is he not answering?*

He ended the call, his hand clutched around the phone, willing himself not to throw it in a rage. *Stay calm. Stay fucking calm.*

The phone rang in his hand, and he drew a breath. Hank. "Where the fuck are you?" he demanded. "And why the fuck didn't you answer your phone?"

"Sorry," Hank said, sounding slightly out of breath.

"I was filling the gas tank. It was almost on 'E' and I knew you wouldn't want to stop. Because of the cameras at the gas station."

"That's true," he said grudgingly. "Why are you so late?"

"It took me a few minutes to get to my neighbor's house so that I could get his car."

That also sounded plausible, but something was off. *Or I could just be paranoid.* "When will you get here?"

"Soon. I'm less than ten minutes—"

Hank's voice was cut off by the loud clanging of bells.

Railroad crossing bells. He clenched his jaw. There were no train tracks nearby. There was, however, a train crossing near Hank's house.

Hank had lied. He wasn't coming.

He was cooperating with the cops.

I need to get out of here. Now. Carefully, deliberately, he ended the call, reminding himself to breathe. *Stay calm. Breathe. Think.*

"He's not coming, is he?" Mercy said, that mocking tone back in her voice. "Your pal, I mean. He's not coming."

His temper boiling over, he shoved the phone into his pocket and opened the van door. He yanked Mercy out of the vehicle, tossing her to the ground, where she landed on her knees in the light snow with a grunt of pain.

"Do not mock me," he snarled.

Twisting to look up at him over her shoulder, she smiled far too serenely. "Oh, I wouldn't think of it. But he isn't coming. Now what will you do?"

His right hand had connected with her cheek before intent to strike her had even registered. Her head snapped back and she sucked in a harsh breath.

"What will I do?" he snarled. "I'm going to kill you, for starters."

"Kill me and lose your leverage," she said with a calm that he wished he felt.

She was right. He hated that she was right. Leaning over her, he grabbed a handful of her hair, yanking her to her feet.

He saw the blade in her hand a split second too late, crying out in fury when she swung her body around, plunging it into his thigh. He knocked her hand away before she could twist the blade or drive it in too deep. He yanked it out, relieved to find that it had only gone in about an inch.

Where the fuck was she hiding that? I should have searched her. Dammit.

But he was relieved to see that it wasn't that bad a wound. The slice was bleeding like a mother, but it was far from mortal.

He moved the knife to his injured hand, sinking his right hand back into her hair and jerking her to her feet. He wound his left arm around her throat, pulling her against him. He took the knife into his right hand and pressed the tip to her throat.

"If I had time, you'd be apologizing to me on your knees," he growled into her ear. She'd gone rigid against him and he calmed at the return of his control of the situation.

Until he heard the engine behind them. Maintaining his hold, he spun them both to see an SUV approaching, its headlights off. *Hank?*

Could I have been wrong? Could there have been train tracks I hadn't noticed?

Warily, he watched the SUV taking each turn of the road slowly, but it was too dark to see what model it was. But an SUV meant the road to Tahoe wouldn't be a problem.

That was one worry off his mind.

Unless he'd been right before and the train didn't run nearby. Instinct had him dropping the switchblade to the ground and pulling out his gun. He shoved the barrel into Mercy's temple as the SUV rolled to a stop and turned its headlights on, blinding him. The door opened and a man got out.

He could see that the man was tall, like Hank. Wearing a white uniform, like Hank.

But . . . the hairs on the back of his neck lifted and he jabbed the barrel of his gun harder against Mercy's head, gratified at the small sound of pain she made.

"Turn your lights off, Hank," he called, but the man kept advancing slowly. Then the clouds flitted by, exposing the meager light of tonight's moon and stars.

The vehicle was blue. A blue Range Rover. That he'd seen before. Frantically he searched his mind for the connection, for the—

The morgue. He'd seen it at the morgue, parked on one side of Reynolds's black Toyota. It was one of the detectives working the homicide of Trish Hart. Sokolov or Rhee. Had to be Sokolov because it was a man in that uniform.

He'd been tricked. This was a trap after all.

Fuck you, Hank. I'm coming for you, asshole.

"That's far enough!" he shouted. "Hands where I can see them, Sokolov, or I'll kill her."

Under his hands, Mercy tensed. *Good.* Maybe she'd go zombie. She'd be easier to control that way.

The man in the white uniform stopped, putting his hands up, still saying nothing.

"I know that's you, Detective Sokolov! Just stop, right there. Tell whoever's with you to get out of the damn car."

"Nobody's with me. I came alone."

He snorted at that. "Right. You never go alone. There's another cop here somewhere." Or more. *Shit.* He looked around him frantically. They could have a dozen guns trained on him right now. He needed to keep Mercy up against him. She wasn't quite as tall as he was, but close. She'd be his shield if the bullets started to fly.

The headlights blinded him. He wouldn't be able to see anyone even if they were out there, but he could see that Sokolov had moved closer while he'd been looking around for the cop's backup. The bastard was *still* moving. The white of the uniform he wore almost glowed. "Don't move! I will kill her. I swear it."

Sokolov stopped, but now he could see the gun in the detective's hand. "What do you want, Carson?" he called.

What *did* he want? "I want you to get everyone away from here. Or I will kill her. I have nothing to lose." He considered it, then added, "Except for you. You stay. Put your gun on the ground and lie down on your stomach." Because he'd have to show his back to Sokolov when he went to put Mercy in the van so that he could get away. He began edging toward the rear of the van, dragging Mercy with him. "I'm not seeing your gun on the ground, Sokolov. I'm serious."

"So am I," Sokolov replied. "If I throw down my gun, you'll just kill us both. Why would I do that?"

Because I told you to, he wanted to shout, but he didn't. He was trembling now and he hated it. Hated that the man could make him so nervous. Hated that the bastard had the upper hand. The last word.

Hated that he was helpless and his options were running out.

"Because I have nothing to lose," he said more calmly.

THIRTY-ONE

PLACERVILLE, CALIFORNIA
TUESDAY, FEBRUARY 21, 4:15 A.M.

Dammit," Frederick hissed. They'd lost Erin Rhee's blue Range Rover. They'd gone around a bend in the road and come up behind two tractor-trailers, struggling up the steep grade. "Erin must have slipped in front of those two trucks before we got to them."

Gideon sat in the backseat behind Frederick, biting back his curse. It wasn't the man's fault. He'd been a damn good driver, keeping up as Erin zipped up U.S. 50 at speeds far faster than the limit.

Daisy muttered a curse. "She made sure we couldn't follow her."

Gideon closed his eyes. Rafe and Rhee were good cops. And Rafe would do his best to get Mercy out alive. Even if his best meant putting himself in the line of fire, and that scared Gideon most of all. He could lose a brother *and* a sister tonight.

"Breathe, baby," Daisy murmured, her hand on his cheek. "You need to breathe."

He tried. He truly tried, but his lungs would not inflate.

"Goddammit, Gideon." Daisy's hands were on his face now and she wasn't gentle. She'd unbuckled her seat belt and was kneeling next to him on the bench seat. She gave his cheeks a slight smack. Not painful, but enough to get his attention. "Look at me."

He nodded, blinking. "You are not safe."

She made another one of those frustrated noises. "And you are not with me." She leaned her forehead against his. "Breathe, baby," she whispered. "With me, okay?"

He got himself under control, feeling ridiculous on top of panicked. "I'm good. Buckle yourself in."

"I'm sorry, Gideon," Frederick said, his misery plain.

"Don't be," Gideon managed. "You've done so much already. Erin never planned to let us catch up to her."

An exit approached. "Should I take it?" Frederick asked.

"Yes," Gideon told him. "If they're close, we'll see the SWAT vehicles go by and we can follow them." *If it's not too late by then.*

His phone began buzzing and Gideon grabbed for it, hoping like hell it was Rafe. But it was an unknown number. Maybe Carson Garvey, calling to negotiate. "Reynolds," he answered, taking care to continue breathing because his heart had started to race.

"It's Tom Hunter."

"Tom? What's happening?"

Next to him, Daisy perked up at the sound of Hunter's name.

"We are not talking right now," Tom said carefully. "Tell me that you get that."

Gideon's pulse shot through the roof. "I get it. Is she alive?"

"I don't know, but I do know Sokolov and Rhee are on their way to Placerville. And I have no doubt that you are, too."

"We are," Gideon admitted, "but they lost us."

"Is Daisy with you?"

"Yes."

"Put me on speaker. Daisy," he said when he'd done

so. "I need you to put these coordinates in your phone's GPS. You know how to do that, right?"

"Um, yeah," Daisy said, then she smiled at Gideon. "It's a property in Placerville. Turn right up here, Dad. Thank you, Tom."

"You're welcome. And you did not get this from me."

"How did you get it?" Gideon asked, his lungs actually filling again.

"Molina has me looking into Carson's finances. Follow the money, right? He'd been looking at this property, trying to get the money together to buy it. It belonged to Sydney. Undeveloped land."

Gideon was nearly speechless. "Why?" he asked. "Why would you do this for me?"

"Because I have a sister, and if anyone touched her, I'd be losing my mind. I've also been on a chase like yours, a long time ago, and I know how it feels to be powerless."

"What number are you calling from, Tom?" Daisy asked.

"I never leave home without a burner," Tom said, the amusement clear in his voice. "And I never said that, either." He hesitated. "Good luck, Gideon. Stay safe."

The call was ended and all Gideon could do was watch and pray as Daisy guided Frederick down a country road.

"There, Dad." She pointed at an access road with *No Trespassing* and *Private Property* signs posted everywhere.

Frederick turned and the Subaru rocked as it went over something big.

"That was the gate," he said, then turned off the headlights, navigating the snow-covered road with care.

Minutes later, they didn't need headlights. They

could see Erin's Range Rover, its headlights shining on a scene that made Gideon's blood run cold.

"Oh my God," he breathed. A six-foot-tall bald man held Mercy to his chest, his forearm across her throat and a gun to her head.

Carson Garvey. Undisguised.

Gideon's stomach lurched. *No. No, no, no.*

Rafe boldly faced the man, his gun aimed at Carson and Mercy, but Gideon knew his best friend. Rafe projected a confidence he often did not feel. Especially when lives were at stake. As Mercy's was.

Frederick rolled down his window so that they could hear, but he kept the Subaru back far enough that they didn't tip off Carson to their presence.

"I want you to get everyone away from here," Carson was saying. "Or I will kill her. I have nothing to lose. Except for you. You stay. Put your gun on the ground and lie down on your stomach."

Carson began to move toward the rear of the van, Mercy in his grasp. He was holding her so that she had to stand on her tiptoes to breathe. Her wrists were bound.

God, Mercy, I'm so sorry. Because Gideon knew Carson had nothing against Mercy. She'd been convenient. *He wanted me.* And Daisy.

"I'm not seeing your gun on the ground, Sokolov," Carson called. "I'm serious."

"So am I," Rafe called back. "If I throw down my gun, you'll just kill us both. Why would I do that?"

There was a very long pause where Carson said nothing, just inched his way to his right. "Because I have nothing to lose," he finally said, his voice now eerily calm.

"Look," Daisy whispered. "Beyond the van."

Gideon ripped his eyes from his sister's face. "Erin," he whispered.

Erin crept up from the rear, her weapon in her

hand, but Carson must have heard her because he turned around, trying to look over his shoulder while Rafe edged closer.

Carson roared, lifting Mercy completely off her feet, when he realized that Rafe was now only a few feet away. Mercy was squirming, her mouth wide open on a silent scream. Raising her bound hands to his arm, she was trying to get air.

Gideon put his hand on the door handle, not wanting to distract Rafe or Erin, but unable to watch Mercy suffer.

"Let her go!" Rafe shouted. "You're not escaping this time, Carson. Let her go!"

"Or what?" Carson taunted, still holding Mercy off the ground.

She was writhing now and even from this distance Gideon could see her face getting red. Carson jerked around and saw Erin, who was only a few yards away.

"I said stay back!" he thundered, then crouched about a foot, making himself smaller, sheltering from Erin behind the van. Making Mercy his shield. At least that put both of her feet on the ground again and she no longer gasped for breath.

But neither of the cops had a clear shot.

Then Carson whipped the gun away from Mercy's head long enough to fire two shots at Rafe, the first hitting him in the gun arm, the second in the opposite leg.

Just like Gideon had done, Rafe dropped his gun, his arm hanging limply. But the second shot cut Rafe down. He stumbled to the ground and didn't get up, his leg gushing blood, falling bright on the snow. His uninjured arm alternated between reaching for the gun he'd dropped and putting pressure on his leg.

Enough. Gideon simply could not sit still a second longer. He removed his gun from the holster at his belt and slid it into the waistband at his back so that Carson

wouldn't see it at first glance. He didn't want Carson
to shoot Mercy because he felt cornered, but as soon as
Gideon got a chance, he was putting a bullet in that
monster's bald head.

"I'm sorry," he murmured to Daisy, then got out of
Rafe's Subaru and began walking toward Carson.

Mercy had been struggling to get away, but Carson
quickly returned the gun to her temple and her struggling ceased. Carson's head was against the van, turned
so that he watched the back corner of it, waiting for
Erin. He was looking away from Gideon's approach.

"I know you're back there, Detective Rhee," Carson said. "I want you to throw that gun in my direction
and then I want you to walk toward your partner, but
stay at least six feet away from him. Then lie down on
the ground. Now! Or the next bullet goes in your partner's head and the bullet after that goes in yours." He
screamed the final command and a gun came flying
past the van.

"Good," Carson said, his voice rife with satisfaction, his body maintaining the crouch, protecting his
head. "Keep walking, Rhee."

Erin stepped into Carson's line of sight, a gun in her
hand, shocking him. His gaze flicked to the gun in the
snow, then flicked back. She'd thrown away her backup.

Erin aimed the gun at his head. "Let. Her. Go."

Carson twisted, now fully facing Erin. He was still
crouched so that Mercy was his shield, his gun still at
Mercy's temple.

Gideon heard his sister whimper as he emerged
from the shadow of Erin's Range Rover, its headlights
still illuminating the space.

"Let. Her. Go." Gideon held his good arm out to
show he was empty-handed. "I'm unarmed," he lied.
"Let her go. You know you want me instead."

Carson chuckled. "How sweet. But you're going to
have to do better than that, Reynolds."

Gideon swallowed hard, meeting Mercy's wide eyes, aware of Rafe bleeding. "I'm sorry," he said to Carson. "I'm so very . . . sorry. Please don't hurt her. Take me instead."

‖ PLACERVILLE, CALIFORNIA
‖ TUESDAY, FEBRUARY 21, 4:20 A.M.

Daisy's heart was in her throat, choking her. For a few seconds she watched in shock as Gideon walked into the line of fire.

"Holy mother of God," Frederick murmured.

"What was that, sir?" the 911 operator asked. Frederick had called seconds after Rafe was hit, describing the scene and asking for medical assistance.

"This situation has escalated further," Frederick whispered harshly. "Where the hell is the SWAT team that the Feds supposedly sent?"

Daisy sat frozen in horror, and then her brain rallied. "Hell, no," she spat, scrambling over the bench seat to the back of the Subaru, finding the gun safe Rafe had mentioned. It wasn't a small gun safe. It was long enough for rifles. *Please, please let there be a loaded rifle in here.*

She put in the code—Irina's birthday—then opened the front to find a rifle and two handguns. She took the rifle and gave her father the handgun along with her own cell phone, then slid from the backseat to stand on the ground.

"Call Molina," Daisy told him quietly but urgently. "Her number's in my contacts. Ask her where the fuck the SWAT team is. Ask her where the fuck *she* is."

Keeping the car door open, she rolled the window down and used the frame to balance the rifle. It was too heavy for her to hold. She was tired and her hands were shaking.

"*What* do you think you're doing?" Frederick demanded, still whispering.

"I'm going to finish what I started on Thursday night. I should have taken his gun, not just knocked it away. Call Molina, dammit. *Now.*"

Frederick let out a breath. "Operator, I need to go." He ended the call as the operator was telling him not to. And then he dialed Molina, just as Daisy had asked.

She steadied her hands, trying not to be distracted by her father's conversation with Molina. The woman and her SWAT team would come in time or they wouldn't. *If they don't, I'll do what I have to do.* But when she looked through the rifle's scope, her heart stopped.

Gideon's loud voice carried easily across the field. "You want me to beg?" he asked Carson, his desperation crystal clear. "Fine. I'll beg. Take me instead. Please."

And then Gideon dropped to his knees in front of Carson.

Daisy's terror ratcheted up, even though she recognized Gideon's action as a distraction. At least she hoped so. *Oh God. Please don't die. Please don't die.*

Carson's eyes followed Gideon's downward motion, his chin dipping, his mouth falling open in shock, distracted for a split second—a second that Mercy used to swing her bound hands up in an arc and squeeze Carson's bandaged hand.

The bald man yelped and Mercy made herself dead weight, dropping from his arms and crawling toward Rafe. Erin stepped forward, jabbing her gun at Carson's back.

Erin's clear command carried to the Subaru. "Drop the gun and hands in the air."

Slowly Carson began to lower the gun, then switched speeds, swinging his arm back and firing blindly. Her grunt of pain confirmed a hit. She staggered back, one hand to her chest. She fired once as her body hit the ground, but it went wide.

"Fuck," Frederick said, moving to open his car door.

"Wait," Daisy snapped. "She was wearing a vest."

"She took that point-blank," Frederick argued. "She'll have broken ribs. Or worse."

"She's alive at the moment. Do *not* walk into my line of sight. Where is the SWAT team?"

"Five minutes out and closing. Molina's with them. They have air coverage, too."

"I don't think we have five minutes," Daisy muttered.

Erin lay on her back, gasping for breath, staring straight up at the sky, and Carson lifted his gun to shoot her again. Daisy had him in her scope and started to pull the trigger, but cursed when Gideon drew his weapon from behind his back as he came to his feet and started to rush forward.

Then gasped when Gideon came to an abrupt halt. His gun was pointed at Carson's head. And Carson's gun was aimed at Gideon's. Both held their weapons in their nondominant hands. Neither had the advantage and they stood in stalemate for several painful seconds that felt like years.

Gideon took a step back and Daisy wanted to scream, *One more step back, just one more.* Because the angle was almost perfect. But if Gideon moved forward, even a little, she'd hit him.

Carson smiled at Gideon and it was a terrifying sight. "On your knees, Reynolds," he said quietly. "You're going to die on your knees."

Yes, Daisy thought desperately. *Do it. Please.* But she knew he wouldn't. Gideon might drop to his knees for Mercy, but he wasn't going to die on his knees. She wanted to run to him, but she stood there, holding position, waiting for the right moment. If Carson moved just a foot to the left, she'd have a clear shot.

And then, to Daisy's shock, Gideon began to sink to his knees once again.

Carson laughed, the barrel of his gun following Gideon's descent.

Daisy pulled the trigger.

Carson died laughing.

||| PLACERVILLE, CALIFORNIA
TUESDAY, FEBRUARY 21, 5:13 A.M.

Gideon fell forward on his hands and knees, sucking in as much air as he could.

"Are you okay?"

The question had come from Mercy, who had used Rafe's belt as a tourniquet on his leg. She sat in the snow, Rafe's head in her lap as she put pressure on the wound in his arm.

"Yes. That was too close." He pushed himself to his feet, holstering his own gun and snatching Carson's before checking for the bastard's pulse. Satisfied when he found none, he pulled his own belt off as he walked backward to Rafe, his eyes seeking Daisy. She was in her father's arms.

"She's fine," Frederick called out.

More than fine, Gideon thought as he made his way to Mercy and Rafe, acutely aware that Daisy had saved his life. Just as he'd expected she would. He could have shot Carson, but the man likely would have shot him, too. And if Carson's bullet had felled Gideon first, there would have been no one to protect Mercy, Rafe, and Erin.

Actually, that wasn't true. If Carson had shot him first, Daisy would have taken Carson out without blinking. *But I like the way it worked out a whole lot better.*

He crouched next to Mercy. "Are you all right?"

Mercy nodded. "Throat hurts. Otherwise, unharmed."

He shuddered out a relieved breath. "Good. Use this on his arm," he said, giving her the belt. "I'll be back in a minute. I need to check on Erin."

He jogged to Erin, dialing Molina as he dropped to his knees beside the detective, who was still gasping for air. He put the phone on speaker and set it on the ground. One-handed, he gently pulled at the Velcro that held Erin's bulletproof vest together.

His boss answered on the first ring, and she was angry. "This better be good, Gideon. You have disobeyed every order—"

"You can do what you need to do later," he interrupted. "For now we need to airlift Sokolov and Rhee. He's got two GSWs and both are bleeders. Rhee was hit point-blank in the chest with gunfire. She was wearing a vest but she may have a punctured lung."

"Already on it," Molina said. "Daisy's father called me once you'd engaged in the firefight. But that's all I heard before a weapon discharged and Mr. Dawson hung up. What about Carson Garvey?"

"Dead. Daisy got him with a sniper rifle." He tried to remove the vest, but couldn't do it one-handed and his right hand hadn't yet recovered enough dexterity to be useful. "Frederick!" he called. "I need your hands." Then to his boss. "I need to go. We have wounded." He ended the call and dropped his phone in his pocket.

He'd take his medicine when the time came. He'd do any and all of it again.

Frederick was already dropping to his knees on Erin's other side. He pulled the Velcro straps free and lifted the heavy vest over Erin's head. She nodded her thanks.

"Better," she said, but she was still gasping. "Help Rafe."

Frederick was spreading his coat over Erin's body. "We'll be back."

Daisy was at Rafe's side when Gideon returned and

had covered him with a blanket. "I found it in Rafe's car with a first-aid kit," she said. "I don't know if Erin has one or not."

Frederick began ripping open the packages of gauze and capably packing Rafe's wounds.

"You have medical experience?" Gideon asked him.

"No. Just lived three hours from a doctor for too many years," Frederick said. "I learned the hard way. The good news is," he told Rafe, "the tourniquets have stopped the bleeding. You'll probably have stitches and then be back to causing trouble like Gideon."

That made Rafe smile and Gideon's heart eased a fraction. He'd come too close to losing too much, but they were going to be okay. He'd keep telling himself that.

Frederick seemed to have the first aid under control, so Gideon turned his attention to Daisy, tipping her chin. She was crying. "Adrenaline?" he asked, wiping her cheeks.

She shook her head, then closed her eyes. "I've never killed anyone before. I mean, I'm glad I did it and I'd do it again in a minute, but . . ."

"Daisy," Rafe said hoarsely. "Thank you."

Mercy smiled tremulously. "Yes. Thank you."

"But it's hard," Gideon told her. "The first time and all the times after."

Daisy sobbed harder. "He made you kneel," she cried. "I'm sorry."

Stroking her hair, Gideon laughed, the sound strange in the aftermath. "I knelt the first time because I knew he'd get off on me humiliating myself and be distracted enough so that Erin could take him down. That was my idea, so it was me manipulating him." He leaned back to tilt her chin up again. "You know why I knelt the second time?"

She sniffled. "No. Why?"

"Because I knew you'd have him in your sights."

Her mouth fell open. "Really?"

"Really. And you came through, just like I figured you would."

"He's dead?" Rafe asked, his breathing labored. "You're sure?"

"Very sure," Gideon confirmed. "It was a textbook headshot. But now we won't know where he'd buried the rest of the victims."

"They're all here," Mercy said. "There's an abandoned mine shaft on this property. He brought them there."

"The property belonged to Sydney," Gideon told them. "So that makes sense." He let Daisy go. "I'm going to sit with Erin until the medevac gets here." He kissed her on the forehead. "Thank you, honey."

She nodded, then held out her hand and he pulled her up. Together they walked to where Erin had pushed herself up on her elbows. "I'm glad you didn't listen to me," she said quietly. "Rafe would have died if we hadn't had help." She nodded at Carson's body. "He might have killed us all." She tilted her head. "Sirens. Thank God."

The first vehicle to arrive was a black sedan and Gideon was unsurprised to see Molina get out of the back. She walked over to them, her gaze taking in the rifle propped against the Subaru and the killer's body on the ground.

She stopped where Gideon and Daisy sat with Erin. "Special Agent Reynolds."

Gideon nodded. "Special Agent in Charge Molina."

Her jaw was tight and anger sparked in her eyes. "There will be consequences."

"I know," Gideon said simply. "But I'd do it again. Mercy is my sister. Rafe is my brother. And Erin, even though she really did try to keep us away, is grateful."

Molina rolled her eyes. "We'll talk tomorrow, Gideon. Daisy, well done. Thank you."

KAREN ROSE

Daisy blinked. "Can't say that it was my pleasure, ma'am, but you're welcome."

Molina nodded, then sniffed at the air. "His burial ground?"

"Yes." Gideon had been too revved up to smell it before, but he could detect the odor of death now. *One of those bodies is Eileen.* "We're going to have to bring them out."

Molina rested her hand on his good shoulder. "Someone will. But it doesn't have to be you. And it doesn't have to be now." She looked up when the sound of helicopter blades got louder. "Call me tomorrow, Gideon. We'll talk. Today, take care of your friends and yourself."

THIRTY-TWO

Do you need anything else?" Daisy asked as she plumped Rafe's pillows. He had more color in his face than he'd had the day before, but he was far from back to normal.

His smile was a weary one. "I'm fine. Just tired. Need to sleep."

He'd been released from the hospital that morning and—against all wheedling, nagging attempts by his mother—had chosen to recover at his Midtown Victorian rather than the Sokolov house, saying he'd never get any sleep at his parents' house. The stairs would have made it impossible to get to his own apartment on the top floor, so he was using Daisy's studio for the time being. Irina had moved into Rafe's apartment so that she could be close and Sasha was just one floor above, so he wasn't truly alone.

That left Daisy temporarily displaced, but she wasn't upset by this. She was staying with Gideon, first at the Sokolovs', but starting tonight at his house. Just for the time being. They'd go back to normal soon, but time with Gideon was what she needed right now.

"Okay." She kissed his forehead. "Your mom's napping, but she has one of the baby monitors with her and the other is at Sasha's. Gideon and Mercy and I will be in Sasha's place for a while, so yell if you need anything. We'll check on you before we leave."

He closed his eyes, nearly asleep already. "I love you, DD, but you're hovering. Go away, please and thank you."

She laughed softly, unoffended. It was fair. They'd all hovered over him, shocked by how close they'd come to losing him. "Okay. Going away now."

She crept from the studio and climbed the stairs to Sasha's apartment, where Gideon and Mercy sat waiting in front of Gideon's open laptop. Sasha had gone back to work but had invited Mercy to use her guest bedroom while she was visiting. Gideon had been a bit disappointed by this but had understood Mercy's need for space.

"He's asleep," Daisy told them. "Are we ready?"

Gideon and Mercy both nodded, their expressions identically grim. Sitting side by side, it was easy to see the resemblance. Same dark hair, same green eyes. Mercy didn't have the silver in her hair, but her eyes seemed much older than his.

"Skype's set up," Gideon said. "We're waiting for Agent Dabney to call."

Dabney was Gideon's colleague in the San Diego field office. He was also the one to have made contact with Lawton Malloy, the university swimmer who had the almost-Eden tattoo. Gideon hadn't been able to travel south and Lawton was in the middle of exams and couldn't come north, so they'd decided to video chat.

Cuddling Brutus in her lap because she suspected she was going to need her, Daisy sat next to Gideon and took his hand. "Whatever he says, we'll deal with it."

"I know." He pressed a kiss to her temple. "Thanks for being here."

Daisy squeezed his hand in answer and together the three of them waited in silence.

The call came in at two sharp. Gideon accepted and

the screen came to life, revealing a fiftyish man in a black suit, who had to be Agent Dabney, sitting next to the young swimmer Daisy had found during her search for the Eden tattoo. He wore a shirt and tie, his hair neatly combed. And his eyes full of apprehension.

"Gideon," Agent Dabney said warmly. "I hear you've had some excitement up there."

Gideon huffed a tired chuckle. "You could say that. Thanks for setting this up. This is my sister, Mercy Callahan, and my girlfriend, Daisy Dawson. Daisy ran the original search that led us to you, Mr. Malloy."

Lawton Malloy's smile was a bit fractured. "I was surprised to hear from the FBI."

"I imagine so," Gideon murmured. "Thank you for talking to us. How much has Agent Dabney told you?"

"Not much. Just that you saw my tattoo and wanted to talk to me about it. Why do you want to know? It's not a gang thing, if that's what you're thinking."

Gideon and Mercy shared a glance and Mercy gave him a tight nod of permission.

"We know what it means. Because I had a tattoo very similar to yours, Lawton."

Neither Lawton nor Agent Dabney could hide his shock. Dabney said nothing, but Lawton gasped, "What? Where?"

"Same place as yours, but I had it covered with another tattoo when I was eighteen. It represented very bad memories. It was given to me against my will."

Lawton's eyes were still wide. "So you came from . . . from Eden?"

Mercy flinched at the name. Gideon didn't flinch but his left eye twitched. His tell. "Yes, I did," Gideon answered, then gestured between himself and Mercy. "We both did."

Lawton's eyes unexpectedly filled with tears. "He thought he was the only one."

"Who did you know who got out?" Mercy asked softly.

"Levi." Lawton's throat worked as he tried to swallow. "His name was Levi Hull."

Mercy sucked in a sharp breath. "Levi?"

Lawton nodded, swiping at his eyes with the heels of his hands. "He . . ." He shuddered out a breath. "Levi killed himself a year ago."

Oh no. Daisy's heart squeezed painfully.

Gideon closed his eyes briefly. Mercy paled. Gideon recovered first and cleared his throat. "You were friends?"

Lawton nodded, wiping away new tears. "More than friends. At least we wanted to be. But that place . . . It fucked with his head. Pardon my language. I'm sorry."

"It's all right," Gideon murmured. "Eden, you mean?"

"Eden," Lawton spat, as if the word left a bitter taste in his mouth. He blinked his tears away, his eyes now burning with unfettered fury. "They preached that homosexuality was a sin, but the men were fucking thirteen-year-old boys."

Gideon went still. He opened his mouth, then closed it again.

Mercy turned to stare at his profile, dawning realization and horror on her face. "Gideon?" she whispered.

She hadn't known. Daisy didn't know what to say. What to do. *Mercy hadn't known why Gideon ran away.*

Gideon shook his head tightly, his gaze locked on the screen. "I got away. But it was close. I guess Levi wasn't so lucky."

Lawton's head shake was slow and incredibly sad. "No. He wasn't."

"How did you meet him?" Daisy asked when Gideon and Mercy fell silent.

"In high school. I'm from L.A. Levi came to live with his uncle when we were fifteen. My mom and his uncle's wife were friends and thought I'd be good for Levi. You know, to introduce him around and hang out. We got along and then we were inseparable. Lawton and Levi." The tears were flowing down his face. "Friends forever."

Daisy smiled gently at him. "And then more than friends."

"Yeah," Lawton said hoarsely. "But Levi had so many demons. He wanted a life with me, but all that Eden shit kept coming back and back and back. He was two steps forward and three steps back, y'know?"

Daisy nodded sadly. "I know."

"And then I got a swimming scholarship," he said miserably. "Levi had been on the team with me until senior year. I didn't know why he dropped out, but then one day I surprised him in his room when he was changing his shirt. He had scars from cutting and fresh track marks. He hadn't wanted anyone to know. That's why he quit swimming. Well, that and he would have failed drug tests in competition. I tried to get him help. Tried to get him therapy. His uncle did, too. But Levi wouldn't go. He was afraid the therapist would get him to tell his secrets and then he'd spill about Eden. It was the first I heard of it and he made me promise to never tell." He looked away. "So I didn't."

Daisy knew that feeling. She hadn't been able to fully open up in therapy during rehab, either. She'd feared divulging their family's secret—that they were in hiding and feared Taylor's biological father. So she'd said very, very little.

She glanced at Gideon, who wore the same far-gone expression that he had the night they'd first met, when he'd blurted out that the man in Eileen's wedding photo was dead.

"Gideon?" she murmured.

He nodded, acknowledging that he'd heard her, but said nothing. Neither did Mercy.

All right then. "Whatever happened or didn't happen wasn't your fault, Lawton," Daisy said, not expecting her words to make a difference, but Lawton surprised her.

"I know. It's the fault of the bastards who hurt him and all the others who looked the other way. But Levi was the one who suffered. And so did we."

"Did his uncle know?" Daisy asked.

"No. His uncle was told that Levi had been abandoned into the system and Levi didn't set the story straight. He told me later, when it all came out, that he couldn't tell his uncle because his uncle would go hunting for Eden and that his mother would be punished, because 'they'd' know. So he never told anyone. Only me."

Gideon abruptly straightened in his seat. "How did he get away?"

"His mother smuggled him out on some kind of supply truck. He finally told her what was going on and she cried. She gave him her brother's name, then paid the driver to get him out and drop him off at a bus station."

She paid the driver, Daisy thought bitterly. Gideon's mother had paid with her body. It was likely that Levi's had done the same.

"Which station?" Gideon asked.

"The one in Medford, Oregon," Lawton said.

"It's about the same driving time from Macdoel as is the Redding bus station," Daisy murmured.

Gideon nodded that he'd heard her, but his eyes were locked on the young man on-screen. "And his mother?"

Lawton shook his head. "She had other kids. She couldn't leave them."

Gideon and Mercy shared a long glance. Mercy let out a slow breath. "We know that story," she said in that still way she had. "I was the child my mother had to stay for."

Gideon's shoulders slumped sorrowfully. "Mercy," he whispered.

"But it's true," Mercy said.

Daisy's heart hurt for Mercy. *What a burden that has to be.*

Lawton looked equally affected. "God, I'm sorry."

"Thank you," Mercy said. "I remember Levi. He was eight or nine when I left, a really sweet little boy." One side of her mouth lifted. "I used to watch him and some of the other kids when the mothers did sewing circle or Bible study. He loved flowers."

Lawton smiled tremulously. "He wanted to be a botanist. He never got the chance."

"Did you go to college together?" Daisy asked.

"No. He graduated, but his grades were poor. He'd missed a lot of schooling growing up in Eden. The drugs had gotten bad, too, so that wasn't helping. When I got my scholarship, I almost said no. I wanted to stay home and take care of him, but he wouldn't let me. He pushed me to go. Came to my meets. Cheered me on." Lawton closed his eyes, visibly steeling himself. "Then he hanged himself from a tree in his uncle's backyard."

There was silence until Agent Dabney broke it with a heavy sigh. He hadn't said a word throughout, just listened, his expression pained. "Does your involvement here indicate that the Bureau is reopening the Eden investigation?"

Lawton's eyes grew wide. "Wait. You mean the government knows about these assholes and hasn't stopped them?"

"That's complicated," Gideon said. "I reported them when I first joined the Bureau and the FBI searched for the community, but the leaders of Eden are very good at hiding themselves. I've been assigned to lead the investigation now that we have some new evidence. We've been a little busy with a serial killer the past week, but now that it's been resolved, I'll be focusing all my time on finding them. Lawton, if you could provide the name and address for Levi's uncle, that would be helpful."

Lawton's mouth thinned. "He died, too. He had a heart problem, and finding Levi's body hanging like that was the kicker. He and Levi didn't get along. His uncle couldn't understand why he'd turned to drugs. He threw Levi out a few weeks before the suicide."

Gideon's jaw clenched and he nodded. "I understand. Thank you, Lawton, for talking to us. Please let me know if you remember anything else."

"I will." His eyes narrowed, glinting with hatred. "I hope you fry their asses. I hope they go to prison and find out how Levi felt."

Amen, Daisy thought, the viciousness of her own thought taking her breath away.

Dabney and Gideon ended the call and the three of them sat quietly.

"Goddammit," Gideon breathed.

Mercy sighed. "What now, Gideon?"

"We keep looking for others who've gotten out." He closed his laptop. "And we have the wedding photos. Edward McPhearson and Ephraim Burton had to have come from somewhere. Hard to believe that men that evil weren't cruel to others before arriving in Eden."

The flicker of true fear in Mercy's eyes was gone so quickly that Daisy wondered if she'd imagined it. Daisy opened her mouth to ask, then closed it when Mercy shot her an imploring look. *Don't ask. Please.*

So Daisy kept the question to herself. And wondered.

"But we have somewhere to go right now," Gideon went on, seemingly oblivious to the silent conversation she and Mercy had shared.

Mercy's smile was wan. "On a date, I hope."

Daisy put Brutus in her bag. "Well, maybe after. I'm going to a meeting. Gideon will wait outside, worrying about me, and then hopefully there will be dinner."

Mercy was frowning. "A meeting? Like a neighborhood meeting?"

Daisy hadn't realized that Mercy didn't know. "No, an AA meeting. Mercy, I'm a recovering alcoholic. Eight years sober," she added when Mercy's eyes widened.

But all Mercy said was, "Have a good time."

"You're welcome to come with us," Daisy offered. "You can keep Gideon company while he paces outside the community center."

"No, thanks. I think I'll go sit with Rafe a bit."

Gideon looked like he wanted to kiss Mercy's cheek, but she pulled away. Schooling his features, Gideon hid his hurt and tried to smile at her. "We'll see you later."

Mercy swallowed hard. "I'm sorry," she whispered.

Gideon stilled. "For what?"

"I can't be touched. It's . . . It's not you, okay?"

"Okay," he said gently. "I get it."

He held the door open for Daisy, not saying a word until they stood outside on her front porch. "She didn't know," he whispered.

He didn't have to clarify. That Mercy hadn't known why he'd escaped was at the top of Daisy's mind, too. "I know. Look, I'm perfectly capable of getting myself to the community center. You can stay here and really talk to her. I know you've been wanting to."

He sighed. "She said she came to talk, but every

time I've tried to start a conversation, she finds something else to do. I figure I'll just wait for her to come to me."

"That's probably for the best." She wrapped her arms around him because he looked like he needed it. He drew her close and rested his cheek on top of her head.

"No wonder she resented me." His voice broke. "She thought I ran off just because I hated it there, leaving Mama to be abused for years."

"I know," she soothed. "Give her time, Gideon."

"I'm trying."

"I know, baby." She stepped back, taking his hand. "I need to go or I'll be late."

He drew a breath and nodded once. "Let's go. Where are we going for dinner afterward?"

She swallowed hard. "Trish and I used to go to this dive. The Forty-niner Diner."

"Would you like to go there?" he asked gently.

She'd been debating it all day but had realized it was what Trish would want her to do. "Yeah. I think I would. I might even have an extra ice cream sundae for Trish."

He squeezed her hand and led her to the sidewalk. "Forty-niner Diner it is."

SACRAMENTO, CALIFORNIA
THURSDAY, FEBRUARY 23, 10:30 P.M.

"I like your house," Daisy said, running her hand over the marble countertop in Gideon's kitchen. The house had clean lines, the decor very simple yet masculine. Very Gideon.

It was the first time she'd been in his house. They'd been staying over at Karl and Irina's, in Sasha's old room, which had a queen bed, so they didn't roll onto the floor. Daisy had wanted to spend as much time with her father as she could before he returned to Maryland. Her father, to his credit, had barely lifted an eyebrow when she'd stated that she and Gideon would be sharing a room.

Karl had told her later that her father was choosing his battles. Daisy could live with that. Especially since they hadn't done anything more than hold each other and sleep.

But tonight, she wanted some alone time with Gideon. She knew that he needed it, too, especially after the afternoon they'd had. Her heart broke every time she remembered the look on Mercy's face when she realized the truth about Gideon's departure from Eden.

But she wasn't going to think about that now, because Gideon was smiling at her from where he leaned against the doorjamb, watching her explore. "I'm glad," he said, "but I have to admit to being a little jealous of my countertop."

She looked down at her hand rubbing the countertop and chuckled. "No need to be. *It* doesn't do anything interesting when I rub it."

He threw back his head and laughed. "God. Daisy."

She feigned innocence. "What?"

He shook his head, still smiling. "You're . . . absolutely perfect."

"Not really." She gladly gave up rubbing the marble to wrap her arms around his neck. "But I'm awfully glad you think so." She kissed him, quick and fast. A teasing peck. "So I've seen this floor. What else is there to see?"

"The bathroom I just finished. The tile has sparkles."

She grinned. "Sparkles? Really?"

"Irina picked it out."

"And did she help decorate your bedroom, too?"

"No," he murmured, kissing her for real, deep and wet, until her toes curled. "The bedroom is all mine," he whispered against her lips, suddenly serious. "Wanna see it?"

"Thought you'd never ask," she whispered back.

Taking her hand, he led her up the stairs and through the door at the end of the upstairs hallway. The bed was the first thing she saw—king-sized, with the sheets turned down. The second thing she saw was the accent wall behind the bed. The rest of the walls were a pearl gray, but the wall behind the bed was a specific shade of blue.

"It matches my eyes," Daisy murmured.

"I noticed that." Standing at her back, Gideon slid his good arm around her waist. "I thought it was a good omen, since I picked that color myself."

He thrust his hips ever so slightly, so that she felt the brush of his erection. He was hard and ready.

She was ready, too. They'd been doing a teasing dance since dinner, lighthearted with the hint of what was to come. But it was past time. Going to the community center without Trish on Thursday night seemed alien and wrong, and most of their AA group had burst into tears at some point during the meeting. It had been utterly draining. She needed this.

She needed him.

She turned in his arms, looping her arms around his neck again. "We're due a good omen or two." She loosened his sling and slipped it off so that she could get to the buttons of his shirt, impatiently pulling them free. But when she pushed the shirt from his shoulders, it was slowly and with care because he was far from being healed.

As soon as his chest was bare, she ran her hands over the hard planes, lightly tracing the outline of his phoenix tattoo. His belt was next and within seconds, his pants and boxer briefs were on the floor and he was gloriously naked. Stepping back, she looked her fill, up and down and everything in between. He was a truly beautiful man.

She started to walk around him, suddenly aware that she'd never seen him from behind. His hand shot out to grip her arm, startling her. Her eyes flew up to meet his.

Where there had been joy and lust, she now saw apprehension.

"What is it?" she whispered.

He drew a breath. "I have scars. On my back. Just . . . be prepared. Okay?"

She nodded soberly and he let her go. Cautious now, she moved around him, grateful he'd warned her. Not because she was horrified. Not because he was ugly.

But the scars were . . . extreme. Had he not warned her, she might have reacted simply out of shock. And rage.

She'd known he'd been beaten, but she thought he'd meant with fists. Not this.

They'd done this to him. *Hurt him.* There were gouges and stripes on his back and the backs of his legs, like they'd used whips and knives. On a thirteen-year-old boy. On his birthday. After he'd already fended off a pedophile.

His shoulders had tensed, waiting for her reaction, making her heart break yet again. She slipped her arms around his waist, laying her cheek against his back. The scars weren't raised, and most had faded, but still they . . . *existed.*

She swallowed hard, praying she'd say the right thing. "I'm so angry right now," she whispered. "They put their hands on you. They hurt you. I want to find them and I want to . . . well, I want to do things that I probably shouldn't confess to a federal agent."

His shoulders relaxed and he chuckled. "You are a bloodthirsty woman."

Sheer relief had her eyes stinging. "I protect what's mine, Gideon. Just like you do." She kissed a line across his back, then traced the worst of the scars with her fingertips. "If you're worried that I'm . . ." She trailed off, not sure which word to use.

"Repulsed?" he asked quietly.

Now she was horrified. "*I'm not.* The scars are part of you and you are beautiful. No 'buts.'" She reconsidered that statement as she studied his perfect ass. "Except for your butt, of course, which is a work of art."

He snorted, shaking his head, and she knew they'd be all right. She came back around to face him. "Put the worries from your mind, Gideon. There is nothing about your body that doesn't turn me on."

He hesitated. "I've never allowed a woman to see my back."

Her eyes widened. "Never?"

His face flushed. "No. I didn't trust any of them, I guess. They'd want to know what happened and it wasn't anything I wanted to share."

But he'd trusted her with it all. The stinging in her eyes returned and she struggled to find the perfect tone. "That means I'm the first to ever see your ass?"

His lips twitched. "Yes."

"Then this makes me happy." She lifted an eyebrow. "Wanna see mine?"

He took a step forward, palming her butt with his left hand. "I absolutely do. Why am I naked while you're completely dressed?"

She smiled cheekily. "I am easily distracted. I may need direction."

His kiss took her breath away. "Take off your clothes, Daisy," he growled, all levity gone. He was serious. A man on a mission. It gave her the best kind of shivers.

She complied, then pointed to the unfinished tattoo on her ass cheek. "See? Brutus."

"I see. I also see a tattoo that I'd prefer you not have filled in."

She blinked, surprised. He was completely serious. "Why?"

"Because I protect what's mine and I don't want a tattoo artist seeing your butt."

She might have bristled had the request come from anyone else. "Okay."

He blinked this time. "Really?"

"Yes. It's a reasonable request."

He cupped her breast and the thread of the conversation frayed as she made a needy, greedy sound. "And if I requested that you get in my bed?" he asked silkily.

She lifted on her toes to kiss him, humming at the simple pleasure of rubbing her breasts against the hair of his chest. She cupped the back of his neck with one hand and stroked his erection with the other, making him groan.

"A *very* reasonable request, but considering I'm going to be doing most of the work while you don't use your arm, you should probably get in first."

His eyes flashed, dark and hot, and he walked her backward until they reached the bed. He let her go long enough to lie back against the pillows. "Come here."

She knelt by his head, laying out her plan in her mind to make sure she could do what she wanted without hurting him. She leaned in for another kiss that left her panting. "I'm wondering if you can make me come without using your hands at all."

His nostrils flared, his jaw going taut. "Come. Here."

Heart pounding in anticipation, she straddled him, placing a knee on either side of his head, checking to be sure that she was nowhere near his shoulder. She'd planned to tease him a little, but he shocked her by lifting his head from the pillow and stabbing into her with his tongue.

Stifling a scream, she reached for the headboard and lowered her body so that she could ride his mouth. Then let herself go. She didn't last long.

Her orgasm was swift and sharp and she leaned into the headboard for support as she caught her breath. *"Gideon."*

He wore a smug smile when she finally got the energy and coordination to swing her leg over his head and slide down beside him. "Well?" he asked.

She could only blink at him. "I want to do that again when my brain stops spinning."

He rolled to his side, his lips still shiny and wet. "I want to see if you can ride my cock the way you rode my mouth."

Her hips gave an involuntary jerk. "Oh God." It was part moan, part laugh. "Yes, please and thank you."

SACRAMENTO, CALIFORNIA
FRIDAY, FEBRUARY 24, 3:10 P.M.

"She looks okay," Frederick said, his gaze locked on his daughter as she and an older woman milled among the people who'd come to Trish's memorial service.

It had been a difficult service. There'd been stories about Trish, some sweet, some funny, and others definitely not safe for work. There had been some laughter, but mostly there had been sadness and tears. So many tears.

Frederick turned to Gideon. "Is she okay?"

Gideon wasn't sure how to answer that. Right now, Daisy wasn't okay. She was grieving so many things—the loss of Trish, the thirty other women who'd died at

Carson's hand, the fact that she'd killed a man—even one who'd needed to be killed—and the time she and her family had lost because no one helped Frederick with his PTSD years ago.

But she'd be okay. Gideon was certain about that. So he went with that, because it answered the question Frederick was really asking—was Daisy's sobriety at risk? "She will be. She's going to meetings and she'll continue using all the coping tools she's honed over the past eight years that she's been sober. You've raised a strong woman, Frederick."

"I know," Frederick murmured. "She's stronger than I am, that's for damn sure."

Gideon wasn't sure how to answer that, either, because he thought Frederick was right. So he told the truth. "She forgives you."

The sudden catch in Frederick's breath sounded suspiciously like a quelled sob and told him that he'd chosen the right words.

"You can forgive yourself now," Gideon added quietly. "Although I know that's easier said than done." Because he wasn't sure he'd ever forgive himself for what happened to Mercy and their mother. *It wasn't my fault.* But it was still so hard.

"That's the truth," Frederick muttered, then turned his head to where Sasha, Mercy, and Rafe sat off to the side all by themselves in the crowded room. Rafe was in a wheelchair because he'd been determined to be there, partly for Daisy, but mostly for Sasha, who sat, quiet and too subdued. She'd be okay, too, but it might take a while.

"Your sister gonna stay?" Frederick asked.

Gideon's stomach clenched at the reality of the Mercy situation. "Not much longer. She only took a week of vacation." And there was still so much to say.

"She'll be back," Frederick said, sounding sure. "Give her time."

"That's what Daisy keeps saying."

Frederick's mouth curved. "Listen to her. She's wise. Oh, look. Miss Jones came."

Both he and Gideon stood when Zandra Jones approached with an older couple that Gideon assumed were her parents. "It was nice of you to come," Gideon said to Zandra. "I know Daisy appreciates it."

"It was the least I could do," Zandra said. "I wanted to introduce you to my parents, Mr. and Mrs. Jones. Mom, Dad, Mr. Dawson and Special Agent Reynolds saved my life."

Mr. Jones pumped their hands and Mrs. Jones hugged them, crying unapologetically. "Thank you," they said, making Gideon feel both amazing and embarrassed at once.

"It was really the dog," Gideon said.

Zandra's eyes lit up. "Abercrombie. That's the name he had when he was Janice Fiddler's. Her family wants me to keep him. He's going home with me tomorrow."

"That's good," Gideon said. "I'll let Agent Hunter know. He was worried."

"Tell him that the dog will be treated like a king," Mr. Jones said.

Zandra nodded, then sobered. "I wanted to tell Daisy something I remembered, but I'm not sure this is the time." She quickly looked over her shoulder to where Daisy was still greeting people up front, before leaning in to whisper. "He was muttering about Trish one of the times he . . ." She made a vague motion at her midsection, then patted her mother's arm when the older lady made a pained noise. "Anyway, he kept saying I was stubborn like Trish. If she'd just told him where Daisy lived she could have made her punishment easier. I got the impression that he tortured Trish, but she kept saying she didn't know where Daisy lived. She died protecting Daisy. I don't know if that will make Daisy feel better or not. I mean, he obviously figured out where she lived somehow, but not from Trish."

Gideon expelled his breath in a rush. The guilt that would heap on Daisy's head was too huge to fathom. "God, I don't think she needs to know that right now. But thank you for telling me. We'll play it by ear."

Zandra nodded. "That's what I figured. Well, thank you again."

When the Jones family was gone, Frederick shuddered. "Don't tell her. Ever."

"I won't. At least not until she's ready to hear it. Which might be never."

Daisy approached then, arm in arm with the older woman she'd been talking to. Both had red noses and puffy eyes, having shed their share of tears. "Dad, Gideon, this is Rosemary, my sponsor."

"You're her dad," Rosemary said to Frederick, then turned to Gideon, her brows hiked to the top of her forehead. "And I've heard *all* about *you*, Gideon."

Gideon felt his cheeks heat, but Daisy chuckled. "It's nice to meet you," he managed.

"Likewise," Rosemary said with a hint of a smile. "We're just so proud of Daisy, Mr. Dawson. She's quite the hero. All the things she's done this week. I wouldn't have been so brave or kept my wits together."

Frederick tilted Daisy's chin so that she looked at him. "Not just this week. She's been brave for the past eight years, staying sober while enduring hardships that would have broken someone weaker. I'm very proud of her, too. I know when I go home that I have nothing to worry about here."

Daisy's eyes grew wide, then bright with tears. "Darn it, Dad. I can't cry anymore." She leaned up and kissed his cheek. "Thank you. That was exactly what I needed to hear."

Gideon felt his heart settle, just a little. Daisy and her dad would be okay, too. He held his hand out to Daisy. "Are you about ready to go? We need to be meeting Molina in an hour and we're going to hit traffic."

Frederick looked surprised. "I thought you were on suspension."

Gideon shrugged. Molina had ultimately been glad that he'd been at the abandoned mine that night, but he had disobeyed her orders. Multiple times. "I got a week's suspension without pay to be served concurrent with my paid medical leave for the arm. So I have a mark on my record, but it won't affect my salary. It was the best my boss could do."

Daisy frowned. "No, she could and *should* have given you a raise and a plaque for your wall *and* a better parking place."

He laughed. "I'll let you ask her for those things. I think she likes you best."

SACRAMENTO, CALIFORNIA
FRIDAY, FEBRUARY 24, 3:35 P.M.

Traffic was heavy so Daisy and Gideon arrived a few minutes late. Gideon's boss sat behind her desk, the curtains drawn to reveal the Sierra Nevada in the distance.

"Please, come in and sit down," Agent Molina said. "I thought you'd want some of the blanks in the Carson Garvey case to be filled in. First of all, we've begun retrieving the remains from the burial ground in Placerville." Her expression softened. "The first body we encountered was Eileen's."

Swallowing hard, Gideon nodded. "You've positively identified her?"

"Yes. Gale Danton up in Macdoel provided us with

items she'd used while staying with them—a hairbrush, toothbrush. We were able to confirm with DNA."

"That was fast," Gideon said, his voice a little hoarse.

"We've made the identification of Garvey's victims our highest priority. I assumed you'd want to receive her remains," Molina added gently.

Gideon jerked another nod. "I'll take her ashes, thank you."

"I'll complete the paperwork for you. You should receive her ashes by the middle of next week. Now, on to the debrief. When we searched Carson's house, we found a treasure trove. So thank you, Agent Reynolds, for saving the house. We found piles of photos under the bed. Carson had apparently been gathering black-mail material on his father, Paul Garvey, for some time. There were photos of his father with mistresses with varying degrees of sexual content. There were also photos of his father with known Mexican cartel members."

"He was running drugs in his planes," Gideon murmured.

"Exactly. This enabled us to get a warrant for Paul Garvey's home and office. We'll be going through those financials for a long time." She hesitated. "We also found his wife's collection of videos. They were . . . difficult to view."

"Carson and Sydney?" Daisy asked.

Molina nodded. "Starting when he was twelve years old. I won't go into detail, but the recording dates are significant. We've matched his flight itineraries with the places and times that each of his thirty-one victims disappeared. Not every video resulted in a disappearance, but before every disappearance there was a video."

Daisy's stomach turned over. "So sex with Sydney was his trigger."

"Essentially yes. There was a six-month gap in the videos when Carson was eighteen. That matches the time frame that his father took Sydney on a six-month European trip. Sydney made a video within three days of her return home. The first of Carson's victims was found the next day. After that, he averaged two victims a year for the first seven years. Last year he killed six."

Daisy did the math. "He killed eleven women in the last year?"

"Yes. And that doesn't include the truck owner in Macdoel or the nurse."

"Or Sydney," Gideon muttered.

"Or Sydney," Molina agreed.

"What changed?" Daisy asked.

"Paul Garvey started traveling more. He was gone for long periods of time." She lifted a shoulder. "Sydney was bored."

"I'm so glad she's dead," Daisy said. "Didn't the father suspect anything?"

"About the abuse? I talked to him this morning and I don't think so. He says he knew Sydney had affairs. He vociferously denied knowing she'd abused his son. He seemed surprised to learn that his son was planning to blackmail him. He didn't know that Carson possessed the initiative to amass so much information."

"Why was his son planning to blackmail him?" Gideon asked.

"One of the reasons that Paul Garvey traveled so much this year was that he was setting up the sale of his charter service," Molina said. "His employees— including Carson—were understandably upset by this. He thinks Carson may have been planning to use his material to keep him from selling."

"Carson used the planes to transport his victims,"

Daisy said. "He didn't want to lose his access to that freedom."

Molina nodded. "I agree. But what Carson didn't know was that the sale was going through, regardless. The other reason Paul was traveling was that he was seeing an oncologist in San Francisco. He has stage four colon cancer. He sold the company because he knew his son or wife would destroy it. The sale of the company is important, again, because of the date. The word came down last Thursday."

"The day he attacked Trish and me," Daisy said.

"Yes. It was the first time there was a victim abducted locally—or in this case attempted abduction, because you got away, Miss Dawson. We think it was the only time he used the stocking mask. He was so worked up about the sale of the company and he'd received a number of provocative messages from Sydney. When he didn't respond the way she wanted, she sent him stills from the videos she'd taken. In every case she hammered him until he apologized."

Gideon sighed. "Say you're sorry."

Molina nodded. "Yes. After his failed attempt on Miss Dawson, where we know now he really wanted Miss Hart, he took Kaley Martell. The next day he flew to Vail, where he took Zandra from the bar. He took most of his victims from bars, actually. The one victim abduction that puzzled me was the victim he took from the Barry Manilow concert after they'd argued about her standing in front of his seat. But then we found a stack of old vinyl albums, all by Barry Manilow. Mr. Garvey was able to shine light on this. He said his first wife was a big fan and played the albums all the time. Carson would sing with her before she died, and sat playing the albums afterward. Then Mr. Garvey married Sydney. He seemed pretty broken up over the videos of her abuse."

"At least there's that," Daisy said bitterly.

"The last thing he said was that the property that Carson used as his burial ground will belong to him—the father, I mean. Sydney left it to him. He's going to sell it and donate the proceeds to a victim compensation fund. I personally think he did that to curry favor with the DA over the drug charges, but victims' families get the money in any case." She looked over her list. "That's all I have. If you don't have questions, you're free to go."

Daisy regarded her levelly, then thought, *Why the hell not?* "I have a question. When will the Bureau reward Agent Reynolds—"

Gideon was on his feet, his expression one of exasperated disbelief. *"Daisy."*

Daisy arched a brow. "You said I should ask."

Daisy swore she saw Molina smile. Just a little.

"I wasn't serious." He held out his hand. "Come on. If I'm on suspension, I don't want to stay here." He pulled her to her feet, then turned back to his boss, sobering. "Thank you for the information, ma'am. We'll be going now."

Gideon marched her toward the rental car his insurance company had provided because the engine in his Camry had to be completely replaced after Carson poured bleach in the gas tank while they'd been talking to Gale Danton in Macdoel.

When they got to the car, he pressed her up against the door. She looked up at him, smiling. "What?"

He laughed. "You . . ." He shook his head. "Thank you. For being willing to ask."

"I still think—"

He cut her off with a kiss that silenced all thoughts. When he lifted his head, she sighed. "I've forgotten what I was going to say. You scrambled my brain."

"You shouldn't have told me that. Now I'll kiss you every time you argue."

She cupped his face, her heart lighter than it had been in days. Maybe ever. "Then I'll have to argue with you often."

"I'm looking forward to it."

EPILOGUE

Gideon pushed away from the wall where he'd been leaning when Daisy came through security in the field office lobby. The guard reached for her bag, giving a blink of surprise when she pulled Brutus out. She cuddled the dog under her chin as she walked through the metal detector, then gave the guard a smile and a "good morning."

Nobody would have guessed that she'd been up at four A.M. after a restless night. Nobody except Gideon, who'd held her when she'd woken around midnight, screaming from a nightmare that had been a near-nightly occurrence. She normally dreamed of finding Trish's body, but last night's horror had featured her father and the torture he'd endured as a POW. That was all she'd been able to get out.

He figured it was tied to the therapy session she'd had the afternoon before—her first. She'd found a therapist and had begun working through the remaining anger she felt at her father for the way he'd dragged them into isolation. That they'd dropped Frederick at the airport on their way to the therapy appointment probably hadn't helped. It had been a teary scene at departures with both Frederick and Daisy completely losing it. Poor Brutus had been petted nearly bald on the drive away from the airport, but the dog just did her job, distracting her before her tears gave way to an anxiety attack and giving Daisy comfort.

A job Gideon now shared. He smiled down at her when she stopped in front of him. "You sounded good this morning," he said.

Blond brows winged up. "You listened to the show?"

"Bits and pieces." Which was a fib. He'd listened to the whole thing so that he could evaluate the DJ who Karl had brought in to replace TNT. The new guy was there on trial. If Karl liked him and, more importantly, if *Daisy* liked him, he'd be offered the job.

"Liar," she said softly. "Did Jack pass muster?"

He laughed, leading her to the elevator. "He did. I reserve the right to change my mind, but so far, so good."

Daisy punched the UP button. "Did you get it?"

Sobering, he nodded, knowing what she was asking. "I did." The funeral home had called to let him know Eileen's remains were ready and he'd picked them up while Daisy had been in the studio. "I also called Mr. Danton. He said it was fine for us to come up this afternoon." Because they'd agreed to release Eileen's ashes in the one place she'd encountered kindness.

"I was sure he would." When they were in the elevator, she gave Brutus a kiss on the top of her head, put her back in the bag, then leaned up and kissed Gideon's cheek. "What's this meeting with Molina about?"

Since he was technically still on suspension, he knew it wasn't about his everyday job. "I think she has news on the search I asked her to run on Eileen's wedding photos."

"Well, good. It's about time."

He bit back a smile. "Don't say that to her, please."

Daisy gave an exaggerated sigh. "I'll try to behave. Who else will be there?"

"Rafe." Who was recovering well but still wasn't supposed to be putting any weight on his leg. He'd arrived in a wheelchair, pushed by none other than

Mercy. "And Mercy. I'm not sure if she's here as my sister, and so connected to the case, or as Rafe's personal assistant." Because the two had spent a lot of time together since everything had gone down at Carson's burial ground. Sasha had to work, so Mercy had shared shifts with Irina, the two making sure that Rafe was well cared for.

Daisy tilted her head. "You didn't ask?"

"I was afraid to," Gideon admitted. "I'm afraid to ask her anything personal. I'm afraid she'll leave."

"It's been more than a week," Daisy said hopefully.

"I know." Mercy had only taken a week of vacation. She should have gone back to New Orleans already, but she was still here. "I guess she extended her vacation."

"And you're wondering if it was for Rafe or for you."

He nodded, not surprised she understood. "I've given her time, like you said."

Daisy twined their fingers together, then kissed his knuckles. "I think she's still processing the truth about why you left the community. It takes a while to make sense of things when you realize the situation wasn't the way you'd always thought it was."

She spoke of him and Mercy, but also of herself and her father. Mercy had been rocked by the knowledge that Gideon had been forced to flee for his life. "I just wish she wouldn't avoid me." The elevator doors opened and he led them to Molina's office, but found himself hesitating when he lifted his fist to knock on his boss's door.

Daisy looked up at him knowingly. "Whatever she says, we'll deal."

He nodded, then drew a breath and knocked.

"Agent Reynolds," Molina said. "Come in."

He and Daisy entered and took their seats between Molina and Rafe. Mercy sat on Rafe's right. She gave Gideon a tight smile, her nerves evident.

So, she's here as my sister. It made him wonder if

Rafe was here as a detective or Mercy's support, but he didn't ask.

Gideon hadn't been expecting the other person at the table—SacPD forensic investigator Cindy Grimes. Gideon's pulse kicked up a notch. Cindy had been working on assembling the pieces of the photograph that Eileen had destroyed. Her presence here could mean that she'd been successful and found something. Or not.

He sent up a prayer for the former.

Molina introduced everyone, then turned to Gideon. "I had a facial recognition search run on the two photographs you provided—the age-regressed photos of the men you knew as Edward McPhearson and Ephraim Burton. We got back more than two hundred hits. And that was after we removed individuals who were either deceased or the wrong age bracket."

Gideon's excitement eroded a sliver. "Two hundred. That's . . . a lot."

"Yes. We would have been investigating for quite some time. However, Sergeant Grimes was independently working." She gestured to Cindy, giving her the floor.

"It took me over a week to put Eileen's photo back together," Cindy said. "Your completed puzzle, Daisy, was instrumental as a guide. I might have needed two additional weeks without it. Anyway, I got two prints on the photo. One is Eileen's." She gave Gideon a look of apology. "The coroner was able to get prints despite the condition of the body."

Gideon nodded tightly, because he understood what she hadn't said. Eileen's body, exposed to the humidity and unpredictable airflow of the mine shaft, had been badly decomposed. "Skin glove?" he asked.

Cindy nodded and prepared to continue, but Daisy stopped her.

"I'm sorry to interrupt, but what is a skin glove?"

When Cindy hesitated, Mercy answered. "It is what it sounds like. The outer layer of skin becomes separated from the body. The coroner removes it intact, wears it like a glove, and gets prints."

Daisy's expression was one of horrified fascination, heavy on the "horrified." "Oh."

"They wear gloves, of course," Mercy added, matter-of-factly.

Daisy blew out a breath. "Thank you. I'm sorry for interrupting, Sergeant Grimes."

Cindy was studying Mercy, curiosity in her eyes. "It's fine, Miss Dawson. Have you studied forensics, Miss Callahan?"

Mercy appeared suddenly uncomfortable because all eyes had turned her way. "I'm a forensic investigator with New Orleans PD. I work in the lab there."

Gideon's mouth fell open. He was stunned. Shocked. "You're what?"

Mercy nodded. "For the last two years."

"But . . ." He shook his head, at a loss. "You never told me that."

Her distress grew and her eyes dropped to her hands. "I'm sorry. I haven't been very good at sharing."

Still stunned, Gideon blinked to clear his head. "No, you haven't." He hadn't known what his own sister did for a living. He felt . . . hurt, he realized. Hurt that it was such a huge area of her life that she hadn't shared. That they could have shared.

Daisy cleared her throat when the silence grew awkward. "You were saying, Sergeant Grimes? About the fingerprints you got from the photo?"

"Right," Cindy said briskly, and Gideon forced himself to pay attention. "The first print was Eileen's. The second scored some hits in AFIS, but like the facial recognition search, there were quite a few."

"But only one name was on both lists," Molina said. "Harry Franklin." She drew a mug shot from the folder on the table in front of her and put it on the table.

Gideon stared at it, his heart now racing like a

runaway horse, his skin gone clammy and cold. All he could feel were Ephraim's fists. All he could hear was Ephraim's voice, saying he was going to die.

"Breathe," Daisy murmured.

The feel of Daisy's hand squeezing his brought him back, reconnected his brain. It was him. Ephraim Burton. He was younger, of course. At least ten years younger than Gideon remembered. But it was him. No question.

Tino's age-regressed photos were uncannily close. So close that Gideon was amazed that the facial recognition software had brought back so many hits.

"Harry Franklin," he murmured, giving a name to his nightmare. "What did he do?"

"Robbed a bank and murdered a guard, a teller, and a customer," Molina said. "He and his accomplice, Aubrey Franklin, who went by Abe, and then later by Edward McPhearson, have been wanted for thirty years."

"Brothers?" Rafe asked.

"Yes," Molina verified.

"They were hiding," Gideon said quietly. "In Eden. Harry Franklin still is."

Molina nodded. "We opened the investigation into the Eden cult on the basis of the abuses that Agent Reynolds reported. But knowing that this 'religious movement' is harboring a murderer supports the formation of a bigger force and, importantly, gives us a place to start. We wanted Agent Reynolds and Miss Callahan to be the first to know."

"What . . ." Mercy cleared her throat. "What do you expect from us?"

"For the time being, nothing," Molina said.

"And for the time after the time being?" Rafe challenged, the tone of his voice making Gideon give him a harder look. Rafe's gaze was locked on Molina's face and he was . . . fierce.

Gideon blinked. *Oh.* Rafe was holding Mercy's hand. Squeezing it, actually. *Ohhhh.*

"Will you expect them to be some kind of bait to draw these bastards out?" Rafe went on. "Because if that's what you're thinking, you need to think of something else."

Gideon leaned back to get a better look at his sister. Mercy was pale. Really, really pale. And trembling.

Molina looked affronted. "I have no intention of using any civilians as bait, Detective," she snapped, then drew a breath, her composure once again intact. "Agent Reynolds and Miss Callahan, I may ask you to speak to our investigators, to answer questions and provide background knowledge. And there may be occasions I'll ask you to speak to the press, if it should come to that."

Gideon winced, but nodded. "We can do that," he said at the same time that Mercy said, *"No."*

All eyes swung to her and Mercy stood, hands shaking as she buttoned up her coat. "I am *not* okay with talking to your investigative team. I am *definitely* not okay with talking to the media. Thank you for informing us about Harry Franklin and his brother. But my involvement ends here." She started to walk to the door, then returned for Rafe, who looked as shocked as the rest of them. "Can we go?" she asked Rafe.

His shock quickly morphed to concern. "Of course."

Gripping the handlebars of the wheelchair, Mercy rolled him out, then carefully closed the door so that it made no sound at all.

Gideon stared. "I'm . . ." He shook his head. "I guess we're not okay with that."

Molina frowned. "I didn't mean to upset her. I should've realized."

Gideon came to his feet. "I need to go after her. Are we done, Agent Molina?"

"Yes." Molina surprised him by grabbing on to the sleeve of his suit coat. "Please tell her that I'm sorry."

"I will. Daisy?"

She'd already risen and positioned Brutus's bag on her shoulder. "Right behind you. Thank you, Sergeant Grimes," she called, reminding Gideon that the forensic investigator was still at the table, watching their private stories unfold.

"Yes, thank you," he added, then took Daisy's hand and they all but ran for the elevator, breathing a sigh of relief as they approached.

Mercy sat on a bench next to the elevator. Rafe sat in the wheelchair, his face filled with helpless worry. Because . . . *Shit*. Mercy was crying, her face in her hands.

Gideon knelt in front of her, panic tightening his chest. "Hey. I'm sorry. I shouldn't have said anything was okay without asking you. Nothing will happen that you don't want to. Please don't cry." *Please don't leave.*

"I can't," she sobbed, rocking herself as she cried. "I just can't."

"I know," Gideon murmured. He hesitated, then, hoping he was doing the right thing, sat beside her and put his good arm around her shoulders, drawing her head to his shoulder. "I know you can't. You don't have to."

She turned into him then, touching him for the first time as she buried her face against his chest, her body racked with sobs that broke his fucking heart. He wasn't sure how long they stayed that way, but finally Mercy quieted.

She shuddered out a breath. "I'm sorry. I cried all over you."

"I don't mind," Gideon murmured, resting his cheek on the top of her head.

"If you want to talk to all those people, you can. I just . . . can't."

"You won't have to. But . . ." He was choking on the words, he wanted to say them so badly. "Will you talk to me? A little?"

She nodded slowly. "But not right now, okay?"

"Okay." He tried not to let his disappointment show.

"What are you doing this afternoon?" she asked, shocking him.

"Daisy and I were going to drive up to Macdoel and spread Eileen's ashes. Would you like to come?" he asked, knowing she'd say no.

"Yes," she said, shocking him yet again. "I think I should."

MACDOEL, CALIFORNIA
THURSDAY, MARCH 2, 5:40 P.M.

"It's beautiful," Daisy murmured, staring out at the mountains, the urn with Eileen's ashes firmly in her hands. Gale Danton had led their little caravan up a small rise to a gorgeous overlook—Gideon and Daisy, and then Mercy and Rafe, who'd driven separately. Gideon had been a little hurt that his sister continued to put space between them, but Daisy had figured Mercy wanted to be able to leave if she changed her mind about returning to land with a view of Mt. Shasta.

Gideon had understood then.

"She liked it here," Danton said gruffly. "Sammie or I'd bring her up here and she'd just sit and stare at the mountains. I asked her what she was thinking about and she said she was imagining a world far away from Eden."

"I can see why," Daisy told him.

At fourteen thousand feet, Mt. Shasta dominated the view, making the surrounding peaks look like mere hills. But the three mountains to the north and east were all over eight thousand feet and covered in snow.

Mercy pushed Rafe's chair up the plywood that Mr. Danton had used to create a makeshift ramp covering the short distance between the car and the overlook. That Rafe would accompany Mercy was not questioned, so Gideon had called the older man on their way up and asked if he could accommodate a wheelchair.

Gideon stood at the edge now, turning a slow three-sixty. "It is incredible," he agreed, and Daisy knew he was trying to reconcile the scene in front of him with the scene he saw in his mind's eye when he remembered Eden.

"Eileen hadn't ever seen the mountains to the west," Danton remarked, and Daisy pocketed that clue for when Gideon set out searching for Eden again.

Because she knew that he would.

She glanced around Danton where Mercy stood staring into the distance, her expression unreadable. Her sobs had ripped Daisy's heart to pieces, back at the field office. But the helpless look on Rafe's face had been almost as bad. They'd held hands wordlessly, she and Rafe, while Gideon comforted his sister.

A truck pulled up behind them and Sammie Danton jumped down, her eyes sad. "Hi, Daisy. Gideon. Rafe." Sammie had spent the day with Rafe, Erin, and one of Molina's agents in Portland. "I read about your adventure. You're looking better than I thought."

"Thank you?" Rafe said dryly.

"Not a problem." She went over to introduce herself to Mercy, who jerked back, as if she hadn't heard Sammie's approach. Sammie instantly changed her posture, her tone going smooth.

Daisy knew the tone and posture. Taylor and their father had used it every time they'd gentled a restless horse. Sammie was gentling Mercy, and Gideon's sister visibly relaxed, shaking the hand that Sammie offered.

"Are we ready?" Danton asked.

Gideon hesitated. "I've never done this before. Spreading someone's ashes."

"Me either," Daisy admitted, eyeing the urn with trepidation.

Danton held out his hand. "Give it to me." Daisy

did and the older man walked to the edge. Daisy and Gideon followed him, their hands tightly joined. Sammie stood at her father's side, tears on her face.

"Do you have anything you'd like to say?" Danton asked.

"Be happy," Gideon whispered, and Daisy's eyes burned.

"Be safe," Sammie said.

Mercy came from behind them to stand at Gideon's shoulder. "Be free," she said.

Danton swallowed hard. "Amen." He slowly emptied the urn, the ashes fluttering to the ground in the canyon below them. "This hillside will be covered in flowers come summer. So she'll have flowers."

"That's nice," Gideon said. "But we asked you if we could spread them here because you were the first and only kindness she ever knew."

Mr. Danton dropped his gaze to the urn, but Daisy saw the tears fall on his coat sleeve. He coughed, then looked up, handing Gideon the urn. "Well, if anyone else escapes that hellhole, they will find my door open." He turned and pushed Rafe to Mercy's rental car, helped him in, then got in his truck and drove away.

"Thanks," Sammie said, wiping her own tears away. "That meant a lot to him. He's been taking her death hard. Eileen was with us for only two weeks, but it was like she was part of our family. You guys take care, y'hear? No more shoot-outs. And give my regards to Detective Rhee. I'm glad everyone on your team is going to be okay."

Gideon smiled at her. "Thank you. I'll tell Erin."

When she was gone, Mercy hesitated, then leaned up to kiss Gideon's cheek. "I'll see you soon."

Smile fading, Gideon turned to watch her get behind the wheel of her rental and drive away with Rafe. "She's leaving, isn't she?"

Daisy's heart cracked, because she knew it was true.

"Maybe. But I think she'll be back. She said she'd talk to you and I don't think she was lying."

When Mercy's taillights disappeared, Gideon turned back to the mountains with a sigh. "I'm going to keep looking," he said.

"I know."

"Even if she can't, I can."

"Yes, you can."

"Hell, maybe I'll keep looking because she can't."

Daisy slid her arm around his waist. "I don't doubt that. Or you. You'll find Eden. And you'll make sure they pay for all the people they've hurt."

"And you? What will you be doing while I'm out searching for Eden?"

"I'm going to be with you, helping you. And writing your story for a magazine which I have not yet identified."

That must have been the right thing to say because a slow smile spread over his face. "And if I tell you that you can't?"

"Then I'll argue and then you'll have to kiss me, but I'll get what I want in the end anyway. So let's just cut the arguing and go right to the kissing."

"Because you'll get what you want in the end anyway?" he asked, pressing a teasing kiss to her lips.

She laughed. "You learn fast."

"As long as what you want is me."

"Yes," she said simply. "Let's go home, Gideon."

Keep reading for an excerpt from
Karen Rose's next Cincinnati novel

INTO THE DARK

Coming soon!

*R*un. *Don't look back. Just run.*

Michael Rowland clutched Joshua tighter and gritted his teeth against the sharp rocks and twigs digging into his feet. And he ran as fast as he could.

Blinking away tears, he focused on reaching the end of the driveway, at the bottom of the big hill.

Get to the road.

And then? He didn't know. He'd figure it out when he got there.

He'd figure it all out when he got there.

Where is there?

Shut up. Shut up and run.

He fought the urge to look behind him. He wasn't sure if he'd knocked Brewer out or not. Even if he had, the asshole could come to, and the minute he did, he'd be coming after them. Checking to see wouldn't make a bit of difference. It would only slow them down and make it easier for Brewer to catch them.

He'll kill me, Michael thought. Of that he had no doubt. But he'd do worse to Joshua. Joshua, who was only five. So Michael kept running.

He was approaching the cluster of trees that Joshua called the "forest." At one time it had been an orchard. Now it was totally overgrown. Branches grew every which way and bramble bushes had nearly taken over.

Damn bramble bushes. Michael's feet were bleeding now. *It doesn't matter.* He ignored the pain, welcoming the cover of the trees. *Move. Move.*

He found another burst of speed, ducking around trees, grateful for the agility drills that his coach had made them do. Michael was fast—fastest on the JV soccer team, even though he'd been the youngest. But he needed to run faster. *Please let me be faster.*

The flickering light that marked the end of the driveway was closer now, barely visible through the trees. He'd run about halfway. Another quarter mile to go.

He felt the yank on his foot, a millisecond before he was pitching forward into the darkness. Airborne.

Joshua.

Michael tilted his body at the last moment, hitting the ground with his shoulder. A burst of pain had him swallowing a grunt, the last-minute tilt giving him enough momentum to continue rolling to his back, then around to rest his elbows on the ground, his arms still clutching Joshua tightly.

He dragged in a breath, blinking as he got his bearings. He hunched over Joshua, in case Brewer had been on their tail. But there were no kicks. No hits.

Nothing.

Michael lifted his head and looked around. No one was behind him. It hadn't been Brewer grabbing his foot. *Must have been a tree root.*

Maybe he had knocked Brewer out. The thought filled him with dark satisfaction.

He glanced down at Joshua. Still asleep. Not dead. Just drugged. He wondered what had been in the syringe the bastard had been injecting him with. Michael said a small prayer of thanks for the extra soda he'd had before bed. If he hadn't needed to pee, he wouldn't have been awake to see Brewer plunging a needle in his brother's arm.

Michael frowned at Joshua's peaceful little face. *Should I take him to the hospital?* He wasn't even sure how to do that. He'd have to figure that out, too, once he'd gotten them away from Brewer's house.

He took another moment to watch his brother's chest rise and fall. *At least he's not dead.*

When he'd staggered down the stairs—his own sight blurry from the punch Brewer had thrown to the side of his head when he'd tried to grab the syringe—he'd seen Brewer carrying Joshua toward the front door. For a terrible minute, he'd thought Joshua was dead. He hadn't been moving.

Michael hadn't hesitated to find out. Whatever Brewer had planned, it wasn't good. Leaping from the third step onto Brewer's back, he'd knocked the man down.

Brewer had released Joshua long enough to punch Michael a second time, this time in the gut. Stumbling backward, Michael had grabbed the iron shovel from the fireplace and swung it with all his might. Brewer had been leaning down to pick up Joshua from the floor when Michael had hit him in the head with the shovel. Brewer had gone down on his knees and Michael had shoved him away from his little brother.

Who *had* been breathing. *Thank God.*

Then Michael had picked up Joshua and run.

Wincing at the pain in his shoulder, Michael pushed to his knees, gently settling Joshua on the ground so that he could do a three-sixty search.

So many times in his life he'd wished he could hear. Never so much as this moment. If Brewer was following, Michael wouldn't be able to hear a twig breaking or the man's labored breathing.

Brewer could be hiding anywhere. Michael didn't trust the bastard as far as he could throw him.

Stop wasting time. Get to the road.

Drawing a deep breath, Michael picked Joshua up and cradled him against his good shoulder. He took a step and had to bite back a scream.

It hurts. God, it hurts. The pain was shooting from his shoulder, up his neck, to the back of his head now. He hoped he hadn't whimpered.

Taking another look around, he started walking again, slowly. Yeah, it hurt. But he'd suck it up. He'd had worse, after all. Lots of times. Thanks to Brewer.

For a moment he wished the man was dead, then shook his head hard. *No.* Not dead. Just in jail. *Where other bad guys—bigger, meaner bad guys—will hurt him every day of every year for the rest of his miserable life.*

That would be . . . What had his teacher called it? *Oh, right. Poetic justice.*

He came to the edge of the old orchard and peered into the night. He could see the flickering light at the end of the driveway again. He was glad he'd known it had always flickered. Otherwise he might be worried that he had a concussion.

He took a step out of the trees, then froze. *Shit. Oh, shit.*

He scrambled back under cover and lay down out of sight, the pain in his shoulder making his eyes tear up. He blinked the wetness away and stared at the car making its way down the driveway toward the main road. It was too dark to see the make, model, or color, but that didn't matter because Michael already knew it was a 2018 BMW 530i. Alpine white exterior with a tan leather interior. Brewer was very proud of his car.

The car was moving super slowly. Maybe five miles per hour, if that. It stopped, then crawled another few feet forward.

He's looking for us. Oh, God. What do I do? Pulse rocketing, Michael tightened his hold on his brother.

He'll kill me. And then he'll take Joshua. To where, Michael had no idea. But it would be bad.

And then . . . another set of headlights pulled into the driveway from the main road. The vehicle was barely visible in the flickering light, but Michael could make out a dark SUV. Maybe black.

The SUV stopped and a man got out. A big man. A big bald man. The flickering light reflected off his head as he strode from the SUV to Brewer's BMW, now at a complete stop.

Because the SUV had blocked its exit.

The man crossed around to the BMW's door and yanked it open. A second later he was pulling Brewer from his car by the shirt collar and dragging him to the SUV. Once they were on the bald man's driver's side, Michael could see that Brewer was oddly limp.

If Michael hadn't been so scared, he would have cheered. Finally someone was bigger than Brewer and giving him a taste of his own medicine.

Michael frowned when Brewer twisted in the man's grip, because he looked like he was moving in slo-mo. Brewer had reached into his pocket when he was thrown to the ground. The man grabbed something from his hand.

Oh my God. It was a gun. Brewer had brought one of his guns. *He would have killed me with it.*

But now Brewer's gun was in the big man's hand. Michael held his breath, waiting for the man to shoot the monster who'd made their lives a living hell for five and a half years—ever since the day he'd married their mother, Stella.

Who was as useless as spit.

But the man didn't shoot Brewer. He pocketed the gun, then yanked Brewer to his feet and pinned him against the SUV. Then he put his big hands around Brewer's throat.

Brewer struggled.

Until he didn't anymore.

Michael's mouth fell open as Brewer's body went limp once again, falling to the ground in a crumpled heap. The big man took a step back, fists on his hips as he stared down, shaking his head.

Oh my God. He'd killed him. The big, bald man had killed him.

Abruptly aware that he was breathing hard, Michael clenched his jaws closed so that the man wouldn't hear him.

Luckily the man was focused on Brewer. He opened the hatch of the SUV and tossed Brewer in, as if he weighed no more than one of Joshua's action figures.

Slamming the hatch closed, he walked to the BMW's driver's side and leaned in. When he straightened, he tossed something in the air and caught it one-handed.

The keys. He'd taken Brewer's car keys.

The man then opened all four of the BMW's doors and the trunk, searching for something. When he didn't find it, he closed the doors, pocketed Brewer's keys, backed the SUV to the main road, and drove away.

Michael let out a quiet breath. *No keys.* He didn't know how to drive yet, but he could have figured it out. Now the car was no longer an escape option.

But now I don't need to escape. Brewer is gone.

And Michael was so tired. His mother wasn't home tonight. She was out partying with her friends, getting stoned again. Which was probably the reason Brewer had been so bold. He usually snuck around to do his dirty work.

But now there would be no one in the house to hurt them.

Besides, Michael knew where Brewer kept the rest of his guns and he knew how to use them to keep his little brother safe. *I'll take Joshua home. Get some sleep. And in the morning I'll figure out what to do next.*

He'd made it back through the orchard when Joshua's eyes blinked open. His mouth curved when he saw Michael's face.

"Hi," Joshua said.

Or at least that's what it looked like he'd said, and Michael was pretty good at guessing people's speech. Especially Joshua's. Michael had been watching his brother speak since he'd uttered his first words.

Michael smiled down at him, despite the pain in his shoulder. "You okay?" he voiced, because his arms were full and he couldn't sign.

Joshua nodded sleepily, his eyes closing once again.

Michael shuddered with relief. They'd dodged a bullet tonight and Joshua seemed none the wiser.

And Brewer? *Good riddance. I'm glad he's dead.*

CINCINNATI, OHIO
SATURDAY, MARCH 9, 2:15 A.M.

The river is high tonight, Cade thought as he watched the churning water flow past his vantage point above the bank. Nowhere near flood stage, but the current was still fast and deadly. Perfect for his needs.

Turning from the river, he stared down at the body in the back of his SUV, glad the miserable SOB was dead. *Good riddance.*

It had been close tonight. Too close. He'd assumed the asshole had been incapacitated by the Taser that he'd fired into the back of his neck, but somehow John Brewer had managed to move his arm enough to draw a weapon.

That hadn't happened before, not in the four years that he'd been performing this service for the community.

He drew the Taser from his coat pocket and held it up to the rear hatch light, studying it. It looked okay. Maybe it hadn't been fully charged? Or maybe it was broken. That did happen from time to time. He'd read the news stories of police being forced to shoot a suspect with their gun after the Taser didn't work, but he'd always figured it was the cops making excuses.

He pressed it to Brewer's chest and squeezed the trigger, causing the body to twitch.

"Well, fuck." The Taser *did* function. At least some of the time. Maybe Brewer had been on something. That might account for it. However he sliced it, Brewer's response had thrown him off his game.

He hadn't planned to kill the bastard in his own driveway. He'd planned to wait. To do it here, on the riverbank, miles from the nearest neighbor, where no one would hear his screams.

He scowled at John Brewer's handsome face. *Son-ofabitch got off too damn easy.* Too many people had been taken in by his fake charm.

My boss included. Normally Richard was a shrewd judge of character. *Me excluded, of course.* Cade was pretty sure that Richard wouldn't condone his extracurricular "service" to the community, were he to find out. Although, who knew? Stranger things had happened.

He'd never considered that Richard would engage in human trafficking, but that was exactly what his boss had done earlier that evening. Brewer had been trying to win back the property title he'd lost before, and Richard had allowed the slimy bastard to add his five-year-old stepson to his stake, when the small stash of heroin he'd brought to the table didn't meet the minimum table requirements.

The super-secret game which Richard hosted allowed no actual currency to be wagered. Instead, a constant flow of unique and valuable items—some legal but most black market—changed hands from week to week. Cade had often wondered what winners did with some of the stuff that had included land, luxury vehicles, stolen masterpieces, and exotic animals— live ones and parts.

He'd concluded that the participants often had their eye on a specific prize and that they probably sold off the rest of what they won as quickly as possible. Usually through Richard.

In addition to running a successful gambling operation on the Ohio River, his boss was also a "procurer" for the wealthy in the Midwest and beyond. Richard knew what some people wanted and what others had. He brought them together, enabling them to trade in a civilized fashion.

Before tonight, Richard had never included people among the prizes to be won. A few times there had been offers of human organs brought to the table, which had shocked him enough. But never people. *At least to my knowledge.*

That was a troubling thought. Cade wondered how many times items had been traded under the table while he'd stood guard outside the door. He wondered if Richard had allowed Brewer to participate tonight because he'd known one of the others at the table would want the boy.

He wondered if he'd have to kill Richard, too.

It was with disgust that Cade realized that Brewer had wanted his house back enough to sacrifice his own stepson. It hadn't even been Brewer's own house. Up until a week before the game, the house had belonged to his wife. Richard nearly hadn't allowed it, but then Brewer had wagered something else that technically belonged to his wife—her little boy.

Richard always said that desperate men played lousy poker, and Brewer proved that to be true. He'd lost big and left the game shaking and pale.

The winner of tonight's game had gleefully arranged to meet Brewer to take possession of the boy, but the exchange wasn't going to happen, because that man was currently . . . indisposed.

Cade yanked away the blanket covering the man lying in the back of his car. Eyes that were wide and full of horror stared back at him. And perhaps a little defiance? *If it is, I'll get rid of it with my first slice.*

He was always glad to rid the world of a pedo. Seeing the pure fear in their eyes, hearing their screams? It made his chosen crusade all the sweeter.

He smiled down at Blake Emerson, the pedophile who'd been bold enough to buy a little boy at a poker game. "Hi," he said to the appropriately terrified man, then pointed to Brewer's dead body lying beside his captive. "You two have already met, so I won't bother introducing you. Not that he'll say much, because, y'know, he's dead. It's true that Brewer had a less painful death than you'll have, but that isn't my fault." He shrugged. "That's sometimes how it goes. But please know that if he'd lived, I would have given you both equal torture. It doesn't really matter at the end of the day, though. You'll both be equally dead."

And Brewer's five-year-old stepson would be safe, as would the other kids who might have been future victims of the monster who was bold enough to buy a little boy at a poker game.

On the other hand, the boy hadn't been in Brewer's car, so maybe the asshole hadn't been planning to make the transfer after all. Maybe Brewer had been planning to make a quick getaway. Which didn't matter because he'd made the offer in the first place.

Cade frowned. Or maybe Brewer had already taken the child. Maybe he'd hidden him somewhere he could easily retrieve him. Maybe Brewer had been on his way to retrieve the boy so that he could give him over to his new "owner."

Bile burned his throat.

"Shit," he muttered. He needed to make sure the kid was okay, but he couldn't drive back to Brewer's house with a live prisoner and a dead body in the back. It was too risky. He pulled the Sawzall from its box in the back of the SUV and waved it in front of the pedophile.

"You want me to saw off a piece of you first? No?" he answered for the man, who couldn't speak through his gag. "Good choice. Now you can see exactly what's going to happen to you. And you'll still be alive to feel every slice."

He dragged Brewer's body from the back of the SUV to the ground and fired up the saw, making sure the bound pedophile had a clear view.

"First his fingers," he explained to his terrified audience, "then his dick, because he was willing to sell his kid to you. I'll start with your dick, though. Because you would have taken that little boy and destroyed his life. From there on, it's pretty standard. Arms and legs. Then, his head. That's where it gets nasty, especially if you're still alive, like you will be. Really a shame that Brewer's dead. I would have liked watching him struggle and squirm. You'll give me that, though."

And when they were through, Cade would check on the boy. Just to make sure he was okay.

CINCINNATI, OHIO
SATURDAY, MARCH 9, 5:40 A.M.

Michael shifted in the chair in the corner of Joshua's bedroom, trying to get comfortable as he kept watch over his little brother, who slept peacefully, unaware that anything had happened tonight. At least there was that. Joshua wouldn't have the memory of being drugged by their stepfather. Of their escape through the old orchard.

Michael had tried to sleep in his own bed. He truly had. God only knew that he was exhausted enough. But every time he closed his eyes, he saw Brewer jabbing Joshua with a syringe and carrying him away. He'd tried to force his brain to see Brewer going limp under the big bald man's hands, but his brain kept seeing the bastard getting up and walking away. That wasn't what had happened, but until Michael knew for sure that Brewer was really dead, he'd be on pins and needles, waiting for his mother's husband to come home.

And watching over Joshua. It wasn't like anyone else was going to. Their mother had never been what anyone would call maternal, but she'd gotten much worse since Brewer had entered their lives.

He shifted again, then froze as a familiar rumble beneath his feet sent an even more familiar bolt of fear through his body.

The garage door. Someone had opened it.

Someone is here.

Michael shot to his feet, fumbling for the gun he'd taken from Brewer's safe. Tucking it into the waist of his jeans at his back, he looked around the room wildly, nearly scooping Joshua up into his arms.

But again he froze. There was no time. Someone was coming.

Brewer? Or . . . He remembered the big bald man tossing Brewer's keys into the air. Had the man come back? Had he killed Brewer and come back? *For us?*

Oh, God. He saw me. He knows I saw him kill Brewer. He thinks I'll tell. He'll kill me, too.

Michael's brain told him to *run*, until his gaze fell to his little brother, still asleep. *I'll keep you safe. I won't let him touch you. I promise.*

Stepping back, Michael hid behind the chair and drew the gun. He'd kill whoever walked through that door. Unless it was his mother. Her, he'd let live. Although she didn't deserve to.

He'd gone to her, terrified and bleeding. Scared. He'd told her what her husband had done, the first time it had happened more than two years ago. And the second. And the third. But she hadn't believed him. Or she'd claimed as much.

You're lying, she'd told him. Michael could still feel the sting of her slap across his face. It was a wonder she hadn't broken any of his teeth. But he hadn't been lying about all the things her husband had done to him.

He shuddered, pushing those thoughts from his mind. *Not now.* He couldn't lose it now. Later, he'd fall apart. Later, when Joshua was safe.

Joshua, the only reason he'd stayed in this house. This hell.

Michael clutched the gun in both hands, willing them not to shake. Willing his eyes to stay open even though he wanted to clench them shut and pretend that none of this was happening. Because the door was opening. Slowly.

He held his breath, his heart hammering in his chest. *No, no, no.* It couldn't be Brewer. Brewer was dead. *Please let him be dead. Please let this be Mom. Please.*

A shadow appeared in the doorway. Big. Hulking.

It was the man. The bald man. The man who'd killed Brewer with his bare hands. He was here. He stepped into the room, the moonlight from the window reflecting off his head as he stopped at the foot of Joshua's bed.

Michael could see his face clearly. Memorized his features. Every detail, so that he could tell the police.

No, no you won't. You can't tell the police. Because they wouldn't believe him. His mother would tell them that he was a liar. Just like she'd done when he'd told her that her new husband came to his bed at night.

She'll find a way to blame me. That's the way it's always been.

He glanced at the gun he held in his shaking hands. *I won't need to tell the police because I'm going to kill him.*

Except the man didn't touch his brother. He simply stood there, his gaze fixed on Joshua. There was no anger on the man's face. None of the lustful leering that Michael had seen so often in Brewer's eyes. Actually the man looked . . . relieved. And that didn't make sense.

The man's gaze jerked up and Michael wondered if he'd made a sound. But he didn't come closer. He just turned on his heel and left the room.

Michael sagged back against the bedroom wall, letting out the breath he'd been holding. A few minutes later he felt the rumble of the garage door going back down.

He crept to the window and peeked out into the night. And sucked in a breath when he saw the big man running down the driveway, toward the flickering light at the road, a suitcase in his hand.

He was gone.

Michael and Joshua were alone again.

Michael's entire body began to shake. He stumbled to the chair just as his legs gave out. He didn't have to wonder what would have happened if the man had discovered him there. He'd have put his hands on Michael's throat and choked him until he'd gone limp, just as he'd done to Brewer.

Oh, God. Oh, God. I would have been dead. And Joshua would be all alone, unprotected. Michael glared at the gun in his hand. He'd frozen. He should have shot the man as he'd stood next to Joshua's bed, but he'd frozen.

I won't freeze next time. If he comes back, I'll be ready.